ER

In the Hydraphur system, crime and corruption run rife, from the lowest echelons of society to the very elite. The only bastion against those that would flaunt Imperial law are the Arbites, tasked with dispensing justice and dealing out punishment. Shira Calpurnia is thrust into this cauldron of lawlessness, and she must deal with danger and intrigue at every turn if she is to survive and discover the guilty...

In *Crossfire*, Shira Calpurnia is a newly-appointed Arbites officer. But soon she finds herself investigating a series of assassination attempts at the dockyards. With so much at stake, she must unravel a mystery that goes to the heart of Hydraphur's elite.

In *Legacy*, Calpurnia is appointed to protect an ancient trading charter. But the document is highly-prized by a number of potential heirs who are willing to go to any lengths to obtain it. Calpurnia and her fellow Arbites must don their armour and fight if they are to see the charter to its rightful place...

Calpurnia must uncover the root of a deadly conspiracy in *Blind*. When a telepath is killed, Shira faces suspicion and mistrust from his disturbed fellows. In a hostile environment, and dogged by her new 'minder', can she solve her most difficult case yet and ensure Imperial law is restored?

Enforcer gathers together all three Shira Calpurnia novels, plus exclusive dossiers on each book and a new introduction from the author.

More Warhammer 40,000 from the Black Library

· EISENHORN ·
Omnibus containing
XENOS, MALLEUS and HERETICUS
by Dan Abnett

· RAVENOR ·
Omnibus containing
RAVENOR, RAVENOR RETURNED and
RAVENOR ROGUE
by Dan Abnett

· BASTION WARS ·
EMPEROR'S MERCY
FLESH & IRON
by Henry Zou

A WARHAMMER 40,000 OMNIBUS

ENFORCER

MATTHEW FARRER

BLACK LIBRARY

A Black Library Publication

This omnibus edition published in Great Britain in 2010 by
The Black Library,
Games Workshop Ltd.,
Willow Road,
Nottingham, NG7 2WS, UK.

10 9 8 7 6 5 4 3 2 1

Cover illustration by Marek Okon.
Map by Nuala Kinrade.

A CIP record for this book is available from the British Library.

UK ISBN13: 978 1 84416 878 1
US ISBN13: 978 1 84416 879 8

Printed and bound in the UK.

IT IS THE 41st millennium. For more than a hundred centuries the Emperor has sat immobile on the Golden Throne of Earth. He is the master of mankind by the will of the gods, and master of a million worlds by the might of his inexhaustible armies. He is a rotting carcass writhing invisibly with power from the Dark Age of Technology. He is the Carrion Lord of the Imperium for whom a thousand souls are sacrificed every day, so that he may never truly die.

YET EVEN IN his deathless state, the Emperor continues his eternal vigilance. Mighty battlefleets cross the daemon-infested miasma of the warp, the only route between distant stars, their way lit by the Astronomican, the psychic manifestation of the Emperor's will. Vast armies give battle in his name on uncounted worlds. Greatest amongst His soldiers are the Adeptus Astartes, the Space Marines, bio-engineered super-warriors. Their comrades in arms are legion: the Imperial Guard and countless Planetary Defence Forces, the ever-vigilant Inquisition and the tech-priests of the Adeptus Mechanicus to name only a few. But for all their multitudes, they are barely enough to hold off the ever-present threat from aliens, heretics, mutants – and worse.

TO BE A man in such times is to be one amongst untold billions. It is to live in the cruellest and most bloody regime imaginable. These are the tales of those times. Forget the power of technology and science, for so much has been forgotten, never to be re-learned. Forget the promise of progress and understanding, for in the grim dark future there is only war. There is no peace amongst the stars, only an eternity of carnage and slaughter, and the laughter of thirsting gods.

CONTENTS

AUTHOR'S INTRODUCTION

THE UNIVERSE OF Warhammer 40,000 is strange.

Well, it is when it's doing its job. It's a dark-tinted, weirdly angled carnival-house mirror that piles distortion on distortion until it's normality that starts to look bizarre. Gloriously over-the-top loopiness? This universe has that in spades. Baroque and dreamlike darkness, the feel of a nightmare you were glad to wake up from but find you can't help trying to recall? That's in the specifications too. Simple, gut-churning grotesquery? Oh, yes. To switch metaphors, it's a weird brew that Rick Priestley first set bubbling back in the eighties, into which many more hands have stirred new ingredients, dark and bloody fruits picked from the writhing vines in the far corners of their imaginations. There's a flavour of strangeness for everyone's taste.

I remember the feeling I had when I took my first real dive into this universe, on a Friday night fifteen years ago, sitting in a below-street pancake restaurant with my new boxed set next to me and the *Codex Imperialis* open with my coffee next to it. I remember studying Rick's background, reading Bill King's short stories and gazing at John Blanche's art, with those haunting, tantalising little quotes in the sidebars. I remember the feeling that I'd become unmoored from familiar settings and quietly drifted into territory I hadn't really seen before.

This was not the SF I'd grown up with: the neat, clean, brightly-lit futures in which dashing space explorers and their thoughtful scientist sidekick zip about the galaxy in some sleekly technological craft, doing cheerfully good deeds and defeating ugly and villainous aliens. Those stories were a pretty straight projection of our own values into a new setting: progress was inevitable, common sense and technology would prevail, the heroes and adventurers who would naturally come out on top were people who looked and thought Just Like Us (for a particularly white, Western, Anglophone, middle-class and male definition of 'us', as unconscious as I was of that at the time).

And now here's this new future. Here's an army of super-warriors, enhanced with biological and mechanical science of dazzling complexity, consulting the Imperial Tarot before they begin their combat drop and marching to war to the chants of their Chaplains under beautiful and ornate banners. Here's a starship on an interstellar voyage whose Navigator shudders as something scrabbles against the envelope of reality that protects his ship, which is riding the churning tides of the warp as phantoms and half-alive things formed from the stray thoughts of the crew swarm along in its wake. Here is a galaxy-spanning human empire which consciously embraces intellectual and scientific stasis, and whose most revered teachings exalt the closed and narrow mind and abhor the free rein of reason. Here are skyscraping buildings beneath skies studded with space stations, along which priests stride with holy books whose pages are holographic memory wafers, connecting to their brains through cybernetic cables.

And this, mark you, was the backbone of the setting. This wasn't the antagonist for the smart, savvy, so-very-turn-of-the-twenty-first-century heroes. The Imperium wasn't a straw target, being set up to be knocked upside-down in time for an inspirational speech and the closing credits. This future wasn't a boys' own adventure waiting to happen. It was cruel, bloody and under siege. And it was exhilarating.

This is what speculative fiction is supposed to do. It's supposed to rudely shove your mind off that comfortable path it's used to wandering along and into new territory. What if we take all those bright, shiny, optimistic futures and turn our backs on them? What if we found ourselves in a universe where all the things we value and strive for today turned into horrible liabilities? What would that universe be like to live in?

I love these sorts of questions. I love fiction that deliberately pulls the rug out from under our assumptions rather than going along with them. And when I was wondering what sort of stories I could tell about this Arbites character I had in mind, I thought about the ways in which the Imperium is so profoundly different from us, and started to wonder: what would trying to enforce Imperial law be like?

The Imperium isn't a society based on rights and freedoms, but on duty and obedience. It doesn't believe that authority is granted by a mandate from the people: all authority comes down from above, from the Emperor, and those who wield authority don't owe the people on whom they wield it a damn thing. Imperial philosophy ascribes no inherent value to human life or dignity: life is given meaning and value by one's usefulness to the Emperor and His divinely ordained Adeptus.

Some familiar constants are going to be pushing their way up into the affairs of these people. There'll be material greed, desire for power, fear for safety, fear of disgrace, the whole human condition. In fact, a theme I've consciously tried to build into the Calpurnia stories is that humans are more than capable of making terrible trouble for ourselves simply by doing what we do, no hostile xenos or sanity-corroding warp entities necessary. It's been important to me that her adversaries be fundamentally human, acting on fundamentally human urges and motives. But even then, those motives will be filtered through a mind and culture that relates to the world in very different ways to us, or at least they will if the story does its job.

I hope they do. If you're holding this book in your hands then I suppose you're at least considering plunging into the stories that follow Shira Calpurnia's turbulent start at Hydraphur. If I can pass on to readers at least some of that strange exhilaration at the unfamiliar that those books brought to me a decade and a half ago, then I can be content.

But watch your step, sirs and mamzels. The Emperor may protect, but the law does *not* forgive...

Matthew Farrer
Queanbeyan
November 2009

NOMINE IMPERATOR
ADEPTUS ARBITES
PATENT OF APPOINTMENT

BE IT KNOWN that;

WHEREAS it is the task and duty of the sacred *Adeptus* to tirelessly protect and defend our great IMPERIUM, to the orders of their most gracious presences the High Lords of Terra and by the will and in the name of his most August Majesty the GOD-EMPEROR OF HUMANKIND;

IN DUTIFUL RECOLLECTION that such duties as have been passed from the hand of the immortal EMPEROR to His servants of the *Adeptus* must by righteous obligation call upon their greatest strength and capability; and

AFFIRMING that it is therefore the most correct and noble duty to advance in office those most deserving, powerful and able of the EMPEROR'S subjects in the ranks of the *Adeptus,* that the reign of the eternal IMPERIUM be forever preserved; furthermore

HEARING the humble petition of the Arbitor Majore and Grand Praetor Judicial of the High Precinct of HYDRAPHUR, the Lord Justice *Krieg Dvorov,* for the advancement of *Shira Calpurnia Lucina,* at this time holding the brevet rank of Marshal of Court and Commander of Court in the Precinct of EPHAEDA, and holding the substantive rank of Marshal Primus in that same Precinct; and

BEARING WITNESS THAT *Shira Calpurnia Lucina* has discharged her duties in the keeping of the EMPEROR'S Laws and Peace with valour and puissance most pleasing to the EMPEROR and to his *Adeptus* in feats of arms, in upholding of the *Lex Imperia* and in faith to the Creeds of the *Adeptus Ministorum* and to the Immortal EMPEROR Himself;

BE IT KNOWN that I, *Giovan Hyashi Raphardi,* Provost General of the Great Precinct of PACIFICA FIDELIS, hereby set my seal and decree to the appointment of *Shira Calpurnia Lucina* to the rank and position of *Arbitor Senioris* of the High Precinct of HYDRAPHUR, there to continue her service to the EMPEROR'S law and the peace and order of our beloved IMPERIUM.

For The Glory Of The Imperium And
The Glory Of Him On Earth

CROSSFIRE

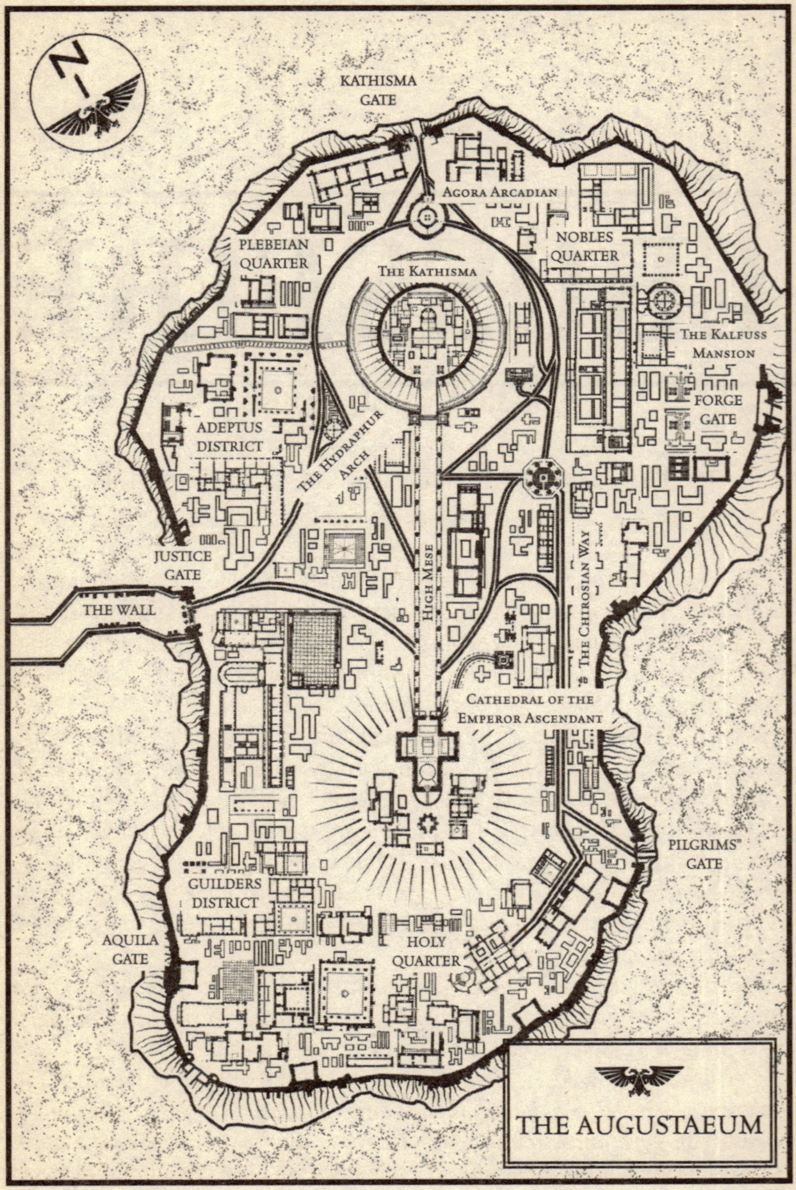
N
KATHISMA GATE
AGORA ARCADIAN
PLEBEIAN QUARTER
NOBLES QUARTER
THE KATHISMA
THE KALFUSS MANSION
FORGE GATE
ADEPTUS DISTRICT
THE HYDRAPHUR ARCH
HIGH MESE
THE CHIROSIAN WAY
JUSTICE GATE
THE WALL
CATHEDRAL OF THE EMPEROR ASCENDANT
PILGRIMS" GATE
GUILDERS DISTRICT
AQUILA GATE
HOLY QUARTER
THE AUGUSTAEUM

Sixth Day of Septista

Twelve days to the Mass of Saint Balronas.
The Festival of the Sevenmark. The Day of Shuttered Tithing (Administratum).

With seven days until the beginning of the Vigil of Saint Balronas, all those with duties, debts, obligations, or any other Imperial or personal business, should be looking to discharge them. The disgrace, both before one's Church and one's peers, of having unfinished business by the beginning of the Vigil should always be borne in mind.

Tradition tells us that this is the day on which masters announce to their servants and workers both the fact and the particulars of the holidays they are to be granted for the period of the Vigil – both generosity by the master and gratitude from the servant are appropriate on this day. Masters should lead their workers, and the heads of households their families, in modest celebrations; the exchange of small gifts and tokens is appropriate. A traditional token is a roll of blank parchment or an empty data-slate to symbolise the clearing of debts.

On this day the halls of the Administratum will be sealed as that order conducts certain devotions of its own. Any tithing or Administratum business must be completed before the halls are closed at dawn.

Celebrations should still be conducted with an air of temperance and deference, and the working day should end with a service or prayer meeting in garb and circumstances traditional to one's duties and station. The evening should be a time to take stock and ensure that the correct devotional items and clothes are ready for the period ahead, and that one's person and home are clean and orderly.

CHAPTER ONE

THE MACHINE-CULTISTS OF the Adeptus Mechanicus are not prone to strong emotions – the beautiful coldness of the Machine is held up as a model for admiration and emulation, even for those orders of the Mechanicus not directly concerned with physical mechanics and the gradual transfiguration of their own bodies into cybernetics. Genetor-Magos Cynez Sanja was of the Order Biologis, with a greater understanding of the emotions of the flesh than most, but this evening the ability to catalogue the exact neurotransmitters that flared inside his skull and how they reacted to and reinforced his thoughts and stimuli, let alone the Cult of the Machine's scriptures and psalms in praise of pure reason, were small consolation. Here in his own domain, in the very shrine of the Adeptus Mechanicus in the Adeptus district in what was supposed to be the safest enclave of the capital hive of the fortress world of Hydraphur, Cynez Sanja had found himself under siege. He was displeased, he was frustrated and he was – to his own dismay – angry.

Noises from the turmoil outside were seeping through the walls as Sanja stood in the forechamber behind the shrine's great adamantite doors, listening with his head bowed and his eyes closed. He had severed his link with the external opticons half an hour before, refusing to watch what was going on outside any longer, but now came a four-second burst of ultrasonic machine-code from the throat-mounted vocoder of his assistant, Brother-Postulant Chaim. Sanja reluctantly decompressed and scanned it; the reports and message transcripts unfolding neatly in his brain.

They were not pleasant. The avenues to the Administratum towers were blocked and the tally-house and the Ordinates' dormitory were ringed in. The bridge over the water-gardens to the Scriptoria was cut off and a brave group of adepts from the procurator-general's tower who had tried to force their way down the hopelessly-overrun Street of Quills had not been heard from again. The Adeptus Quarter, it seemed, belonged to the Adeptus no longer.

As if to underscore the point, there was a ringing thud that seemed to come through the walls and floor at once. Sanja glowered and cycled the tiny augmetic layers in his skull through a precise series of adjustments, but the walls still muffled the sounds to the point where he couldn't pick out much more than a rhythmic, concussive hammering and the faintest traces of hoarse shouts. He wondered again why nobody had thought it necessary to raise the void shields.

He opened his eyes and looked around him, drawing what serenity he could from his surroundings. The forechamber was a shortened rectangle, its measurements calculated to within a millionth of a millimetre to mimic the proportions, if not the size, of the forechamber of the high genetor's own shrine on the Mechanicus heartworld of Mars. The black steel of the floor was inlaid in gold and ruby with illuminated circuit patterns and alchemical forms. The friezes on the walls were burnished brass arrays of pistons and valves, their constant, silent hydraulic motion carrying binary-language catechisms of praise to the Machine-God back and forth. Setting his veiled hood back on his shoulders and tilting his head back, the genetor-magos contemplated the works above him: layers of interlocking cog wheels, the simplest but most sacred icons of the Mechanicus priesthood, hung weightless, slowly rotating in the air, obscuring the roof. Sanja murmured a prayer and felt the circuits tattooed around his eye-sockets tingle as he merged his sight with the opticon in the steel gargoyle on the wall ahead and examined himself through the machine-spirit's eyes.

His own scarlet tech-priest's finery seemed to shine even in the dim light of the forechamber. Behind him, framed by the second set of giant doors that led into the shrine's central cloister, was his retinue, standing with dignity in ceremonial formation and waiting upon his order. Chaim stood two paces behind Sanja's right shoulder. Behind them were four skitarii, the dedicated templar-soldiers of the Machine cult, their burnished carapace armour pierced with cybernetic cables and leads and their power-axes held at arms. Flanking each skitarius, two guardian servitors, mindless vat-grown automata hung about with mechanised implants of their own, weapon-muzzles pointed demurely down. His two luminant skulls, each half-plated with gold leaf and trailing clusters of perceptor vanes and mechadendrites, hung in the air over Sanja's shoulders.

The forechamber was not wide, but its high-vaulted roof was lost in the shadows above the layers of free-hanging cogs. The retinue formation, small though it was, stretched almost the width of the room.

The genetor-magos made a small sound of approval, feeling stronger for his moment of contemplation. He would not be cowed here, in his own temple. Whatever was going on out there, they would meet it as befitted their station.

'It is time, magos.' Chaim routed his speech through his own larynx this time, not the vocoder-plate. 'You asked to be notified.'

Sanja did not respond, as was only proper with a functionary, but simply disengaged himself from the gargoyle, took a quick moment to readjust to his own eyes, then made a single pace forward and, through the transmitter above his right temple, commanded the doors to open.

An avalanche of noise was the first thing to pour in, and Sanja almost flinched before he had the time to cycle down his senses and put up filters. What had been soft thuds with the gates closed was now a bellow of drumming that felt like physical impacts, as though someone were tapping him rapidly in the chest and tugging at his clothes. Underneath that came shouts, screams, squeals, and every so often the sound of breaking glass or splintering plastic. The air was full of smoke and vapour, the swarms of figures milling around the foot of the steps indistinct at fifty metres and an invisible source of yells at a hundred.

How many were packed into the plaza Sanja did not try and guess, but he had seen it hold thousands when Adeptus processions had mustered on the half-kilometre circle of engraved flagstones. That was an inspiring sight, rank upon rank of the Emperor's chosen servants in the rich golden Hydraphur sunlight, but this...

In fact, this almost seemed a deliberate mockery of those processions. Sanja could just make out the row of gaudy trucks and floats that they had apparently all followed here on their damned parade, covered in gaudy foil-and-plastic props to turn them into half-hearted versions of Astartes Land Raiders, Leviathan command juggernauts, Ecclesiarchal reliquary carts, whatever else, their cabs and beds decked with dancers and clowns scattering baubles and sweets. Sanja had no desire at all to recalibrate his cortical implants to see them more clearly: as he and his attendants moved forward in stately ceremonial gait, half-pace and all in step, he was seeing more than enough.

Two diamond-glass pillars stood at the foot of the ramp up to the shrine doors, and each pillar stood on a waist-high metal plinth. On the left plinth stood a pudgy young man with a blond ponytail, dressed in an imitation Imperial Commissar's uniform with the cap sliding down over one ear. He was digging candied nuggets or some kind of stimulant chew out of his pockets and tossing them into the cheering crowd around him. Another equally corpulent boy in a poor attempt at an Ecclesiarchal prayer shawl was trying to scrabble onto the plinth and grab his ankles, but was too drunk to lift himself up. The right plinth was swarming with bodies in varying shades of green: mockeries of Navy uniforms or Scholastia Psykana robes. A woman wearing what she probably thought was an Imperial Legate's uniform brandished a bottle, popped the top with her thumb, and scattered the contents all over her happily shrieking and now sticky companions as a burly man in an Administratum scribe's robe grabbed her around the waist and clamped his mouth over hers.

Nothing in the sea of bodies was any more edifying: everywhere were hideous over-ornamented attempts at Sororitas surplices, arbitor helmets, military and Administratum uniforms of every design. Despite his determination to remain calm Sanja bristled at a brief glimpse of a sequinned, dandified version of his own scarlet Adeptus Mechanicus kimono, the seals and badges placed grotesquely at all the wrong points, before the crowd closed and hid it.

There was no sight of his visitor. It was time, was it? Chaim had miscalculated, and Sanja was not appreciative of having to stand out here watching over this display for a moment longer than he had to.

One or two people below them had noticed the doors opening. They weren't yet drunk enough to think about coming up the ramp, but the whoops and cheers were starting. Sanja was about to march back inside when he caught sight of what had to be the person he was to meet: a wedge of a dozen black Adeptus Arbites uniforms, too stark to be props, forcing their way through the press of glitter and noise. At the bottom step, with only a few more paces to go, they ground to a halt – it took a moment for Sanja to focus his hearing on them and realise what the problem was.

'Stand aside.' It was the voice of the lead arbitrator, a head shorter than her squad and with honour icons on her armour that Sanja had no doubt were real.

'Ooh! Yes, madam! Stand aside for the lady justice!' Giggles. Another woman, much younger and considerably drunker. Sanja guessed it was the one with her back to him, with her hair fluffed and glow-dyed, wearing a lurid attempt at an Administratum Praefecta's formal tunic that was a size too tight for her.

'I'm not joking, and I'm not in the mood. Stand the hell aside!'

Sanja tensed reflexively as his sensors picked up the hum of a power weapon charging.

'Oh, is that real? Wherever did you get it? A real one of those arbitor things, what is it, a power-thing, I don't know. I'm one of these Administr... Administratum thingies... Pref... perf... It's a good touch, though.' More giggles. Someone else was slurring, 'Arrest her! Arrest her!' over and over. The girl grabbed a vial.

'Let's drink to that Arbites thing, and to, to my new friend here, with a very dull costume, I have to say, you know... no, let me finish, you lot, you're really doing the part.'

'I am playing no "part", woman. This is the seal of an arbitor senioris of Hydraphur. You will stand asi–'

'See, now, arbitor seni-whatever, you're starting to just get tiresome. You need to have a drink and–'

Crack. Sanja winced, despite himself.

Ignoring the wails of the partygoers behind her, the arbitor stamped up the ramp to where Sanja was waiting, her squad behind her, power-maul hissing in her hand. On the top step she thumbed its field off and relaxed with a visible effort before they stepped forward to greet each other. Sanja stretched one hand out of his sleeve and made the sign of the Great Engine while his guest clicked her heels and touched the maul to her forehead, then shuffled her right foot a half-pace back and made a slight bow: the short-form salute of the senior Adeptus.

'In the name of the masterful and enduring Machine-God I welcome you to his temple and his benediction. May the miracle of the Machine watch over you.' Sanja had to raise his voice over the din around them. 'I welcome you also in my name, Cynez Sanja, magos and genetor of the great Mechanicus, and pledge my goodwill in the name of the Emperor Omnissiah.'

'I receive and return your greeting and make my humble respects to the Mechanicus,' his guest replied. 'Shira Calpurnia Lucina, arbitor senioris of the Adeptus Arbites, extends her greeting in the service of the *Lex Imperia* and the God-Emperor of Earth. The Emperor protects.'

'Thank you. I think we can agree that this is not the place for high ceremony. Will you accompany me?'

Sanja was itching to get the temple doors between himself and the crowd. The arbitor must have felt the same way: Sanja drew back politely as she gave some curt instructions to her squad, who fanned out into a half-circle with their backs to the door. They remained there in sentry positions as the Mechanicus retinue moved back into the shrine. The arbitor senioris herself fell in beside him as he swept back through the doors.

As the adamantite slabs began to swing shut Sanja risked his dignity long enough to glance over his shoulder: a dozen or so of the revellers were clustered around the glow-haired girl's prone body, most of them gawping up at the temple or wringing their hands. Sanja haughtily turned his back on them and let the doors boom closed.

THE MECHANICUS ZIGGURAT rose above them in precise geometrical ratios and burrowed into the side of the Bosporian Hive underneath them, but everything that Sanja would need to deal with his visitor was here in the chambers ahead. As they walked across the forechamber, the servitor-sentries built into the lintels of the inner doors singing a benediction in binary, Sanja saw that his guest had taken her helmet off and was looking wide-eyed at the tech-arcana around her. Sanja nodded with approval: she was impressed, and was paying him the compliment of letting it show. As the song finished and they moved up the steps into brighter light, he studied her a little more closely.

She was a head shorter than he, with an easy, confident way of moving. Her features were even and her green eyes chilly but bright with intelligence. Dark blonde hair fell to just below her ears, tousled from the helmet, and there were the first suggestions of lines around her mouth and eyes. Her expression was stern – when those lines came, Sanja thought, they would not be kind ones. Three parallel scars, long healed and barely more than pink lines, started in her left eyebrow and ran straight and neat up into her hair.

They passed through the inner doors into the broad cloister that ran to the heart of the tower and branched into stairs at each side. Here the walls and floor were stark grey rockcrete and the contrast with to the richly ornamented forechamber seemed to unsettle the woman somewhat; she fell a pace back as they walked up a long slope of stairs and turned into the passage to the genetors' devotory. Her face was composed and dutiful and he realised she was unsure of whether she was allowed to speak. Deciding to be a courteous host, Sanja dropped back also and walked alongside her.

'We have prepared the fundamentals of the ceremony while you were on your way to us, my lady justice, so we will be ready to begin at your word. However, your trip here was... somewhat less serene than this quarter normally is. If you wish to clear your mind and prepare yourself before we begin, my junior will show you to our chapel. It is small, but quiet.'

'My thanks, master genetor, but I am prepared. That affair outside was irritating, but not fatal to the equilibrium, I think.'

'Dignity and composure are admirable qualities. I commend you on them, Arbitor Lucina. This way.'

'Calpurnia.'

'Your pardon?'

'Arbitor Calpurnia. My apologies, Master Sanja. An act of carelessness on my part. In formal greeting I use Ultramar protocol. The family name is second, the private third. Here I am Shira Calpurnia as you are Cynez Sanja.' She gave a small, contrite smile. 'Once again, I apologise. I intended no slight.'

'No slight is taken, Arbitor Calpurnia.' He saw her relax and then, to his private amusement, tense again as she followed him through the lacquered double doors of the Devotory. The narrow little chamber, its walls red-panelled and ceiling dancing with holo-sculptures of amino-acid molecules, had been prepared just as Sanja had said: two rows of servitors carrying medicae flasks formed an aisle to the little kneeler cushion before the shrine. The relics on the crimson altar-cloth – centrifuge, injector-glove, inscriptions of the gene-codes of Mechanicus saints etched into scrolls of paper-thin steel – reflected the mellow golden lamplight.

Calpurnia saluted the altar from the doorway and then walked to the kneeler without further hesitation, unclipping her half-carapace as Sanja faced her from the far side of the altar. Chaim took and held her armour as she unfastened the top of the uniform bodyglove, holding it against her chest but shrugging it down to leave her shoulders and back bare. Her composure was still good, but Sanja was looking at her now through the eyes of the luminants as well as his own, and in the mosaic of images being fed into his augmented cortex her apprehension showed in her breathing, her body temperature, the acidity of her skin, her brainwaves. The luminants moved down the row of servitors, dendrites clicking as they took and loaded the vials of biotic fluid and extended their injectors, then glided silently to station themselves behind Calpurnia's shoulders, dendrites extending a glittering fan of needles.

Sanja murmured a brief High Gothic blessing, then switched to machine-code and guided the luminants down. Calpurnia's breath caught for a moment as the hypodermics went home, and then the luminants rose into the air again and it was done.

'Walk with me.' Sanja was already stepping down from the altar-dais by the time Calpurnia had stood and fastened her bodyglove back into place. Chaim came forward with her carapace and she turned, shrugged into it and clipped it closed with barely a wince, then fell into step again as Sanja led the way back out through the antechamber, to the gallery that ran around the temple's central hall.

'We shall pace a while.' he told her. 'The movement will help the anointments to integrate faster. Chaim will have given you the tokens–' She held them up. 'Good. The Iron Wheel and the Caducal Helix are strong talismans of the Mechanicus. Grip them well and they will make your blessing a powerful one.'

They walked in silence for several minutes: out of the Devotory, past the stairs they had come up, around a circular chamber full of doors where the half-skull-half-cog crest of the Mechanicus gazed inscrutably down from one wall, back past the stairs to the Devotory doors and so through the circuit again. The skitarii and servitors followed them for the first circuit, then Sanja ordered them away. Calpurnia gave an occasional surreptitious half-shrug, trying to get the armour comfortable on her needle-tender shoulders; Chaim silently trailed them with her helmet. They were halfway through their third circuit before Sanja spoke.

'I would venture to suggest, Arbitor Calpurnia, that this was not the first time that you have had a rite of vaccination performed. You seemed to know your part in it as well as I did.' She smiled.

'My career has taken me through postings across the Ultima Segmentum and now to here, magos. Most of those moves have been across sufficient distances for me to need fortifying for my new position, although the ceremonies were never this involved. They were usually done on board the Arbites ship by one of our own Medicae staff, with a junior genetor overseeing, and they did not involve these...' she gestured behind them with her head.

'The luminants? They are relics as well as servants, perhaps not common on smaller worlds with less distinguished Mechanicus traditions. The honour of continued service to the Machine-God after one's organic death is not earned every day.' He gestured behind him. 'That one is the skull of Clayd Menkis, the chief adept of this shrine just after the overthrow of the Apostate Cardinal. The other is Bahon Sulleya, my immediate predecessor and mentor. I had the great honour of preparing her skull for its mechanisation myself.' Calpurnia shot the luminants another, slightly uneasier look.

'They can act by themselves?'

'I am appointed as their instructor as I am the instructor of my servitors. That privilege accompanies my rank here. The luminants assist me with my work and my studies. Their precision and senses are all that one would expect of idols of the Machine-God. Normally such a rite as yours would not require more than one, but for you to have come so far and to a world like Hydraphur, to which viral and bacterial strains from all across the segmentum are brought, you needed a far more rigorous treatment and I called both of my luminants accordingly.'

'And they are also monitoring my chemical spoor and behaviour to make sure I am who I say I am and that I carry no psychic or hypnotic taint to cast doubt upon your safety in admitting me.'

Sanja snapped his head around to stare at her and she laughed aloud.

'I said that the practices here were different, magos, not that I had never had dealings with your priesthood before. Admission to your shrine is a great honour, and humbling – but when I passed into this shrine with no searches, no weapon-checks or security vigils, I started to wonder how it was that you were making sure I was no danger to you. I'm Adeptus Arbites, remember. We enforce the Emperor's law, pass the Emperor's judgement and enforce the Emperor's peace. We get into the habit of thinking about things like this. You don't need to confirm it if you'd rather not.'

'You are as sharp as my own luminants' needles, lady justice,' Sanja told her, not sure whether to be angry or amused. 'I am sure the Arbitor Majore will not regret sending for you all the way from, Ultramar, was it? A long journey. It's a compliment to you.'

'I grew up on Ultramar. Iax. But my last post was at Ephaeda, north-west of there. But still across a lot of space. I'm a long way from home.' A sombre note had crept into her voice and they walked in silence for a few minutes more. Every so often the bio-augurs on one of the luminants would buzz or click, recording some detail of how the arbitor's metabolism was responding. It did not take long for Sanja to be satisfied, and he led the way to the doors back into the forechamber.

'Am I done, then? Have the luminants given the word?'

'They have, and I have confirmed it through their eyes and spirits. You have not reacted adversely to our anointments, and their eyes show that your body is accepting the inoculations. The preliminary rites and treatments you had before your arrival here laid the groundwork well. My arts are more sophisticated than those of the medicae, and the process will have completed itself within a day or two more. An envoy of mine will visit you tonight and instruct you in the correct prayers and readings to close the day and open the morning tomorrow to ensure this. There should be little problem, arbitor, in your taking your place at the Mass of Balronas and the Sanguinala.'

'Good. I'm looking forward to them. I read Galimet's *Pilgrim's Letters* during my journey here and he describes the mass in spectacular terms. I'm certainly expecting it to be a little more edifying than *that*.' She nodded toward the outer doors as they reached the forechamber again. 'Galimet gave the impression that the period leading up to the mass was one of self-denial and penitence. The dossier I was sent said the same thing.' As if on cue a quick syncopated bass thump came through the walls. 'But I have to say, magos, that if that display outside is Hydraphur's idea of penitent reflection, I'm further from home than I thought.'

Sanja smiled without humour.

'Your first lesson in Hydraphurn behaviour, lady arbitor. Part of the ritual of the season nowadays is the Ministorum's plaintive attempts to have the aristocracy conform to the more general ideal of pious behaviour, but when the nobility assemble and reach a certain critical mass, as they've done here, they obey rules of conduct all of their own. I am given to understand that among less rarefied circles the Ecclesiarchal dictates on behaviour are more strictly followed, if that brings you any consolation. This should blow itself out in another couple of hours.'

'I'd like to have it cleared out before then,' said Calpurnia with a scowl. 'I got caught in the middle of the damn thing when they all started pouring into the area and it was too late to double back to fetch a transport, but I'm sure riot squads will have mobilised from the Wall by now... What?' Sanja was regarding her. 'I mean, apologies, magos. Did I speak out of turn?' He shook his head.

'To speak candidly, Arbitor Calpurnia, although I am part of an order known for its detachment from the day-to-day affairs of the Imperium, I can't help the thought that the workings of Hydraphur are just a little less straightforward than you perhaps perceive them to be.' Before she had the chance to ask him what he meant, the doors swung wide and once again the din of the party piled in.

The fog was thicker now. The still, warm evening air filled with a soup of coloured ornamental smokes and perfumes and some kind of refractor mist that made lights and colours sparkle unnaturally; Calpurnia hastily took her helmet back as Sanja lifted a filter-veil over his face. There was no sign of the girl Calpurnia had struck, and the other revellers were only visible now as a boil of movement through the mist. By the sounds, the party's momentum had not been dented.

'Any further trouble, Bannon?'

'None.' Calpurnia and her deputy had to shout over the noise. Somewhere out beyond the ramp, pyrotechnics were starting to flash through the fog: showers of glowing confetti and miniature starshells flashed and cracked over the heads of the crowd, leaving hazy trails and puffs of hot smoke. Calpurnia fell in with her squad, then turned to salute Sanja in farewell.

The first bullet hit her shoulder at a bad angle, whirred off her carapace and struck a spark off the temple wall, a single tiny chip of black ceramite stinging the chin of the arbitor next to her.

Her reflexes had taken charge before she realised what was happening, sending her darting down the ramp and to one side. The second bullet struck her helmet over the right eye, not penetrating but cracking the armour and staggering her backward in a daze. The third whipped past her ear as her squad pelted down the steps after her, unlimbering shotguns and shields and firing loud bursts over the heads of the crowd.

The movement began like a ripple in grass as a strong wind springs up. The nearest partiers shrieked and ploughed into those further away, until the crowd thickened too much for anyone to force their way through. The mob rebounded off itself, swayed and broke in three directions at once as the Arbites split into two squads and closed around Calpurnia. As she lurched to her feet, groggy and shaking her head, their shields juddered under two more shots and one pitched over backward as a third shattered the cheek-guard of his helmet against his jaw.

Calpurnia tried to will the ringing in her ears away as things seemed to swim around her. It took an age for her to goad her legs into action and another to get into formation behind her guards' shields. They held the foot of the ramp in a textbook Arbites firing line: one row kneeling, shotguns locked through the gunports in their shields to pump out a steady, suppressing fire; the second line standing behind them firing more carefully, aiming shots over their heads. They were aiming high for the moment, trying just to drive the crowd back, but the answering bullets kept coming.

'Bannon! What can you see? Place the shots!' The beat over the vox-horns had fallen silent, and the tumult of the crowd was something the Arbites were more used to shouting over.

'Nothing! We can't spot any shooters, no weapons, no sounds, no flashes!' Bannon's voice had an edge of fear in it. A partygoer, leering with terror, stumbled toward them and two of the squad sent him sprawling with expert shoves of their shields. As that movement parted them for a split-second a third bullet whipped between their shields and scraped Calpurnia's carapace with an impact she felt all down her ribs. She swore and backpedalled. The shots were coming in flat, somewhere at ground level, not a sniper up high. No one she could see had been anywhere near the angle to make that shot. They–

There was a crash from off to her left, a perfume-brazier going over. She glanced at it, registered only a couple of frightened partiers running away, no guns with them. She hung low and kept moving, sideways across the ramp to the left-hand pillar-plinth. The arbitrators broke their shield-wall into a more fluid line for a mobile firefight, some covering Calpurnia and two on guard over the man who'd fallen. A bullet cracked into the armour on her shoulder and she staggered and cursed; the bastards were all around her. She ran the last couple of paces to the plinth and–

But there was nobody in that direction. This was small-calibre ammo, handgun slugs. And there was no one remotely in handgun range.

The plaza roared with the riot the party had become as they surged back and forth trying to find a safe way away from the shooting. But there was nobody to her left, nobody around where the brazier had been knock–

Bannon leaned out from the plinth for a quick glance beyond it and a bullet smacked into the edge of his shield and ricocheted past Calpurnia's ear so that even through her helmet's padded earpiece she could hear the whine. She grabbed Bannon's shoulder and yanked him back in as a second bullet clipped the rim of his shield.

No. Not possible. Nobody could plan a ricochet shot like that. Could they?

She had to move.

'Go. Fan out towards that overturned brazier. Cover every single side. Assume concealment by the enemy. Now!'

They rounded the plinth and raced forward. The space in front of them was empty, the crowd shoving away to the sides.

'Nothing here!' She was whirling on the spot, trying to–

Was that movement?

She ducked to one side instead of standing to shoot and it saved her life. The bullet gouged the side of her helmet and knocked it askew – a second earlier and it would have punched through her top lip. She wrenched off the helmet and scampered crabwise away from the others. Whatever it was, a moving target seemed to give it a little trouble.

With no polarising filters over her eyes the refractor-fog set every light to glittering and sparkling. She narrowed her eyes and almost saw–

She sprinted two steps to the side and vaulted an upended table as two more shots skewered the air behind her. A third smacked into the heavy wood and she put three booming stub-shots through the space where she thought she might have heard firing. She had been careless about placing her feet and the recoils slammed her through almost a quarter-turn; as she turned it into a backward jog to regain her balance there was a roar as three shotguns opened up to support her.

Nothing. Mist and light, echoes and sobs from partiers sprawled on the ground. Her head was throbbing – one of those head shots had hurt, even through the helmet, and it was catching up with her. She willed herself to stay on her feet.

An eddy in the mists. She put a bullet through it as her squad caught up with her, kept her gun high and moving back and forth in front of her face, wanting a shotgun but painfully aware of the momentary lapse in her guard that a weapon-swap with one of the arbitrators would mean. The giant-bore stub pistol she had been issued with was a commander's weapon, a shock-and-terror weapon, something for a senior arbitor to use for great, ruinous shots at high-profile targets to terrify a crowd of rioters, showing Imperial authority in brutal terms while other arbitrators and sharpshooters did the actual combat shooting. Calpurnia was becoming bitterly aware of its limitations in a straight firefight. She kept moving, dodging, reversing her direction. The lack of a helmet made her almost nauseous with nerves.

A woman lying on her back nearby gasped and twitched, and Calpurnia came within a hairsbreadth of shooting her on reflex. It took her a moment to realise that it had been not panic but physical shock, as though someone had stepped on her. She tucked her body down towards her boots, crouching into a foetal ball and sending two shots over the prone woman, aiming high in a last-moment hope that the rounds would pass over any bystanders beyond and letting the recoil roll her over and put her back on her feet. Bannon sent a shot-burst through the same space a split-second later and the little dark-haired party-girl seemed to decide her time was up. She shrieked and scrambled to her feet, frightening the people around her into doing the same, and suddenly a score of people were rising up out of the smoke and running for their lives. The mist between them roiled as if...

As if there were another person there, a shape pushing its way through the crowd, displacing air and bodies.

Calpurnia skittered to one side. The ringing in her ears was turning into a yammering that fought against the screams of the crowd. There was a distant crash as one of the parade-floats went over. She hunted for signs, half-saw them. Smoke moving the wrong way here, there a tremor and backflow in the mob as the moving crowd snagged on nothing she could see. It was moving around the edge of the retreating mob, and she could almost feel its gunsights crawling over her.

Her squad was frantic, desperate for a target. There was no time to instruct them – by the time she explained she'd be dead. She'd have to rely on them to follow her fire when she spotted something. It could be moving into position now, or...

She knew what she was looking for now, and had her pistol ready to bear. The stampede in front of her was wavering, the crowd parted and one man stumbled against something unseen. *Now*. Running on nerves and reflex alone, with barely a conscious moment to aim, Shira Calpurnia put a slug through the clear space and straight through the assassin's heart.

Seventh Day of Septista

Eleven days to the Mass of Saint Balronas.

Feast of Saint Rapanna and Saint Skey. Commemoration of the Second Sacrifice of the Colchans. The First Congregation of Intercessors.

In these days before the vigil the Imperial shrines will station preachers at every street pulpit, with sermons delivered at sunup and sundown. On no account should any be absent from these except in direst straits or by dispensation, for these sermons will have been passed down from the Eparch of Hydraphur himself to strengthen mind, body and soul for the physical and spiritual labour ahead.

It is at this time that the Ecclesiarchy hears certain special pleas and petitions. All those with indulgences to beg should have discussed the matter already with their local preachers and be ready to present themselves either at their appointed shrine, at one of the Imperial chapels on the slopes of the Bosporian Hive or on the High Mesé, or at the gates of the Cathedral.

This is also the first day on which pilgrims hostelling below the Cathedral move through the Augustaeum at the hive peak, and proper respect should be shown to all in the brown pilgrims' mantle. Those travelling to the Augustaeum through the Pilgrims' or Aquila Gates may wish to take a small offering of simple food or distilled water to offer to the pilgrims as they walk past on the paths to the Artisans Quarters or along the Chirosian Way – it is a traditional mark of favour and good fortune to have the food one has set down by the side of the path collected by a pilgrim. The small tokens and devotional items set out in the Artisans Quarter are there for the same purpose, and to interfere with them is a matter of some shame and should not be countenanced.

Those participating in services commemorating the Second Sacrifice should wear a small stone on a thong about their neck or waist. The likeness of Saint Rapanna may be worn by any making devotions to her, but the likeness of Saint Skey is sacred on this day and must only be touched or worn by officers of the Adeptus Ministorum.

CHAPTER TWO

THERE WERE A series of overlapping clacks as the pile of data-slates finally tumbled off the hassock and scattered over the floor, then a thump as the pile of faxcopy collapsed, and then the little suite of rooms, Calpurnia's new home on her new world as of three days ago, was quiet again. She didn't bother to take her hands from over her eyes. Just half an hour more, she promised herself then she'd sleep – better to tackle this fresh tomorrow morning than cudgel herself any more over it tonight.

She opened an eye long enough to pluck the wine-glass from the hassock and drink the last sip of the mellow red. She stayed sprawled on the recliner as she let the taste fill her mouth and then shade to aftertaste, then reluctantly got up and put the glass aside for the stewards to remove. The idea of having servants still bothered her, but just for tonight she was glad to have things taken off her hands. She was wrung out: formal duties, the injuries from the previous afternoon – she had spent that morning being fussed over by the Arbitor Majore's personal physicians – and lingering nausea from Sanja's vaccines. It occurred to her now that she hadn't cleared the drinking of wine with the genetor, and wondered if it might interfere with the inoculations. That rankled – she wasn't used to forgetting things like that. She finally did sigh as she glanced out of the great window at the last of the daylight draining out of the sky, then dropped back onto the recliner and reached for the next slate.

It was her notes from the first full, formal, working meeting with her new colleagues as the freshly appointed and ordained arbitor senioris of Hydraphur. They had met in the ornate chambers of the Arbitor Majore, high in the topmost tower of the great Arbites fortress known as the Wall. Sitting around a table with the three most senior Arbites of arguably the most famous system of an entire Imperial Segmentum had been pressure enough, but one thing she hadn't imagined was that the meeting would be exclusively focused on her. Or to be accurate, she thought as she flicked through her notes yet another time, exclusively focused on the man who had tried, very hard and very nearly successfully, to kill her the previous evening.

'Let's eliminate the most obvious possibility first,' Dvorov had begun, tilting his chair back and stretching his booted feet in front of him. Arbitor Majore Krieg Dvorov, Grand Marshal and Grand Praetor Judicial of Hydraphur, had a long, seamed face and a dry, distracted way of talking. Somehow, he wasn't what Calpurnia had been expecting. 'The first thought into my head, as I'm sure it was yours, was that it was a simple revenge attack for our colleague decking that young lady who wouldn't get out of her way. What was her name again?'

'Keta Merkoli-Ballyne,' put in the man opposite Calpurnia at the little round table. 'Or, as I'm sure she would have me put it, the Distinguished Lady Keta of the Noble Ballyne's most respected Merkoli. Assuming she didn't stand on ceremony and used the short form. But then her behaviour before even such a civilising influence as our own newly-welcomed colleague does not suggest to me that this particular darling of young society enjoys a particularly formal mindset.' Calpurnia gave him a sharp look at his last sentence, but as far as she could tell she wasn't being got at. She sometimes found it a little hard to tell: Arbitor Senioris Nestor Leandro, foremost of Dvorov's three deputies, had a courtly manner and an ornate way of speaking that she sometimes found a little overdone. His theatrical manner went well with his rolling, resonant voice and handsome swirl of silver hair – Calpurnia had not been surprised to find out that Leandro was a patron of dramas and operas, and kept a library of famous Imperial oratory.

'As for what all of that means,' Leandro went on, 'there is no reason you should have heard of the Merkoli, or of the Lady Keta in particular. The Mass and its associated festivities has come at a time when Ballyne would really rather its households be agitating to try and reverse their recent sidelining for close-traffic contracts at Contoscalion, but there has been considerable anguish within Ballyne about whether a good presence here for the Mass will sap their efforts in that direction or reassure their allies that they are strong and in control and build their stock that way. None of this has been more than a background whisper, you understand, it's what I uncovered after peeling back a few layers of disinterest and indifference.

'The upshot, though, is that even if Merkoli-Ballyne had the resources to organise such an expert attempt, and even if they were stupid enough to expose themselves by staging it, and even if they were supremely stupid enough to select an agent of the Imperial Adeptus as a target, there would be no logic behind them doing any of that for a disposable, peripheral flibbertigibbet like the Lady Keta, who as far as I can tell only earned the privilege of a trip here for the Mass because the family didn't know what else to do with her apart from trying to pair her off with some moderately reputable local boy in the hopes of a marginally useful political marriage. All things considered, I suspect a smack across the nose with a power-maul is about the most interesting thing that will happen to anyone in her family all season.'

'I wish you'd pause for breath occasionally, Nestor. By the time you end of some of your sentences I feel dizzy on your behalf.' Dvorov turned to the fourth at the table. 'We have a good idea of somewhere he didn't come from, then. Any ideas about where he did?'

'No.' Arbitor Senioris Ryo Nakayama could hardly have been better calculated to be Leandro's opposite. Squat where Leandro was tall, gruff and raspy-voiced where Leandro was poised and mellifluous. 'Nestor's right, this is something that took a stack of resources. Not just money. Clout, access to rare equipment and highly illegal personnel.' He looked at Calpurnia. 'You remember handing the corpse over to the genetor after you killed it?'

Calpurnia nodded. Her memories of the afternoon were a little fragmented, courtesy of the light concussion that the bullets had managed to give her through her helmet, but she remembered that much. The space in between the partgoers, nothing but smoke and sparkle, became a pale blur which became a brown-grey silhouette which became a tottering, hazy outline which became a collapsing body. She dimly remembered staggering forward and putting two more slugs into its back, and her next memory was of half-lying on the inlaid floor of the Mechanicus shrine while Sanja and Chaim shouted at servitors.

'The Mechanicus have helped us with these kinds of problems before,' Nakayama went on, 'although not often. Their genetor-magi have the finest tools and arts for stripping knowledge out of evidence, bar none, better than our own verispex laboratoria. This time Master Sanja took the remains and set his adepts to work on them without waiting to be asked, or even before we could ask him to hand the body over to us. I think he takes it happening right in front of his shrine as some kind of personal slight that he wanted to redeem. I've read his report – he asked for you, Shira, but you were at the Kalfus-Medell meeting.'

Calpurnia allowed herself a moment's hope before Nakayama doused it.

'They came up blank, of course. They were furious, apparently, or as close as they ever get to it. Sanja was sure they'd missed something at first, but they've cast their best augurs and instruments over our friend and there's still next to nothing they can tell us. Was he a mutant? Yes. A trained psyker. That was how he blocked himself from sight. Was he augmented? Of course. His eyes and the motor parts of his brain were massively enhanced, specialised trick-shooter stuff. Is he traceable? Not a chance. His death triggered a toxin implant in the small of his back which caused massive damage right through his tissues. Sanja invoked his secrecy prerogative pretty quickly when I wanted to get to details, but it's clear we'll never get a usable gene-print. Anti-tracing measures like that need a lot of skill and resources, and they're illegal to boot. On an assassin whose psyker nature put him under an automatic death warrant in any event, they add up to a hell of an investment on a single agent and a single attack.'

'Surprise me, Ryo,' said Dvorov, looking at the ceiling. 'Tell me we're going to be able to trace the weapons.'

'We're going to try, but they don't seem to correspond to any established Mechanicus archprint. So far, anyway. Magos Sanja has a fairly sophisticated medicae chamber there but that shrine isn't much more than a diplomatic outpost when it's said and done. They wanted to send the stuff to one of their bigger Constanta Hive foundries, but I didn't want them trotting out prerogatives again and keeping them. I don't think we're going to get the bionics back as it is.'

'We probably shouldn't push it. Give them an easy time on that, Ryo, just thank them for their help and express the hope that they find the bionics of interest. Frame it so that we're doing them a favour in return for the quick action in going over the body. Level Four delegation.' Dvorov drummed his fingers on the table. 'Ryo's right. Just thinking of the care that went into preparing this man for his mission, and into keeping us from tracking him, makes me queasy. Shira, if it had been any of the three of us we could have gone straight away to dossiers of enemies and with some ideas on what might have pushed someone to that much trouble. But you have been in the system for, what, two weeks? And Hydraphur itself for a matter of days.'

'Which I've spent here in the Wall,' Calpurnia said. 'Yesterday was almost literally my first taste of Hydraphur air. I've been over my movements time and again in my mind and I can't come up with a single thing that might have prompted something like this.'

'Then I trust your judgement,' Dvorov told her. 'We can't rule anything out, but for the present the idea of an opportunistic strike against our order in general should be our primary take. We can't treat this as purely a hive or a planetary matter, either. The Mass of Saint Balronas pulls in visitors from all over the system and a dozen I can think of from across the subsector. For all we know it could be some minerals baron from Stahl-Theta who's avenging an estate impoundment ordered by one of our colleagues four systems away. Just speculating, Shira, that's all.' He had spotted Calpurnia making a note. 'Word of this is already out. I've had a dozen requests for audiences from all kinds of parties wanting to know what's going on, or to put together some case or other to do with this. Kalfus-Medell is probably the most important of them so far but he's certainly not the only one.'

'We'll need to be inventive with this one, my colleagues.' Dvorov had finished the meeting by saying: 'I think we're all agreed that it's Shira's prerogative to command the investigations into her own attempted assassination. I don't need to tell you that you'll need to work closely with these two, Shira. I have the confidence in you that your reputation commands, but this won't exactly be a routine investigation.'

'Local knowledge, sir. I understand.' That was what she had said to him.

And she did understand. She was beginning to suspect that one of the truths of a career like hers was that you never did get used to the wandering from one world to another. From one place to another on the one planet was easy, and within a small realm was easy too: her parents had both had senior duties to the governance of Ultramar and she had travelled more than most before her induction into the Arbites. The training station at Machiun had been bearable because she had been there with seven hundred and ninety-nine other frightened inductees, but her first garrison post at Drade-73 had been much worse. She hadn't been able to get used to the smell, or the constant noise from the pumice floes that came washing down the canals, or the coarse local manners, or the continual grime of ash.

MG-Dyel, Hazhim, Don-Croix, Ephaeda. She was sure she had exhausted the court libraries in each one by the time she had been reposted, but she couldn't remember any treatises about that wrench that came from being dropped into an unfamiliar world where you couldn't take your most fundamental assumptions about things for granted. Perhaps one day she would write one herself.

And one thing she would be damned sure to put in a whole chapter on, she promised herself as she reached for the next slate, was culture shock. *It is a fact to which I would commend my reader's attention,* she wrote in her head, *that although the faith and dedication of the Adeptus Arbites is as steadfast as the Emperor's light itself, as you travel across all the Imperium's worlds you will find our order addressing its duties in ways unfamiliar to you and for this you must be prepared. I shall recite my own experiences in passing from Ephaeda to the world of Hydraphur...*

She made a face, tapped the new slate and watched the text swirl onto it, notes from her other two meetings of the day. Two names, of the double-barrelled sort the Hydraphur bluebloods seemed to like: Tymon-Per, Kalfus-Medell. One in charge of the disaster in the Adeptus plaza, the other the master of the great religious festival that was one of the major pivots for Hydraphur's year.

She tapped the entry for Tymon-Per and made a wry face when she saw she had left a blank area at the top of the note space to record the cell the interrogations would be conducted in.

'Culture shock,' she muttered again to herself. The 'interrogations' hadn't used a cell at all. She had followed Leandro to a gracious audience chamber where the young man she had expected to find in chains was sitting on a chaise and inhaling from a herbal steamer. Her first impulse had been to knock the cur's teeth out, then outrage had turned to bewilderment as Leandro had greeted the boy and she realised that this was not going to be like any interrogation she was used to.

Athian Tymon-Per had been the one behind the 'Adeptus' party-parade and it had been quickly obvious to both Arbites he had nothing much to tell them – every one of Calpurnia's notes was a negative. No, nobody had put him up to annexing the Adeptus plazas for his party. ('It was my idea, you see, the Adeptus theme hadn't been done for *years*, and I thought, well, it would be original, and daring, but festive, too, and it would be, well, you know, pleasingly, you know, *audacious*… don't you…' and he had wilted as they both simply stared at him.) No, nobody had approached him about the parade's timing or its route. No, nobody had told him there would be a senior arbitor moving through the Adeptus Quarter. No, he hadn't checked credentials; the partygoers hadn't been vetted except for someone's half-hearted attempt to make a list for a best-costume contest. No, he didn't know this was the very Arbitor Calpurnia at whom the attack had been directed. No, no, all no.

'No guilt, no help and no clue,' had been her whispered opinion after they had retired to confer.

'I agree, but the hour has not been wasted. The whole hive is always in a ferment at this time of the year, and there's usually a point where we have to put a stamp of authority on it. Word of this will be all over by the end of the day, and whatever its value to the investigation, the account of our giving a young noble such a sharp questioning will show people we mean what we say when we're enforcing the vigil curfew.' Calpurnia looked past him to where Athian was nervously picking his nose and wiping his finger clean on the underside of the chaise.

'Such a – with respect, Arbitor Leandro, I can't help thinking that the message this will send out is that we're treating the matter like a parlour game! If these people have forgotten that the reach of the Emperor's own Adeptus is absolute, then I believe that a roundup of all of those party attendees by Chastener squads would send the message much more effectively. How could it hurt to have so many potential troublemakers penned up for a few days? It would be the lesson that some of these people seem to need.' She was proud of the way she had kept her voice as low as Leandro's.

'The principle of your advice is perfectly sound, Arbitor Calpurnia,' he had replied mildly. 'As to its exact application, well, the affairs of Hydraphur are perhaps more complex and rarefied than that of your previous postings, the position of the Arbites more fraught and delicate. We calibrate our actions to our circumstances.' Seeing her expression, he added, 'And our actions here are quite sufficient. We already signalled our intentions when arbitrators broke up the last of that morass of unruliness that this young man thought he presided over, and we signal them afresh now. The elite of Hydraphur are accustomed to being invited to a diplomatic audience by an Arbites herald, with plenty of notice and due regard for their rank and with any questions we have couched in a dozen layers of protocol. This boy brought here and openly questioned, with none of their own retainers on hand, will have exactly the psychological impact of the roundup you proposed, without the side-effect of stirring up so much hostility to us among the nobility and other Adeptus that any traces of the attack upon you become impossibly kicked over.'

With that Leandro had given the signal for the doors to be opened. Three more young nobles hurried in to form a twittering clump around Athian, who shook in theatrical distress and whispered back at them until Leandro broke in.

'Your presence is no longer required by our investigation, my esteemed young man of Per. It is always hard to know, though, how the twists and turns of our duties may take us. You are to consider yourself available to us, in exactly the manner of today, until we advise you otherwise. For now, a respectful farewell.' The words seemed uncommonly mild to her, but it prompted a fresh wave of hissed conversation that only stopped when Calpurnia, unable to restrain herself, rapped on the side of the chaise with her maul.

'And before you leave, Tymon-Per, I will thank you to clean your snot out from under our furniture.'

All four stared at her, dumbstruck, until Athian finally realised she wasn't joking and bent down, kerchief in hand and white faced with outrage and humiliation. That, at least, had made her feel a little better.

Time and timing, she thought now as she reached for another file. It was supposed to have been slower than this. Dvorov's initial brief to her had been for a clean and orderly appointment period. Time to settle into her surroundings, completion of her medical fitout courtesy of Sanja, a week or so of familiarisation time until her formal appearance at the Mass marked her official commencement of duty, time to learn about Hydraphur and her new position. She snorted and flicked the new slate into life. Learn that suspects here were welcomed to courteous formal audiences and have their hands held while they are questioned. Hydraphur was going to take some getting used to.

Her notes from the second hearing of the day were cross-linked to one of the dossiers she had been issued when she had first arrived. The opening screen was taken up with titles and honorifics that would be meaningless to her until she had the chance to look them up – she suspected they wouldn't mean much even then. The name at the top of the page: Lord Hallyan Kalfus-Medell, ordained Master of the Vigil by the Eparch of Hydraphur.

She and Dvorov had met the lord in one of the formal galleries over the Justice Gate, two hours after Tymon-Per had been shooed away. He was no tenth-rate like Tymon-Per or Lady Keta, but as powerful a man as a civilian could be in the Navy-dominated Hydraphur system, and that was still powerful enough. That called for a different message and a little more ceremony: Dvorov was dressed in the antique, formal robe and high headdress of a Judge; he sat on a dais surrounded by a guard of junior praetors and heralds whose staves carried steel plaques engraved with teachings from the Commandments of Justice. Protocol allowed Calpurnia to stay with her simple black-and-grey arbitrator uniform, but she felt rather self-conscious in it now as she made her way to the side of the dais and saluted. Dvorov gave her a nod in return, and then two of the attendants swung the doors wide.

Hallyan Kalfus-Medell had come striding in straight away, a big man in the prime of middle age, only the first traces of fat about his waist and jaw and a profile like the prow-ram of one of the

Battlefleet Pacificus cruisers orbiting high over their heads. He bore straight down on the dais, all blue and purple silks and piercing voice.

'My Arbites! The earliest messages I received told me that the officer who had been the target of this atrocity had survived. Magnificent news, news to take the edge off the terrible reports that such an attack had even been made. I was en route from Constanta Hive when I heard and I came for an audience with you as soon as I was able. I am sorry it has taken so long for me to be able to meet you.'

We were the ones who granted audience to *you*, Calpurnia wanted to say. Kalfus-Medell had stopped with one foot actually up on the edge of their dais, but Dvorov seemed minded to let that slide.

'The attack was unsuccessful, my most respected Kalfus of Medell. Arbitor Senioris Calpurnia was slightly injured but is already recovered and has assumed her active duties, as you see.' Calpurnia nodded. She noticed a look of surprise in the noble's expression: she realised he had seen her duty uniform and taken her for one of Dvorov's guards. The look turned into one of appraisal. Hallyan's eyes were deep-set and sharp, and as they sized her up they confirmed the impression Calpurnia had already brought away from his file. Kalfus-Medell might be pompous, but he wasn't stupid.

'Arbitor senioris.' He bowed. 'Allow me to express my relief. I was not associated with that... disturbance that coincided with the attack, but as the Master of the Vigil for all of Bosporian Hive I felt responsible for the injury you suffered.'

'I appreciate your concern, sir, but the injuries were minor and fleeting. The would-be assassin is dead by my hand and we are following his trail. Whoever is behind the attack will be brought down, I assure you, and the Arbites will not stand for any further "disturbances".'

'I had noticed the change as I made my way here,' Hallyan said as Dvorov stepped down off the dais. Somewhat surprised, Calpurnia followed a step behind as they strolled back toward the doors. 'There was an Arbites checkpoint at every entrance to the Augustaeum and squads on every street. I trust that this has not damaged your ability to control the rest of the hive and around the Cathedral itself?'

'The specifics of our operations must of necessity remain an Arbites matter, my trusted ambassador of Medell,' Dvorov replied as the two men made a slight turn away from the doors. Calpurnia spun and quickstepped to catch up. 'But I would take no action that would threaten our ability to defend the Emperor's order and the holy Mass. Arbitor Senioris Nakayama is personally overseeing the locking down of controls over Bosporian and his skills at that kind of operation are superb. Delegations have been issued for heightened vigilance in all parts of the system under Arbites jurisdiction. And far from being slowed by her injuries, Arbitor Calpurnia has taken up active duty a week early to command the hunt for those who orchestrated the attack. She is new to our system and its ways, but her record and reputation are of the first order and she will have the support of myself and Arbitor Leandro. I do not expect the hunt to take long, respected Kalfus of Medell.'

They had slowed to a quarter-pace. Hallyan gave her another sharp stare.

'Good news builds on good news, then. You are alive, my admired arbitor, and not only that but you are healthy, and not only that but you are pursuing your enemy with a dedication I can only commend.' He and Dvorov turned to stroll at another angle and Calpurnia, disoriented, turned once more to keep step with them.

'It is a point I hesitate to bring up, esteemed young arbitor,' said Hallyan, 'but my current responsibilities weigh my shoulders and require it.' He paused to allow Calpurnia to answer, and when she simply looked at him he frowned and went on. 'Despite the impression you may quite understandably have gained during your short time here, the time approaching the Mass of Saint Balronas and the Sanguinala is a time of sacred significance. Now, it is my understanding that the Judges of the Adeptus may pursue their quarry in ways that, how shall I say it...'

'I think I understand where you're taking this, Lord Kalfus-Medell. I know that I'm brand-new to the system, and that I'm ignorant of a lot of local protocol. I'm sure I've made a dozen minor gaffes simply in the time I've spoken to you.' She noticed a flicker of placated smugness in his expression before he caught it and erased it. 'But I know that you will overlook them just as I will do my best to track down the assassins without disorder profaning the festival. We have the same objective, sir. The celebration of our devotion to the Emperor and the destruction of any threat to His orderly and united domains. Where is there room to disagree?' He smiled at that, and Calpurnia relaxed a little.

'I am almost ashamed to admit I had concerns, my much-distinguished arbitor,' he said. 'But I am delighted at the chance to enjoy your most eminent company, even for so brief a time as the pressure of both our duties allows us. You have set me at ease that nothing will further trouble us – should unrest and disquiet be kept down I guarantee the Sanguinala will welcome you to your new home with the most glorious ceremony you will have seen!'

He was turning to exit the room; Dvorov remained where he was and gave a miniscule tip of his head for Calpurnia to follow. The etiquette was familiar to her, an important guest being escorted away to blunt any feelings of dismissal, and she walked beside Lord Hallyan out past the double-file of uniformed guards, saw what was waiting for them in the hall and stopped dead, her hand darting toward her gun. She only stopped the move when Hallyan calmly walked over to the monstrosity that towered among shafts of thick yellow daylight from the high windows.

The bodyguard servitor stood a head taller than Hallyan; Calpurnia, helmet and all, would barely have come up to the family crest embossed on its chest-plate. Between the augmetic plates and cables its flesh had the sickly, slablike cast of muscles grown in a vat and maintained by gene and hormone commands rather than exercise and use. Clone-grown skin and filigreed armour shone slick with ornamental perfume-oil, but as Calpurnia reluctantly drew closer she realised that underneath the spicy scent it had the same smell that almost all servitors had, the smell of a fresh-cleaned hospital corridor, antiseptic but somehow still faintly sickening. The vision slot in its extravagantly-worked gold visor was shadowed and there was no way to tell where it was looking.

Hallyan was watching her staring at it, again with that faintly smug expression. No more words passed between them: he spoke a short, stuttering phrase and the servitor pivoted and shuffled after him. Its feet were padded in soft synthetic wads, and the only sound as it fell in behind its master, blotting him from her sight, was a soft soughing sound like the brush of robes against a floor.

Calpurnia barely realised the effect the sight of the thing had had on her until she realised minutes later that her jaw ached from clenching.

Looks like mainly hitter not shooter, read her notes now. *Multiple combat adaptations, heavy duty augmetic claw, bladed dendrite bundles in carapace? Some shooting ability, probably masked/disabled for access to us to be allowed. Voice-only trigger odd – weakness – follow up.*

'Follow up,' she said aloud, dropped the slate onto the carpet and stood up with a groan. The rough knot of scar tissue that twisted the skin of her right hip was stiff and twinging, the way it always got when she was tired, or cold, or had sat still for too long. She worked her leg to loosen it as she paced to the chillplate by the door and poured water from the decanter sitting on it.

As she stood there she could feel the faint prickle at the back of her neck from the energy shields on the other side of the window. Having all Bosporian see an arbitor senioris driven into hiding would be disastrous, so armoured shutters had been out of the question, despite Armourer Thekir's pleas. In truth, she was still a little overwhelmed by having an energy curtain brought to her chambers – before Hydraphur she had seen a void shield exactly once, during a putsch on Don-Croix when elite enforcer squads had come out with the pick of their arsenal to seal the streets to the Capitol Mount. But she still wouldn't feel entirely comfortable turning her back on the window until the initiator of the attacks had been caught.

The initiator. She hated that. The initiator, the organiser, the mastermind. Clumsy to say and frustrating to think about, but Dvorov had been right. They weren't close to being able to put a name to the corpse lying in Sanja's shrine. She still hadn't been able to pick out anything she had done that might spark such an assault and Leandro, their expert in politics and diplomacy, couldn't map out any current power-plays that might benefit from her death. Not that the current state of hive society was easy to read, the time of year being what it was. In the pile of printout next to her were sheaves of report summaries from precinct houses all through the hive and the great city-sprawl that spread out from it to the coast, and fuller reports from the Augustaeum, the enclosed and luxurious city-within-a-city at the peak of Bosporian Hive. The picture they added up to had made her dizzy and despairing of carrying out any kind of orderly investigation. She picked up a handful at random, glancing occasionally at the maps she had draped over the far arm of the couch.

The precinct commander at the Vastener's Spur over in the Nobles Quarter reported a spat between two cartel families from the mill-hives on the far coast over accommodation precedence in the tower they had co-rented for their stay. The dispute had mainly been in the form of intricate snubs that none of the Arbites on-site pretended to understand, but the previous afternoon two young bloods had convinced themselves each had been offended by the other and insisted on holding a formal duel, arriving outside the precinct house with supporters from each family in tow and clamouring for a judge to give the whole thing legal sanction. When the Arbites had refused, both families had taken insult and now had the idea that they could appeal to have the precinct commander's authority revoked.

The family Rhyos-Kauteer had kicked off the social season with a betrothal ceremony of one of its sons to a popular daughter of a highly-thought-of naval dynasty. The young man had taken his new fiancée on a tour of their fyceline foundry at the base of the hive, and when someone impressionable had seen her uniform word had started that a navy press-gang sweep was about to come down. The resulting stampede out of the sector had triggered riots along two major arterial roads, and suppression squads of Arbites arriving to restore order had only reinforced the rumour. The local commanders were counting themselves lucky to have had the area under control within the day, and the hunt for the last of the rioters and looters in the maze of underground freightways and canals was only just gearing up.

There had even been a disturbance involving the Cathedral of the Emperor Ascendant itself. A granddaughter of the Rogue Trader Rannyer Kvan had apparently had a religious awakening and taken vows as a novice in the Order of the Sacred Rose. The first that Kvan had heard of it was when he arrived back in the system for the Mass after a four-year absence, and he had shown up at the Cathedral insisting that the girl was being held against her will and demanding that the sisters give his child back. Now Kvan kept trying to park an air-sled over the Cathedral in defiance of airspace laws and Canoness Theoctista was adamant that they would not, as a matter of principle, let Kvan disrupt the girl's religious duties with even a visit.

Those were just three that had been thought worth bringing to an arbitor senioris. There would be more mundane plots and feuds, petty violence or sedition that the Judges at each fortified precinct courthouse would handle themselves, and the cases that would not even reach the courthouses, the lowest of crimes: defacement of Imperial property, malingering, drunkenness, public affray, killings or injuries among the giant hab-stacks where arbitrator patrols rarely ventured and used the simplest summary street punishments when they did. Conspirators here simply wouldn't stand out as they would on prosperous, pious Ephaeda.

She was starting to understand how hard this was going to be. In his treatise, Galimet had concentrated on the ecclesiastical proceedings and touched on their history: how the people of Hydraphur had lived with years of shame at their system's surrender to the Apostate Cardinal, how Chye Balronas, returning to his home system as Pontifex Mundi after twenty years on Earth, had instituted an annual vigil of fasting and penitence to bring the whole system together in atonement and spiritual cleansing, and how the Vigil culminated in a mass on the eve of the great festivities of the Sanguinala, when the citizens cast off their long fast and ended their penance in joyful celebration of the Lord Angel.

Galimet had recorded in his treatise that it was the custom for the greatest and wealthiest of Hydraphur to assemble for the Mass at the capital hive's great cathedral, and she remembered thinking that this was only as it should be and moving on. As an arbitor, she decided, she should have known enough to deduce what that would actually mean. The month before the Mass saw the place packed with dignitaries: every branch of the Adeptus, Rogue Traders and powerful merchants, officers from the powerful naval dynasties with their spaceborne estates and fief-fleets.

And so naturally, the religious gathering had found other purposes. She had already had an instructive example of how the month leading up to the mass had become a frenzy – a courtly, mannered and impeccably-choreographed frenzy, a frenzy cloaked in so many layers of protocol it was impenetrable even to half of the natives, but frenzy nonetheless as the system's elite packed a year's worth of high-octane intrigues into three or four weeks. Families controlling wealth equivalent to a whole planet's production would haggle and trade favours for the tiniest change in positions at one of the Kathisma's banquets; the right turn of conversation on a morning's stroll might mean an alliance that could make or destroy lives. At the other end of the scale there was the sort of half-spontaneous drunken free-for-all that she had found herself caught up in the previous day. Someone who might want to take advantage of all the confusion to murder an arbitor? Calpurnia gulped water and sighed again. Who knew how many strangers were out there, or what they were thinking or hiding? Guilliman's blood, how would you narrow it down to even a thousand?

She prowled to the window again, ignored the buzzing that the power field made at the base of her skull as she looked out. Her chambers faced away from the Cathedral and out over the slope of the hive as it dropped to the great flat city-plain. She was not new to the great artificial hives that Imperial worlds sprouted when their cities grew too big and concentrated for a simple conurbation to contain. There were no hives on Ultramar, but two had grown up around the orbital freight-launcher silos on Hazhim, and Don-Croix's position astride three well-travelled warp currents had given it a population that had cultivated a respectable twelve hives, jutting up from its ravine-cut surface like tumours.

Bosporian was a modest little affair against the mind-numbing scale of hives on Necromunda or Vanaheim. In fact, technically, it was barely a hive at all, more a place where the sprawl that had paved over the entire alluvial plain below had reached a spur of the mountain range edging it and crawled up its slopes. Bosporian was on bedrock, not artificial, hollow and packed with people as a true hive was. But the view was still impressive enough – a great jungle of spires and towers curved away down the mountain-slope and out into the murkier, more humble city below.

Dropping away directly below Calpurnia's window was the Wall, tall and wide and with enough room in its towers and bastions to house a city and hold off an army on its own. It joined the Augustaeum wall at the towering Justice Gate, swelled into the imposing fortifications that housed the commanders' homes and chambers and the supreme courthouses, then ran down into the thirty-floor-high ridge of rockcrete and adamantium, sprouting towers that were entire precinct fortresses unto themselves, running all the way down to the foot of the hive to one last monolithic keep and gate.

The Wall held trial chambers, interrogation rooms, execution and penance cells, armouries, barracks, training halls, chapels, transmitter towers, generatoria, hangars full of Rhino APCs and Repressor riot-tanks, libraries of paper books and data-arks so vast that searching for a single old record might be a life's work. Around each gate glimmered the camp-lights where supplicants waited weeks or months or years, however long it took for the wheels of the Adeptus Arbites to grind out a judgement or pass on word of the fate of a loved one held in their walls. Breaking up queue wars was a regular feature of gate duties in any precinct house of this size. Calpurnia had even known Arbites who had been born and lived the first few years of their lives outside the gates of the courthouses they grew up to serve in. In most garrisons they were considered good luck to have on a squad.

Just learning her way around the Justice Gate and the upper towers would take Calpurnia a month or more. But learn it she would, she thought, some of her gloom lifting. She had been through this before. However alien Hydraphur felt now, soon place-names would take on meaning. People would stop being faces she passed and names she had to be reminded of. She would start to know who was meticulous and who was slapdash, who could take a broad perspective and who would get lost in details. She would know who backslid in upholding the sacred *Lex Imperia*, and at the other extreme who hid their own deficient judgement behind paralysing dependence on the letter of scripture. She would know the ones who were devout and truly understood the doctrines they practised, and the ones for whom 'for the Emperor' was nothing more than an empty phrase to shout before they swung a power-maul down on some random innocent's skull. She had worked with all those kinds and more and she had done well. The Provost's Wreath and three commendation seals hung on the wall behind her to prove it. She would do well here too.

She turned around and leaned against her chamber wall, rubbed the scars on her forehead as she looked around. The Master of Households and his stewards had thought the plainness of her quarters inappropriate for one of her station, but she had wanted at least something about her surroundings to be familiar and chosen small, spare rooms instead of the richly-appointed fortified tower that her predecessor had lived in. Three rooms, her bed, her books, a small shrine to the Emperor and an icon to Guilliman, a bust of Judge Traggat in a niche over the writing-desk, a clothes-chest and a small personal armoury. The walls were unadorned dark stone, and she relished the coolness and solidity of it through her tunic as she leaned against it – it reminded her of her room in the Ephaeda court barracks.

She had scandalised people there, too, by keeping that little room even after she had been given the garrison command. She had often held command meetings there, sitting on the bed or crosslegged on the stone floor, trying to drive home a lesson by example: their duty was to the Emperor's law and the Emperor's peace, not the worship of their own importance for its own sake. Although, she noted now with a rueful smile, there she hadn't been in the habit of leaving piles of slates and printouts scattered across half the floor. For a moment she thought about leaving that for the stewards too, and then gave herself a mental kick for her laziness. It took another half hour to get them gathered up and filed in order in the racks on her desk, and by that time her eyes were aching with tiredness and the old wound on her hip was throbbing again. Her single short prayer at the shrine was for rest and calm – she already had an idea that tomorrow was going to be exhausting.

Eighth Day of Septista

Ten days to the Mass of Saint Balronas.
The Second Congregation of Intercessors.
Vigil of the Icons Illuminate. First hearing of the Assembly Encarmine (Navy).

This day mirrors the previous one, for it is traditional, after prayers and petitions to the Ministorum are completed, to devote this day to pleading favour with peers and fellows. On this day masters, friends and the officers in the Monocrat's service and that of the blessed Adeptus are expected to look kindly on pleas for favour or intercession in return for prayers and gratitude. Those seeking such favour will usually signal this by blowing a small brass horn at the gate or door of the one from whom they wish it, but to arrange audience in advance is also acceptable. However, no part of the proceedings of the Minor Intercessors must be allowed to interfere with any penance or devotions instructed by the officers of the Adeptus Ministorum the previous day. Those assigned particular duties of worship will be undertaking them at Ecclesiarchal temples and pulpits and it is appropriate for passersby to stop and pray aloud for them.

During this day portraits, icons and statues for the Procession of Further Saints are carried from the Artisans Quarter and arrayed for viewing along the road beneath the south-west face of the Cathedral. When considering whether to travel to see them it should be remembered that the Further Saints are those who spent their lives not only outside Hydraphur but beyond the Segmentum Pacificus, and that this is an opportunity to pay respect and devotion to hallowed servants of the Emperor that may not present themselves at other times. On the road itself anyone holding a certain personage as their patron is free to tend that likeness, keeping lanterns and candles lit through the night, praying and reading aloud the relevant scriptures. It is also customary and appropriate to hand out prayer cards and tracts; the practice of handing out confectionery, sweetmeats and baubles and not to be encouraged.

On this day dignitaries of all the Navy squadrons currently at dock in the system assemble at the space-station known as the Boucoleon Gate to conduct a ceremonial settling of debts, traditionally with the conferring and exchange of honours and the fighting of ceremonial duels. Dealings with Naval officers on Hydraphur itself on this day should be conducted with tact and an awareness of any special circumstances that these ceremonies might create.

Those selected to perform devotions at the Sainted Way the following day should fast from the fifteenth hour, and perform the Maklopin's Second Prayer before leaving their home to travel to the Sepulchre.

CHAPTER THREE

'I JUST WANT you to run me through this walking thing again,' Calpurnia said.

The Augustaeum, nestled within its walls at the peak of the Bosporian Hive, was not flat – its sides kept sloping up to the High Mesé, the avenue that ran along the hive's very peak. The formation of Arbites making their way through the steep, tangled streets of the Artisans Quarter were already high enough up to be able to look over the Augustaeum wall and down at the upper floors of the towers on the lower slopes of the hive. Above them on the left the Cathedral of the Emperor Ascendant speared the coppery Hydraphur sky. Its spire was twenty minutes' walk away and already Calpurnia had to crane her head up to look at it; they were getting close enough for her to be able to see the great statues of the Imperial saints that formed the columns for its upper tiers. Each statue was fifty metres high and carved from pure white marble that shone like gold in the thick butter-yellow Hydraphur sunlight.

Calpurnia and Leandro moved through the narrow byways between the flat-roofed workshop blocks, clustered between the gracious Adeptus Quarter behind them and the pilgrims' barracks ahead. Men and women bustled around them in sober grey and brown garb, many with the aquamarine trim of guild-sponsored artisans, nearly all sporting polished brass augmetics for their chosen trade over eyes or hands. Calpurnia had been looking about for any trace of the religious tokens that were supposed to be set out throughout the quarter but the pilgrims had apparently taken the last of them, leaving only the occasional empty shelf or trestle in the street or against a workshop front. The tinny blare of a ceremonial horn made her jump.

'A custom among the aristocracy,' Leandro told her, sauntering along with his crested judicial helm under one arm and the staff in his other hand swinging and rapping against the cobbles. 'The evolution of a lot of the elites' etiquette and social codes has been documented by Dervick and Ponn, three volumes between them which, despite their last revision being over fifteen years ago, have not dated significantly. It seems the custom evolves from a period when...' He caught Calpurnia's look. 'Ah, well then. To summarise. Less than crucial business on Hydraphur is often conducted strolling through the hall, or gardens, or wheresoever, and subtle changes in direction and pace send certain messages. Moving toward an exit shows the matter is unimportant, the caller inferior. Moving toward seats shows the matter is difficult and intricate, or possibly an advance of friendship, it depends on the context and certain other actions. Pausing before or moving towards a work of art means that a trusted working relationship – not necessarily friendship, you understand – is assumed by the speaking party, although again that can draw all kinds of nuances from the kind of decoration, what is being said, and touches of intonation and body language, all of which make up another layer by which the signals from movement can be reinterpreted.'

'I'm "less than crucial business", am I?' The words had come out sharper than Calpurnia had intended them to.

'Not for a moment, arbitor, you know that. But think like a Hydraphur noble. You rush to talk with Arbites who have just been targeted by assassins, at a sensitive time of great importance to your future. How will they soothe the fears crowding your heated imagination if, for all their airy words that the matter is being attended to, they sit you at a conference table as though discussing a matter of gravest import? As well, try to convince your good self, my arbitor, that an action alarm in the Wall is of no real consequence even while you watch arbitrator squads in full combat gear arming and singing a battle-psalm. The Arbitor Majore simply underlined his assurances.'

'I take it local etiquette is something I'm going to take a while in picking up,' said Calpurnia. Leandro's answering smile had a hint of pity in it.

'My arbitor senioris, "a while" is exactly what it will take you. I spent nearly all of my serving life on Hydraphur, and you will have noticed that the lord marshal tends to bring me to the fore when a situation calls for diplomacy rather than force. And nonetheless I know that I am considered comically flawed and flatfooted on matters of etiquette and manners. I assure you that I have to use the force of my rank to compensate for my social clumsiness in more circumstances than you might credit.'

'My own feelings, Arbitor Leandro, are that the force of our Emperor-given rank is all we should ever need and all the reason to respect us that these people should require. I'm not some thug who looks on cracking bones as her first recourse. I do, though, wonder at the effort we seem to expend courting the favour of people whose deference should be a matter of law. But,' she held up a hand as Leandro started to speak, 'we've already had that conversation. Let's drop it.'

It had been Calpurnia's idea to travel on foot, for the same reason she had refused to have the window to her chambers sealed: to show that this new arbitor would not be chased into a bunker. But now she found herself trying to scan every angle of the crowd at once, looking for a movement that seemed out of place or the glint of weapons, trying to maintain a befitting dignity all the while. She had allowed Leandro to talk her into bringing a small escort – a file of five arbitrators on each side and a proctor marching before them parting the crowds – but she was still tense.

The streets met at intersections that were almost ledges cut in and then built out from the face of the slope: this was one of the steepest faces of the hive, and the traffic around them was made up of pedestrians or little tracked pack-gurneys that clattered along cleated rails in the middle of each road. They stopped at an intersection and took stock: an Arbites checkpoint occupied the central rockcrete island, where a belt-fed heavy stubber nosed the air and cyber-mastiff handlers flanked it, ready to move under the stubber's support. Knots of arbitrators stood at each road surveying the traffic and stopping random travellers for papers and questioning. The setup was repeated at every junction they had passed since leaving the Justice Gate, and on every thoroughfare and public space across the hive, and Calpurnia was pleased with what she had seen so far. Arbitor Nakayama's lockdown had been quick and expert. The duty squads saluted the two seniores and went rather self-consciously back to their work as Calpurnia and Leandro moved on.

'This might be an easier subject of conversation,' Calpurnia said eventually. 'Why is it so important for Lord Hallyan's family that there not be any disturbances during this mass? I won't pretend to have had time to read every one of my dossiers thoroughly, but I couldn't find anything in the man's history that explained why he's suddenly turned up in association with it this year. Not that a concern for proper order is not fitting in a subject of the Emperor,' she added conscientiously.

'Ah, you must build the bridge from both sides of the river, as they say in Constanta,' said Leandro with a smile. 'The key to that is in the organisation of the mass itself rather than a characteristic of the man. You shall need to broaden your studies a little, I think. Were you provided with a briefing slate on the mass itself? I'm sure we've discussed it in the broad outline.'

'Let us just assume, Arbitor Leandro, that perhaps I still have some gaps in my reading owing to recent attempts on my life,' said Calpurnia, nettled. 'What would I be looking for in my file on the mass should I have time to study it tonight?'

'The mass, then.' replied Leandro cheerfully, not ruffled in the slightest. 'It was instituted by Saint Chye Balronas twelve years after Hydraphur was reclaimed from the Plague of Unbelief. It... ah, you know this part? Excellent. Well, as part of its role in reuniting the system in faith to the Emperor, the Sainted Pontifex decreed that it would not belong to any one part of Hydraphur society. It was important that people not dismiss it as simply another piece of high-flown pageantry in a place few of them would ever visit. So he decreed that the Vigil would not be the sole property of the Ecclesiarchy, and that not a single part of Hydraphur's society would be without a share in it. While the Adeptus Ministorum will always officiate at the mass and all the formal rites, the Vigil itself and many of the Sanguinala festivities will be planned and overseen by the designated Master of the Vigil, who is outside the Ecclesiarchy completely. The orders of precedence by which the office is conferred from year to year is a matter of what I would understate to call some complexity, although we have a small office dedicated to tracking and monitoring it and reporting to myself – it is unusual but not unknown for criminal techniques to be used to attempt to push the revered Ministorum's choice in one direction or another.'

There was an abrupt burst of shouting at the top of the street they were walking up, and Calpurnia stiffened and put a hand on her pistol. A pair of heavyset greybeards with glossy aqua-dyed sashes were arguing with the arbitrators, apparently over the street being blocked off while she and Leandro came up it. The arbitrators around them shifted into a wedge formation, the better to keep the two commanders protected, but then one man at the top of the street took his arguments a step too far and the Arbites were onto him. Two of them bent his knees with deft taps of their mauls and slammed him to the ground, and two more kicked over the platform and began breaking the packages open. Calpurnia and Leandro paused where they were and Leandro continued talking.

'The designated Master of the Vigil has some latitude in the festivities, the chance to place their own stamp on them in certain ways. Accordingly, no two years' festivities are quite the same, since it's a point of some disgrace to present a bad one or one too like another year's. It's also the high point of the Hydraphur's year after Candlemas, so you can understand why competition for the honour is rather heated.'

'I'm starting to understand why Lord Medell is anxious that nothing goes wrong,' said Calpurnia. 'So, the Medell are presiding over the Vigil this year…'

'*Kalfus*-Medell. Kalfus is the family, Medell is the syndicate affiliation.'

'Kalfus-Medell, all right. Hallyan's dossier said he was in something of an awkward position in the family: late child, caught between generations with no natural peer base. Being appointed Master of the Vigil must be an enormous coup for him.'

'And for his family, not that they need it. Kalfus-Medell is one of the most powerful family syndicate combines in the system.'

They began walking again. Calpurnia felt vaguely uneasy as their escorts ranged ahead: she had not had the time to speak with any of them, and she was used to knowing the names of her squads. Up in the square the two men had already been locked into heavy strait-capes that covered their heads and pinned their arms to their waists, and were being dragged away. Four other arrestees, two men and two women, had been cuffed into a line and, silent and quaking, followed at shotgun point – they wore tunics and caps of a similar cut but without the sashes, and Calpurnia realised they must have been servants or retainers of the shouting pair.

She turned an eye to the baggage strewn across the cobbles. The bundles had been kicked open, and a young arbitrator was marking them with green paint to show a poison-snooper had cleared them. Most of the plastic sacks had held glistening grey-brown lumps that reminded Calpurnia of melting candy-eggs. One or two held bright metal shavings or what looked like mineral salts. She swung around on the arbitrator who had moved up behind her.

'Summarise the problem, please.'

'Those two men are from a fabricators' collective quartered down against the Augustaeum wall. I'm not sure of their exact line of work, but I think they were hurrying to–'

'Summarise the *problem*, please,' Calpurnia repeated. The man swallowed. She wondered if he'd addressed an arbitor senioris before, let alone two of them standing shoulder to shoulder.

'Yes, ma'am. These men protested our closure of the street and demanded passage. They would not stand away when ordered or move their possessions. Er, their baggage. Ma'am.'

'You saw us coming up the street. You realise that any number of assassination devices could be loaded onto one of these gurneys and rolled down to us.'

'Yes, ma'am.'

'Nonetheless, you allowed it to be brought to the head of the street in control of its owners, where we would have to walk past it, instead of halting it or ordering it diverted elsewhere.' There was a pause.

'Yes, ma'am.'

'You are?'

'Lead Arbitor Madulla, ma'am. Green-Four Echelon, Holdark Precinct House.'

'Thank you, Lead Arbitor. Tighten and improve your efforts, please. You may continue.'

Flushing, Madulla supervised as the two prisoners were stowed on the Rhino, the rings on the backs of the strait-capes clipped to the hooks on the tank's chassis, their feet dangling off the ground. It was a way of transporting and displaying prisoners Calpurnia had not seen before coming to Hydraphur. The servants sat in a miserable knot at gunpoint a few metres away, and what little foot traffic was left in the intersection scurried and shied away from the Arbites. Calpurnia nodded approvingly. It was always useful to drive a lesson home.

'And am I guessing that if anything disrupts the Vigil while Hallyan is charged with presiding, he will be badly disgraced and that will ripple on to his family and his syndicate?' she asked as they began walking again. 'And do I further suppose that the assassination of a senior Arbites officer might be a good way to stir up trouble which popular opinion might hold against him, however illogically?'

'Well done, my arbitor senioris! You're starting to think like a local.' Calpurnia growled and smacked a gloved palm against her forehead.

'Agh, I hope not. These people are insane! They celebrate a Vigil dedicated to penance by drowning themselves in parties and politics, they treat a sacred mass like just another carnival-spectacle and they interpret your whole conversation by whether you take a few steps while you talk! I don't think I was ready for this place, Nestor.' She regretted the last part the moment it had passed her lips.

'Lord Marshal Dvorov thinks you are, my senioris,' Leandro told her as they began to climb the next street. 'And believe me, the lord marshal knows what he's doing.'

Calpurnia threw a last glance at the junction behind her and followed him.

Two more intersections, then a final stretch where the street got steep enough to become stairs. They ascended past etched slabs of iron between friezes of famous and long-dead Hydraphur artisans on their left; on the right, a six-metre gap between them and the walls of the craft-houses, then their roofs, then just empty air. Calpurnia spent the climb thinking of the target she made up here and kicking herself for thinking that the bravado of coming out on foot was a good idea. Amateurish, she told herself, a rookie's mistake, a child's mistake. She took her mind off it by concentrating on Leandro's talk of the Artisans Quarter, which had its privileged place in the Augustaeum through the patronage of the Cathedral and the devotional materials and religious art it made, which was bought by connoisseurs and the devout throughout the subsector. The cargo that the luckless arrestees somewhere below them had been carrying were phyo shells, resinous cocoons of a coastal amphibian whose caustic juices produced a prized burnished effect when applied properly to soft metals. The shavings and salts had probably been to refine the colour and exact tone of the polish and reflection, Leandro had explained as Calpurnia, nodding grimly, put one foot in front of the other and tried to keep her eyes away from the drop on her right.

The stairs switched back and climbed through a tiered series of landings to a broad stretch of paving beneath a thick obelisk, then suddenly they were among people again and on blessedly flat ground. Their escorts spread out as they walked past the obelisk and onto the High Mesé.

This was the high crest of Bosporian Hive, the paved avenue that ran from the gates of the Monocrat's palace at the eastern end across to the Cathedral at the west. It jutted up from the jungle of buildings around it like an axe-edge – or like a chainblade, Calpurnia corrected herself, looking at the pairs of obelisks that marked off the space along its edges. Up here she could look out over the whole sweep of the capital: the towers and roofs of Bosporian, the carpet of industrial city that covered the plain, the mountains behind the Cathedral and the vast ochre sweep of the sky. Even in the daylight, she could look up and see that sky sparkling with the crisscrossing lights of the ships and the great Ring of Hydraphur.

No more earnestly purposeful artisans or pack-carriers here. Up on the high walk Hydraphur's elite promenaded in the early afternoon sun, striking elegant poses, chattering quietly behind copper-lace fans, bowing and flirting, or gazing out to the smog-smudged horizon. There were fewer people here, less hurry and more room between the little groups, but the richness of their clothes and movements still made them seem kaleidoscopic. The dour troop of Arbites marched through them like a black beetle among butterflies.

It didn't take Calpurnia long to start noticing patterns. A common style of skirt and shawl here, a gesture repeated there. She noted and filed away a certain kind of deeper bow that seemed to go with greeting someone dressed in a certain cut of coat, and a particular pattern of jewellery that seemed unique to people accompanying the Navy officers in their elaborate green dress uniforms. (Those at least she had expected to draw comfort from, knowing Navy traditions from senior members of her own family, but Battlefleet Pacificus dress used far more lavish and complex insignia than Battlefleet Ultima and medals she didn't even recognise.) Some were more extravagant: she saw skins that had been inlaid with gems or shimmering electoos, and twice their paths were crossed by packs of young bloods who strutted on shoes soled in stilt-like curls of metal that gave them a springy, prancing, jaunty gait.

She could spot particular rituals in the way certain groups greeted others, or ignored them, or changed their positions to keep certain relative distances. She was sure it was all part of some eye-watering social clockwork which she decided she had no interest at all in learning – until she noticed the subtle little dance seemed to extend to the Arbites too. Every so often one of the strolling groups would turn and salute them, or allow themselves to linger in the way so they could make a show of bustling to make way. After the fourth such encounter, as a group of middle-aged men in particoloured cloaks made into swirling wings by implanted memory-wires extravagantly waved them past, Leandro confirmed her suspicion.

'Word, it seems, has spread outwards and upwards about you, my Arbitor Calpurnia.' Ahead of them, a young nobleman in a green bodyglove and white fur cape waved his entourage – three shrouded servitors and a maid carrying a blue candle in her cupped hands – to a halt and took a showy step out of their path.

'I was going to ask what you mean, but I have the unpleasant feeling that I already know.'

'Would it surprise you, my Calpurnia of Ultramar, to know that the blow you landed on a certain youthful scion – or is "scionette" a proper word? – has done something of a round in the more rarefied levels of the Bosporian Hive?' Calpurnia looked around her. Every pair of eyes she met seemed to have the same appraising look that Hallyan had given her the previous day. Or perhaps she was imagining it.

'Not particularly, I suppose. I'm mildly surprised at such consternation for such a whatever-you-called-her.'

'"Shallow, disposable flibbertigibbet", I believe my words were, for the benefit of any eavescopes that might be trained on us,' said Leandro, and Calpurnia stifled a smile. 'They're a contrary breed, my arbitor, ready to invest a sincerely staggering quantity of energy in undoing each other in the most unscrupulous of ways, but still ready to form a seamless front if they feel one of their own has been slighted.' He considered for a moment. 'In point of fact, I may exaggerate. There is every possibility that the reaction to you is simple wariness. You are a senior officer of the Adeptus, arrived to a position of power and authority here. You agreed yesterday that you have been here barely any time and had no contact with Hydraphur society at all. Thus, many here will be setting eyes for the first time on an unknown and potentially important new player. They may simply wish to see what you're about.'

Calpurnia grimaced.

'A player. That's what I am to them, am I? She tapped the medal ribbons on her chest and the helmet over her scarred forehead. 'I got these at play, I suppose?'

'Their point of view, nothing more.' Leandro was as unfazed as before. 'Well?' he said then, pointing forward and upward with his staff, 'what do you think?'

They had arrived.

Before them was the great ramp to the Cathedral doors. It was the same grey stone as the paving they stood on, but carved into polished frescoes of the deeds of Ecclesiarchal heroes: Uriah Jacobus crushing the genestealers on Solstice, Master Reynard leading the Travian Fire-raising, others that Calpurnia didn't recognise. The carvings looked too precious to walk on and gave Calpurnia a moment or two of hesitation, but their proctor was leading the way up the ramp with barely a break and so she mentally shrugged and followed him, trying not to tread any saints underfoot. Slippery-polished as it looked, the footing was not hard. She peered up at the sheer face of the Cathedral front as it shot up into the clouds, and regretted it: the wall here began at the ramp and rose straight to the very peak of the spire, and looking up at all that carved stone looming over her gave Calpurnia a sort of inverted vertigo.

The arched Cathedral doors tapered to a point fifteen metres high rather than following the smoother curves that Ultramar builders favoured. Calpurnia supposed that there were blast-shutters and defence gates – the Adeptus Ministorum was a warrior church and its sacred buildings were supposed to be military strongpoints – but they seemed to be retracted and sealed and they stood before an open arch.

The arbitrators around them stood to attention, and the proctor rapped his staff on the stone three times.

'The Honourable Nestor Leandro, Praetor and Arbitor Senioris of the High Precinct of Hydraphur, and the Honourable Shira Calpurnia, Arbitrator and Arbitor Senioris of the High Precinct of Hydraphur.'

He was speaking to the armoured forms that stood in a line to block off the arch. These were warriors of the Cathedral's guard, Adepta Sororitas, battle sisters of the Order of the Sacred Rose, stern and proud in sleek white power-armour and black surcoats, gold-embroidered with the fleur-de-lys of the Ecclesiarchy. Their bolters were trained on the Arbites, as unwavering as their gaze, until a hooded sister superior stepped through the line of her squad and gestured for them to put up their weapons. They came to attention with a crash that echoed through the Cathedral's outer vestibule and parted, ceramite boots stamping on the stone as they wheeled and came to attention again. The sister superior clasped the golden aquila at her throat and bowed, gestured behind her to the junior deacon who had appeared at the great doors, and stepped aside into formation with her sisters. Calpurnia and Leandro walked past the sisters and into the Cathedral, the proctor and the other arbitrators fell back to the door. Not a word had passed after the first introduction.

The deacon was young and stocky and ill at ease, rubbing his fingers nervously over his tonsure. He led them through long passages of carving-filled niches and past long lamp-lit walls engraved with the names of Imperial martyrs; another thing Calpurnia was noticing about Hydraphur was the layers of antechambers that official buildings liked to put between their entrances and their cores. The colours around the antechamber changed from the yellow-brown daylight outside to stone walls, forests of ornate pillars and cool grey dimness, statues watching them solemnly from plinths and high galleries. Somewhere deeper inside the building a choir practised phrases and notes, distant fragments of plainsong laying a soft texture to the air. Calpurnia realised she was trying to walk on the balls of her feet, to quiet the noise from her boots.

After the succession of vestibules and anterooms Calpurnia only had a brief glimpse of the great, soaring spaces of the Cathedral proper, a moment for it to snatch her breath away before their nameless guide steered them down a long narrow hall walled in dark tapestries, parked them under a stained-glass mural of Saint Sabbat and bade them wait. Leandro sat on a wooden pew and admired the mural; Calpurnia paced up and down.

'All part of the learning experience, I'm sure,' she said after a while. 'I'm getting a valuable crash course in the front halls and audience rooms of Adeptus buildings all over the hive. I wonder if I'll get shot at coming out of this one?'

'Your first couple of weeks in office were always going to be like this, my arbitor. Such a hub of the Adeptus is not the sort of world where a handful of Arbites can do their job walled up in a precinct fortress that they only ever leave to break a riot. Wait until you get started on introductions to the Navy authorities. There are a great many more of them – Hydraphur is effectively their system, after all. If it eases your mind to any degree, assure yourself that the work we do with Curate Jenner today will most certainly be of value to the investigation of your own assassin.'

'He wasn't my assassin.'

Leandro waved the tart remark away and went on. 'There is, what, a week until the beginning of the Vigil of Balronas? Less, in fact. A matter of days before they ring in the Vigil and all of Hydraphur is bound by the restrictions of the Vigil itself. The goodwill of the Ecclesiarchy will be essential then if we are to continue our hunting, Arbitor Calpurnia. Their edicts regulate even other Adeptus, and their dispensation will allow us a freedom of operation that your conspirators, whoever they may be, might be expected to lack.

'And in any event,' he finished, getting to his feet as they heard footsteps on the other side of the door, 'Clah Jenner is a man whose acquaintance will benefit you. For all that he may strike you as untrustworthily young, his skills as a tutor are admirable. I feel called upon to comment, however,' he added as an afterthought, straightening his cloak, 'that imposing a wait such as this upon guests of what I may immodestly refer to as our calibre is uncharacteristic of him. It lacks diplomacy.'

Every time the subject of her 'tutoring' came up Calpurnia had to stamp down the usual flare of reaction: a first jerk of resentment, then thoughts of how complex the Hydraphur's religious customs actually were. Anything that helped stave off the feeling of being a child traipsing about behind a didactic grandparent was probably worth it, she decided.

Ecclesiarchal Curate Clah Jenner was a slight man, not much more than Calpurnia's height and looking a little weighed down by the heavy brocaded clerical gown he wore. He had little of the youth Leandro had described, nor the softness she had expected: his face was harshly angular, leathery and grizzle-skinned. His hair was tonsured as severely as the deacon's had been, but a thin iron-grey braid ran from each temple back past his ears. As he bowed, Calpurnia saw the braids were elaborately knotted at the back of his head.

'You are not Clah Jenner.' It was a sign of Leandro's surprise that he was stripped of his usual flowery speech. The man bowed again.

'You are correct, Arbitor Senioris Leandro. And you will be Arbitor Senioris Calpurnia. Or is it Provost Marshal Calpurnia? Or Arbitor General? I'm told any of those can apply. Your most respected order has a particularly intricate system of ranking.'

'Any of those titles apply, but the High Gothic seems most common at Hydraphur,' Calpurnia told him, saluting. Leandro was still regarding their interlocutor in mild dismay.

'Arbitor senioris it is, then. Good. And I am Mihon Baragry, Nuncio to the Eparch Hydraphur and Vicar General of the Hydraphur Curia. Come through, please.'

They stepped into a room so small and high-ceilinged it was almost an oubliette, the walls gnarled in scriptural carvings and a great steel sculpture of a warrior-angel leaning out from the wall to hold a chandelier over three small hassocks. Calpurnia didn't doubt that Ecclesiarchal servants would be concealed somewhere and listening in.

'I realise your meeting was to be with Curate Jenner,' Baragry said as he took a seat and motioned the Arbites to do the same, 'but certain circumstances to do with the approaching mass have meant that the curate will be unable to assist you. So I will open by presenting our apologies for such a precipitate change of plans.'

'Precipitate changes of plans do seem to be the order of the moment, Revered Baragry.' Calpurnia could feel herself relaxing. It was refreshing to deal with someone halfway direct. 'I'll apologise for one of my own. I'm aware that arrangements were made before I arrived in the system for detailed tutoring that extended beyond just the specifics of this mass. Jenner was going to go into the broader etiquette surrounding the smaller feasts and ceremonies that the Adeptus were involved in, some kind of vocal coaching, that kind of thing.'

'I haven't had the time to fully check the curate's notes, but that sounds right. The voice coaching would have been for the devotions of the mass. There are differences of melody and intonation required by the pentatonic scale, which we use here, whereas I understand that the galactic South prefers the full octave. It will probably take a few lessons for you to get comfortable with what you'll be required to sing. I might try and arrange a session with one of the choirmasters.'

'Your reverence, my point was that there will be little to no chance of that tutoring going as planned. If you haven't heard about the attempt on my life two days ago I can supply the details, but the lessons here are going to have to go by the board for as long as the investigation lasts. I'll try to make time for a session on the actual mass if I can but that may well be all.'

'We had indeed heard,' said Baragry, 'and your point brings us to mine. You are not the only one who wants to see whoever ran that attack dragged out into the daylight. I speak for the Eparch when I say that the use of a witch-psyker – hah, even the presence of a witch-psyker – practically in the shadow of the Cathedral spire, in the capital hive of a world such as Hydraphur, strikes at all of us. This is a time of great significance to the Ecclesiarchy and our interest in stopping it from being polluted is as great as yours. Possibly, if I can say this without being indelicate, greater.' Baragry was leaning forward on the hassock, elbows on knees and sharp black eyes on Calpurnia's face. 'I want to make it clear that the Arbites will have the full weight of the Adeptus Ministorum behind them in whatever measures they – well, you – take on the matter. Legal, diplomatic, force of arms, anything you require. Canoness Theoctista has stepped up the Cathedral Guard and the Eparch has conferred with his witch hunters. Your work in keeping order within the hive has been excellent; now I think it is time to pick up the trail.' Calpurnia and Leandro exchanged a look.

'This has been an excellent meeting, then,' said Leandro, 'not the meeting we perhaps came here anticipating, but still. Your emphasis on the need for liaison between Imperial Law and Imperial Faith is well-placed, and I believe that such a relationship will move our investigation on at a most desirable pace. Might I inquire, Revered Baragry, if you are the one with whom we shall be maintaining contact to that end? My understanding is that Curate Kaleff of the Eparch's personal officio is–'

'I will be the one working with you.' Baragry held out a small plaswax disc with the mark of a signet ring in its centre. 'My seal. Familiarise your staff with it. Your gate-guard will need to know that I will be calling on you tomorrow afternoon with a formal letter from the eparchal chambers and we can plan our next moves then. The Hydraphur Curia has delegated me as Ministorum representative and your personal aide on matters religious for the duration.'

'The graciousness of the curia humbles us, your reverence, and I am confident your delegation will be met with the utmost generosity of will by our admirable Arbitor Majore, to whom I shall present your name in due course.' Leandro and Baragry were looking steadily at one another. It was obvious sparring was going on at some level, so Calpurnia was a little surprised when after only a moment more Baragry suddenly stood and bowed to them.

'Then duty calls. We both have work to be about and will meet again soon. Go with faith in the Emperor and the blessing of the aquila.' Baragry walked with them as far as the chamber door where a deacon waited – not their earlier guide, but a sallow looking subvicar with an electoo on his scalp that projected holograms of religious maxims into the air over his head. 'The fifteenth hour tomorrow. You may expect me.' He singled Calpurnia out for a bow, and the door swung shut.

WALKING OUT OF the doors and down the ramp carried enough déjà vu to make Calpurnia shiver. The public symbolism of walking up to the front of the Cathedral had been all very well, but she told herself next time she would drive a Rhino. Leandro seemed to have thought on the same lines: he had instructed their proctor to call up three of the squat black tanks while they had been in the Cathedral and now led the way up the boarding ramp of the central one. The well-appointed interior told Calpurnia that this was probably Leandro's personal transport, and the shocked looks she noticed from the people who were hurrying out of their way told her too that armoured carriers were not common on the rarefied streets of the upper Bosporian. Well, that was fine.

'So,' said Leandro, 'what intelligence would you say we can glean from that little exchange of credentials?'

'We're going to have to work out how we're going to deal with active interference from the Ecclesiarchy. He as good as told us that they were powerful enough to do that, and I didn't like that reference to their own witch-hunters at all. And Baragry's no pious catechism tutor and singing coach, although he seemed to have done some homework to appear as one. Not much of the cloister about him. He's a man of action, I think, a field agent.'

'Controlled, businesslike and unafraid to use his authority,' Leandro agreed. 'The idea that the Curia has assigned him to us with their minds solely on our own wellbeing is not one upon which I shall waste a great deal of time.'

'You're right. He's there to monitor us and make sure the Ecclesiarchy knows exactly how our work is going. Notice that mention about keeping order within the hive? Lord Hallyan went on about the same thing.' The Rhino tilted slightly as they began their S-shaped route through the Mercantile Quarter, toward the Kathisma Gate and then back beneath the Adeptus Quarter all the way to where hundred-metre stone eagles flanked the triumphal arch of the Aquila Gate, before they swung back around to the Justice Gate and their own fortress doors. Their visit to the Cathedral had taken longer than she had realised, short as the audience itself had been, and with the relatively slow pace of the drive the afternoon was already dying: the light on the other side of the vision slits was deepening steadily into orange twilight.

'I suspect,' said Leandro at length, 'that this thought may gall you, my arbitor, as it galls me. The thought being that while the desire of the eparchal agents to take their own heads in this matter is something to take up with the Arbitor Majore, the initial fact of Baragry's presence on our investigation is perhaps beyond our ability to change, at least straight away.'

'I'd been afraid of that.' The Rhino slowed, shifted and sped up again, the driver cocking his head to pick up some piece of chatter from the Arbites vox-band. 'I mean, it doesn't surprise me. I wish they'd let us just get on with it, but all right, this is in a different league with Kalfus-Medell wanting to plant a staffer on us. If we can't get them to pull Baragry out without a confrontation let's leave him. It's insane to be picking fights with one another when somewhere out there is someone who raised and controlled an unsanctioned psyker and used him to attack an Adeptus.'

'Raised?'

'Apparently, by Sanja's and Nakayama's report. The kinds of augmetics he was using were delicate, top-notch stuff. The kind that have to tune themselves to their user over years of training. He was part of a stable, not some alley-trash wyrd who earned a favour from an outlaw medicae.'

Their driver leaned over the vox-grille again, and Calpurnia twisted around.

'What's the issue?'

'Some kind of disturbance at the Aquila Gate, ma'am. I don't think it's serious, there's been no alert call. We're just coming up on it now. Lead Rhino reports traffic backups and some kind of dispute at the checkpoint.'

Calpurnia was already strapping her helmet into place and checking her pistol loads; Leandro watched her from his seat, one silvery eyebrow raised.

'Arbitor Leandro. Care to conduct a snap inspection? I wouldn't mind seeing the main Augustaeum Gate procedures up close.' She steadied herself as the APC ground to a halt and the ramp releases clanked.

'I will await your report, my arbitor. One of us should be enough, I think.' Calpurnia shrugged and stepped off the ramp as it finished lowering itself.

The Aquila Gate stood at the head of the Telepine Way, the great traffic artery for the south-western slope of the Bosporian Hive. Its arch was so deep it was almost a tunnel, bright with sodium lamps the same colour as Hydraphur daylight. Layers of galleries and catwalks ran along each wall, crowded with pedestrians who jostled along shoulder to shoulder with worn carvings of parading Adeptus a thousand years dead. At ground level the road to Bosporian proper was combed into lanes, the outer ones thin and filled with bemos and mechshaws, the inner lanes holding giant freight-drays rumbling treads or wheels so fat they were almost cylinders. Arbites were everywhere, blocking every pedestrian walkway and inspecting papers, rummaging through the mechshaw baggage racks, swarming over the drays like ants on a housebrick or prowling in squads the space beyond the gate where queues of vehicles backed up. Drivers hung out of their windows and shouted, or waved paperwork or identity seals, engines revved, arbitrator boots tramped. The din was stupefying.

Calpurnia had thought to slip in quietly, but her habits had not yet caught up with her rank. The escort that had walked with her up to the Cathedral that afternoon were suddenly around her again, the proctor with an amplifier horn from the Rhino's equipment rack: 'Adeptus Arbites! Make way for the Adeptus! Part for the Arbitor Calpurnia!' They moved through the crowd like an icebreaker driving through a polar crust. *There goes the surprise inspection*, she thought ruefully.

The roil around them made it impossible to pick out any kind of order, but it was the central line of drays that had seemed to stop moving and Calpurnia steered her formation through the crowd until she was standing by the proctor who was supervising the dray searches. He was pink and sweating – whether from the close air and exertion or from seeing her rank badges she wasn't certain.

'The drays,' he shouted, having to hunch to reach her ear, 'are hard to search. Their superstructures are built with too many internal spaces. Some of the drivers are indentured servants and don't have the access to let us in.'

Calpurnia was looking down the line of drays. The driver of the one they were standing next to was halfway up a little flight of stairs built into the side of the giant cab, working the hatch on a crawlway that led into the engine space while two Arbites watched. Two drays down a driver and crewman were going through a sheaf of papers with a brown-armoured Arbites comptroller. The one in between, though...

'Why are those two still in their cab?'

The proctor had only heard half the question, and had to lean in again to hear it again. His sweat was sharp beneath the smell of armour polish. In their cab the two crewmen watched Calpurnia intently as she pointed them out with her maul.

'Everyone in the line is down on the ground dealing with you and your squads. Why aren't they? They're next through.'

The proctor was already nodding, and Calpurnia stepped aside as he started gesturing to a knot of arbitrators nearby to fetch the two men down. A bemo drove by in one of the outer lanes, and the squeal of its engine distracted her for a moment, but when she looked back the cab of the next dray was already empty.

Something twanged against her instincts. Too quick. Something wrong.

Reflexively she was running, her escort suddenly pushing to keep up. The drayman was vaulting off the bottom of the ladder and sprinting back through the gate. His companion was nowhere to be seen.

A shake of her maul was all it took – her squad had seen them too. They took off, yelling for troops at the gatemouth. The confusion in the gate redoubled.

Calpurnia had let herself fall a pace back, watching the way the squads deployed, checking for weak points in their advance. She allowed herself a glance up at the side of the dray, and so was the only one to see the very first explosion.

It was a small one, just a *crump* that bent out the metal side of the dray and flared dirty yellow flames out of the gaps between the panels, but it was enough to send her into a skidding pirouette, jabbing her maul frantically at arbitrator and civilian alike.

'Down! Down and away! *Now*!'

The second explosion was bigger, rocking the whole dray on its suspension and sending out a wave of heat that had Calpurnia cringing away, but it was the third that did it. The sides of the dray shimmied then collapsed, falling majestically away, a scorched metal seed-case giving birth to a gorgeous fire-flower that roared up and filled the Aquila Gate with screams and yellow-white wash.

Ninth Day of Septista

Nine days to the Mass of Saint Balronas.
Pilgrims' Devotions. The Stations of the Sainted Way.
The Procession of the Further Saints.
The Master's Pageant.

On this day the pilgrims receive blessings from the chapels on the western slopes of the Augustaeum, and in certain cases will be received into the outer chambers of the Cathedral itself. This day is set aside for those fulfilling their sacred office of pilgrim, and for a resident of Hydraphur to intrude on these rituals is inappropriate, offensive and impious. Those without a specific religious duty in the hive should remain in homes or barracks where possible. The Eparch Lydre's Considerations on the Journey of Devotion *or the first and fifth chapters of* Starfarer's Psalms *are appropriate readings for this day.*

Those favoured with the blessings of the Eparch will have the right to perform the Stations of the Sainted Way. The roads to the Sepulchre and the Way's entrance, and from the Cathedral gates and the Way's ending, will be guarded by the Ecclesiarchy and must be kept clear for the postulants and pilgrims. Remember that by Ecclesiarchal decree, the only sound audible on the Way should be the voices of the postulants as they read the verses inscribed into its surface, so speech and movement must be kept muffled and no engines run within one kilometre.

The trappings of the Further Saints will be taken from their places along the road no later than sunset, and carried in lantern-light procession up along the Chirosian Way to the Confessor's Seat. They are accompanied by those who have been tending them during the night and it is appropriate for those who feel taken by pious sentiments to join the procession. Once the trappings are placed, the pageant commissioned by the Master of the Vigil will begin in the plaza – those unable to attend it in person should endeavour to see it retransmitted by pict-slate through local shrines and temples, and it is appropriate for the heads of households and workplaces to make arrangements for all those under their command to be able to view the pageant as it unfolds or as soon as possible afterwards.

CHAPTER FOUR

Calpurnia awoke, tangled in the sheets from a short and restless sleep, blinking at the morning sunlight which shone in the privacy curtain drawn across the shielded window. She had slept less than five hours, the timepiece on her writing-desk told her, but she felt far more rested than that and in the best mood she had been in for days. Even the silence in her chambers was suddenly pleasant – for the first couple of days in her new quarters she had jolted awake, far too aware that the noise she was used to from living in a barrack-block was absent, fuzzily sure she had overslept.

She scrubbed a hand over her face and grimaced. Although she had let the Arbites medicae team irrigate her eyes after she had emerged from the inferno at the Aquila Gate her skin was still filth-smudged and her hair stank from the thick and oddly bitter-spicy smoke. There would be a lot for her to do this morning, so much to follow up on, their first new lead on whoever was launching these attacks. Two prisoners to catalogue and interrogate, and then the prosecutions would have to be started, and she would need to oversee them. The verispex forensic teams would almost certainly have findings to report to her since she had spoken to them last night, or at least they had better have after five hours. And she definitely owed the other three arbites generals a report, but first she had to bring herself up to speed on–

She stopped herself. If there had been urgent developments, she would have been woken. Consideration number one: an arbitor general did not step out to greet the duties of a new day filthy and stinking like a slum-cat.

Ten minutes later she stepped out of the ablutory cubicle in the rearmost chamber, gasping from the water-jet but feeling newborn. She did a double-take to find a fresh uniform laid out on the bed and a stack of message chits on the desk. The stewards must have come in as soon as they realised she was awake. Another thing to get used to, she thought, laying the chits out and reading them while she dressed.

ARBITOR CALPURNIA – Lord Marshal Dvorov is in receipt of your initial summary report and requests another such from you at such time as is practicable during the morning and as developments continue. In the interim I am authorised to confirm your Level Four delegation to continue with this matter. – Pavlos Calapek, Adjutant to the Lord Marshal

She narrowed her eyes as she buckled her belt. Sleeping in while the others waited on her was exactly what she hadn't wanted to do, but a second reading reassured her. A Level Four delegation meant she could proceed in her own time.

Shira. Most admirable work last night, for 'last night' is what it shall be by the time you set eyes on this, I'm sure. As for myself, diplomatic concerns over the assassin's remains are coming to the fore again. The Ministorum feels it has our approval to attempt a demand upon the Mechanicus for the body. I shall smooth the troubled waters and hold off on a position until I have conferred with you. LEANDRO.

His signature was as flowery as his speech. Calpurnia glowered at it. Politics, politics. The damned psyker-bastard was still making trouble for her even when he was more than two days dead.

Arbitor senioris, we have received a message from the eparchal chambers. The Reverend Baragry wishes to communicate his pleasure at the news that you were unharmed in the explosions during the night and his expectation that your meeting this afternoon will not be affected. Arbitor Intendant Raf Draeger, Clerk of the Watch, Justice Gate.

Security had been raised another notch, then – it read as if the messenger from the Cathedral had been heard at the gates and then turned away.

Well, she was pleased that Baragry was pleased. She was pleased about being unharmed herself. In the chaos after the dray had exploded she had been busy dragging herself out of the way of the sluice of burning fuel: after the initial flare it had burned with a low, smoky flame rather than the white-hot fireball she had been expecting, but that had been bad enough. By the time she got clear the vehicles on either side were splashed and burning, and by the time she had regained her feet the flaming oil had been washing across the gate's rockcrete floor in a shin-high carpet of thick yellow fire.

The barely-controlled bedlam at the gate was suddenly without any control at all. Terrified pedestrians clogged the catwalks overhead and sent one another screaming over the railings into the flames. Drivers tried to bulldoze their way through other vehicles, destroying any hope of orderly escape. The Arbites had been caught as much by surprise as the rest of them, but Calpurnia was proud of the gate teams. With no orders from her, the hivespeople had been driven or dragged through the outer doors by respirator-masked arbitrators while the squads at the inner end of the gate had instantly formed a double line of shields and tanks through which not a single civilian, no matter how frenzied, had escaped into the Augustaeum. If the explosion had been the cover for some kind of mob invasion to defeat the toughened checkpoints then it had failed.

She picked up her rank badges. Someone had polished away the soot and street-grit of the previous night, and she winced a little – that was something she should have done herself, exhaustion or no. And she still didn't even know her chamber-attendant's name.

> *For the Attention of the Arbitor Senioris Calpurnia. Respected arbitor, I now have five prisoners catalogued against your name and assigned to preliminary holding pens – initial cataloguing details are attached. Special measures for the incarceration of the two prisoners early this morning are now in place as dictated by yourself last night. All prisoners are now ready for your judgement or decree as to their handling and I await your instructions. Nomine Imperator. Tranio du Toit, Lead Chastener, Augustaeum Cadre.*

She considered this as she clipped on her holster and weapon-harness. The two men that the message made special mention of were the draymen that had bailed out of their vehicle a few moments before it exploded. Her most vivid memory was of their backs: both powerful and hulk-shouldered, one with his scalp shaved and tattooed and the other with a skinny blond braid bouncing against his tan bondsman's shirt as he ducked and leapt through the crowds.

Her nostrils were clogged with smoke and an indefinable sweet scent; that and shoving her way through the mob had taken her unpleasantly back to the Mechanicus shrine. There had been no time to look back to see if any other Arbites were following her: she had already lost ground to them having to circle and dance around the edges of the spreading pool of fire and she was desperate not to lose either man in the crowd. She had tried yelling for the crowd to part, but the ones who could hear her over the racket were too frightened to pay attention and after a dozen steps she was using her maul on a low-medium charge to bash people aside as though she were beating her way through jungle growth.

Another message from Draeger, the time-stamp less than twenty minutes old.

> *Arbitor senioris, we have word from Lead Verispex Barck at the Aquila Gate. She confirms that the initial inspection of the Aquila Gate event is complete and waits upon your arrival. She has asked that I communicate the fact that others are in attendance. Nomine Imperator.*

And clipped to it:

> *Arbitor Calpurnia, I understand that you will be wishing to attend the Aquila Gate in person this morning. I have taken the liberty of notifying Arbitor Bannon and having a small escort assembled at the Centre Dock. It should be ready to leave by the time of your arrival there. – Hrass. Steward.*

So that was his name, or hers, or at least one of their names. Before the end of the day, she decided, she was going to meet them and speak with them. They deserved at least that.

Her pistol and maul were in a rack in front of the shrine. She touched each of them to the silver aquila with a murmured blessing, then bowed to the icon of Guilliman, tucked her helmet under her arm and was gone.

THE VEHICLE HANGAR in the Justice Gate reassured Calpurnia. Its bright arclights strung from the roof gantries and the barrage of noise, the shouts of squad leaders, the tramp of boots, the roar of engines and the squeak-grind of tank treads. Cranes rumbled and clattered on the rails that crisscrossed the ceiling high overhead, swinging crates of ammunition, canisters of fuel or chained-together bundles of whimpering prisoners through the high space. Before her was a fifty-metre high adamantite slab that stood just inside the gate entrance itself, forcing incoming traffic to weave around it and blunting any rush assault.

Although the scale was greater, it was like most other gatehouses she had worked in, and as always the balance of opposites pleased her. Outside, facing into the Augustaeum, the silent dignity of the gate-pillars, the carved aquilae and inscriptions and the statues of great Arbites past, presenting the stern face of Imperial Law. Inside, the comforting clangour of the Law's servants at their work. She breathed the smell of engine-oil like perfume.

The long rockcrete spine of the Central Dock ran from the main entrance to the Wall barracks out through the middle of the space, splitting it into two half-kilometre hangar floors. Along each side dozens of Rhino and Repressor tanks were lined up like suckling piglets, anchored to the dirty grey walls by fuel lines and maintenance booms. From the walkway on top of the dock, Calpurnia could look down on their roofs as men, women and the occasional servitor scrambled in and out, stopping to peer upwards and salute her as she passed. Finally she saw Dvorov leaning on the rail of the overseers' turret at the end of the Dock, waving her over.

'And a good morning, Shira, pleased to see you none the worse for wear. I thought I'd probably catch you down here. Always leading from the front. Have you eaten yet?'

'Lord marshal. Uh, yes, thank you, I collected some bread and grain-cakes from a commissary I passed back past the, er...' She motioned over her shoulder to the doors that opened onto the Dock. 'My apologies for not appearing before you sooner with a report, sir. I–'

'Not a concern, but thank you for your apology anyway. I trust you to report to me as and when you need to. It'd be quite an indictment of your fitness to be an arbitor senioris if I couldn't.' Calpurnia couldn't quite help the disloyal thought that this hadn't stopped him from checking on copies of the messages that were coming to her, but then she dismissed it, nodded and walked across the turret platform to look down at the Rhinos waiting on the hangar floor. Lead Arbitor Bannon, standing in the top hatch of the lead one, tipped her a salute.

'Of course, now I'm going to go and contradict myself by giving you a direct instruction. Well, not an order as such, but I wanted to drive home to you personally a general matter of procedure I've ordered.'

'Tighter security,' she said.

'Correct. I think I understand the point you made going up on foot through the Artisans Quarter yesterday, and I see the sense behind it. But this new attack starts to make it look like the opening of a campaign, not a single attempted murder. So, no more of it. I won't pretend that you can do your job in a bunker wrapped in void-shields, but no more gadding off on foot with another arbitor general and only a foot squad for security.' He gestured down at the Rhinocade below them. 'Senior Arbites go with full escort and transport. What you have there is a minimum. Junior officers and patrols will be operating in strength. I'm formalising that directive this morning, but I wanted to make sure that you in particular knew it and understood it.'

'Because I'm an unknown quantity.'

'Not entirely unknown, but all right, that might be part of it. In addition, you were the target of the first attack and will be very visible in running the Arbites response. You're going to be a prime target, Shira.'

'I understand, lord marshal.' She saluted him carefully, and then when he seemed to have finished she turned and climbed down to the Rhino hatch.

After a still night the smoke from the fire had been trapped between the Augustaeum wall and the steep upward slope of the land, and around the Aquila Gate the brown haze made the yellow sunlight even muddier, thick with that peculiar bittersweet stink. Just stepping out into the grimy air made Calpurnia edgy again.

'It's from inside the gate,' Bannon told her when he noticed her sniffing. 'The fuel that was coming out of that dray turned out to be scented lamp-oil, for some of the early festivities before the congregation.' Calpurnia nodded and tried to dredge the term out of her bruised memory. The Twilight Congregation, when the Cathedral bell rang in the beginning of the Vigil and lanterns were lit to mark the night.

The Aquila Gate was still blocked. Calpurnia was mildly surprised that there seemed to be no physical shutters for the gigantic tunnel-arch; instead the gate was cordoned at each end by a string of Rhinos parked in a semicircle out into the concourses, with chain-nets strung between them and watchful arbitrators shoving back a constant flow of onlookers. On the other side of the gate the scene was being repeated on a larger scale – from there she could hear engines and klaxons.

'Why hasn't the traffic through this gate been routed away to the others?' she asked. 'Sounds like there's a hell of a congestion on the other side there.'

'I'm not aware of any reports on it.' Bannon said. 'We would have people doing that, certainly, but there may have been problems.'

'May have been?' The arbitrators on the barricade were unshackling the chain-guard to let them through, and she took the moment's delay to stare over her shoulder at him.

'With your permission, ma'am, I'll head through and see. My initial thought is that there's no ready access to the other gates. The hive has not been allowed to extend around the south-west slopes of the mountain to the Pilgrims' Gate, and the Wall runs right the way down the slope of the hive, so a truck of any size would have to reverse down the Telepine Way and right around the bottom of the Wall, then join the queue up the next face. I'd guess that it's jammed up right the way down to the plain.'

'Would you care, then, to head over and see if your initial thought and your guess are correct, and if there is anything more I need to know?' Calpurnia had spotted a lanky middle-aged woman whose insignia marked her as the leader of the verispex team, and changed course toward her as the chastened Bannon hurried away.

The verispex was standing inside the shadow of the arch. A riot of paint-marks and winking marker-pegs stretched away through the wheels of the burned-out tractors and drays. Despite the commotion outside the gate, it still seemed tomblike compared to the previous night. Calpurnia grimaced at the word as soon as she'd thought it, and wondered what the eventual death toll had been. Another thing to find out.

Barck was standing between two of the hulks with a tall man in a thick blue bodyglove, a servitor with vox-recorder wands jutting from its face swaying back and forth to capture the conversation. The man wore no Arbites insignia, and Calpurnia would have felt no compunction about interrupting in any case.

'Lead Verispex Barck. Thank you for your message.' The tall man had not stopped talking. His voice was quiet and throaty, and his back was still to her. Calpurnia gritted her teeth and was about to give the man a sharp rap with her maul when she saw Barck's expression, the face of someone yanked between two points of authority. She took a step around him to glare up into his face, and saw the scarlet rosette pinned below his double chin.

'...must be brought back to me before the trail is cold.' He held Barck's gaze for a moment until the woman had taken a step back. The pause before he turned to Calpurnia was just long enough to emphasise that he was the one deciding it was time to talk to her. He had a high, bony forehead and nose but soft jowls about his jaw and throat. The contrast with his lean body was strange. His brown hair was cut military-short and his eyes were pale and cool.

'You are Arbitor Senioris Shira Calpurnia.' Telling them their name and withholding yours. If there was an older, more basic trick she couldn't recall it.

'Stefanos Zhow,' he added after a pause.

'Of the Imperial Inquisition.'

'Of, as you say, the Imperial Inquisition.'

The recorder servitor would have to be the inquisitor's property – it was not made to any pattern Calpurnia had seen before. The stumps of its arms ended in bundles of shrouded data connectors and data-arks hung at its waist, enough to make it a walking library. Behind it, she saw now, stood another retainer, a chubby man in identical blue, his shaved scalp a mass of augmetic wires and cables.

A pin jutted up above each socket in his skull, each pin holding aloft a scrap of parchment, giving him a bizarre paper halo.

Calpurnia took all this in, then turned back to Inquisitor Zhow. 'Greetings and compliments, inquisitor. I trust that the Adeptus Arbites have been helpful in providing you with whatever you may need from us?'

'So far, yes. My staff and I are examining the site.' Zhow made a brief gesture at his coverall, explaining his workman's attire. 'Meanwhile you will probably want to see to the problems the backflow along the Telepine Way is causing.'

Calpurnia bristled.

'You can be assured that that has my attention, inquisitor, but give me credit for being able to walk and chew at the same time. I am investigating attempts to disrupt the Vigil and Mass of Balronas, beginning with an attack on me and continuing with the explosion last night.' From the corner of her eye Calpurnia could see Barck anxiously lacing and unlacing her fingers. Zhow's fat retainer seemed to be looking right through her. 'I am here to confer with my colleagues about last night's attack. If you are doing the same, then I believe we can be of help to one another.'

'Oh, I am fully aware of your situation, arbitor.' Zhow's gaze had hardened. 'And I will be wanting to speak to you directly about just that matter before too long – rest assured I would have done so already had this not come up.' He gestured to the hulks and smoke filling the gate. 'But by all means, confer. We will need to be somewhere more private for me to talk to you anyway.'

They parted, Calpurnia and Barck walking toward the wreck of the exploded dray, Zhow towards yet another blue-garbed assistant who was deep in conversation with two proctors. Calpurnia waited until they were out of earshot before she growled at Barck out of the corner of her mouth.

'It would have helped to know he was here. Did no one try to get a vox-link to my vehicle, or did he only just arrive?' That seemed unlikely: looking around for more dark blue garments she was able to count four more bustling about the hulks without turning her head. They looked like they had been there a while.

'Ma'am, I did notify you.'

'No, lead verispex, you didn't. And stop wringing your hands like that. Let's get this underway, please.'

The fumes were still noticeable, and they both slipped on filter-masks. The wrecked dray loomed over them, gutted by the explosion and slimy from anti-incendiary sprays. Barck hopped up onto a trestleboard that had been set up along its side and motioned for Calpurnia to join her; Calpurnia had to stand on tiptoe on the board to look through the rent in the dray's side that Barck was peering into.

'It was carrying a consignment of oil, but it's not just a bulk fluid tank. Look.' The dray's carrier was packed with metal drums, a gap in the stacks next to the hole they were looking through. 'The nearest barrels weren't obliterated, we just took them away. But the ones nearest the hole were pretty badly wrecked. From what we've been able to piece together the flames started outside the barrels. There was a spark of some kind within the hopper that got to a leak, going by the burn patterns we found. The actual oil itself burns quite cool and with a low flame.' Calpurnia nodded, remembering the expanding pool of shallow fire. It had been enough, though, enough to cook the legs out from under the hivefolk who'd tried to run and to set the other trucks and drays burning when it reached them.

'So it's the fumes that flared and created the explosion, and from the different characters of the residues I think some extra element may have been introduced along with the induced leak to make them even more volatile.'

'Induced leak?' Calpurnia asked.

Barck stopped and shook her head. 'Apologies, ma'am, I'm getting ahead of myself. There's damage to several barrels that the explosion itself doesn't explain. Weaknesses in the seals and thinning of the metal.' Her voice was getting quicker and more confident as she spoke. 'I sent my message to you because Lacan and his metallurgists confirmed that the damage predated the explosion but was relatively fresh. There were even particles of the barrel-metal in the burnt residues around the barrels themselves, and when we checked with a microvisor it looks like they were scraped, not burned.'

'So someone deliberately weakened the barrels so they would leak flammable oil, then somehow arranged a spark in there.' Calpurnia eased herself down off the trestle onto the residue-slick pavement.

'Correct.' Barck climbed down after her and motioned another verispex officer forward. 'Luxom, did you find what you thought you would?' He nodded and bobbed nervously, holding out a circular ceramic bung.

'The sealant around this got baked hard rather than melted, ma'am, uh, ma'ams. It made it easier to clean away the ash and gunk, which is what we were, uh, doing, uh, finishing while you were talking just now.'

'Thank you, Luxom,' said Calpurnia, taking it from his hand. 'Am I looking for similar tampering here?'

'Those, uh, lines directly across the edges there. Through the sealant residue. That's right, that's one. We may need a microvisor check to be absolutely sure, I, uh, haven't had the time to do one yet. But it looks like someone pushed a needle or something like it through the sealant while it was still soft, not long after the barrels had been filled and sealed, to allow very slow seepage.'

'Can either of you tell me where the spark came from?' The two looked at each other.

'We can find no signs of damage to the dray,' said Barck, 'or at least no damage that seems to predate the explosion. Only the Mechanicus can tell us these things for sure, but we've arrived at a reasonable idea of what kind of decay to a machine causes its spirit to spit and spark. At this stage I think we're looking at some kind of caller-amulet, some kind of machine hidden in the barrels that caused the explosion and either was consumed or blew itself apart to the point that we haven't been able to find any noticeable pieces of it yet.'

Calpurnia nodded, brooded and paced through the wrecks again. Barck and Luxom followed her as she began asking more questions, questions on the pattern of explosions and fires, the crowd movements, how many had died and how they had died. It took over an hour before she decided she had heard enough for the moment and began picking her way back through the wrecks and markers.

'Lead Verispex Barck,' she said, 'I realise you will make your judgement on the matter formally when you place your written report back at the Wall. However, at this point, with what you've seen here over the last few hours, is there any doubt in your mind that this was a case of deliberate sabotage?'

'With what I have seen here… none whatsoever, arbitor senioris.'

'Thank you. When will your full report be ready?'

'By the end of next shift, ma'am. I'll have a runner bring it straight to you.'

'Once again, thank you.'

Bannon fell in behind her as she strode back toward the Rhinos.

'Arbitor senioris, the feeder roads into the Telepine Way are all closed off. Urban Mobility Command reported the last barricade was in place an hour ago.'

'As recently as that? I see.'

'Word seems to be a little slow getting out to the other routes. The drays that are trying to reverse down the Way are probably there for the next day at least. There's already been some violence along the Way's base and Hakaro down at Eight-West is mobilising half an extra watch to patrol. He says there have been a couple of reports of gangs hitting the stranded trucks.'

'Are schematics of the roadways around the bottom of the Wall available?'

'Ma'am? Er, of the major ones, certainly. Do you need me to obtain...'

'When we get back, yes. I'll work out exactly what I need. This inquisitor changes things a little, too. I wish to hell that Barck had notified me that he was here.'

'She didn't?'

'She says she did. The only hint was her original message about "others in attendance".'

'Ah.'

She stopped and glared at Bannon. Arbites got good at reading one another's body language through armour and helmets and he took an involuntary step back.

'Something else I should know, Bannon?'

'Ah. It's local vox shorthand. A reference to "others in attendance" means people from outside the Arbites impinging on our work. Usually in the Augustaeum it's the Monocrat's agents, and up in the docks it's usually the Navy. Sometimes it's someone unusual like the Administratum or...'

'Or the Inquisition.' She looked over to where Zhow was talking to his rotund assistant. As she watched, the inquisitor held up a hand and both men waited while the servitor switched some connections around among its bandolier of data-arks. 'Since I've once again been forcibly reminded of how new I am to this whole quarter of the Imperium, can you tell me whether this is usual behaviour for an inquisitor here? What little interaction I had with the Pacificus

Ordos tended toward rumours and cryptic orders and odd little directives from our high command. I don't remember any of them simply bowling up and flashing his rosette.'

'Perhaps it's because you are high command now, arbitor.' Calpurnia snorted, but it was a pleased snort.

'Perhaps it is. All right, they're coming over, let's not be talking about them. Have the escort squad ready to re-board the Rhinos, please.' Zhow was closing on her now. Calpurnia suppressed a sigh and studied the marks on the ground. The arrows and lines showed where the Arbites had formed their containment line and charted the ebb and flow of the fire and the crowd; the pegs marked where bodies had lain after the stampede ebbed and the fire was out. There were a lot of them. Many had been on fire by the time they had crashed into the shield-wall and by the end the Arbites had been firing into the mob to try to fend it off.

Her left hand crept up towards her head, to rub her scars with her fingertips, before she caught the movement. She hated the way the mannerism persisted even when she had her helmet on – to her it spoke of lack of focus, lack of control. She looked at the pegs again, but each one was topped only by a light-cell and a number, nothing more to tell her who it was that had died on the ground she stood on now.

'Planning your next move?' Zhow managed to make it seem like an order.

'I know my next move, inquisitor. By now the two crewmen of the dray that exploded have spent quite a few hours in pre-interrogation cells. This visit has given me exactly what I need to begin questioning them.' She had to grit her teeth for the next part, but there was nothing for it but to extend the invitation. 'Inquisitor Zhow, if you would like to accom–' but he was already striding away to her Rhino.

'You are right, best that I be present for the questioning. Reassign your escort squad to the other vehicles in the convoy, please,' he told her, 'but make sure there is space for my own staff. Your assistant may ride with us if you insist but that is all.' He marched out from under the gate and into a flurry of murmurs from the crowd.

'I think I'm your assistant, arbitor senioris,' said Bannon helpfully. The rest of the Arbites had already overheard the inquisitor's orders and were distributing themselves among the other carriers in the

Rhinocade. All three tanks were revving their engines and lowering their boarding ramps. 'He is an inquisitor, ma'am, after all. I know the name, although I've never met him. I believe Inquisitor Zhow resides somewhere in the Hydraphur system. They're supposed to have turned old Admiral Invisticone's estates into their own outpost. I've heard Zhow's had dealings with the lord marshal and the Eparch before. He, well, he is allowed...'

'*Allowed* I can deal with, I know what the rosette means. But there's such a thing as basic bloody manners, Bannon. All right then, come on.'

RHINOS WERE NOT made for chat, and Inquisitor Zhow did not appear to be pleased that he had to lean forward off his bench to be able to speak over the engine. The audio vanes on the recording-servitor were constantly clicking and flexing as they tried to sort out the words from the noise.

'This is rather unsatisfactory,' he declared. Calpurnia shrugged.

'It suits my needs, respected inquisitor.'

'Does it now? Most arbite generals of my acquaintance have requisitioned a vehicle for their personal use and have had certain improvements applied. Sound dampening for one, so that the officer in question might conduct briefings and operational discussions on the move. Something I suggest for your consideration.' And he sat back, half-turned towards the vision slot in the hull, and would say nothing more. Calpurnia wished she had kept her helmet on: that slapped expression wanted to creep onto her face again. This time her hand did find the three seams on her forehead and her fingers were still running up and down the scars by the time they rolled back through the Justice Gate.

Bannon must have been right about Zhow working with the Arbites before. There was not even the most perfunctory glance about at the Justice Gate hangar: he simply walked to the base of the stepladder and motioned his tubby servant up it, the man climbing the gritty metal steps with agonising care and frequent stops. The servitor clambered up more quickly and deftly than Calpurnia had expected given its lack of hands, then Zhow himself. Once Calpurnia had climbed up to join him they set off at a stroll down the walkway. As they passed through the doors and turned toward the Chasteners' Tower Calpurnia fell in beside the inquisitor, who had finally condescended to shorten his stride a little.

'Do you think that the sabotage of the oil-carrier was aimed at you?' he asked her. Calpurnia thought for a moment before she answered.

'No. I did at first, because after the shooter this just seemed too pat a coincidence. Too close to me and too soon. It seemed–'

'Do you think the same parties are involved?' he interrupted. She took a breath.

'We still have little to no idea about who was behind the original attack, so it's hard to say. But that's the point, that's what's giving me doubts.'

'Explain.' They rounded a corner into a double column of marching arbitrators. Calpurnia slowed and went to sidestep; Zhow marched down the middle of the formation, the troopers breaking step and shuffling aside when they saw his rosette. The servitor, trying to keep them both in sensor range, shuffled hesitantly in between them until Calpurnia, swearing silently to herself, caught up again.

'The attack on me at the Mechanicus shrine was scrupulously prepared. The assassin had been carefully schooled and his equipment was some of the finest machine-craft that the Adepts at that shrine had seen. And there was enormous effort to make sure that the effort would be untraceable.'

'The gene-prints destroyed, his spoor damped and burnt-out beyond the ability of even my own augur to track,' (Zhow jerked his head toward his assistant) 'and his identity a mystery. I have availed myself of copies of the relevant reports, although I was unable to be present at the meeting where you first discussed all this.' He shot her an amused look. 'Does it surprise you? An assassin operating against an Adeptus officer in a hive in the heart of the premier Naval stronghold of an entire segmentum? What should surprise you is that it took me this long to speak with you directly.'

'I'm sure you had your reasons, respected inquisitor.'

'And you see the contrasts with the incident in the Aquila Gate, do you?' he asked, ignoring the remark.

'The Aquila Gate effort was shoddy and slapdash, haphazard at best. The sabotage to the barrels worked well enough, but it was nowhere near as sophisticated as the preparation behind the shooter. How could they know I would stop at the Aquila Gate? How could they count on my walking to that particular dray?'

'You responded, so I'm told, to the two crewmen running. You seem to have a style of plunging into things that an assassin could exploit quite easily.'

'And they would know this how? They would know that I would be passing at exactly the right moment, how? Traffic was heavy and slow because of the tightening of the checkpoint regimes, it simply wouldn't have been possible to count on the dray being in the right place to catch me. Even assuming that the sabotage got past the inspection point once it reached them. And if the two draymen were supposed to be assassins their conduct was so incompetent it verged on the bizarre.'

'Excellent! Your conclusions match my own.'

And with that Zhow stopped talking again. They were passing down the length of the Wall itself, through the internal checkpoints that marked each boundary. Calpurnia conscientiously stopped for the full identity scan at each point while Zhow, who tapped his rosette and breezed through each one, stood on the far side of it and glared at her while his chubby retainer puffed for breath. They passed through the interior gate checkpoint, the main junction where great stairs climbed away to the high concourse that ran through the upper floors all the length of the Wall, then through the smaller portals into the antechamber of the Chasteners' Tower.

Chastener du Toit was waiting for them. His eyes widened a little when he saw Zhow's rosette but Calpurnia was gratified that he spoke to her first.

'The two arrested in the Artisans Quarter are in the mass cells pending processing. The two in from last night are in individual softening cells, which seem to have worked. One is still quiet but he's had no sleep and is in some pain, the other broke quite early. He fears for his soul – he's been weeping and asking for a confessor for the last two hours or so.' Calpurnia nodded with approval.

'Do you see any reason for us not to start with that one, inquisitor?'

'I do not. I trust you also have copies of the full papers for both prisoners and their vehicle?'

'We will shortly,' said du Toit. 'They were used to track down the shipper to whom the dray belongs. Lead Chastener Klee will be delivering them shortly. As for the prisoner, well, it's a full Ministorum confession he wants to make, so…'

'Do you have a scourging rack?' asked Calpurnia. 'Not one of the standard ones, I mean the kind the confessors set up in public squares when they're raising a purge.'

'Yes ma'am. There's one in the second rotunda, up above us and on the southern wall, for *capita secundus* executions.'

'Good. Have – what's the name of this confessing prisoner?'

'Hiel Jakusch.'

'Have Jakusch brought there along with those papers. And you can show the inquisitor and myself there now.'

Zhow cocked an eyebrow as she finished speaking, but, mercifully, said nothing more.

You ARE A prisoner, arrested at the righteous hand of the Adeptus Arbites. A terrifying, stifling journey in a strait-cape, cocooned blind within tight canvas and crammed into an Abductor-pattern Rhino or simply slung from the carry-hooks on its sides. The cape is taken off in a cell in the giant honeycombed sub-levels of the Chastener's Tower, where the corridors and rooms are deliberately narrow and cramped but of darker stone, high-ceilinged, ill-lit so there's always the sense of being watched from above. How long you live like this, how much food you get, how much water or sleep, will be based on careful Arbites dogma about the breaking of prisoners.

Finally, at some point, bent and weak and exhausted and surrounded by stern brown-sashed Chasteners and their voices and lights, something gives. You beg a confession – and up out of the cramped dimness you come, staggering in shackles, and you stand in a beautiful vaulted glass room full of air and sunlight, looking out over the city and the mountains. The preacher speaks kindly to you and you know that once you have unburdened yourself, the scourging-rack in the centre of that marble floor awaits, and there as the Ministorum has taught you since childhood the pain will cleanse your soul before it leaves your body to stand before the Emperor. How could you not feel joy? How could you not burst out with all those secrets you have locked inside you?

Calpurnia understood the psychology of the chamber and appreciated it. Often the key to the most guarded secrets was the prospect of one final shred of dignity and redemption after the long grind of the cells. If she stood at the window with her back to the rack the room was almost peaceful, even if the sunlight was wrong. Even after several days on Hydraphur, she kept instinctively checking for the smoke-pall or sandstorm that was turning the light that colour.

But anything that got Zhow talking constructively was a blessing, she decided, and taking in the view while they waited seemed to have done that.

'My prediction is that we're going to confirm from this man that that explosion was artificial, but wasn't aimed at you. I doubt he'll know who you are.'

'Agreed. So if it's not an attack on me, are we agreed that it's an attack on the Vigil and the mass? That oil was lamp-oil, and there's a big lamplit parade this evening. The, what is it, further saints?' He nodded.

'Their statues and icons have been displayed in the Pilgrims Quarter for the last day, and tonight they get to the Seat around the other side of the Augustaeum before the Master's Pageant.'

'But the source of the explosion was in the dray, in the cargo hoppers it was carrying. Not the oil itself. If the objective was to sabotage that parade somehow... but I'm getting ahead of myself. Let me think aloud for a moment. The attack didn't need to be on the parade. In fact, it would probably be better if it weren't. From talking to Leandro, to undermine the Vigil is a balancing act. Any sabotage has to cause some kind of disruption to disgrace the Master but too much damage and it backfires. So wrecking that parade would be disastrous, but causing monstrous traffic problems all down one side of the hive is just enough to taint Kalfus-Medell by association. Hell, we probably even helped out by closing the Aquila Gate. It wasn't an assassination, and it wasn't about breaching the Arbites lines to try and get a mob into the Augustaeum, which was the other idea I was playing with. I think the disruptions were an end in themselves. Inquisitor, you understand this place better than I do. What are your thoughts?'

'You're clearly having fun with this, Calpurnia, but it's more your concern than mine.' That slapped feeling again. 'Any attack on the Emperor's peace on Hydraphur is the province of your authority, not mine, as any direct attack on the Ecclesiarchy will be a matter for the Church officers and the Adepta Sororitas. My charter is simply to trace the assassin and destroy his controller and all who had dealing with him, my interest goes no further.'

'I would have thought, with respect, inquisitor, that–'

'Well, yes, you would, but at present the Ordos Hydraphur are keeping our involvement in Ecclesiarchal affairs to an absolute minimum, if you must know. I'm a little surprised that you've chosen to dive in so deep yourself.'

'I'm not sure what you mean, inquisitor.'

'Has Leandro briefed you yet on the conflict between the eparchal chamber and the so-called "flag curates"?' Calpurnia felt her heart sink. Not *again*.

'No, my respected inquisitor, the reference is new to me.'

'Well, perhaps you'd best not be briefed by me, and–'

'And that would be the appropriate course, certainly.' Arbitor and inquisitor spun about at the interruption; neither had heard soft footsteps come through the door.

Mihon Baragry was standing about ten paces behind them, arms folded, flanked by two Arbites Garrison preachers in red sashes and uncertain expressions.

'It is always prudent, Arbitor Calpurnia, to obtain your information at the source,' the Curia emissary went on. 'I would not dream of soliciting information about the affairs of the Adeptus Arbites from a third party, for example. Simply make the request, and I'll acquaint you with as much of the matter as I can.'

'Mind how you go, Baragry,' growled Zhow. 'Insolence to the God-Emperor's Inquisition has a way of coming back around to you. Ecclesiarchal harassment of the Arbites over the body of that assassin is already on our records.'

'Harassment?' Baragry asked, walking calmly over to the rack. 'Hardly. I've just come from a very civil audience with Arbitor Senioris Leandro to explain the charter that the Eparch's witch-hunters operate under. We have a perfectly legitimate authority to be the ones to carry out the destruction of the body according to Ministorum law, of which I know you have a good grasp, inquisitor.'

'That charter originates from the Eparch and has no weight in–' Zhow got out before Calpurnia stepped between them. The effect was slightly spoiled when they simply continued to glare at one another over her head.

'As constructive as I'm sure all of this will turn out to be, gentlemen, can we concentrate on something different for just a moment? Revered Baragry, we have a prisoner due to arrive here shortly to make his confession.'

'Indeed, and I am here as his confessor. He is waiting outside in the company of your Chasteners.'

'You?' boomed Zhow. 'What are you brewing up now, Baragry? Calpurnia, what did you know of this?'

'Exactly as much as I just heard from the Reverend Baragry just now. Reverend, maybe it's just my inexperience of Hydraphur, but is it usual for an eparchal envoy to turn up unannounced and take such a role in an Arbites investigation onto himself?'

'As I said, I came here earlier today for an audience with Arbitor Leandro.' Baragry had finally moved his eyes from Zhow to Calpurnia. 'With that concluded, I took the opportunity to visit, pray and confer with my colleagues in the Justice Gate chapel, with the arbitor senioris's permission, naturally. During our conversation the message arrived that a prisoner required an Ecclesiarchal confessor and the Garrison chaplains paid me the honour of inviting me to take up the duty. Since the prisoner is catalogued against your name, Arbitor Calpurnia, and since you and I are working together in any event, it seemed like a happy arrangement. I assure you no breach of process occurred.'

'You are co-operating with Baragry on the disruptions to the mass, Calpurnia?' Zhow asked accusingly from right behind her.

'We have met on the issue. You indicated that that investigation was not an interest of yours,' Calpurnia told him with a certain amount of relish.

'Reverend Baragry, in order to earn his penance Jakusch will be telling us everything about his part in the conspiracy. Only when we are satisfied that we have every piece of information will he be allowed his scourging and whatever might come after.'

'Understood perfectly,' said Baragry. 'He spoke with me on the way up. I believe he will co-operate.' Zhow snorted.

Calpurnia gave a signal and the Chasteners at the double doors swung them back. Hiel Jakusch turned out to be the tattoo-scalped one, built like a slab but with a soft sheath of fat around his waist and hips. There were generous tearstains on his face and he looked longingly at the rack and then at Baragry.

'Confessor?' His voice was hoarse and high with emotion, and the attentions of the Chasteners had put a lurch in his walk. Zhow's retainer waddled over and leaned close enough to the man to be almost breathing on him, before he turned, went back to the inquisitor's side and whispered something.

'No obvious psyker-taint,' Zhow declared, and the word made Jakusch look around wildly.

Two junior persecutors had brought in stools and a scroll-tube; Calpurnia sat on one and took the papers to look through. Jakusch plopped onto the other one, trembling and staring at the rack. Calpurnia looked at him until he met her eyes and whimpered – she had put a little Macragge permafrost into her gaze.

'The rack is waiting, Hiel,' said Baragry softly. 'The cleansing you crave and the punishment you have earned. But before that you must speak. Tell it all.'

Jakusch seemed to think about this for several moments. Then, holding his quaking hands in the sign of the aquila, he began to speak.

'...*Sanctus*. Went... wrong... we did it wrong.'

'Talk sense. Now.' That was Zhow.

'It was supposed... it should have happened when it was gone. Gone, out of... gone from orbit. Left the world.'

'A ship,' said Baragry.

'Have him start at the beginning, Calpurnia,' said Zhow.

'He will,' she answered, 'we're going to hear everything in order. First just tell me, though, Jakusch. The ship, the one whose departure you said you had to wait on. The name of the ship, Jakusch.'

'*Sanctus*, ma'am. *Sanctus*.'

'*Aurum Sanctus*.'

Tenth Day of Septista

Eight days to the Mass of Saint Balronas. The Festival of Leave-Taking and the Shuttleman's Vigil. The Devotions of the Mariners and the Commemoration of Chilaste the Demi-Sainted. The Declaration of the Precepts.

On this day pilgrims moving on to the sacred stations at Chiros and elsewhere traditionally depart the Bosporian Hive and travel to orbit to take ship. While there are customarily many who are unable to have departed until after this day, pilgrims' business is deemed to finish in the Augustaeum by sunset and after that time pilgrims should not be acknowledged. The Devotions of the Mariners are traditionally recited at the Arch of the Scarii and the Chapels of Konnemahle and of the Revered Vinaphii along the High Mesé. Many preachers outside the Bosporian Hive also make these the centre of their services, so that those wishing to pray for the outgoing ships should determine ahead of time where they will be able to do so.

All pious folk should be in their homes or at their nearest place of worship at the moment of sunset when the Cathedral bell is rung. The roads to each temple, shrine or chapel must be clear for the heralds appointed by the Master to travel out to them – there will be a herald for every place of worship in and around the Bosporian so there will be no need to travel far and those abroad too far without cause may be stopped by the Adeptus Arbites, the Adepta Sororitas or by order squads posted by the Master of the Vigil. Those waiting at home should be alert for the bell or horn of their nearest place of worship, which will signal the arrival of the herald to announce the particular precepts and scriptures that the Master of the Vigil has chosen as the keystone for the observances of the next few days.

The pict-cast of the Master making this Declaration in person at the Cathedral doors is for the benefit of the rest of the planet and the system and should on no account excuse non-attendance at one's own church for the announcement.

CHAPTER FIVE

THEY CAME IN on the *Aurum Sanctus* fast and silent, Calpurnia and Nakayama and Zhow. They rode in the Arbites Indictor-class fast cruiser *Judgement's Clarion*, a squat, blunt-prowed slab of armour and drives around a fat-bellied enginarium, her decks home to a dedicated garrison whose precinct house was their ship and whose specialty was the boarding and sacking of outlaw spacecraft. Nakayama and his personal command team had quickly and easily taken command; Calpurnia had brought no one with her and she had spent most of the trip trying to rest, attacking her first real meal in nearly twenty-one hours and avoiding Inquisitor Zhow.

Calpurnia had never fought in a boarding action before. She had trained for them, and she had led squads through the cramped industrial stacks on Don-Croix in conditions that she had thought were as near to shipboard as made no odds. But an actual ship-to-ship action, storming another vessel outside an atmosphere with life-suits, assault boats, decompression drills, the constant, agonising split of your thoughts between fighting the enemy and keeping the precious, fragile boarding seals intact from stray shots or even blows until the hull breach was secure... No.

So she understood why Nakayama was in charge, why he and Phae, the lantern-jawed Aedile Senioris who seconded him, would lead the storming of the *Aurum Sanctus*. Nakayama had spent nearly his whole career aboard the Arbites fleets that roamed their light-years long patrol beats back and forth across the Imperium, ready to reinforce a beleaguered planetary precinct. It was an arbitrator's life at its most simple, the paramilitary side of their calling stripped bare, and Nakayama had excelled at every aspect of it. It made sense for him to be up here now.

Except that it meant that she had been sidelined, and as much as she tried not to, she hated it. She hated stepping aside from her own investigation, hated the way everything was obviously running so cleanly and efficiently under Nakayama and without needing her, hating most of all the fact that she could understand exactly why things needed to be done like this, but not being able to help hating it anyway.

Her spirits, revived by the overdue meal, had sunk again when Zhow had declared that he and his staff would participate in the boarding. She kept remembering a conversation with Heyd Maliqa, the old marshal of court on Hazhim, years before. 'Though it breaks my heart to host an impious thought about such famously heroic servants of the Emperor, I had four experiences with them when I was posted further to the Southern Fringe and, Shira, nothing plays merry hell with an Arbites investigation like an inquisitor. Emperor forgive me for saying so, but it's true. I hope you never have to put up with it, I hope you never have cause to. But as soon as they set foot beside you the field will belong to them and you'll wind up dumped back on traffic control, regardless of what you know or what you can do. And, Emperor help you, there is just nothing you can do about it.' Calpurnia had listened uneasily to the woman's throaty Hazhim accent shape the words (*Emp'rror hhelp you, thher's yust nodding...*) and had wondered if she should be reporting this to someone. She had never imagined that it would turn out to be so literally true.

And here came Zhow now, marching into the briefing room late and ostentatiously making his way through the assembled team leaders to the front rank of benches and sitting carefully down in the spot that two Arbites hastily made for him. When Zhow was seated Nakayama gestured to the holographic globe by his shoulder.

'The *Aurum Sanctus*.' He indicated a malignant-yellow fixator icon. 'A bonded trader craft operating under direct charter from the Adeptus Ministorum, captained by Vardos del Biel, formerly an officer of the Munitorum bonded-merchant fleet until he was disgraced in some kind of disciplinary matter. Three years after that he showed up on the passenger roster of the *Aurum Sanctus* at the Ecclesiarchal docks at Avignor and was listed as captain for its recent voyages to Hydraphur.

'However, records provided to Arbitor Calpurnia by the Navy system controllers as we passed through the Ring show at least three captains for this ship over the past eight years and crew turnover seems even faster. We know of at least a dozen different brokers and mercantile and legal staff who have conducted business on behalf of this ship just within the Hydraphur system in the past half-dozen or so trading quarters. The major constant seems to be the Navigator, one Peshto Vask Zemlya, who has been confirmed by Adeptus Astra Telepathica records as having been that ship's Navigator for at least the last hundred and twelve years.'

Nakayama glanced down at the faxcopy resting along the rim of the pulpit.

'For the last decade the ship's trading charter has been underwritten by the Adeptus Ministorum. Four times over the last two and a half years the *Sanctus* has invoked special Ecclesiarchal charters to avoid or greatly reduce inspection protocols. The ship has also had more than its share of clashes with the Navy, repeatedly invoking Church sanction for things like course-plan approvals, quarantine audits and access to docks. We have reports of actual armed conflict between the crew of the *Sanctus* and Naval Security, but we don't know much about those – both sides have been keen to keep it between themselves. We know enough to know the *Sanctus* has armed defences that it will use if it feels it has to.'

Nakayama gave a short pause before he made his last point.

'We don't know much about Navigator Zemlya, but both our own data stacks and Inquisitor Zhow's sources confirmed the family's background. From 874.M41 to 912.M41 three other members of the Zemlya family were implicated in a well-established contraband ring within and between the Obscura, Pacifica and Solar Segmentae. They worked through puppet captains and contractual trickery that made them seem innocent dupes, but the craft themselves were traced back to Zemlya holdings in nearly every case. They transported physical contraband through the barriers imposed by quarantine and warzone interdictions, and letters of credit and transaction that allowed them to siphon resources from one system and sector to another and bypass most Adeptus monitoring protocols. A great deal of wealth ended up with some very wrong people. Backtracking data-trails and interrogations of informers suggested that it may have been going on for as much as a century.

'The ring was broken by the Adeptus Arbites, Battlefleet Pacificus and the League of Blackships in 915.M41 and the captains and crews were ceremonially executed by Arbitor Majore Dayn Finegall the following year, but the Zemlya themselves were Navis Nobilite and untouchable. Peshto Zemlya was not in active service with the family then, but who knows what we'll find in another Zemlya-navigated ship? Which brings us to the now.'

He pointed at the string of bright emerald dots strung out around the *Sanctus*.

'For the last two days a carrier battlegroup attached to the Battlefleet Pacificus has been conducting fighter-bomber formation drills in the asteroid fields around the Psamathian Gate. Six hours ago the *Sanctus* appealed against an Arbites directive to change course for interception by the *Praetor Katerina,* citing the usual raft of Ecclesiarchal immunities-by-proxy. At this point Captain-Commodore Esmerian approached us through the Naval envoy's offices in the Augustaeum and volunteered to redirect his squadrons to blockade the *Sanctus* until we could catch up. Captain del Biel has been trying to bully his way through that blockade for the past hour, but he was forced to shed just about all of his velocity when Esmerian threatened to have his bomber wings start an attack run. At this point it's over to us.'

'What authorities or immunities the captain of this craft thinks he might have are nothing you need concern yourself with, Arbites.' Heads turned to Zhow as he spoke. He had exchanged the battered blue bodyglove for an elegant green full-carapace and cloak, his rosette displayed under a little armourglass box fastened to the centre of his chest. Calpurnia had to admit he had a certain presence. 'The mission to intercept this ship now has my own authority, that of the sacred Imperial Inquisition. My stamp is upon this venture.'

There was a brief wave of muttering until Nakayama started speaking again.

'I've distributed all the information we have about the ship's armaments and internal defences – we don't have much to go on, but pay attention to it nevertheless, please. We're hoping for a surrender but we should prepare for the opposite. It's hard to read their intentions: they haven't stopped us from closing but they've made no move to acknowledge or admit us. Remember also that command of the storming operation rests with me, but the investigation that's led to it belongs to Arbitor Senioris Calpurnia and Inquisitor Zhow.' This time it was Calpurnia that the heads turned to. Zhow was frowning, displeased over sharing mention with an arbitor or perhaps just at being named second.

'Take your stations, then,' Nakayama finished. 'There will be a klaxon at thirty minutes to interception, and you have until then to finish muster and weapon checks. Ship's chaplains will be at their posts; prayers and blessings will be by detachment rather than in a single service. *Nomine Imperator, Nomine Legis.*'

As Calpurnia repeated the words after him she was surprised to feel a thrill running through her, then surprised at her surprise. Throne of Earth, but it felt good to be doing something totally on the Arbites' terms for once.

THEY WERE GOING in with the second wave: Aedile Senioris Phae, Calpurnia, Zhow, eight Arbites from the *Clarion's* garrison, two augurs from Zhow's personal staff and six of his troopers, bulky in fully-pressurised carapaces and toting shotcannon and man-high flak-slabs that they used to box in Zhow and his armour-swaddled assistants in a way that would have been comical if it hadn't slowed the team down so much. 'These men are veterans in the service of the Inquisition and myself,' Zhow had told Calpurnia when he saw her staring, 'and experts at keeping myself and my staff from harm.' There didn't seem to be much to say to that.

The main passageway to the front ventral storming-lock branched off in every direction so that the storming-teams could form up in assault files and head straight out in whatever sequence they had to without getting in each other's way. Calpurnia, second from the front of her own file after Phae, braced herself against the juddering as the storm-locks clamped themselves to the locks of the *Aurum*

Sanctus, then with the help of the vacc-armoured engineers who had launched themselves across the closing gap between the two ships they ground and pressed themselves in until they found the right combination of grapples and seals to form a passageway. Like a forced kiss on an unwilling maid, she told herself, and then shook her head and wondered where the hell that thought had come from.

The hatches blew with a *crump-WHAMM*, then a roar of air and popping of ears as pressures equalised. Turbulence from the seam between the two ships' artificial gravity fields sent strange breezes and eddies up and down the corridor as the first detachment stampeded down the passage and into the *Sanctus*.

"Second, *go*!'

At the cry over the vox-band another double file stormed down the passageway past their own branch, then another. Calpurnia murmured 'Emperor protect' to each and realised that Phae was doing the same.

'Fourth, *go*!' If they had their planning right there would be a single long deck beneath this lock, two initial storm-detachments moving down it in each direction.

The communication torc built into the collar of her armour carried no talk, no red Engagement runes. So far, so good.

'First. At our initial waypoint. Layout conforms to briefing so far. Clear.'

'Second. In and at waypoint. Clear so far.'

The third detachment called in, then the fourth. The first wave was through. The command teams would lead the second bigger wave, then verispex and cyber-mastiffs would form the third.

'Clear for the second wave. Command one, *go*!' Nakayama's voice coming out of the torc, and Calpurnia and Phae launched themselves out of the side corridor and into the passageway. It was a pleasure to lose all thoughts and broodings in the simple rhythm of her feet on the decking and the weight of her shotgun and shield. The semicircular lock sucked them in with a burnt smell and a *whoosh* of air, and then there was the leap, the moment of free-floating and the wrenching ninety-degree turn as they passed from the *Clarion's* gravity into the *Sanctus's*. She landed, stumbled and scuttled aside, out of the way of the Arbites dropping through what was now, with the change of orientation, a chute opening into the ceiling of a long, high corridor. She had expected Zhow and his complicated little squad to plummet through in a tangle but inquisitor, guards and even the chubby augur and his companion made the drop neatly and were in formation a moment later.

Phae had an inertial auspex out and Calpurnia, who hadn't seen the need for one, now understood how damaging to the sense of direction that wrench between gravities could be. As they set off down the passageway Calpurnia heard, 'Command two, *go*!' and the sound of Nakayama's squad dropping through the hatch. They had broken in two-thirds of the way down the *Sanctus's* two-kilometre crenellated hull, between the engines and the bridge; Nakayama would oversee the move to the stern, the holds and engineering sector while Calpurnia, Phae and Zhow pushed in the other direction to the squat ziggurat that housed the bridge.

The lights in here were almost non-existent, but by the torches clipped to their shields and shoulders Calpurnia could see that the walls of even this outer passage were elaborately crafted, a non-stop frieze of holy symbols and carvings of grim faces surrounded by High Gothic inscriptions. The outer wall, the one that faced the hull and space, was covered in scriptural banners and purity seals to ward off the dangers of the warp, and gave off the smell of old parchment and stale incense. It was like being in the catacombs of some deserted monastery, she thought as they began to advance, and her mind snagged on that word: *deserted*. No one to meet them? Whether to fight them or anything else? She noticed dust was heavy at the foot of each carved and decorated bulkhead, but thinned and disappeared in the corridor's centre.

'These corridors are patrolled,' she muttered to Phae. 'The devotional scripts on the walls haven't been attended to for some time, but look at that dust. Just the advance teams wouldn't disturb it like that. Somebody moves through here regularly.'

'I see it,' Phae replied. 'Command one to all teams, 'ware possible patrols,' and the string of acknowledgements had still not died away when the team in front of them met the arco-flagellant.

It came first as a burst of exclamations over the vox-band: 'Contact! Single contact, First! Shield and cover!' and then a burst of shotgun-booms in the dimness ahead and a weird, unearthly howl of anger. Then wordless yells and the clash of metal, and the fizzing cracks over the vox-band that meant that power-weapons were discharging too near a transmitter. The cadre team moved into a slow jog, advancing and covering and trying to stamp on the urge to race ahead.

'Fire-call is *hellbreak*,' came the voice of one of Zhow's guards from behind her. 'If you hear it, get flat. At *hellbreak* plus three seconds we open fire.'

'We appreciate the warning,' Phae answered as they came through an arch where the passage broadened to double its previous width and became a succession of archways that stretched away into darkness. Now they could hear the shouts without vox: 'Box it! Box it! Get it int–' and see the intermittent gun-flares as well as two dancing, circling blue lights that sparked and whipped back and forth.

Calpurnia had loaded her stubber with the special low-velocity frangible rounds that the *Clarion* carried for shipboard operations, but she had checked a shotgun and shield out of the ship's armoury as well – in their haste to get spaceborne she had not had the chance to load up on her own kit. Now as she got in formation beside Phae she felt the satisfying chunk of the shotgun locking home into her shield's gunport and watched the red spark, designating an Executioner shell, appear in the corner of the vision slot.

But the advance teams had beaten her to it. Half the squad had formed a rough line facing the thing as it had waded through the other half and now they caught it in a loose semi-circle of shields. This was a shock-team, suppressor charges built into their shields, and their strobing discharges knocked the creature forward into the staggering Arbites it had been tearing at, then the spark-burst of a maul sent it back the other way. By this time the cadre were close enough to see it, a lumbering pale shape whose sickle-tipped arms swung and scissored about it with inhuman quickness, until three point-blank shotgun bursts tore it open and sprawled it, limbs and innards, across the deck and wall. The Arbites put another volley into it as Calpurnia's team closed with them and took up support positions, but now the thing was definitely dead.

'Take stock and regroup,' snapped Phae, but the order was unnecessary: already the uninjured Arbites were reordering themselves into smaller squads while the medicae staff bent over groaning figures on the deck. In the middle of the mess their guns had left was a silver plaque that gleamed in the torchlight. Calpurnia turned it over with her toe: DEFILER OF SCRIPTURE. It was still riveted to a scrap of what looked like the flagellant's breastbone. It fitted. Arco-flagellants were not vat-grown but made, made from condemned heretics who had their bodies engineered with drugs and augmetics into pain-proofed murder machines and their conscious minds ripped away, leaving only a predatory animal's instincts and utter loyalty to the Ministorum.

Calpurnia spoke into her vox-torc.

'Calpurnia, Command one. One arco-flagellant encountered and destroyed on the fore approach. Casualties,' she shot a look at them, 'are three fatalities, three more injured and unable to continue. We need a buttressing team up behind us.'

'*Clarion*. Buttressing team on its way. Five go, Six stand by.'

'Command,' came Nakayama's voice. 'No resistance, but we've found two discarded cassocks, freshly ripped, covered in maxims and seals. Flagellant garb. There will be at least one more here somewhere. Push forward. Move it before the resistance can get more organised.'

The second arco-flagellant appeared two hundred metres on, where the broadened gallery split into an upramp and downramp to the other decks. They had begun to climb the upramp in a careful square when it appeared, running in great silent strides up the downramp and making an incredible arcing leap to crash into the outer line of Arbites. One of them managed to get a shot off that turned it in mid-air, and it was off-balance when it hit the shields. The Arbites were ready and shouldered their shields into it to knock it back out of the air even as the electrowhip bundles sprouting from the stumps of its forearms scored tracks over the rims of the shields and across their helmets and armoured backs. The thing twisted catlike in the air and landed on the balls of its feet, and Calpurnia saw it tense its legs ready for another spring before there was a cry of 'Hellbreak!' from Zhow's team, the flak-slabs swung wide and the shotcannon boomed. It twisted and leapt as they opened up and was actually in time to evade the first two bursts before a four-second volley shredded it. Calpurnia glanced over the edge of the ramp for a moment, but if this one had a plaque on it she couldn't see it from here. They climbed on.

Nakayama found his flagellant as Calpurnia's party found the first portal deeper into the ship. The door had been welded shut, but the welds were old, cold and plastered over with Ecclesiarchal seals. Calpurnia was running her hand over the seams when the burst of chatter came over the vox. The flagellant had crashed through two shield-lines and made for the command squad before a concerted salvo of Executioner shells brought it down. One fatality and three more who wouldn't be going any further. The third wave of storming teams was through the hatch and following up behind them, a fourth was mustering.

'I wonder if this is why there's so little resistance?' Phae wondered aloud. 'They welded these shut to have a complete layer of passages and corridors between the spaces they use and the hull. Then they leave the arco-flagellants roaming in those spaces as a permanent hunt-and-destroy patrol. But it wouldn't stand a chance against any kind of full-strength boarding action, we've taken them apart...'

'It wouldn't need to,' said Calpurnia, 'not if they were so confident about the protection of the Ecclesiarchy. They're not a warship, the most they'd have to worry about is piracy and most pirates don't mount military-scale boarding actions.'

'But they'd still need to come out to see to the flagellants – reconsecrate their machine-parts, make sure their human bodies are fed and properly maintained. There needs to be a way into this layer somewhere. One of these doors won't be sealed.'

'It's still a bizarre response to an official boarding. They let us dock with no signals and no resistance but they don't rein in these things. What the hell?'

'The inquisitor wishes to know why the advance has halted,' came a vox-call from inside the flak-slabs behind them. Calpurnia grimaced and they moved on.

There seemed to be no pattern to the movements of the flagellants, no attempt to organise. Nakayama's teams picked off two more over the next twenty minutes; and another came up the ramp behind Zhow, ran into the buttressing team that had moved up to provide a rearguard and killed two Arbites with a melta torch grafted into its shoulder before it was brought down. But by the time they had passed two more great sealed archways and found a still-functioning one, free of welds or dust, there had still been no other opposition, just these shambling once-human berserkers appearing out of the dark.

Breaking through to the inhabited decks of the *Sanctus* was an anticlimax. Zhow stepped from inside the portable bunker his guards were carrying around him and touched his Inquisitorial signet to a truth-plate by the hatch and there was the immediate rumble of motors in the bulkhead and deck. White-golden light washed out as the thick metal rolled down into the floor: fire-teams from first vaulted the shutter before it was fully descended and Calpurnia followed while Phae voxed for another wave to leave the *Clarion* in support.

The cloisters they were running through, veering left and right by the directions Phae shouted out from her locator, were elaborately vaulted and carved to mimic the design of the Ecclesiarchal buildings in and around the Cathedral complex in the Augustaeum, with a constant smell of incense that must have been deliberately circulated in the ship's internal air. There were even windows, set into the top of each niche and backed by glow-panels providing golden mock-sunlight.

The resistance here was still haphazard. Calpurnia had feared an Adepta Sororitas ship's guard but there were only gaggles of junior armsmen, desperately but incompetently trying to hold the odd set of steps or cargo-crane shaft. The Arbites took each blockade apart almost without slowing down: the shock-teams advanced with lasfire sizzling on their shields, fired a brief suppressing volley through ported guns or tossed a grenade while the second rank got their aim in, then the defenders were broken by quick, precise bursts of shot and any survivors picked off with Executioner shells. Calpurnia could already hear Phae on the vox-channel, organising the cybermastiff handlers in the waves behind them to begin hunting down what few survivors had fled and scattered.

It was beneath the bridge-ziggurat that they met their only real fight. Two dozen armsmen, some bloodied from the earlier skirmishes, dug themselves in amongst serried rows of devotory cases and penance racks, joined by five gantrylike hauler-servitors whose fleshy quasi-human heads and torsos hung incongruously in the middle of their stilt-legs and clanking grapple-arms. They had flanked the door with servitors and flamer-crews, but when the Arbites assault came their organisation began no better than before and quickly dropped to non-existent.

Calpurnia led them through the doors and was knocked sprawling by a servitor's grapple-claw that warped her shield and numbed her arm. Cursing, she kicked out with her heels, pushed herself behind a heavy steel reliquary stand and tried to wrestle the cracked and distorted shield off her arm. Phae, running through the doors a moment later, dived down beside her and pumped three bursts of shot at the armsmen who were clustering behind the servitor and firing spindly laspistols. The servitor reeled forward, one leg-motor already chewed and smoking from gunfire, and tried to grab Phae out from behind her cover. Calpurnia popped up beside her and rapped the grapple-claw with her maul to short the mechanism, leaving the machine waggling its paralysed claw as if giving idiot benediction.

A moment later it tottered and crashed down as Phae shot its organic body apart, and the armsmen fled, yelping. Across the aisle a second servitor was smashed apart by krak grenades and a third began spinning in a mad circle and gouging great strips out of the walls as some minor injury to its organics threw its blank vat-grown brain into confusion.

Calpurnia switched her maul to her left and drew her stubber with her right, she and Phae falling in wordlessly with the fan of Arbites now spreading through the smoke and the maze of cases. The crew had not fled far, but their ambushes were half-hearted and their aim appalling: a lasbeam or an autopistol burst would ring off a shield in the front rank, then there would be a quick shotgun boom and sometimes a single cry.

Calpurnia, shieldless, found herself in the second rank now with little to do: every order she went to say was anticipated by the Arbites around her. They quartered, crisscrossed and flushed the last of them out into a vicious crossfire on the steps at the far end – the fourth servitor was felled by a methodical rain of krak grenades from two Arbites who had come in with the wave behind them, and the fifth simply stopped moving and stood slumped as the last of the armsmen fell and the control amulet he was carrying went rattling across the floor.

It had barely come to rest before the shot-pocked double doors at the top of the steps began to swing open. Instantly they were covered by the guns of more than thirty Arbites and Calpurnia, walking toward the front of the formation, dropped to a crouch and brought her stub pistol up.

But even before they could make out the figure on the other side of the door a voice came through the vox-horns in the ceiling, a soft, tired old man's voice:

'Put up your weapons, men and women of the Adeptus Arbites. I will not fight you, and you cannot fight me. Let this waste and destruction stop awhile.'

Calpurnia stood and with some effort of will lowered her pistol. The cowled figure was grotesquely tall, the shoulders beneath its purple and gold cloak too slumped and narrow, the fingers of the hand it raised too long and thick. A man in the uniform of a petty officer knelt on each side of it, hands stretched out before them with the weapons in their laps bound in white cloth to symbolise surrender, but it was to the cloaked man that Calpurnia's eyes returned. A long, stubbled chin and a quivering old man's mouth, but the cowl hid the rest and that was when she guessed it.

'Navigator Peshto Zemlya.'

'I am he, and I will have no more of... of this, on my behalf.' Heavy fingers gestured out at the room. 'You need not assault me to learn what you need. Come, woman of the Arbites, and I will tell you what you seem to desire to know.'

THEY RODE UP to the bridge in silence, in a glorious jewelled howdah that coasted silently up through a grav-shaft bathed in white light. At every level of the ziggurat the shaft was enclosed by a cage of gold filigree, fanciful wire-work gargoyles forever chasing one another in circles, and beyond it each of the floors, although lit, seemed quiet and empty.

Nakayama had remained down among the decks to take charge of a full-ship sweep, but Phae came with her. Although the two of them stood in front of Zemlya as a mark of trust, two proctors held their weapons on the hulking Navigator from behind where the warp eye in his forehead could not affect them if he should suddenly unmask it. Around them were Arbites that Phae had singled out at Calpurnia's request, cross-trained in space flight, ready to commandeer the ship if they had to. Zhow, who had left his guards behind, and looked as though he were regretting it, stared at Zemlya and gripped a bolt pistol plated in mirror-polished silver.

The ride was uneasy – the beautifully artificed and quiet structure around them was eerie enough, but the Navigator was simply wrong. There was no natural proportion about him: it was as if each measurement had been randomly twisted for longer or shorter. His chin tapered too much but the bulge of forehead under the low cowl was too blunt. His fingers were thick but his hands and wrists slenderer than Calpurnia's. But even over and above his physique, his swaying stance, his wheezing breath and his odd, acrid, smoky smell, there was just a presence about him, something that rankled their thoughts and senses. Calpurnia thought that even if she turned away she would still know which side of her faced him because that was where her skin would be crawling. She wondered if this was how the inquisitor's augurs felt in the presence of warpcraft. Was this how they sniffed it out?

The bridge itself was equally disorienting, in its own way. It was not the forbidding, harshly-lit bunker of an Arbites ship but a stately marble belvedere with armourglass windows framed in graceful arches of precious metals and wirework. Perfume-bowls were set on stands on either side of the captain's throne, warmed by gentle candles beneath them, and silver chains crisscrossed overhead holding lanterns, the filaments in hollow glass figures of cherubs and extravagant heraldic animals. The control plinths were fashioned like musical instruments, miniature buildings or tree stumps and the panels beneath the windows were worked into the shapes of trees and vines with coppery leaves that waved in gentle programmed motions to simulate wind. For a few moments after they reached the bridge she could hear mechanical songbirds chirruping in the metal branches. Calpurnia shook her head. Pampering like this was bad enough in a private home, but what would this place be like in an emergency alert?

Zemlya was stepping down out onto the floor in a rickety, top heavy gait that had her catching her breath waiting for him to fall. Beyond him servitors continued to nod and drone in the control pits but the human bridge crew, in splendid red and gold half-gowns, were assembled in a half-circle around a richly-uniformed corpse that sprawled face down on the deck. Calpurnia took in the dead man's epaulettes and chain of rank and decided she had found the unfortunate Vardos del Biel before she looked again at the officers. None wore pistols or sabres, and all were oddly hollow-eyed and gaunt, with a hunted look to their eyes. All had mechanical pads covering their ears, and looking closer Calpurnia could see filter wads in their nostrils.

Technically the bridge crew had the Arbites outnumbered and trapped, but as Calpurnia looked around them no instinctive alarm bells rang despite the fighting they had done. The officers stood in identical poses like chastised children, hands folded and eyes downcast. She followed Zemlya down with Phae and Zhow behind her and motioned the other Arbites to fan out among the command plinths. There was a little stirring and muttering among the crew, which ended when someone spotted Zhow's rosette and a low moan ran through them. Zemlya swept his arms out for silence, arms that Calpurnia uneasily noticed were of different lengths and set too low on his torso.

'Well?' demanded the inquisitor, trying to take the initiative back from Zemlya's showmanship, beating Calpurnia to it by a moment. Zemlya nodded and pointed to one of the crew, a pallid yellow-eyed man with a drooping moustache.

'I am Jassala Kruthe, the *Aurum Sanctus's* Master of Auspex. My mother and uncle conspired to give shelter and succour to corrupt men who cheated the Sub-Eparch of the Beishi system of part of her triennial tithes. When the plot was righteously purged, my mother was executed. I live in shame for my tainted blood, in thrall to the Emperor aboard the *Sanctus* for my family's betrayal.'

'I am Schacht Eramo, the *Aurum Sanctus's* Lead Astrographer,' said a heavyset woman with hollow cheeks and lank blonde hair. 'I was trained by the Imperial Missionaria on Asherkin and honoured with the gift of a pilgrimage to Chiros, Macharia, Gathalamor and most holy Earth. I vowed that should I finish the pilgrimage in my lifetime I would return and preach of what I had seen. I was seduced by laziness and backsliding, and showed my unworthiness of such a sacred trust. When the Emperor's servants hunted me out in the rookeries of Iata I repented and begged for execution, but to earn that grace I serve the *Aurum Sanctus* on her travels.'

The words had a certain sing-song quality, more recitation than confession. Looking more closely at the crew, Calpurnia could see the edges of penitential chafe-cloths just visible at collars and cuffs.

Zhow was snapping his fingers at the first officer, who answered him in a halting voice. There was a light sweat on his forehead and even in the heavy uniform coat his posture almost shuddered with tension.

'I am Ammon Ginzane, first officer and, uh,' he glanced down at the corpse at his feet – looking at it again Calpurnia noticed blood seeping from its ears and pooling under its eye-sockets –

'Captain-nominate of the *Aurum Sanctus*. I captained the *Voice of Deacis* out of Avignor and Lodesha. My brother was anointed curate in the Eparchy of Crado and required me to speak as a witness at the investiture. For my sins, the Emperor chastised me with poor passage through the warp and I missed the service. My ship was forfeit and my command pledged to the Ecclesiarchy for three years, but in the second year of my service we were gutted by xenos corsairs. For my twofold failures I renounced my claim on full captaincy and boarded the *Sanctus* as First Officer under Captain del Biel and the direction of Curate Majjiah.'

The religious trappings in the outer halls, the relic cases they had fought their way through. A bridge crew of disgraced officers, surrounding themselves with beauty that they cut themselves off from. Perfumed air stopped with nose plugs, birdsong that was blocked from their ears by electronic pads, beautiful, luxurious uniforms but chafe-cloth scoring their skins underneath…

'It's a penance ship.' Calpurnia had said the words out loud before she thought about it, but Zhow nodded approvingly and spoke as if the rest of the crew weren't there.

'You know of the concept, then? It explains the turnover of officers and the arco-flagellants in the outer passageways. Presumably crew are assigned on and off as their expiations begin and end. What I don't understand–' and he wheeled around to Zemlya 'is your role, Master Zemlya. You are the Navigator on a ship of miscreants and sinners, whose yearning to shed their guilt assures their obedience. But the Navigator families are outside almost every law in the Imperium, sir, and can do what they will. You have no need to fear the Church, and the Church considers you a freak whose existence the Navis Nobilite charters barely make tolerable. The fact that you are putting yourself at risk to stand before me here, instead of sealed in the Navigator's tower indifferent to what we do, begs the question, does it not?'

'Then let me make my own confession and set that question to rest,' said Zemlya. 'I am Peshto Vask Zemlya, of the House of Zemlya, grand-nephew of Novator Eskol Zemlya. My misshapen form is simple testament to my legacy of sin. The family of Zemlya are prideful and ever-grasping. They thought to pull themselves to heights of power through a grip on the throats of their rivals. The wretched feud of Belisarius and Ferraci, your own brethrens' pogrom against the D'Kark, all created turmoil amongst our breed that the

Zemlya thought opened the gate for them. My family were desperate for the means to fund their push and found it in wealthy and influential circles who needed secret mobility. My corrupted relatives were righteously destroyed, but their shame endures. That my family laugh at their perdition and spit on the concept of penance only builds upon the foundation that my outlaw forebears laid. I tell you of the disgrace that so few outside our breed know of to show you why I live with this legacy, and why I continue to scratch and deface the great edifice of my family's offences.'

'A Navigator with a conscience.' Zhow's voice was flat and disbelieving. 'A Navigator with a religious epiphany.'

'A Navigator disowned by his family and by all his breed and left with only the burden of expiation to console him.' Calpurnia realised that the hoarseness in Zemlya's voice was emotion. 'Is it so surprising, inquisitor? In my high seat I gaze into the immaterium and see the shadow that our own universe casts into depthlessness. This eye,' and he touched his hood over his high-domed forehead, 'this eye sees gentle flows of soul-stuff where the becalmed mind might starve to death, and tides and churns of genius and hate. The warp mocks the power of words to describe. But what I can never turn my back on is the power and the beauty of the Emperor. I see His soul shine out from Earth and His presence fill every corner of the immaterium. I am scorned for what I talk of seeing, scorned by my family – so be it. Some say that every one of us sees a face of the warp meant only for him, a warp that none other shall ever see, but it makes no matter. I have known from the first time I beheld it that I could do nothing but follow that light with my life.'

There was silence on the bridge for a long moment until Calpurnia spoke. 'If this is a penance ship, and if all your crew have forfeited themselves to serving out their penance as you say, why did you fight? And where are the priests who should have *stopped you*?' She hadn't felt the anger steal up on her but suddenly it was there, cramping her shoulders and fists. Zemlya's great head swung around to stare at her.

'Vardos del Biel is gone into the darkness.' He pointed to the lumpen shape on the deck. 'His orders can do you no more harm.'

'Enough riddles, Navigator,' said Zhow, half-raising his pistol. 'What did he do? What did *you* do?'

'We were to ride the warp tides out to the galactic north,' Zemlya said heavily, 'and then hold ourselves against them while we sent communiqués to Avignor and the diocesan citadels there. Then I was to spy out the countervailing current lower in the galactic plane to carry us southward to Rhanna, Colcha, dark Gathalamor, blessed Chiros. To each we carried an envoy from the eparchal chambers here at Hydraphur. They were sealed into their chambers and I was not told their business, but there was to be one and no more for each of our destinations and they came aboard in secret.'

'I think I can fill in the rest,' said Zhow. 'It's this stupid, damnable squabble between the Ecclesiarchy and the Navy. The senior clergy at Chiros and Ophelia managed to get Baszle into the eparchal throne here as a loyalist to the stricter Terran factions, but the Naval curates all hate him now because he was shoehorned in here instead of one of them. Any communication he wants to make out of the system would normally go through one of the Navy's astropath stations or aboard a Navy craft. Even sending envoys out by civil traffic wouldn't escape the Navy's notice.'

'So if he wanted to send out reports and requests for help with his power base,' Calpurnia said, 'send them out to other powerful Church centres in surrounding sectors and do it without interference, then he would have to do it not just in an Ecclesiarchal ship but in one that had a chance of getting out of the system without any kind of search or surveillance. A penance ship would have all its crew fanatically loyal to their curates and preachers.' She could follow the logic, even if she didn't like it. 'The run in to Hydraphur must have been a dummy, just an excuse to be in orbit to meet the shuttle.'

'No wonder the Navy was so keen to help,' put in Phae. 'They even came to us with the offer before we asked them to intercept. They must have suspected why the *Sanctus* was being so secretive but they didn't have any way to make a move. I wouldn't be surprised if the evidence we have about the *Sanctus* being involved in all that shit in Bosporian was planted to nudge us into doing exactly this.'

'Del Biel thought so,' said Zemlya. 'The place of the penitent is obedience and submission, but del Biel had grown hot-headed. I attempted to remind him of his duty and instructed him to submit, but finally he broke away from me and began giving orders to fight you. When I looked at him I saw a mind like a hot coal.' The

Navigator shrugged his misshapen shoulders. 'Not every spirit has the strength to stand up to its penance. I gave him my unfettered gaze and struck the life from him. He has gone in among the dark tides now. I do not think the Emperor will be kind to him.'

So it was all still politics after all. Calpurnia was not the only one, the anger was in the air now. The Arbites clubbed the crew out of the way and they yielded with a spiritless shuffle; Phae's team stepped to the plinths and began to reverse the security protocols that had locked the ship down. A message went from Calpurnia to Nakayama and an order went from Nakayama to the arbitrators who were still coming off the *Clarion* and onto the *Sanctus*.

'Curate Majjiah. Other shipboard Ministorum staff. Passengers, probably with the Curate, probably Ecclesiarchal officers.

Find them.'

AND OF COURSE they were found. The Arbites sweep was efficient and merciless. The tech-priests in the enginarium had their men muster up and surrender instantly, and the skeleton crews in the cargo levels were quickly rounded up. The *Sanctus* was travelling crew-light and lacked the mammoth manpower of a warship anyway, and the roundup took less than an hour. It was after that that the cyber-mastiffs and their controllers began to comb the decks, armed with gene-traces from the preachers' dormitories and bundles of high-gain snooper auspexes.

As each little group was rooted out of its hiding-place it was marched to the bridge where the Arbites kept the *Sanctus* in the centre of the ring of Navy ships. The preachers were scared but defiant, while the last few armsmen who were guarding them were simply scared. There were three shootouts, all small and panicked affairs. Four more armsmen were dead and two Arbites injured before the priests all stood in an indignant mob on the bridge.

And as the last hours of the day ebbed away Calpurnia, Nakayama and Zhow took ship for Hydraphur again, empty-handed and all in filthy moods. Zhow's rotund augur had been marched, panting, up and down the ship over and over and swore he could find not the faintest trace of witch-taint: the aura of the Navigator found and accounted for, the rest of the ship was clean. The cyber-mastiffs combed the same tunnels and tanks and holds with scent-signatures from Hydraphur locked into their brains and found nothing either.

No trace of scented lamp-oil, explosive or othwise, and no scent-print belonging to the invisible gunman or to any of the prisoners in the Wall. Calpurnia had been so sure, and now all she had were more questions.

Dead end.

CALPURNIA SAT WITH her chin in her hands in a window-gallery on the inner face of the Ring, the great adamantine girdle that hung above Hydraphur's equator. Its wall curved away to either side of the window, studded with turrets and docking towers, glittering like the city that the Ring effectively was. The crinkled face of Hydraphur spread out below them, but the window ran high enough that she could also look beyond it to Galata, Hydraphur's moon, a peach-coloured ghost from the surface but stark and ice-silver from space, studded with glittering clusters of defence stations.

Around them were dark iron walls inlaid with panels of wood, and curling metalwork adorned the furniture, doors and rails. All the chambers of the Ring that Calpurnia had seen had an odd, antique look that didn't seem to match any other ship or building she had been in, but the disturbing atmosphere took her mind off that in short order. Keeping a construct the size of the Ring from being pulled to fragments by the tidal patterns of the sun, Galata and the rest of Hydraphur's bizarre double ecliptic was a challenge that had surpassed even the building of such a thing in the first place: sections of it tens of kilometres long were built to flex and slide, allowing the Ring to gently distort instead of remaining rigid and shattering. At intervals the band of the Ring passed through great square bastions, the most heavily fortified and protected parts of a construct that was itself one giant fortress, housing the gravitic field generators that helped smooth out the roughest of the stresses without interfering with the gravity on the Ring's decks. Someone had told Calpurnia on her way to Hydraphur that the Mechanicus adepts trained there were renowned through the Segmentum for their grasp of gravitic engineering, simply from the experiences of managing the Ring.

The constant flexing and moving of the station was what allowed it to survive, but it meant a constant undertow of noise, soft groans, rumbles, and the occasional high squeal. Veteran crews joked about the Ring's chatter or the lullabies she sang; there was apparently a whole range of superstitions about what certain noises meant to those who heard them. All Calpurnia knew was that it was ruining her nerves.

The locked-together shapes of *Aurum Sanctus* and *Judgement's Clarion* were still somewhere out in space, and would remain so until the legalities were over. Calpurnia refused to let herself think about how long that might take. Captain-Commodore Esmerian, on the other hand, had been in a fine humour once he had heard the reports of the *Sanctus* boarding and had immediately ordered a dromon runner-ship to carry them back to Hydraphur at top speed. The dromonae were in-system boats, cramped and stuffy and with none of the soaring spaces of the interstellar ships, but that had suited Calpurnia's mood just fine.

'We have eliminated an alternative, arbitor,' Zhow told her now, 'and that is valuable.' It sounded as though he were trying to convince himself. Calpurnia thought that he still wanted to believe the *Sanctus* was the culprit – he had left his augurs on board to keep sweeping decks they insisted they had sniffed over thoroughly already.

'I don't know that we have. The timing is still suspicious. That ship may not have brought the wyrd in, but there still might be links to the explosion.'

Zhow grunted. 'My province is the psyker exclusively,' he said. 'Ruling the ship out of involvement with him was my priority.'

'I see,' said Calpurnia. 'You don't think that the Navigator's involvement with the Ecclesiarchy is a little strange? And what about their terror of the Navy? Why would the eparchal envoys be so frightened? Come to think of it, why was the Navy so quick to take our side? I understood all that talk about secret envoys and power bases, but I didn't understand why.'

'That, at least, I can answer,' Zhow put his back to the window, his hands laced behind him. 'That ship was in service to the Cathedral, which is to say to the High Reverend Eparch Baszle, the highest clergyman on Hydraphur. Now, the Eparch in reality has authority only over the world of Hydraphur itself, and some of the outlying civilian-controlled dockings and gates. Which is to say, just a pocket in the middle of the system. That makes the priests attached to the Naval squadrons a powerful force: they are answerable to their own military-religious hierarchy and have their own chain of command up to the Pontifex Militas aboard the Admiral's ship. "Curates of the flag", they're known as, although the title is a vernacular one with no formal Ecclesiastical currency. A powerful faction in the system since their positions can cross the divide between Naval and civil zones better than most. And because they recruit and appoint their own successors, they're self-perpetuating.'

'Sounds like an excellent reason for the Ministorum and the Navy to work together, not undercut each other like this. But there's something I don't know, isn't there? Of course there is,' Calpurnia growled.

'When Lord Admiral Invisticone was assassinated,' Zhow told her with a reproving look, 'the Ministorum on Terra took very swift action. At that juncture the appointment of a new Eparch was about due and with no formally appointed Lord Admiral they saw the opportunity to get one of their own in, someone who had a hard-line view about traditional Ecclesiarchal authority and would be a wedge against the curates of the flag, who in the cardinals' view have taken on a little too much Navy culture to be entirely trustworthy.'

'Which is why you know about all this?' said Nakayama across the room.

'I know it as background. We–' Zhow cut off whatever he had been about to say and began lecturing Calpurnia again. 'Baszle is a relatively recent appointment; it took that long for the infighting over whose choice would be Eparch to finish and the appointment to take place. He's been aggressively trying to build up the authority of the Cathedral ever since. Which is why, I think, his agents feared foul play from Navy ships, and why the Navy were so helpful in assisting an operation they knew would humiliate the Eparch's office. You should probably know,' he went on as Calpurnia got to her feet, 'that Baragry, your designated shadow on Hydraphur, is of Baszle's inner circle. He's certainly been assigned to you to monitor our investigation and to steer it in convenient ways. He will have something to say about being left behind, I'm sure. If you'll excuse me now, I shall check on our flight back to the Bosporian.'

'Thank you for your briefing, inquisitor,' Calpurnia replied. 'If you need me, I'll be out in the hall hitting myself repeatedly in the head with a shock-maul.' Zhow gave her an odd look, but left without saying anything more.

'Don't let it get to you, Shira,' Nakayama said. 'You'll never have everyone in Hydraphur pulling in the same direction, no matter how hard you try.' She sighed, her hand stealing up to rub her scars again: up, down, up.

'The worst of it is that I keep forgetting that this is only the start of my duties,' she said. 'Bosporian Hive is already a challenge. I'm sure I could spend the next ten years of my life learning about half of what there is to know about how that one hive works, and there are how many more hives here?'

'Eight on Hydraphur, not counting the smaller conurbations and the fortified shrines and forges. About twice that through the rest of the system, again not counting fortification clusters, Navy complexes and spaceborne settlements.' She had got used to Leandro's flowery speech and Zhow's lectures, so that now she kept waiting after Nakayama's sparsely-worded replies for more. The stocky little arbitrator sat down in the chair Zhow had vacated; at rest, he gave the impression of a powerful machine packed and stowed. 'Twenty-five hives, who knows how many other communities, sixteen planets, hundreds of space-docks and fortresses, more than forty billion people. That's the permanent population. The Naval and civilian shipping through the system can boost that by anywhere from one to ten percent.'

'It's humbling,' she said. 'I knew this system's scale as I travelled here, but it's only just hitting home at gut level. How do you go about even starting to keep the law in a place this complex?' She inwardly cringed at the question as soon as she'd asked it: it was a rookie's question, and she straight away wondered how it would sound when it got back to Dvorov. But Nakayama didn't seem to take it that way.

'By not trying to do everything yourself,' he said simply. 'Look at the way you handled the Aquila Gate incident. Promptly, correctly and thoroughly. But you did it all in person. Perfect example: fretting over the traffic patterns and keeping order on the Telepine Way at the same time as you were trying to confer with the verispex teams, decide on the processing of your prisoners and co-ordinate your operations with Inquisitor Zhow. Right in line with your style. Oh, you've been studying this system,' he went on as she turned to stare at him, 'but we have studied you too. Are you surprised we studied up on who we were getting? Did you think we won you in a round of seven-deck? Your reputation is sterling, I haven't read of too many finer careers from one of your age. Hell, finer careers full stop. But your reputation is also of handling everything yourself. I bet there weren't even a dozen times in your entire command at Ephaeda when you gave a delegation below Level Three, and I bet you can remember each and every time you did it. That's fine in a precinct house, but not here. Here you won't even have a fixed command. The majore sends us wherever in the system he feels our particular strengths are warranted, to take charge of a particular hotspot for as long as we're needed. You'll have been all around Hydraphur within a year, I don't doubt – Krieg will be picking your assignments with that in mind.'

Calpurnia still couldn't quite stop herself from blinking at his casual use of the lord marshal's first name, but she let it by. Outside the port the sky was still crowded with hundreds upon hundreds of moving points of light, each one a giant, centuries-old warship or defence fortress. Beyond them more points, the nearer planets.

She didn't yet know the Hydraphurn sky well enough to recognise them, or even pick their ecliptic. She had seen maps and models of Hydraphur's system and had dutifully tried to follow the astrographers' treatises on it, but most of them were technical enough to swamp her knowledge of the subject: she had decided to accept that no one really knew how two intersecting planetary planes could form or remain stable, accept that they had and did and get on with her job of policing them.

Hold that thought, she told herself, and turned to look at Hydraphur again. Soon they would board a shuttle and cast off, then the curve of the horizon would barely be visible any more, the drab surface would focus into mountains, shallow seas, hives and forge-towns full of people and plots and enmities and rivalries. Suddenly the descent back to the planet felt to her more like a drop into a mire that was waiting to suck her down to her death.

Eleventh Day of Septista

Seven days to the Mass of Saint Balronas.
The Master's Devotions and the Rite of Common Lamentation.
The Anchorites' Penitence (Ecclesiarchy).

Today marks the final week of preparations for the great mass and the beginning of the Sanguinala. The Master's Devotions are the first of the day's fixed observances, and those who cannot attend the service itself should consider one of the 'proxy' services held elsewhere between Ecclesiarchy and Naval preachers even as the Devotions are conducted by the Master of the Vigil and the Naval curia. Although those with pressing business may be excused from the Devotions, all pious folk should be ready for the Rite of Common Lamentation at noon and dressed in at least one item of green; ideally the hands should be shrouded in green cloth or gauze. Green gloves or green chain or yarn wrapped about the hands is an acceptable substitute.

By today the festive clothes for the Sanguinala should be finished and ready. It is inappropriate to wear these garments between this day and the morning of the mass, so this afternoon is the final opportunity to make sure they are clean and of good fit. This should be done in private and alone where possible, and the clothes packed carefully away afterward, while those caring for children or the infirm should provide whatever assistance is needed in this regard.

CHAPTER SIX

THE WEAPONS RESTED on rich midnight-blue plush, secured by tiny silver wires beneath diagrams and fabricator's charts, painted and embroidered onto silk of the same rich blue. The weapons themselves were a simple gunmetal grey, devoid of ornamentation, and the contrast gave shapes on the thick cloth a menace all their own.

The microwire cutter, mounted in a bracelet and designed to flick out of a sleeve and back in a microsecond. The toxin wand to detect poison-snoopers and auto-immunisers and select just the right cocktail to bypass them. The quarrel-launcher with its deadly flare-winged skewers which could glide along a target's pheromone-trail for an hour before they accelerated in for the kill. And the long-barrelled subsonic pistol, quiet, accurate, deadly. Calpurnia knew she tended to be too straight-backed on such matters, but she was surprised at the strength of unease and distaste that looking at the weapons gave her.

The armourers had set up their display in the chilly grey briefing chamber of the Cross-Four precinct fortress, far out across the city-plain from Bosporian Hive near the sea-cliffs. The fortress-tower served a dedicated Arbites landing-pad, built high above the surrounding slums on great rockcrete piles garlanded with razor-wire and defence spikes, and studded with vox-horns that every few minutes would bellow one of the stern maxims from the Arbites *First Book of Hours* out over the roofs below them. While she approved of the thinking, Calpurnia couldn't help wondering whether anyone in those hab-stacks below them got much sleep.

Half an hour after casting off from the Ring Nakayama had produced a data-slate and told Calpurnia to close her eyes and point to it. Self-consciously she had stuck out a finger, opened her eyes and found she was pointing, more or less, to a map on the slate's display. 'Cross-Four', Nakayama had said, 'as good a place as any.' And they had swung out of their registered course to land at Cross-Four. Calpurnia had seen the sense of randomising their flight path, and anyway the airspace restrictions had been tightened to keep a great column of clear air over the hive and it was best to keep well clear. By coincidence it was also close to the fabricatories and residential towers of the Tudela family, considered some of the finest boutique weaponsmiths in the Imperium, and Nakayama had taken the opportunity to have them rousted out of bed and brought to the fortress.

Now the normally bare chamber looked like a trade fair. The Tudela had recovered from their befuddlement at having to muster their wares for a midnight ride, and set up their displays as though they were in a hive noble's audience-court. Calpurnia and Nakayama received them there – Zhow had commandeered a Rhino just after they landed and had disappeared towards the distant hive, telling neither of them his business and showing little interest in the Tudela audience. Calpurnia had gone along with it, but it wasn't until a full squad of arbitrators marched in around a motor-gurney that she fully understood Nakayama's plan. She had been building up to another one of her brooding moods about the Hydraphur garrison's velvet-glove handling of suspects. The Tudela weren't suspects, they were experts.

Calpurnia was happy with calling on knowledge from other Adeptus – Mechanicus, Administratum, Telepathica – whoever else shared her oaths of loyalty to the Throne of Earth. If anything, she knew that her picture of the Adeptus as unquestioning allies seemed starry-eyed to a lot of her colleagues. But the idea of going cap-in-hand to an ordinary Imperial subject (doubtless a worthy subject, she added to herself guiltily, a worthy and pious citizen, whose type held the Imperium together) was alien. What was bothering her, when she eventually managed to nail the thought down, was her conviction that anything worth knowing should already be known by the Adeptus. The idea that this might not be the case was bothering her.

The arbitrators carried the pannier to the centre of the chamber and hinged the top back. The knot of Tudela, huddled into a clump of midnight-blue velvet gowns, slender silver jewellery and face-shrouding collars and hoods, began muttering and shuffling forward. Dvorov or Leandro must have persuaded the Adeptus Mechanicus to part with their evidence, at least for a time.

There in the unfolded display racks sat another set of killing tools: a heavy augmetic eyepiece, mounted on a steel plate with a skull-fitting curve, trailing the filaments that had joined it to the man's nerves; a coronet studded with perceptor spines and inward-pointing wires that had fed and sped the brain; and finally, sitting on a rack of its own, the pistol itself, skeletal and long-barrelled with a swept-back handguard like Navy sabres, studded as the other two were with feeds and interfaces that had embedded the thing into its wielder. It should have been next to impossible to miss with, and Calpurnia gave yet another silent thanks for the hot fogs and incendiary displays that had cruelled that augmetic eye's aim. Imperial dogma took it for granted that the spirits of previous wielders hung over all weapons, and on each component was a scarlet purity seal and a film of sacred balms to exorcise any lingering presence of the witch-gunman.

The weaponsmiths closed in, weaving in and out between Imperial Gothic and some kind of odd, croaking dialect that she assumed was a House language or tech-cant. Two of them, a journeywoman in a filigreed facemask and a man who had been introduced to her as House Elder Makriss Tudela, with a shock of white hair and a discreet dusting of tiny platinum nuggets across the shoulders and sleeves of his tunic, bent over the weapons to caress them with tiny augmetic microbrushes in their fingertips, taking exact measures and tasting the weapons' forging and composition. The other Tudela looked on solemnly from the rich cloth hoods that stood high above their heads. The augmetics they carried were startlingly delicate and elegant, silver like Makriss's rather than brass like those of the Artisans Quarter. She didn't know if that symbolised anything or not. It probably did.

The analysis didn't take long. Makriss and his offsider both pulled back from the weapons and the whole delegation withdrew to the other side of a display of subcutaneous flick-blades to confer. Calpurnia stepped to Nakayama's side.

'Were you able to hear any more of that than I was?' she asked him.

'Not that I understood,' he said with a slight shake of his head. 'But I think I picked up enough to know that they're stumped and they don't want to admit it.'

'I had the same conclusion,' Calpurnia said. 'Hah, they might be proud of their secret cant but they need to work on masking their body language. Is that significant?'

'If they can't recognise them? Very significant, yes.' Several Tudela had now produced data-slates and Makriss and his journeywoman were stroking their augmetised fingertips over their surfaces. Makriss's eyes were closed, his lids quivering; the journeywoman had begun to sway slightly. 'One of the first things that old Makriss told me was that if he and his staff don't know a weapon design then there's no standard design to know.'

'Is he right?'

'I suspect he is,' Nakayama told her. 'Tudela are the cream, the best boutique weaponsmiths in the system, which means in the sector and maybe the segmentum. They're so respected they've been able to maintain their position without affiliating to one of the mercantile syndicates.'

'Which is why they don't have one of those double surnames, then? I'd wondered.'

'That's right.' Nakayama tilted his head at the weaponry around them. 'Battlefleet Pacificus command commissions Tudela weapons to present to its officers as battle honours if that gives you any idea. And yet he looks at that gunman's kit and says that they're so foreign he can't even pick the archprint they used or what school the designer followed. I don't have quite his expertise, but I can see that these display pieces they've brought in are examples of most of the basic Hydraphur design schools, and that weapon doesn't have much in common with any of them.' He stopped as the delegation approached again and Makriss Tudela bowed.

'Arbitor Senioris Nakayama, Arbitor Senioris Calpurnia. On behalf of the family Tudela we confirm that the weapons and devices are of the kind that we construct – cousins to our own craftsmanship, as it were. But we have bent ourselves to a search lest they bear traces of the archprints bequeathed by the beneficent Mechanicus, or lest they even should reveal traces of our own smiths or even, should I not be too bold in making such a reference, those of our rivals.'

'Your rivals?' asked Calpurnia. 'You can vouch for those weapons not being made in this system? Or are you talking about a bigger or smaller area?' Tudela blinked at the question and gave Calpurnia what she was starting to think of as the 'oh, you're the one who's not from here' look.

'From our own weaponworkers? No,' he replied. Calpurnia could sense him turning the flowery language down a notch. 'Tudela has inherited certain design axioms and privileged archprints which I will not detail, but to which your weapons do not adhere to. As to those occupying our own line of craft? There are only a handful whom I would consider capable of handiwork of this quality. Of those, the Zaphraoi are bonded to Kraegen-Medell for metals and use steels provided by that cartel; there was none of their distinctive taste to the metals we inspected. Durska-Haggan can produce sighting augmetics as fine as this, but their expertise in actual firearms is shallow. To bond the pistol mechanism and the augmentation of its wearer requires a grasp of both mechanical and biometric mysteries that I know to be beyond them.' Makriss pondered for a moment, running a thumb over the fine silver filaments braided into his moustache.

'The weapon shops at the Bescalion Dock – these are operated directly under Navy control in the Gyre Marmarea, you understand. They would have the finesse to produce these, I think, being presided over directly by Mechanicus inductees. But all the major fabricatories at Bescalion operate in zero-gravity. Their microengineering processes quite depend upon the fact. And all the components of your specimens here were crafted under gravity.'

'You can tell that?' Calpurnia asked him.

'Certain minute biases in density and balance correspond exactly to equivalent weapons made by ourselves – that means your specimens were made in Hydraphur-equivalent gravity. Those biases are what gravity-free forging is specifically intended to counteract.'

'It rules out the Navy almost totally,' put in Nakayama. 'They like to keep their ships and stations a fraction below standard

Hydraphur gee. Nothing you'd notice, but it would show up on the sort of scales I imagine Master Tudela uses.'

'Just so,' said Makriss, looking pleased. 'I believe that my original conclusion stands. My own suspicion is that these pieces came from some considerable distance from Hydraphur. Of the most respected armourers in this system, none had a hand in their creation.' He finished his words with a chivalrous little bow, and the sudden change of manner made it Calpurnia's turn to blink.

'Then thank you for your time, Master Tudela, for your help, and for food for thought. The proctor here will arrange an orderly return to your home.'

'The service was entirely the pleasure of myself and my family,' Makriss replied with another bow. 'All I might beg from you, should I presume…?' Nakayama gave a slight tilt of his head. 'I dare say I should not even need to point out that although our skill and our works are our best envoys, a position such as ours must also on occasion be maintained with, how shall I put it… a knowledge of…'

'I think I understand,' Nakayama told him. 'If we do find out who made these weapons and where, I shall see about sharing that with you.' Satisfied, Makriss bowed again, his retinue imitating him and staying bowed over while the two arbites senioris turned away. As they left the chamber Calpurnia heard a sudden, muted burst of activity as the Tudela began taking their display to pieces.

'And once again, we're back where we started,' she growled as the doors swung shut behind them and they climbed the great spiral stairwell that made up the fortress's spine. In the quiet spell between the night-to-dawn shifts the stairs were empty enough for them to hear their footsteps echo.

'Not exactly,' Nakayama said. 'We're able to conclude some things. I don't believe that the killer was smuggled in from elsewhere, I think that was Tudela's way of reassuring themselves that a weapon can't be made in this system without them knowing about it.'

'I wondered about that. Didn't he confirm the weapons had been made under gravity identical to Hydraphur's? How would someone counterfeit that so exactly?'

'Well said. So the enemy has access to a private weaponsmith so secret they can produce high-quality designs that Hydraphur's finest armourer can't identify.'

'And said weaponsmith is also so unscrupulous that they will build those designs into a proscribed witch-psyker,' Calpurnia added. 'The weapons married up too well with the assassin's own abilities for them not to have been deliberate.'

'And we know that they were prepared to risk having all this revealed in the course of taking a crack at you,' finished Nakayama. They had reached the uppermost landing, where galleries led away to the corners of the fortress. Calpurnia paused to look up at the great steel aquila which hung from chains in the dome overhead and was mortified to realise that she was breathing hard – on garrison duty she could have run up and down these stairs and barely notice the effort. She wondered when this investigation would let her get some physical training in. It was just another little thing that seemed to be sliding out of her control.

'So our enemy,' she said, 'is even more powerful than we thought and even more intent on seeing me dead than we had realised.'

'If that isn't progress, what is?' asked Nakayama. His face was still deadpan, and Calpurnia simply had to hope that he was joking.

BEFORE INQUISITOR ZHOW had disappeared he had harangued the Arbites at length about the lack of a skimmer-car to carry him back to Bosporian and demanded a secure voxmat room where he could debrief with his staff. It had seemed to Calpurnia to be as much a fit of pique over not being told about their change of landing place as anything else. Now they were met on the landing by a garrison clerk with a message for Calpurnia that the voxmat link had been kept live: the Master of the Vigil of Saint Balronas, Hallyan Kalfus-Medell, had received word that she was at Cross-Four and requested that she speak with him at her earliest convenience. Normally she would have waited pointedly for a while befor answering, but she needed something to take her mind off the disappointment of the still-untraceable weapons.

The transmission chamber was set into the topmost rampart of the fortress, beneath the dome itself, one of a forest of metal fingers that carried encrypted vox and pict transmissions, anchored the fortress's void shields when they were raised, or were simply dummies to throw off attackers and saboteurs. The chamber itself was meant for private transmissions by senior Arbites, or as a bolt-hole for an arbitor or two to seal themselves in and keep transmitting if the rest of the fortress was somehow overrun.

Calpurnia found herself in a narrow stone cavity with a simple vox-panel at head height (her head, anyway) on the far wall, the space partly blocked by an incongruously soft leather seat. Whether it was a fixture or something Zhow had had brought in was not apparent.

Calpurnia noticed a slight hum from the panel as she composed herself and thought about her opening words. It was time to start dealing with these people in the right way, courteous but not servile. She thought that she–

'Arbitor Calpurnia.' She jumped as Hallyan's voice cracked from the panel. Only slightly, but enough to make her glad the link only carried vox and not images.

'Lord Hallyan,' she replied. 'Your message said you couldn't wait until I returned to Bosporian. If it has you waiting into the small hours to talk to me I assume it was urgent.'

'So you are there, arbitor. I thought I could hear you moving around. I must speak with you about this apparent investigation into the attempts to wreck what is the most pious and holy time of year for the entire Hydraphur system, Navy and civilian alike. This is not something you can be ignorant of. You've been right at the centre of every important disruption since the moment when things started to go wrong.'

Lord Hallyan was livid, it was clear. The niceties of language and the careful manner from their first meeting were dropping away and his voice was snapping with anger, the effect magnified by the slightly tinny tones of the vox-link.

'To repeat your words back to you, Lord Hallyan, I've had a quite personal involvement at every step of the way.' She knew he couldn't see her but she was still adopting a formal stance, feet apart and hands behind her back. 'Involvement with minor things like attempts on my life, things that stick in the memory. What else would you like to remind me of concerning my "apparent" investigation–'

'I would like to remind you of a simple matter.' Hallyan was talking before she had finished. 'This is a crucial time in our religious calendar, and the Adeptus Ministorum has charged me with overseeing it. I believe, arbitor, that myself and those members of the Ministorum who are assisting me deserve better treatment than you have seen fit to hand out. Reverend Baragry and I have both been informed of the treatment of the *Aurum Sanctus*, a ship operating under the direct auspices of the Ecclesiarchy which for some reason the Adeptus Arbites felt necessary to subject to a disgracefully heavy-handed interception! The–'

'Have a care, my lord,' Calpurnia interrupted. 'Remember who you're addressing. Your *temporary* office allows you a certain familiarity of manner, but you are no Adeptus and you are no arbitor.'

There was a pause, long enough for the link to begin crackling and fizzing again. Calpurnia could even make out the faint buzz and clink of the Mechanicus prayer-wheels among the vox gear.

'Very well,' came Hallyan's voice eventually. 'My... my apologies for my abruptness, my duties weigh on me at present. I made the declaration of the Precepts last sunset and will be sharing the conduct of the Common Lamentation today, as well as certain ceremonial responsibilities conferred uniquely on me.' He sounded tired but still pleased at being able to point his station out. 'But I would ask that you recall,' he went on, 'the Ecclesiarchy were generous enough to provide you Reverend Baragry as an advisor because the religious implications of even the smallest Arbites action during this period could be profound. I am at a loss to understand why you have sidelined Baragry in the way that you did. I understand that you deliberately left him here when you took ship to intercept the *Sanctus*. Is this true?'

Calpurnia wondered at the question. If Hallyan was dealing with the Ecclesiarchy he would have known it was. On the other hand, his temporary but quasi-religious office made her baulk at the idea of telling him outright that the last thing they had needed was an Ecclesiarchal agent underfoot while they chased down a vessel operating under Ecclesiarchal charter. Nakayama had made a point of sidelining Baragry as they prepared to launch the interception flight, and Calpurnia had left Bannon behind with him to try to make it look less suspicious.

She thought of the overdressed aristocrats she had seen around the High Mesé and wondered what one of them would come up with, and how she would phrase it.

'It seemed to us, Lord Hallyan, that it was the best thing we could do for the Ecclesiarchy in the circumstances. I understand that there is some friction between the Ecclesiarchy and the Navy over certain matters of religious jurisdiction. We were unsure of the link between the ship and the Aquila Gate – it now seems tenuous, but we had no way of telling that at first. Given the possibility that intercepting the *Sanctus* might embarrass the Ecclesiarchy, we excluded the Reverend Baragry – and yourself, for that matter – so that it would have been that much easier for the Ecclesiarchy to distance itself and denounce the *Sanctus* as a rogue.'

She was not proud of herself. The story, and the ease with which she had plucked it out of the air, left an unpleasant taste in her mouth. But from Hallyan's reaction she seemed to have played it about right.

'I remain somewhat displeased,' he said after a moment, 'but I appreciate the tactics of your decision. You might consider informing us of any future situation, however, my arbitor. I assure you that we can play the part should we need to and still dissociate in the way that you spoke of.' It took a moment for her to understand what he was saying, and when she did her distaste deepened.

'What we can also do,' Hallyan went on, 'is appraise you of the ramifications of any proposed actions the central duty of carrying out the sacred mass. I have overseen much of the preparations myself. At any given moment I will be well equipped to brief you on any proposed course of action you might wish to take in pursuing your own business, on its potential to disrupt the religious proceedings of the coming week and therefore on its advisability.'

'Are you talking about giving orders to the Adeptus Arbites, sir?'

'How you order your own activities and pursue your investigations is probably largely your own affair,' Hallyan told her airily. Either he hadn't noticed the edge in her voice or the vox-panel had dulled it out. 'And I acknowledge the good work you have done on the sabotage of the oil shipment and in pursuing the denounced assassin who attempted harm upon you personally. But as a man of experience in the society of Hydraphur I am in a position to bring your attention to consequences that you, madam arbitor senioris, might have overlooked.

'For example, the sabotage at the Aquila Gate, which I understand you were on hand to witness personally. Now, the destruction of the last shipment of oil was of no great consequence and replacement stocks were supplied to the Augustaeum by the time that the Procession of the Further Saints was due to begin. In the scheme of things the matter may not have been of great import – the damage was not significant, nor were the fatalities. But I believe you were aware, arbitor, of the considerable disruption – indeed the immobilisation – of the freight and traffic up one entire slope of the hive and the disturbances that bred.

'This is a sensitive time, Arbitor Calpurnia. Respectable citizens of the upper hive and Augustaeum are endeavouring to fulfil their pious duties and complete mundane business in time to begin their observances. I cannot find it in me to believe that you do not desire to help them, and to remove from their way any obstacle that you have power over?'

'We sealed off the Aquila Gate for a reason,' Calpurnia said. 'The destruction of that oil-dray was not just the irritating disruption to the mass preparations that you seem to want to treat it as. It was a *crime*, sir, an act of destruction and of loss of life and a gross breach of the Emperor's law and the Emperor's peace and therefore fully within our remit to investigate as we need to. I acknowledge the possible links between that act and your mass and we have told you that keeping order is a priority for us, but the Arbites are not a private security force for the mass. Understand that, please. We are Adeptus, just like the Ministorum who have granted you your *temporary* position, and our charter is Emperor-bestowed just as theirs is.'

So much for subtlety and diplomacy. There was no doubt that her feelings had registered with Hallyan this time.

'I was told, arbitor senioris, that you had familiarised yourself with life on Hydraphur.' The lord's voice was cold. 'In my next dealings with your colleagues and commander and with the Eparch of Hydraphur himself I believe that I shall convey that your familiarity is imperfect.'

'I have never pretended otherwise, but my grasp of my duty is crystal clear. Other than that, say about me what you will. I will be reporting my latest findings to the Arbitor Majore later this morning, I'll be certain to make your feelings known to him then, and I will happily comply with any directive he then chooses to give me.'

'Findings?' demanded Hallyan. 'What findings? The whole *Aurum Sanctus* affair was reported to me as a dead end.'

Was it now? Calpurnia thought. And by whom was that reported, then? But she held back the question.

'Are you familiar with the family Tudela? They maintain a fabricatory spike in the city plain and have a hereditary charter to use certain Mechanicus weapon archprints and lay machining techniques.'

'Give me a little credit. The Kalfus family were patrons-in-chief of the Tudela pavilion at the Martial Exposition at the Monocrat's summer palaces last year.' His tone changed. 'You have not been harassing the Tudela too? To think that they might be involved with something like this beggars belief. I could have told you–'

'Nothing like that, Lord Kalfus-Medell, calm yourself,' Calpurnia cut in. 'Arbitor Nakayama and I consulted them on the weaponry that the witch-assassin used in the first attempt on my life.'

'I thought that the Mechanicus had seized what remained of that.'

'No. We presented the weapons to a Tudela delegation tonight. A Makriss Tudela surveyed them, and says that they correspond to no known armourer operating in Hydraphur – the handful of machinesmiths in this system capable of producing them didn't. It's really only useful in negative terms – we can expand our list of people we *don't* believe were behind it. But it suggests one or two further steps.'

'Which are?' he asked.

'Still being decided on,' Calpurnia bluffed. 'I will ensure you are provided with any information that will be useful to you, Lord Hallyan. We must continue to co-operate in keeping the Emperor's peace through the time of the Vigil and I am sure we will be co-operating in the investigation also. Why don't we discuss the matter when I return to Bosporian? I expect to be back there during the day.'

There was a quick double-gunshot of static and another long pause. Calpurnia was wondering if the link had died by the time Hallyan answered. 'It seems we do still have certain things to discuss and set straight, Arbitor Calpurnia. Very well. You will hear from me.'

There was no click as the link broke, just silence for a minute, two, three, until Calpurnia decided the conversation must be over.

Cross-Four's vehicle hangar sat on a platform between the pilings under the main mass of the fortress, with a tangle of ramps and chain-hoists giving access to the streets and skyways of the city below. Calpurnia disapproved of this setup in the short time she had to think about it: the hangar and ramps seemed achingly vulnerable to sniper shots and missiles from the tower-blocks around them.

Her Rhino convoy rumbled down the ramps five hours into the new day, right at the heart of the patrol changeover. The Rhinos went out one at a time, spaced between the rest of the traffic, then in unison swung and sped away down a broad elevated highway. A squad in the lead vehicle, a squad in the hindmost one, and Calpurnia alone with the two crew drivers in the middle with the benches to herself.

Nakayama was staying on at Cross-Four to audit airspace security procedures; Calpurnia had agreed, but felt his absence now – she had wanted to talk with him again. Casting her mind back over the last few days was almost dizzying: the Cathedral to the Aquila Gate to the *Aurum Sanctus* and back. The dead end at the *Sanctus* meant that the trail was colder than she had thought, and getting colder by the moment. She was even starting to wonder if the attacks at the Gate were connected to the witch-gunman at all.

And there was still fallout she had barely considered. The second prisoner from the dray, the task of tracking down the vehicle's owners. A review of security at all the Augustaeum gates, to make sure the Arbites were better prepared in future. The paralysing traffic snarls up and down the south-west slope of the hive were only just starting to abate after two days. For all its status and odd quirks, Bosporian Hive and its skirt of sprawl were no different from any other high-density Imperial city and so the snarls had created tension, the tension had created unrest, and violence had sprung up along the major traffic roots like brushfires.

Blameless Imperial citizens had also died at the Aquila Gate, trampled in the stampedes or caught in the flames. Calpurnia knew that had she had the whole terrible incident to do again her commands would have been the same and those people would still have died. *Ut iusta esse, lex nobis severus necesse est,* they had taught early and often at the Schola Arbitorum, 'to be just, our law must be cruel,' and also *Lex Imperatoris, quia via vitarum nobis, obiesquat,* 'the Emperor's law be obeyed, even in the manner of our lives' ending'. It was a harsh thing to dwell on, alone on a juddering steel bench in a rumbling tank in a strange city in the pre-dawn dark, but every arbitor knew that the rule of Imperial Law came at a price.

But 'the right to command is bought with duty' was an Ultramar maxim that Calpurnia had internalised by the time she was ten: it was carved into the polished quartz lintel of the Calpurnii's hearth-house, and it had been inscribed below the seal on her father's brief letter of well-wishing when she had been brevetted to the Ephaeda garrison command. In many Ultima Segmentum garrisons, where civilian deaths were necessary in an Arbites action, garrison preachers would visit their families for special devotions to speed the unlucky souls' passage to the Emperor's side. She didn't know if that tradition had spread this far (a resigned little part of her mind clocked up one more thing about Hydraphur policing she didn't know), but if it didn't then that was one little bit of her home culture she wanted to plant here.

There was a brief wash of light through the vision ports and Calpurnia peered out. They had just passed under an arch of rockcrete, arclit in the urban dimness swarming with work-crews blasting away the accretion of pollutant grime. She remembered something in her mountain of briefings about the last-minute rush of building and beautifications that both Bosporian Hive and the plain city crammed into before the mass; around her now she could see other projects dotted about the city, all lit up, all still being feverishly worked on despite the saints-forsaken hour to be finished before the enforced days of rest began.

The little lit patches got more frequent as the bright bulk of Bosporian loomed in the middle distance over the smoke-wrapped city stacks. Within half an hour they passed a procession of statues of Imperial martyrs Calpurnia didn't recognise, but with appropriately gruesome sculpted injuries and saintly heavenward gazes, then a miniature city of temporary amphitheatre-chapels of scaffolding and reinforced sheetboards, standing side by side in an empty pedestrian concourse. After that a pair of triumphal obelisks commemorating long-dead admirals, which workers were shrouding in dark drapes and carefully fitting with auto-launchers that would shed the mourning-cloth and fill the air with scarlet fireworks the moment the Sanguinala was rung in. Further in where the streets narrowed great hoardings were being set up and banners strung between buildings; in the festivities after the mass they would be joyous and bright-coloured, but now they were all in the spirit of the Vigil, sombre and urging repentance. The giant images were simplistic to the point of crudity, but still striking: agonised, wild-eyed heretics stumbling in the dark that symbolised their souls, or stylised pictures of the Emperor with His face turned away and the saints and angels weeping around Him. The localised, lit-up pockets of activity gave the city a strange, on-off aspect as they passed through it. Calpurnia realised they were seeing so many because they were speeding down one of the arterial highways to the base of the hive itself, and that put a thought into her head.

'Randomise our course, please,' she called forward into the driver's compartment. 'Pick a minor patrol route into the base of the Wall and follow that, not this main road. Notify the other two Rhinos in code, even if the vox-band is safe.'

Less than a minute later they swerved off the highway and down into the canyon-maze between the stacks and spires. The lower streets were as narrow as slots and overhung by the towers that boarded them; the Hydraphur fashion seemed to be for sheer walls for at least the first dozen floors and the roads were shut-in and dark. Now they were off the highway she could see more people: shifting, scurrying night-time people who shied away from the lights of Arbites Rhinos, fearful of a credentials stop or an outright curfew-cull.

But even down here preparation for the celebrations was going on, to Calpurnia's uncharitable surprise. The crews were smaller, and she noted with approval that some were dressed in the barbed circlets and heavy sackcloth jerkins of penal details, working under foremen in Arbites or Ecclesiarchal uniforms. The works were more modest, too, fewer giant statues and hoardings, more basic repairs to the roads and buildings and simple devotional pennants.

There was a crackle from the vox-grille in the drivers' cockpit, and Calpurnia shuffled forward to find out what had been said.

'Route up ahead is blocked, ma'am,' the co-driver told her. She had a knotted scar jagging down one cheek and in under her jaw that made her lip move oddly. 'The comptrollers at Lowdock Tower just voxed it through. Pre-Vigil civic works running past due. We didn't know about it until one of the foot patrols for this sector called it in. It just got voxed out to us once the comptrollers realised where we were.'

'How did they know we were here?'

'Convoys are tracked, and we reported in when we turned off the highway.'

'Pick an alternative route at random, then. Now.' The driver nodded and muttered into the short-range vox, and a moment later they veered into a narrower street still, between cliff-like rockcrete walls and sullen strings of lights. 'And no more long-range vox-chatter. I don't care if the dispatcher hails us or not. Short-range only, and only to keep us tight when we change routes and to pass on instructions.'

'Understood, ma'am.'

Calpurnia approved of rules and order, and in her junior arbitrator positions had been very suspicious of the importance that her trainers and commanders put on intuition and the feel of situations. That was a judgement she had been forced to re-evaluate, and she had made an addition to her list of the chief weapons of the Arbites: awe and fear; the shock-maul and grapplehawk and Executioner shell; the Rhino and cyber-mastiff and the Book of Law... and the way that a seemingly innocuous fact weighed oddly in the mind, the way that things struck the senses as being just a little unsettled, like a picture hung crookedly in the corner of your vision, the little unquiet voice whispering, wait... something about this feels wrong.

The feeling got stronger on the second redirection. Their new street was completely blocked with a caterpillar-tracked street-crawler, parked in the middle of the road and supporting a thick web of scaffolding braced against the walls. Their lead driver was alert enough to veer off while there was still a turnoff between them and the workers, but Calpurnia was peering down the street through a darkvisor as they turned. There were men in the gantry it carried, working at anchoring it to the walls. But there was no other equipment, no banners or murals, and they had all stopped working as the Rhinos approached and watched them as they turned aside.

They sped through an alley narrow enough that Calpurnia could have slipped her hand out of the vision slot and lost the skin off her fingertips on the building walls. Then they were into another thoroughfare and intersection, the way ahead blocked by grumbling orange-painted engines just starting to break the surface of the road, and downramps to each side brightly lit but empty. In the one on the left two men ducked out of sight as they passed. A quick, tooth-sharp burst of satisfaction punctured Calpurnia's unease. They had slipped up.

'Turn. Full reverse, now, before the intersection. Back the way we came, retrace our steps. Move. Now.' The knowledge that something was badly wrong had sprung into her head fully-formed and she didn't waste time doubting it. She steadied herself as the three APCs spun in almost their own length and accelerated away again. She was impressed as they shot back into the alleyway – Rhinos were built for toughness and reliability, not high-speed agility, but the crews were making them dance around the corners like pursuit buggies. They came out of the alley, powered away from the scaffold and Calpurnia let them make one more turn, then called a halt and was rocked hard against the driver's partition as the three APCs braked. They were in a silent, empty street, almost overhung enough to be a passageway of asphalt and rockcrete grimed almost black, graffiti and ragged tracts covering the walls. Calpurnia ordered the lights off, armed her pistol and reached for the hatch.

It took three silent minutes to decide that the men from the roadworks were not coming around the corner after them, and another two to firmly override the protests of the convoy's proctor that he should call in backup. Eight minutes after they had halted and powered down the Rhinos they moved out. The first and third carriers each carried ten combat-kitted arbitrators, and with them came the three co-drivers, lighter-armoured and nervous about leaving their partner-drivers behind.

'You three won't come with us,' she said softly, looking at the scar-faced woman from her own Rhino. 'Open the top hatches on your Rhinos and get the pintle weapons up and loaded. What are you carrying? Shotcannon, stubbers…? Storm-bolters. Good. The Rhinos will be the second wave. The rest of you, listen. These work crews are false. They were mobilised to trap us when we left the highway, but we foxed them by switching paths. They've been having to keep moving, trying to keep in front of us. They're good enough to keep spying or guessing the routes we switch into and moving to block them, but they had to move too fast to be able to keep it looking like coincidence.'

'Are we assaulting them, ma'am?' asked one of the squad proctors.

'Not front-on. Whatever they have in mind, it'll be set up to deal with three Rhinos coming at them, because that's what they expected. Every door in this city should have an Arbites override on its seals. Yes? Good. We're getting inside this building and coming out, well, somewhere, wherever we can break out into or behind that scaffold. We'll need a decent number of shock-grenades, have you got–? Good. Once we've got the ambush disorganised, the Rhinos will come round and lend fire support from the street. Report it to the nearest precinct house at that point too and we'll get our own backup on the move.'

'Arbitor senioris, are you sure that we shouldn't get backed up now and make sure we hit them with overwhelming–'

'No. Even if they don't intercept the transmission or hear the backup coming, by the time it gets here they'll have run or tracked us down and attacked on their terms, not ours. This way is risky, but not taking that risk is not going to work. We're taking too long as it is.' She strapped on her helmet. 'The Law commands and the Emperor protects. Let's go.'

The main doors to the tower between them and the streetcrawler were under a shadowy overhang at the far corner. Calpurnia did not yet have a key-signet, but the proctor's signet was enough to override the locks and send the security shackles clanking back into the walls. After a moment they had picked their way up a narrow staircase and into a gallery around over a great chamber that took up the first three floors of the tower and, it looked like, possibly a below-ground level as well. It was the office of some kind of courier-house: the torchlight showed racks of crates and pack-harnesses for humans and servitors down below them, and the gallery was packed with row upon row of narrow, tilted clerking-desks over which the despatchers and ledger-keepers would be hunched during the day.

They were halfway through the gallery when they met the watchman. He was middle-aged and squint-eyed, nervously clenching his hands over a long-barrelled laspistol. Calpurnia doubted that he recognised her rank badges, but he must have realised that she was far senior to the lead arbitors and proctors he was used to.

'I am so sorry, sir arb… er, madam arbitor. I can think of no reason why you would have been called out, I know of nothing that would require you. Not that you, not that you are unwelcome, of course, but I–'

'We're not here for anything in your building, we need passage through it. We need to get over to the…' she tried to get her bearings. The west wall, the south? '…the wall out over one of the narrow streets where a work crew is putting up some kind of scaffold.'

'Oh. I've been keeping an eye on them, ma'am, nothing suspicious to report. I don't believe the watch on this building were told whether they were going to be doing that work tonight, which is a little irregular, but I understand that the procedures for informing–'

'Fine. We need access to a window or a balcony or whatever you have that opens out to near that scaffold. Now.' Guilliman's blood, was everyone on Hydraphur such a windbag?

The watchman scuttled ahead of them through the gallery to a wide lift that buzzed its way up its shaft for an ascent whose distance it was impossible to properly judge. Then they threaded through a disorienting maze of passages and cubbyhole rooms crammed with dim stacks of data-slates and papers, the arbitrators surreptitiously cursing behind her as they manoeuvred their shields through the cramped space. She was almost twitching with anxiety by the time he opened a security shutter and motioned them into an echoing cavity between the inner rooms and outer wall.

Calpurnia could hear nothing. If the men on the scaffold really had been doing anything to the building instead of just keeping up an illusion of it, they had stopped.

'This takes you out onto a ledge we use to maintain the external airwells,' said the watchman from a little metal step below the access hatch embedded in the wall. 'The locks are off now. The ledge runs the way around the building, but it is narrow, ma'am, and with no railing. You'll want to be careful.' He blinked as a thought hit him. 'Perhaps if I go out on the ledge first, spy things out and perhaps–'

'No,' Calpurnia cut him off. 'These people will be quite happy to shoot you off the ledge as soon as they see you on it.' She was amused to see the sneaking relief under his crestfallen expression, and relieved that he hadn't pressed the point. The others were already gathering around the hatch, blessing their weapons and exchanging aquila signs. Calpurnia walked between them to put a hand on the release handle, murmured a battle-blessing and swung it open.

They came out of the building ten floors up and on the far side of the scaffold. The streetcrawler far below them supported the extendable girders of the central gantry and arms had swung out to strut it against the walls, secured to the rockcrete with grapples. Some peripheral part of her saw the racks and pipes on the struts and supposed that this was some kind of cleaning rig, designed to detoxify and wash the pollutants from the building sides. But all her conscious mind was exulting in the knowledge that she had been right. The people perched motionless in the scaffold were no cleaning crew: they were braced in wary postures, hefting weapons, watching the other direction in case the Rhinos came back around the corner.

The ledge was actually a groove cut into the building side, head-high and a metre deep, but the dimness helped Calpurnia forget how high up they were and she was able to move along it easily. They were still at a level where all the other buildings were sheer-walled and windowless, shutting off any view. The others followed behind her as quietly as they could, but Arbites' boots allowed only so much stealth and they had been unable to help the clank of the hatch itself. Some of the ambushers were twisting around to see what was making the sound behind them. No more stealth, no more time to feel precarious and perched here. Time to be Arbites.

'Hailing,' she said, and torches snapped on from the file of men behind her, held up high and away from their bodies. Their would-be ambushers turned from silhouettes into people, stocky worker-types in nondescript khaki coveralls, startled and blinking.

'ADEPTUS ARBITES!' Calpurnia declared into the pickup on her vox-torc. In the small-hours quiet of the street her own lungs were adequate enough, but her voice was also picked up and fired out of the little voxcasters clipped to the shield-rims of the Arbites behind her. 'In the name of the *Lex Imperia*, throw down your arms and surrender yourselves to righteous judgement.'

And of course the men in the scaffold brought their weapons around. The first one to fire had his aim thrown by the lights in his eyes and the krak grenade took a chunk out of the wall over their heads. As she took aim, planted her back against the wall and shot him off his perch, Calpurnia decided none of this surprised her at all.

THE ARBITES KNEW their roles well. The rearmost, holding the lights, kept the torch-beams playing over the ambushers' faces. Those further up wedged their backs against the building and braced their shields in front of them, brought their shotguns to bear through the ports and began a steady suppressing fire. Rounds sizzled and yipped through the air as Calpurnia moved down the ledge with half a dozen Arbites behind her, slamming her pistol into its holster and plucking her maul from her belt.

The ambush crew had been caught by surprise, and they were handling it badly. Too committed to their plan of firing down on a

Rhinocade in the street, some of them had actually strapped themselves into their positions for stability and were struggling to free themselves. Others had panicked and started swinging down through the gantry, dropping their weapons or leaving them hanging from struts and beams.

'Rhinos, move!' she barked into her torc pickup. 'Cover the bottom of the gantry!' They had been waiting on her command and now came around the corner, alarm klaxons nearly drowning out the gunfire. The storm-bolters at each pintle-hatch sent their deadly micro-rocket shells scudding through the base of the gantry, blasting away the top of the driver's cabin and hammering at the base girders.

The ambushers were trapped but they weren't surrendering. The return fire from the scaffold began to get more focused. A frag grenade went off above the ledge and shrapnel crackled against shields and helmets – two arbitrators were dislodged by the blast and toppled, yelling, into space.

'Ware shocks!' came from behind Calpurnia and she hunched and jammed herself home as best she could as three grenade-tubes chugged behind her. There was a moment for the grenades to arc up and in, and she could clearly hear them ringing and bouncing into the gantry, and then there was the flat *ka-whapp* of shock-grenades that compressed her ears even through the muffles on her helmet and more rings and clanks as stunned bodies dropped down through the gantry to the street.

Forgetting the drop, Calpurnia ran to where the gantry reached the wall of the building, grabbed a rail and swung into it. The arbitrators behind her were moving forward a little more slowly, keeping their shields up and firing around her. They had loaded clips of homing Executioner rounds, and now their shots passed Calpurnia with their distinctive buzz as they curved into the scaffold to seek out their targets.

A grenade whistled past, pinked off an arbitrator's shield behind her and exploded in mid-air. Knocked forward by the blast, Calpurnia used the momentum to grab another railing and swing down onto a steel-mesh platform. A bandolier of grenades still hung from a utility hook there; the man with the launcher had retreated to the web of beams below it and was peering up at her as he worked the slide. She wouldn't be able to reach him in time so she grabbed the railing, lunged out and whacked a crossbar with her maul. The blue power-flare made him yelp and flinch and while the after-images were still dancing in his eyes she scrambled down, got her balance as he brought the launcher up and smashed his knee with an unpowered low swing. A chopping return stroke broke his fingers as he shouted and scrabbled for a handhold, and then he was crashing down and away.

Beyond him another shape in the dimness, the sound of an auto-gun clip slammed home. Calpurnia grabbed the support by her side, kicked her feet out and dropped down to sit hard on the beam she had been balancing on as his burst rattled through the scaffolding. To the sound of swearing and shouts from the Arbites above her she danced forward two steps, finding her footholds as much by reflex and faith as anything, and caught the gunner in the gut with an extended fencer's lunge. The power discharge sparked and thudded, doubled the man up and toppled him down.

The Rhinos had pulled up below them and ignited their searchlights. Suddenly the scaffold turned from a dim webwork of shadows, torch-beams and scrambling shapes to a harsh-lit web of yellow and black metal. That broke their attackers completely. With the Arbites on the ledge still in shadow and the Executioner shells homing in earnestly, the firefight became a rout, the last of the ambushers leaping and swinging downward like startled primates, shouting in fear or anger, one or two still bothering to fire wildly until cruelly accurate bursts from the Rhinos' storm bolters blew them apart. Two more landed on the streetcrawler and made to flee until a shock-grenade sent them reeling with blood welling in their nostrils and ears. The handful of others stopped where they were, braced themselves in place and extended their hands to show their surrender. Below them lay their fellows knocked out of position by the fighting, those that could now moaning and calling for help.

Feeling the exertion of the last few minutes in her arms and shoulders, Calpurnia watched as her scar-faced co-driver levered herself out of her Rhino's top hatch, hefting an armful of prisoner shackles. She stepped from the roof of the APC up onto the streetcrawler platform, and that was when Calpurnia, still perched metres above the gunmen below, heard gasps and a strangled cry that sounded like, 'Her!'

That nerve, that *this-is-wrong* feeling was screaming again. Sudden urgency seemed to make her hands and feet heavy and slippery on the beams as she shouted for the woman to get back, get back inside the cover of the stormbolters. Too late, and even as the Arbites above her opened fire for a warning execution and two men propped in the scaffolding twitched and fell, one of the injured ones on the ground gripped the hellpistol that had been slung at his neck and took the front of the woman's head off before three streams of shrill white fireflies from the storm bolters hosed every living thing off the street-crawler deck.

Twelfth Day of Septista

Six days to the Mass of Saint Balronas.
Commemoration of the Innocents of Suelae.

The particular observances for this day will have been laid out by the Master of the Vigil and passed to each place of worship by heralds; accordingly, the three services will be conducted according to each year's selected lessons and texts and few general instructions can be made about them. The service at the Pilgrims' Gate commemorating the Suelae should only be attended by those whose direct descent from the Innocents of the Suelae has been vouched for by the Ecclesiarchy.

Remembering the following day's feast, meals today should be frugal.

CHAPTER SEVEN

THE SHOOTOUT ON the scaffold had cost the Arbites four lives: the arbitrators that fell from the ledge and one more to a lucky round that had gone though the visor slot in the shield. The murdered co-driver from the Rhino – it had taken Calpurnia more than an hour to find out that her name had been Lead Arbitor Vassbin – rounded out the count.

The other roadblocks had been ambushes too, just as she had guessed. The three-way trap at the intersection, the one the Rhinocade had reversed out of, had been set up with machinery across the street and shooters ready to come up the ramps and close the box. The one that they had been voxed about and not gone near had started out as a genuine repaving project, but by the time six arbitrator squads closed in on it the gunners who had hijacked it were long gone, leaving only the rough earth rampart they had thrown up, a box of stub shells and a grenade launcher, still on its bipod, pointing down the street in the direction they had expected the Rhinos to come.

The three-way blockade had not broken up anywhere near as cleanly, indecisive at the sounds of fighting from the next street. They had dithered and argued; some had fled as the last of the gunmen on the scaffold were mopped up and some had stayed at their posts to be cut to ribbons by the first of the backup squads.

They had caught eight of them, six men and two women, none of them in command or knowing anything about who was behind the plan. Some of them had been actual labourers, some even off the work crews whose equipment had been purloined for the impromptu barricades; their orders had come from their crew overseers and none of those had survived. By sunrise, every designated civic worksite was swarming with Arbites, lining confused workers up against the sides of Rhinos and ransacking tool carts and truck beds.

That order had come from somewhere in the city precinct command, not from Calpurnia herself. She could have told them that there was little point – the ambushers had been low-grade muscle, long on quick availability and short on scruples and respect for the Arbites. 'Hookbacks,' the term apparently was here, a reference to the stowing of criminals along the sides of Rhinos. But by that stage Calpurnia was back in the Chasteners' Tower, watching each prisoner being brought in, making sure they were dragged past her on their way down to the cells. She had made sure her helmet was off and that each prisoner had the chance to see her face clearly, and their reactions gave cast-iron confirmation to her suspicions.

She only found out about the second batch of prisoners when their papers were put in front of her and she demanded to know why she was signing for prisoners from something called the Tell-Kerligan raids. While she had been chasing down the *Sanctus*, it turned out, a taskforce had hit the Tell-Kerligan shipping houses where the exploding dray had been based, dragging in two dozen terrified freight-clerks and draymen. They came with a report from Barck that Calpurnia had no time to read and so tucked into a belt-pouch.

Calpurnia had managed to doze in the second half of her ride back to the Wall, despite the noise and the jolting, but she made a point of being in her own rooms before she let the tiredness catch up with her. Stretched out on her bed, carapace off and boots jutting over the edge, she closed her eyes for a moment to rest them and woke with a start two hours later to find fruit, caffeine syrup and chilled towels laid out on the table in the main room. She wondered if it would be appropriate to nominate staff she'd never met in person for medals as she wolfed the fruit and relished the sting as the towel scrubbed across her skin. That was when the door alert sounded.

It was Pavlos Calapek, Dvorov's solemn-faced chief adjutant, dressed in an impeccable dress uniform and official sash and with a message that the Arbitor Majore would receive her in his chambers. She started to frame a reply, something about preparing a report on the prisoner intake to bring along, but the adjutant stood back and made a polite after-you gesture and it became evident that this was no at-your-convenience level-four delegation. She resignedly clipped her carapace back over her bodyglove and then followed him away.

Calapek apparently didn't hold with tramping the corridors on foot, and Calpurnia stood patiently on the back of the little power-sled that carried them through the quarter's levels and into the high-arched chamber in the heart of the Justice Gate bastion, skimming what she could of Barck's report on the way. (True to the Hydraphur character, nobody in this place seemed to start their reports with a summary.) Under the stern gaze of arbitrators and Judges in mosaic, glass and marble she stepped off the sled into the locked and guarded lift that took her into the first of the string of antechambers that led to the Arbitor Majore's audience room. Those didn't help her mood as she stalked through them – she found them gaudy and lacking in gravitas, typically for Hydraphur – and she was only mildly taken aback when Dvorov pulled the last pair of doors open himself.

'Come in, Shira. You need to get used to coming and seeing me here, I think. You aren't so junior any more, you don't need to stand to attention outside my doors like some novice waiting on a lecture from their schola commander.'

The little round meeting table she had sat at on her first trip to this room had been taken away and replaced with a white-shrouded serving bench on which Dvorov's breakfast had been laid out. Beyond it the sun was just lifting its lower rim off the horizon: the bright pinpoints of the lower, brighter orbitals and the silver stripe of the Ring pricked and slit the apricot-coloured dawn sky.

'You have a real knack for running into trouble at highly uncivilised hours, Shira,' Dvorov said from behind her as he caught her looking at the sunrise. 'I'm sure that's what Nestor will say the next time he sees you. Me, I'll just admit to some concern. You're not helping me or anyone else by flaying yourself trying to stay on your feet every hour of the day.' Two stools carved from some dark red-black wood were set by the trestle, and Dvorov motioned her to one as he hooked the other with a foot and dropped onto it.

'I'm doing my duty as well as I'm able, sir,' Calpurnia replied, a little stiffly. 'Apparently I do have a reputation for being bad at delegation, but I think I do have a good reason to want to be at the forefront. It's attempts on my own life that I'm dealing with here, Arbitor Majore. Although I'm sure that Hydraphur has all sorts of convoluted protocols for how one is supposed to go about dealing with such things in a socially acceptable manner.' Events had left Calpurnia not feeling quite herself – she couldn't remember the last time she had spoken to a superior officer like that. To her rather confused relief Dvorov only smiled and pointed to the table.

'Well riposted,' he said as he skewered a syrupy fragment of pastry on a silver needle. 'But give me a little credit. I know that if I hadn't ordered you up here you'd be digging in for an unbroken day of interrogating the people you've just brought in and overseeing the roundup of the construction crews. And you'd be dead on your feet by the time that sun set again. And believe me, I'm worrying about your being dead almost as much as you are.'

'I see, sir,' she said, eyeing the food. She was suddenly aware, as she had been on the trip out to the *Sanctus*, of being ravenous as well as exhausted, but she couldn't spot anything on the table that she could easily identify and was already feeling too self-conscious to start eating an Arbitor Majore's breakfast for him.

'For the first part, Shira, I'd hate to lose such an estimable and promising young arbitor as yourself, particularly after bringing you all this way. Even leaving you personally out of it, I also hate the idea of anyone carrying out such an organised assault on the Adeptus Arbites and the order it stands for. I particularly hate it coming at a time when the working relationship between Imperial authorities on Hydraphur is as strained as it is.' He looked curiously from the table to Calpurnia and she belatedly realised the meal had been set out for more than one.

'You're talking about these conflicts between the Ministorum and the Navy,' she said, leaning forward and trying to identify the least risky-looking dish.

'Well, the Ministorum and this hot-blooded campaign by the Eparch to get control over the Naval investitures is the current flash-point, but it's turned the whole role of the Adeptus on Hydraphur into a sore point again. Hydraphur looks like an Imperial world like any other when you're on it, but don't let that fool you. It's a Navy system, and the Navy have never been happy with having the primary planet denied to them. It's been that way since the Age of Apostasy, of course. The mark that Bucharis and his cohorts left on this whole segmentum was profound. Here, the Administratum's decree of partition was an attempt to create a civilian counterweight to Navy authority in the system and balance them out against one another.'

'The way that the Imperial Guard isn't allowed to have its own fleet or the way Guilliman divided up the Astartes,' put in Calpurnia, picking up a slice of white fruit and chewing on it cautiously. It was eye-squintingly tart.

'Well, the same principle, yes,' said Dvorov, reaching for the caffeine pot on its little spirit-burner in the centre of the table. 'The planet was where the non-Navy presence had always been, what there was of it – a dedicated Ecclesiarchy shrine, an Adepta Sororitas convent, a way station for Navigators, that kind of thing. Even a lot of what the Navy did here wasn't military. Farms to supply the better class of provisions for the officers, estates for the better officer dynasties. Naval parlance still refers to families who lost their planetside holdings as "the Evicted lines", apparently, the same way the prouder Naval families call the Monocrat and the new planetary nobility "transplants". But they found all sorts of ways to delay and appeal the decree. The Navy had holdings on Hydraphur right up until Lord Admiral Invisticone was assassinated about two hundred years ago. After he was dead the Inquisition took over the fortress he had occupied in the other hemisphere and since then the planet Hydraphur has been the pocket of non-Naval authority that it was meant to be.'

'Has it worked?' It had taken Calpurnia a moment to shift gears from talking about the assassinations to the history of Hydraphur, but she was becoming interested despite herself. Dvorov finished pouring his caffeine into an odd little cup, a flattened brass ball with a cavity the size of a shot glass drilled into it, and reached for another kind of syrup to stir into it.

'Not really,' he said. 'I've always been pleased by the idea of the Imperium as a glacier. Powerful, rigid, grinding its way forward beyond anyone's ability to stop. But when you consider our society in the large it's often more like just water. Hard to restrain and always wanting to find its own level and its own way around things.'

'Not sure I follow, sir.' She braced herself and took another bite of the fruit.

'Well, there has certainly been a growth of parallel power on Hydraphur, as intended. Civilian shipping increased, there's a far greater Adeptus presence, the Navigators and the Scholastia Psykana have a much bigger permanent base at the Blind Tower, and the Cathedral has become quite an important centre of power in its own right, the junction of a whole series of pilgrimage routes from the northern sectors through to Gathalamor and points south. The trouble is that it hasn't provided the counterbalance to the Navy that it was intended to. All it did was give the Navy the excuse to insist on even tighter control of the rest of the system. They covered the other worlds and all the major orbital paths in both ecliptics with fortifications and shipyards – as is their right, of course, their perfect right, but the terms of the partition allowed them to run all that territory with even more autonomy than before. And then of course there's all the loopholes through the decree that I was talking about, the intermarriages and treaties and the guilds. Anyone with holdings or interests on the planet isn't allowed to exercise any authority off it, and the mercantile cartels want people in the civil community on Hydraphur they can trade with…'

'The syndicates?' Calpurnia put in as Dvorov took a sip of caffeine. He nodded and poured a second shot for her.

'You'll find this in your briefing dossiers when you have time. Each syndicate is nominally sponsored by interests outside the system under Administratum charters. That provides the access to civilian shipping that the Navy doesn't have, the access to commerce and travel off-planet that the on-planet aristocrats are forbidden, and the navigational privileges and letters of passage that only the Navy can provide and the other two need. That combination made the syndicates an institution within two hundred years of the decree of partition taking effect.'

'To the point where syndicate relationships seem to be as entrenched as family ones. Nobody introduces themselves as Lord Kalfus of the Medell syndicate, it's Kalfus-Medell from the first.'

'Exactly so, although you'll find it's only really a custom on the Hydraphur end of the arrangement. To the outsystem cartels the syndicate relationship isn't so all-defining, and for the Naval families getting too close to the whole thing is a little gauche. And of course even as the syndicates constantly manoeuvre for position among themselves – the opportunities for activity around Hydraphur are wider than the partition meant them to be but they are still finite – the families are also sparring all the time for the leading positions within the syndicate.

'Which makes it interesting that you should ask,' he added as he scooped fruit mash onto a wedge of crispbread, 'about the rules on defending oneself from assassination attempts. There actually are some pretty elaborate traditions about how the parties in those kinds of wars behave, depending on whether it's inter- or intra-syndicate, the relative statures of the parties and so on. How far those traditions are honoured once they stop being convenient is another matter, of course.' Dvorov noticed the piece of fruit in Calpurnia's hand and pointed her to a tureen of stewed berries. 'You should actually start off with those.'

'I hope I'm not supposed to be following these rules myself,' she said, picking up one of the little enamelled bowls from next to the tureen. 'The Adeptus Arbites answer to the Emperor and the Law, or we should. Are we supposed to tie ourselves down to some idiotic noble code? Well, then again, this is Hydraphur.'

It must have been the tiredness talking. She had time for a moment of shocked disbelief at her tone and words before she put down the bowl of berries and turned to him.

'Sir, my apologies for that outburst. I was careless of who I was–' but Dvorov was already smiling and waving her to silence.

'Don't apologise, Shira,' he told her when he'd finished his mouthful. 'This isn't your old post. We're conferring here as two senior officers of the Adeptus, not in some barrack-room bawl-out where you stand at attention and stare at the wall while I shout at you.' He nodded at the bowl on the table. 'You need to eat that while it's warm. Use one of those little ladles from the stack there.'

Letting herself breathe a little easier, Calpurnia picked up a ladle and tasted from her bowl. The berries were faintly tart, slightly reminiscent of the fruit, but stewed in some musky-sweet spice that made her want to sneeze.

'Actually, though, this talk of you adjusting to your new position and me shouting at you does seem to bring us back to why I called you up here.'

'Not to take me from a day of flaying myself alive over the interrogations?'

'Partly. But there's something I do think I need to say to you, and I prefer to make these sorts of points in person.' He caught Calpurnia's look. 'Eat your berries, Shira, I'm not about to strip your ranks or put you on charges. You haven't failed in your duty. In fact, I suppose I want to talk to you about the opposite problem.'

'The opposite? Doing too much of my duty? I've acknowledged that I've tried to stretch myself a little far, perhaps.'

'I'm bothered by a particular aspect of that which came to the fore at the Aquila Gate and in that counter-ambush you led down-city. Shira, the Imperium has a noble and cherished tradition of leading from the front. As you walked through the antechambers out there you would have passed the likenesses of any number of men and women from our own order whose statues honour exactly that. It's not as though I disapprove on principle. Nevertheless, I have to wonder: if all this effort was expended to set up a trap designed to culminate in your death, was it perhaps a little unwise to then rush into the trap and offer them exactly what they wanted?'

'You believe I should have retreated from the ambush?' Dvorov waved the question away.

'I'm not in the business of second-guessing every decision my subordinates make. I'm not going to drag out a map and make you justify every single step you took. I'm not even going to try and tell you that it's always going to be a bad thing that you lead your troops. You're making sure that you don't send the people under your command into a situation without demonstrating that you are prepared to face that situation yourself, isn't that right?' Calpurnia nodded and ate another ladleful of the distasteful berries – she had been about to say exactly the same thing herself.

'I won't claim to know every thought that passes through your head,' Dvorov went on, 'but I can take some guesses. You are very aware of the newness of your rank and position. And you are also aware that you are on a new world in a new section of the galaxy in which very little is familiar to you. It's only natural that you want to conduct yourself impeccably, and that to you means never flinching from danger and standing shoulder to shoulder with the members of your command.'

'Most of the time I haven't even known the names of my command,' she said half to herself, but Dvorov caught it.

'So, it's a difficult situation for you and one you're dealing with well. Really. And I'm not going to try and put a leash onto you and I'm not going to try to take away your freedom to exercise the abilities that brought you to my attention in the first place. But I don't think it will be any great impediment, at least not once you get used to it, to tell you that until the assassination cases are better unravelled you will restrain yourself. Risk is part of the work of the Arbites, combat is part of the work of an arbitrator, but nevertheless you will not fling yourself into the teeth of whatever fresh attacks are sent your way.'

'You're saying, sir, that I should send another arbitrator out into the line of fire while I keep myself safe.' She controlled her voice, but she was knotting with anger inside. Comments about her recklessness didn't feel any better coming from her own superior than they had from Zhow.

'I'm saying that while that may be distasteful to you–'

'*Distasteful.*'

'–you are up against an enemy who wants you dead, and our business is to deny that enemy, not hand him his objective on a platter. You may consider that an order, if that's what it takes.'

'I understand, Arbitor Majore.' Calpurnia took another mouthful of the now-cold berries and made herself swallow it.

'If you're done with those, now's the time to eat that daggerfruit.' Dvorov had switched directions again. Calpurnia picked up the first morsel she had tried and bit into it again. Its flavour was muted a little by the residual perfume from the berries, and she found it cleansed palate.

'Good. Now, pick a syrup for your caffeine – I recommend the Hercus, that's the pale yellow one in the corner there – and tell me what you've been able to find out about the attacks on you down in the city this morning.'

She blinked, poured, and drank – the syrup gave the caffeine a smoky, malted taste that she cautiously decided that she liked – and then began to talk, starting with their departure from Cross-Four and finishing with her overseeing the prisoners' parade. Dvorov listened in silence, cutting small slivers off a half-melon and chewing them thoughtfully as he looked out over the hive.

'Why not a bigger convoy initially?' he asked after he had had a few moments to digest her story on top of the melon.

'To confuse anyone who was monitoring the departure ramps at the fortress. Three Rhinos is the size of one of the routine night-shift patrols. This was before we knew that they'd be able to home in on our actual route.'

'And you selected the scaffold... but no, scratch that, I said I wouldn't micromanage you and I meant it. Do you see a direct link between the sabotage at the Aquila Gate, the flight of the *Aurum Sanctus* and the attacks on you?'

'It's looking tenuous, and we may find it wasn't there to begin with. It would be flattering to believe that someone made incredibly elaborate arrangements to catch me in the dray explosion at the Aquila Gate, but I think it was simple sabotage. The containers were of a sort of perfumed lamp-oil on their way to a storage house in the Pilgrims Quarter. It was either for the Procession of the Further Saints or the big lantern-light congregation tomorrow night.'

'So I understand. There have been some developments there, too, I understand?' Dvorov handed her a silver needle like the one he'd been eating from earlier and nodded towards the pastries.

'The rigged oil containers seem to be linked less to the *Sanctus* than to foul play in the warehouse where they were stored. I haven't had time to go over the verispex report in detail, I only got it when I got back to the Wall this morning. But the freight-house is full, completely packed, with supplies of more oil. None of it has been bomb-trapped the way the first lot was, but the verispex turned up several seals that they say show some tampering. Barck is continuing to work on it.' Dvorov gave her a quizzical look. 'Lead Verispex Barck, sir. The leader of the forensic team at the Aquila Gate. She's taken charge of the freight-house investigation too.'

'Ah. Thank you. I don't normally work at the team-leader level. Move onto the melon if you're done with the pastries.'

The melon was watery and weak-flavoured, but it chased the richness of the pastries out of her mouth in a pleasant fashion. She finished two slices and her caffeine. The strange little drinking-ball seemed to be heavier and she realised fatigue was catching up with her again. She breathed deeply a few times and looked out over the morning-lit fortress-teeth of the Wall and the smog layer that was already settling over the city below it. She was familiar with the first signs of the grey exhaustion that crept up on her during long, tense operations – it wasn't too bad once you knew the signs and could brace yourself for them.

She proved herself a liar straight away by realising she had missed what Dvorov had just said.

'I'm sorry sir?'

'I said you need to remember the order that you ate in just then. This combination of foods is associated with the sacred feasts of the Vigil, and they'll be served at the prayer breakfast you're due to attend with me tomorrow morning.'

'Will there be time for that?' It was the first thing that had come to her mind.

'I believe so. Let's review the threads of the case to date, Shira. You have a verispex team straightening out what happened at the Aquila Gate. The investigation of the *Aurum Sanctus*, after the interception carried out by yourself and Ryo, seems close to disqualifying it from suspicion. An organised attempt on your life last night was foiled and the perpetrators are in custody. The original assassin is dead, and although he is proving hard to trace we now have the aid of the Imperial Inquisition in tracking him down, do we not?'

Calpurnia realised she had not given a thought to Zhow since they had parted ways at Cross-Four. 'The inquisitor declined to meet with me on his own return, but he did condescend to let me know that he wants to be the sole chaser of your invisible friend's trail. We are to suspend our own operations on the matter unless and until he requests and authorises us.' Dvorov arched an eyebrow as he raised the brass drinking-ball to his lips. 'The patrols around the Adeptus Quarter have been reporting that he's been there for the last three hours with that savant of his, pacing back and forth on the laneways leading up to the Kathisma and getting into a lot of quiet arguments.'

'So we do have people with him?'

'No,' Dvorov said cheerfully. 'I told you, we've been warned off. But the patrol teams in that area happen to have team leaders a little more senior than the usual proctors and lead arbitors, and who happen to feel it part of their duties to send reports up through certain direct lines of communication to their Arbitor Majore.'

'I see.' It made sense. 'You have eyes on him the same way the Eparch has had one of his staff appointed to watch us. Lord Kalfus-Medell tried the same kind of thing. Just another part of the way things are here, then?'

'Part of the way things are everywhere, I think you'll find. I'll admit I'm mildly surprised you've never encountered this sort of thing before. You had a garrison command at Ephaeda, didn't you?' Calpurnia sighed.

'I'd like to think that things were different there. Perhaps I'm just not the sort of person to have much to do with them.'

'That sounds more like it to me. Well, you're here to learn, as are we all.' Dvorov drained his caffeine. 'Have you given any thought to a staff of your own?'

'No. There hasn't been time. I remember Zhow talking about custom-fitting a Rhino. Was that the kind of thing he was talking about?'

'Among other things. I'd strongly advise it. You're an arbitor senioris now, Shira. You want to requisition a carrier from the hangars, get the best one out, pick your choice of items from the armoury to go into it for your use and your staff's, select people you need for your operations from day to day. Arbites, Judges, Chasteners, Garrison preachers, Tech-Adepts. Once again, I can't believe that this is the first time you've run across the idea of a commander forming their own staff.'

'I'm familiar with the idea, sir, just short on the time. A standard-pattern carrier and whoever is assigned to me will suffice for the moment.'

'As you wish. What of the lead arbitor who's been accompanying you since the initial attack? Adjutant material?'

'Bannon?' She considered him. 'No. The reason he wound up being my offsider for the investigation is that he was heading my escort squad at the start of it all. He sort of got attached to me by default. He's obedient enough, but he's not up to the work. I won't keep him in that position.'

'Hm,' Dvorov said. 'The Vigil of Balronas begins in two days as the final lead up to the mass. Are you prepared for the problems that religious restrictions will cause for your operations?'

'I will be,' said Calpurnia. She was getting used to Dvorov's sudden changes of tack – she had thought they were to test her, but it seemed to be genuinely how he thought. 'I've been focused on the Arbites side of the operation but if we can get hold of the Reverend Baragry to continue advising me on what I can and can't do–'

'That will be an interesting exercise. How did you manage to sideline him when you took off for the *Sanctus*?'

'How? He had appointed himself the confessor of one of the prisoners who gave us the ship's name in the first place. We left him with the prisoner and, uh, never really told him that we were lifting off to join *Judgement's Clarion*.'

'I do believe, Shira, that you have rather more cunning about you than you give yourself credit for. Although the side effect was that Baragry was utterly livid that he had been left behind. My adjutants had a blistering audience with the man himself and I got two formal letters of reproof from the Eparch's chambers. I'll have to show them to you sometime. Did I mention Nestor spent the time you were in space putting rather a lot of his energy into hosing things down?'

'I'll apologise when I see him next, sir.' Dvorov waved her words away.

'It's his specialty,' he said. 'Anyway, my point was that I think we're going to have to resign ourselves to the fact that you're going to face your first holy season on Hydraphur with a little less instruction than we were counting on. Can you keep the order of the courses here in mind?'

'Berries, daggerfruit, pastry and syrup, caffeine and different syrup, melon.'

'Good. There are certain nuances that, well, never mind, you know what you need to do. This meal is eaten at dawn at the start of the Vigil and on the first day of the Sanguinala. It's supposed to be unique to the occasion, by the way, so don't try ordering it at other times. My stewards were scandalised when I told them to prepare it for today, even after I told them it was for your religious instruction. Which is something that I'm not sure we can expect much help in from Reverend Baragry.'

'I agreed as much with Arbitor Leandro,' said Calpurnia. 'Well, advice on how we can carry out our operations is one thing we probably can depend on Baragry for. I'm getting more confident that I can winnow out the political interference from the genuine direction. If I can keep getting bare-bones guidance like this from yourself and the other Arbites, just enough to avoid actually disgracing myself, then I think I can scrape by for this year. I'll settle for being someone who does her duty over someone who has impeccable table manners.'

'Well spoken. Well then, arbitor senioris. With your delegations in hand, what do you plan to do now?' Calpurnia chuckled.

'I need to rest and get back some energy, sir, and I also need to burn off some tension. I was going to say that I plan to work out how I can do both in one day, but I think I just thought of a way.'

SHE COULDN'T GET a clear look at what had shot at her, but the glimpse of movement was enough to judge its direction and speed and reflexes took over. Her shotgun was locked into the shield's gunport and the gun-grip bucked as the shield juddered against her shoulder and thigh. Her eye had been true: the gun-platform dropped to the floor with a clank as its clamps released their hold on the railing.

She spun back in the other direction straight away, ready to pump out more shots, but there was no movement in the brief flick of the torch clipped to the top of her shield. Four long paces and she was at the end of the alleyway, scowling upward: there were several ways an arbitrator was trained to scale a wall, and all of them were damned awkward if you were on your own, but there was nothing for it. She disengaged the shotgun and flipped it into the scabbard at her back, then slung her shield so that it sat over the angle between the walls.

One hand on the wall and one on the shield grips, she swung her feet up, hung for a moment growling with effort – she was in worse shape than she had realised – then slid and dropped into the space beyond, already swinging the shield back onto her arm and turning to face the shape rumbling out of the darkness.

It was roughly humanoid, an automaton torso built onto a randomly-lurching ring of motorised castors. Chains and control cables snaked from its head up into darkness. One heavy arm finished in a snub gunsnout and the other in a thick piston: two shots from the gun rang on her shield before a blow from the piston knocked the shield-edge back into her face and bounced her off the wall.

There was no time to redraw the shotgun, let alone to lock it back into the gunport so she could fire it one-handed with the shield to steady it. Although the thing was too fast for her to dodge out of its path she was able to quickstep to one side and let the next piston-blow propel her out of the machine's way. She had to bound backwards to soak up the momentum and leave it to faith that there was nothing waiting behind her while she drew her stubber: the reassuring feel of the lock-glove clicking together around its grips was instantaneous and it took a second for her to plant one foot behind her to fire. Her aim was perfect: the round boomed through an armour-seam under the automaton's arm, and after a moment it slumped over as whoever was directing it decided it was out of the fray.

She took a moment to catch her breath and pan the lamp around, then moved forward again. Half a dozen cautious paces. She had just holstered her pistol and was reaching over her shoulder for the shotgun when a rack of searchlights came stabbing down on her. Reflexively she ducked and skittered to one side, pulling the shotgun the rest of the way out and getting ready to shuck her shield – the gunport was good for point-blank shots and suppression fire, but now she was going to need two hands to aim. Even with her helmet visor darkening to counter the lights, she was still blinking from the change in illumination when the floor began to move.

It took her a moment to register the clatter of gears and winches and faint shouts from the machine-crews on the engineering level below, but now she felt the floor vibrating and tilting, tipping her in the direction of the lights as the wall she had pressed her back to slid downward and out of sight.

Change of plan. As the floor steepened she grabbed her pistol again, letting the slope carry her down, body braced behind her shield to let her sock the slab of armour into anything in front of her. The lights still bore down, keeping everything beyond arm's reach in shadow so she knelt, braced herself against the slope and chanced two shots over the top of the shield at the searchlights.

She missed, but there was no chance to re-aim. More clatter came from beyond the retracted wall and she could see lights bobbing down there, red and green, passing before and behind one another as though they were being carried by members of a mob. She fired a shot, then another. The bruising recoil hammered through the glove and up into her shoulder, but the shots told: four red lights went out as each round punched through two of the milling shapes beyond the ramp.

With a grind the floor tilted steeper and she had to scuttle across it like a frantic black-shelled crab, a crab that was desperately trying to stow its sidearm and scrabble for its power-maul. She jumped off the ramp a second before it would have tipped her away completely and careened into the crude shapes beyond, hulking humanoids dangling from chains with arms stretched in front of them and green and red lamps for faces. Four lay motionless on the ground: the chain-clamps had released them when their operators saw they had taken a hit.

Calpurnia swivelled away as the first hulk tried to snap its arms shut on her and into another whose face-lamp was red: she slammed the lower edge of the shield into where its knees would have been, and as it swayed and bobbed she finally got her maul free and drove it upward. Sparks flew and the target dropped from its chain as the red light snuffed out. More servo-arms grabbed at her from behind and another red light glared over her shoulder but she had her equilibrium back now, flipping the maul around and driving the tip backward. The target that had grabbed her crashed to the floor and she turned, danced around a green-lit shape and into the thick of them.

She was aware of how harshly she was breathing and of the way that the shield was starting to weigh on her arm. She brought it close in to her body to minimise the strain but that caused problems too as she slashed at the targets and their reaching arms: it was harder to use the shield as a weapon, to slam it against bodies or smother attacks, and it made a blind spot on that side of her. The hulks could not be knocked off balance with a shield-slam the way a human would – they simply swung away on their chains and back at her. She tried to compensate by always moving away from her shield-arm, circling to her right and redoubling her efforts with her maul, but now that arm was tiring too and her feet stumbled on the hulks she had already dropped. The targets pressed closer even as their numbers thinned.

Eventually she hit a green one, downed it with a wild stroke of the maul that was supposed to knock a red target away from her shield. The error klaxon broke her rhythm and it didn't take long for the shield to be grabbed by two sets of rubber-covered arms. She had to release it, and although she got her maul and pistol switched between her hands in a deft cross-move and began to use both, within minutes she was hemmed in, weighed down by her own exhaustion and a target hulk that had fallen onto her. A pair of arms clamped around her brutally tight and the smell of scorched rubber from the targets she had hit mingled with the smell of her sweat for the twenty seconds it took for the buzzer to go.

WHEN SHE LOOKED from the debriefing platform the little pit where she had been finished off had extruded walls and become a gun-tower. Calpurnia stood on the transparent slab of the platform behind the bank of controllers, watching the emplacement raining high-speed paint rounds on a gaggle of arbitrators who were trying to work their way forward through a graveyard of simulated Rhino wrecks to fire grenades into the mechanism. They hadn't got very far.

'Fresh inductees?' she asked a controller, who was watching through one of the tower's slaved ocular spirits and working stops and levers to aim its guns.

'Oh, and it shows, doesn't it, ma'am?' he replied with a chuckle as another rattling spray of pellets raised shouts of alarm and pain below them. From around them in the dimness came more noises: the bang of firearms and the doublecrack-screech of bolters, the crack-sizzle of power weapons, sirens, voices, and the ceaseless rumble of the heavy chains, pistons, belts and cables under the floor and over their heads that operated it all. Walls and floors moved, attacks were sprung by automata, servitors or practice hulks lowered on chains, areas filled with smoke or were showered with water, light, artificial hail, blasts of sand or disorienting noise.

Calpurnia was exhausted again, aching and her hair hanging in strings, but it was a good kind of exhaustion. It had been far too long since she had trained in a Klavier Maze, and she realised this was the most relaxed she had felt since she first touched down on Hydraphur. The meal with Dvorov, several more hours of sleep and a turn through the Maze had done exactly the kind of good she had hoped it would.

'Perhaps the debriefing of youngsters meeting their paint-spitting nemesis below could include a review of your own most laudable performance, my arbitor senioris.' Nestor Leandro's rich voice rolled over them as he stepped onto the platform, the finery of his Judge's uniform glinting in the lamps.

'Not my best, Arbitor Leandro.' He was holding the printout from the session she had just completed and she had to reach up to point to the lists of hit percentages and target ratios. 'I was sloppy and impetuous,' she said, 'you can see it in the logs for minutes eight, twelve and seventeen to twenty-three, and I've allowed my condition to decline inexcusably during the voyage here. But thank you for your kind words.'

'Not at all. Are the Maze configurations in the Segmentum Ultima garrisons similar to ours?'

'I can only speak for the systems I served in,' said Calpurnia, scooping up her kit before they headed for the exit, 'but yes, by and large. There's more of an emphasis on mobility and reflexes – this maze makes a lot more use of the judgement and target-selection drills, which we used the firing ranges for.'

'Just so.' They had emerged into a tiled hallway, the passage that linked the ablutories with the main entrances to the Maze a level below, the whole training complex cut deep into bedrock halfway down the Wall. The air was damp from the shower blocks at the top of the corridor, and Leandro's judicial cloak looked over-lush and out of place amid the arbitrator and Chastener uniforms.

'Searching for an appropriately poised and witty segue into the news I have for you, Arbitor Calpurnia, I find myself at a loss for one and must perforce present you with developments bluntly, before we reach the ablutories and respect for the modesty of a fellow commander compels me to withdraw.'

I love the way developments always seem to come when I'm doing other things, she thought. Well at least I didn't snap at him out loud this time. What she said aloud was, 'I appreciate your coming down here to brief me in person.'

'Not at all. Well, to be brief.' He cleared his throat. 'The dray full of lamp-oil came from the Tell-Kerligan shipping house, a minor freight broker out past the foot of the Telepine Way. Tell-Kerligan specialises as a dealer in religious artefacts and supplies and the export of a consignment of icons and specially-crafted bindings of religious texts bound for private missions and colleges along the Segmentum border, which had formed the *Sanctus's* official pretext for breaking orbit and heading out of the system, passed through their holdings. The house's ties to the *Sanctus* extended little further than supplying part of its cargo, although a position brokering art-work purchases and transport connections to the Ecclesiarchy was a part of the Kerligan syndicate's activities that the Tell family had been manoeuvring to get into for some time and this represented something of a breakthrough for them.'

'Doesn't the *Sanctus* operate under a direct Ecclesiarchal charter?'

'Such charters,' Leandro answered, rather awkwardly dodging a knot of hurrying Arbites, 'leave a gap between the bonded church storage houses around the hive and loading aboard proprietary Ecclesiarchal ships, a gap within which a number of specialist transporters and orbital-lift operators with close ties to the Eparch's chambers exist quite prosperously.'

'I see.'

'A team of detectives has joined the cordoning taskforce,' he went on, 'and they have been making all manner of requests for lexmechanics and savant staff and access to the data mills in the Wall. The most telling progress, I must however inform you, has been that of a colleague with whom you are familiar – Lead Verispex Barck and her team, who took on the task of examining the shipping houses as an extension of the work you set her in the aftermath of the Aquila Gate. They were initially looking for evidence of machining work, signs that the sabotage that came so close to engulfing you was conducted on the premises. But the sabotage that has occupied them was not mechanical, Arbitor Calpurnia. It was chemical.'

They had reached the ablutory door. The steam and splashes coming through the doorway rather spoiled the drama of Leandro's conclusion, although people were backing up on either side of the doors to give the two commanders space.

'What do you mean by that, Arbitor Leandro?' she asked when she realised he expected it of her.

'Lamp-oil. The warehouse was massively stocked, stocked to the ceiling, with lamp-oil. Consecrated and scented lamp-oil, to be exact, prepared specifically to be burned in the ceremonial lanterns used during this holy period, but in greater quantities than anyone could possibly expect to use. And every cask that the Verispex had been able to tap and test prior to their report back to us had been tainted. Poison, my arbitor. Carefully mixed and deliberately placed. Poison.'

Thirteenth Day of Septista

Five days to the Mass of Saint Balronas.
Feast of the Rhetores. Vigil's Eve.
The Quiet Congregation.

Today is the last day before the Vigil of Saint Balronas begins and Ecclesiarchal strictures conduct come into force throughout the Bosporian Hive and its surrounds. This should be a day of contemplation and fortification. The Feast of the Rhetores begins an hour after sunup and although it is permissible to use the feast to prepare for the fasting ahead, gluttonous conduct is a mark of spiritual weakness that must be reported to a preacher or confessor. When a particular feast is declared done by its host the remaining food should be removed immediately.

Between the end of the Feast and the Quiet Congregation is a time for individual prayer in the home, although spiritual strengthening may be sought from the Ecclesiarchy if urgently needed. Time should be allowed for ensuring that dress is clean and orderly, that lanterns are trimmed and filled with the scented oil supplied by the Ministorum. Dress should be sober and respectable; official garments or uniforms are permitted providing that their brighter colours are dulled with a coat or shawl. Speech should be kept to an absolute minimum while moving to the High Mesé and maintained until the bell is rung. Lights should be extinguished in buildings where there will be no one to extinguish them at the sound of the bell.

This day is a day of particular significance for the Imperial Navy and no communication, social or otherwise, should be attempted with Navy personnel on this day. To do so, or to for example invite a Naval officer at another time to a function that falls on this day, will be taken as a personal slight.

CHAPTER EIGHT

POISON. THE THOUGHT was still weighing on her mind the next day through the prayer breakfast that celebrated the Feast of the Rhetores. The poison in the lamp-oil.

The prayer breakfast was hosted by the Prefect of the Hydraphur Monetariat, a rail-thin woman with nervous, skittering eyes. The service was conducted in the Monetariat Chapel, a side-gallery off the main counting-hall so narrow that the aisle could barely accommodate even one at a time and the pews were no bigger than chairs. The incenses for ceremonies on Hydraphur were sickly and over-perfumed, and smelling them set Calpurnia to brooding on the poisoned oil again so that she kept losing her place among the odd, singsong rhythms of the otherwise familiar Imperial prayers. Outside she could hear the droning of the savants processing their financial algorithms, murmuring the numbers and trigger-phrases that would feed each piece of data through the complex formulae hypnotically implanted into them. As a counterpoint to the sacred liturgies they were saying it struck her as rather impious.

The breakfast itself was more comfortable. They ate on an arboretum balcony that circled the Monetariat tower five floors up, enclosed by a glittering curtain of jewelled armourglass that turned the yellow daylight into an odd, watery rainbow. 'Best not to mention we had this same meal yesterday,' Dvorov had said. 'No harm in no one knowing we broke religious protocol a little.' Calpurnia, who knew herself to be a very bad liar, had not been sure about that, but the subject had not come up.

She had remembered the order to eat in, though, and avoiding any obvious gaffes seemed to be enough – the other Adeptus seemed put off by her arbitrator uniform and spoke to Dvorov instead. She didn't mind: it gave her the freedom to wander over to the glass wall and look out through one of the clear spots, through the sloping forest of towers, to where the Cathedral spiked up from the hive's summit. Beyond the hulking base of the building were the shrine and statue-lined avenues and pilgrims' barracks of the Sacred Quarter, the steep south-west slopes of the Augustaeum that the conspirators in her cells had tried to fill with poison.

The nature of the conspiracy hadn't become properly clear to Calpurnia until she had found a moment the previous night to reread her dossier on the religious stations of the sacred Vigil. (And if, she thought bitterly, the Eparch had seen fit to send her the tutor she had been promised instead of an agent and informant, she would not have needed to piece it together on her own.) It had struck her as odd that such extravagant quantities of fuel for such an old-fashioned kind of lantern had been the subject of so much attention, but now she understood. During the Vigil the lights of the hive and of the city – all across the planet and throughout the swarm of ships and stations that made up the Hydraphur system – were dimmed or extinguished, the nights left dark to commemorate the spiritual darkness of the Plague of Unbelief.

The seaports and spaceports, the docks and military bases would keep their lights, and the Arbites city patrols and the Adepta Sororitas watch in the Augustaeum itself would light their way through the streets. But for most in the Hydraphur system the nights of the Vigil could only have their darkness broken by tiny candles or the low glow of the little brass hand-lanterns, burning the sacred oil made only for the Vigil nights, oil that burned low, warm and with the bitter scent of mourning incense.

The dray had just been the start. Not even very much of the oil it had carried had been tainted. But the Tell-Kerligan warehouse was vast, and nearly all its space was filled with great drums of the poisoned oil. Throne alone, but if that stuff had actually been distributed and burned...

That thought kept her so preoccupied that she spent nearly half an hour at the glass curtain, staring out at the Cathedral compound and the ridge of the High Mesé with its obelisk teeth, brooding about the last few days and wondering every so often why it irritated her so much that the districts of the Augustaeum were still called quarters even though there were more than four of them.

For the past couple of days she had resented the time she would have to take away from the investigation to attend the breakfast, but as she finished eating, made her excuses and slipped away she found herself glad of it. It had done for her mind what the turn through the Klavier Maze had done for her body: grounded her, taken her out of near-total immersion in the investigation and cleared away the cobwebs.

But the break was over. It was time to visit the cells again.

PART OF EVERY young arbitor's career included duty as a penal guard, and Calpurnia had done her share. She had spent an eighteen-month round trip on a transport carrying penal legionnaires from Drade to suicide battalions mustering on the border with the xenos tau, and had finished her tour at Don-Croix as a section leader aboard one of the Arbites picket-ships that kept guard over the hellish in-system prison worlds. Her commendations and her scrupulous reputation had even earned her a six-month stint on the infamous deep-space prison known as Cage Twenty-Twenty, where the most toxic of heretics were quarantined for interrogation or ritual chastisement before their execution.

Even so, she had never seen a system quite like Hydraphur's. Not the physical prisons – she doubted that there would be anything on the planetary camps much different to the bunker-compounds on Don-Croix's inner worlds, and the Cage had been state of the space-borne art. What fascinated her was the Grey Prison.

The Penitential Calculus was its proper name. Hydraphur held its prisoners in a long chain of camps strung across the planet's face, on two giant space stations that stood out from the Ring in heavily-guarded pockets of space, and aboard an endless circuit of shuttles and runner-ships that kept them all linked in carefully patternless migrations. Governing that system was the Calculus, a code, a maze, a cat's cradle of encryptions, double-blinds and randomisations. A cipher for a prisoner here, for a cell or a penal ship there, sentences and transfer times and locations all swimming deep in a lightless sea of false data and ever-shifting code-keys. Even had the Grand Provost Marshal stirred from his palace on Earth to demand the whereabouts of the least of the prisoners held in Hydraphur, he would have had to wait until the name had been passed through the calculus and a coded report brought back out to know whether the subject was a prisoner in Hydraphur at all. She had never encountered anything like it in her career, but the reason for it was obvious: in a system like this, one of the best ways to keep prisoners safe from interference was to make sure that not even the prisoners themselves could ever be entirely sure where they were or where they were about to be moved to.

The role of Master of the Calculus had been gifted to one Arbitor Consul Narranze as a hereditary office twelve hundred years before, and since then generations of Narranzei had carried the rank and title, spending their lives in the lowest chambers of an oubliette beneath the Wall's lowest catacombs. With them were the finest logisters the Adeptus Mechanicus could craft and three families of savants and lexmechanics whose children were indentured to the Calculus at birth. The codes and formulae had grown so intricate with the passing of time that now each generation of savants began their training and mind-conditioning almost from the moment they could talk and count, and the officers who took food and messages into the oubliette were hereditary positions too, oathbound and guarded in turn.

Awaiting judgement were the draymen, the staff of the Tell-Kerligan shipping house and the survivors of the botched streetcrawler ambush. Those who didn't wind up in gibbets would be taken into the maze of penitentiaries. But before their identities vanished into the matrices of the Grey Prison from where it would take months to extract them, Calpurnia wanted to see them.

The Chasteners and interrogators had already spent a day and a night on them, and had told her that they had extracted what they believed was a full account, with as much duress as each accused seemed able to physically stand. It was no less than Calpurnia had expected, and she didn't care. She still wanted to see them for herself. Maybe it was still the unreconstructed street-tramping arbitrator in her, but she wanted them in her memory as a pair of eyes she had looked into rather than as a name on a data-slate display. It gave her a sense of rightness, that things were moving back onto a correct keel, and she sat and read the interrogation transcripts from the previous day as the Chasteners prepared the room.

The Chasteners' Tower had any number of chambers, depending on what environment the interrogators thought would best break their prisoner. For those who had been someone of substance, used to deference and personal space, there were tiny cubicles where an interrogator could loom over them, blotting out the light and swallowing all the available room. For commoners, used to the crowds and claustrophobia of the city-sprawl, there were chambers the size of ballrooms where the soaring spaces would press down on the cowering prisoner more heavily than the visored gaze of the Arbites or the questions boomed over a voxcaster.

Calpurnia was using no such extremes. A room of moderate size sufficed, walls of plain stone and a single bright electrolumen in a grille in the ceiling. They set up a dais for her, with a high-backed judgement seat and a thick stone lectern it took three bull-shouldered Chasteners to lift and position. There were rows of lights on a series of girders and rails overhead, but only the ones behind her were on.

Calpurnia had attended any number of these kinds of interrogations, but this would be the first time she had ever presided over one. She had time to feel a few brief twinges of nerves, which paradoxically were made worse by the quiet obedience that the burly Chasteners gave her, before she ground the doubts under a mental heel and nodded for the first prisoner to be brought in.

'Galpen Tell-Kerligan. Outlaw, condemned in the eyes of the Adeptus Arbites and sentenced by our hand!' boomed Lead Chastener Zimny, and a slender man with his scalp-locks roughly shorn away was marched into the centre of the room and anchored to the ring. His wrists were anchored low, but a shock-maul jabbed into his back when he tried to sit, so that he peered up into the lights from a painful hunching crouch. From the expression on his face, Calpurnia knew the careful tableau they had set up was perfect.

'I am innocent!' His voice was shrill and broken. 'I am wronged! I am a pious man! I will swear it! Only bring me a holy aquila and I will swear–*uhnk*–' The guard behind him jabbed him again, for silence.

'A pious man?' Calpurnia glanced at the papers on the lectern. 'You have confessed to presiding over a house of business which was used to store poison, meant to infect the rites of the Vigil and kill those observing it. You made an attempt on my own life that caused many other lives to be lost. Make no mistake, I came here only to see for myself what sort of blaspheming murderer we were sentencing.'

'No!' His tone was agonised. 'My piety was used against me!'

Calpurnia glanced over at Zimny and stage-whispered 'What's he talking about now?' The transcript was on the paper in front of her, but she wanted Galpen to hear her and keep scrambling to clear his good name.

'I took secret instructions, I confess to that, I've already told you!' he cried out, not disappointing her. 'I received a letter from the Ministorum, the curia of the Eparch! I could not refuse! I am a pious man!'

'A cleric with the Eparch's office wanted you to poison the Vigil-goers?' she asked dryly. 'Oh, certainly, we'll purge the whole Cathedral on your say-so.'

'No, no! The oil, I didn't know about the oil, I don't even know about this poison!'

'He's contradicting himself,' declared Calpurnia. 'I think we're done.'

'No! You have to hear me! I'm not what you think!' Galpen was crying. 'I only wanted to restore my family in the eyes of the Emperor. I wanted to earn back the favour we had! I did no wrong, I am pious!'

'Perhaps not,' Calpurnia told Zimny, who of course had not moved. 'Let him tell me what he needs to,' and for ten minutes Galpen Tell-Kerligan talked.

The Tell-Kerligan family handled shipping from the Sacred Quarter up to orbit, true enough, but these days only texts and religious art. Time was that the family done more than that, contracting with the old Eparch for all manner of duties. They had outfitted Ecclesiarchal preachers and missionaries, accommodated important pilgrims, been people of standing. Then that had all been lost in ructions in the Ministorum, a feud among the clergy, the collapse of something called the Order of the Taper in which

Tell-Kerligan fortunes had been bound. The family had fallen – not quite into oblivion, but low enough for the Galpen to feel the sting when he looked at their histories and heirlooms.

'So it was your separation from the Ecclesiarchy that made you attractive,' Calpurnia mused. 'The Eparch wanted some senior men of the Adeptus Ministorum to be able to move out of the system without Navy knowledge. There's an Ecclesiarchal penance ship in orbit to carry them out of the system, but the carriers who could bear these people up to the Ring are all known and watched. And so who better to use than a family with access to orbital lifters, a record of ties to the Ministorum, and who are desperate to re-earn favour with the Church?'

Galpen blanched at the word *use* and said nothing more – something in Calpurnia's tone had stalled him. She made a gesture for him to be removed, real this time, not a ploy to make him babble. His wrist-irons were unclipped from the ring and onto his ankle-irons and he was taken away in that same stooped shuffle. There was only a moment between the door in the right wall slamming behind Galpen and the door on the left clanking open for the next prisoner.

'Hlinden Fochs. Outlaw, condemned in the eyes of the Adeptus Arbites and sentenced by our hand!'

Hlinden Fochs was a heavy woman whose deep-set eyes glittered in the lights. She stayed silent as she was brought in and manacled. Fochs had thick fingers, callused from dray-ropes, and the brands and electoos of a minor guild official across her cheeks and shoulders.

Silence. And in her eyes, that deep, far glitter.

'Was there a reason for me to sit here looking at this woman?' Calpurnia asked Zimny. 'Who is she, exactly?'

'One of the chief conspirators, madam arbitor senioris,' he told her. 'Fochs was the draymistress in charge of moving the poisoned oil into the shipping-house.' A junior arbitor arranged the papers on the lectern to bring Fochs's interrogation transcripts to the top. The expression on the other woman's face had not changed.

'The interesting thing about this, Arbitor Zimny, is that this criminal outcast was indeed undone by an attempt on my life, but did not actually make one herself.' Was that a twitch in Fochs's face? Calpurnia leaned forward and put her elbows on her knees, staring into those shadowed eyes.

'The poisoned oil was not aimed at me. Anyone cunning enough to set up the poison and the bomb was not going to then use such a sloppy, hit and miss technique as that exploding dray. My death would have been an added cause for rejoicing, I'm sure, but no, that wasn't the object. For a while I thought it was all about snarling traffic down the Telepine Way, causing the greatest possible disruption during a sensitive time, but that wasn't it either.'

Fochs wasn't rising to it. She didn't want to gloat and she didn't want to rave.

'The object was the storage bays cut into the Cathedral foundations at the edge of the Artisans Quarter, wasn't it, Fochs?' Calpurnia asked her. 'That was where those shipments of oil were headed, to the Cathedral's own storehouses to be given out to those who will be attending the lamplight services. By the time that last dray drove up to the Aquila Gate the stocks were topped up, and the doors were due to be thrown open to the first of the faithful the following dawn. There was one last shipment to be added to make sure the stocks were adequate. I don't know yet whether that shipment was genuine or if you, Fochs, manipulated it for your sabotage. I will know soon.'

Fochs's face was a mask, unmoving.

'The flight of the *Aurum Sanctus* was spectacularly badly timed. It meant enough confusion and secrecy in Tell-Kerligan's shipping houses that you were able to poison nearly every drum of lamp-oil. I will know the details of how you did that, too. It went off beautifully. Isn't it a pity that the nerve of your people broke? To break Imperial law is to break faith with the Emperor, Fochs, and both are signs of degeneracy. A mind that can do so is by definition flawed, invariably creating flawed thinking and flawed behaviour, which are symptoms of the essential inferiority of a human being who can set themselves against their Emperor. Criminals err. And when they err, we have them. Is that not the truth, Lead Chastener Zimny?'

'Praise the Emperor! The Emperor's word is the Law, and the Arbites are the voice by which that word is spoken!' Zimny's voice filled the chamber. Fochs did not twitch a muscle.

'This, I suppose, is what you need to leave this chamber knowing. You chose weak, flawed men to crew the dray. They saw my worthy Arbites at the Aquila Gate. They didn't know about the general decree of vigilance, and they weren't prepared for an Arbites checkpoint. They panicked. That bomb was supposed to go off in the Cathedral stores to incinerate their oil stockpiles, wasn't it? Supposed to wreck them and make it look like some kind of accident so that the Cathedral procurators would be too frantic to properly check the replacement shipments that the Tell-Kerligan so-fortunately had to hand and would pass out poisoned oil to hundreds, thousands of loyal worshippers. And Tell-Kerligan would have been the guilty party and would have humiliated the Ministorum even more by their association. They would have had to protect the secret of the *Aurum Sanctus's* passengers, or at least try to. Do you know that one of the dray crew, the first one we broke, was so ignorant he even thought that the *Sanctus* was what we were after? He must have overheard something in the warehouses while he was about your sordid little business.'

Somewhere in the tower, someone wailed – the far-off, anaemic sound came down air-ducts and through vent grilles high in one wall. No one in the chamber acknowledged it.

'I thought I was dealing with some grand and subtle attempt on my life only to find out that what really caused the explosion at the Gate that night was just a pair of criminal weaklings who took fright, blew their cargo and ran for it at the first sight of an Arbites line. Were you as disappointed as I? Had you hoped that you would all hold out a little longer before your flawed, criminal natures caught up with you?'

No answer. Calpurnia wondered if Fochs had been damaged somehow in the cells. She frowned on head wounds during interrogations – they affected the reliability of testimonies.

'The other thing that it will be useful to know, Fochs, is that we are going to find the rest of this little ring you were part of down in the slums. This, what was it?' She glanced at the papers on the lectern. 'Society of the Fifty-Eighth Passage. After we have finished the Ecclesiarchal interrogators will go to work. The Adeptus Ministorum has little patience for assaults on its sacred ceremonies, and when they asked to share jurisdiction over this matter with the Adeptus Arbites we were not minded to say no. We dealt with you as the Law demands we deal with criminals, but they will deal with you as faith demands they deal with heretics. This society of yours has days to live at best.' She glanced indifferently at the papers and tilted her head. 'That's all.' And that was when Fochs spoke, in a dusty croak that took a moment and a cough to be recognisable as a voice.

'Worship of the Emperor is a blessing, the Church of the Emperor is a curse. The Emperor is in all things, His truth suffers no human to carry it but only the blessed Others, and the Society of the Fifty-Eighth Passage will see the dead shell of the false church brought low so that–' When the power-maul found her kidneys Fochs clacked her jaw shut and convulsed silently while the Chasteners dragged her away.

'She lived literally in the shadow of a great Cathedral and all the inspiration it offers, and look at how she poisoned herself,' Calpurnia remarked to Zimny.

'Do you require a moment to compose yourself, arbitor senioris?' he asked, stepping up to the seat, but she shook her head and waved him away.

'Cullos Sclay. Outlaw, condemned in the eyes of the Adeptus Arbites and sentenced by our hand!'

Another arrogant one, thought Calpurnia as the prisoner, gawky, pale-eyed and stubble-cheeked, was dragged in and manacled. His eyes went to Calpurnia, fixed on her face and stayed there, although her expression would be lost in shadows from where he stood.

'Bring the lights onto me,' she murmured to Zimny, and two more lamps blazed on. Calpurnia fought not to blink as they bathed her in light from the front, and when she adjusted to the illumination she saw that Sclay's insolent expression had not changed in the slightest. She reached up and touched the scar-lines over her eye.

'Remember me?' He did not reply. 'I am the arbitor you were sent to kill. The female arbitor with the scarred face you were told to murder. You and your fellow criminals killed the wrong woman, and that made you afraid. I saw it in your faces when I watched you go into the cells.'

'Part of me fears pain and fears for my life. Part of every man does. But I have no fear for my soul.' His eyes stayed calmly on Calpurnia.

'Your record is a good one. You were a lay chemicae practitioner, a mixer of paints. That was what you were doing on the works crew, was it not? You were there to help the painters on a mural of the…' she glanced over at the lectern.

'The mural of the Thesean Martyrs,' Sclay told her. 'Brave men and women of the Imperial Navy who would not bow the knee before the Apostate. I will claim them as my patron intercessors when I stand before the Ecclesiarchal judges.'

'Patron intercessors? You're certainly a different matter from the wretched pieces of work I've just seen. It seems to me, Sclay, that you're bound for the Calculus and eventually an execution yard, but there's also a standing treaty with the Navy to supply convicts for their work crews. Using your skills to prepare the city for a holy ritual is my idea of noble toil. But the Imperium might yet get some useful service out of you before you die.'

'Should I accomplish nothing more before I go to my grave, I have accomplished enough. I stood ready to fight you. I would have fought you.'

Fochs had been hard to crack, betraying nothing despite Calpurnia's gibes at her competence. Tell-Kerligan had been easy, convinced of his innocence and frantic to protest when she loudly assumed his criminality. She had not quite expected this.

'That's right,' she said, 'you weren't on the gantry. You were rounded up a street away, weren't you? You weren't actually party to the murders.'

'You cannot say the same, woman.' There were shocked gasps around her at the words and the guards drove their mauls into his back. He thrashed against his manacles, moaning, but Calpurnia waved the Chasteners away. They all sat in silence as Sclay jittered on the floor and rode out the spasms until his eyes were open and his breathing regular. His eyes wove their way up to hers again.

'None of this came out in your initial interrogation, Sclay. Were you saving it up for when you met me face to face?' He nodded, weakly. 'Well,' Calpurnia went on, 'I shall hear your accusations.' Gasps again, and once more she gestured for silence. 'And all of you can listen. "To stand upon the bedrock of the Law is our great duty." Zimny, finish the quotation.'

'"To presume to stand above it is our worst heresy,"' Zimny replied. 'But arbitor senioris, to allow *this* to accuse you with his words!'

'You heard me,' Calpurnia told him coldly. 'And you and every arbitor in this room can take instruction now in the fact that we are loyal and humble before the Law, and we do not arrogantly hide from accusations. Well, Sclay? You have the chance here to speak accusation against an arbitor senioris before a chamber full of

Arbites. This is not a common occurrence, sir, so I'd advise you make the best of it.'

The expectant silence from the other Arbites was almost palpable. Somewhere on the other end of that maze of air ducts, that anonymous prisoner wailed again.

'Because of you, two innocent men have died.'

'I do not recoil from the fact,' Calpurnia said. '"To be just, our law must be cruel." No arbitor will resile from what is necessary for the rule of Law. When I stand before the Emperor the souls that I have sent ahead will be there and I will face them with a clear conscience. So, these men died at the Aquila Gate?'

For the first time Sclay's eyes flickered with doubt.

'Where the Arbites burned people who had knowledge of their crimes?'

'The place,' Calpurnia corrected him, 'where innocent servants of the Emperor paid the price for the criminality of a pack of murderous blasphemers called the Society of the Fifty-Eighth Passage.'

'No,' said Sclay. 'They did not die there. They were murdered in their beds in our barrack-camp in the plaza beneath Bialtes' Obelisk. You know the one, arbitor.'

'No, Sclay, in point of fact I do not. Zimny?'

It took a moment of whispering with a subordinate before he turned to her.

'A square at the outskirts of the hive proper, ma'am, downslope from the Kathisma Gate. A lot of temporary barrack-camps there for the crews who were working through the night. Those have all been broken up since the attacks.'

'And so you hide the evidence of your crime,' said Sclay, 'as you tried to hide it by murdering the men and women that Robika and Janand worked with.'

'Did I? *You* attacked *me*, and with a moderately sophisticated and well-armed multiple ambush at that. That was a murder attempt by me on you?'

'We knew you were travelling through our city, and we determined to avenge ourselves on you.' Some of the fire was coming back into Sclay's voice. 'Those who came to us who had lost dear ones to your murders, they gave us weapons. We were told that there were people trying to wreck the sacred Vigil of Balronas with murder and sabotage and that we ourselves might be targets, and that a scarfaced arbitor-woman from another world, who came here full of contempt for our ways, would be behind them. And sure enough, within hours of the news reaching us, Robika and Janand, our overseer and our paymaster, were both murdered.'

'How?'

'Burned. Good men, burned like vermin, although they were innocent and faithful. A fuel-bomb into the camp-hutch they were sleeping in. Then others came with weapons and said that they knew when the woman who had caused all of this would be passing within striking distance, and we took our roadworking engines and we came out to stop you and make you pay.'

'Who told you all this, exactly?' she asked him. 'And how did they persuade you to take up arms against an officer of the Law whom you are bound to obey?'

'An Adeptus who hides sin behind an Imperial seal is no Adeptus. I remember my lessons. Did not mighty Dolan himself declare, "I will steal from the plate of decadence to feed the mouths of the powerless"?'

'That was Thor, not Dolan,' Calpurnia corrected him. 'And since you're about to go back to your cell I'll suggest that you think on matters such as the cheapness of your faith and the readiness with which you twisted it. The explosion at the Gate was sabotage, and your attack on me follows one by a mutant witch-assassin just days ago. I refute and reject your accusations, Sclay. Had you reported what happened to you, you might have done the Imperium a service. By embracing half-baked lies you have caused more undeserving deaths than you sought to avenge and weakened what you thought you were protecting. You are the criminal, Sclay, and you will die for it.'

His eyes were still on her, even over his shoulder as he was marched out, but she could not read the expression in them. Maybe he would think on her words and repent, or maybe not. It was, she decided, not her problem any more.

AUDIENCE-ROOMS AND Rhinos. For Calpurnia, the whole of Hydraphur was coming to be defined by audience-rooms and Rhinos.

She stood now in the second antechamber past the Cathedral doors. On her first visit she and Leandro had passed through these chambers too quickly to look around, but now she was trying to get a sense for its shape and layout. The outer building, she knew now, was much larger than the great space of the Cathedral itself. Between them was a great honeycomb of chambers and offices from which the affairs of the Eparch and the Ministorum were run, mazes of cloisters and rooms that filled the walls and met above the Cathedral's vaulted ceiling to fill storey after storey in the spire as it climbed to the sky.

She had ridden up in a convoy, a mechanised echo of the guards she and Leandro had brought on their first visit; this time it was a rumbling square of gleaming black APCs, Rhinos to front and rear and the ominous Repressor tanks on the flanks, the flamers in their cupolas ready to sweep away any sign of attack. Calpurnia had still sat in the cab and brooded on all the ways the convoy could still be stopped and destroyed if someone were determined enough. Apparently, no one had been, and now the tanks sat at the foot of the carved ramp, guarded by their crews and inside a semicircle of black-armoured Arbites and white-armoured Sororitas which cut the ramp off from the crowds on the High Mesé.

Those crowds were not the genteel aristocrats that she had passed among five days ago. Now, with the religious fervour of the Vigil taking hold, all the streets around the Cathedral were full of hessian-wrapped postulants, wild hair streaked with ash, shouting prayers and entreaties. The Cathedral acted as a magnet for the most intense of them, and arbitrator squads had been forced to create an aisle for the carriers and then form a perimeter behind them, the devout beyond them howling in frustration at being pushed away from the Cathedral, the odd one managing to lunge over the top of their shield-wall, trying to touch the shining white armour of the Sororitas for luck, or holiness, or forgiveness.

Calpurnia turned her back on the noise of it, and looked back up at the wall. She was surrounded by mosaics that flooded dazzling colour up the walls. Ceremonial thrones were set into high niches with no apparent way up or down – Calpurnia guessed there were hidden entrances so that curates could be in their seats, arrayed and staring down at whoever was there to beg a favour, without the indignity of steps or ladders.

Ceilings on Hydraphur were sharp-vaulted, not the flat surfaces that Adeptus buildings in the Ultima Segmentum favoured. That meant that the artists had to lay out their works in different ways, with certain consequences for theme and composition. She was craned back looking at the mosaic above her when Dvorov's convoy pulled up outside, and they were admiring the frieze of the Passion of Dolan together when Leandro arrived to complete the delegation. There must have been spy-eyes in the room, because the instant the three of them were standing together the doors on the far side of the antechamber opened and Baragry marched through, Lord Hallyan Kalfus-Medell a pace or two behind him. The five of them stood in a little knot in the centre of the chamber and talked in low tones that made the great space seem conspiratorial, despite the warm afternoon light sluicing down the light-wells.

Calpurnia felt odd, briefing them all in what felt like such a public place, but as briefly as she could, she took them through it: what she knew of the Ecclesiarchy's plan to smuggle emissaries out to the other diocesan centres aboard the *Aurum Sanctus* (Hallyan flared his nostrils and twitch-glanced around him, Baragry simply regarded her expressionlessly); the role of Tell-Kerligan in that smuggling and the disarray it had caused the Tell-Kerligan operations; the way that this disarray had given a cell of heretic saboteurs calling themselves the Society of the Fifty-Eighth Passage an open pass to set up a bomb to incinerate the Cathedral's oil so that the poisoned replacement stocks would be rushed into circulation ('Just what is this Fifty-Eighth Passage, anyway?' Hallyan demanded. 'Who knows? Dvorov told him, 'Secret societies on Hydraphur favour obscure names. It probably only means anything to the conspirators themselves. I'm sure it'll come out in interrogation.'); how the dray-crew's panic at the Aquila Gate had crippled the scheme; and how there were still two fatal blank spots in this whole pattern.

'The connection to the gunman who shot at you that day in the Adeptus Quarter,' said Baragry thoughtfully, 'and the connection to the ambushing forces that mobilised against you as you came back from your landing.'

'The efforts to cover the tracks in each case were quite sophisticated,' Calpurnia said. 'The first assassin had considerable work performed on him to make him untraceable in the event of capture or death. The ambush crews had misinformation fed to them through their supervisors, who were in turn murdered in such a way as to seemingly confirm the lies while making sure that the crews had no way of knowing who was behind them. There is a deftness there which doesn't fit with the Fifty-Eighth Passage operations.'

'It seems to to me,' declared Hallyan, staring at her. 'The infiltration of the Tell-Kerligan house strikes me as skilled work.'

'One was a sabotage attempt aimed at the Ecclesiarchy,' said Dvorov, 'and the other two assassination attempts against an Adeptus Arbites commander. They are different enough that we believe them unconnected.'

'We will confirm it of course, Lord Hallyan,' Calpurnia put in. 'I've given orders for detective and verispex resources to be redoubled to trace the people who incited this. We will know who they are soon enough.'

'Just so,' agreed Hallyan after a pause, and still stood looking at Calpurnia.

'Sunset is not waiting for us,' said Baragry, just as she was starting to feel uncomfortable. 'On to the second reason for your visit, Arbites. This way.'

The more she moved through it, the more comforted Calpurnia was by the Cathedral. In some ways it little resembled the plain Arbites fortresses: the walls bore hundreds of years' worth of inlays, carvings, murals, niches for urns and icons of priests and Sororitas gone by. But as they left the anteroom and began to move through the cloisters she found the formal and purposeful air made her feel at home.

She only had a brief glimpse of the main Cathedral itself, through the great double doors that stood open after three more anterooms. They stepped up to the doors to bow to the altars and pay their respects before they began their climb up through the Cathedral, and that was enough for it to awe her. There was no fussy crowding with pews or sidechapels – the Cathedral was a single vast space whose roof soared away above a crisscross of yellow beams redirected down through giant mirrored light-wells. Two rows of columns, thicker than a Rhino carrier was long, marched down its length, separating the expanse of polished flagstone floor into three aisles each big enough for an Arbites division to march down; concentric rings of steps rose up around the base of each column like an amphitheatre turned inside out. The stone saints and primarchs lining the walls were so tall that Calpurnia would have needed a grapnel and rope even to scramble up onto their feet.

At the far end of the space, beneath a great rendering of the Emperor in gold leaf on the far wall, were the Cathedral's four altars, rearing up just as Galimet had described them. Each was atop a ziggurat bigger than some chapels she had been in: the Altars Dolanite, Sanguinal and Thorian side by side, and the Altar Imperial rising above them from behind. Above each altar hung a marble angel, suspended silently in a gravity column, head bowed and hands folded in prayer. She bowed to each of them and murmured an old Low Gothic blessing from Ultramar, then stepped backwards from the doors and turned away.

They were hours working their way up through the building, as outside the afternoon began to shade to the thick Hydraphur dusk. The tour was part courtesy, part consultation: neither Church nor Arbites could afford to take chances with the security of the Vigil now, and Calpurnia and Dvorov were intent on making sure that the two organisations would be working perfectly in tandem. With Baragry and Hallyan in attendance they prowled through level after level of the giant building in the company of a succession of Adepta Sororitas guides.

The Order of the Sacred Rose garrisoned every part of the Cathedral, and at the corner and end of every corridor a white-armoured sister stood in a guard niche like a statue, bathed in soft white light and with bolter presented. Calpurnia and Dvorov were escorted down wide echoing cloisters and through mazes of tiny passages they had to move through in single file, past great walls of stained glass or tiny vision slits in the thick ramparts. Calpurnia took a minislate from her belt and scratched one name after another into it, fighting to ram faces into her memory for when she met them again. From each they took an account of the garrison and security set out for that section of the Cathedral, and a list of requirements for the Arbites who would complement the garrison for the mass. When they went out onto the terraces Calpurnia kept peering down at the Mesé, the lines of Arbites and sisters and the crowds of worshippers getting smaller and more blurred as they moved further up the Cathedral's spire, and out at the light-spangled slopes of the Bosporian Hive dropping away beneath them in the deepening orange-black twilight. The sisters on the terraces stood guard on circles of armourglass over great spotlights which threw up columns of blue-white radiance, making them shine like stars in the gathering gloom. The white and scarlet pennons on the hafts of their ceremonial banner-staves fluttered and snapped in the evening breeze.

Finally, after climbing more floors than Calpurnia could keep track of, they followed a narrow zigzag corridor onto a balcony with a single chained-off stairway. Up here the wind was chilly and the height dizzying: Calpurnia turned her back on the drop with a grimace. She had not grown up around heights – there were few tall buildings on Iax.

Their Sororitas escort, Sister Iustina, was handing out little half-loops of wire with murmured blessings. Calpurnia stared at hers, and at the intricate little globes on the ends, until she saw the others looping theirs around their heads and followed suit. There was a brief, disturbing moment as the beads writhed and fitted themselves to her ears; the sounds around her grew tinny but no less distinct.

'A tech-arcanum provided by our companions in the Adeptus Mechanicus,' Leandro told her as Sister Iustina unchained the stairway and motioned for them to follow. 'Certain sounds are filtered and certain ones permitted. You will see why in a moment.' And with that they emerged from the stair to the highest platform in the Cathedral's spire.

They stood in a great gallery, two hundred metres long and lined with giant open arches that framed the fiery Hydraphur sunset. From here Calpurnia could see out over the top of even the Monocrat's palace, and the dusting of lights spreading away over the plain beyond it. Behind her when she turned were the silent ranks of the mountains, spreading away in a wedge and disappearing as night slipped forward over them. The height had suddenly ceased to bother her; she felt almost weightless.

'My Arbites.' Hallyan Kalfus-Medell's voice pulled her back to earth, and she turned to face him. He was a black shape against a fire-opal sky in the western arch. His guard-servitor must have been waiting for him here, and it made a monstrous, looming blot beside him.

'Our timing was perfect, and your presence here, my Arbitor Calpurnia, is an honour and a delight. This is something I had greatly hoped to show you, the kind of introduction to the magnificence of my home world that I felt you deserved. It is a delight to be in your presence here.' His voice was gentler than she had heard it before, and he took Calpurnia's elbow to walk her to the arch behind them – she stiffened at the familiarity but saw Dvorov give a quick let-it-go shake of the head in the corner of her vision. She suffered herself to be led to the eastern end of the gallery and the arch facing back over the Mesé; there were no tiers against this side of the spire and the drop to the ground was almost sheer. It was getting on for full night now and the plaza, brightly lit, was a distant haze of colour. Calpurnia realised that it was more than just the mobs that had been around the gate on her arrival. The whole Mesé was packed shoulder to shoulder. It looked as though half the population of the Augustaeum had been flooding in while they had been touring the Cathedral.

She felt another touch on her arm, but it was not Hallyan this time. Sister Iustina checked that her ear-beads were secure and stepped away. She consulted a timepiece on the back of her gauntlet and made a gesture and Calpurnia, seeing the others all drop their mouths open, followed suit. Hallyan said another brief word to his servitor in that chattering code-cant and then pursed his open lips as though blowing a smoke-ring.

The beads cut out most of the sound and so Calpurnia felt the toll of the bell mainly as a physical shock. It was like a weighted punching bag swinging in and hitting her from every angle at once, vibrating her diaphragm as if she had just coughed and setting her carapace armour thrumming and buzzing on her body. It took all her reflexes not to stumble forward a step and all her self-control not to whirl and shout once she saw that the rest of the party had not taken alarm.

And below her, the lights of the hive went out.

For a moment the only illumination was the faint and dimming lights of the hab-city complexes far out on the plain, and then light started creeping back into the jungle of towers and steeples on the slopes below them. Subdued, modest floods began to shine from the palace and the walls of the Cathedral, the Sororitas lit up by their spotlights as if the side of the Cathedral had been strung with diamonds.

A moment later, the citizens' lanterns began to light in the square. At first just a sprinkle, points here and there, but the light grew until the plaza shone like a carpet of fireflies, then like a river breaking its banks as more lanterns were lit in the darkened streets of the Kathisma and more all the way down every road and alley in the hive. In the silence as the single ring of the bell died away, the glittering web was magical, hypnotic.

'Do you see, Arbitor Calpurnia, why I am so concerned for you? Look out over this hive, look at the throngs below us. Imagine what it will be like when the bells ring at the start of the festival of the Sanguinala! Picture what it will be like: the crowds casting the mourning cloaks from over their scarlet festive garb, the red banners unfurling from all the steeples and towers, crimson petals filling the air.' He was almost whispering.

'This mass will be a thing of beauty, my arbitor. I have worked so hard, so long to make such a holy time one that will be remembered and retold down the years. Whoever would harm you, or any of the great Adeptus or myself or even the lowliest servant of the mass, would defile what the Eparch of Hydraphur honoured me with the task of making. I want you to understand that.'

'I think, my Lord Kalfus-Medell, that I do.'

They stood and watched the lights in silence for a time.

Fourteenth Day of Septista.

Four days to the Mass of Saint Balronas. First day of the Vigil of Balronas. Commemoration of Girza the Demi-Sainted (Adepta Sororitas).

As of this day all travel by vehicle in the Augustaeum is prohibited, as it is in the lower city unless on Adeptus business. These laws will be enforced by Arbites and Sororitas, to whom any breaches of these laws must be reported. A religious curfew descends at nightfall and no citizen should be outside their homes unless on religious business. Travel to and from religious services should be as part of an Ecclesiarchal procession, of which there will be dozens for each shrine and chapel in constant motion throughout the night. The only illumination permitted in the home are candles of the size specified by the Ecclesiarchy or the scented lamp that was lit for the Quiet Congregation. Householders should admit officers of the Ecclesiarchy or Ministorum who may by law enter any house at any time during this period to police this edict and pronounce a blessing on the house if all is well.

CHAPTER NINE

BOTH ECLIPTICS OF the Hydraphur system swarmed with Navy fortifications, from the Ring itself, through the necklaces of orbital fortresses that every world in the system wore, the free-stations surfing the shifting gravitic tides between the ecliptics, the lumbering battlegroups of the Squadron Hydraphur prowling the system like panthers in a cage, the tiny sentinel stations and free-floating hardpoints tucked into the curling asteroid belts, the clouds of deadfall torpedoes in the system fringes, and the bunkers and citadels spread across every world and cut into the crust of every moon. But the bulk of the Navy's second-line facilities, the fief-planets it controlled, its forges and shipworks, the Navigator stations and telepathica matrices, the four giant Naval academies and the luxurious spaceborne estates of the officer-aristocrats, were concentrated in the Gyre Marmarea, the larger ecliptic that tilted towards the borders of the Segmentum Obscuras.

At 09.57 on the fourteenth day of Septista, while Shira Calpurnia was sifting through incident reports trying to find links with the attempts on her life, an authorisation code was mistransmitted to *Aventis Sapphire 7*, a dromon runner carrying half a household's worth of dignitaries from the League of Blackships station in the

Gyre Marmarea in for the Vigil. When the ship's astropaths and logisters tried to authenticate their respective halves of the code with the Naval patrols above the Ring, it registered as correct for the first pass and the dromon was cleared to close. Halfway through its approach the code transmissions, despite the layers of security and elaborate fault-tolerance procedures, abruptly began to clash and contradict and the runner arced gracefully into the path of *Highcaster*, a cargo barge accelerating away from the Ring towards an outbound Navy cruiser.

The dromoni were designed to double as system defence boats in an emergency, and the ship had enough agility to turn and glance off the barge and enough structural toughness not to break up immediately. Its starboard side a mass of furrows, bleeding oxygen from its decks and plasma from its drives, the dromon spiralled slowly away as klaxons screamed through the Ring and tugs and emergency boats scrambled through the launching-gates. The barge was less lucky, knocked directly toward the Ring with its back broken by the impact. The roared commands of the Gunnery Control commander for the fortress batteries to wait bought it enough time for about a third of the crew to reach saviour capsules, but the rest, or as many of them as had survived the collision, were incinerated with the ship when the Ring gunners decided they had no more time.

Within fifteen minutes of *Highcaster's* final death throes, the Transmechanics and Astropaths had been dragged from their communications cupolas. Twenty minutes after that the Commander of the Watch was shouting questions at them in his own chambers in one of the Ring's command domes. Over the next half-hour that dome was besieged by the Navy, directors of the line to which *Highcaster* had belonged, furious Adeptus Astropathica envoys demanding to know how their esteemed brethren could have been subjected to this, and rather more discreet representations from the Monocrat's palace.

Two hours after the collision the postmortems of the failsafe systems were coming in. The good news was that whatever problem had caused the collision had been localised, and the failsafes had contained it. The downside of it was that it was starting to point to something darker. Sabotage.

A formal envoy from the offices of the Master of Orbits arrived at the three-hour mark. He walked into the command dome at almost the same moment as two members of the Naval Adjudicature, there with a team of Naval Security invigilators to make their own formal report. One of the first things they found, after demanding to see those involved, was that the astropath who had first broadcast the hails between *Aventis Sapphire 7* and the Ring had committed suicide with a slap-syringe that he had picked loose from the lining of his robe. Talk of sabotage intensified.

At 14.04, just over four hours since the first of the wrong codes had flown into the minds of the *Aventis's* astropaths, Shira Calpurnia took ship at the Arbites Cross-Seven fortress and was carried up to board the Ring yet another time. By the time she stepped through the docking hatch, paranoia was thick enough to be wrung out of the air by the double-fistful. And the entire transmission and astropath crew were in the custody of the Navy.

'THEY'RE WHAT?' CALPURNIA snapped, fighting the urge to step forward and slam a fist down on the desk.

'In the custody of the Navy,' said Hadre Gutamo, Commander of the Watch for the twenty-eighth segment of the Hydraphur Ring. Standing behind the great slab of polished wood in the tiny office in the heart of his chambers, surrounded by rich tapestries and framed Imperial honour scrolls, Gutamo had the bearing of one determined to bravely wear pain and disgrace: formal and straight-backed as though on ceremonial parade, but still somehow giving the impression of sagging, as though his body had gone limp and was only being held up by a harness and wires. One eye was green, the other yellow-orange and surrounded by scars – Calpurnia took it for a tissue graft of some kind – and both mismatched eyes looked dully at his hands, folded in front of his chest. A tiny quaver of misery in his voice and the smallest twitching of his waxed moustache belied his apparent composure.

'I see. This is the boundary area between planetary – that is, full Adeptus – jurisdiction and Naval jurisdiction in open space, is that right?' From what she had heard on her way up Calpurnia had already guessed that the people involved in the mistransmission had been spirited off-station, but she had reined her anger in until she had the word of their commander to go on. Now that she had confirmation her temper was starting to creak for release.

'Yes. The Master of Orbits reports to both the Monocrat and Adeptus and to the in-system Naval Command.'

'And you report to the Master of Orbits.'

'Yes.'

'And did you ascertain from him, or did he tell you, that this may well be related to a string of sabotage and assassination attempts in the heart of the Bosporian Hive down on Hydraphur, aimed at the Vigil of Saint Balronas itself, and that maybe you should bloody well have allowed the Adeptus Arbites access to these people?'

He swallowed. 'The chain of communication that caused the... incident... the crash, it actually began with a Naval station in far-perimeter orbit. The Inner Charisian Gate, under Gate-Captain Sambin de Jauncey. Captain de Jauncey made immediate petition for all guilty parties to be handed over to him so that they could face a court martial along with members of his own crew under Naval protocol.' Gutamo looked up as he finished talking and flinched. 'Green as Macragge glacier-ice', was how one of Calpurnia's brothers had described her eyes when she was angry. His gaze returned to his gloved hands. One of them had developed a slight tic to match the one in his moustache.

'Who will handle the court martial, Commander Gutamo?' Calpurnia's voice was quieter, but the edge had not gone from it.

'There are a number of eligible authorities under the protocols of Naval law.' Gutamo's voice had quietened too. 'The exact strengths of each claim on the trying of this case would need to be weighed in light of the relevant judgements and precedents. It would probably require some consideration by specialist savants and archivists, since the majority of cases would date back to pre-Apostasy–'

'I am sure that such input will be most terribly helpful,' Calpurnia told him, 'but I invite you, commander, to take a guess. I don't doubt that the Arbites will want to carefully examine the role of *every* member of the Ring crews in this incident and I would certainly hope that our working relationship here is going to get off to the best possible start. I hope that nothing in your own co-operation has the effect of prejudicing that examination against your colleagues here.'

Gutamo registered the not-very-veiled threat with the air of a drowning man who has felt it start to rain. He gave a long blink and then lifted his eyes slowly back to Calpurnia's face. She had looked into a great many condemned eyes, but still the weight in Gutamo's bi-coloured gaze almost made her step back.

'From what I have seen in the communiqués from the gate,' he said, 'Captain de Jauncey proposes to chair the hearings himself and make all sentences immediate. There was talk of summary executions, and those may already have been carried out. That is all I can reveal to you, Arbitor Senioris Calpurnia, without endangering myself further with the risk of inaccuracy. As it stands my family will be provided for after I pay the penalty for what happened on my watch. If I make things worse for myself they may not be. I trust you understand.'

She did understand, but she pushed it aside as irrelevant – suddenly she was itching to get to the Inner Charisian Gate before the trail of the saboteurs, whoever they were, was closed off. She gave the briefest of formal arbitrator salutes, which Gutamo returned with the curved-hand salute of the Battlefleet Pacificus, then jerked her head for Bannon to follow.

'Are we not arresting the commander?' he whispered as they double-timed back out through Gutamo's chambers under the eyes of the dome staff. She waited to reply to him until they were well on their way back to their cutter, tramping loudly through corridors of tarnished, raw-looking iron whose walls were run through with heavy girders and studded with great rivet-heads twice the size of Calpurnia's fist. As they came to each new corridor or stairwell she saw little knots of station crew break up with alacrity and hurry away, not wanting to linger in the sight of a senior arbitrator so soon after such a terrible crime.

'Gutamo isn't going anywhere. He understands his duty and I believe he'll do it. And we're close enough to Hydraphur that he's arrestable if he should be found wanting. But doesn't it worry you that the inner gate, that's what you call that ring of way-fortresses just outside maximum orbit, isn't it, the inner gates? Right. The inner gate which might be implicated is the nucleus of the squadron that gave that runner its clearance, and within hours the station commander has arrested every *other* implicated crewmember, to a spot where he'll be able to kick them out of an airlock with a bolt round through the back of the head without anyone else being able to interrogate them or gainsay any report he provides? Nothing about that bothers you?'

'Perhaps we should be co-operating with the Navy authorities in the trial, maybe? Maybe we can send them an envoy...'

'Fine if this de Jauncey is simply being enthusiastic,' Calpurnia replied, striding down an already-moving lift-stair, 'and utterly useless if he's doing what my unpleasant arbitrator's mind is suspecting him of doing. What plan of action did we log before we took off from Cross-Seven? I think I left it to you to word, didn't I?'

'Uh, um. We instructed that we would, um, be conducting immediate questioning of the Commander of the Watch, then conducting what action we thought was necessary aboard the Ring while we awaited a fuller task force of Judges and judicial savants to begin negotiating the overlap of legal jurisdictions.' Bannon's voice firmed as he gradually recalled what he had written.

'Right. Good. I'm countermanding that as of now. No,' she added, catching his expression, 'you didn't do anything wrong, you did just what I needed you to do. It's just that "what action we think is necessary" has just become a little more urgent.'

'We're going out to this station now, without waiting for the taskforce?'

'I know about picking taskforces. It will be hours before they're ready to lift, and I need to be at this station now. Throne alone knows what de Jauncey will be able to get away with if he's hiding something.'

'The jurisdictional issues...'

'In orbit over Don-Croix,' Calpurnia told him coldly as she half-vaulted down a steep grillework staircase to the dock levels, 'we conducted a full boarding action of a Navy cruiser when we had reason to believe that there was a xenos infestation being protected by the crew. Don't try and tell me that there has ever lived or breathed a single Navy officer who is outside the reach of the Law. What did they make you chant on the parade ground every morning of your induction, Bannon?'

'We determine the guilty. We decide the punishment.'

'Damned right we do. And I'm pleased to hear there are some things that are the same the whole galaxy over. Anyway, we seemed to inadvertently generate some goodwill from the Navy when we stopped the *Sanctus*, so maybe that will help when we show up and push our way on board.' I'm talking like Dvorov, she thought ruefully, then barked at Bannon again. 'Go ahead of us and order our cutter to prepare for cast-off. Have the pilot lay in a course for the gate and order the Ring controllers to clear a path for us, on my authority. This is a level four delegation. *Run*!' He shot away from her as though scalded.

For a moment she was alone at the top of the docking-well, and stopped to catch her breath. She realised she didn't even know how much of a trip out to the gate she was in for. Maybe she could requisition a dromon of her own... but no. She'd send a transmission to the gate as soon as they launched and not risk getting bogged down in haggling with the commander if there were no ship readily available. If only the *Judgement's Clarion* had still been stationed at the Ring, but the little carrier had been called from the *Aurum Sanctus* interception to a suppression operation at the edge of the Gyre Aurucon and would not be back at Hydraphur for weeks.

For a moment Calpurnia wished she could be as confident as she had sounded to Bannon, then told herself she was being pessimistic. She was Adeptus Arbites and she had the goodwill of the Navy; that much she knew. And the attack on the Ring was an attack on them both. As she started down the steps, listening to the rumble of launch preparations starting to shiver the walls, she told herself this wouldn't be hard.

'DON'T GO THINKING you'll be allowed to stay here,' snarled the voice on the Charisian Gate's vox-channel as grapples clanged against the hull outside. 'We are docking you on sufferance. Your craft will be refuelled and its anima rested, and then you will be on your way, under armed escort until you reach the Ring. The Gate-Captain issued specific instructions to that effect.' Startled out of any immediate reply, Calpurnia steadied herself in her crash-couch as the cutter was jerked gracelessly toward the Inner Charisian Gate's docks. The crackling voice coming from the grille was a rude bucket of icewater over her earlier optimism. Suddenly she felt stiff and awkward in the couch, and as if on cue the knot of scar tissue in the front of her right hip seemed to tense and stiffen.

In the systems Calpurnia had served in on the south-eastern fringe, the fortresses that rode vital positions in the system's ecliptic were known as points; in Hydraphur they were known as gates. They rode the gravity well at points where the heaviest traffic tended to pass, where it was easiest to slingshot from one Gyre to the other, or to skirt around the largest gas giants or past the dense asteroid belts that looped and twisted through the system. That made the stations gates in more than name – nearly every ship that wanted to pass into the system by a safe and stable route would at some point have to pass through space that a gate station controlled.

The Inner Charisian Gate was one of the smaller ones, not a self-contained fortress but part of an array of platforms and stations that stood out from orbit to form a second, dispersed ring of guns and attack-craft bays. Small it might be by the standards of the giants further out, but it still filled the cockpit window when Calpurnia slipped forward to watch their approach. It wove and tilted in front of them as their pilot threaded them through the stacked minefields and the fire-lanes of the outrigger turrets. The half-glimpsed silhouettes of the dormant mines and the hungry turret gunports were in their own way a powerful sign of entering a new domain. Soon the gate had spread to fill every corner of the port, a fat pitted egg of an asteroid, glittering with windows, ringed with void-shield spines and docking gantries and with great tiered steeples of reinforced adamantium jutting above and below it.

She had left orders at the Ring to inform the gate's astropaths of their arrival, and the hails and counter-hails had been smooth if curt as they closed in. It was not until the approach controller's sudden bark at her from the vox-grille that her feelings about the visit suddenly turned bad. She looked back over the team in the cutter: Bannon, and two Arbites she had collared from Cross-Seven when she realised she should probably have an escort. The cutter juddered and rang as it was pulled taut against the station's docking arm and Calpurnia thought about all the empty space between her and the nearest Arbites reinforcements.

There was nothing for it but to square her shoulders, chill her gaze down to the appropriate authoritative stare, straighten her rank insignia and climb up the ladderwell. To someone outside the station it would look as if the cutter had been seized by a long metal fin stretching out from the station and clamping to its back; from the inside that hollow 'fin' was a high oubliette where the top of the cutter's hull formed the floor. Calpurnia stood on that hull now, boots planted on the frosted metal, and stared upwards.

The docking level was an assault on the senses. The metal around her was as bitterly cold as the hull beneath her, and she could watch her breath pluming up from her lips and the dew turning to rime on the walls and the catwalks, and on the giant chains that had snaked out from the dock mouth and clamped onto the cutter's hull. Squinting past the arclights above her Calpurnia could make out giant cylinders that she took to be the capstan array. The noise of the machinery was like a hammer.

Their pilots had remained in the cockpit, and it was only Bannon and her two-arbitor impromptu escort who joined her in the oubliette. Calpurnia smiled inwardly as they huffed and stamped at the cold air slapping their skin: they were all used to Hydraphur climates, while the chill reminded her pleasantly of the ocean cliffs on Talassar and her one visit – half a pilgrimage – to the poles of Macragge. Then she muttered at them to stop it and collect themselves. She had no doubt they were being watched, and they had to comport themselves properly.

Thinking that in turn made her realise how long she had been standing there. She tilted her head back and called out.

'I am Shira Calpurnia, Arbitor Senioris of the Adeptus Arbites. I wish to make a formal greeting to an officer of this installation so that I can be about my business here. I am being kept waiting.'

Her voice was clear and powerful, ringing up and over the rumble and clank of machinery. And either her tone had made the reception jump or they had been just about to start anyway, because a moment later they could see a grillework carriage come rattling down one hoarfrosted wall. It descended evenly until it was two or three times head height, then ground down a gear and lowered the rest of the way with aching slowness. Lights over the top of its door clanked on and glared at them, and Calpurnia had to take her helmet from Bannon and don it; once behind the polarising lenses she was able to get a good look at the group in the carriage.

They were not a welcoming sight. In the middle of the carriage, taking up much of the room despite the bunched, controlled posture common to constant space-travellers, was a Naval petty officer whose knee-length green uniform coat was adorned with the crimson slashes of decorations for shipboard-combat actions. His sabre and a heavy Naval pistol were hung at his sides and the right half of his jaw was augmetic steel that glittered in the lights. He was flanked by two ratings, faceless in heavy rubberised work-ponchos and hoods, carrying heavy-duty chainblades on the ends of bulky fighting shafts, blades to cut through wrecked bulkheads, tangled cables or enemy flesh with equal ease. A Naval Security trooper in a uniform that was almost a mirror of the arbitrators' rounded out the party, flamer held ready with the igniter jet lit. The intended effect – and the snub it implied – was obvious. Calpurnia gritted her teeth. She was an arbitor senioris, the fourth highest-ranking enforcer of Imperial Law in this damned system, and she was not going to be scared out of acting like it.

She strode forward to the carriage doors and glared at the petty officer through the bars until they ground open.

'My escorts and I are here to carry out arrests over sabotage and deaths at the Hydraphur Ring. Kindly escort us on board the station. Gate-Captain de Jauncey should have been alerted to our arrival and will be expecting us.'

'If you're here, madam, then you know that the people behind that act have already been arrested. Arrested and brought here. You have nothing more to worry about. We will even do the executions for you.'

The man's speech was odd, the synthetic lip on the artificial part of his jaw not quite able to do its part in forming words. His expression was not quite a sneer.

'The guilty parties that you took it on yourselves to arrest are wanted by more than just the Navy,' she told him. 'They are implicated in...' she paused for a moment, long enough to wonder if *implicated* was too strong a word to be truthful, and then to decide that she was not going to justify herself to a junior officer. '...in planetary matters which I will discuss with the gate-captain. If you are not he, then kindly make the arrangements for my admission.'

'You are not a Navy officer. Beyond the Hydraphur Ring, the system is a Naval fief, world, moon and space alike.' His expression had turned sulky, and Calpurnia liked that. It vindicated her: he didn't have the authority to order her off the station, no matter how much he wished and acted otherwise. Keeping her dignity in mind, she simply stared at him as he started to shift uncomfortably in the freezing air, and motioned her escorts into the carriage when he grudgingly stepped aside. With the other Arbites between her and the Navy party she looked out through the bars at nothing in particular until the cage had rattled its way to the top of the oubliette and they were able to step through the series of airlocks into the gate itself.

In spite of their reception, Calpurnia found herself relaxing as they passed through the station. Physically it seemed as exotic to her as much of Hydraphur, with that taper-arched shape to its doors and the passages looking more like a succession of vaulted chambers than plain corridors. But like the Cathedral cloisters or the operational levels of the Wall, this was a *working* place, not a place existing for the sake of its own grandeur. It was full of emerald-uniformed officers, enlisted ranks in coarse grey-green hurrying under the bellows of their superiors, indentured station-hands with their grafted-shut mouths and facial brands. Once or twice she caught glimpses of other adeptus, too, Mechanicus magi on some errand for the system-arcana of the station or astropaths in hoods or psi-dampening metal head-cages, shuffling along in lines with their heads down. There simply wasn't the space on a station to set aside space for ceremonial disuse, and the gate had the comforting bedlam of a place at work.

As they made their way out of the central rock into the steeple and the walls around them changed from stone to steel, the crowds changed too. Here there were more officers, and the enlisted hands had better uniforms and more pride in their gait. These were not the mass-pressganged labour of the lower levels, who would toil until they were crushed in machinery or cooked or electrocuted in system malfunctions and replaced as a matter of routine. These were the skilled crew, the ones who directed the workings of the engines or the aim of the defences, who monitored the dronings of the astropaths or the crackling void-shield generators.

Calpurnia had thought they were being taken to the bridge, but their grudging host instead took them to a double shuttered door flanked by two more ship's security troopers, holding fat-barrelled hellguns on the corridor. He nodded to them and shoved the doors open, motioned the Arbites gracelessly through, and swung the doors shut without another word.

They were in an orrery. The spherical chamber was big enough that the gallery they had stepped into was several metres above the floor, or at least above the lowest pole of the sphere. The walls were painted a midnight blue, and the sun that hung in the middle was a globular lantern of burnt-orange smoked glass. Hanging in formation around it were intersecting silver hoops for Hydraphur's twin ecliptics, metal orbs for the planets and moons gliding along them with a faint hissing sound. The dust clouds were gauzy nets of wire towed between little semicircles of silver; asteroid belts were strings of crystal beads. She stared in frank admiration of its understated elegance as much as the complexity of design.

Gate-Captain Sambin de Jauncey leaned against the railing, his back to them. He was a slender man, not tall but seeming so from his haughty posture. His hair was silky-black and short, his skin dusky, his movements cat-graceful and his eyes, when he turned to face them, cat-alert. He wore no ceremonial sabre, just a slender dagger on a braided gold cord around his neck. The high collar of his uniform bore a richly embroidered emblem that Calpurnia supposed was a family crest.

'You are trying my patience, madam arbitor,' he began without preamble, 'which was not abundant today to begin with. So tell me, what can I do to get you out of my station and on your way?'

'I am here to pursue the perpetrators of sabotage at the Ring which destroyed two ships, cost many lives, endangered many more.' Calpurnia had thought that his snubbing tone was coming and kept her own voice cold and level. 'Those people were aboard the Ring but were removed from it into Naval custody, apparently on your orders, and brought here. There have been similarly callous and destructive sabotage actions on Hydraphur itself, and I propose that the same agency might be behind both. By co-operating we can remove a criminal threat to the Arbites, the Navy, the sacred Vigil on Hydraphur, and an enemy of the Imperium and its people.'

'You're certainly ambitious, but not very attentive. You haven't answered my question.' He had taken a step toward her, dark eyes blazing, and Calpurnia realised de Jauncey was not just being rude. He was furious. 'My question, and I will repeat it for you, is this: what must I do to have you out of my way?'

'Your question, gate-captain, was "what can I do, pray tell me, to get you out of my station and on your way as soon as possible?" Your memory is in about the same state that you allege my attentiveness to be, apparently. And as for an answer, what you can do is accommodate myself and my escorts on the station until my additional Arbites personnel arrive. Then you can join me in interrogating the prisoners, who are most certainly guilty under Imperial law and therefore must answer to the Imperium's premier lawgivers. To show goodwill I am prepared to allow you to co-prosecute once the interrogations and the verispex evidence-gathering is done. Then you can allow whatever sentences and punishments are called for to proceed, participating where you need to, and after that, gate-captain, you will be free of me.'

'Not acceptable.' He turned away and leaned over the railing again. A silver ball representing one of the outermost worlds whispered by an arm's length from his face, twirling a pair of gemstone moons around it. 'This is a military system, arbitrator, and until we were forced off it by politics Hydraphur was a military world. The attack was on space shipping, which is a matter of Naval prerogative. To subject myself to the orders of a planetary authority, to surrender authority over prisoners being held on my station under my orders... I wonder if you fully understand what you ask. What you dare ask.'

'My title, Gate-Captain de Jauncey, is Arbitor. Arbitor senioris. You may address me as arbitor senioris or Arbitor Calpurnia, as you wish.'

'If the best you can manage by way of a riposte is to correct me on some point of formal address–'

'I can also correct you on a point of formal *law*. We are the Adeptus Arbites. The vessel by which the Emperor's laws have travelled down the ages. We light and keep the beacon of the Emperor's Law so that all in His Imperium can guide their lives by it, and we see to it that those who turn away from that beacon and cause themselves and others to stumble are made to pay. We determine the guilty, we decide the punishment. I have witnessed judgements of officers of the Navy and of the Imperial Guard and of planetary and system governors. I have twice helped to pass sentence on men and women of both those organizations, some of them more highly ranked than you, gate-captain. If you wish me out of the way, then I suppose the way is to have me murdered before the ship full of Arbites arrives on-station, and then to have some way of making sure that those Arbites then don't get suspicious enough to declare you renegade and exact the appropriate punishment on you as well as on whatever wretches you have in your brig.'

De Jauncey was gripping the railing he leant on. He was wearing soft gloves that hid his hands, but she could tell from his posture that under the quilted green silk his knuckles would be white.

'Or,' she went on, 'you could join with me in doing what we are both, my gate-captain, supposed to be spending our lives doing.

Combating threats to the Imperium and to its people. Is it really so hard to see what we have in common here?'

'How much do we have in common, do you think? How much do I have in common with some woman who marches onto my own station, the station of which I am the duly appointed captain, to demand that I jump to her tune? Every last one of the crew of this gate would walk out of the airlocks if I ordered it, because a captain, on his ship, and this gate station is my ship, *Arbitor*, embodies final authority.'

'If you do not feel you're answerable to the Arbites, de Jauncey, then fine. You can argue the exact points of law with the savants and locutors when they arrive on my heels. We can all meet back in this chamber and explain your position to you. If you still want to resist the will of the law then, well, I think I mentioned that you won't be the first renegade Naval officer I've helped to take down.'

He swung around again, fists knuckle-cracking tight and eyes alight. 'That was a threat, *Arbitor* Calpurnia. You threatened me. You came onto my gate and you stood there and you *threatened* me.'

'Yes, gate-captain, that is exactly what I did. I'm fed up with dancing around and mouthing fancy words to get the co-operation I should expect by rights. I have the authority and the justification to threaten you and I am using it.'

'You will regret this,' de Jauncey said. He was breathing hard. 'The *Crusader Ascendant* is due to dock at this gate within six hours. I refer, for your information, to the flagship of Commodore Hayl Omenti, commander of the Fourth Hydraphur Squadron and Warden of the Inner Gates. Do not doubt that he will have something to say about the way some,' he made a dismissive gesture, 'some little Arbitrix came scuttling aboard in a planetary-orbit cutter to try to subvert a gate-captain's authority.'

'There's a pleasing symmetry to that, gate-captain, because although I can't quote a fancy name at you, a ship full of Judges is on its way likewise. So, then. You will give me and my fellow Arbites suitable accommodation. When my colleagues arrive then we will sit down with yourself and whoever from the commodore's staff is interested and we will make clear exactly how much authority you have in this matter. And when that is done we will proceed with the trials and the sentences.' She took a step to the door. 'Have someone show us to our quarters, please. Now.'

* * *

THEY WERE GIVEN quarters of a single stateroom and ablutory, that would have been snug for one and was full with four. Calpurnia made a point of talking for a little while to each of the two Arbites she had brought from Cross-Seven: Gomry, a sleek-muscled, almond-eyed young man from Hydraphur's island archipelagos, and Syldati, a woman whose hair and skin were as white as her eyes and lips were dark, with an odd accent that she said came from the DiMattina system two sectors to rimward. Both were relatively junior and feeling as uncomfortable as Bannon with being suddenly trapped in such a spat between their own commander and the Navy. Calpurnia kept talking on and off, as much to relax herself as them, and the uncomfortable silences gradually mellowed to companionable silences as they sat side by side, stripping weapons and kit and trading the occasional anecdote and joke.

Calpurnia wasn't sure how much time had passed before the change of watch was sounded. They all jumped as the horns went off through the corridors outside; it was a harsh, ear-filling sound with an oddly layered quality as horns in passages further away joined in the chorus. The hall outside filled with hammering boots and shouting voices for nearly half an hour before the racket of the changeover died down. She was starting to wonder about organising sleeping shifts when they all jumped again at a bang on the door. It was a station-hand, shifting with discomfort at the unfamiliar duty. Behind him, the corridor was in shadow – the lights, already muted as a nod to the Vigil, had been dimmed further for the night cycle.

'Ma'am, Gate-Captain de Jauncey instructs you to be advised that the dromon runner *Lumen Geodess* has entered the outer reaches of our defences and should dock within the hour. *Crusader Ascendant* has hailed us and will soon be inbound also.'

Calpurnia nodded, snapped her fingers for him to stay for a moment and beckoned to Bannon and Syldati.

'Escort my two staff to whichever docking point the *Geodess* will be using, please. You two, report to the leader of the Arbites taskforce when it arrives. Give him a quick report on what's happened here to date – you were both with me the whole time. Then escort them here. You have a Level Two delegation, reporting to the taskforce leader until you rejoin me.'

The crewman looked nervous enough at that to reassure the two Arbites, who traded glances, donned helmets and stamped away at his heels, in heavy and confident step. Gomry looked after them, and then quizzically at Calpurnia.

'We wait here,' she told him, 'in case there's a new message from the gate-captain. And because I'm fed up with doing every last bit of bolting about myself. I'm going to stay up here, catch my breath and stretch my legs. Lucky you, Gomry, you get to stay here and stretch your legs too.'

The constant traffic and noise of the day shifts was gone, and the cool dimness of the passageway outside their room seemed spacious and tranquil in the quiet. Calpurnia sauntered a short way from the door, breathing deeply. She had no idea whether or not it was just her fancy, but the air seemed cooler. She risked a stretch, standing on tiptoe and tilting her head back, started to run through the list of things she had to go over with the taskforce, then gave up. There would be time to–

There was a soft sound behind her and then a pair of arms clamped brutally tight around her, level with her biceps, pinning her own arms to her body and lifting her onto tiptoe. Heavy arms, a strong and confident grip.

'Got you now, haven't we?' leered a voice in her ear, and a tickle of alcohol fumes curled around to find her nostrils. The voice was husky, male, young, muffled. She was spun around to face back toward the door to her room, spilling light out into the passage; three more men stood there, in Navy uniform breeches and loose shirts with identity pins taken off, dark wraps of cloth muffling their faces, heavy truncheons in their hands. What she could see of their skin looked flushed. Whoever was holding her didn't seem to be the only one to have braced his courage with a bottle.

Gomry stepped through the doorway a moment later, helmetless and unprepared. His eyes widened and his instincts betrayed him: his first reaction was not to spring back into the room to grab a firearm, but to say 'Unhand the arbitor sen-' Then a vicious truncheon swing cracked into his forehead and he pitched soundlessly back into the stateroom.

'You're going to pay for that,' Calpurnia said over her shoulder to whoever held her. 'Up until a moment ago I could have written this off as some kind of stunt by overzealous cadets, but now we've got an arbitor who's going to need a medicae bed or a funeral. Don't think I'm not going to personally end you for this.

All of you. And I'll end de Jauncey, too, if I so much as suspect he's behind it.'

'Full of bragging, aren't you, you meddling little bitch.' The stink of alcohol again, but her captor was managing to keep his voice down to a hiss. 'Think you can come where you're not wanted? Think you can just push your way in here and order us about and disgrace us? We've got a nice idea for a little present for your friends to find. We're going to send a little message about little bitches who push their little noses into places they have no right to be.' His companions were sniggering, and the one who had felled Gomry was slapping his truncheon into his gloved palm.

Calpurnia was taking things in. They were drunk, but probably not enough for her to count on them being slowed or blurred. They were bigger than her, more powerful. Their truncheons were solid bludgeons, either wood or plastic, she couldn't tell, but reliant on their weight and not powered like her maul. The adrenaline they were getting from their own daring was carrying them along. They were badly positioned, taking too long to gloat, not taking her weapons off her.

She was yanked toward the stateroom again. Once they got her in there her chances would be radically worse. Experimentally, she shifted her weight. The hug was still strong, but the man wasn't trying to control her balance or her centre. Ah-ha.

She shifted her hips to the right. Her shoulders didn't move, and the man gripping her had his sense for her movements dulled by his height and inferior balance and by the armour around her chest and shoulders. She pushed the hilt of her maul forward, pivoting it and levering the tip up behind her. He grunted in annoyance, then the grunt turned to a soundless whoop of agony as she thumbed the maul into life. The arms around her vanished, and she ducked away as the man who had held her doubled up so quickly his feet left the deck and he crashed down in a foetal curl.

His three associates were stunned and motionless in their own turn and Calpurnia moved to cut the numbers while she could, taking two quick, graceful steps forward and sideways, angling so that when she drove the maul forward into the second attacker's gut in a textbook fencer's lunge the power discharge sent him retching and cannoning back into the man behind him.

Tangled together, the two of them crashed into the passage wall and Calpurnia turned in time to duck and slip her head to one side to dodge a stroke that would have split her skull. Instinct stopped her counterattacking straight away, and she avoided the backslash that whipped by in front of her nose, but after that the other man had leaned into his strokes too much and given away his balance, so she had a moment's opening to step in and crack his knee with her boot. Then she was inside the third truncheon swing, positioned to catch the man's arm on her shoulder, sock her hip into and under his and let his own swing twist him off his feet. His broken knee folded and he landed awkwardly, yelling in pain and shock and trying to drag her over with him.

She stamped hard on his face and kicked him harder in the ribs and head, then turned and hunched and caught the blow from behind her on her shoulder armour. The man who'd managed to get out from under his half-conscious companion got a double-handed grip on his truncheon for a swing to take off her head.

Calpurnia, who had still felt the impact and was grateful beyond words she had kept her carapace on, didn't give him the chance. Now humming and spitting with power, her maul didn't need a big swing to do damage and she feinted low with it then swatted his hands when he tried to block. She had upped the setting a notch and the crack of power blew the truncheon out of the man's hands and took off the tips off six of his fingers. He yowled and staggered back and Calpurnia, in no mood to be merciful, tilted her shoulder in and made a sharp downward chop that shattered his collarbone and left a scorched, ruined weal from his shoulder to his belly. The maul bucked in her hand as it hit and the man crashed backward, slid along the wall and down it to jitter on the floor.

She slammed the maul back into its clip and ran to Gomry. His eyes were rolled back, his pulse fluttering, and the bruise across his forehead cruel and dark. Calpurnia snarled to herself and would have spat at the prone forms out in the passageway, but there was no point in wasting the energy. She listened to his pulse, talked to him, helped his breathing when she had to, harangued him, ordered him not to die, and she was still hunched over him, doggedly keeping him as alive as she could, when Naval Security arrived.

Fifteenth Day of Septista

Three days to the Mass of Saint Balronas.
Second day of the Vigil of Balronas. Procession of the Thesean Martyrs. Commemoration of Cartigan and of Lucullus Traph.

By this day all food remaining from the feast on Vigil's Eve should have been consumed. Any that does remain by sunrise must be cast away, ideally burned in the braziers before the nearest chapel after being blessed by the preacher there. If the food is burned at a home shrine a reading by the head of the household of the Fourth Ophelian Psalm *or the first ten verses of* Thor's Epistle to the Dannites *is appropriate. It is also acceptable to place the food on the tithing-step at a street pulpit.*

Those attending the Procession of the Thesean Martyrs should fast from sunrise until after the caskets have passed them on the third and final of their circuits around the Cathedral. While the caskets are carried past it is traditional to reflect upon one's conduct before one's masters and the Emperor over the past year. Traditional clothing for this day should be a dark headband or kerchief around the forehead for males, and the same or a dark veil for females. Particularly devoted citizens may wish to wear a blindfold or strap over the eyes during religious observances.

By the end of the day citizens should have decided on the fast they will make to prepare themselves for the remainder of the Vigil. The beginning of the fast at sunset at latest is to be greatly encouraged as a pious practice. During the early hours of the fast, thoughts should be turned to one's sins and misdeeds and the need for repentance and redemption – the keeping of a vigil without sleep until the Services of the Quills is considered a mark of devotion at this time.

CHAPTER TEN

'IT WOULD NOT,' Calpurnia remarked aloud, 'have occurred to me to provide you with medical care. Any of you. I can think of at least one man who had – who has – far better claim on the gate's medical resources than any of you.'

She was standing at one end of the twin-level central concourse of the Inner Charisian Gate, ignoring the curious or sullenly hostile looks of the station crew around her. Stairways curled up on either side of her to the tribunal chamber on one side and the Astropathica suite on the other, and on either side of each stairway was a set of heavy plastic stocks bolted to a plate in the floor.

Leftmost was Station Cadet Gintis, the second assailant to go down in the fight the night before. Like all of them, he had been anchored into the stocks in full uniform from which the rank and identity pins had been ripped. He seemed to be the weak link: the youngest, the least criminal, and now the most frightened and miserable. Across the stairway from him was Senior Cadet Bourdieu, the last one she had taken down. He was slumped badly, his ruined hands swathed in white gauze; the marshals had improvised a metal frame to stop him collapsing and choking himself, since Calpurnia had damaged his torso badly enough to stop him holding himself up.

By the right stairwell was Junior Ensign Cicourel, whose knee she had broken. Her subsequent kicks had broken his nose, cheekbone and two ribs but not, apparently, his insolent spirit: the stare he gave her as he propped himself on his good leg and snuffled through the dressings on his mashed nose was hateful.

'If you have any scrap of honour in you,' Calpurnia told that hot gaze, 'if you are actually capable of building yourself up to worthiness of the uniform that has been taken from you, then you will have the ability to learn from this.'

She walked to the fourth man, Ensign Talgaard. He was the one who had grabbed her, the ringleader, the one who had let his drink go to his head and spawn fantasies about putting the little planet-crawling arbitor-woman in her place and amending the insult done to his captain.

'I don't doubt that your gate-captain wouldn't mind seeing me under a gauze sheet in his station's medicae, a breath away from parting with my life like Arbitor Gomry. But when you four took it into your heads to act, what did he do? What side did he take? Look at where you are now. Your gate-captain took the side of the Law.'

'You... don't understand... insult... honour... must...' It was Talgaard talking. How much of the choked quality of his voice was from the pain of his injury and how much was the constriction of the stock on his throat she wasn't sure. But his words and the curl of his lip were enough to convince her that she was going to be wasting her time standing here and trying to talk him around. Some people were just determined to resist correction.

She walked past him and up the stairs to the doors of the hearing chamber. She would probably have been able to stay inside and listen in, even participate, as Commodore Omenti's staff and the Arbites haggled and argued, but good form dictated that she absent herself while her case was discussed.

The commodore and the Arbites had arrived on the station almost simultaneously. Nestor Leandro had taken charge of the Arbites delegation once he heard Calpurnia had gone on to the Inner Charisian Gate, and the commodore himself had come aboard once he had heard that an arbitor senioris had been assaulted by a gang of junior officers.

By the time they met in de Jauncey's chambers Gomry was lying in a coma in the station medicae, attended by four Navy physicians. Calpurnia had eventually accepted a meal, and slept a little on a spare cot, but Gomry was still comatose when she was woken by a runner-boy from de Jauncey's offices. She took her time, returning to her little cabin, washing and getting herself in order before she set out for the gate-captain's office.

Commodore Omenti, shaven-headed, droop-moustached and with skin as dusky as de Jauncey's, had been the picture of cool politeness, pouring punchy black caffeine laced with brandy into little brass globes like the ones Dvorov used. De Jauncey had remained silent throughout, Leandro had been unusually reserved, for him, which meant that he talked only a little more than the others in the room put together. Omenti made sympathetic conversation about the sabotage attempts at Bosporian Hive and Calpurnia's ordeal, as he put it, aboard the Inner Charisian Gate. Something seemed to have come of the attack on her after all: the fact that de Jauncey's own junior officers had assaulted a visiting dignitary had tripped up his complaints and Leandro was using all his diplomatic finesse to press the point with the commodore while the gate-captain was still wrong-footed.

Calpurnia was much more at ease with Omenti's manner, firm but conciliatory. Although she didn't care for the way his eyes kept dropping to her hip and the line of her thigh in the black arbitrator bodyglove, she was starting to feel cautiously optimistic about co-operation from de Jauncey and access to the prisoners.

Cautious optimism, she would think later, was the bane of her life.

'FINE TIMING, MA'AM' said the Navy attendant who opened the door as she reached the top of the stairwell. 'The commodore and the arbitor senioris wish you to be present. The other arbitor senioris, that is, ma'am,' he added diplomatically.

The tribunal chamber seemed startlingly plain, an affair of simple benches and a horseshoe-shaped table. Leandro and Omenti sat on the far side of the table's curve, far enough apart to acknowledge their differences but close enough to make it a discussion, not a confrontation. By Omenti's shoulder stood a thick-waisted man in the sinister black uniform of the Imperial Commissariat, whose ruddy face and neck seemed to bulge out of his stiff collar as though extruded from it, like paste from a tube. Apart from the commissar, each side's retinue of legal savants and clerks had withdrawn to the corners of the room.

De Jauncey entered through a side door, his black eyes suspicious. Neither Leandro nor Omenti rose, each simply motioned his respective colleague to join him. The commissar stared at Calpurnia, then de Jauncey, his expression unreadable.

'Straight to the issue, then,' Omenti began. His voice was soft and his diction well-educated, but for all that he looked like the kind of man who would never speak below a roar. 'The matter at hand is the overlap and conflict, or at least the question of it, between the Adeptus Arbites and the Imperial Battlefleet Pacificus in the matter of arresting and prosecuting those responsible for what seems to have been a deliberate act of sabotage against our brethren-in-service of the League of Blackships.'

'The question which, in our preliminary and contingent opinion, will resolve carriage of the issue is at whom the attacks, for such we consider them to be, were set.' Leandro took up the thread. 'Such an act of aggression is one that both our orders, and indeed any servant of the God-Emperor, would delight in seeing balanced out with the commensurate acts of judgement. However, discussion of the precedents and accords from several hundred years of interaction between our organisations – scarcely enough to do justice to the full complexity of the subject, but which must needs suffice at this moment – the approach that has commended itself to our attention is that the offices of the good commodore and the estimable Gate-Captain Sambin de Jauncey shall be entrusted with tracking any offence specifically directed at the venerable League of Blackships, while the work done by the respected Arbitor Senioris Calpurnia in the pursuit of the saboteurs who have set themselves against the completion of the Vigil and Mass of Saint Balronas should, in the event that this work is found to bring us to the matter of the attack at the Ring, continue.'

De Jauncey was scowling, Omenti had an eyebrow cocked, the commissar remained expressionless. There was a moment of silence.

'You're saying, sir,' burst out de Jauncey, 'that these people are going to remain on my station, interrogating prisoners I have already given orders on?'

'He's saying that if that attack was directed at the Blackship brass and happened over Hydraphur by coincidence then it's all yours, de Jauncey, and the Arbites back off.' The commissar's voice was a flat rasp that spoke of some kind of augmetic repair to his throat. 'If it's another one of these attempts to ruin the mass which happened to be directed at the Blackships by coincidence, then it's the Arbites' and you give them whatever help they need.'

'And how do we establish that? Don't you think I would have reported anything I learned in my own hearings here? I am a law-abiding and Emperor-fearing man, regardless of what this, this woman might have told you.'

'Your behaviour gives the lie to that, gate-captain. Such a man would show a little more respect to the Emperor's Adeptus than you have shown me.'

'Enough, de Jauncey.' Omenti cut him off. 'Arbitor Calpurnia will be conducting her own interrogations along with Arbites specialists that I gather Arbitor Leandro has brought with him from Hyraphur. The Arbites have more knowledge of the early stages of this conspiracy and they will know more about what questions to ask. There's no question that that's their field more than ours.'

De Jauncey drew himself up.

'Commodore Omenti, I respectfully but formally protest. These Arbites assert that we are all on the same side of a struggle against criminals and the Emperor's enemies, but were that true they would take the word of an officer of the Imperial Navy and depart forthwith. I have given them my formal and solemn word as an officer that justice has been done–' (Calpurnia, who remembered no such undertaking, caught Leandro's eye and gave a tiny shake of her head; he gave a similarly tiny nod of acknowledgement) '–and the sabotage that destroyed the *Aventis Sapphire 7* has been punished. To imply otherwise is not only a subversion of my authority, it is a slight upon my honour. Perhaps the Arbites' concept of such may differ from our own, sir, but this demands nothing less than redress for me.'

'Redress?' asked the commodore. 'You seem determined to make trouble for me, de Jauncey, but if you're going to say what I think you're going to say then let's hear it so we can get on with things.'

'Aye, sir. My honour has been slighted by Arbitor Senioris Shira Calpurnia of the Adeptus Arbites. She has rejected my word as an officer and by her words and actions has clearly implied a suspicion of me in these lamentable events. The expectation that I will co-operate in this outrage only compounds the insult, and on behalf of myself and the family de Jauncey I demand redress.'

'I see.' Omenti turned to Calpurnia. 'You probably followed that, Arbitor Calpurnia, but in any case I am required to inform you that Gate-Captain Sambin de Jauncey of the Hydraphur Squadron of the Imperial Battlefleet Pacificus has claimed insult from you and demands redress. According to traditions within this fleet on matters of honour between officers, he may stipulate that redress as a pre-condition for any future association with you.'

'You're talking about a duel, I take it?' she asked him. Omenti nodded; de Jauncey's expression was triumphant. 'Does this tradition between Battlefleet Pacificus officers extend to members of the Adeptus outside the Navy, then?'

'Honour duels between rival Adeptus orders do have precedent once certain formal preconditions have been met,' Leandro began. 'Two recent examples are the dispute between Kjin Bassonel of the Administratum and Curate Varengo of the Adeptus Ministorum, who exchanged insults over an interpretation of tithing decrees in 942.M41, and–'

'I am sure Arbitor Leandro is correct in his citing of precedents of the planetary Adeptus,' Omenti cut in smoothly. 'My apologies, Arbitor Leandro, I intend no disrespect,' and Leandro inclined his head graciously, 'but precedent is not an issue. Not only tradition, but formal decree that it is not in my power to overrule, prohibits honour duels between a Navy officer and any person outside the Navy. No formal honour duel can be held, and no redress can be supplied.'

Omenti clearly was going to say something more, but de Jauncey straightened, clicked his heels and snapped off a salute, his smile like a white torch. The commissar leaned over Omenti's shoulder and murmured something.

'Calpurnia and de Jauncey will absent themselves for a moment's deliberation,' declared Omenti, and the gate-captain sauntered out of the double doors after Calpurnia rather than away through his private entrance.

'So do you genuinely feel I've insulted you, de Jauncey, or do you just think you've found a way to avoid having to co-operate?' Calpurnia's voice was as cold as the gate-captain's smile was warm, and although she knew that the question could open up the whole honour issue all over again she was too angry to be diplomatic.

'What I feel is that I have found a way to rid myself and my station full of brave and loyal warriors of an insolent menace to our authority, our integrity and our ability to continue performing our duty of watching over the gates of the Hydraphur System and over all those in this system who depend on us keeping that watch. Satisfied?'

'Do you think that I'm going to let you exploit some loophole in tradition so that you never have to co-operate with me over some trumped-up insult?'

'Trumped up?'

'You told the commodore that you had given me your word as an officer that justice had been done. You have not done any such thing.'

'He will believe me over–'

'And you accused me of accusing *you* of being implicated in the sabotage attacks, de Jauncey, and I *know* I never did that.'

His expression grew uncertain.

'You clearly, I mean, the whole way you came onto my station with these accusations–'

'What accusations were those? I came onto your station with the intention of interrogating prisoners you had arrested on the Ring and brought straight here.' She remembered her words to Bannon about her suspicions over that action and knew she was uncomfortably close to lying. 'Show me where I slighted your honour by making an unfounded accusation against you.' That, she was slightly more at ease with. It had scored, too. De Jauncey simply stood and stared at her.

'Well, gate-captain, what's one insult more on top of all you claim from me already? I had no reason to think you were involved in anything before I came here, beyond an arbitor's normal, free-floating suspicion.' She cursed the truthfulness that had made her add that last, and bulled on regardless. 'I do now. I think you have something to hide, and it's making you nervous and you're overdoing the efforts to get us off the station. That makes me as suspicious as hell, de Jauncey.'

'Suspect all you like. You will think twice before you lock horns with the Pacificus Fleet again. You should be glad I am the man I am – were I of a level with so many of you planetcrawlers, I might give those men another crack at you.'

She was readying a reply to that when the doors swung open for two black-clad figures: Leandro, cloak in place and judicial head-dress under one arm, beamed at her from beside the commissar.

'Gate-Captain de Jauncey, Arbitor Calpurnia, I can announce that only the barest discussion has proved necessary for a solution to our impasse. It was a small matter to bring the particulars of the issue – the concepts, rather than the facts – to the scrutiny of legal resources on both sides of the debate. It pleases me as much as it must surely please the both of you–' his eye twinkled '–that we have found that on any interpretation that we can muster the judgement deriving from the prosecution of war crime allegations against certain elements of the followers of the renegade Fleet-Admiral Krayle in the century previous to our own supports a way forward.'

'*War crimes*?' For once Calpurnia found herself in agreement with de Jauncey, whose tone was incredulous. 'Are you seriously alleging war crimes now?'

'Calm down, de Jauncey, nothing of the kind,' snapped the commissar.

'I stand corrected and admonished by the good Commissar Modjeska's bluntness,' said Leandro with a bow. 'The news I have for you is not, I reassure the gate-captain, news of charges or prosecutions. The news is that there is not the deadlock we thought there was. The precedents in question are to do with the mechanisms of Imperial justice within an organisationally self-contained body such as a Segmentum Battlefleet, and the role of the Fleet Commissariat.'

'What he's saying,' put in Modjeska, 'is that Commodore Omenti has ruled that law allows for a proxy in cases where an honour duel is not resolvable in any other way, including where it involves a disputant from outside the fleet.' De Jauncey's eyes widened, and Calpurnia could understand why Leandro had been smiling. 'The challenged party in this case is not able to participate in the duel, which means she's precluded from nominating a Naval proxy, but precedent says that a member of the Fleet Commissariat provides the proxy in a case like this. Accordingly, gate-captain, your duel for redress will be with me as a proxy for Arbitor Senioris Calpurnia. Commodore Omenti has volunteered the use of the duelling-floor on board the *Crusader Ascendant* as acceptable neutral ground, and will preside over the engagement. As presiding officer he has set the time of the duel at an hour into the third watch, two hours after the conclusion of the service to the Thesean Martyrs.' He saluted de Jauncey. 'Thank you, gate-captain, I shall see you on the duelling floor.'

And with that he spun on his heel and marched back through the doors in a swirl of black storm-coat, back ram-straight and boots clanging on the deck. Leandro and Calpurnia both turned calm, level gazes on de Jauncey, but he too had spun and marched away, through a throng of station crew who suddenly were busily about errands that had, by remarkable coincidence, required them all to be standing within earshot of the stairs until a moment ago.

'The dromon I came here in is a semi-dedicated Arbites one, Shira,' Leandro told her as they stood under the silent stares of the four young men in the stocks. 'I ordered your escorts onto it for a little rest and some food – shall we step that way to treat ourselves to the same? Perhaps even something a little unusual and rich. Despite the austerity that is supposed to accompany this time of year I can't help feeling that we perhaps deserve some self-awarded latitude.'

'More of that brandy-laced caffeine? I noticed you enjoyed that a great deal.'

'Ah, perhaps no intoxicants, but yesterday I managed to acquire two pitchers of syrups from the Shequa Archipelago, each suitable for a slightly different caffeine brew. I confess to being indulgent enough to have brought them with me.'

'I think it would be wasted on me, Nestor. I have a very uneducated palate by Hydraphur standards.'

'The syrups are something of a trademark of Hydraphur cuisine,' said Leandro. 'Not always so, of course. There was an extended period which seems to have ended about the time of Ecclesiarch Thor, where particular brews were allowed to crystallise and served as powders or resins. That resulted in certain cooking techniques becoming favoured, but the change to syrup-based seasoning can be traced back to the migration in from the Colonna Sector's outlying worlds which saw the introduction of – am I holding forth again?' Calpurnia smiled.

'A little. And I have business elsewhere on this station. But one of these days, Arbitor Leandro, I'm going to manage to find an aspect of Hydraphur about which you actually can't launch into a seminar on the spot.'

'A challenge to which many aspire but none have vanquished,' said Leandro happily. 'Well then. We are not invited to the devotions in the Navy chapels and so shall be conducting a short service to the Thesean Martyrs aboard the *Geodess* in honour of the day. I would encourage you to come aboard for that, my arbitor, if you possibly can – I worry that the rush of events has seen you falling behind in your religious duties. But if circumstances do not permit, I shall set eyes on you again at the *Crusader Ascendant's* duelling floor.'

They saluted one another, and Calpurnia couldn't resist a last satisfied glance at the men in the stocks before she marched away to the medicae chambers.

THE GALLERY CONTAINED wooden pews so steep and narrow that the head of the person in one row would be practically wedged between the knees of the person behind them, and the heads of the top row would brush the low ceiling. There was a deep drop from the railing in front of the foremost pew; after a metre of empty space there was the *Crusader Ascendant's* duelling floor, a strip of pitted plastic, soft and rough to give traction to boots, four metres wide and stretching about ten from one little doorway to the other. It was bathed in deep yellow spotlights that Calpurnia presumed were there to reproduce Hydraphur daylight; on the other side of the strip she could see the glint of braid and medals as an identical gallery filled with officers.

On her way over Calpurnia had been too preoccupied to be nervous. She had a little experience with duels in Ultramar, where such wasteful infighting was considered contemptible, and Arbites internal laws on duelling were iron-hard. But she knew about the reverence that ceremonial duelling was held in elsewhere and knew this was an earnest event, even without de Jauncey's co-operation at stake, and she was fretting that she would make some gaffe that would disgrace Modjeska or damage the conduct of the duel. All she had been able to get from her hosts so far was that Modjeska was to be given 'the forward advantage', whatever that was, and that the two men would be using lethal weapons despite the duel officially being to first blood or to yielding. She looked around now ready to zero in on the actions of those around her and make sure she conformed.

She needn't have worried. The first thing that had hit her when the door had opened was a wave of chatter, pungent cigar smoke and the clink of glasses. The rows of officers were all deep in jocular conversation at the tops of their voices, twisting about to call up and down the gallery to one another, passing little silver platters of sweetmeats, tobacco and snuff back and forth and pouring decanted liqueurs whose scents alone made Calpurnia's head spin. She had to push her way to Leandro through a crowd of green uniforms all bent on cheerfully ignoring her, but she decided as she sat down that it was better than the hostility she had been bracing herself for.

'And how is your wounded one?' Leandro asked her.

'His name is Arbitor Gomry, and he's better than he was, which is not saying much. He's deeply unconscious, but the station medicae are good at their jobs.'

'One might be forgiven for placing a certain amount of faith in the ability of medics aboard a military station to handle combat injuries.'

'Just so. Well, the next step is trying to get him strong enough to travel. If they do a good job of it, and there's an Apothecarion aboard your dromon–'

'There is such.'

'Good, well, we might be taking him back to Bosporian with us. It would be good for him to come around in the Wall, among friends. If Modjeska wins, I wonder if we can push for those four bastards to be–' Leandro motioned her to cut the sentence short and tipped his head back at the crowd of officers who had all but filled the pews behind them.

Gate-Captain de Jauncey had emerged at one end of the duelling floor and was standing with two others Calpurnia took to be seconds, talking quietly and sipping from a brass drinking-ball. The gate-captain was stripped of his long uniform coat and wearing a close-fitting white vest that emphasised his slender build. He made no sign that he registered any of the rowdy mobs of officers on either side, and the reaction was mutual: if anything the clink of utensils and the cigar-smoke had thickened. The general conversation seemed to have turned to elaborate puns about the duellists and other fleet personalities. Calpurnia guessed that they would still be meaningless to her even if she knew the system – she was aware that she didn't have much of a sense of humour, and that she tended to vaguely distrust people who did. She supposed that pointed to some kind of terrible character flaw, but she had never got around to worrying about it.

The lights over the two sets of spectator pews dimmed as though they were at a play. Calpurnia saw that de Jauncey's seconds had retreated back through their door and the gate-captain himself now held a weapon. A moment later the far door slid back, Modjeska strode through it and the duel began.

Calpurnia expected elaborate pre-duel formalities after all the talk of tradition and custom, but there was not even a salute. Modjeska simply marched up to de Jauncey and began swinging in short, brutal arcs. Stripped to boots, breeches and singlet like his opponent, he carried a single-edged hacking-blade, part falchion and part hatchet, the blade flared and weighted at the head to allow vicious, limb-severing strokes. His other hand held a weighted baton, meant more as a parrying device and shield than as a weapon by the way he used it.

De Jauncey was fending him off with something longer, a ludicrous-looking weapon that put Calpurnia in mind of a double-handed axe with a bizarre tuft of hair like that on a comic tumbler in a circus. It wasn't until she had watched them trade lunges for at least a minute that it clicked home from a long-ago weapons seminar: it was a shipboard weapon, the whippy bristles on the end needle-tipped fibres that drew a charge from a power pack in the counterweight at the far end of the shaft. It was a weapon for boarding action when quarters were too close for firearms or flamers, designed either to swing and cut into the enemy or to be thrust forward so that at least one or two of the bristles would find their way through a weak point in the heavy reinforced suits and hoods that ship-to-ship boarders wore for protection. Watching de Jauncey use it that way now, skilfully keeping the bundle of spear-sharp quills between him and each attempt of Modjeska's to close, Calpurnia realised that it must be charged now. Either or both of these men could easily be carried away to the hospice or morgue at the end of it.

The duel was a deft contrast of techniques: de Jauncey's elegant, dancing poses, the thrusting jabs his weapon as quick as a lizard's tongue, and Modjeska's aggressive, brutal style that concealed a cunning offence behind a veneer of crude aggression. De Jauncey's technique was classic aristocratic fencing, emphasising poise, skill and finesse, and Modjeska's was the classic Commissariat style, designed to make a political point as much as win a fight: an assertion of the commissar's savage authority to impose Imperial discipline by whatever means necessary.

De Jauncey had given ground. He had been a third of the way out onto the floor when Modjeska had entered, but now another step backward would see him barking his heels on the door behind him. He needed space, and made it with a complex pattern of lunges and swipes that forced Modjeska to give ground to his right, swatting the electrified quills away with the baton in his left hand. It must be ceramite or plastic, Calpurnia thought, watching sparks spit between the quills but nothing come down the baton to the commissar's arm. Then de Jauncey spun the haft around and sidestepped cat-quick to his own right, trying to shuffle around Modjeska and away from the door. He almost made it, but he had to correct himself to keep away from the drop off the edge of the duelling floor and Modjeska, who had obviously seen the move coming, used the moment of distraction to wind up and whacked the haft of the long axe with a backhand hit that crushed de Jauncey's knuckles and almost shuddered the weapon out of his hands.

His mouth twisting in agony, de Jauncey frantically backpedalled as Modjeska kept the turn of his body going and aimed a forehand slash at de Jauncey's other arm. Sliding his grip down the haft the gate-captain tried to create some distance with long, whooping swings of the axe-head that needed less of a fine grip, but Modjeska had the timing to press in just a little further behind each swing, forcing de Jauncey back if he wanted to control the space he needed for the big strokes. Finally he gave up and tried to drive the Commissar back with a series of deep, low lunges that forced Modjeska to give ground or bend down to block and expose his head.

There was complete silence in the chamber now, except for the scuff of the duellists' boots and the sound of their breathing. Both men were shedding sweat: de Jauncey's smooth dark skin gleamed while Modjeska's, rough and coated with coarse red hair all down his shoulders and arms, trickled and dripped.

De Jauncey's nerves betrayed him yet again. He had become carried away with his low lunges and was trying the same thing, over and over again, not registering that Modjeska's defence against each one was growing more and more assured and that the commissar's footwork was getting shorter, tensing him for a return sally. The officers had realised it too, and Calpurnia heard a murmur of 'Mistake there' from somewhere.

A moment later Modjeska moved. De Jauncey was telegraphing badly: a certain placement of the feet, a small backward swing. Modjeska watched him as he placed his feet, swung his weapon backward, then moved forward in a step-pivot that spun past the bundle of quills. He was suddenly on de Jauncey's blind side, behind his shoulder, and as the other man frantically tried to reel in his lunge and take control of the space between them the head of Modjeska's cleaver bit into the bicep of his good arm and a second later the baton cracked into his head. De Jauncey staggered and drooped, Modjeska swatted the axe-head down with the back of his cleaver and stamped it out of the gate-captain's hands, then grabbed de Jauncey by the arm before he could topple off the side of the duelling floor and dragged him into its centre.

They held still in a tableau for a long moment, the slender officer sprawled on the floor and the heavy commissar standing over him, boot on his chest, and then de Jauncey tremblingly raised a hand. The doors clanked back and attendants came flooding out onto the floor and, as Calpurnia and Leandro saluted Commissar Modjeska and began to make their way to the door, the officers of the Battlefleet Pacificus rose to their feet to applaud.

DE JAUNCEY CO-OPERATED. He had to. The duel had been the last shot in his locker, as Calpurnia inelegantly put it to Leandro as they had crossed along the slender, vibrating and frankly alarming docking bridge. At least it had gravity, which was more than the link to the *Geodess*. Leandro accompanied her back to the station medicae, but Calpurnia suspected it was more to do with putting off the passage through the shifts in gravity and orientation. Leandro, it turned out, hated the sensation even more than she did.

'He'll submit to being questioned?' Calpurnia asked as they made their way to the Charisian Gate's upper medicae bay.

'He will. I think I managed to achieve sufficient rapport with the commodore and to consider myself informed, and I can inform you that Omenti has strengthened his views on the matter. You may have noticed that the most respected commodore has a different attitude on co-operation with the Arbites than does a certain gate-captain under his command. Said gate-captain is considered to have brought quite enough disrepute to his battlefleet, never mind unfavourable attention from an order of the Adeptus who, as you have apparently pointed out to the gate-captain, is capable of exacting perfectly legitimate penalties from the Navy should it see the need. He has proved himself unable to control his station to the point where a member of that same order of the Adeptus was forced to fend off a vicious attack from no less than four of his subordinates. And now a matter of honour for which he insisted redress has instead brought him low–'

'He lost the duel, Omenti has told him he's out of options and to tell us what he knows.'

'Ah, my Arbitor Senioris Calpurnia, your words cut to the heart of the matter with the swiftness of Macharius's own sword.'

'Did Macharius use a sword?'

'I believe he is shown with one in most of the historical illuminations in my library. In all candour I had taken the matter on faith from those.'

'My father kept an excellent collection of military histories. I used them to teach my brothers to read and orate. I had the impression he leaned more toward firearms and some kind of power weapon.'

'The sword I have seen him illustrated with may well have been a power weapon. I shall have to inspect the colour plates again. After all, we are far closer to the areas of Macharius's actual conquests than Macragge.'

'The books I read when I was younger were sourced from this Segmentum, though, Nestor.'

They bickered amiably enough in the medicae outrooms, while the doctors came and went around them. They were still disagreeing over the issue when the report came that Gomry was drifting between coma and dazed, disconnected waking – Calpurnia refused to leave without looking in on him but he was unconscious again.

'It must have been a terrible strike,' said Leandro softly as they came away.

'It was,' said Calpurnia, 'and he was struck down because of me.' She was very quiet during the walk to de Jauncey's chambers.

The gate-captain had already begun talking by the time they got there. Pale and tired, he sat in a padded chair by a half-metre-thick window of armour-glass that looked out over a cluster of lance muzzles and the dim shapes of two docked dromoni.

Commissar Modjeska was sitting in a chair opposite him. A second commissar, younger and thinner and with a certain resemblance to de Jauncey himself, nodded to the Arbites when he was introduced as Gate-Commissar Chalce. Halfway across the room was a a clerk perched on a stool with braided leads trailing from his skull augmetics to a data-slate perched on his knee, and another green-coated officer whose aquila-and-balance badges marked her as part of the Naval judiciary. She introduced herself simply as Lieutenant Rybell, and went back to staring at de Jauncey. The whole scene looked casual enough – with de Jauncey's arm-sling and dressings and the attentiveness of the others an observer might have thought they were well-wishers there to pay respects to the injured captain. But the fact that it was a questioning session became apparent soon enough.

'Lyze-Haggan,' the gate-captain said, and Leandro was instantly galvanised.

'What did you say?'

'The House of Lyze-Haggan. I have told the commissar what I know about the setting-up of the sabotage. I had no hand in it myself. My... my wrongdoing was in not lifting a hand to stop it when I knew it was being planned. I thought it would form a strike against Kalfus-Medell. The Kalfus family and the de Jauncey...'

'I am aware of and understand your history,' said Leandro. Calpurnia made a sour face that only Rybell picked up, and the other woman looked at her curiously.

'Then I will not dwell on it,' de Jauncey was continuing, 'except to say that the hereditary postings of commands in the Gyre Aurucon, the same ones that have brought us into conflict with the family Kalfus, have also given us reason to monitor movements and dealings of members of the Adeptus Astropathica. What goes on between those folk when they congregate at the Blind Tower is anyone's guess, but because they must spend time around the officer corps when at their posts it is not hard for us to track them.'

He was getting into his stride, now, and Calpurnia fought down the urge to thump the cut on his arm to remind him that this wasn't a mess-hall anecdote. But she knew enough about interrogating not to interrupt a man who was picking up momentum. This interrogation was what she was starting to think of as a 'Hydraphur special', all kid gloves and etiquette.

'The Haggan syndicate is now influential on a great deal of the inner-system civilian routes. The Lyze family, I understand, Arbitor Leandro, is senior within the syndicate, wealthy but boorish and barely considered among the gentry.' Leandro made a noncommittal nod. 'But over the last two years they have been everywhere on the Ring and as guests aboard as many Naval stations as will have them visit. Since they became of interest to the family de Jauncey we have had the opportunity of watching them build diplomatic ties to half a dozen leading astropath cabals.'

'A fact which didn't seem to concern any of you unduly,' put in Modjeska. He had shifted so that de Jauncey had to look back and forth between himself, Calpurnia and Leandro, a basic questioner's tactic.

'The purpose of the exercise was to outflank Medell interests in the civilian docks, which would chiefly have disadvantaged the family Kalfus.'

'You're saying that your feud with Kalfus meant it was expedient for you to sit by and watch these people get their hooks into who knows how many astropaths,' finished Calpurnia, unable to quite hide the contempt in her tone.

'Astropaths are not infants, bald and bulbous though they are,' replied de Jauncey. 'They were capable of understanding the Lyze-Haggan motives perfectly well on their own. As far as I was aware the Adeptus Astropathica enjoyed formal, excellent and honest relations with Lyze-Haggan.'

'Excellent and honest?' Modjeska sounded like he was grinding his teeth. 'Does that extend to–'

'To sabotaging transmissions to engineer a collision?' The gate-captain's eyes were steady and solemn. 'No, sir, it does not. The infiltration they effected to create that disaster was deep enough that it slipped beneath the net that any of my family's agents were able to track.' De Jauncey put a slight emphasis on *my family*, and Calpurnia had to grudgingly concede the point: it should not have been up to the private efforts of a single Naval family to uncover a plot like this. 'My family have held commands in the Imperial Navy for more generations than I can remember. The thought of countenancing such an act as took place on the Ring is repellent to me. I will confess that I was motivated in my behaviour toward the Arbites by the desire to preserve my own name, but do not doubt that I wanted punishment for the guilty ones as much as they do. That was my reason for exerting my authority to have them brought off the Ring, no other.'

'And what were you able to find out from those people you had brought here, de Jauncey?' Calpurnia asked him. 'Did you interrogate them when they arrived?'

'I stood and watched them when they were brought off the dromon I had sent,' he replied, and it must have sounded ridiculous even to him because he immediately shifted onto the defensive. 'Your own rather abrupt arrival was hot in their wake, if you will recall, Arbitor Calpurnia, and once I had word that you were inbound I felt I had certain other matters to attend to. I had to simply muse on what I had learned from seeing them marched up the docking bridge.' His defensiveness had sharpened, and Calpurnia had to remind herself that he was only co-operating at all because he had been beaten into it by the commissar.

'And what were you able to conclude from these observations?' Leandro asked him in a gentler voice. The change of tone worked, as it almost always did.

De Jauncey turned toward Leandro and spoke more quickly.

'I recognised several of the astropaths brought on board. I believe that is where this all originates, with the astropaths themselves, not the tech-adepts or transmechanics. My officers reported that several attempted suicide on route to the station and one has successfully killed himself since his arrival here. Their behaviour is odd – yes, I know, but even for astropaths it's odd – bodily twitches, facial tics, false starts at conversation directed at thin air. I had my own astropathic representatives watch them over a pict-link and they recognised the signs immediately. They demanded the opportunity to re-enter their trances and send a message to the Blind Tower immediately.'

Both Arbites and both commissars were leaning forward intently.

'They told me that these are the symptoms of a psyker-trick,' de Jauncey went on, 'a mind-command bored so deep into the brain the victim himself may not know of it. These can be built subtly by an experienced psyker to make the catspaw almost impossible to detect, or they can be hammered into an otherwise untouched mind full-force. Such a command will echo inside the mind and soon burn out the one it has been forced into, but until that happens it will be irresistible.'

Psykers. Calpurnia saw the image for a moment, clear behind her eyes: wreaths of smoke, panicking, screaming crowds, and a tottering, collapsing shape that seemed to fade into existence out of the air...

'To drive a command into a mind as strengthened as an astropath's takes a powerful will,' de Jauncey went on, 'such as is not found among the lower orders of the Adeptus. I did not interrogate any prisoners, Arbitor Calpurnia, but I had my astropaths give me an idea of the ranking that such a feat would need and then compared that to transmission logs and movement notifications such as are my right to access as a gate-captain.' His jaw lifted a little at that. 'I may not be an agent of the Arbites, but I found a name. Would you like to know who, and where he is?'

Calpurnia stayed silent, allowing him his face-saving little moment of pride.

'Master Astropath Yannod Dwerr was the leader of the Astropathica cell for that segment of the Ring. All three of my own senior astropaths confirm that Dwerr is easily powerful enough to force an embedded command into a strong mind, a command such as to engineer a collision and commit suicide afterwards. They have told me that reports they have received from their brethren aboard the Ring seem to point to Dwerr spending time alone this morning with the poor wretch who sent the tainted transmissions. My astropaths also confirm, although reluctantly, that Dwerr is also involved in some kind of internecine intrigue against members of the League of Blackships. And according to my transmechanic and logister savants, Master Astropath Yannod Dwerr was recorded as leaving his post in the Ring three hours before the collision, on his way down to Hydraphur. His destination was listed as the outskirts of the Bosporian Hive. The Lyze-Haggan family citadel.

'There, now, Arbites.' De Jauncey looked at Calpurnia again and all the arrogant fire was back in his voice. 'I trust my assistance to you has been worth all your trouble?'

Sixteenth Day of Septista

Two days to the Mass of Saint Balronas.
Third day of the Vigil of Balronas. The Service of the Quills.
The Dedication of the Scourges.

Three hours from midnight priests and deacons will travel through the streets calling to the pious to make their confessions ready. This is the time to light the lamp from the Quiet Congregation, and by its light all members of each household or barracks write out the matters of which they wish to unburden themselves and atone for during the Vigil. These must use parchment of the type decreed by the Ministorum and perfumed with the required incenses, and be sealed with plas-wax tablets given out by the priests.

The clergy who travel out to spread the call to begin writing carry this paper and wax but the shame of being unprepared and having to request it of them should not be taken lightly. It is appropriate for scribes and clerks to assist the illiterate, but this must only be permitted where that person has taken oaths before their preacher and bears the corresponding seal. During the Service and afterwards, reading one's list of misdeeds should prompt thoughts on repentance and redemption. The Creed of the Gyrae *is an appropriate communal reading for the evening once all the confessions have been written.*

Confessions must be recorded by dawn, and then sealed to the outside of the home or to a pulpit or shrine. From dawn, citizens should walk the streets with eyes on the confessions and thoughts on guilt and salvation. The clergy will continue to process through the streets and any who wish may follow them or join them in prayer.

One hour from sundown, all citizens should present themselves at a chapel with the blades for their scourges for the following day. These must be blessed and ritually sharpened by a member of the Ministorum or Sororitas. Children too young for scourging should assist in sharpening their parents' blades as a way of preparing them for the age when they will participate. Those who have not begun to fast must do so after their blades have been blessed.

A downcast demeanour and quiet voice are essential for this day, especially when travelling outside the home. Plain cloth or sackcloth garments are appropriate for this day and all until the Mass itself.

CHAPTER ELEVEN

RUSHING TO INTERCEPT the *Sanctus*, rushing to investigate the Astropathic sabotage, now rushing to chase Dwerr down to Hydraphur. Calpurnia suspected that for the rest of her career she was going to associate the groaning halls and curling black ironwork of the Hydraphur Ring with desperate haste.

They came bulleting back from the Inner Charisian Gate with the engines on the *Geodess* open to the fullest, unable to converse for the noise over the voxcasters. The magos overseeing the plasma core had declared this was an ill-omened time for high-speed, high-output engine settings and his congregation of tech-priests were broadcasting their chants through the entire ship in an effort to keep its anima appeased against the strain. The buzz and rustle of machine-hymns wove in and out of the plainsong of the organic adepts in a blend of sound Calpurnia found disturbing.

They had been careful to keep all their astropathic communications as routine as possible, but it was not possible to disguise the the code-red overrides that had yanked normal traffic out of their way. If there were still astropaths in the Ring implanted with Dwerr's deep-buried commands, commands they themselves would not know they carried, they could not be allowed to know something was amiss.

Once they were aboard their lander things became easier. Calpurnia was bent over a tight-beam vox-station, shouting to make herself heard over the engines and the wind-friction scraping the hull, ordering patrols to change course, storming-teams to mobilise, Chasteners to ready weapons and cells. Her orders went to the Wall, then to the precinct fortresses out in the sprawl, and gradually the net was thrown around the great family citadel of Lyze-Haggan.

By the time they were in the lower atmosphere she was starting to get collated updates from the precinct controllers. Exhaustion was dogging her heels as always and having to concentrate over the noise was giving her a headache, but even when she had the reports repeated they made no sense. Two patrol teams barricading the streets to the citadel had come under vicious attack from its walls, but then the attacks halted as suddenly as they started and Lyze family militia came filing out to surrender. On another approach storm-teams had heard gunfire and rushed to break in one of the fortress doors, to find them unlocked and the barricades beyond them already wrecked by explosive charges. Some kind of autogyro had tried to take off from a landing-shelf halfway up the citadel's northern wall only to be shot down by a stream of rocket-grenades from the very shelf it had taken off from, and it had then steered itself around and rammed its own launching-pad rather than crash.

After forty-five minutes of this Calpurnia gave up, crumpled the notes she had been trying to make in one gauntleted fist, and started to run pre-battle checks and blessings on her weapons instead. Whatever insanity was unfolding down there, she knew where she stood with a maul and a stub-gun.

At first approach, the Lyze fortress looked daunting. It stood far from Bosporian, at the shore of the polluted lagoons that ended the sprawl's northern and eastern march. Three thick towers, gnarled with external skyways, overhangs and habitation-shelves big enough to hold houses, reared up over the fifty- and sixty-storey minnows around them, and the elevated bridges between them had become thicker and heavier until now the three spires simply formed the cornerposts of a great triangular hulk whose curtain-walls left a bizarre fifty-metre gap down to the ground.

The Lyze household guard had commanding positions, good weaponry and, at least at first, determination. Arbitrator weapons tended to be for crowd suppression and storm actions rather than the building-levelling artillery of the Imperial Guard, and so the cordon had retreated from the walls, particularly when precinct records showed that at last inspection there had been two layers of minefields under the gap and deadfall grenades built into the walls' undersides. The commanders dug in and waited for the siege weapons.

But that was before madness took hold. By the time the lander carrying Calpurnia and Leandro went bellowing overhead some of the erstwhile defenders had thrown open doors and remote-detonated some of their minefields to allow the Arbites in. Suspicious at first, then frantic to grab the opportunity, arbitrators by the tank-load surged to the doors, and by the time the lander had managed to set down nearby the lower floors were breached a dozen times over.

The fighting was quick, vicious and fragmentary. Arbites found themselves here battling mobs of household staff swinging pieces of furniture and table-knives, there pinned down in firefights with skilled and tenacious Lyze militia gunnery teams, elsewhere in bewildering three or four-way skirmishes, fought at a flat sprint through the fortress between the Arbites and rival gangs of householders.

By the time Calpurnia and her escorts walked through the wrecked doors into the south-eastern tower, the descriptions coming over her vox-torc most often were 'insane', 'demented', 'brainless', and 'bizarre', mixed in with Hydraphur expletives that she didn't recognise and didn't want to. By then occupation of the lower levels was uncontested, leaving level after level strewn with smashed furniture and the slumped forms of householders, dead or too injured to move, shoved gracelessly aside for the Arbites mop-up teams. The battles with the invading Arbites had been around the kitchens, plant rooms and workshops. Calpurnia was starting to think that was because the arbitrator forces had taken it for granted that those would be the objectives and sought them out early, drawing the fighting there. The worst of the internecine violence seemed to have broken out in the dormitories and mess-halls, and only migrated outwards as the violence had spread.

She was on the eighteenth floor when the word came that the storm-teams were in action, and ground her teeth with the urge to be up there shoulder to shoulder with them. She thought of Arbitor Gomry, comatose on a Naval medicae bed because of four men she had let sneak up on her, placed his face side by side in her mind with Dvorov telling her she was not to rush blindly into traps. It occurred to her that her determination not to back away from difficult duty was mis-aimed: courage to put herself in harm's way was something she had never lacked, but remaining behind the lines while others fought under her orders was turning out to be cruelly hard.

She stopped, blinked, and turned back toward a knot of corpses at the entrance to a freight-lift. Bannon and Syldati, who had nearly run into the back of her, hefted their shotguns and looked around; two Arbites engineers who were working to excise the fused locks on the lift doors under the eye of a proctor doubled their speed on the assumption that she had stopped to look at them.

'Look at those bodies.' She pointed. On the other side of the corpse-pile the proctor barked at his charges to keep working.

'That one. And the woman, there. And that white-haired man with the boning-knife.' All three had the front of their thin tunics soaked with blood, and Calpurnia traced the outline of one of the blood-smears. It was oddly regular in shape, oddly clean in the centre, oddly similar to the other two. She hooked the tip of her weapon into the old man's shirt and yanked it downward, breaking the button-snaps, and the other two peered over her shoulders. The man's chest had been cut, lightly as if with a small belt-knife or a kitchen tool, in a crude outline of an aquila. It looked as if the thin material of his clothes had been deliberately pressed against his body for the blood to soak through and create the same image on his shirt.

'Either of you remember odd-shaped bloodstains on any of the other bodies? Or on any of the ones who've surrendered?'

'I hadn't registered it as a pattern, ma'am,' Syldati said. 'Shall I speak with the command post and try to verify how widespread those marks are?'

'Good thinking, arbitor. Let's keep moving.' They set off again, Syldati muttering into her torc. Calpurnia noticed Bannon fidgeting sheepishly at not having thought of it first.

In the central tower, where mechanised screw-stairs clanked and ground between the floors, the Arbites had set up a staging-post: a first-aid Apothecarion, a mustering point, caches of ammunition and fresh supplies of the articulated manacle-trains that would lock captured prisoners into long lines for herding away.

Surrounded by black armour, the tramp of boots and battle-smells – gunsmoke and the ozone of discharged power-mauls – Calpurnia felt in her element, at home again. She watched dispassionately as two prisoner-trains were goaded out of the stairs, stumbling a little as the metal steps moved under their feet. Both at first glance were a random gaggle of Lyze householders, until she looked more closely and saw that the second column all had blood-stains covering the fronts of their clothes. On most the stain had smudged out and was unrecognisable, but when she ordered an arbitrator to tear the cloth loose the aquila outlines cut into the skin were clear.

'We had to separate them, ma'am,' one of the handlers told her. 'Even after we had them chained up they were still trying to get at each other. I don't know what's got into these people but they're just feral up there.'

'How far does the fighting extend?' she asked him, eyeing the rows of prisoners. She could catch occasional flickers between them still – a poisonous glance or a spit in the direction of the other line.

'How far? If I understand you, ma'am, then it seems to be through the whole citadel. I don't think we've yet found properly organised resistance that hasn't been broken up by this fighting. The Emperor has been provident, ma'am, and set them against one another.'

'I actually think you may not be too far off,' said Calpurnia half to herself, with another look at the cuts in the nearest prisoner's flesh. 'All right, so what have they been saying? To you and to each other?'

'Saying?' He looked puzzled for a moment. 'I can't say I've been paying all that much attention, ma'am. Was there anything in particular that we should have been listening for?'

'No way to tell now, is there?' Calpurnia asked a little more sharply than she had intended. She weighed up staying here to question some of the prisoners, but odds were it would take too long to try and break them here. She called Bannon and Syldati to her; suddenly she had an idea of where in the building to head.

THE SCREW-STAIRS finished at the fifty-fifth level with another foyer, almost indistinguishable from the one she had left but for fewer prisoners and injuries, more combat teams and ammunition carriers, and an arbitor with the red badge of a lay tech-adept who had overridden part of the citadel's vox-system. Calpurnia took the speaker-wand from him a little tentatively. On the one hand, she had been raised to believe that the Machine-God of the Adeptus Mechanicus tech-priests was at most a subordinate, and more probably just one aspect of the divine Emperor, so that the rituals of a duly ordained member of the Emperor's Adeptus ought to subjugate the system. But she couldn't quite shake off the dark superstitions about renegade machine-spirits that she had heard whispers of on Hazhim and at Machiun – what if the forces that ran the communicators had retained some blasphemous loyalty to the Lyze? How could she trust them with her voice?

The mechanic seemed to have had the same thoughts, because he began a new check of the system with a device of his own, examining the tuning-dials and murmuring abjurations as the transmission shifted. After a minute the vox-officer at the command post responded; a moment after that she was talking to Leandro at the command post outside, through the hisses and cracks of the resentful transmitter.

'The prisoners here?' He seemed a little surprised by her question. 'Lacking the knowledge of my own eyes, I will hazard a guess that they are behaving as prisoners do, remaining in their chains and awaiting sentence, since I have heard no alarms to the contrary. My time has been occupied chiefly with monitoring the fighting through the citadel and briefing the commanders on the interest of the Arbites command in this matter, a courtesy the initial haste of our landing did not permit us.'

'Very well. How is the fighting going? I'm at – you there, where is this? – the upper mech-stair foyer on the forty-fifth level just off the second core.'

She had to wait for a minute for Leandro to answer, through a bark of static and then the distant sound of voices and the distinctive clinks and buzzes of an Arbites command holo-tank updating its display.

'You are below and behind the fighting,' he told her when he came back to the link, curt and businesslike now. 'The third core from level eighty and above is where most of our combat and shock teams are mustering, and the advance teams report great crowding and more violence from about the eighty-fifth level on. Levels ninety and upwards of the third core are wilderness to us as things stand now.'

'Is that all? No other major activity?'

'Not at present, although the room-to-room scouring has not yet begun. Two detachments of cyber-mastiff handlers are on route to facilitate hunting out any pockets but they won't be here for another half hour or so, as they estimate it.'

She leaned away from the console and shot another look at the prisoner trains. Something she hadn't noticed before: the prisoners without the aquila cut into them, who from their more battered condition had put up more of a fight against the Arbites, all still bore Lyze family crests on shoulders or chests, some on headbands, some as belt-buckles. The ones with the aquila cuts did not – but she could see rips where the crests had obviously been torn off. She spoke into the wand again.

'Where is the main chapel in the citadel?'

More hissing, more chatter and clinks and beeps and what sounded like data-slates being docked and read.

'Arbitor Calpurnia? Are you there?' Leandro's voice came through a sudden buzzing on the line.

'I'm here. The chapel?'

'Is at the highest-but-two of the levels on the core that you are in. There is a thoroughfare up to each of its side gates, along the top of the hundred and eighteenth floor of each of the wings. A screw-stair will take you to within ten floors of it, and a spiral ramp, some kind of ceremonial concourse, runs to the main chapel gates. There has been next to no fighting in that area... wait–' there were faint voices behind him '–and the combat teams met no resistance in that part of the building. The urgency of the fighting below and beyond them in the far wing drew them away. Has the chapel itself been swept?' That was directed to someone away from the pickup. Then, back to her: 'No. There has been some lamentable oversight regarding the securing of the chapel itself.'

'We'll look into that later,' she told him. 'In the meantime, please have the operational command relay orders to all combat teams in that area of the tower. All routes up to the Chapel are to be held and watched. How many shock-teams are nearby?'

Another pause, more voices. Another sharp hiss-crack-rattle made her eyes want to water.

'None,' Leandro's voice came back. 'They have all moved into the northernmost wing to begin breaking the stairwell barricades around the ninety-second levels. There are two squads that had to stop to allow reloads and fresh grenades to reach them and should be about ten minutes' travel from the major stairwell. Shall I hail them?'

'If you would, thank you, arbitor senioris. Have them at the foot of the ramp you mentioned, with as many combat teams as can be comfortably spared. Leave–' She was about to start specifying numbers and deployment patterns to cordon the chapel before she caught herself. Leandro at the command post had the maps, and the Arbites already in the upper floors had the direct knowledge. 'Leave it to the Aedile commanding that section to determine who is needed where. Pass on a Level Four delegation, please, Arbitor Leandro, until my arrival.'

Honouring and preserving the family name, yes, remembering and paying respect to family achievements, yes, dedicating libraries and galleries to the works and memories of respected forebears, yes. Calpurnia could understand all these things because she was from a family that prided itself on its service to Ultramar and the Imperium and saw nothing wrong with teaching its traditions to younger generations. Once or twice she had even dared imagine her own likeness, in paint or marble, in the upper of the hearth-house on Iax, and then, typically for her, had fretted at length over whether such dreaming was conceited and unworthy or whether it was part of a desire to perform commendable service and therefore noble and justified.

The ramp to the chapel gates was a useful reminder, she decided, of what happened when such thoughts decayed into self-aggrandisement. The approach to a sacred place should inspire faith and devotion, or warn of the consequences of failure before the God-Emperor, but here the great space on the inside of the spiral ramp was full of the busts and masks of great members of the Lyze family, hanging from the dome high above on gilded chains, and the outer wall sported tastelessly lush murals in silver-leaf, blue and green velvet and opal, religious only as an afterthought. Lyze-Haggan on pilgrimage to Dimmamar, Chiros and Ophelia, Lyze-Haggan presenting rich gifts to the Ecclesiarchy who were always shown with expressions of rhapsodic joy at such beneficence, wealthy Lyze-Haggan helping fund regiments of Imperial Guard or arm Missionaria Galaxia crusades, who were then shown standing on heaps of dead heretics or aliens directing adoring looks back at their patrons.

There would be time for a ritual scouring of this place later, but Calpurnia's first urge was to have a flamer or a few blasts of shot ruin this walk of vanity just to make a point before she found someone had beaten her to it. The fine trappings of the ramp had been ritually scarred, the faces of Lyze grandees scorched or ripped with blades. The higher they marched, the worse the damage became. Calpurnia's suspicions about what was behind all this were firming with every pace.

She came to the head of the ramp with two shock-squads walking behind her and three combat-squads behind them. Up here the inlays on the walls were shot through with gold and threads of tiny diamonds, and the sculpted likenesses hanging in the central well were crusted with sapphire. The high-peaked doors of the chapel showed the Golden Throne attended by angels carrying shields and scrolls, all decorated with the Lyze family crest, now crudely defaced. To Calpurnia the Emperor sitting on that Throne seemed to be scowling, but she thought that probably hadn't been the sculptor's intention. Two more combat squads were spread across the ramp to block the doors at its top, in a basic double-rank shield-wall. A thickset arbitrator with the wreath-and-pistol of an arbitor aedile on her carapace saluted Calpurnia as the rest of the Arbites drew up behind the line.

'We've checked the doors as much as we can without alerting whoever's inside, ma'am; we made no other move pending your authority. They're unlocked and unsecured as far as we can tell. There has been no sign of resistance, but we now believe that there are numbers of people within the Chapel.'

'Your reasoning?"

'We can hear singing, ma'am. Er, prayers and catechisms and suchlike.'

'Any that you recognise?' Calpurnia asked. The other woman thought for a moment.

'Some from the *Sancta Adeptorum*,' she said, 'mostly the second book. Some common hymns, common on Hydraphur anyway, ma'am, excusing your presence. And a couple of old militant psalms I haven't heard since my schooling.' Her tone was a little baffled, and Calpurnia could tell these weren't the questions she had been expecting. No matter. It was time to gamble on her instinct about what had happened here, on what she was sure now was a winning hand. She drew her pistol and took a place in the second rank behind the shock-squads, took a moment to give a few terse orders and make sure they were understood, then ordered the doors shoved open.

And oh, it was nice to be right. The chapel was a little amphitheatre, a semicircle of softly-padded gilded seats, enough for maybe fifty at a time, looking in and down on an altar adorned with what had once been the Lyze coat of arms. That had been smashed and scorched and now a gold devotional aquila had been propped up in its place. As Calpurnia looked around she could see that the act had been repeated all around the walls and over each set of side-doors. The replacement aquilae were often little more than silhouettes scraped on with ash or burned on with a hand flamer at low setting. The lowest parts of the walls, from eye to floor level, were covered in crude handwritten sheets plastered hastily to the walls.

Before the altar, the foremost and richest seats had been broken up for pyres, and smoke filled the space of the chapel and stung Calpurnia's eyes as she moved in. Beneath it was the smell of flamer gases and the thicker, greasier stink of burning meat. And around the pyres were the congregation.

Not more than thirty strong, they were ragged, deliberately ragged, their clothes and skins torn. They held shards from the broken Lyze crests and were using them to bruise and gouge their own flesh in time to the chants and hymns. They barely registered the Arbites filling the aisle-tunnel and pouring out into the open area before the altar, not stopping their singing and if anything only redoubling it if they happened to catch a glimpse of an arbitor out of the corner of an eye.

Calpurnia cautiously moved through the crowd, ducking this way and that to avoid swaying bodies and swinging limbs. Differences in the penitents began to become clear: they were of all ages, both sexes. All were ragged, but the clothes of some of them had been of far richer fabric and cut than others. Some had combat wounds, powder and las-burns, as well as those they had inflicted themselves.

Silent, her pistol back in its holster, she made her way through the half-circle to look at the pyres, both now burning strongly, each just big enough for its flames to engulf one body. On one, an obese form whose skin and clothes had been scorched away but whose rich jewellery was still visible through the flames as it cooked into the flesh underneath. On the other, likewise half consumed, a spindly figure with the high cranium of an Astropath and the glint of metal plugs and neurocerebral augmetics still visible through its blackened flesh. The reek of cooked fat was intense.

The singing died away as the figures before the pyres made a gesture. Two women, both hard of eye and regal of bearing, had been leading the singing in clear, powerful, trained voices. They regarded Calpurnia now amid the crackle of flames and the intermittent metallic sounds of the self-punishment of the congregation. Both wore holy aquilae around their necks, and the fleur-de-lys insignia of the Adepta Sororitas. These were not the power-armoured Sisters Militant of the Order of the Sacred Rose who guarded the Cathedral; rather, they wore the elaborate gowns, cloaks and veils of the Order of the Sacred Coin, one of the Orders Famulous, appointed by the Ecclesiarchy as teachers, chatelaines and spiritual overseers to the great families of the Imperium across the galaxy. Calpurnia nodded, and when the sisters took that as a greeting they both made deep, formal kneeling curtseys to her and the confused Arbites behind her. Calpurnia responded to that in turn with a parade-ground-sharp Adeptus salute. Oh yes, it was nice to be right.

THEIR NAMES WERE Sister Mimetas and Sister Superior Gallans, and while the congregation took up its hymns again they briefed Calpurnia in quiet voices out by the chapel doors. She had been half-expecting another little ritualised speech like the ones aboard the *Sanctus*, but the two Sororitas gave her a quick, thorough summary that, Calpurnia decided, one of her own staff could have been proud of.

The Haggan syndicate, they told her, had attracted the suspicious eye of the Sororitas a hundred and fifty years before when the Inquisition found cause to purge one of its families' holdings towards Hydraphur's southern pole. And within the Haggan syndicate, the ruthlessness and declining piety of the Lyze had prompted quiet but increasingly urgent efforts by the Order of the Sacred Coin to contain it as two generations of Sisters Famulous found that efforts to inculcate Imperial faith and ideals were less and less successful. Gallans and her own mentor had begun their own subtle manoeuvres twenty years before. They had diligently worked to counter the expansion of the Lyze power-base into space by nurturing relationships with planetary families with impeccable religious records, and quietly redirecting as much of Lyze's economic efforts as they could into ventures that involved contact with Ministorum officials. When the Lyze had begun actively courting astropaths as allies and contacts the suspicious sisters, in careful collaboration with their counterparts elsewhere in the city, had begun to lay a fifth column, arranging marriages of lower-level retainers with devout deacons and ex-missionaries who moved into the Lyze fortress and began to inoculate the population of the citadel with loyalty to the Golden Throne and the Holy Emperor above its masters' loyalty to themselves and their coffers.

They had recieved word from the Cathedral to be careful as soon as word of a well-resourced assassination attempt against a senior arbitor had flown around the hive. They had kept their eyes open as much as they could, but despite the sudden flurry of Lyze activity around the orbital docks they could find nothing that firmly pointed to the attempts on Calpurnia's life or the deaths at the Aquila Gate.

That had changed with the sabotage at the Ring. Word had come back to them quickly that Yannod Dwerr had been the Master Astropath in charge of that segment, and hot on the heels of that Dwerr himself had arrived in secrecy in the Lyze household. Sister Superior Gallans had politely asked paterdomus Therion Lyze whether she should report Dwerr's visit to the Administratum and the Adeptus Arbites, as was the requirement on Hydraphur, and was told that that had already been seen to by Therion's own staff despite Gallans' own informers telling her to the contrary. At the same time word reached Mimetas that the family was preparing some kind of secret bolthole for Dwerr. That was when Gallans had begun overseeing discreet thefts from the House armouries to her own chambers, and the sisters had used the schedule of religious observations dictated by the Vigil to assemble and arm their own partisans, ready for their signal.

When Arbites APCs had appeared on the avenues outside, that signal had been given as the voice of Therion Lyze was broadcast through the citadel exhorting family retainers to stand against the forces of a corrupt law (Calpurnia blanched when Gallans repeated the words) with their lives while the unjustly-wronged Lyze family made good their escape. Then the sisters' own loyalists began deserting their posts, sabotaging the attempts to resist the Arbites, collecting weapons from the chapel and receiving the aquila symbol cut into their chests (and Sister Mimetas held up the little finger-knife she had used to make each mark), as a sign of their blessing and as a mark by which the loyalists could recognise one another.

The Lyze retainers had been stunned by the sudden attacks from within their own ranks, but the family militia had maintined the discipline to recover from their dismay and launch a furious internal scouring of their own. Confusion over exactly who had betrayed them and why slowed them down enough for the two sisters to personally intercept Therion Lyze and Yannod Dwerr as they fled from an autogyro bay that two of the sisters' partisans had martyred themselves to sabotage. The battered and terrified pair had been quickly dragged to the chapel.

'We had planned a short rite of excommunication and certain ritual chastisements, perhaps confessions given the significance of the day,' the Sister Superior said, 'but the psyker began to lash out with his mind and three of my congregation were given up to the Emperor before we had to perform the execution impromptu.' She had tilted her head to biers set in the Chapel wall where three bodies lay under pale mourning cloths. Spots of dark red had soaked through where the psychic violence that had killed them had brought blood from their eyes and mouths. So Therion and Dwerr had been shot through the face and thrown onto the pyres.

'And so matters are brought to rights in the sight of the immortal Emperor and his Adeptus,' finished Gallans, and Calpurnia followed them in the sign of the aquila.

'You have acted with bravery and resolution, sisters, and I present the salutes and the respect of the Adeptus Arbites.' They both bowed slightly. 'Although,' Calpurnia went on, 'perhaps our respective orders of Adeptus should confer on matters such as this in the future so that we can act in greater unison on this kind of threat. Had the Arbites known what was happening in this building we could come to your aid and those two criminals could have died under a full sentence of Court.'

'We felt that the pronouncement of a duly-ordained member of the Adeptus Ministorum was sufficient,' Gallans replied a little stiffly, 'and we can cite the condemned ones' breaches of Ecclesiarchal law if we have to.'

'I intended no offence, Sister Superior, simply to fulfil my own duties to my own order', Calpurnia said, trying not to sound hasty about her rejoinder. But she was unable to stop herself. 'I was accompanied here by Arbitor Senioris Nestor Leandro, whose knowledge of the nuances of legal scripture and dogma will be more refined than my own. I am an arbitrator by training, not a Judge. Arbitor Leandro will be able to supplement your own executions by confirming your sentencing retroactively so that Dwerr and Lyze will stand condemned by the *Lex Imperia* as well as the decree of the Church. An outcome we can agree is desirable, can we not?'

Their agreement was still chilly, and Calpurnia allowed herself a moment to think, well excuse me for trying to do my duty as she left the chapel in the care of the squad leaders and left to oversee the last of the Lyze citadel's scouring. Her anger, though, was partly at herself – listening to the accounts of the two sisters of their activities in the Lyze-Haggan had given her an idea that she was suddenly kicking herself for not having thought of before.

ONCE THE WORD went out about the loyalties of those with the aquila design cut into them, the cleansing of the citadel went faster. She must be getting the hang of delegation, Calpurnia decided: after trailing behind a leapfrogging formation of shock-squads and manacle-toting arbitrator mop-up teams and watching the speed and skill with which they worked their way through the citadel she decided she was satisfied, let the commanders get on with their work and made her way back down through the citadel to where Leandro was waiting. She found him standing at the foot of the metal fold-down steps to the extended-chassis Legatus-pattern command Rhino with its forest of transmitter vanes, looking benignly out at the crowded, chaotic Arbites encampment that the Lyze main gates had become.

'We have been listening to the directions you have been voxing over the citadel's systems, my arbitor senioris, now that our own adepts have managed to tame it.' Leandro had donned a surcoat of heavy ballistic cloth over his judge's robes as a precaution, although the last shooting at the main gates had been hours ago now. 'The taking of this place seems to have been the model of thorough method and efficient execution. And what I have been able to understand of your messages to the command post from this citadel's chapel lead me to believe that you have good things to impart to those of us who must lurk behind the line of battle?'

'A few things,' she told him, 'some of which can wait until we're back at the Wall. I think we've closed the matter of the wrecking of those two ships, with the help of the Adepta Sororitas, but from what they have told me, and their inside knowledge of what's been happening with the Lyze family seems good, Lyze had nothing to do with the attacks on me.'

'A regrettable lack of involvement, then,' Leandro said as he watched the first of the aquila-marked prisoners submitting to fingermark scans, eye-readings and stinging blood-samples. 'Not that I would wish the enmity of anyone on you, my arbitor, I merely regret that this whole chain of events seems to have brought us no closer to the essential problem of an assassination directed at yourself.'

'Now as to that, I think we may well have a very useful little avenue of inquiry opened up to us. When we have a moment in a slightly less hectic setting–' they shuffled back against the Command Post hull as a file of arbitrators double-timed past leading clinking, hissing cyber-mastiffs '–I'll fill you in. It will involve some diplomacy with the Adeptus Ministorum, or at least the Adepta Sororitas.'

'I see. Well, the Sacred Rose Preceptory is attached to the Cathedral and therefore to the chamber of the Eparch, but although the initial approach should by protocol be made to the Eparch it is Canoness Preceptor Theoctista who will then make the decision. She has the autonomy to do that, you see.'

'I trust your skills, Nestor. I don't think that co-operation will be an issue.'

'Good. I believe we will need the help of the Ecclesiarchy in any event, in the matter of–'

'Oh, Throne alone, how did those two get here?'

Walking towards them through the milling formations of Arbites and crowds of prisoners and rumbling APCs were Lord Hallyan Kalfus-Medell and Inquisitor Stefanos Zhow.

'IT'S NOT THAT I don't enjoy your company, my lord,' Calpurnia said, 'but I have to question the wisdom of coming from the Bosporian to here in this.' They were sitting in the lord's litter, a slender carriage on a gravitic cushion a metre above the ground, with a driver at the front and a shelf-seat for Hallyan's giant guard at the back. The body of the litter was enclosed by a silver-blue ribcage that arched up from the chassis underneath them to support rich blue velvet curtains and chains of tiny blue-tinted lanterns, and which now at a gesture of Hallyan's created a shimmering privacy field that blanked them out from anyone outside. Hallyan had instructed his driver to begin a slow circuit inside the perimeter that the Arbites had created before the citadel, and Calpurnia could feel the slight rocking of the seat beneath her cushion as the team of elegant, stilt-legged servitors tugged the carriage into motion.

Zhow was not with them. He had pushed past Calpurnia and Leandro, spoken to one of the marshals in the command Rhino, then disappeared into the citadel. His staff were apparently on their way, probably to examine whatever the pyre had left of Yannod Dwerr. Calpurnia didn't care. Let the inquisitor ignore her and chase his own ideas if he so insisted, she was sure that Dwerr had nothing to do with the psyker-gunman or the roadwork ambushes.

Privacy-screened the litter might have been, but armoured and shielded it was not. Calpurnia felt naked sitting in it.

'We are starting to understand the scale of resources the enemy is mobilising against us,' she went on, 'and in future I would ask that you bear that in mind. If the objective is damage to the Vigil then you are leaving yourself horrifyingly open to attack. A privacy veil is no protection. What if our enemy simply decided to detonate an incendor round over the litter?'

Hallyan, who had been about to say something when Calpurnia had started talking, was now simply watching her through hooded eyes. When she finished he gave a stiff, jerky bow of the head.

'Well-chosen words and excellent caution, my arbitor, although in my defence, for an opponent as distinguished as that behind the attempts on your good person, well, had I been the target as well as yourself do you not think that I would have seen something directed at me? I have been all over the Augustaeum over the past few days overseeing the Vigil, and nothing has come against me. Nothing.'

* * *

His voice had been getting harsher and harsher but Hallyan caught himself and softened his expression. 'My... apologies, Arbitor Calpurnia. Two things, perhaps, made me forget myself to a degree. I have observed the Arbites being deployed throughout the upper hive with a commendable degree of caution – I have met and conferred with Arbitor Nakayama and his senior adjutants and your stringent security. Now that the Adepta Sororitas are supplementing them and guarding the sacred places of the hive according to their own duties the guard is doubled.'

The litter tilted as it made a sharp turn, back the way they had come. Calpurnia couldn't quite understand why Hallyan hadn't just left the thing standing if all he wanted was the privacy shield.

'You should also remember that we are in the last stages of the Vigil,' Hallyan was continuing, 'a time when the people of this hive are enjoined from purposeless or distracting tasks. An Ecclesiarchal curfew is in place as well as your judicial one, and there are bans on dining and drinking-houses, gaming, theatrical entertainments, any manner of public association other than certain religious processions. You stood by my side, Arbitor Calpurnia, and watched the hive's lights extinguished in the signal act that began the Vigil proper. Any activity launching another assassination attempt now would be too obvious and out of place and your Arbites and the Cathedral's own garrisons of sisters are too alert to allow such an act to get far.'

'Arbites are Arbites the Imperium over,' replied Calpurnia, returning his gaze, 'and I would and do trust their vigilance with my life. But these are exceptional times, and I believe my advice stands.'

Hallyan made as though to look out of the litter's doorway, although there was nothing to see except the shifting, depthless greys of the privacy field. Looking at it made Calpurnia's skin creep: she could understand the aristocracy's liking for such things but it made her feel furtive and underhand. Besides, she hated the idea of not being able to see what the other Arbites were doing and what might be happening. Her fingertips traced the scars on her brow.

'You said two things, my respected Kalfus of Medell,' said Leandro, and Hallyan replied with the air of one who had been patiently waiting to be asked.

'The second matter, my Arbites, was one which I believed could not be allowed to grow stale once I thought upon your mission to the esteemed Tudela.' He tugged a slender braid of blue-white silk, and a floor panel rose on rods to become a table. On it Hallyan placed a silken bundle bound in cords of aquamarine velvet.

'It is now well known in good circles that you are trying to ascertain the source of the weapons used in the attack on the noble Calpurnia.' Hallyan's voice was more animated now – Calpurnia was still fairly sure she had offended him at first, but he seemed to have ridden over it. 'I fell to discussing a certain unfortunate war of assassins between families among the Medell and certain nobility of... well, the details, my Arbites, would only be tedious. But consider this.' He untied a cord and unrolled the bundle, and for the second time Calpurnia found herself staring at dull metal parts on a rich cloth bed. Augmetic plates with a certain pattern of flesh-clips and filaments, half of a phylacterial headband radiating slender perception spines. And a long-barrelled assassin's pistol with a swept-back grip.

It took a few moments for the details to sink in, but when they did suddenly the feeling of potential that she had experienced at the start of the Tudela audience flooded back. Leandro was already turning one of the parts over in his hands. They were not identical, certainly not identical, but the similarities...

'I have never had much of a military sensibility,' Hallyan was saying. 'But I do recall being shown these items in the Kalfus trophy halls and told we had kept them for curiosity value. I gather, my Arbites, that my family's counter-assassins were never able to track their creators conclusively. When I heard that the trail of your assassin's weapons was of importance to your investigation, naturally I thought that I could provide you with something of value.'

'What specifically was their origin?' Calpurnia had picked up a grip-and-feed system that seemed very similar to the one that they had showed the Tudela smiths. Leandro was holding the stripped-down pistol frame and peering at the housing. Hallyan was shaking his head.

'These weapons were seized from certain retainers of my opponents' households, their creator never traced for certain. There are traditions in this kind of matter of which you, my Arbitor Calpurnia, would not be aware, but there are established practices in this kind of conflict...'

'No there aren't.' Hallyan's smile slipped a notch at Calpurnia's words. 'I may be new to Hydraphur, Lord Hallyan,' she told him, 'but I already know enough to know better than that. And I know aristocratic politics, too.'

'Really.' The noble's voice was flat.

'Really,' said Calpurnia. 'The streetfighters on Drade-73 had their traditions, too, when I was an arbitrator there. "Trenchman's Honour", they called it. You never struck an opponent who couldn't see the blow coming, you never drew a blade against bare hands, there were a dozen other rules. And it never stopped any of them from lunging at your back with a bottle-fragment or ganging up five to one if they thought no one was looking. So pardon my cynicism, Lord Hallyan, but I don't believe with the kinds of things at stake in a place like this, people play their feuds out as courtly chess-games except when it suits their exact purposes to do so. If you were about to tell me that Kalfus-Medell deliberately never went looking for who was providing these weapons, I have to wonder if it's simply that no-one admitted they'd done it.'

Hallyan's face was expressionless and paler than usual. Calpurnia met his gaze until Leandro interrupted them in his smoothest, richest tones.

'Why, my admired companions, shall we not wait until we have more to go on, until more light has been shed on the path immediately in front of us, before we dispute how sure our footing is? My Lord Kalfus of Medell, I trust you brought these pieces to place at our disposal?' Hallyan's eyes narrowed, but he could hardly do anything other than agree. 'Why then our own Verispex have tremendous skills to bring to bear and I am sure if they share an origin with the instruments of assassination that Calpurnia's abominable assailant bore that this will be known to us very quickly. Why we have not only the resources of the Adeptus Arbites but no doubt those of the redoubtable Inquisitor Zhow.'

'We may even take them back to Tudela,' took up Calpurnia, 'there will be measures of design and workmanship that I want to go over. And detectives will come to you, sir, to discuss the conflict in which you came by them.'

'Pardon me, my arbitor, but I must be clear.' Hallyan was pointedly addressing only Leandro. 'You are going to confirm that these were crafted for a noble family?'

'That,' Calpurnia said, 'and we can use your accounts to piece together which families issued their agents with weapons like these and see about tying them in to anything we can draw a bead on about the initial attack. Not to mention adding a little extra surveillance to those families' representatives in the Bosporian Hive.' She smacked her gauntleted hands together. The agenda struck her as impossibly ambitious even as she spoke it, but that feeling of potential, of a breakthrough almost in her grip, bore her on. 'I'd appreciate a list from you, Hallyan, of what you consider to be the central possibilities. I'd like to start drawing up cordons and search teams, even if we won't be able to mobilise until tomorrow morning. Hah, having everyone go about by lantern-light certainly adds to the atmosphere of the Vigil, but it will complicate our movements just a little.'

Hallyan's jaw had dropped.

'I cannot permit this! I am the presiding envoy, appointed as Master of the Vigil by the Eparch of Hydraphur himself! Do you have any idea of the consequences for the Vigil if this, if you…' He shut his eyes for a moment, collected himself and then fixed Calpurnia with a pale-blue glare.

'It would befit you to learn at least a little of how things are done here, rather than in the gutters of Drade. Despite what you may think of us, the Vigil of Saint Balronas is no idle conceit. The edict of restrictions on the hive is very real, and there are similar restraints on every other city on this world. No-one may go about trade. Affairs other than bare necessities and devotional duties may not be conducted out of doors. Not only that but the Vigil demands devotions and worship! Look at the streets around you, from here all the way to the Bosporian Hive and the Augustaeum itself! Look at the confessional screeds sealed to the walls, and at the devout of the Emperor preparing for the scourging of the Passion Redemptor! Need I remind you also that these are equally binding on the Adeptus, however much you might like to think yourself above piety? If you have no respect for my own rank, are you still so ready to antagonise the supreme Ecclesiarchal ruler of this subsector?'

'Your command of religious detail is admirable, Lord Hallyan,' put in Leandro as Calpurnia forced her fists to uncurl. 'So I won't need to quote the Vigil of 198.M41 when an overloaded venting station in the lower Bosporian threatened a major fire and toxin leak and the laws of the Vigil prevented the Mechanicus crews from working to repair it. I'm sure you'll know that the then Eparch granted indulgence and absolution to the magos-engineers who took charge of the operation and the Canoness Preceptor of the Sacred Rose who skipped the Mass and spent the day by the station. You should know that the Arbitor Majore and I are making the case to the Eparch in a letter today that such a potent assassination attempt implies a potentially equal threat and circumstance. Arbitor Calpurnia will be at the Cathedral tomorrow to swear an oath and be given a seal of absolution so that she and her staff can continue to do the Emperor's work during the strictest period of the Vigil.'

'And make no mistake, sir, the Emperor's work is what I am about.' Calpurnia hadn't known about any absolution, but she grabbed Leandro's point and ran with it. 'Did you have any other questions?'

Hallyan grudgingly lowered his eyes and kept them lowered while Calpurnia tucked his bundle under her arm, then gave a flick of his hand. The privacy field faded into a sudden rush of sound, and the two Arbites climbed wordlessly out of the litter and walked away to the command post. Calpurnia did not turn and look back until she heard the clink of the servitors' long augmetic legs on the paving and turned to watch the litter being towed away. Either those servitors had a hell of a turn of speed once they hit their stride, Calpurnia thought, or it had some other engine – it would have had to have taken a day to cross the city at the pace they were going.

Hallyan had engaged the privacy veil again and the litter's silver ribcage was filled with grey. On the back the servitor still sat, its massive shoulders rounded and its head bowed. Calpurnia pointed at it as the litter glided away and said 'Ah-hah,' and Leandro gave her a questioning look.

'That servitor,' she said, 'that enormous bodyguard construct. Did you see it? It was in some kind of cradle on the back of the litter. That means it has to have a more sophisticated trigger than those phrases he uses. I knew it had to.'

'Interest compels me to be so rude as to ask you to explain your reasoning.'

'I've yet to see Hallyan without that monster tagging along somewhere. It's obviously something he'd rely on heavily for defence if he's attacked. And yet he had the privacy field between him and it –

there was no way to activate the thing verbally. There had to be a more advanced signal that he could activate through the field. I didn't think anyone would be impractical enough to set up a guard that sophisticated with just a spoken command pattern.'

'Ah, well, an accurate observation so far as it goes. That would indeed be considered the logical, practical way to set about it.' Calpurnia's expression soured.

'Don't tell me, I can guess. This is another one of those damned local-knowledge things, isn't it? Wonderful. Tripped over my own feet again. What have I missed out on this time?'

'Ah, now, be easier on yourself, Arbitor Calpurnia. Hydraphur's idiosyncrasies make it a tougher place than most to settle into.'

'I used to think I was up to tough jobs.' She was still scowling. 'All right, so what did I miss?'

'Just an aristocrat custom, such as is found all over the sector and I have no doubt further afield still, in different forms. The custom of setting about a task, whatever it may be, in an inefficient way as a matter of deliberate choice, the intention being to present and emphasise the symbolism of that inefficiency.'

'I understand,' said Calpurnia as they threaded their way between two arbitrator squads marching from the command post to the citadel doors. 'You rub everyone's noses in the fact that you're too privileged to have to worry about being practical. You're right, it happens everywhere. The deep-space foundry masters at Hazhim used to wear loose robes that were impossible to work in if you were weightless. That was how they advertised that they were above menial work.'

'Exactly so.' Leandro tipped his head in the direction in which Hallyan's litter had disappeared, beyond the outer lines of Arbites and through the crowds shuffling along the paper-lined streets. 'And now you have observed the selfsame principle in operation on Hydraphur. Much of the supposed honour and gentility of the armed conflicts in amongst the aristocracy here is a façade, as you have accurately perceived. What really counts is that certain factions – and I might nominate Kalfus-Medell as an instructive example – grow so powerful that their best weapon is the sheer terror of what they can do in retaliation, what you might consider a reverse show of force. The carefully calculated message is: "My power and position is such that the mighty servitor you see before you is programmed with a clumsy verbal activation code... and still I walk in safety that you can only envy." The true cream of the elites won't even put in autoreactor commands, you know. One could walk up and punch them in the teeth and the guard would stand there and watch you until they actually told it to kill you. We might presume that to be the configuration behind Lord Hallyan's guard too. You'll see versions of that gesture around as you deal with the local elites some more.'

Calpurnia sighed, stared up at the bulk of the Lyze citadel for a moment and then followed him the last few steps to the command post.

'Does any of this bother you?' she asked as they walked up metal steps.

'Bother me? That foolishness with the servitor commands?' Leandro tilted one black-cloaked shoulder in an elegant shrug. 'I think it's pointless, as I see you do. And I could discourse for a week and a day about matters of historical law dealing with the rights and obligations and expectations that a Judge might have of a citizen at any given rank regarding that citizen's use of force of arms. There are enough conflicting judgements and precedents and decrees for an army of counsel-savants to weigh and debate on, and every shipment of new volumes of the *Book of Law* from Terra adds more of them. Where were we?'

'You were talking about that foolishness with the servitor commands,' Calpurnia said, suppressing a grin.

'It's what they do,' Leandro said simply. 'They behave in a way that suits them, and we perform our Emperor-given duty to the best of our ability and in due service to the Adeptus and the Law. What else, really, is there?'

They walked into the command post and the hatch shut behind them.

Seventeenth Day of Septista

Mass's Eve. Fourth day of the Vigil of Balronas.
The Service of the Taper. The Passion Redemptor.
Commemoration of Master Reynard
and of Saint Chye Balronas.

All citizens must be in the streets an hour after dawn, although ideally the practice of walking the street with the priestly processions throughout the night is to be encouraged. On the hour mark the clergy in the streets will give the order and each citizen should put the confession they previously sealed onto their home to the torch. Priests, deacons and the heads of households or masters of barracks will lead the prayer once the confessions are alight. Members of the Emperor's flock must remember that their souls should be unburdened of sin as their confessions are burned away, and the small blades blessed the previous day should already be bundled on the end of the scourge lanyard ready for the prayer to end. The scourging should bring on collapse by the time the confessions are burned away, and those too physically or morally weak to achieve such a state in time may plead assistance from members of the clergy who will be patrolling for this purpose.

Citizens should attempt to return to their homes as soon as they are able; all doors and shutters should already be closed. During the night no lights should be lit at all. Now the cleansed soul may mourn for the weakness and fall of Hydraphur all those years ago, and for the good souls who perished beneath the rule of the Apostate and the unbeliever.

CHAPTER TWELVE

CALPURNIA HAD MANAGED to get her first good rest in over a week, sleeping for eleven hours and waking with the heavy stiffness that exhausted, motionless sleep brings. But the rest had reawakened an appetite placated mostly with morsels grabbed on the run, and the fact that now she had time for a proper meal she was bound by the fasting edicts of the Vigil was an irony she was in no mood for. She felt stretched and snappish as she polished her rank and honour pins and cleaned her weapons to prepare for another trip to the Cathedral.

Leandro had not been bluffing about Ministorum absolution, or if he had he had turned bluff into action. Today Calpurnia and a small handpicked team would be granted indulgence to work unimpeded by the edicts of the Vigil, able to ride in a vehicle, speak with impunity, enter houses, fight. And now she had a whole new line of investigation to launch. Ultramar being a fief of the Adeptus Astartes, her own family had never experienced much of the attention of the Sisters Famulous, but the conversation with the two sisters at the Lyze citadel and Hallyan's evidence that nobility was behind the first attempt on her had her twitching with excitement. Between them they pointed to a rich vein of information that she had simply not thought to tap. She had been gratified when Leandro had agreed with the approach.

Zhow was another matter. After an hour of futile vox-hails at the Lyze citadel she had given up and set off through streets full of crowds silently studying the fluttering confession-scrolls that covered every wall or trotting behind the priests' palanquins, yelling pleas for benediction and tearing at hair and clothes.

Then the report came that Zhow had marched into the command post and ordered every single arbitor off the site, then stationed Inquisitorial militia at every entrance, each team holding up elaborately-worded interdiction scrolls nailed to staves and ready to shoot to kill at anyone who tried to enter the fortress. Finally he had visited the nearest precinct houses and had servitors carry away every data-slate, pict-capture and note-sheet on the raid. The Lyze fortress and the recent activities of the late Yannod Dwerr were now under the direct aegis of the Inquisition. While Calpurnia accepted that this was as it should be, on behalf of all the Arbites she was also starting to feel taken advantage of. As a final, winning touch the message chit told her that Zhow's staff had mentioned formal warnings and reprimands to be served on all four of the Arbites commanders for not notifying Zhow of the assault in advance.

She was no better off with Baragry, who was indifferent to the details of the assault but had sent messages disapproving that Calpurnia had not been part of the Passion Redemptor. The Arbites were not under obligation to take part in the great self-scourging that had filled the streets that morning, but Calpurnia got the impression that she was supposed to have done something mildly symbolic for the occasion. She knew she was lagging in the observances she was supposed to be making – she hadn't even made sure of the fit of the ceremonial uniform she would wear to the Sanguinala, which was supposed to have been done days ago – but she covered her irritation with herself with irritation with Baragry, whose dedication to his supposed role as her instructor seemed rather selective.

What had stuck in her mind was the last thing that Syldati had said to her before she had returned to her own precinct house, an hour after the news that Arbitor Gomry had died in the Inner Charisian Gate's medicae ward. Syldati had hovered after her dismissal until Calpurnia had asked her what she wanted.

'I just wanted to say, with your permission, ma'am, that, well, we won't forget what you did up there.'

'Did? I don't follow.'

'What you did for Gomry, ma'am. You stayed with him in the medicae, wouldn't leave him.'

'Of course not. He was under my command.'

'There are commanders here who wouldn't have, ma'am. What you did… it's all over the barracks. We won't forget it.' And she had saluted and retreated, leaving Calpurnia puzzled but vaguely pleased.

To Rhinos and audience chambers, Calpurnia added another thing that was defining her picture of Hydraphur: smoke. The coloured and scented smokes of that terrible masquerade in the Adeptus plaza, the still, sickly haze that had filled the Aquila Gate, the reek from the charnel-pyres in the Lyze chapel. Every time she thought back over the past two weeks her memories were always shrouded in it.

And now here she was again, marching through smoke. That morning the people of the Augustaeum, and of the rest of the hive and of the city beneath it, and throughout Hydraphur, had leaped and cried and wept and thrashed their backs with clumps of sliver-blades as the great flapping sheets of parchment coating every building had caught and burned, burned slowly as they were treated to do, burning away each penitent's account of their sins while the pain of the scourging burned the sins themselves from their souls.

Now the flames were long dead, only echoes in the grey haze in the still air, the flakes of paper-ash that scurried about their feet like strange snow, and the scraps of paper and dribbles of melted plas-wax that still stuck to the scorched building walls. They would remain, someone had said to her, until the first rains of the wet season sluiced them away in a month's time.

There was human detritus left in the streets too: sprawled and moaning, their backs bloody messes, men and women who had thrown their whole hearts into penance and were too weak to rise. Calpurnia had not been sure of how to react until she had seen the ghostly forms of Sisters Hospitaller moving through the streets, directing bearers to carry the stricken ones away. The only other people they saw were squads of Arbites or Sororitas, moving with slow dignity through their watches, the black-armoured Arbites looking for lawless acts, the white-armoured sisters for blasphemous deeds, the two orders nodding to each other as they crisscrossed in jointly planned patrol routes. There were no voices, no engines.

Calpurnia marched at the head of her score-strong formation, uneasy in the empty, eerie streets, looking around her at the shuttered buildings and remembering her own words to Hallyan about caution, telegraphing movements, persistent assassins, bullets and bombs. She almost cursed the planet whose tangle of rules and customs made it so damned hard to follow her own advice, then cut the thought off. The laws had been made by the Ecclesiarchy, just as much a part of the holy Adeptus as she was, not some puffed-up planetary aristocrat. And besides, she told herself as they marched down the length of the Mesé to the Cathedral ramp, the Adeptus Arbites do not hide. And neither does Calpurnia. The great spire towering over the end of the Mesé made her feel humbled, uplifted, braver.

Some citizens had enough strength left to crawl and stagger to the Cathedral ramp and more than a hundred lay there, running their hands over the ramp carvings or sprawled on their bloodied backs looking up at the spire, protesting feebly as the Hospitallers carried them away. As the Arbites came marching up the Mesé two sisters detached themselves from the door guard and led the way down a street that narrowed to a high-walled alley around the side of the Cathedral, leading to the fortified quarters of the Hydraphur Preceptory of the Order of the Sacred Rose.

The Preceptory was nothing like the ornate Mechanicus chapel or the imposing maze of the Cathedral proper, and more like the barracks in the Wall, bare and functional. But the ritual quickly brought her visit to Sanja to mind: it was quick, it was strange, it was certainly not what she had expected. White-gowned Sororitas met them as soon as they had entered the gates, their badges of office and eye-prints coolly and thoroughly checked while armoured Sisters Militant took their weapons. From there they were shepherded deeper into the building, where Calpurnia was smoothly separated from the others and steered down a long, echoing hall and down a narrow flight of steps which ended, rather against her expectations, in a garden.

'Welcome.' Canoness Preceptor Theoctista's hair was as white as her habit and hood, her skin lined and coppery, her voice soft. 'Kneel, please.'

Kneeling in the clipped grass with her eyes down, Calpurnia felt the Canoness's hand on the crown of her head. She put her own right hand on her armoured chest and repeated the lines of the oath as they were recited above her.

'I am Shira Calpurnia Lucina of the Adeptus Arbites, and I take this oath in devotion and duty to the God-Emperor of Earth. I beg His absolution for my actions and will, and I swear that this absolution shall be a weapon in my hands for the service of the almighty Emperor and no other. This is my oath in devotion and duty.'

'Rise.'

She stood, and the Canoness leaned forward and pressed home her badge of absolution. A traditional Ecclesiarchy seal, crimson plas-wax with fluttering streamers of white silk covered in illuminated High Gothic script.

'When the Vigil is completed you will return here and I will take the seal back. All of you must display those at all times until then. The Sororitas know to aid and obey you if you bear that seal and to... sanction you if you do not.'

'Reverend Canoness, my other staff, the ones who came here with me...'

'Their oaths and absolutions are under way elsewhere. Do not concern yourself, their blessings will bear a different seal but carry no less authority. You were separated at my instruction. There is a matter I must discuss with you.'

The Canoness rose slowly, leaning on a cane of pale wood. Two novices, their faces invisible beneath white veils, spirited away her seat and the little lectern that held her signet and the heated pot of plas-wax. Calpurnia wondered if one of them was Rogue Trader Kvan's granddaughter.

The little garden was circular, totally enclosed in a round stone shaft that opened out to the sky two storeys up, laid out in concentric arcs of lawn and path. The order's heraldic white roses grew in simple stone-rimmed beds, shaded a delicate yellow by the sunlight. In the very centre of the garden, another heraldic piece: a statue of the order's device, a gauntleted hand holding a rose aloft, done in the same bare stone as the garden walls. They began a slow circuit of it.

'You are in pursuit of assassins, powerful and unknown, with the unclean and the mutant in their fold.'

'The psyker gunman, yes.' Calpurnia noticed that at the word *psyker* the canoness touched the white-gold aquila at her throat. 'We may have destroyed the one who sent him at me, though, Lady Canoness. We now believe that an astropath psyker–' that touch again '–led some kind of cabal against other Adeptus members, members of the League of Blackships, myself–'

'No certainty, just belief?'

'Just belief, Lady Canoness,' said Calpurnia, wondering if *just belief* was an incongruous expression to hear from a Canoness Preceptor.

'Hm,' the other woman said, and they made half a lap of the sculpture. Eventually Theoctista spoke again.

'During your pursuit of those who are attacking you, you have been dealing with one Hallyan of the family Kalfus and the syndicate house of Medell.'

'Yes.'

'You should know that at some time during the night Sister Arlani Leyka of the Sacred Coin, assigned by the Order Famulous as chatelaine to the household of Lord Hallyan, was murdered.'

They walked a few more paces in silence. To Calpurnia the air she was breathing suddenly seemed icy cold.

'Sister Leyka contacted me by a sealed message late yesterday,' said the Canoness. 'She told me she needed to confer with me, and that only a face to face audience in one of our sealed chambers would be sufficient. She said that she would provide me with more information then. I felt you should be advised.'

Calpurnia's mind was whirling. A strike at her, a strike at Hallyan. Or Hallyan's household. One dead, and the canoness had said, 'murdered' so it couldn't be a large-scale raid, not a pitched battle. She would have heard if that had happened, wouldn't she? Did this mean a shift in strategy by Dwerr's allies, or something different? Another strike by the Society of the Fifty-Eighth Passage? It would certainly fit with their desire to wreck the Vigil.

'Arbitor?' Theoctista's eyes were on her own; Calpurnia realised she had been silent for several moments.

'I'm sorry, Reverend Canoness. I was trying to factor this into our own investigations. Clearly it's related. We're going to have to find out how. Depending on some final tests on some weaponry that Hallyan made available to us, we think we can narrow it down to a selection of noble families on Hydraphur. That was why I wanted to start putting requests out to all the Sisters Famulous, but if this is connected things become uncertain again and we…' She collected herself. 'My apologies again, my thoughts are skittering a little. The last few days have not been... restful.'

'Collect yourself, then, arbitor,' the canoness told her crisply. 'I shall pray for the Emperor's hand to guide you.' Calpurnia took a deep breath.

'I should see for myself the message that Sister Leyka sent you yesterday. The body, too. I may be able to–'

'Out of the question. The affairs of the Sororitas, the orders Famulous in particular, are a sacred trust.' Theoctista's voice was so quiet that Calpurnia had almost wanted to lean in to listen to her, but the simple authority in it made her feel she should be standing to attention at the same time. Somewhere in the building a gong rang, and as it faded a high, clear voice sang a call to afternoon prayers from the cloisters above the garden. 'Remain here or come to pray with us, arbitor,' the Canoness told her, 'and I will give you what assistance I can when I return.'

Canoness Theoctista turned away, her two novices reappearing to attend her. As Calpurnia watched their stately walk to the stairway arch she finally became consciously aware of a sound that had been pushing through the last notes of the prayer-call, an odd, gritty sound from above and behind her. At first she could see no other movement in the garden, then the sculpture rocked on its plinth and that sound came again, not from the base but from the tip, and rock chips spat from the carved hand and flower. And then, finally, the stone cracked to fragments and fell away and the buzzing black mass the statue had held poured down towards them.

NOT A SINGLE mass, Calpurnia realised. It was a swarm, a swarm of fat metallic-black insects, now writhing down the statue like grubs, rushing like ants, hopping like ponderous crickets. They made a buzzing that began as a cicada-chirrup and deepened to the sound of a chainsword grinding into rock.

At the base of the statue the swarm puddled in place for a moment, and Calpurnia could hear an odd and almost mechanical clicking as the little black shapes bounced and crawled over each other. Then, as she began to cautiously back away, they began to wriggle forward, tracking her steps across the grass.

Calpurnia was motionless for a moment, then grabbed a small stone from one of the rose-beds and skated it into the swarm. There was a slight sizzling sound as it passed through the cloud and fell to the grass on the other side. The swarm seemed to follow it back and down, as though it were a piece of cloth that had become snagged around the stone, and for a moment Calpurnia could clearly see the grubs crawling over it were leaving scored trails in the stone. Then they flowed forward again.

'Get the Canoness to safety!' she shouted over her shoulder, but the novices were way ahead of her: she looked around to see a flash of white cloth disappearing up the steps. She thought about following them for a moment, then pushed the idea away. She didn't know what she was going to be able to do to this thing, but she wasn't going to leave it here unwatched.

The little insects advanced on her, grinding and chattering. Calpurnia danced two steps to the side, expecting it to move to head her off, but instead it accelerated to where she had been standing and then curled around. Looking back over its path she saw that the swarm had turned the grass into stripped, pulped wreckage in its wake. Somehow she wasn't surprised. The creatures had sped up slightly too, and... yes, the swarm was definitely growing. It was broader, denser than when it had first poured down the side of the statue. Calpurnia had an idea of where the mass from the stripped grass and earth had gone, but how could anything reproduce that quickly? Fear gnawed at her belly and she stamped on it, crushed it, tried to think.

Her back was against a row of roses and she shoved her way back through them, thorns squeaking against her carapace. A moment later the swarm reached them and for a split-second Calpurnia could see the trunks of the rose bushes fray and evaporate under hundreds of grinder-jaws before the bushes toppled over and into the swarm. It increased its speed another notch and traced her steps.

Again she pushed fleeing out of her mind. It was tracking her, she couldn't draw it into the cloisters where it might go after the Canoness, an innocent novice, Emperor knew who. The alarm must be raised by now, someone would be back before this whole garden was ankle-deep in scuttering, chirruping black shapes.

She misstepped and had to correct her balance, and a lunging vanguard of the swarm made it to her foot before she could pull away.

Calpurnia hopped backwards and up onto a stone bench and kicked the instep of her foot into the bench and into the back of her other boot, praying for the sound of crunching shell. The rest of them piled around the bench legs and fat armoured bodies began to climb over each other to reach her. There was a faint sensation as of a fingernail lightly scraping the top of her boot, and she could feel a similar vibration coming up through the stone of the bench as the things ate away its supports. A frantic shake of her foot dislodged the grubs that had crawled onto it, but each had left a part of itself, a head that kept drilling and champing at her armoured instep. Calpurnia fought off panic, gave it a moment more until she was sure they were as tightly packed around the base of the bench as they were going to get. Then she squatted, pistoned her legs out and dived over the pile of insects to roll to her feet on the grass.

Her foot thrummed, and the instep of her boot was crumpling – she could feel it about to give. She needed time to unbuckle it, get the boot off, but the swarm had pulled the bench down into itself and the chewing ant-grubs were starting to sway in the air as though they were sniffing for her. Calpurnia's blood chilled as she watched the pile fold over on itself to follow where she had arced through the air. Now the black of the carapaces shot through with streaks of grey and silver and she thought she could see different shapes of creature – worms, grubs, ants, flies – as they came after her again, close to running speed now. She crashed through another row of roses as one end of the swarm found her trail.

The material of her boot parted and jaws began to pinch and bite at the fabric underneath. Her skin crawled at the thought of them on her skin, but she couldn't stop moving to take the boot off. She tried to think. They were blind, they had to be, they didn't see her movements but followed her trail. (The skin on her foot began to itch and sting.) They had trouble getting up into the air. Could she use that? Could they climb? She eyed the garden walls: rough, but not rough enough for footholds, and the things had chewed away the base of a stone bench. (The itching on her foot was becoming a burning, and in another moment the swarm would widen enough to start encircling her. She had to *move.*)

'Why are you still here?' a voice snapped from across the garden and Calpurnia tried to limp-run back on an angle to the tall, power-armoured sister standing at the base of the steps.

'Needed to contain them, watch them,' she yelled back. 'They're tracking me somehow. Don't let any contact you! I may be contaminated!'

The sister regarded her for a moment, then raised a bolt pistol and fired a careful shot into the middle of the swarm. The bolt disappeared into the black and they both heard the *bamm* as it detonated just under the topsoil. The creatures roiled as the explosion flung up dirt. The sister grunted, fired three more quick shots. The swarm ignored her, condensed and closed on Calpurnia.

'It's too thick, I can't blast a path for you.' The swarm was sending a column straight toward her injured foot. The sister raised the pistol carefully, this time at Calpurnia's head. Calpurnia realised what her intention was and swallowed, closed her eyes and began to stumble through the prayer she had been taught as a child, taught in case she ever needed the Emperor's Grace to put her out of...

The bolt shell yowled overhead and slammed into the wall behind her. The sister snapped again:

'Open your eyes, woman, I've shot you a handhold but it's only going to buy us a moment.'

The pain in her foot was searing now but she spun, ran two paces and jumped to hook the edge of the little crater in the wall with her fingertips. The swarm washed up against the base of it underneath her feet, and Calpurnia planted her toes against the stone and braced herself, wondering how long she could hold on.

Behind her, the sister's voice said 'Here, hand it to me. *That's* better' and then the crawling mass under her turned to yellow-white as the whoosh of a flamer and a thick, scorched-metal smell drenched the air.

'ARBITOR! ARBITOR CALPURNIA!'

The top of the garden steps was surrounded by Arbites and sisters, the sisters were grim-faced and hefting weapons and the Arbites peering down to try to see her. The tall sister had grabbed her foot and jammed the hot flamer nozzle against it, scorching the little metal ticks under her skin into immobility before handing a combat knife to Calpurnia to dig them out. They came out easily, but now Calpurnia was hobbling on that foot and the instep was weeping blood through the cauterised skin. She stood swaying for a moment in the babble of voices, then tried to answer them.

'No, I don't know what they were. sister, were they familiar to you? I said I don't know. You saw them, some kind of predatory creation, self-reproducing. Alive? No, I don't think so, Because look at what got into my flesh. Here. That's metal. Those things were *built*. Some kind of killing device. They moved faster the longer they were… out, or there, or whatever. They tracked me, but ignored the sister. No, I don't know why.' She shook her head. 'Wait, stop, all of you.'

She looked around at their faces.

'Let me tell you what we're going to do next. Canoness Theoctista, you tell me you cannot reveal details of Sister Leyka's message to you. Save it, Bannon,' she waved his question away, 'I'll explain later. Can you confirm for me, canoness, that it was something to do with the Vigil?'

Theoctista's eyes widened. 'I have said nothing to that effect.'

'No, but Sister Leyka was of the Order of the Sacred Coin, an Order Famulous. You're of the Order of the Sacred Rose, an Order Militant. I know Sororitas order structures are rigid enough that Leyka wouldn't have come to you instead of her own Canoness without an extraordinary reason. And the extraordinary thing your sisters are involved with at the moment is policing the Vigil and standing guard over the Mass. Well?' The other woman gave a grudging nod.

'There were things that she said had come into her possession. Some information, something that I think she wanted to show me. She wanted my guidance about how it affected the Mass. I was surprised – Sister Leyka was not one of my own charges but I had heard of her as intelligent and resourceful. I decided that if something had forced her to depart proper practice I should find out what it was.'

'But you never did.'

'No. The next I heard from that household was when one Master Nomikros, Lord Kalfus-Medell's major-domo, visited to tell me of her death. He seemed to be aware that she had planned to see me that afternoon. I saw him not long before I received you, Arbitor Calpurnia. He sat before me in the same garden, he insisted on it being a tranquil place because the news grieved him so.' She waved a hand at the smouldering mess below them. 'And he did seem grieved. He brought in a cushion from his lord's litter and insisted on sitting in the garden with it. He kept wringing it in his hands. It bespoke a certain lack of composure, I thought.'

'Thank you, canoness. Bannon, the rest of you, we have our dispensations, our target is the Kalfus household. She looked down at her foot. 'I won't try and walk there. One of you can get a message to the Justice Gate and requisition a Rhino, no, wait, we're the ones with dispensation to drive. A team of you, then.' She scowled, trying to focus past the pain in her foot and come up with a plan.

'One moment, arbitor.' The tall, dark-haired sister who had saved Calpurnia's life in the garden stepped forward. 'As to that, with the canoness's permission, I may have a better idea.'

THE SORORITAS RHINO's interior was a copy of the Arbites transports Calpurnia had ridden in for nearly twenty years, but different too. It felt weirdly spacious with no lockers, racks of stub guns, mauls, grenade and net launchers, grapplehawks, shotguns, shields, no riot gear stowed around the walls and ceiling. But it had been designed with power armour in mind: narrow benches, friction-taped to stop armoured bodies sliding on the metal, the seat-backs studded with couplings for armour connections. Those had made the benches unbearable, and Calpurnia had soon given up on them and wedged herself into a standing position by the transport's rear ramp-door. The wrong size and shape for seats designed for broad armoured shoulders, the other Arbites were all squirming and jolting as they slewed around corners, sped up and slowed down at intersections: the crew were coupled into the controls and drove faster and more brutally than any Arbites crew could.

Peering through the vision slit at her shoulder Calpurnia could see a second Rhino following them in perfect formation. The Order of the Sacred Rose had its own particular freedoms during the Vigil, and Theoctista had not hesitated to order her sisters out to take Calpurnia straight to the Kalfus mansion.

Five Sororitas sat on the far benches, heads down and engrossed in their work of praying over each shell as they loaded it into bolter clips. At the front of the compartment sat the dark-haired sister from the garden, who had introduced herself as Celestian Superior Aurean Romille. Romille had already loaded her silver-filigreed bolter and latched a sarissa to its top, a short heavy power-spike with a razor tip. That tip was now scabbarded and braced against the floor as Romille sat with her forehead resting on the stock, eyes closed. She had a round, pale face and a nose almost as long and sharp as

Hallyan's, and Calpurnia was reminded disrespectfully of the auspex dishes arrayed by the landing pad at Cross-Four.

The notes of the Rhinos' engines changed as they swooped down a terrace-drive, with a cliff-face on their left and a hundred-metre drop to the next street on their right. Calpurnia braced herself as the Rhino slewed through ninety degrees and the ramp ground down and open. They came out of the tank quickly and quietly and Calpurnia led them through the Kalfus gates without another word, limping on the wounded foot in its chewed boot but her face expressionless.

The Kalfus household blocked the end of the drive like a rockfall across a mountain road. It was not the spire or palace that Calpurnia had been expecting, certainly nothing like the raw might of the Lyze citadel, but a clump of ungainly grey-brown boxes and domes spilling down a kilometre or two of hive-slope sheer enough to be almost another cliff-face. The heavy steel shutters that sealed the compound off from the roadway were slid back into the cliff. Seeing them, Calpurnia turned to Bannon and Romille.

'The gates are open. There may have been more trouble. Be wary.'

'That's local law, ma'am,' Bannon corrected her, and Romille nodded.

'It's part of the Vigil,' she said. 'The Master of the Vigil represents all the faithful of the system and must never place barriers before them. It dates back to…'

'Thank you, Sister Celestian, I get it.' Calpurnia limped through the gates and boots crunched on gravel behind her as the Arbites and sisters fell in behind. Romille strode forward to catch up.

'I was going to say, though, that I agree with your warning. A sister is dead and that law about no shut gates has been exploited before.' She had matched actions to words and charged her sarissa: the speartip was surrounded with a hazy blue power field, and Calpurnia thumbed her own maul into life so its energies cracked and spat.

'Ready for anything, arbitor?'

'Halfway hoping for it, sister. I'm in a killing mood. I'm so sick of trotting up and down the hive as someone's moving target, running after shadows when I'm not jumping at them. Every lead we've found has just withered away and disappeared up itself and I'm no closer to knowing who wants me dead than I was ten days ago. Guilliman's ghost, I just want something I can shoot!'

'Raised voices in public are not fitting during the Vigil, arbitor. Sorry.' Calpurnia was trying to think of a retort as they reached the steps of the house itself and marched up them to the open doors and the figure in deep blue.

Calpurnia had picked up enough Hydraphur manners to know that navy-blue was the traditional colour of senior members of an aristocrat's household, not of the nobility itself, but the man's robes were of fine cloth and cut, rather finer than the harshness of the Vigil's laws was supposed to allow. She took a guess.

'Major-domo Nomikros?' He blinked and nodded. 'I am Arbitor Senioris Shira Calpurnia of the Adeptus Arbites. This is Sister Celestian Aurean Romille of the Order of the Sacred Rose. We travel with members of our respective orders and commands. Good of you to meet us in person.'

'I... well, it was by chance, arbitor, in all candour, since much of the household went to the public shrine at the Ascension Arch to mourn the terrible passing, the, well...'

'The murder.'

'The *murder* of the dear Sister Leyka. She and I prayed together only the previous evening, madam, and she spoke of the terrible events of recent days and the magnificent way in which the Arbites had risen to the occasion. And then this!'

'She was on her way to the Preceptory, then?'

'Did you not know of this, arbitor? She took no one with her but a maid I had assigned her myself, but the servant told me that the attack had come as she passed along the Second Imperial Way, below the Savants' hall.'

'She got about a third of the way, then,' said Romille. 'But on one of the smaller, more winding streets.' Calpurnia felt her expression harden.

'We had patrols on every corner. Someone should have flagged us down.'

'The laws–'

'I know about the laws! No vox-link contact, direct speech in hushed voices only when in public. I knew about them when I vetted plans to rework the policing of the whole damned Augustaeum when we thought we weren't going to catch the assassins in time. Every patrol was instructed to keep visual contact with at least one other so that we could transmit information without breaking the

Vigil. Someone should have flagged us down.' She collected herself. 'But all right. We're here now. Nomikros, I take it Sister Leyka had her own chambers here in the household? Good, we'll start there. Show us, please.'

The major-domo drew himself up.

'By no means! Have your senses deserted you, arbitor? Does the sacred Vigil mean nothing to you? Must you rifle even the household of the Master himself and disturb the serenity of the Vigil with less than a day until the very Mass itself? Lord Hallyan will hear of this!'

'The sooner the better, then. Where is he?'

'He... if you wish to speak with him you will need to await his return from the shrine. My lord is a pious man, arbitor, and has led the household in the mourning of Sister Leyka's terrible death. Although I think that he will be rather more interested in taking your conduct up with your superiors. I trust you have a formal delegation from the lord marshal to behave in this way?'

Calpurnia pointed to the seal at her chest and tilted her head at Romille.

'I have all the authority I need, Nomikros, and yet again I find myself tiring of talking to an upstart local who doesn't know his place.' And she shoved past the man and marched through into the house's atrium, the others with her.

The place did not look palatial from the outside, but inside it lived up to its owner's station. They were in a vaulted space of green-veined marble, lit by soft free-floating suspensor lamps and threaded through with intricate lattices of vines, treated to grow along invisible patterns of micro-wires. The splash of water came from fountains out beyond the vine-curtains that made up the aisle into the house's centre courtyard-hall, and now a quartet of servitors at the far wall registered their arrival and began a light melody on harps and tap-bells. Over the melody came the sound of booted feet not their own: a half-dozen Kalfus retainers in glossy dark-blue tunics had appeared out of the greenery. They wore no uniforms, but their bearing was familiar – Calpurnia recognised household guards when she saw them. Each had a hand resting casually near a pocket or on a belt-clip, and she had no doubt that their weapons would be as expensive as the rest of the setting.

'This is utterly impermissible!' Nomikros was spluttering behind her. 'What next, will you want to cancel the holy Mass itself? Rifle the reliquaries of the Cathedral?' Responding to his tone, the servitors changed to a faster, harsher tune, full of minor keys and percussion, until Nomikros waved them furiously to silence. 'You impose grievously upon the Lord Hallyan's authority and good nature!'

The muscles of the lower chest and upper stomach are important to the breathing. On its lower settings the Arbites power-maul, when tapped lightly against the solar plexus, will carry just enough charge through a layer or two of clothing to painfully convulse those muscles for several seconds. Nomikros doubled over and staggered back, whooping for breath, and Calpurnia kept her maul raised as she turned and stared down the closest of the household guards. All of them now had pistols out and pointing, and she could hear quick movements behind her as her party took firing positions.

'I am done playing games, believe me. If you all are as loyal to your master as I would expect, consider how much harder it will go for him if the Arbites and Sororitas had to fight their way into his house while attempting to safeguard the Vigil he himself presided over.' There was silence for a moment, then the weapons cautiously started to lower. Calpurnia motioned behind her for her own side to follow suit. 'At ease,' she told them, 'there are still people in the household of Hallyan Kalfus-Medell who know where their duty is.'

The point was lost on Nomikros, who was on all fours in front of her drooling and retching for breath. She walked around him and pointed at a guard.

'You. Show me to Sister Leyka's rooms. Appoint someone else to show Lead Arbitor Culann to the rooms of the maid who accompanied her.' She pointed to the two squad leaders in her escort, Bannon and a young man from the Justice Gate command. 'Culann, your particular objective is anything that Sister Leyka had with her on the trip that the maid brought back after the murder. This is a Level Two delegation. Sister Celestian, you might want to send some of your own with him.'

Her judgement had been good: by the easy, low-key way he murmured orders the man she had picked was the ranking officer in the guards. The sister's chambers and the maid's were next to one another in a long terrace that jutted out of the slope of the main building like an upside-down shark fin, and the two parties ended up walking down the long halls of the household together.

Nomikros had stayed in the atrium, sitting on the floor and groaning softly. The doors to the two chambers led off an arboretum whose stained-glass walls made kaleidoscope palettes of the sisters' white armour: Calpurnia whirled at the double-crack of a bolter behind her but it was one of the sisters shooting the locks out of the maid's door.

Her own grim-faced guard had unlocked the door to the sister's chambers and Romille insisted on entering first with an intricate Ecclesiarchy amulet in her hand.

'What did you touch?' asked Calpurnia when the sister opened the door a minute later. Romille didn't answer but motioned them inside.

SISTER LEYKA HAD had three rooms assigned to her, and she had kept each of them spare and eye-wateringly neat. The walls were covered in charts and lists, some obviously of Kalfus family genealogy and holdings and others that Calpurnia didn't begin to understand. A rack of books and slates by the hard little futon was obviously religious, topped with two incense holders and a silver aquila on a stand, but the other rooms were crammed with filing stacks and slate-holders and the desk held reams of notes and memos in the sister's neat, rather impersonal hand. Calpurnia sighed.

'We should have brought another Sister Famulous or two and some Arbites detectives with us.'

'We've got a place to start,' Romille replied. 'In answer to your question, arbitor, this is the only thing I touched, because you wouldn't have found it otherwise. You haven't been trained in our concealment protocols.' Romille held out a small document case, then stood at Calpurnia's shoulder while she opened it, glaring at the Kalfus house guard until he retreated out into the arboretum again.

Through the archway to Leyka's bedchamber there was the thump of furniture being moved. There turned out to be nothing under the bed, but there were still the private religious books in the bedside shrine and a quiet but vehement argument broke out between Bannon and Sister Rea Mankela about whether it was proper to go through the dead woman's lectionary.

After several minutes they agreed to take the matter back into the study and let the Sister Celestian and the arbitor senioris argue it out, but by that time the point was moot: Shira Calpurnia was hunched saucer-eyed over Sister Leyka's journal and Aurean Romille was outside rounding up her sisters and shouting at them to get reinforcements and block off every exit from the Kalfus household that they could find.

THE NOTEBOOKS WERE plain vellum, with a neat aquila and 'Nomine Imperator' handwritten at the top of each page. She had skimmed the summary of attempts within the Medell to wrest the position of Master of the Vigil off the Kalfus family, and then attempts within the Kalfus to seize it from Hallyan. Leyka had simply commented that Hallyan had moved to keep his prize with 'far in excess of even his usual ruthlessness', a dry statement with implications that chilled her increasingly the more she read. Leyka had documented his obsessive drive for perfection in the performance of every rite and function, and her own role in helping his initial efforts, and added her commentary on his growing paranoia too.

No one within the family may now move to block him, for it has reached the stage where the fortunes of all the Medell are bound up in what Hallyan will accomplish and they are committed to his support lest they share the disgrace should anything go wrong. But H. knows full well that other interests will work to undercut him, disrupt and disgrace him by bringing the Vigil undone. He fears the Haggan, particularly the Lyze-Haggan, and certain Naval dynasties who will be attending the hive for the mass, but also…

More names, but ones that meant nothing to Calpurnia. She flipped ahead.

A new commander in the Arbites has come into the system and there was an attempt on her life today. I have been able to find little more so far, but I will record that H. was tense and moody throughout the morning as he is when there are risks or threats in the making, and when he heard news of the attempt he went into a rage and locked himself away. I have sent word of this to the preceptory but no reply yet.

But the first message Hallyan had received had told him that she was still alive. He had said so himself.

She skipped ahead again.

H. has ordered a consignment from his personal weapons gallery in secrecy – the couriers were instructed not to reveal this to me but the pilot was one who had often petitioned me to hear confessions of unholy thoughts and I was able to use this to get the intelligence from him. The casket was locked but he said that he knew it to contain weaponry, something that H's own grandfather in the Kalfus had used in an internal war two generations ago. I believe it is this that H. has prepared to take with him when he goes to meet the Arbites. He is well pleased with the harsh measures they have taken to keep the hive and the Augustaeum quiet but there is something in their actions that has disturbed him. He will not confide in me and I must be careful to conceal my knowledge and suspicions.

The weapon parts. The components Hallyan had told her came from an enemy. No. They were his own family's, his own grandfather's. His own.

Another page.

H. no longer has what I now know to be gun parts. The Arbites must have them. He returned in a rage but the household guards are armed and the locks will not respond to me. H. must plan crimes spiritual as much as temporal if he wishes to keep them from me and from the Sisterhood. Whether he has watched me in ways I have not known about or whether I am betrayed to him I do not know, but I believe he knows he must move against me. He has used the laws of the Vigil as a pretext to shut off vox-traffic and the guards are watching my movements. He brought a cushion out of the litter and spoke to Nomikros about it, something to do with the new Arbites commander but I could not get close enough to hear what they said.

The last entry.

Nomikros is planning to take the cushion to the Chapter House. He has talked to one of the House armourers about some kind of scent-sign. Emperor protect me, by their words this vicious House has managed to extend its reach into our own sacred cloisters, there was talk of some trap for the arbitor to be triggered there. I do not know what it will be. H. has donated servitors, weapons and artworks as tithes to all the Orders, perhaps it is in one of those.

I cannot delay. I must reach the Chapter House before Nomikros. The Canoness of the Sacred Rose knows I am on my way to meet her. Nori will accompany me, and I go in haste and armed. Nomine Imperator.

The exchanges outside the chamber were growing more and more heated. Nomikros must have got his breath back; she could hear him shouting that a message had been sent to his lord. Calpurnia saw Bannon peering around the door and spoke to him, quiet and deadly earnest.

'Go and talk to Sister Romille, then commandeer one of the Rhinos we came in and drive like hell for the Justice Gate. Bring back a full suppression detail equipped for a massed prisoner drive. If they move on foot and come straight here they should be within the laws of the Vigil, but order it how you need to so they can get here without any Ministorum problems. Get Romille and Culann to finish locking down the house as best they can. Order the household guards to co-operate. Execute any who resist. You and Culann both have Level Four delegations.'

Bannon hurried out and Sister Mankela followed him. Alone in the chamber, Calpurnia took deep, careful breaths and stared at the journals again.

She said the name out loud, the name of the man who had sent them against her. The psyker with his ghost-trick and pistol, the ambush crews blinded by lies, the hidden devouring-machines.

'Hallyan. Kalfus. Medell.'

CHAPTER THIRTEEN

Eighteenth Day of Septista

The Mass of Saint Balronas. The Sanguinala.

ON THE MORNING of the Mass of Saint Balronas, three of the four most senior Adeptus Arbites of Hydraphur met at the Justice Gate an hour before dawn. Shira Calpurnia had been up for an hour and a half, too nervy and distracted to sleep. She knew that Dvorov, Leandro and any number of other senior Arbites were groomed by valets from the moment they awoke but she had resisted the practice until today, when her ceremonial clothing arrived with two attendants and she dressed in it while they fussed about her. Now she wore her formal dress uniform duplicated in brilliant scarlet, the insignia and braid in bright cloth-of-gold instead of silver-grey on black.

Calpurnia kept getting taken by surprise by the flashes of colour when she moved – she couldn't remember the last time she had worn something so extravagant. They had given her clothes to wear over it, too, for the last few hours of the Vigil: a sober grey skirted tunic that fell to her ankles and a cloak with a hood of mud-brown hessian. Almost as an afterthought she had fastened Theoctista's absolution seal at her throat beneath the cloak-pin. She walked out of the gate into the pre-dawn dimness of the unlit Augustaeum, Leandro walking ahead at the lead of a procession of Judges and a dozen armed arbitrators and Dvorov beside her.

'You're still nervous, Arbitor Calpurnia.'

'Shows, does it? I know we're walking because walking to the mass is Ministorum law, but I received absolution from that law and I'm sure you could have too, sir. We could have ridden out in one of our own Rhinos or talked Romille into ferrying us again, kept a guard up, checked on some of the patrols on the way.'

'The street presence is doing fine, Shira. There are plenty of excellent squad commanders making sure no one can repeat what happened to Sister Leyka.' Dvorov gestured to the black-armoured arbitrators standing in long lines down the centre of every street, facing alternately left and right, shotguns ready.

They passed through the Avenue of the Defenders and met up with more Adeptus, likewise walking, likewise cloaked and shrouded. By the time they had passed the Arch of the Scarii and passed up the Titheman's Way they had joined a modest stream of other mass-goers coming up from the Kathisma Gate, and the growing crowd was swallowed by the flow of people from the Nobles Quarter so that they finally entered the High Mesé in a great, slow-moving tide of dark-dressed figures that filled the avenue from side to side, all walking with heads down and in silence. Occasionally one would glance up at the Cathedral towering overhead and Calpurnia would catch a flash of crimson under their mourning robes. To her, the walk was almost dreamlike in its silence and stateliness. The rich fabric of her new uniform felt oddly soft and heavy on her skin, and it seemed strange that she would not wear this again for a full year.

A twinge from the still-tender wounds on her foot brought her back to earth, and she grimaced and tried to walk more carefully. Pain she could deal with – it was part of the ritual of this occasion, after all – but she didn't like the idea of being slowed if anything happened. In the formal robes and regalia of a Judge, with his mourning cloak over it to boot, Dvorov was having to take care with his step too. The mantles worn during the morning had to be treated with care: the pins that held them were designed to break so that they could be cast off at the moment the Sanguinala was rung in at noon, but to have them come away before that and stand there in scarlet festive dress would be a deep disgrace.

'It still chafes at you,' he told her after a moment, 'I can tell.'

'The new boot? No, it fits fine.' It came out thin and flat. She had never been good at jokes. She stepped in closer to him and dropped her voice a notch. 'Having to be here while Nakayama and Zhow are on the other side of the planet sacking the Kalfus-Medell holdings? In honesty, sir, it does. Two assassinations were aimed at me. Hallyan's slimy mock-solicitous speeches about my safety were directed at me. His attempts to order us around and his sanctimony about keeping the Vigil sacrosanct were pointed at me. So yes, I'd like to be over there. I feel I *should* be over there. I want to turn his rock over and drag him out into the light in front of all the other members of his so-fine family and his damned syndicate and sit them all around him in chains as Leyka's notebook is read out at his execution. I've been running back and forth playing shadow-games ever since I arrived, and I wanted to get some proper Arbites work under my belt.'

'You'll get your chance, Shira. Nakayama's good at his job and he has a taskforce of almost a thousand and a Level Five delegation. Zhow is backing him up with the Inquisitorial seal and his own staff and militia. The Kalfus family were broken as of the moment you found Leyka's notes, their allies have deserted them, there's no way they can keep hiding him even assuming they want to for much longer. They're coming to the point where cutting their losses and handing him over will be by far the easiest course. We'll find where Hallyan has disappeared to.'

'It's...' Calpurnia sighed as she tried to find the words. 'It's just the feeling of being so out of place. Like I'm an adult in a world of children playing incomprehensible games, except it's with each other's lives. They bury themselves in these twisting little intrigues and lavish so much on themselves and their Emperor and their Imperium just disappears from their memory. I think it's ironic. I'm from Ultramar, a world that isn't even governed by the Administratum, and here I am on a planet renowned as one of the greatest fortresses in defence of the Imperium and I'm the one talking about due deference to the Adeptus and these puffed-up skankwits around me are the ones convinced that they're somehow born outside and above it.'

'A Hydraphurn might quote a local saying about rank having its privileges.'

'And the privilege of rank is service. That's what they teach us at home, and I used to think they taught the same everywhere. If you serve well you are rewarded with rank and the privilege of being allowed to perform greater services. By the manner of that service you show that those privileges were not wasted on you.'

She looked at Dvorov sidelong – he was smiling under his cowl.

'Tell me you sympathise with me at least a little way, sir. I took you for someone who saw through all the blueblood crap.'

'Be at ease, Shira. I was smiling at another irony that I don't think you've picked up on.'

'Oh?'

'I know a reasonable amount about you, Shira Calpurnia. I selected you and oversaw your appointment myself, it could hardly be otherwise. The same quirk of the immaterium – the Shodama current, I think it's called – that brought you to this Segmentum so quickly allows message traffic to come the same way, of course, and it is customary to share dispatches among Arbites of a certain rank. Your background has certainly not escaped my attention. The Calpurnii are not well known here, but then we are almost on the other side of the galaxy to your home. But yours is a remarkable family, prominent in the governance of Ultramar ever since records have been kept and part of every elite one cares to define – mercantile, scholastic, military. And outside Ultramar, once I started looking, I found illustrious Calpurnii in every arm of the Adeptus. Imperial Guard commanders, officers in the Battlefleet Ultima, Arbites like yourself, servants of the Ministorum and Sororitas, high posts in the Administratum, one with a Rogue Trader charter. I even consulted rosters of the Adeptus Astartes, and there's a Scaero Calpurnius serving in the Ultramarines' Second Company...'

'My great-great-grand-uncle.'

'...and a Phaedrus Calpurnius is listed in the roll of dead for the First Company during the First Tyrannic War.'

'From a cousin's side of the family. Not a direct relation.'

'Nevertheless, there you have the irony. I was smiling at the way you were talking about the nobility and the aristocracy, walking beside me there with a pedigree that probably half the nobles in the Augustaeum would give an eyeball for. But you really don't think of yourself as high-born, do you? You see your lineage as a responsibility to live up to, not a mark of superiority. It says a lot about you, my arbitor. That's why I was smiling.'

Calpurnia walked on beside him, trying to favour her good foot and not knowing what to say. Around them the crowd was thickening even further as more joined them from the Alabaster Well and the Avenue of the Saints, and along the iron roadways from the Forge Gate. As the press became close the two Arbites gave conversation away and Calpurnia's imagination put a knife in every hand and a pistol under every cloak. She silently gave thanks for the absolution seal at her neck that allowed her to keep her own weapon.

She had read that in most years the walls of the Cathedral before the Mass were surrounded by supplicants and penitents in a rapture that bordered on frenzy, packed fifty or more deep, howling out the Emperor's name and begging visions and divine blessings. This year the Arbites were taking no chances and they had been cleared away, the ramp and that whole end of the Mesé empty and sealed off until the dignitaries had all processed into the Cathedral. From around her Calpurnia heard one or two murmurs about how quiet the morning was before she and Dvorov moved up the ramp, through the doors and into the darkness beyond.

THE CENSER SMOKE was bitter and almost chemical, crafted to recall the stink of flamers. Skeletal mock-angelic servitors glided overhead on suspensors, trailing ragged scrolls of dark scripture and transmitting grief-stricken groans over their voxcasters. The Cathedral was in dimness, the columns and the vast statues disappearing into high shadow. The choir, massed like an army in lofts to either side of the altar steps and over the doors, sang a low, discordant chant of lament and despair. The angel-statues hanging over the altars were swathed in black sackcloth.

Calpurnia had gone over it in her mind over and over again. She wanted to be sure she had left nothing out, but every time she tried to convince herself of it she could not. Hallyan had not been at the chapel. He had left as the rest of his household prayed for Leyka's soul, telling the retainers at the doors that he was going back to the house to speak with the arbitor. And then he had vanished, simply walked down one of the paths from the Gate and, as far as anyone could tell, just dissipated into air.

The congregation had assembled on the flagstoned floor, herded by Ministorum attendants into four thick masses with three empty aisles running through them. Now down each aisle came a shuffling procession of black-robed deacons with the tattered banners of all the Houses, the Navy ships, the guilds and regiments and orders that had bowed the knee to Bucharis. The first had already reached the steps of the little ziggurat on which the main altar stood, the end of the processions were still lost in the shadows behind them. The Chief Commandant of the Hydraphur Naval Commissariat stood on the steps below the Altar Sanguinal, reading each disgraced name from a scroll as its banner arrived in the growing press before him.

There had been odd sightings from Arbites patrols all over the Augustaeum, reports from different streets of him heading in conflicting directions, but when the orders had gone out to bring the man in… nothing. Romille's Rhino was the only vehicle to have driven the streets all day; the Gate watches monitoring the exits from the Augustaeum to the rest of the hive reported that Hallyan had not tried to exit it. The Arbites at the airpads and landing-crosses out in the city-sprawl reported no launches of aircraft, not even attempts. How had he managed to flee?

A high, fast song sprang up from the choir, sharp and urgent soprano notes, fierce words, pain and sacrifice, penance and contrition. Fires sprang up around the walls as Sororitas guards lit sacred braziers, and in the flame-lit Cathedral Canoness Casia of the Order of the Lexicon walked to the base of the Altar Dolanite and began to read from the *Dialogues of the Confessor.*

Calpurnia was at floor level, toward the front of the congregation among the more prestigious worshippers, but she could imagine how the rows of braziers would look to those in the high tiers behind them. She thought again of standing with Hallyan atop the Cathedral's spire, of watching the lights go out and the soft ghost-lanterns of the Vigil light up the square below. She remembered his descriptions and those she had read of what the square was like at the moment when the crowd at the Cathedral doors threw off its mourning robes, remembered him talking about the care he had taken over that pivotal moment of the festivities. A pity he couldn't see them.

And it was so simple she wondered how she could ever have missed it.

Shira Calpurnia stepped from her place and edged her way out of the line of Arbites. Dvorov and Leandro stared after her but did not interfere as she backed into a clear space, gave a salute in the direction of the altar for safety's sake, then walked as fast as dignity permitted toward the back of the Cathedral and the passages to the vestry chambers. A bow-wave of scandalised sound spread out from her path, almost too low to hear over her footsteps: no one dared talk aloud, so the susurrus was made of intakes of breath, muttered questions and exclamations, the rustle of cloth as heads hurriedly turned back to watch the ceremonies at the altars. Two deacons stepped out from one of the tiered column bases to block her way, but glanced at one another and stood aside when she pointed to the seal at her throat.

A drumbeat, and the braziers went out. Calpurnia clamped her lips together to keep in a curse and sidled out of the aisle she stood in, right into a clump of startled Navy officers. Through the darkness, each under a single lamp carried by one of the gliding angel-skeletons, came three processions, at their heads priests robed in black, with leering masks representing the traitors of the Apostasy: Bucharis, Sehalla and Gasto. A column of Sisters Repentia followed each priest, keening and raking their nails across their crudely-shaven heads and emaciated faces. Calpurnia shifted from foot to foot until they had passed a respectful distance, then began walking again. She was sure she could feel the gaze of the people around her on her shoulders like a weight. She reached the vestry chambers at the same time as the processions reached the Altar Thorian, and the booming dirge of the choir followed her through the doorway.

Her entrance very nearly got her spitted on two honour-blades until the sisters at the door saw the seal and put up their weapons. Beyond, a shocked senior pontifex in dazzling white and cloth-of-gold stared at her over the mask of Dolan he had been about to put on to lead out the next procession. Calpurnia ransacked her memory for the name of the people they had placed in charge of security for this area.

'I need to speak to Sister Superior Zafiri and Proctor Essker.' The pontifex was still staring bug-eyed at her as a deacon hurried her through the vestry and into the marshalling rooms beyond it.

'Arbitor senioris!' Essker looked as shocked as the pontifex had, spinning away from the far window and snapping to attention so fast Calpurnia half-expected him to wrench something in his spine. Fed up of the constricting layer of cloth, Calpurnia snapped the pins and the cloak and tunic dropped away as they were designed to do. The junior arbitor gulped.

'Ma'am, you shouldn't go about in Sanguinala dress before–'

'Don't stand on ceremony, Essker, we haven't the time. Where is Sister Romille stationed? Celestian Superior Aurean Romille. And I think Lead Arbitor Bannon is outside, get him in here too.'

'I don't know. Uh, I'll find out.' Essker was collecting himself.

'Do that and get me whatever squad is on duty as floaters at the moment. Have someone get me the security journals for the Cathedral garrisons, too, both ours and the sisters'. But first show me where you've got the equipment dump, I want a carapace to put on over this.'

She was glad they had decided to keep an equipment stash, and gladder that there was a body-carapace there that fit her. By the time she had clipped it on Romille, Essker, Bannon and half a dozen Arbites were standing and watching her. She supposed she looked a little odd in the scuffed black battle-armour over the gorgeous red and gold of her uniform.

'I'm giving you the benefit of the doubt, madam arbitor, because I have some respect for you,' said Romille coldly as Calpurnia reattached her holster. 'Walking out of an Ecclesiarchal ceremony, let alone the Mass of Saint Balronas, is not something my order or anyone in that Cathedral takes lightly, however they might want to do things wherever you came from.'

'I am fully aware of what I just did, sister. In a moment I'm going to show you my reasons.' She took the log-slates without looking at whoever handed them to her and began going through the information in them with quick, careful taps of a forefinger. If I'm wrong about this, she thought, then I am utterly and undoubtedly–

But she wasn't. She cut off a triumphant smile before it could show and held the slate up for the sister to see. It took a moment for Romille to take in what she was pointing to, another moment to understand it and snick off the safety on her bolter. After a moment more her face split in a grin.

'What,' she asked Calpurnia, 'are we waiting for?'

'ARE THESE DELAYS wise? I want to get up there and see if your hunch is right.' They had stopped again for Calpurnia to pass contingency instructions to the sentries in the cloisters. It was the fifth such stop as they worked their way up through the building: they had gone almost high enough now to be level with the ceiling of the Cathedral space itself. Two floors ago they had passed a window that looked out into the central chamber where the mass was being held: the swathing was gone from the marble angels and they blazed in white searchlights as the Chief Confessor Militant led the congregation in the Second Psalm of the Martyrs.

'The bells will ring in fifty-three minutes,' Calpurnia said, checking her timepiece. 'I'm positive we'll have at least that long to get into position and I want to make the most of the time. But if it makes you any happier…' She reset her timer into a reverse countdown. 'Does that match yours? Can you pinpoint to the minute when the end of the mass is rung?'

'To the microsecond. It's written into the laws of the mass itself.'

'Silly of me.'

Romille simply grunted, checked Calpurnia's timer countdown again and led them on.

They picked up two more Arbites from one of the balcony details; Romille had commandeered three more sisters. Calpurnia was pausing them at each level, methodically making sure that each area knew what was going on, listening as Romille gave out orders to the Sororitas and collecting Arbites from their liaison checkpoints. Romille had eight white-armoured sisters behind her now, and the impromptu arbitrator squad following Calpurnia and Bannon was a dozen strong. She was being careful to leave a good guard presence behind, and she was being careful to have the passages between each level sealed behind them as they climbed. Flight back down through the Cathedral was going to be impossible. Not that it would come to that, she corrected herself grimly. Not at all.

Another five-second lift ride. The forty-second level, ecclesiastical libraries, bare teaching rooms and devotories. Two edgy Arbites in the lift foyer and another twenty sisters moving around the floor. The two women gave their orders and moved on and upward. By the sixtieth level they had fifteen people apiece and Calpurnia began spacing them back along the corridors, fearing that things would get too unwieldy if there were trouble. By the ninety-eighth level there were twenty-two minutes to go, Romille was grinding her teeth and Calpurnia had started to bark her orders and eye her timer. At the moment that she stepped out of the little corridor to the foot of the bell-colonnade steps and gestured for the squads to assemble, her countdown read exactly fifteen minutes.

* * *

At thirteen minutes and forty seconds to go, Hallyan's servitor came down the stairs from the bell-chamber with the fluid, silent speed of a closing shark. Its crusher-claw arced in like a wrecking ball and Proctor Essker flew up and out past her, dead from the hit even before he cleared the balcony railing and began to fall. The flesh-machine used the momentum of the swing to turn and drive its other arm forward and rammed a bundle of high-velocity drill-spikes through Sister Iustina's chestplate. The drill teeth buzzed against the ceramite as the fat little pintle-stubbers on its shoulders whined and tracked and spat bullets out of barrels no longer than Calpurnia's little finger. It seemed to be squealing, but Calpurnia realised it was coming from her vox-torc. Something was jamming their transmission band.

Romille shouted a battle-blessing and the crackling sarissa-spear on her bolter slid effortlessly through the thing's armour plate; she might have been bayoneting air. It was a perfect killing stroke, neatly through where the heart should have been, but the servitor slammed Iustina's body into Romille's with a swipe of its arm and she went sprawling, her weapon clattering on the stone. By that time Calpurnia had her pistol out and was placing careful shots, trying for the base of the neck where the helmet visor stopped, her shots tearing gouges out of the thing's shoulders. The servitor lunged and crushed an arbitor into two with its claw. The arbitor and sister behind him got off two shots apiece before the drillspikes in the thing's right arm retracted, a triple-chainblade array extended and sheared them both in two in a terrifying double stroke. The gold visor was spattered with red, its blankness more frightening than a living, snarling face would have been.

Calpurnia shifted targets now, backing away and firing at the thing's hips and legs as Bannon stepped up beside her and pumped scatter rounds into its face to try and blind it. Her shots tore into its knees, but it barely slowed as it twisted about and put a bullet from each shoulder-stubber through an arbitrator's face. Bolt-shells from two sisters blew red craters into its side before it dropped one with another headshot and the other with a drill-lunge, then smashed a third with the claw. Romille was on all fours, shaking her head and trying to stagger to her feet until it knocked her flying into the wall at the other end of the balcony hard enough to crack the stone where she hit – she collapsed and lay still. Bannon ducked away, trying to place another shot into the thing's side between its armour plates, but the drillspikes were too quick. They skewered Bannon's chest and hoisted him high, then retracted to drop him onto the chainblades. A swipe of the arm sent the wrecked corpse tumbling wetly back down the stairs.

Calpurnia, the only one left now, wove her maul in front of her before the crusher-claw plucked it out of her grasp quicker than she could follow and snapped it. She spun to flee and get some room to reload her pistol when the claw hit her on a downward angle that shattered her left shoulder and arm like porcelain and drove her to her knees. She had time to watch the gun drop from her hands before her vision washed red and she shrieked. No second blow came and she tried to half-stand, to look around for a weapon, until a second, lighter hit buffeted her against the wall and a third sent her sprawling back towards the final set of stairs. For a moment she lay there, retching and gasping at the raving storm of agony that was eating her left side whole, before somewhere underneath it she realised what was expected of her. White with pain and staggering on her feet, Shira Calpurnia climbed the stairs to the gallery beneath the Cathedral bell, to meet for the last time in her life with Lord Hallyan Kalfus-Medell.

HALLYAN STOOD WITH his back half to her at the north-eastern end of the gallery, looking out over the Mesé as they had done on Vigil's Eve. He wore drab mourning-grey as she had been doing, although she could see scarlet at his collar and ankles where the mourning robe did not quite reach. Hallyan was dressed for the mass. Calpurnia tottered to a stop and her left leg gave out; at the sound of her toppling to one knee Hallyan spoke.

'You thought I wouldn't know.'

'Wouldn't know what?' Her own voice sounded thin and stretched to her ears.

'Wouldn't know, you little sow, that you were coming up here after me. I have eyes and ears keener than yours, you know.' He turned and gestured at the servitor as it padded up beside him. The damage it had suffered in the fight appeared not to have slowed it at all. 'A step ahead of you, little Shira. A step ahead of you every single time. A step... Little Shira-bitch.'

For a moment she was back in the dark passageway on board the Inner Charisian Gate. She found herself sniffing for the smell of alcohol on Ensign Talgaard's breath.

No. Mustn't lose touch... mustn't lose track... She tried to regain her feet and couldn't. Hallyan's posture was haughty, his clothes neat, but his eyes...

She made herself gasp out words.

'You didn't get ahead of Sister Leyka, did you, Hallyan? You barely managed to catch up with her before she could let anyone know what you were doing.'

'She... questioned me. The same as you are doing. *She* tried to judge *me*. She tried to judge me. I am... you know who I am. And you people, you are... you think that I should... *justify*...' His hand twitched, and again, and even through the fog Calpurnia realised what iron will it was taking for him to keep himself composed. His eyes were ragged with near-madness. 'The words don't matter. Anger, anger is done with and you wouldn't have what it takes to understand me.'

Hallyan's gaze wandered again and Calpurnia took the moment, lunging and getting her left leg under her and taking a step towards him. He caught the movement and spat a code-phrase; the servitor took a step forward and raised the drillspike arm until she stepped back again. *Emperor help me, Emperor help me*. 'Never understand,' he said as though he had not been interrupted. 'The rest of them will all talk about how terrible I am, and my family will tell that peasant oaf Nakayama that I acted alone, that I was a rogue, their undoing with mine ...' he tailed off and seemed to shake for a moment.

Her arm and shoulder sang, and colour swung in and out of her world, but behind it her thoughts were becoming weirdly clear.

'That's... that's why you showed us those gun parts,' she said. 'I wondered why you gave us something that would lead the search closer to you. But that wasn't how you thought, was it? You didn't realise that we–' she heaved a breath and it was like breathing hot metal '–felt the same way about the nobility as you do. You pointed us to it being a noble family at the root of all this so that I would remember my station and call off the investigation rather than harass my betters.' She made herself stand straight, although she could not stop herself swaying as her shattered bones yowled. 'For whatever it's worth now, that was never even close to working.'

She had been wondering if that would provoke him; it did not, and suddenly another thought sailed by on the hazy swells of agony. She couldn't provoke him, not yet. She had to bide her time.

'It didn't work, no. You clung on like hive-mud. Hah! You are hive-mud. Mud. Mud and disease!' He spat on her, on her broken shoulder. She looked muzzily down to see his spittle mingling with her blood. 'No doubt you're so terribly proud that you eluded a device that cost me any amount of time and resources to secrete?'

'The swarm in the garden.' She blinked sluggishly as another connection slid in. 'The litter-cushion. It was…'

'Nomikros took the cushion you had sat on in my litter to get a pheromone trace of you into the garden for the nest of machines to pick up. A tech-arcanum that is beyond our production now, you know. One of the few left in the whole sector, the only one my family had at its disposal, do you understand that? Of course not. What can you understand? You can't even understand *obedience*.' His hands were twisting in the cloth of his robe. Hallyan was starting to come apart. 'I had originally placed that swarm with the intention of using it for something considerably more important than you, you wretch. I had wasted my prize wyrd-shooter on you as it was.'

Her eyelids felt heavy. Shock. She was going into shock. She couldn't. She couldn't go into shock she couldn't she couldn't. Her thoughts raced around in a bewildering rat-maze of agony. *Holy Emperor, beloved Protector, by Your light do I walk unafraid in the bleak places…* She cradled her broken left arm in her right, gritted her teeth and jogged it. She mewed and hissed with the pain, but the dazed feeling ebbed. Hallyan hadn't noticed. She looked at the servitor, took a step forward. She remembered what Leandro had said. Oh, Emperor grant him right, Emperor…

Keep him talking.

'You didn't start anything more against me until you realised we were going to specifically come after you. We spent days on a lock-down of the Augustaeum, the whole hive, but you didn't care.' She took another step forward. Her lips felt numb and her words sounded sludgy to her ears. 'But I think I know why. It was never us at all. It was your rivals. The Lyze-Haggan, the people in your own house and syndicate, the aristocracy. I know enough to understand what they had to gain by disrupting the festival while you were appointed to preside over it. If they could disgrace you they could undo you.'

He was staring at her. She wanted to drop her eyes to the timer but she forced herself to hold his gaze.

'That's what started it all. The assassination of the fourth most senior arbites officer in the system would... give all the Adeptus the jitters. Stir us up. Killing some other local noble wouldn't. I was newly-arrived and from far away, easy target. And my death would have forced the Arbites to lock down the whole place so tightly that none of your rivals would have had room to try anything, and you'd be safe because who would ever have thought that you would undermine your own Vigil like that?'

'And it worked. You did exactly what I wanted. You did lock the hive down, there were no plots able to take hold against me. And step back, please, arbitor, before I instruct my guard again. It will place a shot between your eyes if I tell it to.'

Fighting off despair, she shuffled back a pace, gasping. Blood was flowing steadily out of her arm and the floor seemed to be rolling softly under her.

'So you got what you wanted, Hallyan. You got the Arbites dancing to your tune, you get to stand on top of the Cathedral and watch them ring in the Sanguinala.' She cursed herself for using the word, hurried on before he could pick up on it. 'You never dreamed, though, that we'd keep following you, that my fellow Arbites would be so... loyal to me. You don't realise people think like that, do you... Hallyan? Except for the trifling matter of underestimating... the Emperor's Arbites, you have come through this... remarkably well.' She managed a glimpse of her timer.

'Underestimating.' Hallyan's hands were balled into fists in his robe. 'I am an idealist. I thought I lived on a world where people behave as they should, where a little guttertrash such as you had respect enough to leave those born her betters alone. You're smiling!'

She was. She wondered if she was delirious. Her left eye seemed to only see blurred reds and greys. 'You remind me of something the lord marshal said. No matter.' Hallyan took a deep breath, and she looked at the timer again. *Not long, not long. Emperor please, oh holy Guilliman lend me your strength...*

'But I am a man of will and a man of my word. I swore I would see you dead and that I would see the Vigil end and the Sanguinala begin. I swore it.'

'And I realised it.' Calpurnia could hear her voice getting stronger. *Not long now, not long. Keep him talking.* 'Down there on the

Cathedral floor. There was no way you would allow anything to get between you and your triumph, you had to be here to see the end of your Vigil with your own eyes. Once I knew that the security logs for the Cathedral entrances confirmed it. You never fled after we took your house. You cut a zigzag path through the hive so that your movements would be hard to predict, got here before word of your crimes did, strolled by the guards and hid. Do I have it right? You're as brave and ruthless as your reputation told me. You might have made a good arbitor if someone had taken you in hand.'

That scored, and Hallyan had to squeeze his eyes shut for a moment. She noticed that his mantle was speckled with dried blood, blood that was not his own. He caught her looking.

'What? You think I liked having to do this? You think I liked sitting in a rathole somewhere in this place looking at that scrawny old man's corpse all night? I should not have had to... someone like me... someone in my, my station... Even after I killed him his eyes mocked me and he wouldn't listen.'

That was where he had hidden. He had murdered one of the anchorites in their meditation-cells somewhere in the Cathedral spire and he had sat in the cell all night with the corpse and his silent servitor. Talking to the corpse. Throne of Earth, the man was coming apart at the seams. She wondered how long this side of him had been bottled away as he smiled and made polite words and bred his plots, the pressure eating him alive. She should have stopped him, should have seen–

Calpurnia groaned in pain and dropped her eyes; her timer display blurred in her vision and she came close to panic again. She squeezed here eyes shut and made them focus. Hallyan cackled.

'Unlike you, I need not sully my own hands with the labour. I will kill you. It will be this weapon beside me but my command and therefore I will be killing you myself. Another concept that only my kind can understand. But I will not kill you yet, woman, I will make you see that square light up with–' He stopped dead. He had seen her staring at the timer on her wrist, and he snarled. 'What are you doing, bitch, what have you cooked up? Very well, to hell with you. I'll kill you now and die happy when the mass is done.' He turned to his servitor, pointed at her, and spoke the words that would send it lunging to end her life.

Calpurnia's countdown hit zero.

She had barely heard the whoop of air behind them as the hammer flew into motion, but now the toll of the Cathedral bell slammed into them as though the bell itself had been hammered down onto their backs. Calpurnia felt the sound drive into the sides of her skull, was sure she felt it buzzing in her splintered bones. The noise was monstrous, the noise was the whole world.

She had seen Hallyan's mouth move, knew he had spoken the trigger phrase. And it was swallowed, buried, beaten down by the god-voice of the Cathedral bell.

She forced herself to move, felt herself lurch forward and struggled to not pitch onto her face. As she ran forward, shouting noiselessly at the pain as she dropped her left arm to free her right, she was sure that any moment the servitor would leap at her, but even Hallyan's second call was barely more than texture against the fading ring of the bell. He spun goggle-eyed to face her and Calpurnia drove the edge of her knuckles forward and upward, crushed his voicebox and left him staggering against the parapet choking for breath.

She could have killed him there with a single good shove. He was stunned, gurgling and could not have resisted. She thought about it for a long moment.

No. There was only one right way.

She left Hallyan wheezing and gobbling against the side of the arch and walked unsteadily back down the stairs. Her pistol was where it had fallen in the litter of bodies. She picked it up and wondered dimly how she was going to load it, managed to fumble it open somehow. She worked the loader in, groaning as the pain seemed to send stealthy wires across her body, down into her legs, up into her head. The snick of the lock-glove helped her focus as she gripped the gun and stood up again. She walked back up, gun-arm heavy and hanging as limp as her ruined one. Her head wanted to sag, her body wanted to faint. *No. Must be done right.*

Hallyan was still up against the little parapet over the Mesé. He was leaning on his servitor, staring imploringly into its visor and making pleading gurgles to it. It stood impassively, staring into the distance ahead of it, ignoring his clawing hands on its arm, waiting for its command. Hallyan's mourning-cloth had come away and the red of his mass silks mingled with the blood from his servitor's wounds, and the blood of arbitrators and sisters that slicked its weapons. She saw his ears were bleeding and realised hers must be too. Her hearing was full of hiss and din, she could only hear her steps as faint, gravelly sounds and her voice, when she addressed him, barely registered at all.

'Lord Hallyan Kalfus-Medell of Hydraphur. With the evidence of my eyes and the proof in my hand I condemn you as is my right as arbitor senioris of the Adeptus Arbites, in service to the law of the God-Emperor of Earth. I condemn you for murder and for unholy conspiracy against the God-Emperor of humankind. Blessed be the God-Emperor, in His name do I carry out sentence.'

Hallyan looked at her, paralysed and seeming to only barely understand, as she took careful aim and shot him once between the eyes.

The bell had rung at the moment the dawning sun cleared the horizon, and down on the Mesé and in all the streets of the Augustaeum and the Bosporian Hive and its great surrounding city and in every place across Hydraphur the crowds had shed their mourning robes and were leaping and shouting in their scarlet festive clothes: the Vigil was over, the Sanguinala had begun. Red pennants had unfurled from every tower and red streamers spilled from every window; bright red pyrotechnic showers brightened the already rich dawn light.

Calpurnia watched as Lord Hallyan's body, its head gone above the bottom lip, tumbled off the gallery and away, turning end over end, disappearing from view in air thick with confetti, fireworks, shouts and exultant hymns. She reeled and lurched a step backward, then another. It dimly seemed to her that this wasn't right, that there had been a party on already. She knew this next part: there was a party and then someone she couldn't see would shoot at her and then she would meet nobles and fly into space and be chased in a garden. She shouldn't have to do all that again...

It caught up with her, finally, and Calpurnia crumpled slowly to the floor of the gallery as her mind slid down into the dark.

EPILOGUE

JUST AFTER NOON on the twenty-fourth day of Septista Shira Calpurnia, in dress uniform and a dusty-black funeral mantle, waited by the outer doors of the Cathedral of the Emperor Ascendant. The other mourners were gone into the bright day outside. In the middle distance across the Cathedral floor she could see men and women in the yellow-brown gowns of penitents, citizens who had been carried away and committed some minor infraction at the Sanguinala feasts for which they were now atoning. They bustled about the column steps and the altars, sweeping and polishing and fanning away the funeral incense. Calpurnia knew that the air needed to be sweet for a procession that afternoon, but she still wished she hadn't seen this. There was an impersonality about it that saddened her.

The Eparch Baszle had performed the funeral rites himself at the Altar Thorian. The noble families had sent representatives to the service because none of them had dared not to, and none of them had looked happy about such a distinguished ritual for what they thought such lowly functionaries. The Cardinal had filled his eulogy with references to the greatest nobility in humility and duty, heroic deaths and true worthiness, and Calpurnia didn't imagine the assembled upper crust had taken that gracefully either. The only person to approach her after the service had been Inquisitor Zhow, who had presented his condolences and congratulated her stiffly but apparently sincerely on her 'victory'. She had accepted both graciously, and Zhow had stalked away with no more ado. Calpurnia had heard no more about the reprimands he had threatened after the Lyze-Haggan assault, and she suspected he was going to let it slide.

There was a discreet cough from behind her. Baragry was standing there in a simple black and red clerical gown, proffering a black linen scroll. Unrolling it awkwardly in one hand – the arm shattered by the servitor's claw had been rebuilt on grafted bone but it was still strapped to her body while it healed – she looked at the neat column of names in white ink, the names the Eparch had read from this scroll during the funeral, the dead Arbites and sisters from the fight below the bell chamber. Arbitor Essker, Sister Iustina, more. Bannon's name was second from the bottom and she closed her eyes and bowed her head for a moment when she came to it.

'The Eparch sends you his personal blessings, my lady arbitor,' said Baragry as she rerolled the scroll and tucked it into her belt, 'and he hopes that he may meet with you in audience soon. But he is curious – and I will say that I am also – about the roll of names. We happily make you a gift of it, but what will be its use?'

'The prayer book I was given at my induction instructs us to reflect upon service and sacrifice, Reverend Baragry. I will place this on the shrine in my chambers and read these names along with my scriptures. I can think of few better scriptures than the names of the men and women who died alongside me because that was their Emperor-given duty.'

Baragry nodded, understanding straight away, and blessed her with the sign of the aquila. Calpurnia returned it as best she could and walked out of the Cathedral. She had dismissed her guard when the service had ended and now walked alone down the ramp, studying the carvings under her feet. She had decided she was going to learn the stories of all the Segmentum Pacificus saints they depicted. Maybe Leandro or one of the precinct chaplains could teach them to her. There was a clean cool breeze coming in from the mountains – wet season on the way, people were saying – that lapped around the Cathedral spires and tousled her hair, and for the first time in three days the micro membrane repairs to her eardrums seemed to be itching a little less as they healed.

She stowed the scroll in her belt and rested her other hand on the hilt of her maul. Her new maul, presented by Dvorov from his own armoury to replace the one the servitor had crushed, the one that she had first been given at Machiun. That had been a classic Ultima pattern maul, short and heavy, unadorned, best for choppy strokes. The new one was a Hydraphur style, longer, lighter and slenderer, with a spiked handguard that made it impossible to perform the grip-reverse manoeuvres she had been trained in. Her old maul had been blunt and powerful, effective as a truncheon even without the power field, able to break bones with choppy strokes; the new one carried less weight of its own and needed greater finesse, almost a fencing technique, lightly jabbing with the tip and letting the power field do the rest. She supposed she would get used to it.

Her Rhino waited out beyond the ramp, engine idling, ready to carry her away down the Mesé and back to the wall. She could see her guard around it, one at each corner, and caught herself wondering which one was Bannon before she pushed the thought away and kept walking.

There was a knot of subdued colours at the foot of the slope, a pack of funeral-goers who had stopped to talk before they went on their way. They noticed her, and the conversation fell silent. Arbitor and citizens regarded one another for a moment, then the group parted uncertainly to let her through.

She knew they would never forgive her. She knew as well as they that Hallyan Kalfus-Medell had died an excommunicate criminal, officially unmourned. And she knew as well as they that it didn't matter – she was a crude outworlder and he had been one of their own.

One of the last to move aside was a young girl in purple-black with an odd dark mask – not a mask at all, Calpurnia realised, but a catastrophic bruise, a ridge of swollen black flesh across the bridge of her nose, fading to deep yellow on her cheeks and forehead where it had begun to heal. It was several seconds before Calpurnia realised who it was.

'Lady Keta,' she said, and tipped up her new maul in a token salute. The girl flinched, and Calpurnia looked into her watery grey eyes.

She wondered if she could ever explain it to the girl. She doubted it. She could even see herself through their eyes, all cruel smile and weapon flourished in their faces, the new bully revelling in their submission, the new power who had destroyed her enemy and was setting herself up in his place. That was how their minds worked.

One day, she promised herself, she would sit down with Keta, or Athian Tymon-Per, or whichever of them she thought she could persuade to listen, and try to make them see. She would read them the maxims she had learned on Ultramar, get out her old children's primers if she had to. She would talk to them about her duty, about Law and honour. That the Law could be cold and the Law could be cruel but the Law was their guard and guide and peacekeeper and protector. She would try to talk to them about doing what was right.

All of this passed through her mind in a long, silent moment there before the Cathedral. But right at this moment she had work to do. Silent, eyes streaming, the other woman stepped aside and Shira Calpurnia, Arbitor Senioris of Hydraphur, walked proudly past her and away to where her Arbites were waiting.

CROSSFIRE

A DOSSIER

Excerpts from A Pilgrim's Letters – Journeys Along the Roads of the Faithful by Jendro Galimet.

Jendro Galimet was a product of the gentry of Bunikel's World, whose aristocratic traditions decree that one child of each family generation forgo entry to the Imperial officer corps and pursue a religious vocation instead. After his schooling Galimet chose a life of pilgrimage, vowing to perform his family's traditional obeisances at Ophelia, Chiros, Hydraphur and Avignor before he died. He kept up a prolific correspondence and his collected letters, published by his family after his death in M37.878, remain a popular religious and inspirational treatise.

We broke warp at Hydraphur early in the second shift, and about our staterooms there was an excitement and a vigour, not only for the lifting of the oppression of the transit but with our proximity to our goal. The new shine to the air was shared among all except P, who had expressed much desire to visit the lower decks and see the festivities among the massed travellers but was constrained by myself, with S and her sister and I being required to take inventory of the blessed tokens we had brought from Avignor and from Mere's Reach, for which I commanded his assistance. P made much of his surly mood during the exercise, with the intention, I have no doubt, of putting the rest of the company out of countenance, and once a second inventory confirmed the first I struck him and instructed him to recite his litany by his cot. As we were obliged to remain quartered and I could not send him to the deck's chapel.

The ship's officer-at-arms and two of his company visited us nearly two hours after the klaxon to take our measure and confirm our safe passage, but even once we were declared untouched we were still to remain in our staterooms. S's sister was vexed by this and shared her sentiments with some others who had come out of their own quarters into the central processional, the whole conversation in such strong voice as to catch the ears of the armsmen, and to earn a thick ear in return for one young gallant of Ciskura Tertia who was minded to try to get his own way with them. Such an order, so strictly enforced, has been outside my experience, even for rough transits such as the Peacock Breach. Nor is the *Rose of Gathalle* a craft burdened by age, such as my uncle had described to us from his travels on the Ghydd Passage, in which you will recall the Mechanicus adepts had been obliged to conserve the craft's strength by rationing the ship's gravity for some of the voyage.

We remained in such confinement for both of the following shifts, our spirits in increasing distress, until word came that we were standing off from one of the major outer Gates - such is the term for the great fortified stations that throng the twin ecliptics of Hydraphur. We made some haste and pains to render ourselves presentable, thinking we were to meet with officials of the fleet, but the *Rose* was not boarded for another three shifts, or full ship-day, which saw us voyage further in-system and moor at another Gate for our inspection. This was much upon the order of such affairs throughout my travels: clerks and servitors of the Administratum passing among us to take our measures and business, but with them came a corps of men and women of the Battlefleet in such finery as to make themselves the centre of the spectacle, in uniforms of glossy green silk with braids and chains of all styles and colours in great variety, the meaning of them beyond my grasp. I had made to greet them, thinking this to fulfil what courtly manners might desire, but upon my approach their demeanour became fierce and proud and they made clear by the set of their stances and the jut of their jaws that they wanted none of me.

Such was our experience at three more Gates, the names of which were not divulged to me. Our movements between these Gates made up four more ship-days, during which my impatience tested the nerves of my companions greatly, we being confined first to quarters, and then allowed only about a small portion of the deck. It brought not a whit of cheer to know that others were taking the matter equally as hard, and in fact on the third day I observed armsmen descend upon a suite at the near end of our deck to carry off the sire of a noble petitioner's family who had taken this regime very much ill and attempted to duel none other than his infant son. S and I did pray for boy and man both, but I will confess that S lifted our spirits by composing impish accounts of how such a duel might have turned out.

By the fifth day we were permitted forward into the gallery decks, and availed ourselves of the sight of the world of Hydraphur and its encircling Ring. This latter is a wonder to compare with any I have seen on my travels, striking in my mind the likeness of the curtain-walls that surrounded the great temple fortresses of Gaer Boll against the greenskin, but wrought on so much larger a scale, hanging in space and disappearing from view as it curved away around the edges of the world. We marvelled at its great bastions and towers, marching along the Ring and jutting out into space, and at the great ranks of lights, the banks of weapons, and the statuary and gargoyle-work to fend off the malignities of space and please the all-seeing gaze of Him on Earth. In amongst these, visible between the great ships moored at the docks with which the Ring is surrounded, we made out stranger constructions, brighter and more angular than the familiar shapes of the bastions, and I was able to explain to S that these were the homes of the Adeptus Mechanicus priest-engineers whose Emperor-appointed gift and duty it is to forge these structures and tend the machine-mysteries that keep them alive.

Much though we were chattering amongst ourselves at its first sight, I can record that all the company fell silent as we approached the Ring. We had expected to take shuttle to travel to it and thence to the Bosporian Hive, but truly we had misapprehended what with the God-Emperor's blessing the human hand can make. Our ship, which even at station at Avignor had had to stand off from station and receive her passengers and provisions through her craft (if, Emperor willing, my letter from the start of the journey has reached you then you shall have my account of it) came in to moor directly at the Ring, as though she were naught more than a lander shuttle or a ship's pinnace! Later in our descent I was to learn that even the mightiest warships of the Fleet Pacificus are able to dock directly at the Ring, which can moor and sustain a squadron of them with ease, and that Navy crews consider it an omen of good luck to spend a shift docked at the Ring before their craft strikes out on its new voyage.

The letters of passage, which we had been furnished with by our kindly and excellent Reverend at the Cathedral of Avignor, were already known to the Naval officials who govern the outer fortress of the Ring and we were met by an officer of the watch who greeted us by name and gave warm and pious thanks to Him on Earth for our safe emergence from deep-voyaging (this being the Hydraphur idiom for that part of a star voyage undertaken through the warp). The fact of the letters now being properly known to the authorities of the Ring, our interlocutor, a subaltern G, being most attentive in conveying us through the scrutiny of the dock guards. We passed from the ship's boarding pens amid great clamour, the pilgrims and travellers from the mass-transit decks being mustered in a great press through the docking assemblies and raising great shouts and imprecations at the armsmen who were keeping them in order with some force while our own company and those from the upper decks debarked. Our subaltern informed us as we moved through the Ring that many such travellers leave the mass decks under the misapprehension that they are already at Hydraphur, and offer fight to the officials in their path in the belief that the gates of the Cathedral lie just beyond their ships' portals, so eager are they for the ease of their souls.

The ease of our own souls was somewhat disturbed by the passage to our shuttle on the Ring's inner docks. No sooner were we past the commotion of the boarding pens than we detected a high keening sound, at first so faint that we were barely sensible to it, but then becoming lower and guttural. S and I looked at one another in some perturbation but our guide appeared to pay the sound no mind, and nor to my surprise did P, from which I took reassurance, remembering the voidborn's intuition for such things. Next came another note, a deep thrum similar to a drawn bass bowchord note, with an unexpected music such that I found myself looking up and down the narrow little passage for vox-horns, thinking that a hymn was about to play to mark the hour. Our subaltern noticed our disconcert, however, and explained to us as we rode a small railcar through to the planetary docks that the mighty Ring has been fashioned to flex and yield with the tidal forces that Hydraphur's moon and fellow-worlds exert upon it, and such a motion often causes sounds and winds as the great fortress subtly adjusts and deforms. He observed that the Ring had been 'in fine voice' for the previous four planetary days, and that 'she had good news'; we drew from this that some aboard the Ring read omens and portents from the constant sounds around them, a thought which was confirmed by our subsequent conversations.

[*The more moneyed or connected pilgrims tend to take shuttle at the Ring and proceed directly to land at or near the Bosporian Hive. Galimet, thorough as always in his devotions, took the more common route, riding down with his companions on the mass haulers down to the equatorial archipelagos to make ritual ablutions in the sea. The route then travels up the tablelands of the northern continent to the conurbations at the Dardanne cliffs, which form another staging point before the next leg of the journey up the specially-built pilgrims' highways to Constanta Hive and thence across the mountains to Bosporian. The next excerpt picks up on this latter approach.*]

We travelled up the side of the Bosporian Hive along the Telepine Way, a sturdy road cut sharp into the side of the mountain, and mountain it is, Bosporian being not a hive after the style of our own stately towers on Bunikel nor of those of Leyate (from which your letter had informed me that my cousins have lately been wont to travel for their selection of spouses, upon which I shall await our father's correspondence with interest), but indeed a simple city, dense though it is, spreading up the side of the mountain to the enclosed keep at the peak. It had been the subject of some humour among our hosts at Constanta Hive that the Monocrat should be so determined that the planetary capital should be named a hive, in the face of this physical fact, and even the Adeptus following his suit.

Although the condition of the canopy prevented us from a proper view, as we ascended we were able to make out the fringe city spreading out from the hive foot and around the arms of the bay. The city is a fine one, thick with towers, steeples and the firestacks of many forges and manufactories. I described in my last letter the orange colour of Hydraphur daylight, and the smoke layer over the city combines with the light to shade it in perpetual twilight. While I have seen grander constructions in my travels, there was something quietly marvellous in the building lights and beacons glowing beneath the smoke layer like tethered sparks, and the dark shapes of airships hanging in formation over the bay, with the gigacarriers moving beneath them in the water among crane arrays that put me in the mind of the bare-limbed trees in our own chapel gardens at the season's turn toward winter.

Of the flank of the hive itself we could see little, the whole side of the mountain from foot to crown being covered in towers and blocks with their foundations sunk deep into the slopes, or sometimes built out from the sheerer faces on great buttresses. The great roads up and down the sides of the hive are most commonly used by the plain traffic of the city, but our Way was that which led to the pilgrims' quarter and here it was thronged with our fellow travellers. P was amused (to a degree not altogether fitting, in S's sentiments) at the manner in which the joyous energy with which the pilgrims had flocked to the foot of the road had been exhausted by the steep climb; the movement of the crowds around our carrier was sluggish and their postures stooped. Bustling among them, discernible both by their brighter garb and their higher spirits, came merchants and hawkers of all descriptions, shouting their wares to the climbing crowds. Many were holding up the manner of trinkets and talismans which have become so familiar to me on my travels, and which I am sure will be likewise familiar to you from my relating, but in addition to the aquilae and dolmeni terra I saw many works peculiar to the system and to local customs of worship. One device which I saw repeated in many forms was a crown-like emblem of three lesser points and one greater, which I understand to echo the design of the hive's peak, with the spires of the Monocrat's palace and the Cathedral spire overshadowing them. Another was a pair of oval hoops joined at the base and spreading in the manner of an eagle's wings, representing the twin ecliptics of the Hydraphur system which form the echo of the triumphant eagle when viewed from the direction of Terra. This device was often worked in gold or bronze to a great artistry by the crafters who make their home on the hive-flank, as well as on banners and phylacteries. We saw at least two traders plying their trade with a small gas-torch and a branding-iron, rendering the emblem directly onto pilgrims' skins for a small coin.

As we ascended and the exhaustion of the pilgrims around the carrier became more noticeable, S became distressed at a practice we saw several of these hawkers using, selecting a climbing pilgrim and blocking their way further up the road, relying on their mark's fatigue to prevent them from quickly stepping up and around them or offering resistance. My own ire at this matched S's distress, and at my direction P leapt from the carrier and belaboured the hawker with both his words and his staff, driving him to the edge of the road and allowing the pilgrims to climb onward.

I should remark upon the great variety of travellers with which we found ourselves surrounded, for as we climbed I had my data-slate upon my knee to record them.

Transcript from mid-trial conference in the prosecution of Shemmerik Lyze of the House Lyze, called by Praetor-Declamator Secundus Yoss Durrandi; eighth day of Umberi/day six of the trial.

Present: Praetor Durrandi; Detective-Intelligentser Falk Doberak; Detective Hurshant Holg, representing the near-orbit garrison command; Senior Chastener Koswin Bura. Also in attendance: Praetor-Laureate Umry, staffer to the Arbitor Senioris; Lead Arbitor Carthes, staffer to the Praetor; Savant Blohemm, scriptor-adjutant to the Detective-Intelligencer; Savant Mowir, court scribe.

Meeting convened at conference chambers of the upper fourth Praetory in the Wall at 17.30 hours.

Transcript begins.

DURRANDI: I formally convene. All obedience to Him on Earth.

ALL: Praise and obedience.

DURRANDI: I shall not have this running long, colleagues; I expect to have a lot to cover in this evening's trial session and I haven't eaten in nearly nine hours. I propose we quickly make sure our offices are in step on the prosecution and adjourn with minimum fuss. Speaking of our various offices, let the record show the attendance of Praetor Umry on behalf of the Arbitor Senioris Calpurnia, and my appreciation that the arbitor senioris is active on this matter so soon in her recuperation from her injuries. Thank you.

UMRY: Thank you, sir. Noted for conveyance.

DURRANDI: Well then. Strategy so far has been to remain fairly quiet and let Lyze go through his initial self-denunciations and pleadings. Done on his behalf by professionals, of course, but you'll note that the Lyze have hired very much from the middle rank, not the sort of divas you'd expect their resources to command. His family's disassociating from him, and they're not being subtle about it. They're scrambling to try and quarantine the knowledge of the senior family's conspiracy, and they haven't yet realised how much we've uncovered about the rot through the whole household. It smacks of desperation and sloppy strategy. Intelligentser, I'd like your judgement on how likely the Lyze are to switch to a turncoat strategy as we start peeling Shemmerik's defences off in the dock.

DOBERAK: I'll make a fuller report on this after today, but actually our assessment is that House Lyze is going to stick by Shemmerik. They've been badly hobbled by this and they need assets like him. Established, connected, politically capable. They'll salvage him if they can.

HOLG: Impudent bastards, aren't they?

UMRY: A similar thought was going through my mind, by your leave, Praetor. There'd been something of the feel in the arbitor senioris's offices that the Lyze family wouldn't survive.

HOLG: Mamzel Calpurnia's feeling on the matter or your own?

UMRY: Her, well, I mean both. She was there to see Therion Lyze's corpse being cremated by the Sororitas. That seemed to us to be a lethal disgrace on so many levels. I for one wasn't expecting a family to be able to come back from it. We were taking the implosion of the Kalfus family as our example.

HOLG: But Kalfus arguably *was* the Medell syndicate. None of the other family groups have what it takes to prop up Medell on the Hydraphur side, and everything I have on the outsystem half of Medell says that they'll just cut their losses. Lyze-Haggan is a different matter. They're trying to make a display of the fact that they can handle a body blow like Adeptus scrutiny – you probably need to write this down, Umry, it'll bear on your briefing.

UMRY: Getting it this way, sir. Cortical augmetics. With respect.

HOLG: Hm. Well, the power equilibrium in the Hydraphur half of the Haggan is much more evenly distributed. Lyze being disgraced won't end the syndicate. Dreiter-Haggan and Kotzuka Haggan are both potent enough to keep the syndicate powerful. Even if it's a lethal disgrace, as you called it. And Lyze are useful because they're twined so deeply into the orbit-lifting business.

UMRY: So they're a spacegoing family? The senioris has asked me about this in some depth. She wants to know if they've had a hand in any of the related incidents we've had further out in the ecliptics.

DOBERAK: I'll not be thought disrespectful to my Emperor-instated superiors, Praetor, but how is the senioris's grasp of the Hydraphur partition and the nature of the syndicates?

UMRY: She understands the partition clearly. It's just that the operations of the syndicates tend to be idiosyncratic and I think that with Lyze's close ties to outer-orbit interests the details are harder to–

HOLG: Idiosyncrasies or no, House Lyze have no direct interests in anything outside the orbit of the Ring. Partition is partition. Since the day of the decree the Arbites have–

DURRANDI: That's enough, both of you. Your zeal in defending your respective commanders and operations is noted for the records. Be satisfied. The Throne Watches.

UMRY: The Throne Watches. Thank you, sir.

HOLG: The Throne Watches. Very well. Lyze are highly active in space operations on the Hydraphur side of the partition. They operate shuttle runs and cargo lifts to the Ring and have controlling interests in planetside final-stage fuel refinement and landing-dock operation. They have heavy influences in most of the inner-orbit pilot guilds. The Coydo-Haggan family have the contract to tend to the needs of the six biggest Mechanicus enginewright cloisters on the inner Ring, but they got that through Lyze manipulation and they're so totally beholden as a result that it's effectively a Lyze operation.

DOBERAK: That's all within the Ring. If the arbitor senioris is interested in business further out, you may wish to mention to her that House Lyze have been steadily cultivating connections into the Administratum satrapy for planetary Hydraphur, lobbying for a commission to aggregate and ferry up the Hydraphur tithe. That's their corridor through the partition laws to be able to deal with the Navy procurators. That makes the Lyze family the crucial connection for the whole planetside Haggan syndicate.

DURRANDI: Your command sent me a breakdown on this, Hurshant, but it's useful to hear it so succinctly. Thank you. I expect that the Praetor shares my sentiments.

UMRY: The... Yes, of course, thank you, detective. If the arbitor senioris requests a copy of the breakdown brief you just mentioned, what may I tell her?

HOLG: I'll have a copy delivered in the morning, per yourself, if that suits.

UMRY: It does, thank you. The aquila provides.

BURA: Speaking of providing, sorry, do I understand that the Lyze are going to be controlling the tithe-flow to the Navy as well as via the Administratum? That wasn't in the interrogation parameters that came with the family prisoners after their compound got purged. Do I need to change them?

DURRANDI: Not yet. I've been reviewing the transcripts from your castigation sessions and I think that you can continue as you are for the time being. Once the denunciation phase of the trial is over we can confer on whether the Lyze pleadings require any shift in the work you're doing.

BURA: Understood. Thank you, sir.

DOBERAK: By way of context, however, so that we're all aware of the broader pattern, Lyze don't and can't tithe directly to the Navy. The output from all the other worlds and stations in this whole system go straight into the Battlefleet Pacificus stores because they're Battlefleet facilities. Or they're owned by hereditary officer household concerns with exclusive contracts to the Fleet, but it's the same thing. The partition laws excise the world of Hydraphur from the military so it tithes to the Administratum exactly like any other world, technically.

HOLG: Technically is right. The Administratum classes a lot of the trade that comes up through the Ring docks as part of Hydraphur's tithe. Anything the planetary producers funnel to the outworld half of their syndicate and from there to the Battlefleet squadrons: wines from the Heshmara lowlands, silks, optics from the Constanta Hive foundries, syrup-spices–

DURRANDI: You're reminding me how long ago my last meal was, Hurshant, and it's getting longer.

HOLG: Apologies for the digression. So a lot of that manages to get aggregated into Hydraphur's general tithe, which makes it cheap for the Navy who pick it up off the out-of-orbit half of the syndicates, and still fantastically profitable for the in-orbit syndicate halves. And that wealth has a way of percolating back out through the partition. It's a constant job digging into Administratum affairs and rooting out the trades that have gone too far. There's a fashion coming in for importing goods from all over the sector to 'tithe' back out as part of the syndicate trade, too.

BURA: Which has been restricted too, correct? I'm sure I have a couple of people on my prisoner rolls…

HOLG: Correct. Anyway, it's why Lyze were hatching the plots they were and it's why the blasted little ring that Dwerr was part of went and helped them. Each one was trying to prove they had what it took to play at the biggest table.

UMRY: And to hark back to the beginning of the discussion, by continuing the Lyze prosecutions, we're allowing them the chance to show that off even more by surviving our attentions. Do I have that right?

DURRANDI: The potential for that exists. You observe acutely, Praetor, thank you. With that, please accept an adjournment until after Trial Part Thirty-Two when we'll reconvene this group. This has been valuable, thank you all. *Vox Legi, Vox Imperator.*

Meeting adjourned

Preface from a pre-inaugural briefing prepared for Master Ordinate Yakulius Bo of the Administratum, shortly before his accession as Grand Master Ordinate of Praefectural Logistics (Acting) in the Kunvazi Sector.

This briefing is intended for Your Serene Presence to re-familiarise yourself with those elements of the Adeptus Arbites with which the Grand Master Ordinate *etc., etc.,* may be called upon to interact. In accordance with Your Serene Presence's request, a focus is kept on differences emerging between the planetary and subsector level.

It is understood that Your Serene Presence's previous post in the field logistics of tithe collection and acquittal has included interaction with arbitrator garrisons, particularly during the Baello-Beukin hive culls and the Second Queue War on Hougeran Tertia. The central brief will therefore not presume to offer further detail of the on-ground operations of Precinct-based arbitrator forces. (Should Your Serene Presence wish this information for purposes of completeness, your attention is respectfully directed to Section K, and to Appendices B and G as well as attachment F.) The duties of the Grand Master Ordinate *etc., etc.,* will more generally require dealings with the Judicial arm of the Arbites rather than the Militant.

I) A structural overview

I-a) It is respectfully recommended to Your Serene *etc.,* to have in mind that these two types of Arbitor referred to hereabove are indeed formal divisions, whose separate natures are as clear to the Arbites as the differences between an Ordinate Executor and an Ordinate Parajunct are to ourselves. Passage out of the organisation's base ranks places an Arbitor onto the lowest rungs of one of the central *cursi:* the *Aedile* (Arbitrator) or *Praetor* (Judge). The full structure of ranks of the Arbites is of a complexity that rivals some of our own Administratum bureaux (a map of observed ranks is respectfully submitted at Attachment B and a conjectural full rank map based on the work of the Intradeptine Directorate is at Appendix P), but the two central cursi form its foundation and core. As these two diverge from base ranks, so do they re-merge at the topmost echelon, the Arbites General, a supreme command structure which intermingles Arbites from both specialisations.

I-a-i) (Your Serene *etc.*, may wish to also familiarise yourself with the abbreviated rank map at Section A-A2 of the full briefing, and the commentary offered at Attachment D, concerning the sub-specialisations that branch off from the central *cursi.* Of note because of their visibility may be the Chasteners, whose speciality is the capture, interrogation and punishment of prisoners. Of note because of their involvement with other Adeptus are the Detectives, whose activities are more heavily protected by the Arbites' secrecy measures but who are believed to control surveillance, infiltration, intelligence, and the informant and agent provocateur networks. It is humbly recommended that briefings on known Detective activity be made face-to-face under certain privacy protocols with which Your Serene *etc.*, is understood to be familiar. The Arbites also maintain sub-specialisations along familiar patterns such as garrison chaplains and preachers, ordained tech-ministers and armourers, savants, medicae and similar.)

II) Precincts and their Hierarchy

II-a) The Precincts of the Arbites follow an organisational principle broadly similar to those laid down in our own tithing and governance structures, although it is asked that Your Serene *etc.*, pardon the personal observation that without the traditions and insights of the Administratum to guide them, their organisation must inevitably lack the inspiration and elegance of the structures laid out in the *Res Demograf* or the *Principia Administrata.* Nonetheless, their essential cell, their Precinct, will generally correspond to the divisions of population, moderated by demographic and political assessments. The attention of Your Serene *etc.*, is humbly drawn to the information at Annexes D, N and V in Appendix K, detailing examples of observed Precinct organisational principles and conjectures as to the policies on their variations, principally the relatively sparse Precinct structure for the low and scattered population of Kedunis Mundi (tithe grade Invidita Secundus) and the considerably denser network of Precincts that govern the hives and force-farm stacks of Spaaken (tithe grade Copis Optima). Further briefings on these or any other Precinct organisations within our Subsector are available upon Your Serene *etc.*,'s request.

II-b) It is humbly and respectfully submitted that Your Serene *etc.*'s needs may centre more on knowledge of the higher Precinct structures, and therefore on Sections B-D97.7 to C12 inclusive, G557 and T8 to T93-V5 inclusive of the main briefing. For brevity, the Precincts within a system will generally interlock to form a *Precinct Superior*, which it is understood is often referred to in Arbites circles with the Low Gothic of a 'System Precinct'. Lacking the fine mastery of organisation and co-ordination displayed by our own Emperor-blessed traditions, the Arbites choose to impose an organisational break point at the point in which transit *per immateria* becomes necessary for contact with the broader organisation. The Arbitor who constitutes the highest rank in a Precinct Superior will take on the honorary Low Gothic title of 'Commander of Court' in addition to whichever title their rank currently earns them.

II-c) A network of Precincts Superior will form a *High Precinct*, which may make up several systems but which does not necessarily (and frequently will not in actuality) be congruent to the subsector-sector hierarchy which delineates our own splendid works. (An analysis of known exceptions is presented at Attachment L.) High Precincts interlock in turn to form the *Great Precinct*, whose boundaries, like the High Precinct's, will often defy our own Sector boundaries, and the *Grand Precinct* continues to build upon the

Great Precinct before the Arbites at last submit to the inevitable order and divide their penultimate commands according to the Imperial Segmentae before the pinnacle of command in the person of the Grand Provost Marshal.

II-d) A subsidiary structure which it is considered worth holding up to the light of Your Serene *etc.*'s attention is the Arbites fleet. It is regretted that organisational details for this body are difficult to confirm with certainty, although Section E-44 of the main brief and Attachment S and its annex B2 contain observed and conjectural details respectively. The fleets constitute mobile forces able to reinforce the work of the planetary precincts with resources both of judicial expertise and scholarship, and considerable military and paramilitary force; observations suggest that the fleets operate very much within the arbitrator *cursus* and their primary function is the exertion of armed might in support of their planetary colleagues. Fleet commands follow a command hierarchy not dissimilar to the fixed hierarchy discussed elsewhere, and it is respectfully suggested that they might usefully be considered as spaceborne Precincts in this regard.

II-e) By the general disposition of Arbites ranks the commanders of the Precinct Superior and upward will be drawn from the highest echelon of ranks, the Arbites General. The pattern we have most commonly observed is for a Precinct Superior to be commanded by an arbitor senioris, a High Precinct by an Arbitor Majore, a Great Precinct by an Arbitor Imprimis and a Grand Precinct by an Arbitor Majestas. The most common Low Gothic titles matching these ranks are High Marshal, Lady/Lord Marshal, Grand Marshal, Lord Grand Marshal, although by the indulgence of Your Serene *etc.* a case study of known variations and exceptions to this pattern appears at Annex II to Attachment S with associated and annotated references at Appendix 4-W and a connection is respectfully pointed out to (III), below.

★ ★ ★

III) The Hydraphur High Precinct

III-a) While it is confidently speculated that the sphere of administration to which Your Serene *etc.*'s attention will most worthily reside is the Kunvazi Sector. It is humbly raised to your attention that the Kunvazi Precinct Superior has tended to be the secondary Arbites power-base for consideration in matters pertaining to the work of the Grand Master *etc., etc.* Due to a confluence of traditions, historical circumstances and conjectured power balances within the Arbites hierarchy of the Pacifica Fidelis Great Precinct (a thesis on the details of such circumstances is present at Annex IV to Attachment S), the Hydraphur High Precinct forms both a symbolic and actual power base for Arbites operations throughout their own Sector and the bordering Sectors, including our own.

III-b) A full account of the physical and organisational disposition of the Hydraphur High Precinct Command, as prepared jointly by the Satrapic and Supradeptine Cloisters of the Transmilitant Prefecture Bureau under co-ordination of the General Directorate of Transcommunicate Data Preservation, is presented at Attachment S-15 and the relevant attached annexes V through XII shall be brought before Your Serene *etc.* upon direction. It is humbly suggested that the following particular aspects are those which may benefit the most from Your Serene *etc.*'s early attention.

III-b-i) The Hydraphur High Precinct's jurisdiction is complicated by the partition of the Hydraphur system itself, under which edict the world of Hydraphur is excised from Navy control while the remainder of the system continues in its military function. The Arbitor Majore must therefore not only run a command across two very different populations, but administer the laws of the partition itself, ensuring that the activities of planetary concerns onworld, and both Naval and civil concerns offworld, interact in a manner becoming of, and obedient to, Imperial law.

III-b-ii) The Arbitor Majore of Hydraphur, Krieg Dvorov, was promoted into the Arbites General from the Praetor ranks, although the observation is made that his administration displays what might be considered a reckless disregard for the established and continuous practice. Three arbitor senioris report directly to the Arbitor, although in breach of convention these are not attached to a specific geographic command or function but are utilised for a variety of tasks on an ad-hoc basis. Currently two of these positions are filled, namely by Arbites Nestor Leandro and Ryo Nakayama. It is understood that processes to appoint a candidate to the currently vacant third position are under way. A list of likely appointees will be made available to Your Serene *etc.* as soon as it is made known.

III-b-iii) Both the Judicial and Militant arms of the Arbites operating in this sector have been heavily influenced by procedure and loyalty to the Hydraphur High Precinct. Grand Praetor-Dignitary Liomu and many influential members of her staff all began the substantive part of their judicial careers at the scholastic facilities at Hydraphur, either contained in the command fortress known as 'The Wall' or at the separate campus of 'Trylan Tor'. Fleet-Marshal Laureate Treneal has commanded fleetborne precincts under now-Arbitor Senioris Nakayama and served on Arbitor Majore Dvorov's staff. Both are understood to have notable personal loyalty to the Arbitor Majore, complementing the command chains that pass through Hydraphur on their way to the Pacifica Fidelis Great Precinct command.

Prepared for the seal of: Acting Chief of Staff to the Head of Office to the Grand Master Ordinate of Praefectural Logistics.

LEGACY

PROLOGUE

THEIR LORD AND master had been carried into the trees at the opening of the day, and instead of the morning clarion, the halls of the flotilla's spacecraft had rung with a single soft mourning-chime. Those appointed to it followed the catafalque into the arboretum deck, through the shin-high mint-grass with the insects around them chirruping in the morning air. The creatures had been chosen from a dozen worlds for the beauty of their sounds, both individual and in choir, and although the lord was too close to death to be able to hear them he would have been happy with the sounds in these his last hours.

Galt stood one rank back from the catafalque, head bowed, the white linen of the cover-cloth glimmering like summer cloud across the top of his vision. He wore the white gown and black shawl that they all did; his face, as all of theirs, was painted with the intricate downward-curving black and white patterns of mourning. The paint was mixed with an anaesthetic that deadened the face and numbed his skin to the feel of the warm artificial breeze, but he could still feel the stir of the cloth and the brush of the grass against his legs and his bare feet. He stood looking at the grass below and in front of his laced hands, and now that the moment they had all been preparing for had come he found that his mind was empty and calm. He welcomed the sensation – he was too tired to carry any more emotion after the past year.

They stood and waited. The two black-hooded senior medicae standing on either side of the catafalque were the only ones to move, following the movements of their diagnostor, a silver replica of a human heart with spidery mechanical hands growing from its sides, as it glided slowly to and fro about the lord's head.

Time passed. The singing of the insects was a soothing counterpoint to the lazy sounds of the carefully-choreographed breezes in the arboretum's trees.

And finally, after who knew how long, Galt blinked as the medicae took a signal from the diagnostor and dismissed the machine, sending it coasting away. Those present stepped away in silent synchronisation, turning their backs to the catafalque and the body upon it. A sigh seemed to run through them all. There were no cries, no staggering or tearing of hair, just that slackening and release. They had all known too well for too long what was coming to respond any other way.

Galt's thoughts were still quiet and empty with the same exhaustion that he sensed in the others. Something had ended, something had moved on, and now they themselves were free to return to their own lives. For now it was enough to stand in the warm still air of the arboretum and sink into reflection, but soon everything would begin to change.

Their lord and master, Rogue Trader Hoyyon Phrax, was dead. It was time to set course for Hydraphur.

CHAPTER ONE

The Avenue Solar, Outskirts of Bosporian Hive, Hydraphur

THEY WALKED, THE arbitor and the priest, in an amiable promenade beneath the great shoulder of the hive. Cool moist breezes set the cages overhead creaking on their chains, and the occasional shower of excrement pattered down around them.

At this end of the Avenue Solar, the footbridges connecting the towering urban stacks had grown together into a roof over the crowded truckways below. It was ungainly and humpbacked, following the arch that most of the footbridges had originally been designed with, a jigsaw of rockcrete, gritty asphalt, flagstones and tiles. Here and there were odd-shaped gaps where the space between intersecting bridges hadn't quite been worth covering over and, even at this distance, Shira Calpurnia could hear the never-ending rumble of traffic beneath them.

A splat against the cloth over her head reminded her that it was not what was beneath their feet that concerned her today, and she looked up. The canopy was embroidered with devotional scenes and Ecclesiarchal livery, held above them on poles by six impassive Cathedral deacons. A thick blob of muck had landed on a panel showing an angel of the Emperor blessing the battlefleet. It was taking more and more effort for Calpurnia to keep the disgust from her face.

'We'll be clear of them in a moment,' Reverend Simova told her, anticipating her thoughts. 'It's a little uncomfortable to see, but then a citizen who behaved as they should wouldn't be up there in the first place. Soiling a sacred image is simply one more thing that they will pay for.' As they moved toward the edge of the bridge the deacons shuffled away with the canopy and they looked at the scene above them.

Calpurnia could see why the Eparch had chosen the Avenue Solar for his display. It was a place for awe. Here at the foot of the Bosporian, the capital city-hive of the world of Hydraphur, the towers of the sprawling lower city were the highest and most forbidding, rearing into the copper sky towards the pale band of the orbiting Ring. Classical Imperial architecture had a pattern and a purpose: it existed to symbolise implacable might and everlasting grandeur, and the sky-scraping towers to either side presented sheer cliffs of wall, intimidating overhangs and the stern gaze of statues to cow anyone who looked up at them. The design had been repeated all the way back down the avenue, making it a great deep canyon full of engine-noise that boomed off the high buildings.

And then in front of them, greater and taller still, the sloping side of the Bosporian itself, tier after tier of wall and buttress, glittering windows and polished statues, the steep zigzag of the Ascendant Way climbing up to the walls of the Augustaeum at the mountain's crown. From here the paired spikes of the Monocrat's palace and the Cathedral of the Emperor Ascendant were invisible, but the great mass of the hive was sight enough.

With that sight to arrest the eye, the cages shrank to an afterthought, a cluster of flyspecks. They were strung like party-lanterns on great swoops of black chain, each link so large that Calpurnia could have put her fist through its centre without touching the edges, held up by girders that Ministorum work crews had driven into the skyscraper walls. The metal was still smooth and shiny, the rivets and padlocks on the cage doors bright and new. The Eparchal decree that had ordered the cages strung up was less than a fortnight old.

'There seems to be something about this tradition that brings out the very worst in some of the penitents. I was with the Eparch during his tenure in the Phaphan subdiocese, and we had exactly the same problem. Hence...' he made a gesture with a red-and-grey-sleeved arm. Calpurnia looked off to her left.

A narrow set of bleachers had been set up at the foot of the arching bridge and when Calpurnia looked at them, she had to rein in a smile. Thirty Ecclesiarchal officers in dark red and bone-white cassocks, Wardens of the Cathedrals Ordeatic Chamber, were crammed in ten to a bench, packed almost shoulder to shoulder, their poses identical: hands laced demurely in laps, faces staring ahead in earnest concentration. By each man sat a little tripod bearing a brass casing no bigger than a pistol-clip, and from each casing a single unblinking metal eye stared. Each was fixed on a different cage, and every man on the bleachers had had their right eye replaced with a receptor for the cable feed; the flesh around the sockets was still raw from the newness of the graft. She suppressed a smile again – as soon as she had seen them she had thought of a row of birdwatchers, all sharing the same cramped hide and now fixated on a flock of some rare specimen preening itself in front of them.

'One for each cage.' Simova expanded his gesture to point at the chains and cages behind them. 'The mechanical eye keeps a pict-record – that's kept in the Cathedral permanently – but the controlling elements are members of our own clergy, not servitors. That's important. Before anyone in the cages is deemed absolved and brought down, the Warden watching his cage has to confirm that they have not compounded their sins in any way. That's how whoever was pelting us with filth is going to be made to pay. I wish I knew what it was about this punishment that makes people do that.'

Calpurnia didn't respond immediately. She was looking at the cages, hands behind her back, face expressionless. In the near cages the penitents were visible, some grasping the bars to peer down at them, some rocking back and forth and setting their cages swinging, some slumped down, the occasional arm or leg hanging through gaps in the floor-bars. One, the nearest, whose cage was hanging above the most soiled stretch of paving, was crouched over the little slop-bucket bolted to the bars and busily scooping something up in its fingers. Higher up the figures were just grimy, ragged silhouettes against the distant hive wall; the furthest cages were no more than dots. She took off her helmet and squinted at the highest, hanging in the centre of the street, but it was impossible to see what, if anything, the person inside it was doing.

It seemed there was still some time left, and keeping Simova talking was as good a way of passing it as any. She pointed to where a knot of junior deacons stood donning rubberised cloaks.

'What exactly are they listening for? A particular chant or prayer? Or does it vary?' As if on cue, the priests began their procession under the cages and the penitents above them let off a chorus of shouts and howls. The one who'd been grubbing in its slops leapt to the cage bars and began scattering filth out and down onto the ground. The priests kept their hoods low over their faces and walked impassively beneath him.

'It varies with the offence, as you imagine. That determines what they have to make heard as well as where their cage is positioned. The ones down the bottom have committed trivial offences – careless misconduct during a religious service, minor disrespect to an officer of the clergy, you can guess the sort of thing. All we require from them is a short oath of contrition. Most of the time they're able to call it out to the priests' satisfaction on the first pass and they're down from the cage within a couple of hours. A little longer for the ones who are tongue-tied or have trouble speaking up. There was a throat-fever in Phaphan one season, and I remember that even the most lightly-sentenced penitents spent days in the cages before the priests reported that they had heard contrition.'

'And that was considered acceptable?'

Simova gave the arbitor senioris a sharp look. The cries from the cages and the deeper rumble of engines under their feet floated through the silence between them for a moment.

'The answer to that is the whole premise of the cages, Arbitor Calpurnia. You people deal with the *Lex Imperia* and a traditional system of penalties, but the traditions of trial and sentence by ordeal are almost as old. They remain in the cages until their oath of contrition is heard in full. That's the law of it, pure and simple.'

'You're saying that there's no such thing as being sentenced to six hours in a cage, or a day, or what have you.'

'Exactly. It is not for any lowly servant, no matter how pious, to judge whether a sinner's contrition has outweighed his crimes. That is decided by the Emperor and by the infallible natural moral order that flows from Him. The ordeal simply reveals the truth to our own lesser eyes so that we can act on it.'

'So if someone in the cages has a throat disease and can't make themselves heard, they might spend a month in the cage for stumbling on the altar steps during a temple ceremony.'

Simova gave a polite anything's-possible nod.

'And, hypothetically, someone who'd stood on the High Mesé for an hour screaming blasphemies against the Emperor and all the Saints and primarchs while giving the fig to the Cathedral spire with one hand and wiping his behind on the Litanies of Faith with the other–'

'–would be confined in the highest cages,' Simova finished, pointing at the speck that Calpurnia had been looking at herself earlier on.

'Where it wouldn't actually be humanly possible to be heard at all, I'd think. I can barely even see them up there, and didn't you tell me that the cages on Phaphan were hung even higher?'

'The ones we used for the most serious of crimes, certainly.'

'Was anyone ever heard from those highest cages?'

'Not during my own tenure there.'

'And that to you demonstrates…'

'…that the Emperor looked into their sinning hearts and saw fit not to give them the voice to make themselves heard so that their penance could end,' Simova finished smoothly. 'The received tradition of the Ecclesiarchy teaches us that the blasphemer and the heretic may find absolution in death, and so we may observe that death was the absolution that the Emperor required of them.' Simova's voice had taken on a ringing, pulpit-style quality, and the thought caused Calpurnia another inner smile. The man's tonsured head and broad chest were unremarkable, but where his ribs began the reverend bloomed into a great swell of fat in all directions which held the hem of his cassock well clear of his legs and feet. A ringing voice was not inappropriate for a man who so resembled a bell.

She looked up at that furthermost cage again, squinting as she followed the lines of the chains back to the walls. The chains were invisible by the time they reached their anchor points, but she could just see the metal catwalk that ran along the girders that held the chains up. She thought of taking the magnocular scope from her belt to look in more detail, but that could wait. Best to play it safe and dumb until things were under way.

'You have nothing to worry about the construction of the cages, arbitor senioris,' said Simova, who had followed her gaze and misinterpreted it. 'The girder supports are driven an arm's length into the rockcrete. I'm told that we could safely hang one of the holy Sisterhood's Rhino tanks up next to each cage. You don't have to fear anything falling on you. Well, except for...' He gestured to the filth splattering the walkway. The priests had left tracks through it as they walked about to listen for confessions.

'So this whole array was put up under direct Ecclesiarchal supervision?' It was hard to see, but there seemed to be some kind of disturbance on the catwalk where the uppermost chains ended. Calpurnia felt her shoulders tense.

'Of course. I will not say there isn't much to admire about the Hydraphur Ministorum, but this is not a religious practice that ever took root here. The Eparch wanted to make sure when he instituted it here that it would be done properly.'

'Really?' Calpurnia strolled towards the bleachers where the wardens sat and stared upwards. The identical expressions on their faces had not changed.

'And done properly it was, arbitor,' said Simova, pacing alongside her and once again misunderstanding her interest. 'The only significant blemish on the whole affair was one particular inhabitant of the upper stack levels, who insisted on an above-market rate of payment as well as the granting of Ecclesiarchal indulgences in exchange for the privilege of driving our bolts and rings into the walls of his building. You can see him in that cage there, the one third from the edge.'

Calpurnia made a small polite sound, but she wasn't looking. Two Arbites were walking up to the rows of benches, one with an adjutant's badge and carrying a compact vox-case, one in the brown sash of a Chastener.

'I trust this isn't the call of duty just yet, Arbitor Calpurnia?' asked Simova, misreading things again. 'I had hoped you would have time to see the priests arrive back from walking beneath the cages. I'm sure that at least one of the prisoners will have had their full contrition heard, and it's instructive to see the whole process of–'

He broke off. Arbites helmets could make it difficult to tell where their wearer was looking – it was part of the design – but it had become very obvious that the black-armoured figures were staring over his shoulder. Simova gave a disapproving frown and turned.

The blimp coming down the avenue was about fifty metres long, bulbous and dirty. The metalwork along its scooped nose was a clumsy attempt to duplicate the lines of an Imperial warship's prow, and clusters of auspexes and magnoptic emplacements jutted from the long gondola. Its engines were a loud, insectile buzz that counterpointed the seismic rumble of the traffic below.

'How singular,' Simova said. 'Is that an observation gallery built into it there? The Cathedral certainly was not notified of anything like this. I think we shall have to have words with the Monocrat's court. I'm assuming that it's his propagandists who are behind this. Look, you can see the pict-lenses. They must be capturing the cages. Don't you agree, arbitor?'

'No.' Calpurnia's voice was distracted rather than snappish, but it was enough to annoy Simova.

'I'm sure I'm correct. Although I wish they had–'

'The identification numbers on the sides there are from the nautical traffic directorates down past the lagoon. It's one of the blimps they use to monitor sea traffic off the coast and report to the harbourmaster. Haven't you seen them out over the bay?'

'I suppose I must have, arbitor, but what's such a thing doing flying up to the hive like this? Throne preserve us, look! It's barely above the level of the cages! What if it drops?'

'Not *exactly* the problem I'm anticipating,' Calpurnia said calmly. Simova, wrong-footed, gulped air and watched her unholster, check and arm a stub pistol that looked impossibly large for her slender arms.

The arbitor holding the voxer tilted his head as it broke into a terse series of staticky messages. 'East and west teams report that anchors are seized, ma'am,' he said after a moment. 'Repeating that, both anchors are seized.'

Simova looked around and upwards.

'What anchors? What are you talking about? I see no anchors, the thing's... wait, do you mean... Yes, it's lowering a chain, look! How dare they? Where's... Emperor's eyes, there should be a deacon on duty here, where... you. *You.*'

A nervous deacon, who'd been gawping up at the blimp from several metres away, hurried over. 'Give me a magnoc, or bring up a reader so we can look at what that idiot in the blimp is– What? Emperor's light! You improvident lackwit! There is *always* supposed to be a sighting device available at the cages for members of the priesthood to–'

'Use mine if you wish, reverend.' Calpurnia passed across a stubby tube, smaller and plainer than the ornate Ministorum devices Simova was used to. He conscientiously said a small benediction for its machine-spirit and put it to his eye.

It was not a chain that the blimp was lowering but a cable and hook, from a heavy winching scaffold on the rear of the gondola. The blimp lurched back and forth as the pilot tried to keep it in one position in the cross-breezes, and the hook swung in wilder and wilder arcs as it descended. The ragged figure in the cage was standing with its back to Simova, gripping the bars, watching the hook descend. The sheer enormity of what he was seeing stopped the words in Simova's throat for a dozen seconds, and it made an undignified squeak of the voice he eventually managed to find.

'The man's being *rescued*. Golden *Throne*, don't these people realise what they're doing? Have they no idea of the *consequences*?' It took a moment for him to realise that he was talking to himself – the Arbites were conferring with one another and with the rustling voices of their companions on the voxer.

'Anchors cutting, repeating, ma'am. Anchors cutting, both sides. Mast on the move, ETA four minutes.'

'Do we see Helmsman?'

'Tentatively placed with Mast, but not confirmed.'

The hook swung over the top of the cage. The magnoc make it look almost close enough to touch; it was odd when there was no audible clank when the back of the hook bounced off the top of the cage bars. Simova started as the sound of traffic-alert horns blared up through the gaps in the rockcrete.

'I take it someone's going to tell me what that was.' Calpurnia's voice had only the tiniest traces of an edge.

'Mastwatch reports in, ma'am. Mast has developed engine difficulties, probably fake. The horns were from the traffic backing up behind it. They hit their mark exactly, though.'

'I'd expect no less,' said Calpurnia. 'Anchors? If they're too enthusiastic up there then they may save us having to be involved at all, although I'm not sure I'd call that satisfactory.'

Her words crystallised Simova's suspicions, and he rounded on her.

'This is not a surprise to you, is it, Arbitor Calpurnia? What do you mean by allowing this to go ahead? Do you plan on intervening before these prisoners are all loaded up and flying to saints-know-where?'

'I'll have my magnoc back from you, reverend, if you're done with it,' was her reply. 'I'd like to see if that hook has found purchase. Culann, raise Anchorwatch please.'

'Both anchors still cutting. They're... wait... Anchorwatch reports anchors away! Repeat–'

'Thank you, Culann, no need.' She was not looking through the magnoc, but up at the building walls. Simova realised with a sick sensation in his gut what 'anchors away' must have meant. One of the chains had been cut. He watched it curl and flap loose down the rockcrete face of the stack, shattering a row of gargoyles and gouging chunks out of the ledges and balconies it lashed against on the way down. Before it had landed he jerked his gaze back to the distant cage, but Calpurnia had been right: the hook had found purchase and the cage now swung back and forth from the blimp. But the cage was not being raised, as Simova had expected, but lowered.

'Mast still in position,' reported Culann. 'Confirming just one vehicle. No definite sightings of Helmsman. We're having trouble intercepting their vox-bands so we haven't placed his voice yet either.'

'Keep everyone back, Culann. I don't expect anyone to see Helmsman until Captain is... you know, I think we can dispense with the code-name. I didn't like that one anyway. I don't think Symandis will pop his head up until Ströon hits the ground.' Simova gaped.

'That's Ghammo Ströon? That's his cage? Damn, from this angle I didn't...' The curate remembered where he was, and rounded on the ranks of Wardens behind him.

'Who is monitoring Ströon's cage? How is... what...'

'The penitent Ghammo Ströon has not been heard to express contrition,' came the toneless reply. 'My humble judgement records forty-eight offences before the sight of the Emperor and by Eparchal decree, for which penitence must also be made.' The man was silent for a moment, and then corrected himself: 'Fifty-one.' Calpurnia looked through her magnoc: the figure in the cage was making an indistinct but definitely obscene gesture in the direction of the Cathedral spire.

'The... why have...' Simova was trying his hardest, but discoursing about punishment in the abstract in the Chamber of Exegetors had not prepared him for seeing action first-hand. He stepped forward to try and lay a hand on Calpurnia's shoulder but the Chastener, who was a head and a half taller than Simova with shoulders as broad as the curate's waist, stepped forward and silently blocked his way. Simova finally managed a sentence:

'This rescue must be *stopped*!'

'Mmm.' Calpurnia folded the magnoc with a snap and stowed it back at her belt. 'I don't see Mast yet, but it won't be long.'

'Mastwatch and Noose are still standing by, ma'am.' Culann's voice was showing an edge of tension.

'Thank you.' Calpurnia had donned her helmet again. 'The cage is on the ground, and I can see Ströon at the door. They had to know that there would be alerts by now. When they move, they'll move fast.' She drummed her fingers against her leg for a moment. 'I think we need to be closer.'

At her words Culann began stowing the voxer in his harness while the Chastener gestured to the Arbites who had been waiting in the pavilion that Simova had put up for the Ecclesiarchy's own staff. The curate's mouth went dry as he watched them move up: more Chasteners, massive and broad-shouldered in heavy carapace armour, hefting shotguns and grenade launchers. The tramp of their boots was countered by the metallic *tik-tik-tik* of cyber-mastiff feet as the dog-like attack-constructs paced beside their handlers, and the last two Chasteners carried shining steel grapplehawks in their heavy launching-frames, the suspensors in their ribcages whining as they warmed up.

As he watched their armoured backs spread out and move towards the hanging line and the beached cage, Simova felt eyes on him. It was the little delegation of priests who had been walking under the cages to hear the confessions. There could not have been a lot to hear: the other penitents had all fallen silent as the shadow of the blimp had passed over them.

Curate Simova did not consider himself a coward. His duties had taken him to more cloisters than battlefields, but the Adeptus Ministorum was at its heart a militant church and its doctrines never shied from violence. Nevertheless, at that moment he felt glad to have the line of Arbites between him and what was about to happen. He snapped his fingers for attention and beckoned the priests over.

'Join with me in raising your voices,' he told them. 'The Adeptus Arbites need our battle-prayers.'

SHIRA CALPURNIA HALF-HEARD the little chorus of plainsong from behind them, and it soothed her. There was always a need for prayer – to believe otherwise was prideful and sinful. The stranded cage was still a good four hundred metres away, and she upped the pace a little.

She flexed her left arm and shoulder and felt a sharp twinge run through her. It had been more than half a year since it had been rebuilt after her shattering injuries atop the spire of the Cathedral, and Calpurnia knew she was healing quickly as such things went. Quickly, but not yet completely. She unsnapped the power-maul from her belt and gripped it tightly in one gauntleted fist.

Three hundred and fifty metres. There were more figures around the cage now, busily working at it. Her detectives had reported that the clique had bought an oxy-cutter with false credit and doctored authorisation, and stolen breaching-charges from a shipment to the Monocrat's personal militia. She had personally suspended the investigations into both crimes: if Symandis had suspected that the Arbites were onto rescue preparations he might have become suspicious.

Three hundred and ten metres. Vox came in, simple and coded. Anchors both locked. The saboteur teams that had blown the chains loose had all been rounded up. That was where most of the breaching-grenades had gone, she would bet. The four teams represented almost the clique's entire field strength, and all of its best, and with the teams codenamed 'Anchor' taken out two of those teams were down.

Two hundred and sixty metres. No one had been able to give her a sure guarantee that the bridges would take the weight of a Rhino, so the strike force spread out on foot, the cyber-mastiffs on the flanks, the grapplehawk tenders in the centre. Two hawks, one for Symandis, one to recapture Ströon. Easy. There was a Chastener at each of Calpurnia's shoulders, and it took an effort of will for her to slow her pace to allow the line to overtake her.

Two hundred and twenty-five metres. The targets' discipline was excellent. They had to have seen the force of Chasteners, and she was sure they knew the saboteur teams had been taken. But they bent to their work still, and Calpurnia could see the glare of the cutter at the bars of the cage. Let them try. All she needed was for–

'Helmsman!' cried Culann from a pace behind her, but they were close enough now that the vox-torcs in their carapaces had picked it up as well. 'Helmsman! All Arbites, we have Helmsman and Captain! Helmsman and Captain!'

'Maintain pace, please, don't speed up. Remember your orders.' Calpurnia kept her voice level, expecting any moment to have to interrupt herself with the next order. If both Symandis and Ströon were confirmed as being ahead of them, then she didn't think she had long to wait.

A couple of the men around the cage were shooting panicky looks over their shoulders now. They would not have expected the Arbites in such force or so soon, perhaps not at all. Calpurnia gritted her teeth. Their orders were not to open fire until her mark, and she trusted her Arbites to hold that order absolutely, but she hoped that the rescuers would not start shooting before–

There was a blue flare ahead of her – not the steady pinpoint of the cutter but the flicker of a power weapon. It flared twice more and the side of the cage fell away. Ströon was free.

'Captain's free!' Calpurnia barked. 'Ströon's free! Close the noose. Go!'

And then everything happened. The Chasteners sped up into a run. Lead Chastener Vayan boomed through his vox-horn for the men to surrender to righteous judgement and overhead four krak missiles drew sharp white trails from the building heights. Their impacts blew out the blimp's engines and it began a slow, undirected drift; the cable, still attached to the cage, grew taut and dragged the cage away. And then, after a moment, the cage dropped and wedged itself tight in the gap through which the rescuers had climbed, blocking it and anchoring the blimp in place.

And so the Emperor shows His hand for His servants, Calpurnia thought with only a little smugness, before she called into her torc again.

'Mastwatch, the hole is blocked. The cage fell into it. Our targets are trapped, no need for main force in disabling Mast. Take as many alive as you can.' And then, heeding the warning twinges from her arm, she slowed to watch the Chasteners close.

Symandis's own little taskforce was armed too. They carried punch-daggers, home-machined blades, little foldaway laspistols and stubbers you could hide from the crude traffic-control auspexes if you knew the trick of it. But the Arbites' armour was tough and their wills were tougher: they began weaving as they ran to spoil placed shots to armour-joins and held their guns in a high shoulder position that kept an armoured vambrace over the half of their faces the helmets didn't cover. Not a man so much as staggered as they ran towards the crack and pop of the enemy's small-arms, and then two grenade launchers chugged and the fire stopped completely even before the heavy double-*wham* of the shock grenades. The people they were facing knew more than enough to take cover when they heard launchers.

Not that they had any intention of making a last stand. The burly figure of Symandis was already running up the slope of the pavement. Calpurnia didn't need to give the order: the first grapplehawk went screeching out of its frame, weaving on its suspensor as its handler thumbed the studs on the controller to steer it forwards. It only took a few seconds for its cortex, patterned on the preying instincts of the Avignoran black eagle, to lock onto its prey, and then send it swooping with metal hooks and taser-spikes unsheathed.

Calpurnia swore as Symandis spun at the sound of the suspensor and shore it in two with a stroke of a crackling power-axe.

'Culann! Stohl! Even as the words were leaving her mouth she was in a flat run, champing her jaw shut and ignoring the warning tautness in her shoulder as her power-maul sizzled and spat. She jinked to the left and around the wedged cage, barely registering the shots and sirens echoing up from the roadway below as the stolen scaffold-truck they had codenamed Mast was stormed by Arbitor Odamo and the Mastwatch teams.

Symandis had taken a moment to draw a bead on her, but his snub-barrelled pistol could not give him the range – the shot didn't even pass close enough for Calpurnia to hear it hit the paving. Then he was running again.

'Mastiffs! Two mastiffs on Helmsman, breaking left. Two mastiffs *now*!' She hated to take strength from the fight behind her, but Symandis was just as much a target as Ströon had been. The whole reason they had let the cage be lowered was to make sure Symandis was there before they moved. 'Mastiffs on Helmsman!'

With a clatter of claws two of the hunter-constructs loped past, narrow metal faces fixed with inhuman intent on the criminal ahead of them, their handlers racing to keep up. Running ahead of them, armoured boots sparking off the pitted and uneven paving, Calpurnia resisted the urge to draw her pistol: the mega-bore rounds would wipe out any hope of capturing the wretch alive. The grapplehawks were supposed to have achieved that – where the hell had Symandis got a power-axe from?

The handlers must have directed a secondary attack pattern: when Symandis whirled with a low sweep of the axe timed to decapitate the lead mastiff, they both shied away and passed one to either side of him. Suddenly Symandis was between the two mastiffs and the Arbites. When he realised this he tried to break right and make for a different paving gap. One mastiff darted in and there was a sound like metal shears as its mechanised jaws snapped the air behind Symandis's heel, a microsecond away from severing his Achilles tendon. The other ducked under a stroke of the axe and managed to rake its teeth along the side of Symandis's knee before he knocked it scrabbling with the axe haft and put two rapid bullets into the side of its torso. It lurched drunkenly away as Symandis backpedalled, sweeping the axe to and fro pegging two more quick shots towards Calpurnia.

As the first bullet whistled overhead, something crashed into her from behind, shoving her to one side. She growled and tried to drive an elbow back until she realised…

'Damn it, Culann!'

'You were under fire, ma'am, I was trying to interpose myself!'

She opened her mouth, but this wasn't the time. The two mastiff handlers and Lead Chastener Stohl pelted past her after Symandis and as she stood she took a moment to look over her shoulder.

These were no hysterical rioters or brainless slum-thugs. Ströon was weak from three days in the cage, but a circle of his men were bearing him in the other direction as fast as they could, trying to make the most of Symandis's diversion and the way the Chasteners had to sight through or fight past Ströon's own men: they had obviously worked out the Arbites were trying to take Ströon alive.

Mast was crippled, and there was no way they could get down through one of the other gaps without the fall splattering them across a busy roadway... but Calpurnia saw in her mind's eye Ströon clambering down his followers as they made a groaning human rope of their interlocked hands – it would only need to hold for ten, twenty seconds – or simply having them hurl themselves through a gap to form a soft pile of bodies on which to land. However unlikely, she wasn't going to take the chance.

'Anchorwatch, do you see captain and his guard? I want you to put a missile in his path every time they make for one of those gaps. Frag load. Well ahead of the pack, we're trying to deny him ground, not kill him.' She nodded with satisfaction at their confirmation – missile launchers were certainly not regular Arbites field kit, but the gunnery teams were turning out to be well worth the trouble she had gone through to borrow them off Arbitor Nakayama's armoury echelon.

The first missile boomed on the rockcrete in the middle distance as she advanced on Symandis again. He was staggering now, on the defensive, unable to face two groups of enemies at once: the Arbites moved in further every time he swung his power axe at the mastiffs, and the mastiffs lunged for his legs every time he tried to snap a shot at the Arbites. One mastiff was missing a leg, and Stohl was bleeding from a bullet-crease to the side of his arm, but Symandis's legs were gashed in half a dozen places and he was treading his own blood into the ground at every step.

Calpurnia shot another look back. Ströon was being forced towards one of the sheer building walls, pressed by the Chasteners, hemmed in by cyber-mastiffs and carefully-placed missile explosions. She would be needed there soon.

She doffed her helmet, switched her maul to her other hand and drew her pistol.

'Are we going to play this out to its finish, Symandis? I can kill you now, or we can take you apart piece by piece. Or you can–'

'Or I can surrender and go to exactly the same fate in your cells that I'm ready to meet here now,' he panted. His voice was hoarse. There was sweat on his eyeglasses and sweat slicking the dark curly mop of his hair. 'You want me alive so you won't shoot me. You'll keep trying to knock me down while I make sure I damn well take as many of you as *uhhh*–'

The sentence finished halfway between a grunt and a scream as the mastiffs took advantage of his distraction to scissor through the backs of Symandis's knees, collapsing him to the ground with his hamstrings severed. The hand with the pistol waved in the air and Stohl clubbed it down with an efficient swing of a gun-butt. The power-axe swung wildly and Calpurnia swung her maul in an elegant twisting stroke that came in behind the axe-blade, blew the circuitry in the haft and knocked the weapon flying. Then the mastiffs clamped onto his wrists, razor-teeth retracted but jaws as powerful as ever, and that, finally, was that.

CHAPTER TWO

The Avenue Solar, Outskirts of Bosporian Hive, Hydraphur

STRÖON, BLASPHEMER AND seditionist and the teacher of blasphemers and seditionists, was almost in hand. The mastiffs had broken up the men surrounding him and carefully aimed Executioner rounds had picked off any who got too far from their leader. From inside the clump he was shouting slogans in a voice even more sore and cracked than Symandis's and waving a combat blade someone must have given him. The running fight had left a trail down the side of the humped bridge-slope: blood-spatter, shell cases, four outlaws sprawling unconscious or dead and two Chasteners, one lying on his side cursing softly as blood seeped from the shoulder-joint of his carapace and a companion knelt by him trying to jam a pressure-pack into place. Calpurnia slowed down to make eye contact with the wounded man and give him a nod, then spoke into her torc.

'Calpurnia to lead Chasteners. Helmsman is taken. Both Anchor teams are taken. Mastwatch, verify...' she waited for their confirmation. 'Mast is taken. All that's left is Captain. Push them into the wall and let's finish it.'

It took only minutes. A volley of shot sent low to ricochet made the knot of enemies scramble backwards down the slope with blood starting from their feet and shins. When they had spilled down to the flat pedestrian concourse along the stack wall a choke grenade burst on the rockcrete and filled the space with smothering vapour. None of the Arbites even needed to clip rebreathers into place: the cyber-mastiffs didn't need air to pull down the three of Ströon's bodyguards who had managed to stay on their feet, and the grapplehawk didn't need air to glide in on Captain himself. Jittering from the taser-hooks, hoisted up by the hawk's suspensor so that his bare toes just scraped the ground, Ströon was dragged forward into the half-circle of Chasteners to where Shira Calpurnia waited to put him in chains.

Simova and his priests had not moved from their spot by the time Calpurnia walked back to them. The prayer-songs were over and Simova simply watched her as she had Culann vox a report; she let him wait, grimacing as she rolled her shoulder to try and work the kinks and aches out of it, not letting on that she had noticed the tiny tremor in Simova's hands from second-hand adrenaline or the quick glances he kept shooting toward the empty space where Ströon's cage had hung. The fighting seemed to have cowed the other penitents for a while – the air was now clear of cries and excrement.

Finally, she sent Culann down to the roadway level to make sure her Rhino was ready for her and turned to Simova, sweeping her damp hair back from her scarred forehead. It was the end of Hydraphur's wet season, cool enough to make people want to move around a little to keep warm but humid enough to make you sweat as soon as you did. The sensation was not pleasant.

'You didn't come here today by accident,' Simova said. He wasn't asking a question, and Calpurnia didn't bother to pretend that he was. 'That was as careful an ambush as I can imagine,' he went on. 'Set up to cancel out every detail of the rescue raid. You knew exactly where those people were going to be and what they were going to do.'

Calpurnia went so far as to nod.

'You knew their plans to the letter. You must have detected their approach, well, how long ago would–'

'A while. Symandis wasn't as good at keeping his activities secret as Ströon. He was too clumsy about getting hold of his equipment and hijacking the surveillance blimp. Things like that find their way to informers.'

'Who were your informers in Ströon's cell?' demanded Simova. It only took a few moments of Calpurnia's level ice-green stare for him to think better of the question and try to soften it. 'Arbitor, if there had been just a little co-operation, well, we could have removed Ströon from rescue's way, or had the Adepta Sororitas guard the cages.'

'Symandis was good enough to know exactly how the Ministorum had set up the cages. You don't think a guard would have alerted him?' Something in Calpurnia's gaze was making Simova uncomfortable again.

'It, well, arbitor, I realise that this is your own, er...'

'We needed to make sure that Symandis was confident enough to attempt the rescue himself,' Calpurnia continued calmly. 'We needed to make sure they believed such a daring exercise would pay off.'

'And look how this turned out!' Simova jabbed a finger at the spot where Ströon had been taken. The choke fumes had left yellow stains on the rockcrete that would take days to fade. 'Ströon was on the ground and running before you got to him! Think of what could have happened! If you had arrested them when they showed their faces they would be safely in irons now and we would not have lost a cage from the array!'

'And Symandis would be free, we would not have their collection of henchmen and dupes dead or slung off a Rhino and Ströon would not be in proper custody.' The louder Simova's protestations got, the quieter Calpurnia's voice became, to the point where he had to take a step forward to hear her.

'I will not have you talk like that to me, arbitor. Ströon was a prisoner of the holy Adeptus Ministorum, as you might remember if you would like to cast your mind back to seeing him hanging over the Avenue Solar in a cage. In fact, by Eparchal decree those cages represent Ecclesiarchal premises just as much as the altars and nave of the Cathedral itself. Ströon should have been no business of yours while he was incarcerated there.'

'Our grapplehawk did not, you will have noticed, pluck Ströon out of his cage,' Calpurnia said levelly. 'In fact, we did not even begin active engagement until Ströon was free of the cage. And a known seditionist running free after exploiting the failures of his captors is most certainly an Arbites matter.'

'It is the role of the Ecclesiarchy to embody and spread the divine word of the Emperor–' Simova began.

'And the role of the Arbites to *enforce* laws and decrees and to ensure that all of the Emperor's Adeptus are in full command of and service to their duties,' finished Calpurnia calmly. 'Which I am quite sure you and your Ministorum colleagues are, of course. All the same, I do not believe in being less than thorough. Although I myself am called to other business, I have deputised Praetor Imprimis Dastrom to prepare a full dossier of inquiry on the business. I won't insult you by lecturing you about co-operating, but I will mention that Dastrom will hold you accountable for the co-operation of all external labour you engaged to put up the cages.'

'You let the rescue happen.' Simova had gone pale, his lips very thin. 'You knew that they had a plan that would get Ströon free. And you allowed it to happen so that Ströon would be out of his cage and into your own hands.' His words were confident, but the confidence was leaching out of his tone. Calpurnia had found that a steady look could do that.

'The Eparch will hear of this. As will Canoness Theoctista.'

'I shall count on it. The Eparch and I have intended to meet and speak in person for almost six months now, but the opportunity has eluded us. And it will be good to speak with the reverend canoness again. There's no need to delay on my account if you need to set off for the Augustaeum now, sir, I have my own transport waiting.'

And after that it was just a matter of meeting the curate's eyes until he turned and walked back the way they had come.

The Wall, Bosporian Hive, Hydraphur

'IT SOUNDS LIKE he took it well, ma'am,' said Culann, 'considering.'

'He was smart enough to realise that he didn't have a choice,' said Calpurnia, 'especially not outside the hive and with the Arbites outnumbering him. I should have kept some of you up there, actually, to drive the point home. But never mind.'

The giant fortress known as the Wall formed the Arbites barracks and courts for all of Hydraphur and whole systems around. It began amid the building stacks that crowded the base of the Bosporian and ran up the entire side of the hive-mountain to finish at the great fortified Justice Gate, set into the wall of the Augustaeum high above. Calpurnia didn't know how long it would take to travel on foot from the lowest entrances at hive bottom to her own rooms in the Wall's highest bastion, and she didn't think anyone had ever tried. She and

Culann were riding in one of the cable cars that ran the whole length of the great bastion, rattling along in the highest space of the building, just below the vaulted roof. Calpurnia was standing at one of the car windows, looking out and down; Culann sat on a bench along one wall

'And he didn't challenge you on the law of it?'

'No. Either he knew we were in the right – and he's a specialist in religious law, after all – or he wasn't sure of his ground and didn't want to force the issue.'

'Do you think the Eparch will? Force the issue, that is?'

'I don't believe so. I hope not.' Calpurnia sighed. 'I don't like playing law games, especially over vermin like Ströon. The Ecclesiarchy were so rapt at catching him for spreading his schismatic books, but I don't think they knew the half of what he was up to.'

'Was that why you wanted him personally, ma'am?' Culann gulped. 'To personally arrest him, that is.'

The cable car was passing over one of the high-roofed drilling concourses. Sixty metres below her, squares of infantry, a hundred arbitrators to a side, stamped and clashed through a weapon drill, whipping heavy *Vox Legi*-pattern shotguns out of the scabbards on their backs and aiming from the shoulder, from the hip, kneeling, then into the scabbard, out, kneel, shoulder, turn, kneel, scabbard, turn, hip, kneel... The drill was one so old that it had not changed between here and where Calpurnia had trained in the Ultima Segmentum, and although she wouldn't have performed it in at least five years she found her muscles twitching along with the remembered moves as if her body still wanted to join in without asking her.

She blinked and realised she owed Culann a reply.

'No. Well, part of the reason, I suppose, but I hope I'm not prideful enough to personally insist on taking in every single outlaw whose warrant declares him dangerous. That's all of them, for one thing.'

'For symbolism, then?' Culann seemed to be taking the conversation for an examination. Calpurnia smiled. The question was not frivolous – the idea of the symbolism and pageantry of the law, that Imperial justice should be seen by the populace to be bearing down in full and unstoppable force, was a philosophy expounded by generations of distinguished Arbites scholars.

'An object lesson for the populace, well, perhaps,' she said, 'although there wasn't much of an audience there today. To focus the minds of the Ecclesiarchy, too, as you probably picked up. I made it very clear to Simova that Dastrom's investigation wouldn't go soft on him because of his office. I don't think they'll find anything – I think Ströon's people got the schematics for the cage anchors and all the rest through their own devices, but I'm uncomfortable with how pushy the Eparch is getting about having Ministorum agents conducting hunts and arrests. The Arbitor Majore and I have been waiting for the right occasion to make a point about knowing their boundaries.'

'A political operation,' said Culann, nodding.

'Not quite,' she corrected him a little stiffly. 'Just the performance of our duty as Arbites that extends some lessons in more than one direction at once. Anyway, that's the second reason.'

'Is there another, ma'am?'

'My own peace of mind, since you ask.' At the words 'peace of mind' Culann noticed her gloved hand creeping up to touch the scars on her forehead. It didn't take most people long to notice the mannerism or recognise what it meant. 'This rogue trader business is going to swallow up a lot of my time, and I wanted to see Ströon and Symandis scooped up with my own eyes so I didn't have to fret about them while I'm supposed to be concentrating on this bequesting I'm signing, or presiding over, or whatever the hell I'm doing with it. And in all honesty, Culann, since I know you're a dependable and discreet adjutant, "bequesting" means taking on those seditionists was the last chance I'll have for quite a time for some good solid boots-on-ground Arbites work. If I'm only going to have one chance to stretch my muscles and see how I'm healing between here and Candlemas then I'm bloody well going to take it.'

Culann took this in solemnly. Another thing that most people found out quickly about Arbitor Senioris Calpurnia was how much she hated leading from anywhere but the front. Opinion on this in the arbitrator barracks further down the wall had been evenly divided between approval at a commander willing to put themselves on the line with their troops, and disapproval at an arbitor senioris who put herself at risk instead of riding in an armoured pulpit in the second rank of Rhinos, reading from the Books of Judgement over an amp-horn as befitted her station. Culann had heard there was a small but vocal third faction who contended that the control-freak bitch wanted to be on hand to make sure the arbitrators kept their boots polished and their kits neat while they were being shot at.

'And if I may ask, ma'am, your injuries...?

The cable car passed from the drill hall into a tunnel, and onto a steeper slope that would take them up to the next bastion level. Four more of those to go before they reached the Justice Gate itself.

'Not bad. Thank you for asking, Culann.' He thought that she perhaps was worse than that: they were passing under a series of light-wells in the thick ceiling above them and the brief bursts of yellow Hydraphur daylight made her look tired and hollow-eyed. He knew that she had been on her feet very soon after the confrontation at the Cathedral had wrecked her shoulder and arm. Cynez Sanja had made it a personal point to have his Magi Biologis work minor miracles on her flesh and bones, but her convalescence since then had not been easy. Culann's impression was that Shira Calpurnia did not deal with being a patient very well.

She dropped into a seat opposite him.

'It's the smaller things that bother me, not the big ones,' she said suddenly as though she had seen his thoughts. 'I know I can't carry a shield, my left arm just isn't strong enough yet. Well, fine. What gnaws me is things like having trouble buckling my armour because the fingers on that hand won't quite work the fasteners yet. Or having to spend the time I thought I was going to spend getting back into physical training in the medicae chambers instead, feeling weak and stiff instead of running around a drill-hall like I should have been doing.' Her expression soured. 'Anyway, complaining won't make me heal any faster, even though I know it's said that I never do anything else.' Culann kept gallantly silent. 'Anyway, the Arbitor Majore had a suspicious sort of a "let's see you get into a gunfight on this assignment" air about him when he gave this rogue trader matter to me.'

'Legal theory work, you mean, ma'am?' Culann felt a twinge of relief at the conversation moving to less personal grounds. He had seen the arbitor senioris at her forceful best when she had hunted down plotters and saboteurs just before the great Mass of Balronas, and to hear her sound so worn was oddly disturbing.

'Not even that, as far as I can tell. Ceremonial, more like. This man's ship, or is there more than one? I think there is. They're bringing his rogue trader charter back and his son's being summoned from his home by the Pyrmondine Spur. As far as I can tell most of what we're doing is providing a nice warm room where the one can meet the other, and clapping everybody on the back afterwards.'

Despite her air of disdained detachment, she already seemed to be more familiar with the basics of the Hoyyon Phrax affair than Culann was, and he was the one who had prepared the briefings for her.

'Are we overseeing the Naval judicature, or Administratum, or the Monocrat and planetary authorities, or our own, ma'am? I've not studied the underpinnings of Letters of Marque in the *Lex Imperia*.'

'Neither have I, Culann. Because we're Arbitrators, not Judges. It's their job to know the cumulative effect of ten thousand years of Imperial decrees on the law we apply, and it's our job to know the cumulative effect of a hundred-shell Executioner volley on a line of rioters.' She smiled at her own turn of phrase for a moment. 'On the other hand, take my advice, Culann, pay attention to any opportunity you have to see how the other pillar of the Arbites works. I like to think I'm versed in both of them, but I get caught flatfooted more often than I'm pleased to admit. Having Judges on my staff doesn't make up for everything.' She blinked. 'Throne alone, listen to me ramble. I've been around Leandro too long. Where was I?'

'Imperial letters of marque, ma'am.'

'That's right, and why this isn't one. We're dealing with something a little over and above the usual planetary governors' marques or the Adeptus wildcat warrants. I'm talking about the true rogue trader charters, the old decrees for the captains who used to fly right clean out of Imperial space, often as not. They would go to places where they never knew what they would find or what they would have to do to survive, so they were given the power to do whatever they needed to.'

'Whatever they...'

'My home was on the Eastern Fringe, you understand. Wild space zones and the Imperial frontier were a lot closer than they are here. There were a lot of stories about the great old rogue traders in the histories of our segmentum. There was one who used his charter to lead a fleet into wild space and raid and strip two xenos factory ships that were mining its asteroids. Then his son used the wealth from that to return and outfit a whole flotilla of ships and return to those systems to drive the xenos out completely. Then his granddaughter used the charter to recruit colonists from half a dozen Imperial worlds and found a permanent fief of her own in this system they'd taken. There was another one who struck a pact with the Ecclesiarchy to transport a missionary taskforce out beyond the Imperial border – the accounts said they loaded an entire prefabricated temple into the hold of his largest ship to deposit whole onto the first habitable world they found, if you can believe that. He went out beyond the border and his grandson came back into Imperial space a hundred and eighty years later with a giant pilgrim fleet in tow. They had found two human worlds lost to the light for more than a thousand years, and turned them into an Emperor-fearing part of the Imperium. That'd be something to be remembered for, wouldn't it?'

They passed out of the tunnel, and Culann blinked at the sudden light. The car rattled up through the high reaches of the spinal concourse of a barrack level; beneath them Arbites bustled in and out of dormitory entrances.

'So these are the rogue traders. The real ones, the grand old ones, the ones that these little pissants with a decommissioned Munitorio hauler and a life warrant from a local governor want to be mistaken for when they boast they're a rogue trader.'

'And so this man, this Hoyyon Phrax…'

'Not Hoyyon Phrax, not any more. His age caught up with him somewhere out past the Anseelie Drift toward the Segmentum Solar.' She stretched and winced. 'There was a riddle in the margin of one of the dossiers that some old clerk apparently thought was funny. "Rogue Trader Phrax never arrives at Hydraphur, but uncounted Rogue Trader Phraxes have left."'

'I think I follow it, ma'am.'

'Well, do some of the talking then. I'm tired.'

'Well, if each new Rogue Trader Phrax receives the charter of trade at Hydraphur, it means that none of them arrive here with that title. And if they all die away from Hydraphur it means they never return here, the charter does, without them.'

'Well done, although I don't see what's so witty about it myself.'

'It's related to the way the hereditary charter works. There seems to be a different principle in operation to the usual Imperial laws of heredity.'

Calpurnia, who had been leaning against a seat back with her eyes half-closed, fixed Culann with a cool, slightly amused stare.

'You anticipated my advice, then, you've been studying already. Carry on then, proctor. Explain to me how it's different.' Culann managed to catch himself a split-second before he audibly gulped.

'Most offices where the Imperium gives a decree of heredity transfer instantly when the previous holder dies. I know that there's often a ceremony or something to cement the transition in, but not like the one that's going to happen here.'

'Go on.' Calpurnia had leaned forward, and the light made the scar-lines in her face look livid.

'It's a quality of those charters, the grand old charters you mentioned, ma'am. No two of them are alike. We police the way governors issue charters far more strictly now, so they never contain anything too outrageous, and the wildcat warrants the Administratum gives out are churned out by a hundred servo-scribes at a time according to templates laid down by the Adeptus, with a space for a name at the top and a stamped-on seal at the bottom. But the old ones, well, they were tailor-made for whatever circumstances led to a rogue trader being necessary at the time. So there were some that gave the traders power to raise troops and make pacts with the Astartes–'

'Well observed. There are at least two famous families who have pacted with Astartes Chapters.'

'–and some that appointed them as de facto officers of the Ecclesiarchy, like the missionary you described.'

'Not entirely the same thing, but parallel, I suppose,' Calpurnia said. 'I keep interrupting. Go on.'

'And there were some that bound the charters, their bearers I should say, to particular areas of space,' Culann went on, feeling a little more sure of himself. 'Possibly to make sure the new rogue trader remained in the area where his influence and skills were needed, or so one might think. And those clauses in the charters have never been amended or repealed, or at least not in most cases, because the charters were originally drawn up by the warmasters, or sometimes by primarchs or members of the Emperor's court or His crusades. So there's no one senior enough to repeal or amend them, and they don't expire on the bearer's death like most of the new ones do.'

'Hence all the rather disreputable folklore on the subject,' Calpurnia said, 'stories of rogue trader charters being stolen, or sold, or forged, or gambled with, which is a disgusting thought. When a charter can be... but I'm interrupting you again.'

'All I was going to add was that the intent of the succession clause was that this charter can only ever be legally transferred in a ceremony conducted within the boundaries of the Hydraphur system. So no matter where else in the Imperium their interests take them, every generation, the Phrax family have to come back to Hydraphur so that a new rogue trader can be appointed.'

'So they do. Don't feel slighted by this, Culann, but I had Praetor Minoris Zbela search some of the oldest records we have in the Wall as well as your own briefings, tracing the Phrax Charter as far back as it would go. That's a long way, too. This charter is for all intents and purposes an Imperial decree and the Arbites oversaw the actual drafting of it, from what sense I've been able to make of the records. Hydraphur was on the very edge of Imperial space back then, and apparently the intention was to use rogue traders to push forward towards the Rim so that the Crusade itself could travel on to Caliban. That was when the line of Phrax was granted its eternal rogue trader charter, bound to Hydraphur. I suppose that the plan was for a few generations of Phraxes – Phraxae? – to have civilised the fringe domains through trade by the time the Crusade returned ready to take them into the Imperium itself.'

'A Crusade-era document,' Culann said. 'I had seen accounts that mentioned its age, but I didn't think about what that meant until now. Ten thousand years. Imagine what the document will be like to look at! Imagine what it would have been like to be there when it was signed! To see, who? Ma'am, do we have a record of whose hand the charter is signed in? One of the Crusading Saints, or the original Lords Militant? Maybe Lord Marshal Wiertalla, they say he was one of the very founders of the whole order of Arbites!'

'Guess again.'

'Ma'am, I'm not sure I know of too many other names. The stories that survive of those times are so broken up anyway, and I remember even at the schola halls they said there was so much myth mixed in that we can't, I mean, guess...'

'This actually isn't a hard one. I doubted the first accounts I read, for exactly the same reasons you just described. But all the later references to the charter in all the old data-arks that Zbela dug up seemed to point to confirmation, so I'm taking it as true. And who are we to question the received word of our predecessors and betters?'

'I don't follow, ma'am.'

'As I said, Culann, it isn't a hard one. Come at it this way. Think back to all the legends and scriptures and gospels and sagas and paintings and pageants you've ever seen or heard about the Great Crusade. Who's the constant, Culann? If the Crusade was resting in Hydraphur at the time that the very first Rogue Trader Phrax was appointed, then who is the one person we can say for absolute certain would have been there to put their hand out to sign it?'

It only took Culann a moment to think of the name, but that moment another dozen times over to realise that she wasn't joking. He felt the colour drain from his face, and the skin on his shoulders and palms start to tingle.

The change on his face must have been visible.

'That's right, Culann,' Shira Calpurnia said. '*Him*.'

CHAPTER THREE

Shexia System

AT SHEXIA, THE flotilla of Hoyyon Phrax came into port to take on certain supplies, make certain arrangements, purge the old trader's possessions and ceremonially kill his concubines.

Disposing of Hoyyon's not especially large harem was a matter of routine for the flotilla and its acting masters. It had been flotilla custom since time well out of mind to greet a new heir with none of their predecessor-parent's possessions of significance. It had been the custom for almost as long for the Phraxes to take concubines – the first that the flotilla histories officially recorded had founded her harem late in the thirty-second millennium – and if the whole flotilla could be considered to be essentially the personal transport, homestead and entourage of the current Rogue Trader Phrax, as the wording of the charter indicated, then it seemed logical that the members of the flotilla who entered the harem of the trader should go one step further, become literal possessions, and be disposed of as such as part of the funerary routine.

So the thinking went, at any rate, and only the occasional malcontent saw any problems with it. Of course, the practice was seen rather differently by the Imperial citizenry at large, whom the flotilla people referred to as 'tikks' (the origins of that term had been lost to memory, the contemptuous way in which the flotilla people used it had not). The fact that almost every tikk who heard of the custom reacted with shock or disgust irritated the flotilla no end. It was the job of tikks to go about the business of being tikks: having things to buy, or things to sell that other tikks wanted to buy, or coming on board to perform the rare piece of maintenance or repair that the flotilla's considerable resources could not manage. It was not their job to pry into the Phrax family, whose job it was to pursue whatever the charter allowed them to pursue, which was, within a few token limitations that the flotilla observed out of tradition, almost anything. The Emperor Himself had said so, had he not?

While the tikks saw the Emperor as some kind of distant but demanding god, the people of the flotilla tended to view Him as a benevolent former patron, the source of a very valuable signature on a document. That was another little fact that it seemed best to keep to themselves: new inductees to the flotilla's petty-officer class were shown bulkheads near the bridge of the *Bassaan*, the flotilla's flagship, where bolt-shell craters had been left unrepaired as a reminder that one of the few things the Phrax Charter did not grant immunity from was the Imperial Inquisition. Folklore had it that whenever the *Bassaan* broke into the immaterium the fifteen-hundred-year-old bloodstains from that terrible affair would for just a moment become fresh and visible again, but then few such communities are without a story of that sort.

So as they flew among the dust clouds and barely-big-enough-to-be-called-planets that made up most of the Shexia system, the *Bassaan* and its little formation-mate the *Callyac's Promise* manoeuvred up side by side. *Bassaan* was the more powerful ship, home to commanders, officers, brokers and fiduciars, a sleek and elegant ram-prowed cruiser. The *Promise* was nothing more or less than a floating palace pushed through space on a tail of plasma, a fat-nosed little block of hull sporting a coxcomb of steeples down its back. To some it looked like a claw, to others a small mammal arching its back and bristling its fur. It had been the private estate of successive Phraxes since the thirty-seventh millennium when Olendro Phrax had decided that sharing any of his other ships with pilgrims (even the fabulously wealthy, ostentatiously pious pilgrims he was doing rather well out of transporting) was beneath him.

Once the two were flying close enough for the crewmembers clustered at the high-arched windows to wave to one another, the shuttles launched, crossing the tiny distance between the hulls quickly and cleanly, avoiding the usual bravado and fancy flying as a mark of respect, their doomed passengers wrapped in shrouds woven with refractor-wires that created fuzzy shadows over each stooped form and painted face. They had all known Phrax was dying – the man's final coma had lasted for more than a year – and most were resigned. Only a few were weeping, and only one needed to be physically helped out of the shuttle and down the corridors into the funeral chamber. The air was quiet and solemn as for any unpleasant but serious duty – similar, perhaps, to Marking Day, when all the babies who had been born in the flotilla over the past year were rounded up to be presented to the trader and receive a ritual brand across their stomach.

The armsmen stationed in the hall and chamber made sure that the whole business went quietly enough. The elaborate and gruesome ceremonies of earlier generations had been dispensed with, and the concubines knew their role. None fought, in the end, and after their ashes were fired into space they formed for a while a faint haze over the *Bassaan* before vacuum and momentum dispersed them. And so it was finished.

Or so it was thought at the time. It was not until the flotilla was in orbit over Shexia itself that one of the watch officers of the *Bassaan* realised that the concubine inventory was not correctly notarised by his counterpart on the *Callyac's Promise*, and it took the two of them together more than an hour to realise the document had been doctored rather than just sloppily prepared. Two concubines were unaccounted for, and over a dozen shuttles had travelled between the flotilla ships and down to the planet's spaceport already. Already working out excuses to their superiors in their heads, they began organising a search while the word went up to the flotilla masters that the purging had been botched.

It was not unheard of, of course. Concubines recruited from outside the flotilla had a particular tendency to flout tradition and try to run, although most of the flotilla people did not understand it. Concubines, no matter the gender no matter the age, were always given plenty of time to prepare themselves. Fighting or fleeing seemed ungrateful, not to mention graceless and unprofessional. The flotilla had even dispensed with the old rites of live spacing or slow incineration: the concubines had been sent after their owner with a slender needle of instant-acting neurotoxin, as a mark of compassion. It wasn't as if the flotilla were savages, after all.

Foundry Level, Shexia City, Shexia

'As a mark of *compassion*?' Karmine Mitrani was finding it hard to believe his ears.

'Oh yes.' The young man pacing the catwalk beside him took a deep breath. 'Compared to the old ways, which I think we can both be glad we don't have to think about too much, it's remarkably compassionate. That was what everyone kept saying.' He swallowed hard.

Mitrani didn't say anything more, but walked alongside the man, his features downcast. There was something odd about Flag Ensign Nils Petronas's manner that made Mitrani think that more obvious sympathy or horror might be misplaced.

Karmine Mitrani was an orbit-clerk in the service of the Shexia Dockmasters' Guild, and he was good at his job. He should have been – selective augmetics, deep hypnotic therapy and conditioning for fifteen of his most formative years, and repeated physical and chemical surgery to carefully selected areas of his brain, had hardwired and super-sensitised his social reactions. His sense of mood and nuance was uncanny, his ability to grasp and understand odd customs and adopt them seamlessly was confounding. He could keep up hours of the dry, borderline-abusive banter that the farmship syndicates from the Novanjide sub used to test anyone they planned even the smallest commercial dealings with, or remember every tiniest detail of the family affairs of a fiduciary courier who had last come to the system five years ago, and ask after them in the man's own planetary and continental accent, reproduced so perfectly as to bring his guest to tears of homesickness. He could count on one hand the number of times he had had to deal with people whose ways he truly did not understand.

He was having a little trouble with this.

'That's why we're down here, you see. Two of the damned little dollies ran away. Spat in the face of the rest of the flotilla. Pissed all over the respect the rest of us were showing for the funeral rites for old Hoyyon. So now we have to grub around here to make sure they get what we promised them.' Petronas stepped to the edge of the catwalk and peered over it.

Back when this had been a foundry first and a spaceport second, great mazes of gantries and pipes had spread out from the railheads, becoming higher, denser and more intricate over the centuries until now the whole outlying city was a rat-warren of metal lattices rising high above the basalt, endless jungles of pipes and laddershafts and walkways in constant vibration from the pounding of the furnace sublevels and the craft passing overhead.

The two men stood on a viewing platform with a semicircle of exhaust tubes half ringing like organ pipes, echoing the roar of the machinery deep beneath them and radiating dull heat. The air was close and smelled scorched; the valley's permanent ceiling of black cloud and ash looked low enough to be scraped with the fingertips.

After a few more moments of surreptitiously watching the ensign, Mitrani tried again, with a carefully-judged change in tone.

'Are they even worth the trouble? Should you not treat the matter dismissively?' He weighed his words; they were well away from the arclight arrays of the central pyramids, and the perpetual twilight was making Petronas's body language hard to read. 'Perhaps the best punishment,' he went on, 'would be to let them lose themselves in a substreet pit of Shexia?'

'They belong to the flotilla. They are its property, which is to say ours. I've been tasked to make sure they die as they were intended to, and to forfeit three square centimetres of skin from the back of each of my hands without numbing-drugs if I have not done so by the time we cast off for Hydraphur. I wouldn't expect a t... I wouldn't expect you to understand.'

Petronas untucked an infrascope from the oversized cuff of his elaborate uniform tunic and scanned the platform underneath them again. Mitrani thought he saw a slight tremor in the hand holding the scope that Petronas couldn't quite control. Or maybe it was the heat-haze spoiling the infrared view of the platform that made him grunt with annoyance and stuff the scope crudely away again. Below them were bulky, prowling figures: troopers of the dock watch, loaned to Petronas by Second Dockmaster Paich as a gesture of goodwill to his distinguished clients. When Mitrani had been placed in charge of keeping the flotilla officers happy, he had not seen this coming.

As they stood amid the rumble and the low red light, a pair of prop-carriers passed overhead and by their lights Mitrani saw Petronas scrub a hand over his eyes and face. His shoulders slumped for a moment, and then he gasped in a lungful of the smoky air and snapped himself back to attention when he remembered he was sharing the platform with someone else. In the better light the orbit-clerk got his best look at the ensign's face since they had left the ornithopter: pale dun eyes, lantern jaw, a birthmark curling under one side of the mouth. It wasn't hard to see where the tears from Petronas's eyes had left marks down both his cheeks. Despite the ensign's crude attempts, their tracks were still as clear to read as the cocktail of expressions he was trying to hide. Agonised frustration, grief, and poisonous rage.

During his career Mitrani had encountered behaviour that he understood in a cerebral way but knew he could never fully feel in his guts. He knew about the intensity of emotions within families, and there were times when he had visited client ships and seen families together that made his own feelings ring like a bell, but he himself had been taken from a foundry crèche at five to begin his conditioning and could not imagine what such a life might be like from the inside.

Master Paich liked to amuse himself by locking Mitrani away by himself every so often, where the lack of human company was torture as the clerk's heightened social cognition starved for input. Each of the nights that he wept himself to sleep in an empty room, Mitrani knew it amused Paich to see how much isolation hurt him. But that was not the same thing as knowing what made such casual cruelty so appealing. Mitrani had tried to imagine inflicting cruelty on another person and the thought had revolted him.

So it was easy for him to know what the ensign was feeling, but Karmine Mitrani was still trying to understand how that meshed with his words when there was a shout below.

'Hear that?' cried Petronas. 'The lift-platform, they're trying to get down the shaft! Run, come on! I knew the little bitches couldn't have gone far!'

The metal lattice under their feet rattled as Petronas bolted across the platform and down the narrow stairs. Mitrani, wishing not for the first time that he had not drawn this assignment, picked up the hem of his ash-coat and ran after him.

* * *

The *Callyac's Promise*, Docking orbit, Shexia

THEY NEVER TALKED about the little vault in the depths of the *Callyac's Promise* as a conference chamber. The conference chamber was where old Hoyyon had called them together to wait upon him, the place where all their advice had to be pitched to his ears, the place where they all were required to begin every meeting standing in stylised positions around Phrax's throne so as to reproduce exactly the earliest known painting of a Phrax delivering orders to his underlings. As the whims of traders went that had not been the worst, and it had been bearable while Hoyyon had been younger and lucid and still full of steel, but as he had aged the conferences had changed, and not for the better.

So now they met here instead, a little room where the truth was told between colleagues and equals. None of the masters brought in their retainers, none attempted formal greetings or rites. They all understood that the flotilla required traditions and ceremonies – but occasionally it also required this.

'Have we got the last of them yet?' Halpander asked. He was the flotilla's Master of Logistics, the controller of provisions, loading, unloading, crewing, repairs. Things being out of place bothered him.

'We haven't had the final report yet, but it won't be long,' answered Kyorg. Kyorg controlled the Office of Envoys aboard the *Arrow of Magritta*, supervising diplomacy with whatever authorities the flotilla was required to deal with. Most of the others had a low opinion of him: as rogue trader, Hoyyon had been his own figurehead and first envoy and had left Kyorg with little more than formalities to take care of. With Hoyyon dead, Kyorg had shown little inclination to pick up the slack, and always had a delegate to blame for anything that went wrong. 'I gave Rachen the job of getting authorisation to hunt them down and he said the dockmasters had waved us in and given us a clerk to help it all go smoothly. I think he sent an ensign down to finish it off. I'm sure they've got it in hand.' The others around the circle exchanged glances.

'We must have the full account of the escape documented for punishment and suppression, too. And quickly.' That was the papery voice of Mistress Zanti, skin as white as her tunic and eyes as black as her skirt and shawl. The grey silk scarf over her head showed the outlines of the ridges of data-sockets that covered it from ear to ear.

Zanti had the unusual ability to genuinely unnerve most of the flotilla masters: she was as cool, ruthless and unerringly precise in her thoughts as one of the logic engines she presided over. Her craft, the *Kortika*, was the newest of the flotilla, added seventy-eight years before, all from the way she had built up her own agencies and her own turf. Nobody could remember the last time someone had become that powerful in the flotilla through nothing but their own efforts. 'I have not ordered the eidetor-savants to begin the scribing processes yet,' she went on, 'and I will not do so until I can know that they can record that the escapees were brought home and their accomplices punished.' Such a statement in such a tone should have been grossly out of line for someone in Zanti's position, and it was a measure of the force of her personality that the rest of them simply stared at their fingernails or at the table.

'We have managed our affairs for centuries, I think we all know,' put in Galt smoothly after the silence had stretched out for several minutes. 'This is an unfortunate untidiness that will soon be over, and which I am sure we do not need to spend any more time on. Perhaps the charged situation we have found ourselves in since the death of our old trader is persuading us that such setbacks are larger than they are?' Looking around the table, he saw that he had hit on it. They had spent so much time on the minutiae of the escape because no one wanted to come out and say what they knew they were all here for.

Galt had been Hoyyon Phrax's major-domo, his master of chambers. Officially he was probably the least powerful man in the room, even with the fluid, personality-driven way that the flotilla masters measured rank, but in personal terms he had been closer to the old man than any of them. So, he supposed, it came down to him.

'It's time we admitted it,' he said. 'Not all of you may know how strongly the feeling runs, but I have spoken now to every one of you and I know that all of us here feel the same way.'

He watched them look at each other. The masters of the Phrax flotilla were tough and seasoned. They had been in their jobs for decades at the least; many could remember a change of trader, some of them two. Between them they had seen the flotilla through warp-tempests, radiation and meteor storms, excursions into wild space and through Imperial interdicts, pirate ambushes and xenos raids, the attentions of rival rogue traders and rare internal intrigues. They had even bluffed, connived or deceived, or on one occasion outright assassinated, their way through clashes with Imperial governors, the Adeptus and the Inquisition. But the introverted little microculture of the flotilla could be oddly sensitive about certain things. Like...

'The matter of the succession.' It was no surprise that the voice was that of D'Leste, the man with whom Galt had spent the most time in secret talks. A squat man with the craggy red face of a brewhouse thug and the deft hands of a born surgeon, D'Leste commanded the flotilla's Apothecarion and had been Hoyyon Phrax's personal physician. 'More specifically, the matter of the heir.' There were uncomfortable stirrings around the table, but no one contradicted him. Galt would not have allowed the subject to come up had he not made sure that everyone at the meeting would hear the matter out. But they went one better.

'Phrax the Younger. Varro Phrax.' Behaya's thin, mobile face and reedy voice always made her seem nervous, even when she was simply thinking aloud as now. Her title, according to the old and quaintly-worded flotilla documentation, was 'Supervisor of Pertinent Bodies and Labours'; she was universally addressed by the shorthand title of 'Crewmistress'. 'I suppose we've all had time by now to form an opinion of him.' Behaya had charge of the network of 'friends and correspondents', as the flotilla referred to its spies and informants through the major systems of a dozen sectors. The responsibility had technically been Kyorg's, but he had been outwitted by Behaya and had lost the responsibility to her after he had not displayed the wit or ambition to retain it. By that stage Hoyyon had been entering his final illness and one of the first things Behaya had done with her new powers was to establish a dossier on Varro Phrax. Neither she nor any of the other flotilla masters had liked what they had heard.

'The man's useless,' ventured Trazelli, the flotilla's captain-at-arms, once again voicing the room's opinion. 'I don't remember him as a child the way I suppose some of you do, but let's be honest, we've all read the reports from Behaya's people. The little wastrel's done nothing but drift and spend since he parted ways with his father. No stomach for the role. Oh, I don't doubt he's got a gut hanging to his knees, but no stomach for the role.' That was what passed for humour with Trazelli. The others ignored it.

'I do remember Varro as a child,' said Galt. 'He left the flotilla at ten. His father thought it would do him good to grow up on

Gunarvo. There was talk at the time of a major migration into the worlds beyond it in the Deunoff Sub-sector after the second Hadekuro Crusade cleared the orks out. Full Imperial colonisation and reconstruction edicts, very profitable for rogue traders providing we moved in time. Hoyyon wanted to make sure there was a way in for us if we needed it, so he left Varro and his mother there so the boy could grow up making some good contacts.'

'He's wasted his life, then,' snapped Zanti. 'Literally.' One of the things she also handled was the flotilla's contracts and commercial bonds; if anything at all had come of the Deunoff Sub she would have known it.

'Admittedly it's been forty years,' said Galt as though he had not been interrupted, 'but I remember Varro as being a very... *passive* boy. He wasn't short on brain, and he seemed to like pleasing his father, but I watched him carefully and I never saw him with that light in his eyes. Never saw him want to reach out and clutch something and change it.'

'A withdrawn little man, would you say?' asked Halpander.

'Not as a child, no. In fact, I remember him as not being shy in making use of the finer things we provided him with. No qualms about making sure his life was good.'

'Has that changed?' Zanti asked Behaya.

'Not at all,' the crew-mistress answered. 'He and his mother became quite the darlings of Gunarvo, by all accounts. That push into the Deunoff sub never came about, but Gunarvo grew prosperous anyhow. And Hoyyon made sure Varro and his mother were very well set up to begin with – he wanted them sought after so they could get established in the right kind of way. Pity we never got around to going back there, really. We might have made a difference.'

Zanti flicked her hand as though she could physically brush the irrelevant thoughts away.

'So it's out in the open, then, isn't it?' she said. 'We don't want him. We're without a trader and in the shit, because our trader-in-waiting is an indolent little playboy who's going to come on board with favourites he's built up after forty years of being allowed to indulge himself.'

More thoughtful silence.

'We were not always a flotilla,' said Galt, who had often heard Hoyyon talking about this. 'We were a single, small ship. Then we were two, then three, and as the line of Phrax built itself it built us. But how many times have we talked about this? How many of us have not had the dream that our grandchildren or our great-grandchildren will not be masters of a flotilla but of an armada? Other rogue traders have commanded them. Is the Phrax Charter not the equal of any and the superior of most?'

'I know what our charter says,' said Kyorg, as if everyone else didn't. 'It might let us look down our nose at the Imperium, Galt, but it won't let us spit in their eye. Remember those craters on the *Bassaan*? Our trips back to Hydraphur are the one time when we're really under the Adeptus' thumb. We don't get to pick and choose which successions we like and which we don't. The charter says that–'

'Thanks, Kyorg, we follow you,' D'Leste cut him off with little grace. 'We know this is not a good succession. We have had bad successions before. There are sometimes ways around them, but not this time. Varro's not old, so just dropping out of communication for however long it takes him to die and blaming it on a warp storm won't work.'

'We did that?' asked Halpander.

'Succession of Saitiri Phrax from his brother Rukkman, 347.M37,' said Zanti. 'The fleet wasn't able to reach Hydraphur until after Saitiri had passed away. His daughter Mietta succeeded.'

'Letting Varro succeed and simply running him as we run... as we administer the fleet in the temporary absence of a trader is not an option either,' said D'Leste. 'I won't bother with details now, but it's clear from Behaya's reports if you want to read them. He's not the man Hoyyon was, but he's no pliant little custard-brained figure-head, either. He'd fight us if we tried anything. Even if we kept control, the flotilla might not last in any form we recognise.'

'You and Galt seem pretty confident you know your succession problem inside and out,' said Kyorg, giving D'Leste an appraising look. 'If I said "I suppose you have an answer for us too", would I regret it?'

D'Leste's and Galt's eyes met, and the same thought was in both of them. There was no point in dancing around it any longer. D'Leste fingered an amulet at his throat and the room lights dimmed; a holo-cage of tiny wires hissed down from the ceiling to hang in the air and wove a net of light-threads that grew into a picture. A holo-pict of a young man's head, pale dun eyes, a lantern jaw, a birthmark curling under one side of the mouth, the collar of an ensign's tunic just visible where the picture truncated.

'Well then,' said D'Leste, 'I would like to move the discussion on. And so here, my colleagues, is our subject.'

Foundry level, Shexia City, Shexia

THE ALLEY THEY had found themselves in was a hewsink, which came from 'HW-sink', which came from 'human-waste sink.' The human waste was humans themselves, outcasts whose age or injuries stopped them working in the foundries, and who had so far eluded the Urban Purity Patrols who chased unproductive citizens out into the sewage marshes to die. As the pursuit party stampeded down the narrow space the shadows around them were full of furtive shapes slipping between the pipes and pylons – in a hewsink, if you saw a weapon or a uniform you ran without another thought. As Mitrani gritted his teeth and followed the troopers through the slippery muck underfoot, he could hear scuffles breaking out behind him as the braver outcasts emerged again to fight over food scraps or heat-taps abandoned in the rush.

Underneath the ash and warm mud the alley floor was a bundle of broad pipes with not even a grid laid over them, and Petronas and Mitrani both found themselves slipping and stumbling. The troopers, who had the advantage of cleated boots and experience moving around the lower levels, were pulling ahead of them, and that meant that they were drawing closer to their quarry. Mitrani's guts knotted at the sound of a woman's voice, a young one, sobbing out prayers and pleas ahead of them.

The alley suddenly dipped down into a slope and zigged through a ninety-five degree turn. Their quarry was already through it and the troopers, laughing and calling to one another as though they were on a treasure hunt, rounded it easily. Petronas, just behind them, skated on the ash-mud and clanged into the pipes in front of him, then went down on one knee, cursing, as he tried to pull away from the hot metal and unholster his pistol at the same time. Mitrani, almost piling into him, saw the pistol come out and before he could help himself blurted 'oh no.'

'Oh yes, clerk,' Petronas snarled. His eyes and teeth shone in the ruddy foundry-light. 'Don't think you can do a damn thing to stop this. If you do I'll kill you myself and tell your oily little boss that someone down in the slums had a pistol we didn't expect.'

Ahead of them one of the women was caught, crying out as she kicked armoured shins and bit gauntleted hands. Petronas regained his feet and walked towards her, and the light was bright enough for her to recognise him. Mitrani heard her scream 'Nils! Nils for pity's sake, you of all of them–' and then there was the snap of a las-round and her voice cut off. The troopers, finally starting to be disturbed by the work they were about, let her body slide to the alley floor as the second woman was dragged back.

The trooper who had her in a brutal hammerlock was also a woman, her face grim under the uniform bandanna and ash-goggles as the concubine talked quietly and urgently to her. Finally, when they were alone in a clear spot of mud together and the trooper still had not answered, the prisoner spat full into her face.

'Look at me,' Petronas told her as he walked up to them. Neither woman moved. 'Look at me, Aralye,' Petronas said again, and when she still refused, walked around behind her, put the hellpistol to her head and pulled the trigger. Then he stepped away, faced the alley wall, and stood there for a moment shuddering so violently that the muzzle of the pistol chattered against the gemstone edging of his holster when he tried to put it away. He pulled two heavy plastic parcels from a satchel at his hip, fumbled with them for a moment trying to open them, and then let them drop from his shaking hands and made a curt gesture for the troopers to pick them up and unfurl them.

'Corpse-sacks,' he said to Mitrani. 'Flotilla custom says they have to be burned onboard ship, so we need them easy to carry. Get on with it, we gave you orders!' The last was a bark at the troopers, who were standing and staring at him; after a moment, two of them drew serrated combat knives and knelt down by the first corpse.

'One of them knew you,' Mitrani whispered. 'I heard it in her voice, there was no mistaking it.'

'We knew... each other. She was a friend... of my mother's.' Petronas's voice was dry; he had to gulp and lick his lips before he finished each sentence.

'Then *why*?' Mitrani was almost screaming, all thoughts of service and diplomacy forgotten. He had never, never seen anything like this. 'Why did you kill them? Why hack them limb from limb? Nobody would have known! Why didn't you help them?'

Suddenly Mitrani was half-sitting on the warm ash-slurry, blinking at the way his mouth suddenly felt wet and stung. He had never been punched before. Petronas stood over him for a moment, then crouched down to glare into the shaking clerk's eyes.

'Because the third of the women to walk into that chamber aboard the *Bassaan* was my mother. Do you understand that? My mother. Walking in there with her head high. And there was nothing I could have ever done to help *her*. So if I have to lose my mother because that old bastard saw fit to finally die, well then no one else, *no one* else is going to go running away from their duty. Do you understand?'

He stood up and turned away, shouting at the troopers again, and Mitrani rolled over, scrabbled away on hands and knees and vomited again and again as from behind him came the sound of knives sawing into flesh.

The Flotilla of Rogue Trader Phrax,
Docking orbit, Shexia

'Do you think he'll do it?' Galt asked D'Leste as they walked away from the meeting room. They both understood what the question was. Galt was asking if their subject would manage the deception. The question of whether he would decide to co-operate with them would have puzzled both men. What the subject thought he might decide to do was irrelevant. But D'Leste was not going to be drawn.

'It's something to try,' he said, as he always said when he was unsure of whether the thing to be tried was going to succeed. The look they exchanged said all that was needed: a select circle of pragmatic people had considered their position and taken the only option they felt they had. What else to say?

As the ships began to vibrate with the power of the plasma coils and vox-hails flew from ship to ship and from ship to dock, they went to their posts. Halpander stood on a platinum pedestal surrounded by a holo-sheet of green crystal on which fiscal and logistical algorithms flashed and swam butterfly-quick – it was traditional for the Master of Logistics to begin every voyage surrounded by the signs of his post. Zanti's spindly frame settled into a deep-cushioned linkage niche as the ports on her skull spoke to the ship's logisters and sent transmissions sleeting through her skull like chilly white lightning. D'Leste, no longer needed on the household decks of the *Callyac's Promise,* retreated to his chamber and began planning his letter to Magos Dyobann. He knew that the Mechanicus cabal would be on the flotilla's side, but the magos would be insulted were he to simply assume it. Certain formalities had to be followed.

Galt was left on the *Promise,* the only one of the conspirators with no traditional or required place to be, but there was one thing he thought it fitting he should do. And so he walked down the ramp from the speaking room, weaving slightly every so often or adjusting his gait without conscious thought as the ship's gravity didn't quite cancel out the ship's manoeuvres. As the flotilla powered away from Shexia and out to where they would break warp, Galt walked down the long promenade that ran down the spine of the ship, connecting the base of each of its spires with a tunnel of crystal-clear armourglass reinforced with rows of carved rockrete arches like ribs.

In the heart of the tallest spire he sat on a stool of pink and grey marble while thrumming augmetic drones analysed his scent, gene-print, walk, breathing patterns, brainwaves. When they were satisfied they flew ahead of him down a hall of chilly, unadorned steel and spat the blood and breath samples they had taken into the eyes and mouth of an intricate gargoyle embedded in the hall's far wall. The trial was passed, the terrible devices in the walls spared Galt's life. There was a hiss as parts machined to near-miraculous tolerances slid over one another and then one of the steel walls was gone.

Galt walked forward to stand on a little square of black steel on a floor polished to mirror-brightness. In a steady voice he began reciting each of the oaths of loyalty he had taken to the line of Phrax, begun on his tenth birthday and added to in each of the twelve decades since then. He found himself wondering, as he spoke each ritualised line, whether his doubts were showing in his voice, whether the listening machines were capable of deciding that what they were planning to do would trample on those oaths. But if there was anything to show in his voice, the machines did not hear or did not understand. The automata at the far end of the room, patterned after great men and women of the First Crusade whose names no one now remembered, bowed in unison and said his name in flat voices. There was a crack of power as the void-shield lowered and then the final wall parted like a curtain. And after so many trials and barriers the space beyond it was comically simple: a little metal nook with a table sitting under a bank of polished glass.

Galt knew the stories and the rumours, and knew they were stupid. No dire curse-runes, no pages of human skin or ridiculous incantations to appease dead spirits. It was a small, plain parcel of cloth cover and creamy paper, the writing across each page the regular, even hand of a competent scribe. What ornamentation imaginable by a human mind could go a hundredth of the way to doing justice to what was inside?

The book was held in a neutral gas formulated to prevent the material from ever decaying; the stasis field that filled the room whenever there were no visitors made sure of it. It had acquired scuffs and creases in its days as a working document, but it would acquire no more. Fine wires rested between the pages and in theory the machine could turn the book to whatever clause a reader needed to look at. Galt could not remember it ever being used. The flotilla had plenty of transcripts and copies to use day to day, the masters knew the whole document to the letter. There was only one thing worth coming into the chamber to see. Galt crouched down and looked at the last page of the book, the expanse of stiff paper untouched but for three marks.

At the top of the page, in an antiquated hand that made the letters barely recognisable, the signature of Beleusa Phrax. And below it…

…below it, a single letter, written down the dead centre of the page with five beautiful, elegant strokes of a nib: a cross-slashed letter *I*.

And below that, a little mark, a smudge, a dot on the page. Looking at it, as always, Galt seemed to feel the air shudder around him, growing close and thick as though before a storm.

He stayed there for nearly an hour, crouched before the case that held the Phrax Charter, staring with meditative intensity at the page and the twofold mark that signed it: the *I* of *Imperator* and the single pressed-in drop of blood.

CHAPTER FOUR

The Phrax Manor, Asterine Lock, Gunarvo

VARRO PHRAX DIDN'T seem to want to talk about business, but Domasa Dorel found that less irritating than she had expected. That morning she had risen early and taken an hour longer than she usually did to go through her physical and mental exercises. And if all else failed she had brought a little flask of sweet-perfumed liqueur concealed in the fold of her mantle, a sip of which she knew would relax her if she needed it. But she had been lucky: the visit to Varro's estates had been exactly the diversion she needed after nineteen dolorous months as a junior Navigator with an Adeptus Ministorum pilgrim fleet, surrounded by pious mutant-haters who refused all contact with her whenever they could and kept staring at the bulge on her forehead and making the sign of the aquila when they couldn't. Varro seemed barely to have given her genes a second thought, and his home offered far more diversion than the cramped cell aboard the *Song of Righteousness*.

The giant enclosed garden they were strolling through now, fully half again the size of the manor itself, was a case in point, even if some of its diversions were more than a little unnerving to a spacefarer unused to wildlife.

'Now this,' Varro said, 'this is the sort of thing that the charter will be very handy for indeed. Take a look here.'

'I see a very interesting stretch of churned earth between two large, rather dull trees,' Domasa replied. She was confident enough now to make wisecracks; something about Varro tended to put people at their ease. He laughed delightedly and pushed a hank of hair out of his eyes.

'Just earth now, Domasa. But here's the thing. The Emerald tripleaf – that's those two plants on either side of it – they're very social plants. They try to co-operate when they sense another growing nearby. They produce waste as a result of metabolising their prey – you remember the picts I showed you of them in their native system? – and they pump that away through their roots. Careful!' Cherrick, one of Domasa's entourage, had stepped closer to look at the tripleaf. 'See how the leaves are quivering? That's how the higher-order mammals on Stavron know to back off. You saw the way they lunge on the picts.' Domasa shook a playful finger at Cherrick, and he went red under his visor and made fists as Varro waved at the empty ground. 'So they've spotted the empty ground and they're pumping out the exhausted haematic fluids they can't use, and guess what the Tygranese pufferfruit uses?'

'Uses as in eats? Hmm, could it be the kinds of, er, things found in exhausted haematic fluid from the, er...'

'Emerald tripleaf?'

'Of course, there's no way I could have guessed that.'

Varro was laughing again.

'The pufferfruit are amazing. I've only seen one myself apart from in picts, a tiny little one in a glass bell in a botanical exhibition on Lynia three years ago. Then last month I paid through the nose for an original copy of Euseby Riva's book on Tygranese plant life, and you should see the size they can grow to. There are all sorts of edicts about what flora you can transport to where, of course, and the Imperial mercantile controls are pretty strict. One of my best agents in the Kozya sub has told me that he won't be able to send me specimens any more, because the whole quarter has been closed off by some kind of quarantine. But with the family charter, you see, well, what's the limit on what I can do?' He grinned at Domasa and clapped his hands.

'Almost ready!' called Rikah from behind them, making Domasa jump. Rikah was one of Varro's close retainers, tending to the same sort of uncritical jolly humour as his master. The sides of his head had been implanted with vox-receivers, the receptor vanes incorporated into ornamental frills that ran from his face around to the nape of his neck. Domasa thought them tacky beyond words, but Rikah was obviously tremendously proud of them – he had confided to her that when Varro had the charter he was hoping someone on the flotilla would put in augmetic muscles that would let him flex the frills up and down. Domasa had smiled politely while she doubled over with laughter inside.

'Hear that? We really should get going. Do you all have your cards? Have you all given your picks in? Everyone?' Varro looked past Domasa to her retinue, who were unused to being directly involved with their mistress's conversations and shuffled nervously. 'Dreyder's been after me to organise another of these for months, we can't let it start late. All ready to go up to the gallery? Rikah, let them know to bring some more drinks to the gallery, will you? Kolentin knows what we like.'

The twisting skyways that ran this way and that through Varro Phrax's rambling garden of horrors were not directly reachable from the ground, and they had to wait for one of the little platforms to come rattling down on its silver chains before they could be winched up to the nearest one. Gripping the railing to steady herself, Domasa finally took an opportunity to talk business.

'Varro, we're going to need to talk about the charter at some point.'

'I'm looking forward to it,' he cut in. 'I know it probably looks like I've been dodging my responsibilities here, you know. When I lived on the flotilla they made sure I knew every day that I was going to grow up to be Rogue Trader Varro Phrax.'

'Good. But–'

'I don't take it lightly. But don't you think I deserved a breathing space before I take it up? I think it will make me a better trader, don't you? Living in that weird flotilla, I can't see how that makes you a rounded person. Wealth for its own sake, I mean, it's stupid. I think I should use those resources *for* something. Do you have a garden, Domasa?' She shook her head and went on quickly before he could start up again.

'I know you're excited about the possibilities it gives you for all this,' and she swept a hand out over the garden, 'but I'm worried that you're making too many plans too soon. I'll be honest with you, Varro, you're going to have to give some more serious thought to your succession.' This was the kind of conversation she was used to having in sealed rooms that had been swept for auspexes and spy-flies, wrapped in privacy fields with an astropathic choir drowning them out to any scrying or spellcraft. But she was proud of her adaptability.

'The trip to Hydraphur, do you mean? I don't believe there will be any problem with getting there in time. Anyway, the ceremony can't start without me, can it?' Varro stepped onto the elevated gallery-path that snaked through the garden and held out his hand. After a moment's surprise she took it and was impressed when he didn't flinch: like most of the Navis Nobilite her physique was skewed in more ways than just the warp eye in her forehead – her hands had only three long fingers each. It was the only oddity of her appearance she was really self-conscious about – the others were all invisible under her gowns and robes, and most other Navigators didn't care about them.

'No, the trip wasn't what I meant,' she said, looking around. Like all of Gunarvo's trading gentry, Varro kept a manor embedded in the ravine wall over the Asterine Lock and it loomed over them now. But his garden ran on over kilometres of canal-bank, an ungainly range of arboretae and ribbed domes on the outside, a lush mass of plant life on the inside, all of it hostile. Further on there were domes of elaborately engineered climates for dangerous flora from the more exotic worlds which she was hoping to avoid seeing; walking the elevated paths over the predatory greenery in the main gardens was more than enough for her.

Now some of the plants below were starting to quiver as the gardeners began to stimulate their attack responses with scent-puffs, electromagnetic shadows, tiny patterns of vibration on the ground. The tripleaf thicket they had walked past was shivering, the edges of the plate-sized leaves hitting against each other with a faint chinking sound.

'The laws, then? I don't imagine that dealing with the Arbites will be a problem. Nobody told me it would. Rikah, is everyone ready? Is Dreyder ready?'

'He's bounding about like a puppy, Varro. He's been sprinting in and out of the garden for the last two hours. He's told everyone he's scouting for the runners, he's been taking them little tips and reports. They're playing along. He's fine.'

'You let him run in and out of the garden like that?' Domasa asked, curiosity getting the better of her annoyance. The dynamics of Navigator families were very different to those of mainstream humanity, and sentimentality towards children was something she didn't begin to understand, but she found it interesting nevertheless.

'Dreyder's seven,' Varro told her, 'and that's more than old enough to know his way around the south wing. The plants there are all passive hunters, so he's in no danger if he keeps clear of them. The gardeners won't let him anywhere he might be in over his head. He'll own this garden one day, remember. He needs to start young! I was twenty before I discovered predator-plants.'

'Speaking of inheriting, though, Varro...'

'Yes, the Arbites. I looked at the last succession when father got the charter. There was some kind of ceremony with a general.'

'Arbitor General Actte.'

'That sounds right. Have we written to him?' They stepped aboard a little viewing-carriage, barely more than a flat platform, designed to skim along right at the edge of the gallery. It glided toward the southern end of the garden; the viewing levels were all packed with chattering spectators and drums were beating.

'He's no longer on Hydraphur. Arbites change more often than rogue traders do. There are four Arbites General commanding on Hydraphur now. One Majore, three Senioris. But no, the problem isn't with them.'

'I see.' Varro was waving to a slender woman in yellow who was carrying a squirming little boy through the throng. 'Ksana! Here, come up on the car with us.' Ksana and Domasa exchanged cool looks – she did not have her husband's expansive nature, and had kept at arm's length from the Navigator ever since her arrival. The boy Dreyder paid no attention to her, although when he had first seen her he had cried and complained about the 'cold ice lady'. Domasa had shrugged and avoided him as much as she could after that. Being around Navigators affected people in different ways, that was all.

Watching them now, Varro bent over the boy exclaiming over his accounts of the 'scouting' he had done, Ksana smiling at them both and adding details that Dreyder was too excited for, Domasa decided that she wasn't going to be able to get the man to concentrate on business matters any time soon. She looked down into the garden again.

Ten athletes, eight men and two women, had emerged from the staging-rooms and stood in a rough line while the starter capered up and down before them: his glittering suit included suspensors just powerful enough to let him dance on his toes and turn oddly slow-motion backflips. The racers' hair had been dyed to match the clinging gymnastic uniforms they wore, brief and glossy affairs that finished just short of elbows and knees. They jogged on the spot, ready for the signal.

Domasa idly wondered how many variations of this were being played out today across the Imperium. Navigators tended to quickly acquire rather jaded palates for entertainment, and Domasa liked to pay attention to how the connoisseurs amused themselves wherever she went. Wearyingly often, 'elite entertainment' boiled down to cheering people on while they tried to kill each other. But apparently these people were volunteers, and the race was only through those parts of the garden that would be challenging rather than deadly.

The runners got a round of applause, and Dreyder got another one when he was hoisted on his father's shoulders to give the signal. Domasa slipped her pick-card out of her sleeve. Not knowing anything about any of the runners she'd chosen orange and black, the closest to the russet-and-black robes of House Dorel. Orange was a thick-necked man with a great shock of hair and skin the shade of creamy caffeine that rather clashed with his running colours, and black was a slender, snake-hipped young man who was finishing off his pre-race stretches with some poses that had moved several of the female spectators to thoughtful silence.

Domasa had come prepared to bet extravagantly – normally that was the way to a host's good books on occasions like this. She had been a little surprised to find that it wasn't expected. All she was supposed to do was give a small token if one of them finished. Well, she was equipped for that, too. Another old trick was to bring arrays of flashy but basically expendable jewellery and trinkets to meetings like this, to be given away as presents if that looked like it was going to make things easier. Domasa's appreciation for physical beauty had been stunted by a life spent among Navigators, whose appearances tended to range from odd to grotesque, but as she watched the runner in black finish off his exercises she found herself thinking that perhaps getting up close to him to hang a gem-thread around his neck might not be such an ordeal.

Then Dreyder suddenly threw both of his arms in the air and screamed 'GO!' The drums gave one almighty beat and Domasa grabbed the railing as the car surged forward to keep pace with the runners.

IT WAS HALF an hour before they all came back down the gallery, the younger spectators trotting ahead and laughing, the more sedate ones walking behind with drinks in their hands. Varro's little son was with the six runners who'd finished, riding on the shoulders of the tallest, kicking his heels and crowing. Domasa walked a little behind the slowest of them, keeping a stately gait, hands shrouded in her long sleeves and tucked demurely at her back. When Cherrick met her the disgust in his face was the first thing she saw – she shot him a warning look and he had the wit to keep his voice low when he finally fell in alongside her.

'No fatalities! What the hell was everybody supposed to be betting on? What sort of nursery school have we fallen into the middle of, lady? What next, are we going to take turns making each other flower-chains?'

'No, no fatalities. I made the mistake of talking to our host as though there were going to be and he gave me this look and said "I'm not a savage, you know." But it was diverting enough and it's put our host in great good spirits and therefore I will *not* hear you take that tone again while we are here and in earshot of anyone, Cherrick, you or anyone on your team. I don't care what the provocation, there's a flogging in it for you the next time at the very least.' Despite the venom in her words she had kept her tone light and conversational: anyone standing over a couple of metres away would have thought she was sharing an exciting moment from the race.

'In fact, just to make a point about diplomacy and to make sure we stay at the front of our host's mind, I believe I'll take you with me to meet the runners. Paste on a smile for me, now.' A smile seemed to be beyond Cherrick – he made do with cordial nods to the people they passed, while Domasa silently wished she'd been born with too many fingers instead of too few, so it would be easier to count the days until she could start a new assignment on which he would not be tagging along.

Although Varro's physicians were waiting back at the starting line, none of the runners had been seriously injured. The woman in green had welts running across her thighs and shins from the stinging tendrils of a lasher plant she'd been too slow to hurdle, and cords stood out on her neck as a nurse plucked out the little thorn splinters and squirted on a sterilising mist. The man with the dazzling silver suit and hair had misjudged the reach of a scissorleaf creeper, and a quick shoot had caught his ankle. Once the rest of the field had passed him the gardeners had gone in to help, but by that time the horn-plated leaves had succeeded in twisting his foot to a nasty angle – he now sat and stoically watched as the swollen joint was bound up.

Over by the garden door itself the lithe young man in black whose card Domasa had drawn was sitting on a bench surrounded by nurses and well-wishers, all female. Domasa had missed whatever it was that had happened to him but it didn't seem all that serious. On the other side of the gate the wounds on the finishers were being tended to – the winner, the man in blue, was the only one unscathed.

Varro and his wife and son were sitting around the last of the non-finishers, a man in early middle age, stocky and sallow, dressed in bright white and riding out the last of the jitters from the stingmoss juice that still stained his hands and bare feet. As they came off the bridge over the garden's central pond the runners had had to run holding their breath for about half a minute through a cloud of soporific pollen. The runner in white was the only one to have misjudged and taken a breath, which had sent him staggering over the stingmoss to fall to his hands and knees. Dreyder sat cross-legged in front of him and watched with huge eyes as the man's legs and arms jumped and shivered. For some reason the movements reminded Domasa of the shivering of the tripleaf when they had gone too close to it.

'Domasa!' Varro called as they drew near. 'I was wondering where you were! I hope you enjoyed the race. These people are quite something to see, eh? Aetho here is one of the trainers at the Whitroc Citadel up on the Escarpine Lock, where they train the PDF officers.' Varro shot a grin at the twitching Aetho, whose answering smile was a little strained. 'I'm sorry your corps colleagues had to keep pace on foot. Hopefully we'll be able to arrange a spectators' car for them if you're here for the next meet.' Varro caught himself and laughed. 'What am I saying? We've got a voyage ahead of us, haven't we? Ridiculous of me.'

Instead of agreeing, Domasa gave Aetho a regal nod.

'Your race certainly made an impression on Cherrick, my head of entourage,' she said. 'He claims never to have seen anything like it.' Both statements were technically true, she thought, wondering what Cherrick's face looked like at this moment. 'Varro, the part of the classic business-obsessed, world-hopping trade envoy is one I hate to play at a...' she blinked as the stung woman behind them let out a pained yelp '...happy occasion like this, but I really would like to continue the conversation we were having before the race. There are things you need to be thinking about.'

Varro nodded earnestly and gave Aetho a reassuring clap on the shoulder.

'Perhaps Cherrick can wait here and go over the finer points of the garden race with Aetho?' Domasa suggested sweetly, steering Varro away from the other guests with no particular subtlety.

'Will you navigate my ship?' Varro suddenly asked, catching her by surprise.

'I... no. No, I'm far too junior for the responsibility of a voyage as important as this.' She'd made herself sound like a bloody novice, too, which hadn't been her intention, but if playing the helpless-junior card was the way to keep Varro's guard down, then fine. 'I'm here for *you*, Varro, to help and advise you and to make sure that my family helps you too. You've got three whole Houses of the Navis Nobilite and their allies and friends looking after you, Varro. Don't you go doubting your ship will have the keenest eye we can provide.'

'Three Houses? I thought you said it was just yourself and some associates.' Varro was looking back to see what his son was doing, and Domasa ransacked her memory for anything she might have said that she couldn't contradict now. She had only had a few hours' notice of her change of assignment, and she had been too taken up with skipping out on the pilgrim-hauler and actually getting here to be able to concentrate on her story.

'There are a lot of people who want to see this charter pass smoothly from hand to hand, Varro,' she said before he could notice her concentration. 'My own family as well as the Krassimal and Yimora. I won't pretend that we are great Houses in the scheme of things, certainly not with lineages like yours, but we are working hard on your behalf to–'

'Really?' She had his full attention now. Varro wasn't stupid, she reminded herself, however he might appear. 'What needs doing on my behalf, exactly? I had assumed that a little thing like ten millennia of tradition would be enough.'

Domasa's family had been founded before anyone named Phrax had even heard of a charter and had survived the toxic politics of the Navis Nobilite by never, ever assuming anything. Oh, Varro was a puppy all right. But puppies could be trained, provided you didn't get too sentimental about them. Now, how to word this...

'The spacefaring class is one of the oldest in the Imperium,' she said after a pause. 'The Navigators, the rogue traders, the officer classes of the Imperial Navy and the explorators and others. The regrettably spreading habit of granting low-level charters and so-called "wildcat warrants" is creating a callow breed who don't really grasp the ventures they're taking on, but I believe the core of the Imperium's essential travelling aristocracy remains. We remain because we... understand things. We have values like tradition. Continuity. Order. We believe that there is a way of doing things.' She was quoting from one of her uncle's lessons, back in her days in the Segmentum Solar when he had been her tutor. 'The inheritance of the charter is important to us just because of those values, as a point of principle. You want it to pass to you at Hydraphur, and of course you are fully entitled to do so, and so that is why we are on your side. My family and my associates and I.'

Varro was staring at her. Behind them there were cheers and shouts: the second stage of the entertainment had begun, with acrobats leaping and swinging and vaulting around and over spiny cacti and thorn trees. Coloured paper lanterns were appearing overhead, strung from tiny wires, and the drumming was back: a light, fast beat that the guests could clap to. Domasa and Varro walked deeper into the garden again, where the light was dimmer. When they reached the point where the plants were starting to rustle at their approach, Varro stopped and turned to Domasa again.

'I'm not completely naïve, you know,' he said. 'I am a member of the Gunarvo Mercantile Chamber and I'm a rogue trader-in-waiting, too. You've told me that yourself enough times, Emperor knows. So come on. You've been so frantic to talk business to me all night and now you won't get it out. What aren't you telling me?'

There was a cry behind them as an acrobat did something amazing. Or maybe fell on his face and died. Domasa didn't care. She was watching the look on Varro's face.

'There's been a counter-claim.'

Varro blinked once, twice, then stared back at the party. Domasa looked the other way, less trusting than Varro of what the assortment – five hundred and sixty-eight species, he had boasted – of carnivorous greenery was doing.

'Impossible,' he said, finally.

'If you think so,' Domasa replied, 'you only have to wait a day or so until the message reaches you. It's an Adeptus communiqué, authenticated by the Arbites command precinct on Hydraphur. The flotilla will go before whoever the Arbites have appointed to oversee this thing, as they're supposed to. But what they're going to do then is announce that there's someone with a better claim on the charter than you who should become the new Rogue Trader Phrax instead.'

'Impossible.' Varro's voice was not angry, just disbelieving. 'How idiotic do these people have to be to think that someone else can walk in and have the charter handed to them? The Arbites supervise the succession to stop exactly that.'

'The charter stays in the Phrax family, Varro. That's all. What do you think happens when more than one heir contests the succession? That was why the Arbites were written in. If there's more than one viable heir the ruling between claimants is theirs.'

'Yes. Well, maybe that's so. I never really paid much attention to how the succession would work with more than one heir, Domasa, because I am the *sole* heir. The one and only.' Varro's voice had risen enough to set a nearby Kendran feather-tree groaning as it tried to spit still-unripe spores in the direction of the noise. Domasa shot a warning look over at the party, and Varro took a deep breath while he got his equilibrium back.

Finally, Domasa spoke: 'Sole heir you might have been, Varro, but you're going to have to change your thinking. You're going to have to get a lot less comfortable about the idea of just putting your hand out and taking the charter. Now I'm going to say this again. Some very powerful people believe you are the rightful heir whose claim must be protected. They found out about this communiqué and they arranged for me to see you, to let you know that we're on your side and to make sure you're ready for your voyage. You're going to be facing a challenge from Hoyyon's other son. Your half-brother. Petronas Phrax.'

CHAPTER FIVE

The Flotilla of Hoyyon Phrax,
Deep Space outside the Antozir Proxima system

THERE HAD BEEN chop and eddy in the immaterium on the long, looping route from Shexia towards Hydraphur. Not enough to be dangerous, but the flotilla masters were grim about taking any chances at all, so at the great empty shell of Antozir Proxima with its beautiful, sterile garlands of gas clouds, the flotilla broke warp and rested. As always, the vox-traffic danced between the ships as they drew in and coasted through Antozir's fringes; the occasional shuttle, too, as those with errands or cargo that couldn't wait to move between vessels took advantage of the freedom of real space.

Two teams of cooks and slaughtermen had come over to the *Bassaan* from the *Proserpina Dawn* with a shuttle-hold full of fattened verdikine from the sprawling pastoral decks, to be slaughtered in the *Bassaan's* own kitchens. Eight of those cooks had visited the *Bassaan* for a single day just before the flotilla broke warp on the outskirts of Shexia, and that made them the targets of Flag Ensign Nils Petronas, who waited hidden in the shadows in the flagship's vast galley with vomit down the front of his uniform coat and his right fist taped shut around the grip of a punch-dagger.

Two hours ago he had haltingly, blearily looked over the weapons rack in his stateroom and decided that he was too sick to reliably use a gun, and he had nearly lost his balance when he took a test swing of his rank-cutlass. The dagger was the least risky, the hardest to miss with. Petronas could tell his vision was beginning to blur, so he probably would not have been able to see to use a pistol anyway.

It had started within hours of the dinner for two dozen or so flotilla personnel, all about Petronas's age and including several of his friends, hosted by Petty Officer Intendant Gensh.

Gensh, the vain little poisoning bastard with the little blond beard he was so damned proud of. Petronas squeezed the dagger grip until his hand tingled. He could hear the man's voice in his head, wet and smug as though he were gargling his words through cream.

'Why've I invited you all here?' he'd asked. 'Isn't it obvious?' No, a couple of voices had answered. Few of them knew Gensh personally. 'Meetings like this are a new directive from the masters of the flotilla, Crew-mistress Behaya is enthused by the idea.' Rubbish, they had agreed later as they ate. The fact would have been better known. 'The flotilla goes to meet its new trader,' Gensh had said, 'and Emperor bless Trader Varro! This is a time to come together as crewmates and brothers and sisters,' he had said, sloshing drink. 'We shall make sure that every soul on this fleet knows he is part of a brotherhood, a united crew...'

That was what had struck Petronas as the lie, although he didn't think at the time that Gensh knew it was a lie. And all the stirring, wine-fuelled talk of the golden days of Trader Varro soon to dawn only served to keep his mother's face hanging in the front of his mind. He hadn't dared let his anger out at the dinner, but walking back to his quarters afterwards he had found a pair of deckhands he didn't know and roared that they had been looking at him insubordinately. His friends had held one of them back while Petronas had torn into the other, and he had finally returned to his room with his knuckles raw and bleeding and his head ringing with exhaustion. There was none of the beautiful calm he normally felt after finishing an evening that way, but with the state his thoughts had been in since the alley on Shexia a night of dreamless sleep had been reward enough.

The verdikine meat in the pot flared and the cooks laughed and clapped at the bursts of yellow flame. Petronas started shuffling between the two slop-chutes, but his knees folded and the dagger point squealed against the chutes as he toppled over. He lay slumped in the cramped space, feeling his stomach roil – the last of the food had come up two hours ago, but he had still been bringing up bile every few minutes. His eyes felt like coals, and no matter how many times he squeezed them shut or worked the eyelids with his fingers he could not get them to water and give him some relief.

Waking up like this, he had known straight away Gensh was responsible. When he had lurched out of his bed, throat bubbly with vomit, he had realised even through the cramps in his gut and the spike that twisted behind his eyes that it had been deliberate. Rengill, Rengill his dear friend since the days they had played along the ornamented garden-decks of the *Callyac's Promise*, who had sat beside him at Gensh's dinner, was sprawled in the doorway of her own stateroom, convulsing. Her own mouth and chin were smeared with bile, but it was mixed with blood and mucus, and as Petronas had staggered toward her blood began to drip from her nostrils and ears as well.

Beyond her, Lead Ensign Omya sagged against a wall and wept from the pain that was doubling him over as pretty, dark-haired Atith tried to help him move. Omya had sat opposite Petronas and argued with him about the merits of the wines, and had helped hold the unlucky deckhand's friend back while Petronas had worked off his anger afterwards. And behind Atith, a sprawled shape that Petronas barely recognised as Nimmond, against whom he had boxed until they both collapsed from exhaustion and with whom he had learned the strange lilting Low Gothic dialect they spoke on Spaeter Relixas so they could read the stirring warrior-poems of its militant priests. They had even given a recitation at the dinner, clanging their pewter wine-cups together as they roared out the verses. He recognised Nimmond by the swept-back way he wore his long hair and the broad gold belt he had won for his gunnery – he would not have recognised the young man's distorted face, bloody where muscle had torn the skin apart and twisted itself free of the bone.

His surroundings now matched those grim memories, as bloodied scraps and bone were dumped into the chutes with clamour and echoes from the metal walls. The racket shook Petronas back out of semi-consciousness and gave him enough energy to drag himself to his feet. His balance was still bad, though, and he could not stop his forward lurch. But the interruption had been timely, because ahead of him, walking around the seasoning tubs, was the moustachioed senior steward who had served them their dinner. Their poisoned dinner.

Petronas erupted from his niche in a wild-eyed run, the kitchen crew yelping and scattering out of his way. In the hot fog of his vision the steward turned, his eyes widened and he scrambled backward. The point of the punch-dagger caught in his tunic but only made a shallow gash from hip to shoulder. He howled and grappled at Petronas's arm as the ensign made graceless stabs at his face and eyes.

Petronas heard a voice, cracked and crazed, screaming over and over again and when he saw the man's mouth move in reply he realised it was his own. When he stopped to suck in a tortured breath he had a chance to realise that he had been shouting, 'Your life for Gensh! Your life for Gensh!' over and over.

The steward, groaning, hit the side of a tall carving-block and slid down it as a sudden burst of hot, liquid pain in his abdomen made Petronas double over with a cry and go down on one knee. When it slackened again he spiked the point of the dagger into the floor to steady himself and looked the steward in the eye.

'Gensh... Officer Gensh... I can take you to him! We didn't know! We didn't know! Please! I bear you no ill-will, sir, you know that! I was *pleased* for you, I was happy that such a fine young man...' the steward gulped and clutched at the wound across his torso, 'such a fine officer had been invited...'

'You poisoned me.' Petronas knew his words were coming out slurred, but there was no time to slow down to try and talk properly. So many of them must have been involved, there were so many of them to track and find. 'You all did. Rengill and poor Nimmond. Why Nimmond? Who poisoned...'

'No, no, not we! Food and celebration are our, our, *calling*!' The steward was gabbling, his hands held out. Dimly, Petronas realised why no one was coming near them: to the ones who knew no better he was carrying the marks of disease. Better to let him stab a colleague than get close and risk the flotilla's ruthless internal quarantines. He drew his arm back and the steward screamed.

'No! We were driven out of the kitchen, the red-robed man, that was him! He never eats! The red-robed man and the trader's doctor! They came in with staff and–'

Petronas let his weight drop forward and aimed the dagger carefully at the steward's eye. It went in true; the man shivered and died.

After a moment slumped against the corpse Petronas pushed himself back and staggered upright to look at a grey-uniformed blur in the centre of his melting, throbbing vision.

'Gensh.' For a moment Petronas was thankful almost to the point of prayer that his nemesis had been miraculously placed here for him. But he was confused. There were more? The trader's doctor, D'Leste, an ugly man Petronas had only seen once or twice, and the red-robed man who never ate, that, that had to be... Suddenly Petronas saw everything clearly.

'Here's the last one. Light of Terra save us all, but look at what he's done! It's a good thing we got to you, Petronas. When we heard you'd gone over the edge we feared the worst.' The blur that was Gensh turned to the indistinct masses behind it. 'Get him down and restrained, and get that grox-sticker off his hand. We're lucky we were vigilant, it looks like he only got one.'

The thing about the punch-dagger was this: Petronas already knew that he could kill with a simple forward fall to put his weight behind it. He tottered a step, then another, then as someone started to say, 'It's all right, sir' he let his final collapse pull his arm forward and heard the shocked whoosh of air out of Gensh as his weight bore them both over in a cascade of cries and shouts from around them.

'Two,' Petronas gurgled contentedly into Gensh's face. And although he felt strong hands gripping his arms and hair, he was deep in unconsciousness and never felt them dragging him clear of the dying officer's body.

Private Offices of Shira Calpurnia,
The Wall, Hydraphur

'So what the hell is this about a counter-claim?'

Normally the briefing conferences of the senior Adeptus Arbites followed a detailed and traditional protocol, which was why when Shira Calpurnia needed to get quickly to the pith of an issue she held a less formal and more forthright meeting somewhere away from the meeting-vaults around the Arbitor Majore's tower. The Arbites who made good use of the freer, blunter-spoken environment tended to be the ones who found their way onto her growing personal staff; the ones who were scandalised by it or allowed it to make them sloppy were quickly and firmly rotated out. Now in her little set of chambers were three of the staff she liked and trusted the most: Culann, her personal aide, the grizzled Arbitrator Odamo and Umry, the quick-witted praetor-cognatis who'd distinguished herself in the Anstoch trials the previous year.

'Received by communiqué sent by flotilla astropaths from Shexia system, repeated again at Antozir Proxima. Authentication reads "Zanti", that's one of the flotilla masters. Shexia and Antozir-Prox are successive steps on the route to Hydraphur from the border sectors where the old man died. Time-stamps on each of them show the flotilla making good time.' Leaning against the table by Calpurnia's door, Praetor-Cognatis Umry was twirling the data-slate in her fingers but rattled off the report without referring to it.

'Good time? Hurrying, are they?' Kyle Odamo was a heavy-jawed aedile senioris with thirty-two years on arbitrator strike teams, including eight on an Arbites intercept cruiser until a shipboard accident had cost him both his legs. The augmetics hadn't taken well enough to return him to full combat assignments, but on his planetside posting he still took an interest in spacefaring. 'Don't know much about that direction firsthand but I've heard it's not hard to hurry through. They'll have an easier time of it than that other poor fellow. Fearful rough it gets coming up the well past Knape and straight out from galactic centre.'

'We can't know,' Umry replied, tossing the slate and catching it. 'That message is pretty much all we've had out of them. We've got no informants on the flotilla. The really old traders have had these whole sealed communities grow up around them. Just try getting one of your own people in or turning one of theirs. Next to impossible, I'd think. Unless the Emperor willed it,' she added piously.

'But someone's got an insider,' said Calpurnia. She was out of armour and in simple duty fatigues, sitting cross-legged on a soft mat in front of her bookshelf. 'We know that because we're monitoring the Varro end, or so Culann tells me. Culann?'

'Yes, ma'am. Things are as rough between here and Gunarvo as Arbitor Odamo said, and our communiqué from the commander of court there took a few attempts. But, well, the flotilla may not be hurrying but the heir, this Varro Phrax, is moving like a scorch-arsed blasphemer. A representative of Navigator House Dorel visited him and he was making tracks out of the system within twelve hours. Rather a lot got spent to make sure he had a ship in a hurry. More than we think Varro can afford, although he's not badly off.'

'Is this House Dorel behind any of it?' Calpurnia asked. In her experience, very little that the Navis Nobilite did was as it appeared on the surface.

'I don't know about that, ma'am.' Culann was the only one to still call her ma'am in the private meetings – he seemed to find the habit hard to get out of. 'But we do know that the rush-requests on some of the exit permissions for the ship that they're taking out of Gunarvo weren't paid for by Phrax himself. One of the astropaths travelling with them is part of the precinct commander's collaborator networks, so we have a couple of insights from what he was able to send. The money came from an exchequer to a shipping syndicate with ties to the House Yimora, not Dorel. There's been more money moved around in the financial houses at the Gunarvo docks that the Courthouse there is starting to pull out into the open, but it looks like bribes may have been paid to get the right traffic patterns for the *Gann-Luctis*, that's their ship, to get out of the system and break warp as soon as it possibly could. No formal communiqué is recorded in Gunarvo's astropathic logs about any counter-claim.'

'And I assume we didn't tell him ourselves?' Calpurnia asked. 'Of course we didn't.'

'We didn't,' said Odamo. 'I used your delegation to demand confirmation of that. Our own Astropathicae chambers certainly didn't pass anything on, and the Chancellor of the Witchroost confirms likewise. Oops,' he added.

'Oops is right,' Calpurnia told him. 'I've made my feelings on that clear. Use one of its more respectful names, please.' She looked over at Umry. 'So... This counter-claim...?'

'I'm sorry to say it, but I think at this moment we know exactly as much about it as has just been aired in this meeting and we're going to have to wait to find out any more. The older a charter, the cagier its holders tend to be about letting any Adeptus hooks into them.'

'That notwithstanding,' Calpurnia put in, 'I wanted us to sweep for information. How far along is that?' Umry glanced at the slate and tapped a key.

'Transmissions have gone out to every Arbites leader on the list I gave you and the secondary list is with the Arbitor Majore's cryptomechanics prior to transmission.' She turned to the others. 'To keep you up to speed, the prime list is every taskforce and precinct head on every world and patrol route that we know the flotilla has had dealings with in the last thirty years. The secondary list is a range of possible but unconfirmed stops. We're asking all of them for any records or observations that may give us an idea of who this new mystery counter-heir is and how strong his claim on the charter might be.'

'What we need,' said Odamo, half to himself, 'is some way of forcing these people to share their records with us. Now, if they had to supply us with information on every change in events that might impact the charter…'

'I believe there are some like that,' said Calpurnia. 'There were several major rogue traders in the Ultima Segmentum whose charters required them to co-operate with inspectors and archivists. Unfortunately, that provision tends to have to be built into the charter from its creation.'

'If we have the authority to oversee the charter, ma'am…' Culann began, but Calpurnia was already shaking her head.

'Oversee is exactly what it is. We can enforce the possession of the Phrax Charter by the rightful successor, and where the succession is unclear we can judge and rule and enforce our ruling. That's it.'

'It's kind of the point,' said Umry. 'It's the exact things about the old charters that make them so sought after – antiquity, tradition, exalted legal status – that make them so hard to interfere with. And they're next to impossible to amend. I don't think alterations to any of the really old charters have ever even been considered.'

'Whose mark do the oldest charters bear?' asked Calpurnia, and the question hung in the air for a while. For a citizen of the Imperium, a subject of the Emperor, a worshipper at the altars of the Adeptus Ministorum, how could the idea even be countenanced? How did you set yourself up to rewrite and tinker with words penned and sealed by a walking god? Calpurnia watched the same thought go through the minds of the others: Odamo's eyes had gone hooded, Umry was staring at the floor and Culann was actually shivering. She knew exactly how they felt. She had only been able to concentrate on the details of the succession ceremonies because she had kept the nature of the charter out of her mind. When she allowed herself to think about it the weight of it was almost physical. It made her feel too small, too young.

But duty was duty, and only in death did duty end. She picked up the jug and refilled her water glass, poured more for the others and picked up her data-slate.

'Well,' she said, 'whatever the details of the claimants and their cases, the fact of it is we're going to be conducting a hearing, not a ceremonial handover. So let's start getting ready for one.'

The Flotilla of Hoyyon Phrax. In transit

'–USELESS IF HE–'

Blackness.

'–INK HE'S GOING to be able t–'

Blackness.

'–ATCH WHAT YOU'RE doing, I don't kn–'

Blackness/a moment of pain/blackness.

'–E THOUGHT IT best, magos. But Doctor D'Leste, sir, I should tell you that the codes–'

Fading away more slowly this time, but still…

…blackness.

SLOW FADE UP, blurry light. Something wedged in his mouth. Needs to get it free, needs to–

'Gods, but he's thrashing! Get over here! I don't *care*, just get over here and hold the little bastard down, get him, get his arm!'

Blurred movements in the blurred light. Pressure bearing down on tender muscle and skin. Pain. Have to get the pressure off.

'How can he be so bloody strong, look at him! Damn it, get D'Leste! No, get the magos. Yes, bloody well disturb him! Do it! Give me that slapneedle–'

A startling cold sting through the fog of raw pain.

Blackness.

Dreams, for the first time in a while. Not good dreams. Wandering through the decks and halls as a child again, dead bodies bleeding through their skins littering the floors and piling up in the arches and hatchways. Mother's voice echoing through the ship. She's singing a lullaby, except that she's trying not to cry at the same time. Hearing her aches.

Blackness.

* * *

LIGHT. NOT BLURRED this time. A white, concave ceiling and figures, way up in the distance, looking down on him. Faces he knows from shipboard musters and officers' gatherings. He knows there was something about them that was so clear, so clear, back before all the light and the blackness and the dreams and the pain.

There is still pain, though. His brain seems to float in a strange, unearthly cup of it.

Rich red at the foot of the bed. Hard to see. He knows he stabbed someone. Did they live? Couldn't have. Did they die and come to tell him they're dead? They must have. In the tilted fever-logic that is all he can think in now, he decides this must be the only explanation.

'Can you hear me? Can you understand me?' The voice is odd in cadence, beautifully warm and soft, but soulless with it, like the voice of an actor who can reproduce all the appearances of a human voice but believes none of them.

'Ensign Petronas, can you understand me?'

A rich red robe with odd, geometrical gold trim, characters that he doesn't recognise. A steel chain at the neck. And above the neck, the face, the face of pale flesh and glittering metal and a single red-rimmed eye...

'His cognition seems to be returning,' says the voice from that face as he thrashes and the hands grasp his arms again. 'Sedate him. Another day of rest and we'll see if he's ready to meet with us.'

Blackness.

Council Chambers of Kostazin Baszle, Eparch of Hydraphur. Level 47, Ducatine Spire, Cathedral of the Emperor Ascendant, Hydraphur

REVEREND SIMOVA GLOWERED about him as they filed through the door and each priest touched the amulet at his neck to the feet of the marble statue of the Emperor set into the far wall. As was the habit in many Ministorum chambers it had been set deliberately off-centre so that it could watch over all the room, not stare out from behind the Eparchal chair. Moving from the statue, each kissed the aquila stitched into the end of the Eparch's prayer shawl. It was done in green thread on blue at the moment, reflecting the sacerdotal colours for the celebration of the Hydraphur's wet season and the turning of the year.

It was four minutes before they were all done and kneeling before their seats, repeating the Eparch's brief High Gothic blessing. Then they rose, settled into their seats and waited to hear what was on their master's mind.

'No, it isn't about Reverend Simova's continued clash with the law,' Eparch Baszle said, to dutiful murmurs of amusement from everyone except the man he had named. 'Although perhaps, brother, you could hazard a guess as to exactly how long that affair will take?'

'There is little left for them to do,' Simova said with as much dignity as he could. 'This arbitor they have set in charge is obviously anxious to prove himself to the Calpurnia woman, and he seems to feel that the way to do that is to subject the Adeptus Ministorum and her priesthood to all manner of pointless legal delays. Their real targets are the cell whose leaders we were punishing.'

'Or leader, at any rate. You only had one in the cages, didn't you?'

'One, yes,' said Simova, bristling inside. It had been the Eparch's insistence behind the reintroduction of the old Phaphanite cages, but anything going wrong of course was Simova's fault alone. But he knew better than to start trying to defend himself in front of all the other clerics. He would wait and plead his case another time. Except that the Eparch did not seem minded to let it drop.

'The matter I want to discuss is an important one, important enough to require you all away from your afternoon duties. It will involve placing this Cathedral in the way of a certain amount of attention from the other Adeptus. In particular,' Baszle turned his handsome, angular head to stare at Simova again, 'it will bring us the attention of Imperial law. And will involve questions of law both spiritual and temporal, so I must say, Simova, this is a particularly poor time for one of my senior exegetors to lock horns with the Arbites.'

'I am not on trial, your eminence,' Simova replied, flushing a little. 'Praetor Imprimis Dastrom has made that clear. The investigation is into the infiltration of the construction and guarding work on the cages. Aspects of it that do not concern myself,' he added after a moment, conscious that he had been the one technically in charge of the whole affair. The supercilious Dastrom had made no secret of the fact that he considered Simova at least a little culpable. 'But I am faithful according to my powers, and what they lay in my way I shall overcome since I know that the Emperor is with me.' He sat back in his seat, a little happier. 'Your eminence, I must say that I am curious about this important matter that you say you wanted to discuss with us.'

The Eparch's deep-set eyes stayed on Simova for a moment before he too decided to move on.

'Brother Palomas, will you please list for me the latest additions to the reliquary of our Cathedral?'

A short man in a simple brown habit at the far end of the semicircle read from a faxscroll.

'Two shell casings from the pistol of Saint Csokavi of Tamar, obtained as tithe from the Diocese of Chigand. They await their reliquary case; Demipater Ushiste will be blessing it at tomorrow's sunset mass in the Bell Chapel. A vial of soil from the landing-field where the Four Bishops of Phael were martyred. It's been authenticated by the Chamber Pronatus you authorised at the end of last year, your eminence, and the ship carrying it broke warp at the edge of Hydraphur yesterday. It should be here within the week. Lastly, the Reverend Baragry has sent word from Iskaza-Maru that he has recovered nearly all of the fragments of the skull of Sister Elidas the Demi-Sainted. I understand he will be returning here as soon as he is able.'

'Excellent, and thank you for the news of that last, brother. Our sisters in the Order of the Sacred Rose will be pleased that a relic of one of their own is on its way back to them. And I convey the Reverend Baragry's apologies to this meeting, of course, but you all knew he was absent on my errands. Apparently there were certain parties on Iskaza-Maru who were reluctant to allow such a relic to be taken off their world.

'But all things unfold for a reason, my friends and brothers, and we can reflect on our brother's exploits under a different sun to remind us that the ways of worship are often harsh and must at times be ruthless if our faith is to spread its wings and raise its spires.

'I know I've spoken to you all about my desire to make Hydraphur the brightest beacon of the Imperial faith in all the sectors around. Hundreds of worlds and billions of souls, all looking back to us as we reflect the Emperor's light to them as Luna shines the sunlight down on holy Terra. I want the walls of the Cathedral to groan with the trophies of the Ecclesiarchy and the relics of her holiest saints. And I have said that there is much that the Emperor will smile upon in such a holy cause.'

Ah, Simova thought. That was why Baszle had gone off on the tangent about Baragry. It wasn't a tangent – he was preparing them. There was something they were going to have to do.

'Let it never be said,' Baszle told them, 'that I saw glory for my Cathedral and my Emperor and turned my back to it. We have the chance now to take a wondrous relic of the time when the Emperor Himself set His eyes to Hydraphur, to fetch it from hiding in a prison of iniquity and set it high in the Cathedral where it belongs. A token of the Emperor's true life, that will have our faith strengthened as steel. Something that will place us at the head of an army of the faithful, pilgrims and priests and crusaders, as it ought always have been.'

The priests shifted in their seats and looked at each other, but Baszle himself had fixed his eyes on Simova again.

'We will not be tithing for this. It will not be brought here by a war of faith and force of arms. No matter what we demand of our Eparchy it could not furnish us with this.

'No, the way we are going to acquire this relic is through *you*, Simova, you and your chamber. There is a very precious relic being brought to our very doorstep here at Hydraphur, and the Emperor, all-providing, has seen fit to set its owners against one another. They will come before the Adeptus and they are going to try to argue that the Arbites should rule them the rightful owners of this relic, as if there could be any kind of rightful owner but the Emperor's own Adeptus Ministorum. That is what we are here to plan. Curate Simova?'

Simova was about to cross his arms defensively and argue when he realised that Baszle was no longer accusing him but appointing him. He ran through the Eparch's words again and blinked. A great relic, a relic that was to be fought over by law. The importance of his new task hit him so hard he almost gasped.

For a horrifying moment he thought he had run dry of words. And then, as it had so many times in the days-long debates in the chamber, his mind clicked smoothly into motion.

'I will begin,' he said, 'by outlining the writings of Pontifex Militant Orgos Arnck concerning the right of the Adeptus Ministorum to take possession of any object, person or territory which meets the definition of a holy relic. We shall also consider the definition of a holy relic as originally addressed in the writings of Ecclesiarch Chiganne IV and formalised by the Four Thousand and Eighty-Second Ecclesiarchal Conclave. We must also consider the Eighth Edict-Spiritual of Terra and its implications for clashes between religious and temporal law;

there are over a dozen recent and relevant precedents in the Segmentum Pacificus. And I believe, your eminence, that I should also touch on the epistles of Confessor Luzaro of Sirius which, according to the deliberations of the Eparchs Solar in M38, is considered canon for Ecclesiarchal actions where holy items must be claimed from fellow Imperial subjects by brute force of arms.'

With the Eparch's permission, he stood, then closed his eyes for the few breaths it took for him to find his orator's voice and lay out the points of law in his head. This was what delighted Simova as few other things did: he could almost see it in his mind, an interlocking web of points and counterpoints, tracts of text and decrees of religious law, forming constellations and webs of duty and obedience.

He opened his eyes and began to speak. They listened, they questioned, they discussed, as outside the yellow Hydraphur sunlight ebbed away into a long, chilly, rainy night.

The Flotilla of Hoyyon Phrax. In transit

WHAT HAD BEEN simply and luminously clear to Nils Petronas while he was killing Officer Gensh was not clear any more. It had come back to him with time, as treatment brought the spasms and pain under control and thinking was no longer like trying to pick up spilled oil in his fingers. He remembered the realisation clearly: the purging of the flotilla went far deeper than he had believed, that he and all his friends had been sentenced to death by some arcane tradition that the seniors and masters had kept from all the rest of them. It wasn't as though there weren't plenty of those.

That insight had had the force of a hammer. All he had been able to think of was striking back, taking as many with him as possible. If there was to be a hole in the flotilla where he and his friends had been, then he would make that hole a little bigger, leave a scar that the masters would have to remember.

But he no longer thought that was true. He no longer knew what was happening or why. He still knew something was going on – the scraps of memory of what he had heard in the kitchen and the Apothecarion saw to that. But he could look around him now at the luxurious chair that they had shifted him into from the survival-bed, the diagnostor hanging silently in the air over his right shoulder (it was built into a beautiful butterfly sculpted in silver and stained-glass, a holdover of an infatuation old Hoyyon had had with insects some decades ago), and the slender weave of tubes and lines that were nourishing his ravaged muscles and strengthening his flesh. He could not believe that they were nursing him so extravagantly just to put him to death again. If he were so valuable to the flotilla masters, that gave him power. At some point he was going to have the chance to hurt them.

Just that morning (as far as there were any mornings in the whiteness of his chamber) Petronas had found that he had enough strength to make fists of his hands again. They were weak, and he could not maintain them for more than a few moments, but when he made them he could see the last of the red roughness on his knuckles from the beating he had given the deck hand, and that made him feel better. He had even started to grin when he found that out, until he realised that someone was probably watching him. So he kept the grin but hid it inside his head, stoked like a little hot coal, and bided his time.

CHAPTER SIX

The Sanctioned Liner *Gann-Luctis*. In transit

THEY HAD RUN into trouble right from the start.

Gunarvo lay at the edge of a band of perennial riptides and whirls in the immaterium that followed the line of worlds trailing out of the Broadhead Cluster. To accurately scry and catch those tides was work for a skilled Navigator, and most craft that left the system took on extra supplies and endured a ten-week haul through real space before they broke warp where the conditions were calmer. The Navigator that Domasa's backers in House Yimora had assigned for Varro's voyage was tough and skilled enough to make even Domasa feel deferential, but it had still taken three attempts to properly break through into the currents that grabbed them from Gunarvo into calmer warp flows where they could come about and lay in course for Hydraphur.

Ksana Phrax had travelled between the stars exactly three times in her life, and had counted herself lucky for it. Not just because her husband had told her so, either. Although she remembered him picking up a tiny pinch of gravel from the riverbed at the bottom of the Asterine Lock one night before their first voyage and holding it out to her. 'If the riverbed is everyone on this whole world for the past hundred years,' he had said, 'then this is the number of them who will ever manage to look down on Gunarvo and see it hanging in space, let alone how many of them will ever look down on another world the same way. The people who never travel between worlds never think about it; the people who do usually take it for granted. But it's an incredible thing, my love, to look on a world so far from yours and taste its air. You'll see.'

Ksana had believed him, and remembered her privilege. This should have been a greater privilege still: she still had to tell herself that, after so much anticipation, she was leaving Gunarvo as the wife of a rogue trader-in-waiting, to return, if she ever did, a merchant princess with a flotilla and a ten-thousand-year old legacy behind her. Varro had once told her about how the charters had been signed and sealed by the Emperor Himself, and although she had thought he was exaggerating she also believed she was coming into whatever destiny the Emperor had for her.

Alone in the beautiful stateroom, with its blue velvet drapes and cushions and its purple-trimmed furniture of ebony and gold, she told herself again that she should not be so disturbed, that there was no reason for her nerves to be so taut or for her hands to want to lace and unlace themselves – she had even put on gloves of thin blue silk when the skin between her fingers had become red and sore.

But there were things to disturb her. Plenty of them. Varro had told her with a smile that they were in good hands, that Dorel and Yimora and the rest were worthy allies who understood how important the charter was going to be to him. He had shown her letters from the first controller, the Imperium-appointed governor of Gunarvo itself, who would help them make the case for his proper succession. As they were leaving they had been joined by another delegation, Imperial Administratum representatives bearing seals from the subsectoral prefect on Baryatin II. The delegation leader, haughty in his formal gown and high, intricate collar, had told her that the Administratum would be pleased to place its resources 'at the disposal of the Phrax succession and its orderly and correct resolution.' They had not said much else to her after that, and that had not surprised her. She knew how most of Varro's new associates thought of her: the little heir's trophy-wife, ignorant of the Imperium beyond the walls of the family compound, standing well back and smiling benignly at whatever her husband did.

But Ksana Phrax was the daughter of a Gunarvite merchant guilder and the sister of two doctors-at-law to the planetary Congress of Selectmen. She saw much and suspected more.

There was a plate of meats and spices on the table next to her, but she had little appetite. Her nerves had robbed her of it. She slipped off her shoes and padded carefully to the sleeping alcove to move the drapes carefully aside with a hand: Dreyder was still asleep, more quietly than he had been when they had been trying to break warp and he had twitched and cried out from the dreams. Ksana resisted the urge to pull the blankets up around him – the room was warm enough, and she didn't want to wake him. She let the drape fall back into place.

What she had seen was the way that Domasa Dorel spoke to her husband, either artificially gruff as though she were a better friend than she had the right to consider herself, or a contrived singsong lilt as she pretended a respect for Varro she clearly did not feel. And that bright, steely, calculating look never left her eyes. Ksana had watched to see how Domasa dealt with the way she frightened their son – and there had been no reaction at all. The look in her eyes as she had watched Ksana consoling her son after he had cried at their first meeting had been cool and dismissive.

She knew about the whispered conferences between the first controller's men and the delegation from the Administratrum. She had gone walking the decks and visiting what few diversions the ship offered – the little library, the promenade stairs around the base of the bridge-tower, the rows of idols to the Machine-God that lined the halls leading to the enginarium – and time and again she had come on them, little knots of turned backs and low voices, that broke up to shower her with sunny greetings and then silently waited for her to move on. She knew that message-runners had been working the corridors between their suites night and day, special Administratum-trained couriers who were hypno-conditioned to remember nothing of what they heard and recited. She knew that she and Varro had dined with the *Gann-Luctis's* officers at a table half-empty because the others were meeting privately in rooms that even the ship's personnel had been barred from.

She knew that the first controller's men wanted a copy of the charter's wording, and resented Varro for not providing them with one. She suspected that they were looking for ways to distort those words:

she knew enough about the controller's dreams for Gunarvo that trying to tie the charter to their world instead of Hydraphur seemed natural when the prism of ambition was applied to one's vision.

She knew that Maghal, the Adept Prolegis who was second-in-command of the Administratum delegation, was already trying to negotiate with Varro to attach a ship to the flotilla under an Administratum charter. The ship would have a captain appointed by Maghal or his superiors and its relationship with the rest of the flotilla would be governed by contract – it would collect tithes of populations, resources and data from the Imperial worlds the flotilla visited and the Administratum adepts on its crew would have a voice in determining the flotilla's itinerary. And in return, subsidies and favoured-trader status on merchant routes all through the subsector. Ksana could well imagine what they were planning: get Varro fat and comfortable on a regular run across routes the Administratum already controlled, use his charter to flout the vigilance of the Arbites, use him to venture into the wild space south of Gunarvo where the prefect desperately wanted tithe-paying Imperial rule to spread again.

And the Navigator. Even the memory of her pallid face and her fierce, somehow feverish eyes chilled Ksana. She did not know and did not want to speculate what Domasa Dorel might want, but she did not think that it would stop with taming a rogue trader to a pet run in a favoured subsector or to a certain world. She did not think that at all.

'THAT PRYING LITTLE rodent of a wife is going to be a problem, too, you mark me,' said Cherrick, hefting his hellgun.

'What makes you think so?' Had they still been back on Gunarvo Domasa would have dismissed the remark out of hand, but even this early in the voyage she was uneasy. The turbulence in the warp was bad – as a Navigator she understood just how bad, and what that might mean for the voyage. She was trying to put it out of her mind: the man who was navigating them was far more accomplished than she, and she had other priorities. Hers was the thumb that the thrown-together syndicate wanted on the pulse of whatever was going on around Varro and that was what she was trying to concentrate on.

With the glimpses her third eye was showing her of what was going on outside the hull, she had a feeling that was going to be hard.

'I don't like her. I don't like her at all. She's got this nasty, ratty, watchful look to her. I bet she's got it all planned out in her mind, wants the charter for herself. It fits, doesn't it? And she doesn't like you.' Cherrick grinned.

'I suppose I see why. She's smart enough not to trust me, and I think she's got a good idea of what I want out of her husband.' Domasa shrugged. 'Plus, I scare that little brat of hers, so I suppose she dislikes me for that. Rather sweet of her, really. Have you got the conduit covered?'

'What?'

'The crawl-way. There's meant to be a crawl-way along the roof of this whole corridor.' Domasa's voice slowed and dropped into an ice talking-to-an-idiot cadence. 'So. Do. You. Have. It. Covered?'

Cherrick glowered upwards, trying to think of something smart to come back with. The two of them were standing at the head of the central utility corridor that ran through the *Gann-Luctis's* lower decks, whose maps Domasa had spent half a day memorising: it would not be wise to walk about the ship with blueprints under her arm that she was not supposed to possess. She stood patiently as Cherrick muttered into a vox-set and watched as two armsmen came hurrying down the stairwell. She had obtained an amulet-key that could speak to nearly every security plate on the ship, and when she directed it at the hatch above them there was an avalanche of screeches and clatters as it slid aside and a rickety metal ladder unfolded. The two men exchanged a sour look, ignited shoulder-lamps and began climbing.

Domasa closed her eyes and brought up her mental deck plan again. The crawl-way was the last way out of this level. She and Cherrick blocked the corridor, other armsmen were guarding the liftwells off the utility deck and covering the compartments to either side. Domasa had experienced a single small flash of annoyance when they had found their quarry gone from the Psykana dome, but it was something she had been prepared for. It was fine. She had control.

'So, were you listening?'

'Hmm?' She hadn't been. She needed to concentrate. If they didn't do this seamlessly things could get messy.

'The wife. She's going to get in the way. I think we can run him, but we might not be able to run him with the wife around.'

'Leave the diplomacy to me, Cherrick, you've already proved that you can't do it. What you can do is make sure that toy of yours is charged so we can get started.'

'If weapon-handling is something I'm meant to be better at, my lady, then maybe I should just check to make sure you're properly equipped yourself?'

Domasa glared at him and slipped her sleeve back. A bundle of fine golden rods rested against her forearm and the back of one malformed hand: her long fingers were curled around a trigger-grip and the ammunition tank was anchored at the inside of her wrist. Cherrick sniffed.

'Useless if he's armoured, of course.'

'He won't be,' snapped Domasa, 'and this is much better for taking him alive but incapacitated, which I'll thank you to remember is our priority.'

'Fine.' Cherrick tapped the chime-stud on his glove for the teams to start moving and got half a dozen steps down the corridor before he realised Domasa was still behind him. 'Are you coming, ma'am? You're the one with the non-lethal weapon, after all. Are you really going to let me laz him full of holes?' Domasa began to follow, slowly, weaving back and forth to make sure Cherrick was between her and door or alcove they passed. She was confident that Symozon was no fighter, but physical confrontation made her edgy.

Oafish as Cherrick was most of the time, now he was silent and focused, his steps so controlled that Domasa realised she had to listen hard to hear each footfall. Domasa tried to do the same – her feet were as elongated as her hands, only touching the floor at the balls and toes of her feet, her heels jutting like a big cat's, and that made it easier.

From Cherrick's vox-plate she could hear the faint rustle of voices from the other men. The whole formation was moving now, slowly, thoroughly, unstoppably. Domasa almost tripped on the leading edge of her gown, and realised she was walking hunched over. This was stupid. She found herself wanting to straighten up and shout out. How did the man think this would end? Where did he think he was going to go? How long did he think he could hide?

As long as he can, she thought to herself, and when he's brought out of hiding then we can damn well expect him to want to take a few of us with him. So be careful, Domasa Dorel, and don't give him the chance.

The Flotilla of Hoyyon Phrax. In transit

ALTHOUGH HE HAD been expecting it ever since he had properly regained consciousness, Petronas's heart still gave a lurch when they came filing into the room. He was still in the chair, still nauseous and always tired, but his thoughts were razor-sharp and he could make fists and hold them for a count of seventy-three before the pain made him stop.

He recognised Crewmistress Behaya straight away – he had spoken to her once or twice before, on special occasions when she had toured the lower tables at feasts. And after a moment he was able to place Kyorg as well, the old fool who purported to run the Office of Envoys. It had been Kyorg's orders that had led to him going down to Shexia to – to do a thing he didn't like to think about. He tucked his hands under the blankets so that the masters would not see him making fists.

Halpander he had dealt with a few times, when he had been assigned to run loading of cargoes and provisions. And there were faces he couldn't quite put names to: the lipless woman in the black and white shawl, the little bald man with the sad-hound face... and the figure in red. Petronas's eyes locked onto it and did not move.

'I find it difficult to believe that you never knew anything at all about Magos Dyobann.' That was D'Leste, who was dragging a stool over to sit by Petronas's chair. 'He's a regular associate of mine, of course, but aren't I right in thinking that the whole fleet knows about the monster-man who lives on board the *Gyga VII*?'

Petronas kept staring. Just like all the other flotilla children, he had listened to, made up, embellished and passed on the myths about the *Gyga VII*. It was the ship that almost no one travelled to and that anyone who had seen inside was not allowed to discuss. Although he had scoffed at the stories of the red monster-man, those stories had still kept him awake after lights-out, and when N[illegible] mond had made up extravagant fantasies about what lay in t[illegible] he had listened along willingly enough. When he was o[illegible] learned that the ship was something to do with e[illegible] workshops and had barely given it another thoug[illegible] full of things it was useless to wonder about.

But now the red-robed monster-man was here, and Petronas was surprised to feel no fear in the presence of the flotilla-children's favourite bogeyman. He kept staring.

'Time for you to be introduced, I expect,' said the sad-looking little man. 'This, Mister Petronas, is an honoured member of the flotilla, a member of rather more years of service and standing than yourself if I might say so. As Doctor D'Leste has said, he is Magos Dyobann of the Adeptus Mechanicus. He joined us as a magos errant after the Explorator fleet of Pontifex Mechanis Hvel was disbanded some, what was it, one hundred and twelve years ago, by my count. Near the beginning of my service, in fact.'

'I thought we were supposed to be independent from such as that.' Normally Petronas would have stopped at the thought, but the words were out before he realised. He wondered if the drugs in his system were blunting his edge.

'Our great flotilla could travel the galaxy for a long time on our own resources,' said Galt, the reproach stronger in his voice now although Magos Dyobann had not reacted to the shot at all. 'Perhaps a lifetime. But there come times when we must conduct rites of engineering or medicine or other things that are simply beyond us. The Adeptus Mechanicus knows this. And even as we have need of their services, there are things that we offer in turn. We are a rogue *trader* flotilla, after all.'

'Our contract with the Adeptus Mechanicus is a simple deed of exchange, with no date of expiry,' said the woman in the shawl, pinching each word off with her lips as though she resented having to expend the energy on it. 'We have the right to call upon the services of the Mechanicus to meet what needs our own lay techmen are incapable of meeting. In exchange, the magos errant... travels with us.'

'There has to be more to it than that,' said Petronas. The realisation that he had not been punished for the way he had first spoken was making him bolder. 'What is your stake in this, Magos Errant Dyobann?' His voice, he noticed, was still weak, even hoarser than the woman's had been. Then his gut lurched as suddenly the magos bore down on him with a disturbing, gliding gait.

'There is much all across the cosmos to interest and draw a disciple of the Omnissiah,' came the voice from under the scarlet half-veil hid the magos's lower face. It was the voice Petronas remembered from his sickness, simultaneously warm and affectless. 'And its charter allows this flotilla to travel in places that might attract attention or be simply forbidden. There are certain discoveries that my ancient and holy order consider are better studied in privacy.' The magos bent over and then, to Petronas's revulsion, the corner of the man's right eye bulged and birthed a slender metal worm that stretched from the place where the eyelids joined. It swayed in the air for a moment, then lunged out to meet and snap onto one of the antennae of the butterfly-diagnostor at Petronas's shoulder. The machine began to quiver as though the magos's tendril were sucking it dry.

'There will be the occasional need, for example,' Dyobann went on, his face centimetres from the ensign's, 'to ensure that a… setback for the Imperial military does not lead to the loss of rare and consecrated technology. There may be times when a traveller of independent means such as a trader flotilla comes into contact with devices fashioned at xenos hands, or specimens of value to our Order Biologis, which it is prudent to extract and place into Mechanicus custody as a priority. Fortunately the flotilla has permitted the construction of excellent laboratoria aboard the *Gyga VII*, over which our treaty allows me full control. Or perhaps there is an artefact of our own construction, lost in the way that so much of what the Imperium once was has become lost, rediscovered by our scouts and agents or by purest chance…'

'I think I see,' said Petronas as the worm suddenly uncoupled from the butterfly and snaked back into Dyobann's face. It did not completely vanish, he noticed now that he knew to look: it still hung at the very corner of the eye like a tiny silver tear. 'That detour we made out into that dead cluster a couple of years back. Fourteen-month round trip to a world none of us were allowed off the ships to see. Was that you?' The magos didn't respond. 'And that xenos meeting post out in Lucky Space in the Segmentum Obscuras, and the stop at the Wulanjo system forge-world straight after. All right.' He suddenly winced, looked down, and could not stifle a cry.

The magos had brought his arm up and the sleeve of his crimson kimono had slipped back to his elbow. His arm was a tangled braid of metal cables, twisting over and around and through one another, of some dark metal that gleamed with scented ceremonial oil. The whole array was in subtle motion, each cable pulsing and shifting against its neighbours. Petronas looked down in panic. At a point a little past where the magos's hand would have been the cables plaited together and locked into a shining gold collar then splayed out like a hand: the dozen metal dendrites that were its fingers had slid under the thin sheet covering Petronas's body. The ensign gawped silently into Dyobann's augmented eyes as each tip slid coolly over his skin, then stopped, pinched and slid a needle home.

'You demonstrate a perceptive and assertive nature, ensign. I approve.' The magos's tone had not changed in the slightest. 'Yes, the missions you have mentioned were performed at my request. The decision to keep the nature of the *Gyga VII* from the rank and file of the flotilla was made by your own masters, but I admit to occasional curiosity as to what the crews of the other ships made of the errands that my own masters occasionally require us to make.'

Petronas fought to control his breathing and think. Every instinct he had told him that something big was about to happen to him, something *big*, and that he had to get onto the front foot and be ready for it. With an effort of will he pushed away the sensation of the needles wriggling in his skin.

'And I'm no longer rank and file, am I? They've brought you out into the open and introduced you. So you're about to kill me or about to promote me. Which is it?'

There was silence in the room. The dendrites squirmed and left pale-orange oilstains on the sheet; the needles withdrew and the magos dropped his sleeve over his snakes' nest of a hand, then straightened up and stood there with his eyes closed. Looking at him, Petronas thought of one of Galt's sommeliers tasting a wine before pouring it out for a dining-party.

'The diagnostors are correct,' Dyobann announced a moment later. 'The preliminary doses have all taken and been absorbed. You did well to recommend this one as the most likely, D'Leste. I approve.'

Petronas fought down another wave of revulsion. He had been right. The magos had been tasting his blood, with whatever inhuman senses he could extend through those cables.

It took a moment for the other word to hit.

Doses.

Under the sheet, his fists were white and aching.

'What do we have to straighten out?' D'Leste asked. 'Didn't he cause a little trouble before we got him?'

'He thought it was the cooks who were behind what was going on and went after them,' said Behaya.

'Killed a couple of them, didn't he?' asked a tall, stately man Petronas recognised as Captain-at-Arms Trazelli.

'A steward named Rheo and a junior officer named Gensh,' said Behaya. 'Nobody important.'

'More importantly,' put in Kyorg, 'how many of the other potential subjects actually survived the dosage anyway?'

'Technically?' D'Leste asked. 'Four. To all practical purposes, none. Two are comatose and fading fast, their metabolisms have lost the ability to process nutrients. They won't last two more days. One will probably be gone by the time we get back. Every single cell in his body seems to want to become a tumour. And there's one last one, Omya, another young officer. He has developed some rather interesting instabilities. The magos and I are going to keep him on the *Gyga* as long as we can, out of curiosity.'

'We cut it very fine indeed, then,' rasped the woman in black and white. 'You ought to be thankful that this one survived. I didn't realise we were going to be taking this much of a chance.'

'Omya...' Petronas whispered. 'Omya. My friend. He's not dead?'

D'Leste snorted. 'I'd forget him were I you, my young friend. You're not going to see him again, and you're going to have plenty of other things on your mind.'

Petronas stared at him until Galt finally stepped forward.

'Spite's sake, let's just out with it and tell the man, shall we?' He turned to Petronas. 'We have a duty for you, my young ensign. A new office we want you to take on. One that perhaps won't be pleasant at first, but which is vital to the survival of the flotilla as we know it now and which will reward you in ways you cannot imagine.' He stopped, made to speak again, stopped again and laughed.

'And even I find myself balking at saying it outright,' he said to the rest of them. 'You'd think we'd all be a little numbed to the enormity by now.' He turned back to Petronas and took in a deep breath.

'Nils Petronas, how would you like to be the new Rogue Trader Phrax?'

The Sanctioned Liner *Gann-Luctis*. In transit

'He was hiding in the winch-wells on the utility decks. He hurt a couple of Cherrick's troopers but we flushed him out with a microshock grenade and gave him a needling for good measure.' Domasa Dorel's normally flat, hard eyes were shining and her voice was excited – she looked as though she should have been flushed, but her skin was as pale as ever. Behind her Cherrick, the man in charge of her bully-squads, held a leash whose other end was cinched around the wrists of a kneeling man with the sunken eyes and green robes of an astropath. Behind them, one of Cherrick's men quietly closed the door of the *Gann-Luctis's* ready-room.

'Hurt? How did he hurt them?' Varro looked past her for signs of injury among Cherrick's men. Domasa waved the question off.

'They're not here, they're off resting up. He didn't have any weapons, nobody but the ship's own complement is supposed to carry weapons during a warp-voyage,' said Domasa, cheerfully ignoring Cherrick's hellgun and belt of grenades and the needler whose trigger-grip she was still clasping. 'But psykers don't dare work their wills too hard on a warp voyage either, there's only the thickness of a Geller field between them and the Worst of Seas.'

'And the beneficence of the Emperor,' put in Ksana Phrax, standing behind her husband's shoulder with her arms folded.

'All right, and that too,' Domasa conceded. 'But still, grabbing up power with your mind on a ship at warp is like firing krak missiles back and forth when you're sitting in a shuttle. That was why we waited until we broke warp to go after him, except we got to the Psykana dome and found he'd already gone scuttling off.'

'What did he do?'

'We were taking a bit of a chance with the microshock, weren't we Cherrick? But it was worth it, we needed to make sure that his concentration would be scrambled.' Domasa was almost gabbling – it was the most excited Varro had seen her.

'What did he do?'

'But I don't think it was really too much of a chance, I mean, if he had been somewhere else, but the winch-wells, that's pretty heavy machinery and the microshocks would barely scuff the metal, we judged it a worthwhile risk.'

'That was my judgement, yes,' put in Cherrick, with a not particularly subtle emphasis on 'my'.

'What did he *do*?' The snap in Ksana's voice was finally enough to register with the others. Domasa caught her reflexive sneer and bowed.

'Apologies, my Lady Phrax, events have me a little keyed up. He sent an astropathic transmission just as we passed the cometary zone. Not enough of the signal was caught by anyone actually *loyal*,' her speech turned into a spit for a moment, 'for us to know about it word for word. But we know that our friend Symozon here has been harvesting information on our voyage and our ship's complement, and he was careless enough to leave some ghosting around the telepathica chair he used that one of our *loyal* astropaths was able to catch before it evaporated, so we know at least some of the names in the transmission.'

'I don't see why you're doing this,' said Varro. His hands were clasped in front of him, taut with distress. 'What have we to hide? You told me yourself that this counter-claim is just rubbish. If we have the stronger claim, then who cares who knows what about this? About us?'

Domasa's mouth opened and closed for a moment.

'Prolegis Maghal has shared some of the Administratum's knowledge of our destination with me,' she said after a moment. 'And one of the things he said was that this arbitor who'll preside over the succession – at which she'll judge whether you even succeed to the charter, I'll remind you – is a straight arrow. Not like some of the Arbites my House has encountered, the ones who love their secret informants and midnight raids. This Calpurnia's apparently a fussy little bitch. If a woman like that wanted to know our complement she'd have an Arbites herald bang on the hull until we handed over a list. She just loves barging in where she's got no right and throwing her weight around, that's what I heard.' Domasa turned, and the hem of her russet skirt twitched as she jabbed Symozon with her foot. 'No, if our friend here was doing any spying then it wasn't for the Arbites. It was for whoever is trying to pull your family's legacy out from under you. Is that honestly the kind of thing you'll sit back and take?'

'How are you going to confirm all of this?' asked Ksana as Varro stared at Symozon's slumped form. 'What has he told you? Wouldn't there be some sign we could find that he has ties to... to some possible other interests?'

'Nothing on his person, nothing in his cell,' volunteered Cherrick. 'But he came on board as a last-minute transfer by the Telepathica chambers at Gunarvo. It's not the kind of thing they do too regularly. Strings got pulled, you mark me.' Domasa nodded agreement.

'We have to deduce, because of where we are. If we were out of warp, then this would be a lot easier. We could peel back the little rat's brain until we found what we wanted. There are certain ways to use a warp-eye that I've even been keen to try out myself, although I'm no psyker in any kind of way that would let me do a thorough job. But we're in warp at the moment, and it's rough out there too.' Her face grew sober and she took a breath. 'Things can ride in storms like this. Pulling a mind, especially a psyk-mind, inside out in conditions like this, when our protection is already strained... no,' she said more loudly, as if convincing herself. 'We're not going to risk that. I don't even want to take a chance on a mind like his in pain or drug-weakened, not when the warp's like this.' She flared her narrow nostrils. 'And I'm certainly not taking the risk of having him fire off some kind of distress call after we break warp. He's not going to be communicating then.'

'I think that this ship has psyk-cages,' Varro began, 'so if we need to imprison him...'

'Imprison,' snorted Cherrick, cutting him off. 'Did you hear what Lady Dorel was saying?'

'We need to be able to confront these counter-claimers with him as evidence for what they've tried to do,' said Varro. His mouth was dry. There was something in the eyes of both the Navigator and her trooper that he didn't like. 'I would have thought that the evidence of wrongdoing, espionage, like this, would weaken their case at law. If this Calpurnia is such a stickler for above-board legality...'

'It would have about as much effect on them as their producing evidence of a spy of ours would have on us,' said Domasa. 'And if the arbitor-woman is surprised that it's happening then she's even dumber than Maghal's reports made her sound. If he just doesn't transmit again then we've got them wondering. Did we catch him? Did he get left behind? Did he turn? Has he just not got much to report?'

'So it's the psyk-cage, then,' said Varro. 'I'll have one of the stewards paged and they can make the arrangements.' He stood up from his seat, but no one else moved. Domasa was staring at him. Varro looked to his wife for support, but she had gone pale and was looking away.

'I think, Varro, that I need to provide a demonstration of the way your mind is going to have to start working from now on,' said Domasa, raising her needler. One of her elongated fingers curled around to work a stud on the trigger-grip nestled in her narrow palm.

'Lethal dose,' she said briefly, and lowered her arm. There was a tiny sound, no louder than a sniff, and Symozon slumped forwards. As Varro watched, his gorge rising, he saw the little sliver of crystallised toxin that had embedded itself in the back of the astropath's high-crowned head melt and soak the rest of the way into his skin. He dropped back into his seat as the strength seemed to go out of him.

'The nature of my mission here has been made very clear to me by my backers,' Domasa said. 'I am to help you in whatever way I can to fight the counter-claim and have you succeed to the Phrax Charter and the mastery of the flotilla. You need to travel there, so here is a ship and a Navigator. You need protection for your own good, so here am I and here is Cherrick. You will need aid and support for your future work as a trader, and so worthies of Gunarvo and of the Administratum are with you.' She raised her arm and Varro flinched, but she simply released the grip of the needler and folded it back into her armband. 'All you have to do,' she told him sweetly, 'is claim your inheritance and remember your friends. That's all you have to do, Varro. We'll take care of everything else.'

They left him, then, left the silent tableau: Varro Phrax, pale and clutching the arms of the seat; his wife in her yellow gown, turned away with her face in her hands, and at their feet the sprawled corpse of Astropath Symozon.

CHAPTER SEVEN

Arbites Fortress of Trylan Tor, Hydraphur

THE ADEPTUS MINISTORUM arrived at Trylan Tor on the fifth day of Shira Calpurnia's stay there, on an afternoon when she was distracted and irritable and in absolutely no mood for uninvited visitors at all.

It wasn't the tor itself that she disliked. Both island and fortress were rugged and powerful: like all Arbites architecture the tor fortress was designed so the mere sight of it intimidated any onlooker. It took up the whole crowning plateau of the tor for which it was named, sitting on an almost sheer-sided pillar of rock that jutted three hundred metres above the waves. Even from the air it radiated power and immovability; she thought it would be even more impressive from the sea.

Inside, away from the constant wind and the booming of the waves, the warm air and narrow corridors made the place feel almost like some giant burrow. Through most of the building the halls were only just wide enough for two Arbites to pass, and even then it was only Calpurnia's slender build that meant she could move through them easily. Even Culann, not a heavyset man, was noticing the cramped quarters when he was in armour and Odamo, manoeuvring his broad shoulders around the tor on two canes and his sticklike metal legs, had resigned himself to having to wait while anyone he met coming the other way either backed up to a niche or a cross-corridor, or plastered themselves against a wall.

The tor was not a conventional precinct fortress. The archipelagos were lightly populated, and the sea and all the surrounding island-tors were kept empty for a hundred kilometres around by Arbites interdict. Some long-ago Arbitor General had decided that the Arbites presence on Hydraphur could not be crippled by a decisive strike on the Wall: pockets of strength were carefully cached around the planet and the system so that, should the unthinkable ever happen and the four thousand year-old citadel at Bosporian fall, the surviving precinct houses would not be without their most essential tools: weapons, personnel and the *Lex Imperia*. The fortress at Trylan was one of those specialised bases, keeping within its thick black walls copies of the most vital core of Arbites scripture and dogma.

It was the custom for Arbites to come there to study or teach, the fortress becoming over the years a kind of miniature university. There were texts there of which copies existed nowhere else in Hydraphur except for the Wall itself, and while the tor had its garrison of arbitrators guarding the walls, crewing the sentry posts on the surrounding tors or patrolling the interdiction zone in armoured flyers or snub-nosed submersibles, most Arbites on Trylan spent their time by lamplight in honeycomb of tiny reading-cells in the lower levels of the central bastion.

Judges were the most common, bent over bound papers or flickering data-arks as they explored ten millennia of ever-expanding, ever-complicating Imperial laws. But there were Chasteners there, too, standing out from the rest in their bulky uniforms and brown tunics, usually posted to Trylan to build their knowledge of the rarer and more obscure treatises on the capture, handling and breaking of prisoners. Verispex officers came to wade through the forensic notes of cases a thousand or more years old. Garrison preachers studied the texts of their forebears, sharpening their understanding of their religious duties to their fellow Arbites. And the arbitrators themselves would go down to the reading levels when they were not walking the walls with magnocs in hand, to read about techniques the Arbites of generations past used to break a crowd, or a bunker, or a seditious parade; the weak points of a house, a palace, a tank, a cargo-dray, an unarmoured rioter; how formations of arbitrators could best work to lock down a hab-block or bring it down in rubble, storm a spaceship or commandeer one, defend a power-plant or detonate it from within.

Calpurnia approved of the bookish atmosphere. Two Calpurnii five generations before her had both been Arbites General in border systems on the Ultima Segmentum: she had read their diaries and the remark of one of them that force without understanding was of no more service to the law than understanding without enforcement had stuck with her. Under almost any other circumstances at all she would have found a spell at Trylan tor restful and inspiring. But not when she was being badgered by uninvited visitors on a day when her hands were full dealing with her invited ones.

'Arbitor Senioris Calpurnia, I fully understand, I assure you, that I stand on sovereign ground of the Adeptus Arbites.' Genetor-Magos Sanja spoke carefully and formally. 'But arbitor, you must understand that I just do not have licence to throw off the laws and traditions of my own Adeptus, which are not only binding by decree of the Mechanicus but sacred in the sight of the Machine-God. This *must be* how I work here. There *can be* no other way.'

'But I have to respectfully repeat my question, magos. Can I know, please, the specific requirements on your rituals? If your laws are against anyone outside the Cult of the Machine setting eyes on your–' she had been about to say equipment, but she knew that some Mechanicus considered such a term for their sacred devices derogatory '–on the homes of your machine-spirits, then we have no conflict. A screen can be erected, or curtains, or a simple veil or blindfold on all the non-Mechanicus present in the room whenever the machines are in the open. I'll allow one of your own servitors to do the blindfolding. I'll stand in the room and allow myself to be blindfolded first–'

'The matter is not one of beholding,' Sanja told her. As far as Calpurnia could tell he was accoutred identically to the first time she had met him on the steps of his own shrine in the Augustaeum. He made a vivid splash of colour in the fortress's dark, austere little courtroom: a crimson Mechanicus kimono, his head hooded and veiled with only his bright blue eyes and hooked nose visible, a skull-cog emblem around his neck in black steel and diamond, the red and white sash decorated with the helical livery of a genetor in tiny gems. Behind him stood one of his junior acolytes, also in scarlet, his head completely hidden by a hood of red chainmail and his hands bulging with shrouded augmetics. Shoulder to shoulder behind him in turn were four dwarfish servitors, resembling obese, blank-eyed children balanced on hoofed, reverse-jointed augmetic legs that gleamed under the lamps. Sanja's luminants, the gold-plated skulls of Mechanicus dignitaries that accompanied him around his shrine, had not followed him here.

'The ark of the Helispex is one of the most revered engines of the Genetor cult on the whole of Hydraphur,' Sanja said. 'To consult with it is to perform an act of religious significance. Even on consecrated ground, the rituals of calibration and initialisation take over an hour to please its anima to the point where it will bring the engine to bear. To remove it from our shrine is something I have done before, and the engine itself is built for travel, but in every case we travel to ground that has been sanctified by a member of our cult before our arrival.

'That is the issue here, arbitor. I don't care to think about what might happen to the Helispex engine should we attempt to rouse it on unsanctified ground. The possibility that its spirit might be angered or damaged beyond our ability to repair does not bear contemplating. If this is where you wish me to examine the gene-samples from these two heirs, then some part of this fortress must be handed over to one of my liturgical mechanics for consecration as sovereign Adeptus Mechanicus ground. There is no other course of action. If this is impossible,' he went on as Calpurnia opened her mouth to reply, 'then I shall provide every assistance that I am able without the engine. Or, if you prefer, I shall return to the Augustaeum and rouse the Helispex there, so that the work you require can be done and the results communicated to you here. I shall do this with no animosity and with my respect for you undiminished, as it goes without saying.' Sanja finished his words with a bow.

'What we have here, you see, magos, is a clash of sovereign territories. I am just as bound as you are. Every precedent for a contest between heirs has said that the claimants remain in the courtroom while their blood is taken, away, brought before the Helispex and the engine's verdict brought back before the court by one of your order. Trouble is, all the precedents are for trials conducted in the Wall, where your shrine is not much more than walking distance.'

She sighed. 'You don't want to be the man who broke the Helispex engine for all time, and I don't want to be the woman who created the precedent for an outside organisation to claim sovereignty over an Arbites fortress.' Her fingers had found the scars over her eye and were lightly tracing them. 'I can't lie, even by omission, and leave something like that out of the records. And once it's recorded into precedent, magos, it's a devil to get out again. Things don't just unhappen.'

'I understand. We are at an impasse, one that is the creation of neither of us.' Sanja had nothing against the arbitor senioris, and his willingness to help was genuine. But for a moment he could not help but be amused. While its control over its own jurisdictions was absolute, the Mechanicus had little ability to simply move in and overrule other arms of the Adeptus as the Arbites did, and he suspected that such impasses happened to him more often that they did to her. He tried again.

'Where are the engineering functions of the fortress carried out, arbitor? Do you have tech-priests ministering to your systems, or laity?'

'Laity. It's the same here as in our other fortresses, there are lay tech-adepts granted indulgence by your priesthood for the duty. There's no tech-shrine on the tor that will meet your needs, I thought of that.' She looked around.

The room was probably the biggest one in the whole fortress, and it was barely bigger than some of the meeting chambers back in the Wall. That was unusual for an Imperial building, which tended to have at least one soaring, vaulted space in it, although at first it seemed bigger than it was because the ceiling and far walls got lost in the dimness of the light. The light at Hydraphur's equator was brighter and less fusty-yellow than further north at Bosporian, but they were far too deep inside the fortress for windows. Although while she thought of it...

'Is outdoors out of the question? The surrounding tors have sentry posts on them, but nothing else. There should be enough open ground to put up some kind of tabernacle...' But Sanja was already shaking his head.

'The engine's physical form is as delicate as its temperament,' he said. 'I cannot chance exposure to the elements, even under conditions better suited to it spiritually. I suspect, arbitor, that if I am to use the engine to verify this succession as you wish me to, then it will have to be done either back at Bosporian or at one of our shrines on the southern coastline of Nyherac. There are perhaps some there that would be suitable, although I would be obliged if your own arbitrators would assist with fortification and security while the Helispex was housed there.'

'Hmm.' Calpurnia was brooding as she took a message chit from a runner who had shuffled in and was looking nervously at the tech-priest and his retinue.

'If I may be so bold as to wonder, Arbitor Calpurnia, I can't help noticing that no similar problem to this appears in the Mechanicus's own archives on the Phrax succession, although I confirmed that we assisted in verifying the genes of contesting heirs. Now although I don't wish to be less than tactful…'

'No offence taken, magos. As I said, the precedents are for hearings at the Wall, and holding the hearing there is one area of tradition that I want to get away from. There are already signs of possible foul play and I want this hearing somewhere we control absolutely, not where both parties can play hide-and-go-backstab through the Augustaeum for days before and afterwards. I found out the hard way how much potential there is to be mucked around by all sorts of interests when you're sitting in the middle of Bosporian Hive, no matter how safe you think you are.'

Sanja, who had been caught up first-hand in Calpurnia's experience of the Bosporian's brutal intrigues, bowed agreement.

'And I got caught out,' she went on. 'Had I thought about complications like this I might've stayed there.' She grimaced. 'Actually, no I wouldn't. But I wouldn't have had you fly a third of the way across the planet on an errand that turned out to be a non-starter, magos, and for that you shall have a written apology over my seal. I had no business being that careless.'

Sanja waved the words away. 'Fault attaches to me, too, since I should certainly have made sure before my departure that you understood everything that the Mechanicus would require of you.' They were moving towards a narrow hall door; the arbitrators standing guard there presented arms as they passed through.

'And I am sure that the problems need not be fatal to the endeavour, in any event,' said Sanja as they turned into the passage outside. It was narrow enough that only the four little servitors could comfortably walk two abreast. 'There are a number of ceremonies of diagnosis that I could perform in the fortress as it stands. They will not have the ceremonial weight of the Helispex, whose formal stamp I accept is a traditional part of the succession. However, if you are after simple genetic confirmation so that you can move on to legalities, I should be able to meet your requirements. Who are these two again?'

'One a son by his late wife, one a son by a concubine on board the flotilla itself, according to our information.'

'Well, I can guarantee that given a day or two with their samples I can – arbitor?'

Calpurnia had come to a halt in the middle of the corridor and was reading the chit under one of the brighter ceiling lamps. As she finished her arm twitched as if she wanted to throw the thing away down the passageway.

'I don't believe this. What does the idiot think this is, some kind of bloody carnival? What the hell is he doing all the way out here?' She set off again, at a pace that Sanja found difficult to match with dignity. 'Why isn't he back where I told him to be?'

'Arbitor, may I ask who you're talking about?'

'Simova! That pompous, gawping Reverend Simova.'

The *Gyga VII*, In the flotilla of Hoyyon Phrax, Batrista midsystem docks

SOMEONE HAD TOLD him they were in-system again, one last stop at Batrista, as much a regrouping stop as anything, before the ride down a cascading warp current to Hydraphur. Nils Petronas, no longer ensign but rogue trader-apparent Nils Petronas, didn't care. He had almost forgotten there was a flotilla, a system, an Imperium out there. His world had narrowed to the vaulted ward-chamber on the *Gyga VII*, and the wide four-poster bed on the dais in the centre of it, directly beneath the tall dome in the ceiling, and his own body, and pain.

He tried to tell himself every so often that not truly knowing what was happening to him before had made it worse, that now he knew what was wracking his body he could deal with whatever else might happen. But there were times when it got so bad that this didn't help at all, when the pain got worse and he lost the ability to think clearly enough to tell himself anything. They would not help him through the pain, either. Your system must grow into its changes, they had told him. If we numb you even a little your body may lose the ability to govern the changes, they had told him. We will not risk you, they had told him.

Maybe that was it, and maybe it wasn't. Petronas thought it wasn't all of it. The magos didn't seem to care, but Petronas had seen D'Leste's eyes light up and his tongue creep into the corner of his mouth while he watched the spasms light Petronas's nerves up like a sun-flare.

When there was no pain at all he would sleep as much as he could; indeed, those times he often dropped straight down into exhausted unconsciousness, or at least into a blissful drowsiness in which he wanted no troubling thoughts at all. It was when there was just enough pain to run along his nerves like a whetstone and make his thoughts cool and sharp that Petronas closed his eyes gently and worked on his plans.

Once his treatment was complete, he would succeed to the charter and become the new Rogue Trader Phrax. On that he believed them. The guests at that fateful dinner had not been selected to help the flotilla bond – as Gensh the (dead) idiot had told them all – it had been a way to get all the promising subjects that D'Leste and Behaya had identified between them, a way to administer the first stage of the serum.

Nobody in the flotilla knew if the gene-treatments Dyobann had designed had been tried before, anywhere, ever. The magos had based them on scriptures he had found in the wreckage of an explorator ship that had been studying a mercenary xenos breed, combined with treatises on the transformative gene-seed of the Astartes that no one outside the bio-forges of Mars was supposed to own any more. But the treatments themselves were an unknown quantity, and they had needed an inconspicuous way of exposing their candidates to the trigger-serum.

And Petronas was the one who'd survived, although D'Leste had told him in a less guarded moment that they had clawed him back from the edge more than once. He was the one they had been the most confident of, the one that they had actually been hoping to work with: the fact that he looked more than a little like the young Hoyyon Phrax was a bonus.

'Does that mean I'm really Hoyyon's son?' Petronas had asked hesitantly when he had heard this. There had been a bundle of serum tubes running into his mouth at the time, making him careful as he shaped his words. But D'Leste and Trazelli, who had been watching over him at the time, had both burst out laughing.

'No, you cheeky little..., you're not the child of the trader,' Trazelli had told him. 'Didn't you know that his whores were allowed to roam a little in the old man's later years? He was never very randy in the first place. I've heard tell in some quarters that Galt even needed to proggle him along a little to make sure there was any kind of heir at all, although if he'd known then what we all know now I suppose he wouldn't have bothered.'

They had all fallen silent for a little while as one of Dyobann's servitor-aides detached the tubes from Petronas's gullet. When the coughing had died down and the water he swilled and spat no longer had any red in it, Petronas had dabbed at his eyes and cautiously asked what Trazelli had meant. They told him amiably enough – by now they didn't seem to care what he learned. What threat could this sweating, gulping little creature in its thicket of medicae devices be? And that was fine.

'Varro Phrax, you've probably heard his name,' said D'Leste. 'He's the target here, or at least his claim to the charter is. It's a claim that has to be knocked over, for the sake of the charter and the Phrax name and the flotilla. Harsh decision, maybe, but our first loyalty is to the line of Phrax as we see it. Varro is unacceptable. An overindulged little playboy who has not done a thing to earn a claim on the charter other than have some Phrax genes sloshing around in him. And if a succession is so weakly constructed as to be based on that rather than true worthiness, well then we can challenge in the same way.' The look on the apothecary's face had been just a little too carefully composed, and as he had listened to him Petronas had realised that D'Leste was forcing himself to believe in what he was saying. Since that moment Petronas had no doubt: this was a power-grab, nothing more. And that was fine too.

'Anyway,' said Trazelli, 'if there were no other direct heirs this'd be a lot easier. The key is blood proximity, do you see? You're a reasonably bright boy. Now I don't know much about this – well, I know about drawing blood, but not playing with it, ha – but the idea is that if we show blood proximity then we're all but there.'

Blood proximity. It was a good term. Petronas had remembered it and held onto it as he lay in the four-poster now and watched

Dyobann's servitors, with their spidery limbs and inlays of pearl ivory and ruby. They glided between biotic vats and sample-vials, centrifuges and arrays of pipes and dishes. Occasionally one would extrude a worm from a limb or face and slide it into one aperture or another in the banked lecterns that housed the cogitator engines. Petronas understood that then they were talking to the engines beneath their fingertips, and maybe more elsewhere on the ship, although he didn't fully understand how. Dyobann's pulpit was behind his head, although the bed and his own weakened body meant that he had not been able to twist around to see it. The magos stood there when he was overseeing the servitors and some kind of machine-witchery allowed him to see from their eyes and control them without any commands that Petronas could hear.

Beyond his feet, hanging over the door to the chamber, was a great pict-plate that showed a constantly rippling mosaic of images: elegant patterns of lines and circles etched in green light, strange greyish ovals and ellipses that seemed to move and swim, and strange strips of oscillating colours and spinning runes that Petronas couldn't read. On Dyobann's previous visit he had mustered the courage to ask what those images were and the magos had replied, 'that is how I see your blood.' Something about that had disturbed Petronas so much that he had lain back with his eyes closed and not opened them again until he knew Dyobann had gone.

Had there been no direct heir, no son Varro, the flotilla could perhaps have escaped with little or no tampering and this whole exercise might not have been necessary at all. But contesting the succession in a court of the Adeptus meant they would have to produce not just a tissue sample but a challenger whose blood would show gene-traces of Hoyyon Phrax himself. He supposed, then, that it could be expected to hurt when artificial viruses and alchemic serums were working their way through his metabolism, twisting and rewriting his fundamental blood-print to show that he was the son of someone whose son he was not.

So he let Dyobann and D'Leste work on him. When they were satisfied, he was told, he would be moved to the *Callyac's Promise* where Galt would work on him too, making sure he could talk about Hoyyon as a father, talk about the flotilla as his own, and never arouse suspicion even from one who really had spent his first ten years living with Phrax as a father. When it was over he would be the little merchant prince, decked out and properly primed, ready to dance on the flotilla masters' strings while they got themselves a charter and to be their pretty figurehead after they had it.

And that was fine too. Really. All of it was fine.

Nils Petronas as-was, Petronas Phrax as-was-becoming, didn't know if Dyobann could pull it off. He had taken in more through the pain and the occasional delirium than he had allowed them to see, and he knew the flotilla masters were taking a roll of the die on whether his rewritten blood-prints would fool the Arbites and steal Hoyyon's legacy away. But he had already decided that, whether they got away with it or not, whether they got the charter or not, he owed something for his mother and Rengill and Nimmond and Omya and all the others.

Petronas lay under the sheet and made his hands into fists. He could hold them, now, for a count of five hundred and he grinned as his nails sank into his palms and drew little red arcs of his strange, changing blood.

Nils Petronas would ride with the flotilla masters to Hydraphur. And at the end of the voyage – this he vowed to himself yet again – Petronas Phrax would kill them all.

Arbites Fortress of Trylan Tor, Hydraphur

Reverend Simova was standing on the sloping top of a tor at the edge of the interdiction zone, underneath the high grey walls and watchful gun-slits of one of the Arbites' observation strongpoints. Beside him stood a herald from the Eparch's Nunciate office, without much to do except hold up a scroll since Simova seemed to have decided to do most of his own talking. Behind the herald was arranged a single rank of white-armoured Adepta Sororitas, Sisters of the Order of the Sacred Rose that Simova must have drawn from the Cathedral garrison back in the Augustaeum, in full-face Croziat-pattern helms that hid their faces from the stiff sea-breeze.

Calpurnia leaned over the holographic pict-relay and watched the scene as it was captured by the sentry-post's opticons, eyes narrowed with anger as the little holographic Simova jabbed a finger at the miniature arbitrator in front of him. There was a sound pickup at the post, but the wind on the tor and the natural noise of the transmission swamped the voices into incoherence.

'Do we have any idea what he actually wants?' she asked, and Arbitor Thesalka, the comms technician, shook his head.

'Our visitor is rather insistent on his protocol, ma'am, so once he was face to face with the senior officer of the post – Proctor Ammaz there – he went through a presentation of credentials and so on first. Full and formal. Now he's demanding passage to the tor itself. He says he's got letters of errand from the Eparch. Ammaz told him no, but the priest didn't look like he was gong to take that for an answer. Started talking about how his office was divine and wouldn't stand for mortal sanction. Then Ammaz told him that if they flew into the interdiction zone without express grant of passage and an escort they'd be shot down before they'd gone two kilometres...'

'Good.'

'...and so now he's back to trying to talk his way in again. He's saying that he is here to follow up business with you and that you're going to punish the crap out of Ammaz when you find out he kept the priest waiting.'

'Good work Proctor Ammaz, and more fool the priest. Are you passing instructions back to him while he's out there?'

'Yes ma'am,' said Thesalka. 'His torc is active but he's got a helmet pickup that the priest can't hear too.'

'Good,' said Calpurnia, straightening up. 'Tell him he is not to give any ground. Literally. Not a millimetre. If they try to force their way forward then he's to react exactly as he told them he would. No arbitor ever makes an idle threat.' Her left hand rose uncertainly, moving to touch the scars over her eye, then her expression firmed and the hand dropped to rest on the hilt of her power-maul. 'Culann? Have the transport flier we came in prepared for departure, please, and notify our respected guest Magos Sanja that he should make similar preparations. Have one of the patrol fliers prepared too, for a trip out to that sentry post. You'll be flying in that one, by the way, so you might want to take your pick of the hangar in person. The Reverend Simova didn't appear to take a point I made to him when we last met. I think I'm going to have to add a little emphasis.'

CHAPTER EIGHT

Coronet Triatic MRA-47; Imperial Navy sentry gate, Outlying Hydraphur system

The first person to see the flotilla break warp on the outskirts of Hydraphur was an opticon rating named Jarto, who saw the tiny, distant pinprick of light as the ships came spilling through the gap in reality, surfing their momentum and setting their prows toward Hydraphur's bright sun.

Jarto dutifully slid the bronze measuring rods into place and charted the co-ordinates of the sighting, called them up the speaker-tube to the Opticon Intendant's control cabin high above him, and punched them into a grey card that was sucked into the slotted mouth of a gargoyle on his viewing-deck's central pillar and carried smoothly to the gate's archive stacks. He never thought any more about it, as he never thought any more about any of the tiny warp-flares he recorded. Everyone knew Hydraphur was too well fortified and too deep in the Imperium for hostile traffic – Jarto's priority was earning enough commendations for a transfer off this crowded, Emperor-forsaken little pocket of tedium and back to one of the big planetside bases, where the fortifications went deep under the crust and there were warm rooms, and women, and forgotten little passageways where a man could run a still.

So if the first man to see the arriving flotilla did not, perhaps, accord it the importance its masters would want, that would not last for long. The astropath in the top spire of the gate's slender metal spindle sent a hail to the flotilla which was courteously returned, and then a message by both astropathy and vox to the naval squadron of Captain Irian Traze, the nearest node in the complex web of warship patrols that prowled all through Hydraphur.

The Navy's goodwill toward the Phrax flotilla tarnished quickly. Despite an invitation, then a request, then a demand that it halt one hundred and fifty kilometres out from Coronet Triatic MRA-47 to await escort, the flotilla grudgingly dropped its velocity to a little under cruising speed and set a course that would take them between Hydraphur's two ecliptics, around the star and toward the planet itself. Offended by the flotilla's rudeness and unimpressed by the repeated and unsubtle references in its communiqués to the privileges the charter granted it, Traze took the opportunity to give his squadron a little live close-manoeuvring drill.

So the observers on the flotilla decks were startled to see the high, crenellated prows of half a dozen Battlefleet Pacificus warships bearing down on them, fast enough for some of the more nervous flotilla commanders to issue orders to brace for collision. The Navy formation speared into the side of the Phrax flotilla and then, in a beautiful display of piloting and discipline, the powerful warships wheeled around onto the flotilla's course, effortlessly matching speeds. The flotilla crews, used to looking out of their viewports to the comforting sight of other flotilla ships blazing with light, now looked out at the pitted grey hulls of the battlefleet vessels, their arched gunports and the venomous, hulking shapes of lance turrets.

This time there was no invitation, request or demand, but an order. Navy pilots would come aboard with data-plaques and vox-links to guide the flotilla through the maze of minefields, sentry gates, gravitic tides and patrol squadrons that would, it was made very clear, wipe out every one of the Phrax ships if they tried to fly into Hydraphur on their own. Flag-Captain Traze boarded the *Bassaan* himself, and the first thing he did was walk onto the bridge and up to the captain, and send the man sprawling on the deck beside his own command pulpit, his lips split and bleeding from the swipe of Traze's pistol barrel.

The Navy, as a rule, did not like rogue traders much.

The Flagship *Bassaan*, Flotilla of Hoyyon Phrax, Hydraphur

AND THE FEELING was mutual.

'Interfering grox-loving...' growled Zanti. She stood with Kyorg on a catwalk before a great circular window, looking out at the great flank of Traze's flagship *Diarmid's Redemption*. A runner had brought them news of the orders and of the indignity the Navy man had inflicted on their poor captain. 'I don't understand why we're letting them do this. The charter means what it says. We should be able to sail through their lines and be damned to the lot of them. You people lack spine.'

The flotilla masters had conducted a brief but heated meeting when the Navy squadron had closed in. Zanti, who had been listening carefully to Dyobann's reports on Petronas's health, had wanted to speed straight to Hydraphur and demand the charter. She was none too pleased at being outvoted, and less so at getting one of Kyorg's lectures about diplomatic realities. Zanti was a woman who lived by the letter of the law, and the human complications that surrounded it were things she had never mastered.

'On the contrary,' Kyorg told her, 'I have a spine. And guts, too, which was the other thing you said I didn't have any of. Oh, and brains, you made remarks about those. I have brains.'

'Pah.'

'I also have bones, eyes, lungs, muscles and even toenails, and I'm fond of all of them, and that's why I wanted us to co-operate with the Navy and not try to bluff any outrageous behaviour with a charter that they resent having to honour in the first place. I'd rather that all those parts of me stay parts of me, and not end up floating around Hydraphur in a cloud of vapour.'

'I told you,' snapped Zanti, 'the charter's passive protection is considered to apply to the flotilla even when a trader is not present to wield it. The codicils referring to–'

'Yes, but do the Navy agree with that interpretation? You admitted yourself, that particular boundary of the charter has never been tested.'

'It doesn't matter,' snapped Zanti. 'Our interpretation is *right*. The whole point of having the charter in the first place is so that the *tikks* can't boss us around.'

'I don't even understand why you're impatient,' Kyorg told her. 'Explain to me where there's a hurry. We're here now, we're at Hydraphur. We'll be shaking hands with the arbitor before you know it.'

'I know this full well, thank you.' Zanti was suddenly trying to understand why she had allowed herself to be drawn into conversation with a man she so detested.

'And has anyone told you that the real heir is still labouring through warp storms off Santo Pevrelyi? Storms bad enough to send out ripples that even made our own astropaths nervous.' Zanti glared at him. The flotilla's astropaths were one of her responsibilities. 'They're going to be ages yet, Zanti. Think of all that time we'll get to work on the Arbites. I'm sure we'll come up with some way to lay the groundwork in our favour.'

'You're the Master of Envoys, Kyorg, you're supposed to have plans to lay the groundwork now. And backups and contingency plans. What preparation have you done, exactly, to make the most of the time?'

'There's plenty of time yet,' Kyorg told her loftily, sauntering away.

He had done nothing, then, as usual. She wondered if he understood how precarious his position in the flotilla was, and how he seemed to be wilfully making it worse.

She shook the thought off, made an irritated flap of her hand at the giant warship outside the window and stamped off in the opposite direction. If he wanted to make such a poor bed for himself, let him; after he was gone the role of Master of Envoys would sit neatly within her own portfolio. She just didn't see why people had to be so stupid all the time, that was all.

The *Gyga VII*, Flotilla of Hoyyon Phrax, Hydraphur

D'Leste watched the shape under the veil uneasily. Petronas's eyes seemed to be getting more sensitive, and he had demanded veils to keep the light on the bed dim. D'Leste was rather grateful for that now. Dyobann's retrogenetic treatments were taking a toll on the boy – he was barely recognisable as the arrogant young ensign they had looked at in the speaking-chamber's holographic display.

'He's stable,' came Dyobann's voice as a tickle in D'Leste's ear. They had taken to using microbeads around the bed, especially when they were discussing their patient's condition. 'If you obey my teachings, allow my servitors to do their work and stay vigilant, then he will remain stable.'

'For how long?' D'Leste asked. He was not looking forward to this. Something he would not have admitted to anyone was that he was frightened by the idea of being in charge. He had become used to the magos's sure touch and preternatural calm. The idea of having no one to take a problem to was bothering him.

'For long enough. Until I return,' Dyobann informed him coldly. 'You will not need to initiate any new stages of treatment. Should I be delayed, we have in fact brought our subject to the point where his tissue will at the very least be able to contend as a Phrax relative. We shall not know specifically what this Arbitor Calpurnia will require until we reach the moment of her decision.'

'We're trying to find out what that will be,' said D'Leste, although he didn't hold out much hope. Kyorg's handling of it so far had involved delegating a clerk whom D'Leste was pretty sure was his mistress to send a message ahead. He wasn't even sure if the message had gone.

'If she does require a live tissue-draw then I leave it to yourselves to improvise a solution,' said the magos. 'I, however, shall do my best to lay the groundwork for it. This is why it is best I go. I trust myself more than I trust Kyorg.'

'Don't we all.'

'That is not my affair,' said Dyobann. 'I am no envoy, but I am best placed for this errand. Genetor-Magos Sanja is the one who will conduct the rites of analysis and he will be flattered by the fact that I have made a point of bringing him a sample in advance. The fact that I only need to alter a small sample rather than a full living being allows me to make more comprehensive alterations on the specimen I shall bring before him–' he held up a metal flask in one gleaming hand '–but should my additional work be insufficient to convince him, I am also best placed to make the case for the flotilla's continued ownership of the charter. The relationship between this flotilla and the Mechanicus has been most constructive for us both and Magos Sanja will realise the new heir cannot be trusted to let that continue.' D'Leste felt proud to hear that. Nobody had any idea what Varro would make of Dyobann's status in the flotilla, but he had told the magos that Varro was known for antipathy to the Mechanicus and apparently he had been convincing. He pointed to the bed again.

'Galt will not be delayed any longer, I understand?'

'He won't,' D'Leste confirmed. 'Navy protocols will mean a delay of quite a few days travelling into Hydraphur, perhaps more, and Galt says he needs all of that time to make sure Petronas can comport himself like a proper trader-in-waiting. He's more than a little angry that he's had to wait as long as he has. That's why I need your word that Petronas will be fit.' He glanced at the bed. 'Will he be fit to deal with people? Learn things? He's no use to Galt if he's in a haze all the time.'

'The subject,' said Dyobann, starting to move towards the door, 'is lucid and in control. I have had him perform certain verbal, physical and logical exercises, and used pain relief to provide small rewards. You may convey to Galt that he should need no concessions to any supposed dimunition of our subject's capacity.'

D'Leste grunted. He hadn't known about the exercises.

The double doors swung wide for Dyobann, and the magos marched away from D'Leste with two servitors behind him. The apothecary didn't know what clout Dyobann had had to use to commission a dromon system-ship to carry him ahead of the flotilla, but he was glad of it even as he was nervous about the wrecked man behind him being left in his care. It meant something was happening, at last.

He turned back to the white curtain and put his face up to it, but all he could see was a faint hint of sluggish movement in the bed. He supposed he should go and notify Galt that his pupil was ready. Petronas would have to appear before the Arbites soon, after all, and Galt had promised he would have him acting the part.

From inside the curtain, Petronas Phrax watched the burly doctor walk away. He lay half in and half out of the covers: his lower body had developed regular, painless spasms that were continually dislodging the bedclothes. Even through the curtain the light was unpleasant for his eyes, which had become almost black, tinged with yellow, but he made himself stare after D'Leste until the doors had closed behind him.

Something had happened to his hearing, and words often seemed to pick up an odd, metallic, double-echo, but he had made out the conversation well enough. D'Leste's part of it, anyway – the man hadn't got the hang of subvocalising into the microbead link.

Soon he would be out and among the other officers. Soon he would be back with his brothers and sisters in uniform. Odd, discoloured tears seeped out of Petronas's eyes at the thought, staining the pillow beneath him. He did not doubt that he would be able to make his plans and his needs clear to them. He did not doubt that they would side with him, not Galt.

He did not doubt that they would help him have his revenge.

The Sanctioned Liner *Gann-Luctis*, Docking orbit, Santo Pevrelyi

Domasa Dorel, normally chilly of emotion and tightly controlled of gesture, wanted to throw back her head and howl.

She clutched the communiqué from Hydraphur in one malformed fist, written out onto flimsy ricepaper in the same coded syllables the astropath had fielded it in. The cipher was a custom one, designed for this particular informant; learning it from the file her Navis Nobilite backers had provided her with had kept Domasa from fretting during the turbulent warp-passage it had taken them to get here.

The news was bad enough that Domasa had suppressed the urge to shred the paper in her fingers out of spite – she wasn't sure that she wouldn't need to show it to Varro at some point. If he wasn't yet convinced of the voyage's urgency, this would do nicely.

So where the hell was Varro? Domasa had spent half an hour prowling the upper passenger decks under bitter mental protest: a minnow she might be in the world of the Navigators, but she was not accustomed to having to run errands like this. She had rousted Cherrick and his squadmates out of bed and set them to checking the lower hab-decks and the utility levels, and haranguing them over their private vox-link helped her mood a little. But too much was starting to go awry, and she hated the feeling that her assignment was going off the rails in ways that she seemed to be powerless to stop.

She tried to keep from pointless fretting, but as she passed like a robed shadow down the arched passageway to the formal dining hall, she found her thoughts returning to the problems like a tongue to loose teeth, like fingernails to a scab.

The warp storms were the greatest and least of her problems. She did not take lightly the fact that turbulence between Santo Pevrelyi and Hydraphur was building into a tempest of a kind she had never had to navigate anywhere near before. She trusted old Auchudo Yimora. He was a good Navigator. But no matter how good the man was, Domasa thought darkly as she stood in the shadowy forechamber of the dining hall, there came a point when even the keenest warp eye was useless except to set its owner to soiling himself with fear at what his ship had caught itself in. No matter how skilled the Navigator, he could no more steer them through a truly lethal storm by sheer skill than an athlete could learn to run through a brick wall by agility alone.

She thought she heard a movement behind her where the long passageway stretched off into the gloom, but when she turned it was empty. Domasa gritted her teeth and gave herself a mental kick – this was no time to let her nerves get the better of her.

It didn't help that she knew better than most of the other passengers on the ship what sort of shape they had finished the last leg of their voyage in. Domasa had felt the great surges and rips of anti-reality that the ship had tried to ride with and push through, which had sent it swooping back and forth, on and off its course, sudden churns that had tried to twist the ship apart like a crepe-paper party-favour, blunt surges of power that had pushed the Geller field in almost to the hull and caused the warp engines to stutter and yelp in protest. Yimora's skill had been breathtaking, the skills of the pilots in obeying him barely less so: they had turned the ship to surf the most powerful swell, spun it back to drive through the slightest gap of calmer passage in the walls of storm, ridden out every swirl in the energy flows that had seemed sure to tear the ship in two. But Domasa had sat in her cabin, hands clutching fistfuls of her robe in tense double handfuls, trying to remember prayers and charms that she had not used since childhood. It was what nearly every Navigator had experienced and what few non-Navigators were ever privileged to hear about: the sensation that you had looked out into the heart of the deadliest storm-cells out there in the immaterium – and something had looked back at you.

There was a sudden jab of sound in her ear, and Domasa whirled and skittered two steps to the side, spinning around to stare into the darkness around her. But it was her vox-piece, and after a moment of spitting anger at how stupid she was being she got herself under control and keyed the link on.

'Cherrick here. Utility deck, nothing. Nothing in the corridors. Nothing in the compartments we could get into. Crew habs ditto. We haven't tried to force our way into the flight sections or the enginarium, and we haven't started going through the cabins. The whole ship's on night-cycle, so if we search more thoroughly than we have done we're going to start waking people up and that's going to mean having to answer questions about what we're up to.' She ignored the sourness in Cherrick's voice. 'So unless you want us up there to help you with whatever this is...'

'No,' snapped Domasa. 'Fine. Forget it. You didn't find him, forget it. Go back to whatever you were doing.'

Cherrick broke the link without further comment and the clunk of the severed connection sounded even louder in Domasa's ear in the quiet of the deserted deck. She thought about pulling the vox-receiver out of her ear and stamping on it, stopped the thought and forced herself to get a grip again. This wasn't over yet, and she was going to need all her wits about her.

Yimora had invited her into the Navigators' perch that morning, and with the shutters safely sealed behind her she had stood beneath the armourglass bubble, carefully undone her hood and bandana and looked out towards Hydraphur. Looking into the immaterium from real space was more difficult than from a ship that had broken warp, and Domasa had only recently caught the trick of it. What she had seen from the *Gann-Luctis's* observation port had turned her guts to ice.

Santo Pevrelyi stood in a relatively small disc of calm warp space: in some places the weight and movements of planets seemed to roil the immaterium on the other side of the membrane to them, in some places such as this the effect was the opposite. But to galactic north-north-west and forty-five degrees above the ecliptic was the storm they would have to ride through to Hydraphur.

Every Navigator, it was said, saw the immaterium in a different way: some as clouds, some as swirls of colour like bands of glowing ink floating in clear water. The great Ayr Shodama had described it as a brilliantly lit room full of thick steam, swirling this way and that. Others 'saw' it in ways that presented to their senses as patterns of sound or even music; others saw nothing at all when they unveiled their warp eyes, but were overwhelmed with tactile sensations and perceived the movements of the warp as breezes or cloth or fingers against their skin. For some the warp even manifested itself as an elaborate dream, their minds presenting what their warp eye saw as a detailed landscape of jungle, or city, a treacherous mountain range, or an underwater reef through whose bright coral a ship had to make its cautious way.

Domasa Dorel saw the warp as simple, depthless blackness when it was calm. Her visions of its depths and movements were subtle, and it had taken her time to learn to properly interpret them – her learning was incomplete even now. She saw eddies and currents in the immaterium as brief, slight swirls and flashes of light and colour, often hard to pick out against the dimness, gone almost before they were there; the kinds of patterns that anyone could see by closing their eyes and pressing against the lids with their fingers. She was used to navigation being difficult for her, taking care and concentration.

It took no care or concentration to see what was ahead of them now. Towering over her in Domasa's warp-vision was a wall of sheer coalescent chaos, not the darkness of her normal warp-sight but a somehow living blackness, shot through with angry, opalescent discharges of light and power. Streaks and spots of red and green stuttered in her warp eye when she looked that way, and flares of strange non-colour seemed to give the thick, knitted darkness meat and movement. Even from here both Navigators could feel the power rippling out from it.

'There's power in it,' Yimora had said. 'Whether it's living power I don't know. There's a feel to the really bad ones, Dorel, I don't know if you've ever been close enough to a high-calibre storm to know. A kind of clenched, hungry feel.'

'What caused it?' asked Domasa. 'Do we know?'

Yimora had given her an odd look. You're old enough to know that there's no easy answer to that. The idea that for every little stir and gust in the warp you can point to a single thing and say "that did it" is a myth for the warp-blind. Waves and echoes have been rebounding back and forth through the immaterium since the

Emperor Himself was in swaddling robes. Every thought that every living creature has adds to them, or interferes with them, or breaks them, or makes new ripples of their own. Who can disentangle what does what? I've been checking the logs and speaking to some of the others around the high docks. It's been growing steadily over the past few weeks – just chop and eddy to begin with, but there have been tides coming up from the Rasmawr Gulf that have fed into the thing and been trapped in it. It's been building up energy ever since. Three days before we came into dock it sent out a shockwave that unhinged a dozen of the more sensitive astropaths in the Pevrelyi Psykana station and gave nearly everyone on the planet screeching nightmares.'

Domasa hadn't known about this, but it explained why the shipworks had been so slow to get under way. She had been told by the captain that there had been riots down on the planet and a rash of suicides on the docks themselves. She had heard of severe warp storms leaking out into reality like that.

All she could hope for now, she thought to herself as she jerked herself out of her reverie, was that whatever menial slobs the Santo Pevrelyi dockmasters had got working on the ship were going to do good work.

Domasa pushed open the dining chamber doors and peered around. Had this been a ship belonging to the Navis Nobilite, there would always have been servants in here, ready with confectionery and soft music to soothe whichever of their masters had found themselves restless, but there was nothing here now but stale uncirculated air and more dimness. She pushed the irritation out of her mind and began a circuit of the room.

The storm ahead would have been frightening enough under any circumstances, but the storms they had already weathered between Gunarvo and here had weakened the ship. The reactions of the ship's drives had been strained and the machine-spirit that raged in the heart of its plasma furnaces had become weakened and angered. It was all the ship's own engineers had been able to do to contain and placate it, and that meant that they had found little time to examine the Geller field, whose generator had also been taxed to its limits keeping the surges of the warp away from the hull.

The toll on the field engine would not even be known for another day or two – the ship's crew could perform the rites of initiation and maintenance usual to a warp voyage but the ship's officers were unanimous that the field needed the attentions of the Adeptus Mechanicus before it would be ready to break warp again. The master engineer had told her of other things: hull stresses and power depletion, anomalies with some of the internal gravity systems that had injured several of the crew, minor things that she had not cared about. All she cared about was when they would be strong enough to face down the monstrous storm that straddled all the quickest routes to Hydraphur.

There was a whisper. Domasa stopped, cocked her head, took an experimental step. No, it had not been the sound of her skirts on the hide-skein matting that framed the rich carpets in the centre of the room. She put a finger to her vox-piece, checked the settings. No, it hadn't been anyone trying to hail her. She listened, and heard it again, grinned, and marched toward the trio of doors in the rear of the chamber behind the high table: the private dining rooms.

Varro Phrax, his wife, his chief attendant with the ridiculous metal head-frills and two others that Domasa didn't bother to try and put names to were all perched on the dining-couches. They all started up guiltily as though Domasa were a dormitory-mistress who had caught them at some kind of little game after lights out. Later, Domasa would think back on that analogy and laugh, but for now there was too much to do. She jabbed a finger at Varro.

'Master Phrax. The ship's Apothecarion, if you please. Now.'

Ksana put a hand on Varro's arm, but he, to Domasa's disgust, had already stood. He really was like a puppy – snap an order at him in the right tone and he couldn't help himself.

'We were having a…' Varro shot a look over his shoulder. 'We were having a private conversation, Domasa. It's nothing you need to be present for, I assure you.'

'You may resume your *private conversation* at any point that pleases you, Master Phrax,' Domasa said. Warpspit, but the man was transparent. 'Only not right at this moment, I regret to say. You are needed at the Apothecarion. Now.'

'What's wrong?' Varro's face suddenly twisted. 'Dreyder? Has something–'

'Your son is fine, I am sure. It's you we need. You're in no danger, don't worry, I'll explain on the way.'

Phrax gave what he probably thought was a knowing nod to the rest of them and stepped out of the room; Domasa could feel the others' eyes boring into her as she went after him.

'What is so urgent?' he asked as they marched away. 'Surely nobody will be there?'

'One of the ship's medicae staff is being roused on my instructions,' Domasa said, 'and he should be there and waiting for us. It took me a little while to find you, Varro, after I realised you weren't in your stateroom.'

'I'm sorry. Well, I mean, I thought we'd go elsewhere for our, er...'

'Your private conversation. Of course, Master Phrax. This is your voyage, after all, when one thinks about it.' She caught him in her peripheral vision, giving her a dark look. Well, score a point for the man, she thought, he had more about him than she had credited him with.

'Quite right. How long have you been looking for me?'

'Some while. We checked the other decks too, or at least the main compartments. We weren't sure where you were.'

'Well, I'm sorry to have put you to the trouble. I assure you I'm safe with Rikah and Malon. And what could happen in the depths of the ship anyway?' His expression changed to something Domasa couldn't quite read out of the corner of her eye. 'Do you mean to say that you suspect more traitors in the crew?'

'It's nothing like that. Read this.' She pushed the communiqué paper at him. 'That should convince you that this is worth running about in the middle of the sleep shift for.' Varro took the paper and carefully uncrumpled it. He peered at it one way and another for the time it took them to walk down the passageway and down the forward well, where a wide curl of ramp led down through three layers of passenger decks, all deserted after Domasa's syndicate had taken exclusive charter of the ship. The walls of the well were strung with slightly brighter lanterns, in ornate spiked cases fashioned to resemble sunbursts, but even these had been dimmed for the sleep shift and Varro handed the paper back.

'I can make out references to Hydraphur and my father's flotilla. Does any of this matter? I'm sure I remember that the succession hearings wouldn't be able to start until I arrived. What's changed?'

'Did you even read the–' Domasa stopped short. After so much time clutched in her hand, the lower paragraphs were smeared into one another, and even in good light the scrawls would have been a challenge. With a small impatient noise she stuffed the paper into the sleeve of her gown and set off down the long passage, twin to the one they had just descended from, which led to the ready-room and the Apothecarion.

'All right. Our informant tells us that the flotilla has sent a sample of blood from their counter-claimant ahead to Hydraphur so the examinations to prove their half of the case can get under way. There's a line about a Mechanicus escort or something, but the message had trouble with the warp storm so some of the details got lost.'

'They must be sending it to the Mechanicus temple at the Augustaeum. That's where the tissue samples are traditionally examined when there's a contest of heredity,' said Varro.

'You knew that already, did you? Well here, Master Phrax, we do indeed have a contest of heredity, as I believe we've been at some pains to make clear to you. That's why we're marching down to the Apothecarion at this damnable hour.'

'You want a sample of my blood, then. That's what this is about.'

'Well done. Presenting you in person will be a trump card for whenever we manage to arrive there, since we now know that the bloody flotilla has beaten us to the system. But we are not, mark me Varro, we are *not* going to let them have the whole thing their own way. My associates have a fast warp-runner ready to go, something that has enough power in it to skirt the worst of that storm and still make it to Hydraphur within ten days. What it's going to be carrying...'

But he had guessed. 'A tissue sample of my own.' Varro was puffing a little as they quick-marched.

Domasa had discreetly picked up the hem of her gown.

'Blood is all it should need. We've got a flask of the same pattern the Mechanicus use to transport samples so we're pretty sure it's going to arrive in the system in good condition. Given that we know for a fact that you're the Phrax firstborn, your blood should tell enough of a story to at least stall whatever the flotilla are trying to pull.' A door slid open ahead of them and white light poured out, making them both blink. 'Not nervous about having your blood taken, are you, Varro?'

'With an occupation like mine? I can't exactly afford to be, you know. Hah, all they need to do is reopen some of the weals that that

Invus glasswood left me when I got careless the day before you arrived.' Some of the animation had come back into Varro's voice, and Domasa found herself smiling, rather to her own surprise.

'Before too much longer, Varro, your occupation will be rogue trader and merchant prince. You won't have to do any undignified rushing about like this, but I fear I have to warn you that you will still have people waiting around corners to draw your blood, albeit in more figurative ways.'

'That's a fact I think I'm starting to get used to, Madam Dorel,' said Varro, and walked forward into the whiteness of the Apothecarion where a white-and-green-shrouded servitor was already moving forward with a syringe in one delicate hand.

THEY STOOD AT the lock and watched through the narrow port as the shuttle carrying the flask in which a vial of Varro's blood nestled slid backwards out of its berth with a brief spray of white frost as the remnant of the air in the lock escaped and froze. For a moment before it pushed itself into a new trajectory with bursts from its altitude jets they could see the distant shape beyond it of the *Noonlight Phoenix*, the fastest ship anywhere near Santo Pevrelyi, a sleek four-tiered hull with a flared prow like a snake's head.

'Wish her well,' said Domasa. 'She's carrying the opening of your claim. Throne knows I'll be sending my thoughts with her tonight.'

'I've been thinking, Domasa.'

'Oh?' Now she had her counter-gambit launched, she felt her tension lifting. She suddenly felt that she could use a good sleep herself.

'Has the charter ever been held jointly? I mean, have two members of the Phrax family ever owned it between them? I've been thinking back over what I know of my family history and I can't think of it happening, but that doesn't mean it couldn't.'

'One charter, one hand, one Phrax, one heir. I trust I'm being clear,' said Domasa as they walked away from the lock. She thought she knew where this was heading, and she had a mind to tread on this line of thought as soon as she could.

'It just seems so... stupid.' Varro sighed. 'You know? I had this whole childhood on the flotilla and then I came of age on Gunarvo and it was all wonderful in so many ways, but... well, I keep thinking that there's this other Phrax, my half-brother, blood of my blood, another son of Hoyyon that I've never known about all this time. And now that I do know about him what's the first thing that's happening? We head straight for opposing camps and get ready for war over the spoils from my father's death. Doesn't this strike you as wrong?'

'Try growing up in the Navis Nobilite,' snorted Domasa, surprising herself a little with her candour. 'The family affairs of Navigators have probably not given me a very good yardstick to judge questions like yours, but if you're thinking of letting down your guard and throwing open your arms, then I'll say think again. Stop and think, really think about what's at stake here.'

'I've thought about it. My son. That's what's at stake. *Who's* at stake.'

'Thinking about the way you will pass on the charter is very noble, and perfectly fitting for the position you aspire to, but before you can get too far with plans like that we need to make sure–'

'No. Not my son's inheritance. My *son*. He's the one I look at and remember what's at stake. As you say, Madam Dorel, perhaps your own family circumstances stop you from really understanding.' There was a tone in his voice that set her teeth grinding. Perhaps there were things in the universe she hated more than being condescended to, but she hadn't found one yet.

'After all the work that I've done for you, Varro, after all the work my associates and backers and I have done to help you to reach Hydraphur and mount a case against this ridiculous counter-claim, I must say that we perhaps expected a tiny degree more co-operation and gratitude.' Her back was ramrod-straight and her shoulders back, the way she always held herself when she was angry. 'The effort we are making to help you is perhaps something I need to remind you of rather more often.'

'No, Domasa, you don't.' He had stopped, now, and waited until she drew level with him. 'I am very aware of all the work you have done. The ships you have obtained, Navigators, the medicae help, the support against my half-brother Petronas. And information about him, too, and on the progress of the counter-claim. I've noticed that. I've noticed that all your talk about treachery and honour when you found what you told me was a spy in our own midst didn't stop you from cultivating this informant of yours in the flotilla. There seems to be a lot of help that you and these backers of yours – whom you still haven't fully named or described to me, either – are giving me that even I don't know about. How else are you helping me, Domasa Dorel?'

'By putting your spine straight and ready to contest your succession,' she came back without missing a beat. 'You don't know your own best interests, Varro Phrax. If someone doesn't take you by the hand you are going to sit there with that amiable smile on your face and let a rival you've never met stroll by, pluck what is rightfully yours right out of your hand and walk away laughing at you, because you're somehow worried that reaching out to stop him makes you a nasty person. I didn't think there really were people like you in the Imperium, Varro. I have trouble believing that you mean all this pious brotherhood stuff even now. But if you do, then you're luckier to have fallen in with me and my syndicate than you know.' The lateness of the hour was finally starting to tell on her. It was the kind of private thought that Domasa would never have given voice to normally. But Varro only stood there, silent; he gave the Navigator an appraising look that was very unlike his usual one.

'I know enough to guess, Domasa, what form of gratitude you and your syndicate will be expecting. I do know that much. I believe, in fact, that we understand each other possibly a little better than you realise.'

The two of them looked at each other for a little while in the dim corridor. Domasa had seen such face-downs on rare occasions in the past, and could usually rely on the strangeness of her features to unsettle the other person enough to get them to walk away first. But, she remembered, Varro was one of the few non-Navigators she had met to whom her appearance didn't seem to be strange at all.

'Good,' was all she said in the end, and took her leave of him. It wasn't until much later that she realised she had never thought about what Varro and his wife and his staff might have been having a private conversation about, in a private room on a deserted deck in the middle of the ship's artificial night.

CHAPTER NINE

The Bastion Praetoris, The Wall, Bosporian Hive, Hydraphur

Reverend Simova's appearance in the court of Praetor Imprimis Dastrom was insultingly brief, an anticlimax. He had been marched into the court to testify and answer questions about how the cages had been commissioned and hung over the Avenue Solar, how Ghammo Ströon (now chained with Symandis in the dock) had been apprehended and sentenced, how the whole ordeal and the handling of prisoners worked, what his own role was. He was stunned and mortified that his mission to Trylan Tor had ended back here, scant kilometres from the Cathedral where it had begun, in a courtroom full of harsh lights and steel fittings with the cadaverous Judge enthroned high above him.

Simova was not stupid. The Ecclesiarchy worked as hard at keeping citizens' minds in line as the Arbites did, if not harder, and he knew the rituals, the settings, how to place an accused in awe. The Judge on high, the booming orders and decrees, the quieter tones of the junior examining Judges who unrolled in front of him a clever mix of what the Arbites already knew and what they suspected, lines of questioning hidden inside one another, hunchbacked scribes and blank-eyed auditing servitors recording every word. Why, had he not presided over the trials of heretics and blasphemers using exactly the same strategies?

The true humiliation: it was working. Simova had walked into the courtroom full of anger at the coarse treatment he had received at the sentry post, and disdain at the Arbites' belief that the tricks they used on common criminals were going to work on him. But still he found himself reacting the way he knew they wanted him to: wrong footed, over-anxious to explain himself and fill in the gaps in their knowledge. 'You are not on trial here, reverend,' they kept telling him, and he knew that it was a lie. This was a trial if ever he had seen one.

And it didn't help that the arrogant thug of an arbitor senioris seemed to be able to pluck his thoughts out of the air, because the first thing she said to him when he emerged from the courtroom through the four-metre-high courtroom doors was: 'That was not your trial, reverend, but it so easily could have been.'

She was standing in a carefully careless way in amongst a knot of black-armoured Arbites in the centre of the corridor. Facing her, still alone as the door swung silently closed behind him, Simova touched the gold aquila on its chain around his expansive waist, for confidence.

'Do not presume, arbitor, to even speak to me, much less to hector me about trials and what you might or might not do to me. I do not back away from a single word I have said about what will come of this. There are some things I took care to make clear to your subordinate on the flight back from that wretched tor–'

'Indeed there were. I understand that your eloquence was matched only by your stamina. There were vox-pickups in the ornithopter that brought you and your Sororitas back to the hive, did you know that? I have every point you made to my long-suffering Arbites in a data-ark on the desk in my personal chambers. I haven't listened to them yet. Perhaps I should ask one of the Bastion clerks to make a summary.'

'You are doing justice to the absolute worst of your reputation, Arbitor Calpurnia,' said Simova coldly. 'You show all the worst tendencies of the arbitrator: the oafish reliance on force, the tendency to think with your fists and boots and the barrel of a shotgun, the belief that the *Lex Imperia* is nothing more than whatever you feel like doing to whatever devoted servant of the Emperor is unfortunate enough to–'

He had scored a result, although not the one he had intended. Suddenly the tip of Calpurnia's slender power-maul was buried in

Simova's navel, the spines on its tip pricking him unpleasantly through the brocade of his robe. Her black-gauntleted thumb hovered over the power switch.

'Here you stand, in our courthouse, and you lecture me on the law of the Imperium and how I may or may not go about enforcing it,' said Calpurnia. 'What an interesting thing to witness.' Her words were light but her eyes were locked on him like emerald lasers, and only now did Simova realise how furious he had succeeded in making her.

He took a step back, and she a step forward: the maul remained dug into the swell of his belly.

'You have presided over punishments for blasphemers against the Emperor, Simova. You know how literally damning words can be. Except that you forget it. You assault with words the authority of an Arbitor General of the Adeptus, something that will condemn you under a hundred different codes with every sentence you utter, and then you decide that you will lecture me on the law that I know and enforce? You forget yourself most grievously, reverend. I could execute you on the spot for what you have just said to me and my actions would be clad in iron by every letter of the law. There would even be cases, were you any other man, reverend, by which I myself could be placed on trial for *failing* to execute you. Do not test me again.' The pressure on his gut was suddenly gone; there was a click as Calpurnia returned the maul to its belt-clip.

'Is that why I was brought here, then, arbitor?' Simova made sure his tone was respectful and mildly curious. 'I do not believe that at the time that two dozen Arbites... removed me.' He still could not quite say *arrested*, although that was obviously what it had been 'and my escorts from that tor, I had said anything at all about you or your authority, arbitor. We had not even broken the interdiction around your fortress, although our errand was no more and no less than to submit a claim in a matter of law that you are currently overseeing. An action with deference to the authority of your office built into it, you will notice. I have co-operated and ordered co-operation at every step. Do you think the Sororitas would have put up their weapons had I not expressly ordered them to? They were ready to fight for me on that tor.'

'Where you had no right to be, incidentally, reverend. You were required to remain here to be ready to appear before Dastrom's tribunal.'

'To provide testimony, Arbitor Calpurnia, not as an accused party, despite your performance to the contrary. Read the testimony I gave in there. I am not the guilty party, and I do not see why you needed to pretend otherwise. Or do you seriously think that you're going to find my fingermarks on the hijacked blimp and the crane-truck and Symandis's power axe?'

'Let's say for the sake of the argument that I don't find you actively complicit,' said Calpurnia with a considering look. 'The responsibility for setting up and overseeing the ordeal was still yours. If one of my Arbites dozes off on watch and an assassin gets past him to murder me, he'd be sadly mistaken to think he wouldn't be found at fault even though he didn't pull the trigger himself. Take note and take instruction. If it weren't for your particular mission and the Eparch's feelings about it you'd be in a cell already.'

'Must you drag the Eparch into this, arbitor? If you are alleging some kind of failure then kindly allege it of me alone rather than trying to besmirch the whole Cathedral.'

In reply, Calpurnia snapped her fingers and Culann placed a message scroll into her hand. Simova's nerves, which had relaxed when Calpurnia had put her weapon away, tensed again when he saw the Eparchal seal on it, already broken.

'I've had a letter,' she said, 'from the Eparch apologising for your actions in leaving Bosporian and trying to bully your way to Trylan Tor. He also says that you were merely trying your best to perform an errand that he had asked of you. I'm assuming that this is something to do with the matter of law you mentioned to me earlier, is it?'

Simova nodded, still staring at the Eparchal seal. Eparch Baszle himself had been forced to intercede on Simova's behalf, to allow him to finish the mission Baszle himself had sent him on. One little part of his mind was bidding a mournful farewell to the gold statues and lush tapestry of the Chamber of Exegetors: after this, the rest of his career would be spent supervising the cleaning rosters in a roadside shrine on some dung-splat little agri-world in the ugliest corner of the segmentum that his rivals at the Cathedral could find.

For some reason Simova always became aware of the soreness of his feet when he was nervous, and they were aching badly now. He took a breath.

'You, Arbitor Calpurnia, have been appointed to rule on the succession of the rogue trader charter passed down through the merchant family of Phrax. This charter bears not the imprimatur but the personal inscription of the Immortal God-Emperor, investing it as a relic by the hand of Him on Terra. And so in the name and by the power of the Adeptus Ministorum, I claim it as a holy relic for the greater glory of the Eparchy and Cathedral of Hydraphur.'

Culann cocked an eyebrow and looked sideways at Calpurnia's face; the other Arbites were motionless as before. There was silence in the hall while a pair of scribes hurried nervously past with armfuls of data-copy and rapped on the door behind them. The door opened to admit them, and then swung closed.

'Do you know, Reverend Simova,' Shira Calpurnia said in her most conversational tone, 'I believe that your claim is, quite possibly, the very last thing that this whole affair needed.'

The Shrine of the Machine-God,
Adeptus Quarter of the Augustaeum, Hydraphur

THE HERALDS HAD gone back and forth in the form of data codes, servitors and the occasional junior adepts. The formal invitation had been, issued, received and confirmed with all due protocol. The meeting between the two respected magi of the Machine-God unfolded as flawlessly as two perfectly maintained logic engines working through a data transfer handshake.

Sanja knew that there were those in the Mechanicus who distrusted people like Dyobann, considering that tech-priests spending too long in the company of extraneous influences tended to develop miscalibrations of their sacred doctrines and corruption of their liturgical beliefs. But Sanja was a genetor, a studier of biological systems that were both incredibly complex and less predictable, and such a field of study had left him a little more flexible of temperament than those of his colleagues who had embraced the inorganic for their studies.

And so when Magos Errant Dyobann came down from the Ring, alone but for two servitors and carrying an engraved flask of red-tinted steel, Sanja had met him amiably enough.

He had chosen to receive his guest in the Helispex Chapel itself. The much put-upon engine had already been dismounted for the move to Trylan Tor before it had turned out that the aforesaid move was out of the question; it had now been re-mounted in its ark in the centre of the chapel. Had there been no more pressing business at hand Sanja would have ordered the room filled with incense and a solid-state vox looping through psalms of placation, then locked with a seal placed on its door for seventy-three standard hours and fifteen seconds; this being an appropriate rite of appeasement for a machine that had been forced to endure some kind of insult to its operation. But duty and obligation awaited, and so the placation of the engine would have to wait too. Sanja had a binary translation of the Omnissiah's Catechism of Subjection loaded into the ancillary data engines that attended upon the Helispex itself, and now they circulated it constantly through the data cables lining the walls to create an atmosphere of prayerful obedience. Sanja hoped it would remind the engine's spirit of its responsibilities, at least for as long as the business of the charter took.

The chapel itself was narrow and long. Buttress-columns curving up from the floor and meeting overhead turned its sides into a procession of niches, the walls and pillars holding complex patterns of inlaid power- and code-lines ornamented and illuminated with rare metals and gems. The top and side of the ark were folded out to expose the face of the engine; the power cables running to the engraved bronze panels in the floor were adorned with ribbons, seals and strips of parchment bearing Mechanicus blessings. Behind it Genetor Sanja, in bright ceremonial robes, sat in a suspensor throne two metres above the floor. His luminant skulls hung in the air by his shoulders and his hands cradled a jewelled data-slate reader bequeathed to him by thirty-seven generations of forebears.

Dyobann left his servitors at the door and advanced with slow, deferential steps. His own garments were much plainer: red for the Mechanicus, with rows of patterns stitched into the fabric at sleeves, collar and hems to show the many disciplines of the magos errant: genetor, alchemys, metallurg, more. His head was bowed and his patchwork face was hidden by his hood.

The two luminants took the flask delicately from his hands in their webs of metal dendrites. As Dyobann knelt and prayed at the foot of the steps, Sanja's throne lowered and circled the ark, always facing in so that his back was never to the engine itself. The luminants gave little twitches of their dendrites and flicks of red light from their optics as they inspected the metal and the seals: their report, beamed into Sanja's brain through the receptors in his skull, showed all was well.

Sanja stepped from the throne and walked to them. Standing before the Helispex Engine, he felt the awe he always did: this was as great a relic of the Machine-God as he would set eyes on in his lifetime. For a day and a half now he had been anointing it with oils, circulating precious incenses through the housing and meditating to clear his mind for the ritual – the preparations had left him in a state of religious concentration that bordered on trance. But now the faces were clear and cold, the air purified so that nothing might enter the engine except what he begged it to take into itself and show to him.

On the top step Sanja abased himself and set the flask down.

He closed his eyes and the world became a mosaic, a composite, like a series of images painted on layers of translucent curtains. He looked at the flask through all the senses of his luminants and through the eyes of the machine gargoyles that watched over the ark from the top of every column. He watched as the luminants' dendrites, whose grace and delicacy no human could match, carefully broke the seal on the flask and lifted out the vial inside. Then, floating no more than a few centimetres off the floor and with their skull-faces turned downward, they approached the silvered face of the Helispex Engine.

The face of the engine was just that. Engraved on the silver slab of its side in breathtaking detail, detail so fine that without his augmetics there were elements to the picture Sanja would not have seen at all, was a stylised reproduction of the sacred emblem of the Adeptus Mechanicus, the half-skull, half-cog of the *Machina Opus*. But that had been superimposed over a larger design, another skull, this one drawn with augmetics to the eye and cranium that suggested a servitor or certain patterns of junior acolytes. The skull was distended and stylised, its mouth open, and it was into the maw of the skull that the luminants slipped the vial.

Sanja's breath caught. He had heard the quiet click and hum of moving parts within the engine, the sign that its spirit remembered its duty. Moved by that spirit, the luminants moved back and outward and the doors to the chapel swung shut. The Helispex Engine was about to begin its operations, calling down the mind of the Machine-God into its circuits and nanostacks, bringing the unknowable intellect of the Arch-Mechanicus to bear.

Sanja and Dyobann both set up a buzzing, chirruping prayer in machine-code that echoed through the chapel. The lights in the chapel flickered and the luminants bobbed in their places. And then, with a still and small sound like a sigh from the depths of the engine, it was done. The magi straightened up and looked at one another, and the doors to the chapel, and the outer doors beyond them, both opened again. Dyobann's servitors stood there exactly as before.

It was time for the engine to rest before the revelation of data. The two magi stood at the base of the dais and waited.

'I acknowledge gratitude,' said Dyobann at length. 'I have seen many things in my travels with Phrax, but none compare to this. To be present at such a ritual is an experience such as I had never expected to have.'

'Genetors come from three sectors on pilgrimages to this shrine,' said Sanja with a trace of smugness. 'Seven months ago the arch-lexmechanic of the Twelfth Tech-Guard Fleet came here with gifts of servitors and scriptures and machine-parts blessed on Mars itself, for the right to pray at the foot of the dais for one hundred minutes and look upon the engine itself. The clarity of the engine's communion with the Machine-God is such that it can perform seventy-six billion calculations and observations in a second, and process them in five seconds more. This is the traditional honour that the Mechanicus pays to the line of Phrax, that no less a device than the Helispex shall confirm the bloodline at each succession.'

'You are to be praised for your custodianship, magos,' said Dyobann. 'And you honour me in turn, permitting me to see the invocations for myself.' He had seemed to tense at the reference to the confirmation of the bloodline.

'Knowledge is holiness, the Omnissiah teaches us so,' Sanja replied. 'To pass on knowledge to the select and the anointed is a great sacrament and elevates us all in the service of the Machine.'

'It is as you say.'

They both stood there for a moment longer, each one reluctant to break the gravitas of the moment. Then there was a tiny sound that made Dyobann look around: the slabs of carved stone that made up the ark of the Helispex were slowly closing around the engine itself. As both magi watched they locked into place and sealed themselves, the join lines now barely visible.

'It rests now,' said Sanja. 'Tonight I will lead my acolytes in the ceremonies of cleansing as we refresh its spirit, and then we shall leave it for a time to restore itself. It has had a taxing time of these last days. Magos Dyobann, if your other duties permit you, do you wish to attend upon the engine when we do so?'

'It would be an honour, genetor-magos, thank you.' Dyobann's voice bespoke a trace of nerves, Sanja thought, but that was only natural. Then he turned as two jointed metal arms wrapped about with transmission wires emerged from the dais: the engine had passed on its insights to its attendant machines, and these in turn were ready to pass them on to the two magi. Sanja and Dyobann walked to the dais steps and knelt, each connecting to it in their own way. Dyobann extended the tiny tendril from the corner of his eye and stroked the tip of the arm until he found a receptor and slid the tendril home; Sanja had one of the luminants move forward to take the end of the other arm in one of its own and begin transmitting back to him. For a quiet moment the attendant engines performed last-minute collations on the data that the Helispex itself had vouchsafed to them, and then both magi closed their eyes and submitted to the flow of information.

In the space behind Sanja's eyes, colours exploded and swirled, sonic codes cracked and buzzed in his ears, senses no unaugmented human possessed all began to sing. The Helispex had held Petronas Phrax's blood up to the glare of the eternal Machine-God's gaze, and now he saw what it had seen.

Dancing through the imagery was archive-data, the parallel records back through every generation of the Phrax bloodline. The engine remembered every operation it had ever performed, every petition that had ever been made to it. It had known it was being asked to look once again at the bloodline of Phrax, and so now the knowledge of the tests it had done on the family's every generation blossomed silently in the backs of the magi's minds as the bloodprint of this new heir danced through the fore of their consciousness. Gene-prints, chemical analyses down to the molecular, down to the sub-molecular, microchemical forensics that showed every influence and impact on the heir's blood from the genes he had been born with to the food he had eaten, diseases he had had, the kinds of sunlight he had been exposed to, the kinds of vaccinations, the...

...the...

Wait.

With speed born of fear, Magos Errant Dyobann wrenched his consciousness out of the coded swirl, hissing at the flare of pain in his eye from the sudden disconnection of his tendril. At the door his servitors swivelled as he ran between them and then they fell in behind him, the sculpted metal hooves he had made for them clashing on the stone floor.

Out of the chapel they fled, through one set of doors and then another, down a reliquary hall where two young acolytes gawped at them. Dyobann fixed grimly on the end of the hall where it met the two other main halls and became a tall cave in the rock beneath Augusteum. If he could make it to the ground level there were only three sets of doors to the plaza where the mech-carriage that Phrax money had bought him was waiting. Then, alone with two lightly-armed servitors in a whole world on which he had never set foot before today–

They reached the lift-car, with a junior priest riding in it. He made to say something and Dyobann ordered him out with a gesture; he made to argue and Dyobann flicked a curt, silent message to one of his servitors which snapped a stiletto out of one of its utility-arms and stepped forward. The blade punctured the priest's skull five times in two seconds and then the car doors were closing behind him and they were on their way up to the surface.

–but he would get out, he would survive, so many years of travel with the Phrax flotilla had meant the one thing he had learned to do was survive. And here they were, the lift-car doors opening: Dyobann gave thanks that the shrine was not one of those that extended kilometres down. Had the lift ride been any longer it would have become a trap.

They ran up a ramp and through the rear hall of the shrine's central level. Could they fight their way out? He didn't know, but maybe they wouldn't have to. The circuits around the Helispex must be closed off from the rest of the shrine so the engine's contemplations would not be sullied with the mundane data. It would take Sanja some time to realise what he was seeing, more time to disengage if he took the time to do it properly, then he would have to realise Dyobann was gone–

Through the portal to the stairs, they were almost at the forechamber.

–and then he would have to leave the chapel himself to reach a system from which he could raise the alarm. If Dyobann could just survive in the hive until the flotilla arrived, he could get a message to Trazelli and have–

He reached the inner forechamber doors just in time to see the great outer doors crash closed. As he cycled up the auxiliary photoreceptors built into his eyes to make the most of the dim light, Genetor-Magos Sanja's voice boomed into him through his own ears and through every mechanical code-frequency he had open, boomed from the devices built into every wall of the chamber. The force of it nearly drove him to his knees.

'You *dare*!' the voice roared. Dyobann triggered neuroregulators inside his skull and shut down the fear impulse. Sanja was no mightier than he, he told himself. Sanja could not possibly have had to survive the things Dyobann had seen and done.

'You *dare* to bring this, this filth here? Into the place where our cult is in most abject service to the God of the Machine? This is how you serve Him?'

'...rve Him?' There was a pale echo of Sanja's voice coming from somewhere, but Dyobann didn't have the time to pay it mind. He turned, looking around him at the soaring forechamber, the bronze pistons in silent motion around its walls, the ceremonial cogs hanging in gravity fields high overhead.

'Yes,' he called back. 'Yes, this is how I serve. Do you understand, Sanja, do you have the first conception of what I have done for our order with the freedom that the charter gives me? The things I have seen? Found? The relics I have brought away? I have performed works for our high priests that no magos without that flotilla to support them could ever have performed? The pieces of tech I have carried through Imperial domains with never a report or a tithe? The sacred sites I have been able to direct our explorators to? The species I have been able to treat with out of sight of Imperial eyes? The enemies with whom the flotilla has given me the resources to deal?'

'So this is the Magos Dyobann,' came that shattering voice from the walls ('...gos Dyobann,' came that slurred echo). 'A scavenger-rat in a red robe, a smuggler and thief? A murderer and a consorter with murderers? A friend of the xenos, the alien whose form mocks the pure genetics of the human template? One whose contempt for what is sacred leads him to poison a sacred engine of the Mechanicus with lies and betray the trust its keeper placed in him?' ('...in him?')

'How could you understand, rattling through endless prayers in a sealed shrine, locked away in ignorance!' Dyobann was fired with anger now, barely aware of the magnitude of the insult in the word he had just used. 'How do you dare to judge me?'

'Knowledge is holy,' bellowed Sanja, and now there were two organic voices joining in the flood of input from the walls. One was from Sanja's own throat, and Dyobann whirled: the genetor-magos had appeared in the doors behind him, flanked by luminants and servitors. 'Knowledge is holy and information is holy. We live our lives in the quest for it. The purer the data, the purer the lifeblood of the Machine and the Machine-God. Purity of data is the greatest sacrament a priest of the Machine-God can hope for. And now you come here with this.' He raised a vial in one shaking hand.

'...here with this.' Dyobann realised with a shock that the echo was the voice of one of his own servitors, the one he had killed the priest with. It had half-turned to him, blood and machine-oil dripping off its blade arm, and was repeating every word of Sanja's as the other magos spoke them. He'd found a way in, into its systems, had some override code that had bypassed the programs Dyobann thought he had embedded beyond all possibility of breaching. Without even a physical connection. Dyobann for the first time realised what a dangerous enemy he had just made.

'You falsified knowledge. You tampered with the data. You came here knowing that you yourself had created these impurities. You thought that you could deceive the Helispex Engine, may its spirit recover. You attempted trickery on the holy engine, attempted to use it to create untruth. An untruth which itself distorts knowledge and moves us away from the perfect knowledge of the Omnissiah. *You tried to trick us.*'

'...us,' the servitor finished. The delay in its speech was growing shorter as Sanja's control over it tightened. There was no way to tell if he had found a way into the other one. Dyobann's thoughts spun ever faster. 'Your blasphemy against the Machine-God is doubled and compounded,' Sanja went on, 'and your betrayal of your holy office is nothing less than total. I strip you of your office and your name. You are forfeit.' The genetor-magos threw the vial down onto the stone floor, and as it shattered Dyobann spat a coded command at the bloody-handed servitor: *'Tikk!'* It was a word from the flotilla, the word for outsider, and the command was for the servitor to kill everyone present who was not of the flotilla. This was only the fourth time he had ever had to use the command, and the secret he was protecting here was probably the most terrible one he had ever kept.

In his heart Magos Dyobann knew that Sanja was right. He wondered if he had ever had a chance: those short minutes coupled into the data-stream had shown him the sight of the Helispex was clearer and more powerful than he had ever anticipated. But he was not going to stand here and let them cut him down.

Sanja had almost total control of the servitor, but the *tikk* command was buried somewhere he still had not reached. The servitor loped toward the magos before Sanja was able to halt it with a frown and a gesture, and while it swayed there Dyobann spun and wrenched off the other servitor's tunic-shroud. The flesh-machine tensed as Dyobann brought it to combat-readiness and reached for the stubby cylinders around its waist. To all appearances they were part of the pneumatic mechanisms in its legs, but falsely so, a disguise.

Dyobann flicked back his sleeve as he heard Sanja'a own servitors clatter down the steps, and the round collar on the end of the thick roll of mechadendrites that had so revolted Petronas Phrax unclipped and clanged to the floor. Dyobann's arm unplaited into a hydra-cluster of metal snakes that plunged and snapped into housings on the top of each cylinder. Loadout data, weapon specs and targeting reticules unfolded themselves across Dyobann's mind and vision as he pulled the weapon modules free.

The servitor Sanja had controlled was spasming wildly: Sanja must have found its combat subroutines and was trying to suppress them. But the genetor's own weapons were just a few strides away now, three heavy servitors, cloned muscles reinforced by layers of exoskeleton, iron plates carved with the *Machina Opus* or leering gargoyle visages grafted to the front of their skulls where their faces had been. Chainfist blades rumbled and revved; a drillspike spun so fast it was just a blurred length of shining metal in the yellow light of the lamps.

Dyobann's hydra-arm flared and writhed like an anemone and the first servitor was pitching forward, lifeless: one cylinder held a pressurised reservoir of a vicious nerve-toxin that Dyobann and D'Leste had brewed up two years before.

The second servitor hurdled the body straight into a tight-burst haywire pulse that blew out its cybernetics and sent it into a mad jerking dance. Its exoskeleton smoked and froze. The weapons in its limbs accelerated past their tolerances and began to burn out.

Dyobann backpedalled, circling out and around the floor of the forechamber. The forest of tentacles sprouting from his shoulder snaked in the air, searching for the luminants; another snapped forward and fired a chaff-pellet into the doorway where Sanja stood. There was a tiny crack as it exploded and then the doorway was full of metal-dust, heated by a tiny melta-charge and throwing out magnetic static. The sentry-servitors built into the pillars on either side of the door had been shut down as a mark of respect for Dyobann's position, something that Sanja was probably bitterly regretting now. And now, even if he reactivated them they would be blind and useless.

The third of Sanja's killing machines was grappling with Dyobann's own, and there was no time to shout out the codes: he had to use his tight-beam coder and gamble that Sanja would not detect the frequency and override it. Dyobann flicked his perceptions across the beam-link and was looking through his servitors' eyes. His vision split, the shrine-servitor doubling on itself, filling his vision as it rushed straight at him at the same time as he watched it barrel toward his servitor from four metres away.

Then his vision took a strange half-lurch, disorienting him even with the compensators built into his senses, as his commands pitched his servitor over on its side. In the second it took Sanja's machine to adjust, Dyobann's servitor had hamstrung it with a low sweep of a wire-fine blade that slipped out of a finger. A homing-dart flew from the tip of one of Dyobann's outthrust tentacles – it hung motionless in the air for a split second before it lunged forward. For a moment a third layer appeared in Dyobann's already doubled vision: the sight of the gap between the servitor's face and shoulder plates growing wider and wider as he guided the dart home. His vision flashed white, then dropped to black, and he snapped the connection back from his servitor as his dart – its outer layer of microflechettes, inner core of pyro-acid – burst deep in the last enemy's abdomen. Smoke and the stink of evaporating flesh shrouded the wreck of the servitor as it fell.

And then just silence, but for a low hoarse sound that Dyobann realised was his own breathing. He muttered a verbal command and his servitor clambered to its feet and loped towards the doors. Dyobann backed after it, fixing every mechanical sense he had on the thinning chaff-cloud between the door-pillars. Runes danced in his vision to show that a second homing-dart was armed and ready, that the neurotoxin reservoir was still at eighty-seven per cent capacity, that the tentacles tipped with diamond-claws and tiny sawblade arrays were running at combat revs.

There was a crackle behind him as the powered spurs built into his servitor's forearms and wrists snapped into operation and charged up the destructive energy-fields that sheathed their blades. If they gave him even sixty seconds for the servitor to work on the shrine doors they would...

Red figures poured out into the forechamber, moving with quick, deadly precision. Their flak-gowns and cowls were a dark, dusty red and bronze augmetics glinted and flashed where their garments did not cover: skitarii. Tech-guard. Not servitors but the elite military of the Cult of the Machine.

Three of them threw short, slender carbines to their shoulders and banged off quick bursts that broke against the subcutaneous flex-plates that armoured Dyobann's torso and against the servitor's back as it hacked at the doors. The renegade magos experienced a flash of hope: they were using lightweight shatter-rounds, slugs whose breakable design could not damage the forechamber but which also robbed them of stopping power against the armoured bodies of Dyobann and his servitor.

Regaining his balance, Dyobann lunged forward to bring the two nearest skitarii in range of the one-shot microflamer in another tentacle-tip, but the burst of white-hot vapour only splashed across the front of their gowns. Both men dived and rolled to efficiently snuff the flames, one of them firing another burst at Dyobann as he came up onto one knee. The magos errant spent a second, precious homing-dart to crumple the man's head like a gourd and flung another chaff-pellet at his feet. That was when he realised that the complex web of transmitted data dancing and tickling in one sector of his vision and in the back of his head had gone, gone at the same moment as the sounds of bladework behind him had ceased. He suddenly realised why the shots from the skitarii had died away, why they had not thrown grenades.

Magos Dyobann spun around, the tentacles of his hydra-arm thrashing the air for a target, his non-modified hand hooked into a claw, his transponder augmetics bellowing defiance on every frequency. Even the data tendril at the corner of his eye was extended and sniffing the air.

In a flash of gold and a glimmer of bone, the two luminants whipped up and away from the servitor they had just killed. They had flown into the forechamber high over his head, hidden by the hanging cogwheels. Dyobann snapped out the tentacle that held the haywire grenades…

…but the luminants were angels of the Machine, made from components engineered to the purest of tolerances and the skulls of the most pious of the Mechanicus priesthood – dare he strike them down with such a terrible weapon?

The hesitation wrought by that last scrap of his old piety undid him. By the time the haywire detonated over the prone servitor the luminants had arced up four metres in the air and swooped smoothly down again. One jinked to the left, and even with Dyobann's vision guiding it the third homing-dart could not turn in time to follow it and it flew on to spend itself somewhere in the darkness high overhead. The other luminant corkscrewed and rolled in the air. Dyobann's claw-tentacle snapped on air and skated by a millimetre away from its gold-leaf skin.

There was noise in Dyobann's ears, noise that hit the translator augmetics and unfolded into data: the luminants were broadcasting a simple packet of code, over and over, three times a second: nothing more than the data-seal of Genetor-Magos Cynez Sanja, so that Dyobann would know who was watching through their eyes as they delivered sentence. As one of them extended mechadendrites whose adamantine tips drove through the magos errant's armour like paper and hoisted him onto his toes, the other extruded a humming power-pack from the base of its skull. The code changed, sending a high-speed data signal on every auditory and vox-channel Dyobann possessed.

The communication fed itself directly through his translator layers into his brain, so the message in all its detail unfolded in his consciousness in an instant. The message was not complex. A list of charges and four declarations. Accusation, condemnation, excommunication, destruction.

One point eight four seconds after the transmission completed, the second luminant clamped Dyobann's eye-tendril between the thick grips on the end of its power pack. There was barely time for pain: the power-pulse coursed through the tendril and through the webs of micro-augmetic filament spread through the magos's cerebellum, flashing them to white heat and incinerating Dyobann's stunned, disbelieving brain.

CHAPTER TEN

Ready-room atrium aboard the flotilla flagship *Bassaan*, En route to Galata, Hydraphur system

GALT RARELY FELT comfortable aboard the *Bassaan*. He was acutely aware of how firmly his role on the flotilla placed him aboard the *Callyac's Promise*, where shipboard routine emphasised an unhurried pace, comfort and tranquillity. The *Bassaan*, businesslike and functional, run by a curt, quasi-military crew, made him uneasy.

And that was on the better trips. With Hoyyon himself a step and a half ahead, he was always ready to serve as he watched the old man's gaze sweep back and forth and the crew blanch as though his face were a searchlight, painfully fierce.

If I could go back there, he thought, see that contented Galt and talk to him, I wonder what he would think of what I would tell him? I wonder what the old Galt would think of the reason I'm here now?

He watched the officers file past him down the corridor, reflections dancing across the engraved metal walls, checking their dress uniforms and fiddling with their hands. It seemed to take longer than it should – there were only half a dozen or so of them. He and Behaya had put their foot down about that: no more than a small group, and making even that concession to the travesty of an heir-apparent had driven home to both of them how bad their predicament was getting.

D'Leste stood further down the corridor, shuffling his feet fretfully. He and Galt had not spoken since Dyobann had flown on ahead to Hydraphur, and as days had passed and they had both become sure the magos would not return they had taken to avoiding each other. The flotilla meetings in the speaking chamber had given way to bitter, whispered little conferences between the masters two or three at a time in secret places. Rumours and uncertainty were spreading through all the crews. Galt wasn't surprised. A tikk could have come on board now and known straight away that something was wrong, it was that bad.

The doors to the room swung shut behind the last of the officers and Galt exhaled. They had commandeered a room near the Apothecarion, near enough to get Petronas onto life support very quickly if he took a turn for the worse. What nobody was admitting was that they were nearing the point where it might not help. Dyobann was gone and D'Leste's attempts to keep Petronas stable without the magos's help had been increasingly ham-handed. Zanti and Trazelli had already promised the doctor to his face that if Petronas didn't last until the hearing they would take it out on his hide.

The hearing. That was their magic threshold, their event horizon. Just keep their heir-apparent alive until the hearing; whatever happened then would happen. Galt looked gloomily at the closed doors of the ready room. He felt the floating, fatalistic calm of someone who has made a terrible choice and is now waiting for the consequences, whatever they may be, to fall.

'How did we get to this?' murmured Behaya beside him, and neither Galt nor D'Leste had an answer.

Ready-room aboard the flotilla flagship *Bassaan*,
En route to Galata, Hydraphur system

ATITH WAS THE only one who could speak as the seven of them stood around the white-shrouded bed. Phyron had fallen a place back as if what he was seeing had physically hit him, and Trichodi had put her face in her hands. Kohze, hands knotted behind his back, whooped for breath despite the smell that the perfume-mists couldn't hide.

'Nils,' said Atith in a small, broken voice. 'What have they done to you? Oh, Nils, what's happened?'

'Not Nils,' the twisted shape on the bed said. 'Not Nils Petronas. Halfway right, though, halfway. Half-right, about a half-man. Hah! Half-man. Half-man, becoming half-something else, becom–' The figure suddenly doubled over with a burst of wet coughing, trying to expel something from its chest that its muscles were too weak to shift. A medical servitor, one metre high with mask and augmetics designed to make it look like a fat ground-bound cherub, slipped through the ring of officers and snaked a drainer into Petronas's mouth. There was a short, grotesque sound and the drainer was withdrawn, slathered with something pink and translucent. The servitor shuffled back on its cloth-soled feet, awaiting the next fit.

'Petronas Phrax, that's me,' said the wreck on the bed. 'Haven't told you yet, have they? Keeping me alive for the hearing, that's what they're doing. Heard them talking, heard them all the way down here.' One of Petronas's stick-arms moved sluggishly up and pressed against his ear, then dragged itself across his temple and down over his stomach. It was impossible to tell what he was trying to point to.

'Petronas *Phrax*?' That was Kohze, who'd been one of Nils Petronas's shooting-partners when they had visited worlds with huntable fauna. 'Nils, my old friend, you can't know what you're talking about.' He looked around him. 'He's delirious from the taint. It's a miracle he's survived this long.' He took a reluctant step towards the bed. 'Nils, do you know where you are? Do you know who we are?'

The eyes were suddenly on him, and Kohze found he could not look away from them. They were clouded with sickness but glittered with energy, they danced with madness but stayed locked on his with a terrible focus that Petronas had forged by sharpening that very madness into a razor-keen, steel-cold obsession for survival.

'I know who you are, Kohze.' Suddenly it was the Petronas they all knew – all the snap and fire – lying in this bed and speaking through the wreck he was hiding in. 'I know who you are. Atith, Phyron, Trichordi, get your paws down by your sides and look at me. Omali, you tikk-loving little milquetoast, stop backing away and be a man. I need all of you. I need the help of all of you.'

'Nils, what's going on?' asked Atith. 'They told us you'd been given some kind of command dispensation, and we were going to be your crew. They said you had asked for us and that we were to... to indulge you.' She dropped her voice a notch as she finished and shot a look at the servitor as though it were writing her words down. The others took the message and began glancing apprehensively around for spy-ears.

'Forget that,' spat the Petronas-thing. 'They told you some stupid lie to make themselves think they are in control. You listen to me, now, all of you. You listen the way they are, the way they are all going to listen, the way we're going to–' Suddenly the thin body jittered and went rigid for a moment, and droplets of thick yellow liquid ran from the cracked skin at the corners of its mouth.

'I don't think I have a lot of time,' that mouth wheezed as the servitor dabbed the liquid away with a contraseptic pad, 'and that means neither do you. Those shit-gobblers outside think they're giving me a gift. I'm supposed to cry and say how glad I am to see you. I'm supposed to forget, forget all they–' Petronas spasmed and screamed reedily for nearly thirty seconds before he could ride out the pain and speak again. By that time there was a black stain seeping through the cloth beneath his legs and the gagging, sour stink of excrement filled the air.

'They think I've forgotten everything they've done. Think it's all gone the way I'm supposed to be. Hah! Hah!' The laughter made him cough again. 'Supposed to be gone but still here. Supposed to be treated and changed, treating and changed to a tumour instead. Tumour-worm, that's me. Hah! If I can go wrong in one way I can go wrong in others. Wrong plan all over. Shouldn't have been born to a whore, but even if she was a whore my revenge is still for her.'

Petronas's voice had drifted, as though he were talking to himself, and a frightening, slow-tongued slur had started to creep into his words, drifting in and out again.

'Nils, what revenge? Please, tell us what's happened to you!' Atith's voice was breaking. 'Who is this "they"? What do you want us to do?' She flinched as Petronas's eyes snapped onto her.

'Ah, little Atith. Never wanted to flirt with me, did you, even in my better days.' Petronas managed to force his face into a smile at her. Five of his teeth were missing; two of the sockets still bled. 'Nice to see you doing what you're told now, though, little girl. All right now, no more time for pleasantries. Draw in, all of you, draw in, little children. It is time for Daddy Phrax to start explaining what he needs of you.'

And the figure on the bed bayed laughter as the junior officers, the survivors of a circle that had once considered themselves the friends and colleagues of Nils Petronas, shuffled forward to listen.

Ready-room atrium aboard the flotilla flagship *Bassaan*, En route to Galata, Hydraphur system

'WHERE THE HELL are you going?' snapped Behaya, and D'Leste cursed himself for his guilty start. He had told himself over and over that he had nothing to feel guilty about. The treatments had been experimental to put it mildly, they had all known that, and they had been Dyobann's doing anyway. How was anyone to know that the damn cogboy would see fit to disappear right at the point when the flotilla – the flotilla masters, anyway, same thing – needed him around to keep their heir stable?

He turned to face her.

'They're either going to gawp at our wonder boy and be in there an age,' he said, 'or they're going to be disgusted by him and come running out of there in a minute. Either way, the three of us standing about out here is stupid. Things haven't gone wrong enough yet for the rogue trader's chief apothecary to wait on a bunch of spotty junior officers like some damn valet. I've got things to see to before we arrive, and I suggest you might look at yourselves waiting on those people's beck and call and consider the dignity of your offices likewise.' It was hard to tell from their expressions, but he thought he'd scored a point. When in doubt, attack, attack.

And anyway, he really did have some business to transact. He had thought of something. If Dyobann was out of the picture, and D'Leste had reluctantly accepted that he probably was, then their gamble with the extra-modified blood probably hadn't worked. But with audacity and subtlety, he thought, there might be a way to smooth that mistake out.

The Sanctioned Liner *Gann-Luctis*. In transit

DEATH HAD COME to the *Gann-Luctis* late in the voyage, as the ship tried in vain to force its way through a great thunderhead of force towards a momentary break of calm Yimora thought he glimpsed somewhere ahead. There had been pressure, crushing pressure that had made the ship's astropaths howl and claw at their clothes and skin, begging for sedation and crying out prayers. Domasa Dorel had felt it in her warp eye, like a finger jabbing into her forehead, and she had covered her brow with a phylactery containing hexagrammic inscriptions by House soothsayers on Terra, written in tattoo-ink on strips of her own cloned and cured skin. It usually helped. It didn't now.

Death came in as the ship burst free of the thunderhead and catapulted into the space beyond, not a calmer passage as it had seemed but a tight corkscrew of energy spinning through dimensions that no human sensibility could comprehend. The ship began to tumble as Yimora desperately looked for a way through and the Geller field rippled as the riptide struck it, closed on it, seemed to bite at it. It bowed further and further inwards and then, for less than a hundredth of a second which set off klaxons and bells throughout the *Gann-Luctis's* besieged hull, it flickered out.

Death came in through that tiny gap, while Varro Phrax stood in the doorway of his stateroom and watched his wife hold down their yelling, thrashing son. Even the most ignorant ship's labourer knew in a basic way that the immaterium somehow resonated with emotions: drawn by them, feeding off them, feeding them in turn. Varro and Ksana had been ready for the warp dreams, knowing what was waiting for them when they slept, and they had said the right prayers and hung the purity seals at the corners of their bed. But Dreyder must not have been paying attention when he said his prayers and allowed his words to wander, and some time after they had closed the drapes on his bed he had pitched away the little pewter aquila they had given him as a charm, playfully, absent-mindedly or in some transient pique. Warp-dreams were bad, but Varro remembered from his days on the flotilla that for a young mind they were worse. For a young mind that did not understand to expect them they must be far worse still. He remembered how blasé he had been back on Gunarvo, saying, 'He'll get a few bad nights and then he'll be used to them,' and felt sick.

'Go,' Ksana told him. 'I'll take care of him. He's awake now, but the dream got him so frightened he doesn't know it yet. I have him. You go on.' Varro closed the door.

Rikah was waiting in the passageway, leaning against one of the mosaics of capering nymphs and cherubs that lined it. He was twiddling the end of one of his implanted vox-vanes, his usual sign of nerves. That was when the klaxons went off again and both men flinched at the sudden clangour.

Death found itself born inside the *Gann-Luctis*, inside the re-established Geller field that cut it off from the beautiful warm fluidity of the immaterium outside. It had found itself born through no conscious effort of its own: in the moment the field had flickered, its essence earthed itself quickly and painlessly into a mind inside like a spark jumping across a circuit-gap and then it was in a dry, cold, glaring straightjacket of a universe, surrounded by minds imprisoned in meat that jabbered and flapped.

It didn't like the way the meat behaved, so it did certain things that its instincts suggested and the meat took on new shapes and patterned itself through this horribly constricting cell of dimensions differently and then there was no more behaviour. It did not like the way that there were ways in which it could not move, but it found it could do things to change the little physical universe it found itself in. It could unravel things and part things, and it found that rending and breaking was far more delicious here than manipulating the soft stuff of the warp. And so it went looking for more meat to break, meat whose little droplets of spirit would puff so exhilaratingly into nothing when it pushed on them.

The noise of the klaxons barely registered with it, but they terrified Varro and Rikah. Varro was three steps down the corridor before the horrifying thought hit his mind's eye and he doubled back. But inside their room his family were still alive and unpossessed: Dreyder now crying steadily instead of screaming, Ksana cradling him. Rikah touched his shoulder.

'We need to arm, Varro. Ship's drill. We're able-bodied personnel.'

'What about getting our own–'

'Best to use what's in one of the lockers,' said Rikah, glancing around them. 'Let's not show our hand yet. If we don't think we're going to get through this otherwise, then maybe. For now, just come on.' Varro followed him away. Twice he broke his promise to himself and looked back at the stateroom door.

Adeptus Arbites precinct fortress of Selena Secundus, Galata, Hydraphur system

'"THE HEIR,"' CULANN announced from the message chit he held, '"is unwell, and will not leave the *Bassaan* until the opening of the hearing. He will not be able to remain in the courthouse for longer than a certain time." What a strange way of putting it. What "certain time" do you suppose they mean?'

'I don't know,' replied Shira Calpurnia, 'and I don't care. What it means is that the heir will be out of our hair... *Stop* that, Culann, it was a slip of the tongue, not a joke. I'm not in a joking mood.'

They were standing in one of the V-shaped defensive buttresses of the Arbites fortresses on Galata, Hydraphur's moon. This was Calpurnia's second attempt at a place for the hearing, after ornithopters and air-sleds with Ecclesiarchal markers had started circling Trylan Tor just beyond where Arbites flyers were authorised to engage them. Then sea-platforms carrying squads of Sororitas had begun to appear around the tors at the borders of the interdict zone, and nervous proctors at the sentry posts had started to ask for extra squads and ammunition. Then Arbites informants in the portion of the Ring orbiting above the tor reported that more Sororitas had begun commandeering launch bays and hardpoints, and were clashing with the Ring's military crews over control of two of the giant barrage-cannon barbettes.

Calpurnia's initial, furious thought had been to simply shoot down every last one of them and haul Simova and a couple of random clerics into cells until they told her who had given the order, and she'd stepped on the urge. That the Cathedral thought itself able to make such openly threatening moves against the Adeptus Arbites showed a need for correction that Calpurnia fully intended to deliver. Later. Now, she had another duty to perform, so something else was called for.

'Guilliman could circle like a mountain-cat as well as spring like one,' was an Ultramar proverb that was supposed to date from the holy primarch's conquests that unified his domain. It meant there was no shame in manoeuvring. If head-on confrontation would cost you more, then where was the shame in marshalling and directing your strength another way? Calpurnia had muttered it just before she sent orders to the tor to batten itself as though for an attack, for the picket and sentry forces to be visibly enlarged from whoever was stationed at the tor and could put on carapace, and for the flyers to get as aggressive as they could in their flying, doing their best to unnerve the pilots the Ecclesiarchy had roped in.

Meanwhile, in one quiet shuttle-hop, she had arrived at the great adamantium tower that the Arbites kept on Galata. It jutted out of the silver dust of the surface and drove down deep into the cold bedrock, the winged gauntlet of the Arbites glittering from the slab-roof out into space. While Simova, or whoever was running the Ecclesiarchy's bid for the charter, was busily trying to intimidate a non-existent hearing at Trylan Tor, Shira Calpurnia would sit in judgement at Galata and the charter would leave in the hands of the rightful heir.

Everything about the Ecclesiarchy's campaign for the charter made her angry. She believed in the law, the holy *Lex Imperia,* not in the idea that the tools and processes of the law were there for a flawed case – for so she knew it to be – on behalf of personal ambition rather than any belief in a right cause – for so she strongly suspected it to be. It unsettled and angered her. It wasn't just the in-principle objection to legal games, either.

She dreaded the practical implications of such a case if it got under way. Flawed or not, there would be enough points of order, enough contradictions between religious and temporal laws, enough overlaps and grey areas of authority between the two Adeptus, enough odd precedents and historical incidents to illustrate anything that one wished to have illustrated, so a mind as cunning as Simova's could keep proceedings running indefinitely until the Eparch or someone working for him thought of something else to try.

The street justice of the arbitrators was bent on brutal control and swift consequences, but the long, slow work of the Judges focused on enacting the most insignificant letter of the least of every law, as decreed by the High Lords in the name of the Emperor. Every arbitor knew the sight of the great camps stretching away from the gates of a precinct fortress, where supplicants lived out the months or years it took a Judge there or on some more distant world to decide their case. Some went into the decades as books of precedent and case histories had been shipped in from a thousand other worlds to make sure the verdict stood foursquare on the rock of Imperial law. Calpurnia had even heard of Judges and advocates who had had been given leave to raise a new Arbites on a case so successive generations could take over the arguments when their originators had died: mere mortality would not slow the great engine of Imperial justice.

Had the Ecclesiarchy a stronger case, Calpurnia would have heard it. The idea of overriding valid law for her own convenience would have revolted her, had she taken a moment to entertain it. But after Simova had been shipped back to his Cathedral he had sent an envoy straight back with a written copy of his claim, which had gone to Calpurnia's chambers and then to the great complexes of archivists and lex-savants in the Wall's second bastion. Her initial appraisal of it had been that there was no case, and every fresh examination by savants and Judges reinforced it.

That helped her feel better about having faked them out and slipped away to Galata to hold the hearing. But not so much better that she wasn't spending more time than she should have running through her analysts' latest reports on the Simova claim and muttering the Guilliman proverb to herself over and over.

For a moment she wondered what the shape blotting out the left side of her vision was, then she realised to her embarrassment that it was her hand. It had crept up to run a fingernail down the scar-lines on her forehead. She put it down, feeling the twinge in her shoulder: she had fallen behind on the exercises she was supposed to do to keep it limber.

'Ma'am, one more message, and then I'll go and check on those dock-security protocols you asked me to look at. A reply from Genetor-Magos Sanja. It begins with the same formalities as the last one, and–'

'I'll take your word for the phrasing and the formalities. Is he telling us anything we wanted to know?'

'No. Um, he makes it pretty clear that he's not going to, either. He repeats what he said after that first blood specimen went to him. Circumstances which he may not reveal have placed the Helispex Engine beyond the reach of these proceedings, but the oaths and duties of his office prevent him from explaining why. He also says that he's empowered to offer some kind of compensating obligation by the shrine and will meet with you to discuss this, but not for ten days from the sealing of that message which was about an hour ago.'

'And an explanation of why exactly the Helispex Engine is unavailable for the first time in thousands of years?'

'No ma'am.'

'An explanation of what happened to that blood sample from this heir who came in with the flotilla?'

'Nothing, ma'am.'

'A clue as to what's going to happen to this second blood sample from Varro Phrax, which is apparently coming in on a dromon from the Higher Tetrajin Gate?'

'No clue at all.'

'And I suppose I don't even need to ask what he says about the tech-priest from the flotilla who went marching into his shrine with the heir's blood and hasn't been seen since.'

'Indeed, ma'am, you do not.'

'What do you think happened, Culann?'

'I couldn't say, ma'am, I've been with you the whole time.'

'I was being serious, though,' she said, turning those green eyes on him. 'I'm interested in hearing it. I like to know how my colleagues' minds work. Go on.'

'Something happened, ma'am.'

'Oh?'

'The Mechanicus are zealous about their privacy and their mystique. If something had happened to the Helispex there's no way any of them would come out and say so even to many people inside their own order, given the disgrace it would mean to Sanja as its custodian. I don't think it's because of that trip out to Trylan. He was worrying about what effect travel and non-consecrated ground was going to have on it, but I don't think the engine itself left Bosporian. I think something happened after he got back, maybe related to the flotilla cogboy, sorry ma'am, tech-priest going there to visit him. Unless he left by some way we don't know about.'

'We have a pretty good idea what goes on around most of the Augustaeum, Culann, and I'm as confident as I can be that the only way out of that shrine is through the main doors. Me, I think Dyobann is dead, either because he had something to do with why the Helispex is unavailable, or because he found out something about it and the other adepts killed him for it. I'm fairly well-disposed towards Genetor-Magos Sanja, but I have no illusions about what he might be capable of if he gets his blood up. Did I tell you about the Mechanicus cell we had to deal with on Don-Croix?'

'No, ma'am. But your thoughts about what happened to Dyobann match mine.'

'They do? Then you should have said so, Culann. Candour between an arbitor senioris and her staff is important. I need to know I'm getting every thought that passes through your mind.'

'Yes ma'am,' said Culann, standing at attention, his spine vibrating with pride.

'All right, then. Go and check those protocols. There apparently are appalling warp storms between here and Santo Pevrelyi and it's holding up the heir's ship. The other one, that is. But meanwhile, I have to go and announce that the blood vial of Varro Phrax that this emissary brought through those storms is actually of no use now. I'm sure he'll enjoy hearing that. Apparently the passage here is not one to wish on your worst enemy at the moment.'

CHAPTER ELEVEN

The Sanctioned Liner *Gann-Luctis*. In transit

'You're staying back here,' said Domasa Dorel. 'Cherrick, get in front of him.' She would have blocked the way herself, but the hellish storm outside the hull meant that too much of her strength was spent keeping herself upright and her thoughts her own. There was thick, migranous pressure on her temples, and the flashes of power against the Geller field showed in her warp eye like a flash of red through closed eyelids. She sagged against the plain metal wall of the crew-deck.

'No ma'am,' said Cherrick and, after the initial disbelief Domasa's burst of anger on top of what was already in her head made her dizzy. 'All available able-bodied hands have been ordered to hunt this thing down,' he went on. 'One of the oldest shipboard disciplines there is.' Cherrick eyed Varro and Rikah's short-barrelled lasguns as he spoke, his words underlined by the clanging alarms in the corridors around them.

'And you're not going to order me away from this, Madam Dorel,' Varro put in. Behind him the mini-squad of the *Gann-Luctis's* troopers muttered and looked at each other. 'I left my son in my wife's arms eight decks above us. Believe me when I say I'd rather be with them than here. But Cherrick's right, this is an obligation.'

'You're the heir,' said Domasa, but with little spirit. She hadn't the energy. 'Anything happens to you, the whole point of the voyage gets flushed. Won't that be nice?' A dozen ratings, white-faced and gasping along to a prayer their overseer was chanting, clattered by, heading down the ramp behind Varro. They mostly clutched ships' tools to fight with: oxy-torches, heavy wrenches or tool-hafts, buzzblades on heavy forearm mountings. For all the good it would do them.

'It's an obligation,' Varro repeated. He was pale with fear, but there was no give in his voice at all. 'That's all. Now if you're coming with us, Domasa, then let someone help you. Otherwise we'll see you to somewhere safe.'

'Nowhere is safe at the moment,' she said, and as if on cue there was a momentary shudder as the ship bucked in the warp flow faster and harder than the gravity plates in the deck could smooth out. The tremor boomed through the dim halls all around them: where they stood, at the intersection of four great fifth-deck thoroughfares, it was like muffled thunder welling out of the darkness on every side at once.

'You're right,' said Rikah, 'and as long as this thing is loose inside the hull we're less safe than ever. And we're still standing here talking.' He tilted his silver-frilled head towards the ramp down to the second-order crew-decks. 'Let's not allow it any more time, shall we?'

Cherrick nodded with grudging respect, wheeled and strode to where the ship's soldiers, overhearing them, were going over their weapons once again. Most wore bulbous combat bridles holding the targeting visors over their eyes, vox-pickups at their jaws, and dangling amulets and purity seals at their temples; their faces, what could be seen through all the hardware, were grim. Cherrick knew they had been trained and conditioned to trust in one another, and having to follow him and Domasa around was galling. Cherrick himself was no better off: distrust of anyone but his own hand-picked people was ingrained so deeply in him that he had insisted on having at least one of his own troops at a dozen strategic points across the ship. He was feeling their absence now, though, and he muttered obscenities under his breath as they readied themselves to move.

'Can somebody tell me,' slurred Domasa as she leant on Rikah's arm, 'why we all have to club together like this? I thought it was only bad melodramas where any dangerous mission required all the most irreplaceable members of the crew to gang up.' The ship lurched again and a tight, coherent current of warpstuff scraped down the side of the Geller field. Rikah and two of the ship's troops jumped and looked around as though they had heard a voice calling to them, and strange transparent spots danced in Domasa's vision.

'We're not leaving,' Rikah countered by reflex, and then calmed himself. 'Varro and I are here because we're able-bodied personnel and we're obligated to do what we can to defend the ship. The troopers are here for the same reason. Cherrick, well, I suppose he's here because he's the chief of your staff and he's responsible for you, but you, Domasa, if there's anyone here who should be somewhere safer–'

'She's here because she's our bloodhound this evening,' called Cherrick over his shoulder. 'Except with an eye in her head instead of a nose on her face. So to speak. She's how we knew to follow the thing down here.'

'What it is,' Domasa condescended to put a little more weight on Rikah's arm as she spoke, 'is... like a little, thing. A piece of what's out there all bundled up with what's in here.' She swallowed as the ship bucked and the internal gravity lurched for a sickening moment. She wasn't sure, but she thought they might just have been tossed end over end. 'It's like... little fine threads working their way in, then being tied into a knot. Or something from outside seeping in and then crystallising in here. Or something from outside spurting its seed in, which grew into something in here. All of those things and none of them, I can't... *Ahhii–*'

Two murder-black whirlpools of force had merged right on the ship, and the force of them wanted to wring it like a yard-fowl's neck. Every man on the deck around Domasa felt his skin crawl. Cherrick was suddenly caught in the memory of his first kill and realised that he was a murderer. Varro remembered the first time he had truly feared for his son's life, in a watercarriage crash on Gunarvo's canals. Domasa thought nothing at all, the thoughts chased from her mind by bursts of filthy urine-yellow light, hot and sour as old hatred.

'Are you all right?' asked Rikah as he gripped her arm. A tiny drop of blood trickled down from his nostril. 'Can you stand?'

Domasa muttered something. 'I'm sorry, Madame Dorel, I didn't catch that.'

'I said Throne protect Yimora. If this is what this is doing to me in here, then... eagle's beak, he's perched out there in the Navigator's roost. Throne protect him.'

Rikah helped her stagger down the ramp after the rest of them. Two more ship's troops ran past, one toting a flamer and one pulling an outsized fuel-cylinder on a trolley.

'Can't... afford,' she said. 'It's up ahead. Strong one. Saw it clear as day. It flared up in sympathy when we hit... that last... whatever it was.'

'If it's that strong, Domasa...' Rikah began, but Cherrick turned and interrupted him..

'If it's that strong we need to weaken it and damned soon,' he snarled, 'because if it's that strong then by the time it uses up all its own punch it's going to have gutted the ship from prow to tubes and any of us left alive will soon wish we weren't when it breaks down the hull and we get our souls torn out of our bodies. You want to wind up in some nightmare's gullet before you get a chance to come before the Golden Throne, Rikah, then find your own way into it. Domasa?' She nodded, wearily.

'He's right, Rikah. We're going to finish it off. It can't be more than a few compartments away, coming towards us. Let's find it and get this over with.'

It didn't seem like much longer before they were close enough to hear the screaming.

A man ran back past them, one of the ratings they had seen earlier. The buzzblade he had carried was splayed out into streamers of metal, some of them threaded into and out of his flesh in a way that stitched his arm to his body. He was howling, scorched, almost naked, insane, and Cherrick felled him with a point-blank hellshot. Varro groaned, but nobody argued: broken minds were a threat in a warp storm.

The ramp brought them to an assembly area, rows of benches across the hall and order-sheets pasted to the walls. Now the benches were overturned and broken and a crowd of crewmen were coming the other way, screaming and shoving, trying to have someone, anyone, their enemy or their best friend or the man from the shift-crew whose name they barely knew, anyone to get between themselves and death.

Death came behind them, framed in the archway where the assembly area split like the arms of a Y into two low corridors. It capered and flopped on the red-slicked deck, pausing with each little leap or stamping step as though the sensations of its lacerated feet slapping against the metal were odd and delicious. It had been unfamiliar with the limitations of the meat it had somehow become snagged in at first, and by the time it had learned that the pitiful little extremities the meat owned were supposed to move only in certain ways most of its joints had been broken or dislocated by the inhuman will moving its muscles. There was a point when it had wanted to pass through a hole it had managed to make in a bulkhead that the meat had to run around, but the hole had been barely wide enough for one extremity to fit through, so it had crumpled the hard little bone frame the meat was strung up on and fed itself through the hole like a snake. The frame had not reassembled on the other side, and trying to hold it in place through will was tiring. Now its skeleton was a mass of bone fragments and splinters all clicking and grating as it moved. Its feet either splatted on the metal with the sound of raw meat or clicked like a dog's foot from the bone jutting through the sole.

The midshipman's uniform it had worn when it had still had the human mind it had been born with was soaked red and dripping, but not all of the blood was its own. With a crackle of tearing flesh it shot out an arm, the skin popping as the limb distended, and a hand that looked like a cudgel spiked with bone thudded into the back of one of the rearmost crew. Only Cherrick, standing his ground at the head of the formation and clubbing crew aside as they ran at him, actually saw the red shape drag its catch back. Suddenly more bone splinters sprouted through its skin: first just their points like droplets of hard white sweat and then their whole length like bloodied cactus-spines, and it took the screaming crewman into its embrace. He screamed for a moment longer, then the red thing let him drop and gave out a gargling wail that could have been triumph, disappointment or something else beyond human thought.

The sound was enough to redouble the panic, and in another moment most of the hunt-and-destroy squad had disappeared up the ramp, all thoughts of drill and duty forgotten. Perhaps half a dozen were left, knocked sprawling or tangled in the benches or cowering by the walls. One shrieked and writhed in Cherrick's arms and two more were grappling with the troopers. Varro and Rikah both backed away, trying to protect Domasa from the brawling before the troopers realised it wasn't worth the trouble for people obviously so determined to run. They let them go and two sprinted away, one cannoning into Varro and then on up the ramp. The other curled against one wall, weeping.

The metallic scratch-click of shells being rammed into a shotgun snapped Varro's attention back onto what was in front of them. In amongst the wrecked furniture, three crew were making a stand. The two they had seen with the flamer-cart crouched behind an upturned bench and worked frantically on a fuel connection – they had lost their trolley, but a little metal egg that must have been an emergency reservoir hung from a hose on the side of the casing. The sound he had heard came from the woman next to them, frantically reloading a snubby, wire-stocked shotgun as the red thing loped out of the arch.

Varro walked shakily forward, feeling as though his body was going to tear itself apart in the way the red thing's seemed to be: the instincts branded into every cell of his body wanted to propel him back up the ramp even as his horrified, disbelieving mind told him he had to go forward. His gun trembled as he raised it.

The red thing took a half-step and reached for the men with the flamer, but this time its arm seemed to have trouble stretching and a shower of blood and bone splinters pattered down onto the deck. The woman with the shotgun panicked and set off one blast, stunningly loud in the low metal space. Shot rattled and stung off the metal roof and blew out two of the lamp housings; two more began to flicker and spit erratically, and the sudden sporadic light gave everyone's movements a staccato quality that only added to the dreamlike horror.

The red thing staggered another step. Even with his ears ringing from the shotgun blast Varro could hear the sickly tearing sound its neck made as its head tilted up to look at the flickering light. One of its eyes was gone, a wet flap of skin and hair from its exploded scalp hanging over and partly sucked into the empty socket. The other eye, turned glistening black like a basalt pebble, bulged as though some unimaginable pressure from inside was about to burst it and it glittered madly in the light from the broken lamps.

The crewwoman took a breath, steadied herself and fired again as the snaking, wavering arm veered towards her. This time her aim was true, and the arm turned into a blood-spray that painted the ceiling and wrecked the half-broken lamps. Suddenly the room was almost lightless. The thought that the red thing might be advancing on them in the dark threw Varro into a panic. His hand clenched the trigger, more fear-reflex than aim, and the room was lit by a quick flurry of dim red stabs of light as Rikah joined in. At a shouted order from Cherrick two of the ship's troops opened up too, and then the rest of them, with Cherrick at their head, darted ahead into the assembly area proper, fanning out in a line, planting their feet and adding their own fire.

'Split!' Cherrick was shouting. 'Split up! Make sure if it gets near you it only gets near one of you!' And indeed, the other troopers were spreading out. Varro, his nerves and instincts screaming again, forced himself to move into the room and around the opposite wall, aim and fire again.

The thing in its coat of blood watched them silently, the single black ball of an eye catching the light of the las-bursts as they struck it. They did not knock it backward: normally even a laspistol shot would feel like an impact as explosive vapourisation of part of the target's surface imparted backward momentum. But the shape in red stood there, its jaw hanging slack on broken and dislocated hinges, as shot after shot burst puffs of vapour off it. They did not seem to be penetrating as they would a human body, they simply cratered its front, as though something were binding its meat into a barrier far more dense to the bursts of incinerating light.

The shotgun did better work. Under cover of the las-fire around her the crewwoman crept forward through the wrecked and tumbled benches, clamped the stock to her shoulder and sent three more booming, flaring shots ripping into the already stippled flesh. Domasa could see it happening, see the hurt, although she could not communicate it: the thing throbbed in her vision like an ulcer and it was all she could do not to drop onto all fours. But her warp eye could see it starting to come apart. The shotgun was what it needed: las-fire was a weapon for living creatures, a way to inflict trauma on a live metabolism to the point when it could not continue to function. But to fight something like this you needed a weapon that could not only break up a body but demolish it, physically rip it apart until the knot of will that held the flesh together was exhausted. The clot of warp stuff inside the corpse opposite her was starting to leak and lose cohesion: already it was having trouble stretching its limbs and the shredded flesh of its neck and shoulders was starting to settle and slump. The wretched heir was still playing the damn-fool hero, though, the way she had specifically tried to stop him from doing. Who did he think he was?

The barrel of Varro's gun was smoke-hot and icons were flashing down the length of the case: power cell low, mechanisms overheating. But he still ran forward. The shotgun woman was reloading again and the daemon-corpse's attention was on her; the flamer crew would not get there in time. Las-fire and shouts from Cherrick and the troopers passed over his crouched back; Rikah was two paces behind him, his own weapon approaching overheat level as he tried to cover them both. The corpse still had not moved. Its other eye had taken a hit and ruptured; its front had been cooked black as the bolts hit it, and Rikah saw places where the bone had started to show. All Rikah could think was, 'How can it not die?'

It wouldn't die, and Cherrick hated that. The thing stood there, flesh sizzling and crackling, and didn't waver or fall. He had spent a long time learning how to break bodies and take lives, and with his mind charged and twitchy from what was going on outside the sack of meat in his sights was starting to look more and more like a calculated insult, a rebuke to his skills. Roaring wordlessly, forgetting what this thing was and what it could do to him, he advanced. He wasn't going to be resisted by the mockery in the spreading red pool, and he wasn't going to be shown up for a fool by the merchant-brat who was rushing right through the field of fire. He spat, and his saliva sizzled on the heat-sink fin of his custom-crafted hellgun as he ejected the spent cell, kicked it away across the floor and slammed in another. He stepped over a broken bench as the two flamer-men were lugging their weapon into position, kicked one of them in the ribs and bellowed at him to move faster.

The thing in the corpse had noticed the nature of things around it change. It could not understand that this was because its eye had gone and with it the last crude analogue of physical sense, and that it now possessed only psychic sense blunted by its looted flesh. It had never had the experience of material form, knew no way to differentiate one material experience from another. But it was starting, in some way, to sense a danger: it was now an effort to move and hold the meat together. It wanted to pop open these new bundles of inflamed emotions that were surrounding it, but it did not like the sensation of having to grip and hold the stuff of itself together – every last aspect of that sensation was utterly alien.

So it turned, but it was hard to move. It realised after a moment that there was something in the way, and just as the line of humans firing at it were starting to think that perhaps it was weakening as it walked face-first into the bulkhead, it twitched and heaved and stroked one ragged forearm-stump down the metal. The steel bulkhead parted and peeled back at the motion, like stretched cloth parting under a knife, and the meat-shape stepped through.

On the other side of the bulkhead was just air, the upper half of a double-high passageway through to the mess and to the lower decks' chapel. Tearing open the bulkhead had opened a hole in the upper part of its wall, and the thing from the warp made its meat-vehicle fall slowly, end over end, what was left of its crude senses relishing the curve and tumble – only a sad echo of what its home had been like, but good enough. Then it stopped, and what little the thing understood of the rules of its new home seemed to mean that it would have to get up and move under its own power again. It got its arms and legs under it, lurching and slipping on broken joints forced to work at inhuman angles, and found out that it seemed to move much better now. It liked being away from the attackers and their odd sensations, but it hated being away from the strange, exhilarating taste of their souls. It tried to think of a way it could do both, but making its thoughts work in the sack of meat was hard so it picked a random direction and wandered in it, waiting to see what would happen.

Rikah had been first to the breach it had made in the bulkhead, and at first Cherrick and the others thought that he had been attacked by the way he staggered back from the opening with his mouth working. But each of them when they looked through the opening had to fight down the same visceral response at the sight of the once-human body walking away from them in a kind of dragging scuttle, its palms flat on the deck and its knees and ankles both bending through right-angles in the wrong direction to bring the soles of its feet onto the floor. Its head hung limply down, almost brushing the floor as if it wanted its ruined face to watch the bloody prints its hands and feet left on the deck behind it.

'Can't,' gasped Rikah, breathing harshly in between dry heaves, 'can't we wait? It... has to be dying.' But Varro and Cherrick were already shaking their heads.

'Not an option,' said Cherrick without his usual unkindness. 'They sometimes die, they sometimes get stronger. And if there's another accident and this happens again there is no way that I'll have two of them about at once. I've never heard of anything like that happening on any ship that survived its passage. See to Madame Dorel if you can't come with us.' He turned to the crew and troopers behind him. 'Who's got climbing line?'

One of the troopers started to reach for the kitpack at the small of his back, then froze, arm twitching and mouth gaping under his combat-bridle. The others were reacting the same way. Varro had taken a convulsive step back and Rikah had clapped a hand to his mouth. Cherrick registered this in a half-second; a half-second later he heard the sticky sound of something wet encircling his helmet and smelled blood and burnt meat. A half-second after that he punched the quick-release on his helmet strap and sucked his body down toward his boots, and as he toppled into a clumsy roll and came up scrabbling he heard the splintering sound as the warp-thing crushed his helmet between splayed and distended fingers.

It had disappeared from sight below them, then wriggled about and walked easily up the wall and back to the tear it had made: now the sac that had been its head hung in the gap while its fingers snaked around the helmet trying to find why there was no mental death-spasm as the ceramite and fibroc shattered in its grip.

There was a boom and hand and helmet both vanished: the crewwoman had reloaded her shotgun again. Too confident, though, and too far forward. The thing's head split open like a lamprey and sprayed hot blood and flechette-sharp fragments of skull with every bit the force of the shotgun blasts. The fountain of red decapitated the crewwoman and three slivers of bone went through the face of the trooper behind her: both pitched backward as Varro jumped forward with a yell and jammed his gun into the dripping stump. The barrel sizzled in the meat, and then he began to pump the trigger as Rikah and Cherrick both tried to drag him away.

Varro was lucky that the cell of his gun was so low, because when the clogged and overheated barrel finally hit flashpoint and exploded there was little enough power behind it to be soaked up by the warp-thing's body. The thump of power was still enough to send him staggering back, though, his face, chest and hands painted with blood.

What came swarming through the hull breach behind him was no longer remotely human. It leaked and stank and moved on a collection of limbs, some its old human ones and some sucking tendrils of flesh that it had extended from its torso.

The thing hurled itself out of the breach, past Varro, Rikah and Cherrick and straight at the troopers who were the ones right in front of it, knocking them flying. One died immediately, gouged in a dozen places by bone claws, one thrashed two metres backwards with his throat open before he gave one final kick of his legs and lay still. There were three quick las-shots in succession that sent bursts of reeking steam up from its skin, then it leapt again.

The slow, almost thoughtful pace of its moves was gone now, now it was all predation and deadly speed. Two more dead by the time a third shot had been squeezed off. Cherrick leapt up and pelted back toward the ramp, Rikah dragging Varro away from the wails and crackling bone. The flamer crew were both screaming at them to get aside, and as Varro passed them they managed, finally, to produce a spurt of white heat that lit the assembly area ferociously and brought the stink of melted plastic to the air as three benches slumped down into pools of slag.

Acrid smoke made a wall across the room, and as the firelight died the after-images added to the dimness. There was only silence, and Varro had time enough to collect himself and look around for a replacement weapon before the thing flew out of the dimness and sprawled over the flamer crew. They screamed in unison, their voices sounding eerily alike, like brothers, and then Cherrick took careful aim and snapped off a single hellshot.

He hit exactly what he was shooting at, the weak spot where the hose coupled the flamer to its reservoir. There was a tiny flare as the seal was breached and then Cherrick flung himself flat as a roaring orange-white cloud filled the room. The flamer crew didn't scream – they didn't have time. But something howled as its flesh was incinerated and the lattice of thoughts it had tried to hold together were left with nothing to anchor them. Domasa and the three men felt the scream begin in their bones, build through their forebrains and finish somewhere in the writhing subconscious – on nights to come that scream would still reverberate through their nightmares. As Domasa saw the knot of force finally untangle and melt away, the flames swirled and all but guttered: weaving in and out of the pools of burning plastic, paths of hoarfrost glittered in disturbing patterns before they evaporated. The last of the lights blew out, and in the darkness the whispering echoes of that death-scream seemed to echo and slink through the smoke for a long time.

Lower decks of the sanctioned liner *Gann-Luctis*. In transit

'WE HAVE TO find out who he was,' Varro Phrax said dully. He was sitting crosslegged on the deck, head bowed. 'There won't be anything left of him here but we can piece it together somehow.'

'Why?' asked Cherrick. Varro couldn't see him, except in occasional silhouette from his shoulder-torch as the man prowled about the scorched wreckage.

'We all need to pray for him. It frightens me to think where his soul must be. We need to pray the Emperor will find him in the warp and carry him safely home.'

'There are some dead people around here who might suggest that that's being a little gentle, Varro.' The sneer was back in Cherrick's voice. 'And I personally don't believe in praying for the souls of things that have tried to crush my head like a chew-seed.'

'That wasn't him and you know it!' retorted Varro. 'You know it as well as I do. That man was the thing's first victim, as much as the rest of us!'

'I don't care.'

'Well, I do. And I don't care if you don't care, because we're going to break warp and hold a funeral for these people. All of them. Even the ones it didn't kill itself.'

The torch-beam swung around and Varro blinked as it fell on him. The disc of white grew larger as Cherrick stamped closer until Varro was sitting and looking up into the light like a schola progenium child waiting to be let out of a repentance closet.

'That sounds like an accusation. Don't you think that sounds like an accusation, Madame Dorel? I think it does. And I think it's odd that there's an accusation being made here, considering I did exactly what needed to be done to save us and the ship.'

'Think what you like, Cherrick,' Varro told him. 'I'm the heir apparent. I'm the leader of this mission and the reason for it. And I say we break out of this storm and hold our funeral, and do whatever work we can to make sure that we can travel the rest of the way safely.'

'We go on.' Domasa's voice, unexpectedly firm and strong. It made Varro jump, and Cherrick gave a hoarse laugh. Her face, swimming out of the gloom and into the torch-beam, unnerved him even more. The shadows emphasised the mutated, distended bones and the pallor of her skin, the feverish hostility burning in her eyes. 'We came into this storm knowing the risks, and those risks have not changed, and I say we go on. If we broke out now it could mean months of drifting in real space, and months we do not have.'

'But we–'

'No, Varro. No. My backers are keen to help you, as am I. But my backers are keen to help because they know you are going to help them in turn. And you are going to help them,' and Varro cringed at the feel of Cherrick's gun-barrel pressing into his temple, 'by going to Hydraphur and getting your damned inheritance. And after that we shall go on to decide what our working relationship is going to be. And if you are good to us, and behave, and your charter is useful, then we will even allow you to do the occasional deal or authorise the occasional trip yourself, Varro, won't that be nice? And if you *really* behave, if I am left with no doubt about your desire to co-operate with House Dorel by the time we come away from Hydraphur with our little document, why then I will even have Cherrick control his baser urges and let your wife and brat continue to live with you instead of aboard a Dorel barge as my guests and hostages. And I know you'll agree that that will be nice.'

There was a long silence. Rikah watched, his skin cold and crawling, until Varro quietly dropped his eyes to the deck between his feet.

'I see,' said the heir. 'Well, then. At least we have certain things out in the open now. The cards are all played now, at least.'

'I didn't want to have to get so ugly with you,' Domasa told him with no real regret that Rikah could see. 'But if you're going to pull at the collar and force things, well, I don't have much alternative, do I?' The ship twisted and groaned again, and she winced. 'We're still in the storm. I'm going to my quarters. Cherrick, report this in, will you? And you two, it's quarters for you, and quickly, please. See how trusting I am? I'm not even going to send someone with a gun at your back. Don't let me think you're having second thoughts about that co-operation we discussed.'

They walked away from each other in the gloom, and as they came up the ramp Varro and Rikah exchanged a look. Behind them Domasa said something quietly and Cherrick brayed with more laughter, but neither man flinched. They held the look for a moment longer, then Rikah gave a tiny nod, imperceptible to the two at the bottom of the ramp, and Varro returned it. Then they walked away, not speaking, faces thoughtful, as the ship twisted and the warp storm howled and flared.

CHAPTER TWELVE

Adeptus Arbites precinct fortress of Selena Secundus, Galata, Hydraphur system

AFTER ALL THE angst and preparation, thought Shira Calpurnia, it seemed odd to finally look through a window-slot and see the *Callyac's Promise* seeming close enough to reach up and touch, its spine of steeples raking the black sky. Above the *Promise* in turn loomed the grey bulk of the Punisher-class cruiser *Baron Mykal*, keeping watch with gun bays open and batteries armed. The rest of the flotilla had been herded by the Navy to dock at Hydraphur's Ring, putting almost the whole of the moon between them and the fortress, and Naval patrols combed the space in between.

The fortress itself was in lockdown by Calpurnia's orders, and Odamo, who had spent half a day prowling the upper levels with a team of his own auditing every security feature he could think of, had reported himself satisfied. The lower levels were sealed and guarded, the courtroom itself garrisoned by arbitrators from the fortress and the Wall. The levels between the hangars and dromon docks, the courtroom itself and the surface, had been stripped down beyond even their usual ascetic furnishings and filled with guards.

And somewhere out there, according to the message chit Culann had just come in with, the battered and bruised liner *Gann-Luctis* had finally lurched out of the warp and into a long, exhausted coast toward Hydraphur, in formation with a watchful Navy escort. And something else too, apparently.

'A dromon runner carrying an Ecclesiarchal delegation, if you believe that,' said Umry, who had spent some time monitoring vox chatter from the Ring and requisitioning travel papers from the airspace and orbit controllers.

'Oh, I believe it,' Calpurnia replied, still standing at the window with her hands laced behind her back. She was enjoying the view. Hydraphur sunlight made everything orange-yellow and hazy; she liked the way that the airless surface of Galata gave everything outside a bright and knife-sharp precision. 'The bad blood hasn't gone away, Umry, it's just in remission. At the moment they don't feel that they can stop the Ecclesiarchy flying out on such an obvious mercy-mission to a vessel in distress.'

There was a faint satisfaction in her voice: Calpurnia had been intimately involved in the events that had seen the long feud between the Cathedral and the Navy chiefs fall off into a grudging truce. 'Innocent though I'm sure they are, I trust you got a full passenger complement.'

'Of course, ma'am. As registered at the Ring on departure, there's a party of preachers and lower-order acolytes from the Vicariate Astral, a full pontifex in charge, appropriate religious supplies for purification and benediction masses. And a dozen Sisters Hospitaller with a respectable load of medicae supplies. Exactly the sort of mercy-mission you'd expect in the circumstances. If the reports of what they flew through to get here are a tenth correct then I'd be wanting to hear some hymns and smell some incense at the end of it too.'

'Is that all?'

'One here that I don't recognise. A Sister Palatine of the Sororitas. Sister Elouera Krovedd. Order of the Eternal Gate. Don't recognise them as a Hospitaller order. And not Militant, either, not on Hydraphur.'

'The Eternal Gate. Hmm.' Calpurnia sorted through her memory for a moment until it hit her. 'One of the Orders Pronatus. They're a minor order, or a minor range of orders. Their responsibility is tracking down and obtaining relics and sacred items to bring back into the Ecclesiarchy's care. I knew I recognised–'

Umry was ahead of her: Calpurnia saw the expression on the other woman's face a moment before she caught up with her own words and realised their import.

'*Damn* it,' said Shira Calpurnia as she motioned Umry to pick up a data-slate and began giving out a new set of orders.

Rogue Trader craft *Callyac's Promise*, Low docking orbit over Galata, Hydraphur system

'THIS GETS WORSE and bloody worse,' muttered Kyorg as they waited for D'Leste to show up. The others looked at him with barely-concealed contempt and said nothing.

'Well, don't you agree? I mean, is this how it was meant to go? Am I the only one who realises there are going to be whole swarms of tikks tramping about here? What are we doing about this?'

He had meant the question for Trazelli, but it was Beyaha who answered.

'I suppose,' she said sweetly, 'that we were rather trusting that our Master of Envoys was up to the job of meeting with this Arbitor Calpurnia and persuading her to rethink this ridiculous idea. Wasn't that foolish of us? Trusting you to be up to doing your job, that is, Kyorg.'

Kyorg flushed. He had never had any illusions about what the rest of the flotilla masters thought of him, but there was an etiquette to what one did and did not say. A line had just been crossed. He made sure his expression betrayed nothing and ran his fingers over the heavy rings on both his hands. It wouldn't be long now.

Then portals from the docking bays rumbled open and the first of the Arbites stepped over the high threshold. The floor of the reception deck was beautiful polished bronze, the walls gold leaf, the ceiling overhead great sheets of softly lit amber, and all inlaid with wire-fine lines of jet to form a line-drawing of the view from the High Mesé at Bosporian Hive, facing toward the Cathedral. It did not usually fail to make an impression, but the arbitrators paid no attention.

'Who presides here?' demanded one of them, with a pistol and silver trim to his uniform, as D'Leste came hurrying from the stairs that led up to the primary deck. Like all of them, he was in full and formal garb: an ornate grey and white tunic that fell to his thighs, soft black boots and frock-coat with silver braid in which threads of scarlet, denoting him a physician, caught the light. Like all of them, he wore a tapered black hood-cap decorated with chitin-quills from a Vassilian spark-glider and a rosette with the Phrax emblem.

'No one of us presides, respected arbitor,' said Galt, pointedly ignoring the apothecary's entrance. 'We are the masters of the bureaux and offices within the flotilla, operating in a caretaker capacity for the voyage back to Hydraphur. We meet and welcome you aboard in that capacity.' He bowed, as did they all.

The head arbitrator thought about this for a moment, then muttered into a vox-pickup and more Arbites poured into the *Callyac's Promise* like black beetles. Kyorg winced at the way their hard boots scuffed the finish of the deck. To the flotilla masters, used to even their lowest menial being uniformed and decorated with fastidious care, the Arbites were underdressed to the point of being comical in their simple carapace and flakcloth and their impassive mirror-visored helmets. The smell that came through from their ship was metallic and sharp, the smell of armour and efficiently-filtered air, coarse after the delicate perfumes circulating through the *Callyac's Promise*.

'Is this necessary?' That was Galt again, making a second small bow. 'My recollection of previous inheritances is limited, but I do not recall an Arbites presence on our own craft on previous occasions. When the late and mourned Master Hoyyon succeeded the charter, we carried the charter down to the very surface of Hydraphur ourselves.'

'Special circumstances,' said the arbitor curtly. Eye coverings had never been in fashion aboard the flotilla, and it was disorienting to Galt to hold a conversation with someone whose eyes he could not see. 'Attempts to interfere with the succession are at a level without recent precedent and Arbitor Senioris Calpurnia has ordered an Arbites watch on each claimant's ship for the duration. Notify your crew.'

'The crew in this matter fall under the fiat of my colleague, Madame Behaya,' Galt replied coolly, and Behaya took a step backwards and closed her eyes. A loose silk scarf was wrapped around her neck but Kyorg could see her throat working as she subvocalised into the microbead in her neck. A second whisper from another direction confused him until he realised it was D'Leste trying to attract his attention.

'It's all under control,' he muttered to Kyorg under the tramp and clank of boots as the Arbites began spreading out through the deck and the ship.

'I'm sorry?'

'All handled. I knew I'd find a way to balance out the advantage.'

'D'Leste, what exactly are you trying to talk about here?' Kyorg looked over his shoulder: Zanti, Halpander and Trazelli were walking over to them as well. D'Leste gestured to them and the little group shuffled out of the way of the flow of grim arbitrators.

'Dyobann!' said D'Leste in an urgent, pleased murmur. 'Whatever happened to the old freak, I don't think that doctored blood sample he took on ahead did very much to help us. There was another sample due from Varro, of course, but the warp storms helped us there. It got delayed and I don't think–'

'It got delayed and it's not necessary anyway,' snapped Zanti. 'Because the Mechanicus got something stuck up them in the last few days and brought the shutters down. No blood-printing, barely any of the tissue-printing we were bracing ourselves for, for us or the heir. Dyobann's scam may not have done the trick, but I think that he somehow got things so stirred up down there that he's done just as well.'

'But anyway,' put in Kyorg, delighted by the apothecary's crestfallen expression, 'what was this thing you had taken care of, D'Leste?'

'I used some connections from your resources, Kyorg,' D'Leste answered, returning the sally. Kyorg tried to make it look as if he had known that D'Leste had been giving orders to his people. 'It wasn't too hard to find out when the ship that was carrying the blood ahead of Varro came in and where it docked. It flew right in and disembarked at the Ring itself, I don't know who had the contacts to pull that off, but we should have the same ones.' D'Leste's voice was picking up as he got excited again. 'Kyorg's office had all sorts of contacts and getting an agent who could move around the Ring was no trouble.'

'I think we get your drift, D'Leste. You took care of things.' Trazelli gave a meaningful tilt of the head to the Arbites swarming around the rest of the room. None seemed to have heard them, but D'Leste saw the point and moderated his voice.

'All I wanted to pass on was that I made sure that a particular possibility, presenting a possible if minor threat, has now been closed off. I shall so inform Galt and Behaya when they have finished conversing with the, uh, commander over there.'

'Here's a better idea,' said Zanti. 'You go back to the heir's bed and make damn sure that he manages to stay alive until the hearing. All this closing-off of possibilities is no good to us if our claimant's dead by the time we walk in there.' D'Leste, chastened, touched his cap and hurried away again.

'What happens if he dies?' Kyorg had assumed that even if Petronas wasn't going to recover from the treatments, at least he would still be around to contest the hearing.

'Then we improvise,' Trazelli told him. 'As far as we can tell, Varro's built up quite a syndicate of his own, too much of a power base for us to housetrain him. We may have to bring him in anyway by force, and break that power base somehow. Zanti and I both have plans for that. Maybe you'd like to consider whether you have any capacity to assist.'

'Of course, colleague,' said Kyorg, bowing and ignoring the open insult. 'Everything depends on having the successful heir in the right hands. I shall, as a matter of fact, pursue the possibility this instant.'

He walked away, his mind revving and whirring, barely noticing the squads of arbitrators filling the halls and decks of the *Promise*. He didn't have much time. It wouldn't be long until the hearing, not long at all.

The dromon *Omicron's Dart*, En route to Galata, Hydraphur

IT WAS NOT the arrival Varro Phrax had dreamed about.

He had fantasised about flying down to the Augustaeum in a richly-appointed shuttle, his wife on his arm and his son running ahead of them as they walked through the Adeptus Quarter, admiring the minarets of the Monocrat's palace and the great spire of the Cathedral. They would stand before the Arbites the way his father had done, the way one of the giant paintings in his manse on Gunarvo showed: Hoyyon Phrax standing in a ray of gold light that lanced down through a high window, head back and noble profile tilted into the light, one hand on the crystal dome beneath which the book of the charter lay open.

The reality never stood a chance. He looked around him now at the long, narrow passenger hall of the dromon that the Adeptus Ministorum had sent out to collect them. Only four metres wide and two levels high, the walls opened into regular flights of steps up to the outer galleries, from which windows looked into the passenger deck in turn. The furnishings were mainly benches along the walls –

it was more like an alley between buildings than a room on board a spaceship. There was still a residual taint of incense in the recycled air, left over from the clergymen and sisters who had filled the ship on the way out.

Their presence had seemed like a true blessing at first, a mercy mission. There were plenty of systems where mission-ships circled the outer reaches ready with healing and spiritual strength for crews coming in from bad warp-passages, and Varro had been delighted to find one here.

He had been surprised but not alarmed when the fat priest had come aboard and addressed him by name, but he had felt a chill when a sharp-eyed, shaven-headed Sister Palatine had followed him and he saw the pistol holstered under the shoulder of her purple-black robe, its grip and barrel matching the gunmetal grey of the aquila at her throat and the chain of office around her waist. He had not led his wife and child into the court on Hydraphur: 'Do your duty, my husband, I am proud of you,' Ksana had said, and Dreyder had hugged him, and then the sisters had escorted him away.

Now he sat despondently at one end of the compartment with Rikah next to him. Further down was Domasa, silent and hunched over: the start of this trip was the first time he had seen her truly afraid. The Sororitas and their grim reputation toward mutants, Navigators or no, had her pulling her cowl over her head and her sleeves down until barely any of her was visible under the black and russet cloth. She looked almost as though she were praying; more likely, Varro thought, she was regretting having left Cherrick back aboard the *Gann-Luctis*.

'Domasa,' Varro hissed, to no answer. He moved closer. 'Domasa!'

The cowl slowly turned toward him.

'Shut up, Varro, I'm thinking.'

'What about?'

'About a way we can manage this situation, you little pissbrain. I can't believe that the issue hasn't arisen before, and it must have been dealt with because the charter is still in circulation, but I don't know enough history to know, so I have to improvise. If you don't have anything useful to add you have my cordial permission to leave me the hell alone.' Varro had heard no news about Yimora but he had seen Domasa recover from the warp-voyage with terrifying speed, and this was a Domasa Dorel he barely recognised. Not the courtly and obliging woman who had come to him on Gunarvo, and not the sick and exhausted woman of the voyage. This, he supposed, was the Domasa Dorel that had lived underneath those two, all steel and poison.

'The Ministorum, you mean? I remember my father carrying relics for them once, when I was very young. We flew into a war zone in the Ophidian Sector where the sanctioned traders couldn't go and brought stones from some old shrine back to Avignor to be made into altars. That's all I know of.'

'And they didn't try to snatch it then, at least not in any way obvious to a toddler. So there probably won't have been any clashes recent enough for a decent precedent.' Domasa was talking half to him in the way one might use a child or a pet as a token listener while they sifted ideas. 'All right then. If they were really confident about the charter they wouldn't have come for us, they would just have taken it. If they're here with us it means they think they need us. And that means we can make them negotiate. And if they'll negotiate…' Domasa took a deep and satisfied breath, 'then they won't know what hit them. At least until we're safely away with the thing, methinks.' She glanced at Varro and shrugged, half to herself. 'I'll have to keep improvising, but that's all right. Nothing about a bunch of pious little cloister-monkeys that I can't handle. And I've had news that the stupid fake heir the flotilla crew are putting up may even keel over dead before long. They're panicking, and that's good. Just *you*, Varro, remember not to try anything on with them. You owe it to yourself to bear in mind where your wife and son are, and that Cherrick is there with them.'

'I know the situation,' Varro said softly, and backed away. He thought again of Ksana and Dreyder, and wished he could have left Rikah back aboard the *Gann-Luctis*. But Rikah was his aide and retainer, his close companion for the whole voyage, and leaving him behind would have been suspicious. And they could not afford suspicion, not now. After all, it would not be long now.

Adeptus Arbites precinct fortress of Selena Secundus, Galata, Hydraphur system

'Do we separate them, ma'am?' asked Odamo, slapping his gauntleted hands together. 'We've got more than enough boots on deck to be able to face the Sisters Militant down. And this rock is tough enough to fend off anyone who comes after them, too, until we choose to give them up. Just let them try and stand over this place like they did with the tor.'

Odamo had been offended by that, Calpurnia knew, and had been looking for a way to bend the Ministorum's nose by way of retaliation. And then – she smiled at this – there was the gravity. The fortress used deck-plates to boost the moon's weak gravity, but they were still a little below Hydraphur gee. Odamo was finding it much easier to get about on his usually stiff augmetics, and it was making him feisty.

'He's got a point,' said Umry, walking alongside. 'Simova's not stupid, and this Sister Krovedd won't be either. They'll be using the flight to try coat-tailing their way into the hearing, but if we know that that's what they're doing, as we do, then why should we allow it?'

Calpurnia did not answer for a moment, but touched her signet to the Arbites icon in the centre of the door in front of them and stepped through into the courtroom.

This was a smaller, plainer court than the great chambers in the Bastion Praetoris, there because every Arbites fortress was required to have a courtroom within it. Unlike the more grandiose chambers it was built for function, not pageantry and exalted spectacle. It suited Shira Calpurnia perfectly.

'I believe we will let them enter, and speak their case,' she said, walking out onto the high pulpit from which she would oversee the trial. She stood five metres above the courtroom, above walls of smooth black metal at seventy-five degrees to the floor – had she wanted to walk to the far side of the court from here she would practically have to rappel down first. 'One heir will stand on each side of the centre-aisle, with whatever retinues they have brought, and Simova and his delegation central and further to the back.' She turned to face the others, whose rank did not allow them to stand in the pulpit: they peered in from the other side of the door.

'I didn't think this could be the first time that the Ecclesiarchy would have made a grab for a relic as precious as this,' she said, 'and I was right. Umry, it was you who made the report on the last documented fighting, wasn't it?'

'Yes ma'am. The Ecclesiarchy tried to bail up the flotilla while it was in orbit over Mayinnoch about a century and a half ago, and had a confessor and a quasi-independent order of warriors called the Fraternal Order of the Aquila try and demand the charter. The Arbites garrison stopped that attempt in its tracks.'

'Because...?' Calpurnia asked.

'It took any number of years before a ruling was sealed – went up to the high precinct command for judgement. But the verdict was that while there's a pretty damned complicated stew of law and tradition that allows the Ecclesiarchy a heavy hand in acquiring sacred objects, this particular sacred object contains express direction as to how it is to be disposed of and controlled. Express placement in the hands of temporal law and the Arbites takes precedence over its origins including it in the broad subset of things that mostly-implied law gives the Ecclesiarchy control over.' Odamo was nodding, Culann was blinking.

'Thank you,' Calpurnia answered. 'And the fact that this current attempt seems to have been made with no knowledge of the previous one is heartening. It strikes me that Simova, and the Eparch too, are blinded by ambition for a unique relic and haven't done their research.' She looked out over the courtroom again, with its high-sided boxes and dock, the aisles cut into the floor, the stacked galleries around the walls. As an arbitor senioris she was at the lowest rung of the arbites general, where the Judge and arbitrator hierarchies recombined. Just as arbites generals promoted from the Judges had to get used to donning armour and commanding actions in the field, she was having to get used to presiding over trials and ceremonies. She, she thought, had the better deal.

The doors to either side of the pulpit swung wide and bailiffs from the courtroom garrison saluted up to her and began setting up the dais on which the charter would sit. She was prepared and confident of herself against the Ecclesiarchal claim now. She had the counter-arguments and the precedent, whatever Simova might think. And once his interference was cancelled out, the heirs could put their cases. And when she had heard those, she was confident that the right judgement would be obvious. Whatever had happened with the flotilla tech-priest might have traumatised or scandalised Sanja into seclusion, but that was a loss she was sure she could handle. It was nothing she couldn't handle. She was starting to feel eager for the courtroom to fill up, eager for the hearing to start.

Patience, she told herself. It wouldn't be long now.

* * *

Main landing hangar, Selena Secundus, Galata

HER UNIFORM WAS grey silk that whispered when she moved; her hood-cap was of the same grey as her eyes and the veil that fell across her face made her look at the world as though through a fog. The other nine were dressed alike, in paler, simpler versions of the ceremonial uniforms the flotilla masters were wearing. Through the veil, when Atith had looked around, her companions looked like ghosts.

The ten of them stood in the cold air of the hangar bay, breathing the acrid smell of propellant smoke from the tubes of the ship's boat that stood on six landing-legs behind them. They stood with antique long-barrelled autoguns, held outward to show where the ammo clips had been removed, and slender formal daggers thrust through their grey silk cummerbunds at precise angles. They stood in a ring, all facing outwards, and in the centre of the ring: a simple dome of dark metal, perhaps a little over a metre across, catching the light dully.

None of the ten wavered or looked around as the circular platform on which they stood began to move. On growling treads it carried them to the broad hangar doors, to the broad passage leading deeper into the fortress. It was lined with black-armoured Arbites, all with shotguns held at arms, their faces as invisible behind helmet visors as Atith's own was behind her veil. For the first time, she wondered if she would come out of this alive. Ten of them, only ten. The seven who had come out of the soul-branding meeting with Nils in the medicae, three more they were sure they could trust. Ten of them, ten whom Nils (Petronas Phrax, she corrected herself, he was Petronas Phrax now) had insisted on for the charter's ceremonial guard. Ten to help him get his revenge.

She breathed out and snapped through the motions of the drill, dropping her empty gun into the ceremonial position in the crook of her arm and falling into step as four heavy servitors, their thick augmetic limbs shining with filigree and fluttering with ornamental grey silk, lifted the dome and began carrying it toward the courtroom.

Not long now, she told herself. Whatever happened, she would help Nils. They all would. That was all she had to remember. Not long now.

* * *

The dromon *Omicron's Dart*, Low orbit over Galata, Hydraphur

THEY WERE BEING flown straight to Selena Secundus, and Simova was delighted. Arbitor Calpurnia didn't seem to want to stand on formality, and the charter was being conveyed to the courtroom as they were flying in. It meant that they would be able to walk almost straight into the hearing in the company of the heir, and although Simova had spared some time for a moment of dutiful indignation at such an offhand treatment of such a precious relic, the whole affair couldn't suit his purpose better. Or the Emperor's, he assured himself, or the Emperor's.

Sister Krovedd had seemed confident, too, when he had instructed her in the basics of the case as his second, and he more than trusted the Sisters Militant to emphasise the Ecclesiarchy's determination. He was even willing to let the heir make a statement or formally hand the thing over or whatever he felt like doing, if propriety allowed. He wasn't sure why the horribly deformed Navigator woman was tagging along, but that was probably why there were guards with them, so that Varro could order her contained if she tried anything. Not that she would; he was sure the abhuman knew her place.

He gripped the landing harness in sweaty hands as they coasted in under the giant shape of the *Baron Mykal* and towards a docking bay in the side of the fortress. He was looking forward to this. Not long now.

Not long at all.

CHAPTER THIRTEEN

Adeptus Arbites courtroom,
Fortress of Selena Secundus, Galata

THE HONOUR GUARD from the flotilla, ten young officers in pale uniforms and veils, stepped aside with empty weapons pointed down, and the servitors removed the metal cover and carried it away. Shira Calpurnia leaned over as far as dignity and the high-collared formal uniform would allow, but there seemed little to see: a small square of cloth, a closed book. It was only knowing what was in those pages that made her breath catch.

'Bring in the heirs and claimants,' she said. She had been mildly surprised that the terms of the charter laid down no formal legal liturgy for the hearing itself, but she was taking advantage of it. No ornate ceremony. Respectful, plain, functional as an arbitrator's kit. It was her way of paying the charter her respects.

Simova was first to bustle in, of course, at a pace that had Calpurnia expecting him to trip over his robe at any moment. His arbitrator escorts halted him well back from the two raised boxes and he stood there, scowling, stymied.

Varro Phrax came in next, a tanned, nuggety man with cropped black hair, wearing a suit of deep green that Calpurnia considered a little too dishevelled for an occasion like this. He had a broad, likeable face full of deep laughter lines, but his expression was tired and haunted. He was followed by two retainers in heavy armoured shipsuits and a slender shape in a deep-cowled rust-brown gown that Calpurnia took to be one of his Navigator backers. A third retainer, with odd silver ridges inlaid into his head, had turned away at the door and walked back out into the atrium as Varro and the cowled shape stepped up into the box.

The third party, the second heir...

...the second heir was nothing like she had expected. Three junior flotilla ratings, in simple bodygloves with blinker-harnesses and mouth-stitches to show their indentured status, pushed in a medicae carriage on silent suspensor cushions. There was something behind its curtains, something that twitched and wheezed. The man hurrying beside the carriage, with the face of a slum-thug and the elegant uniform of a flotilla master, had his eyes riveted to the flickering life-sign runes on the diagnostors floating by the curtains. Others in the same uniforms filed in behind the carriage: two women, one tall and gangling, one hunched and sour-faced, an elderly man with a lugubrious hound-face and a slender metal staff, the next bald, with a blade of a nose and darting, suspicious blue eyes, the last a bull of a man with a plaited red beard.

They were grim, tense, and when the curtains retracted Calpurnia understood why.

'THAT... THAT'S MY half-brother...' Varro's words were disbelieving, and not quiet enough. Domasa heard him and snorted. But most of the court's attention was on the wasted travesty nestled amongst the soft white cushions.

The thing was dressed in Phrax livery, more ornate than the flotilla masters'. But surely no uniform had ever been tailored for a body like that.

Its lower limbs were fluid-swollen and elephantine. On its torso weeping tumours strained against the cloth, ribbed or folded like brain coral. The arms were sticks, the hands gripped into fists that the thing began to flail in the air: the skin and flesh on one seemed to have melted the hand into a single uneven lump. The other opened into a hand, but the flesh between the fingers had split so deeply there was barely even a palm now, just cracks where the hand was splitting right up to the wrist, lined with a red-black crust. The head above the ruffed collar looked like a skull covered in runneled and melted white wax, clouded eyes glaring blindly. The final touch, which nauseated Varro all the more for its banality: such a head should have been hairless, not bearing such a mane of tawny hair.

A shudder seemed to pass through the flotilla guards. Varro heard someone cry out. The female arbitor with the green eyes was leaning forward again, staring down.

WHAT WAS LEFT of Ensign Nils Petronas beneath the hate and the tumours and the agony-induced psychosis could dimly make out the woman leaning over to watch him, high, high above. He idly wondered if it might be his mother looking down, or one of the women he had killed in that alley. He was trying to focus on her when he heard D'Leste's voice buzzing in the aural feed they had fastened to his head to make sure he could hear them.

'They're looking at you, Petronas. Be careful. Can you understand me?'

Somewhere in his mind, down past the dreams and hallucinations, a switch was tripped. This was it. The moment. Mad, scrambled thoughts spun and tumbled. Then, rising up through his fevered mind like an iceberg surging to the surface of a stormy sea came lucidity, clear thoughts forced together by a monstrous effort of will.

D'Leste moved a vox-pickup in front of his face.

'I... am...' His voice was a death-whisper, barely his own. For a long moment his thoughts wandered and he tried to remember whether his mother's eyes had been as green as this woman's. Then he shuddered and coughed and squeezed his eyes shut.

'I am Petronas Phrax, the son... the son of Hoyyon Phrax, Phrax the... the elder.' It was broken up by wheezes, but he recognised it. It was his own voice. His own body and mind had been taken away from him, but he still owned his voice. That pleased him and he grinned, and above him Calpurnia flinched: his teeth were a gapped and snaggled ruin, but white new teeth were trying to push themselves out of the fronts of his gums. 'I am here... here. For the inheritance. Father's charter, mother's... mother's, mother's satisfaction. My doctor knows about that, although he doesn't know really. That's what my friends are here for.' Petronas giggled and his split hand rapped and drummed on the coverlet. D'Leste, face white with nerves, bent over his equipment and muttered orders to the diagnostors. 'It all makes sense if you know what... what...' something seemed to puzzle him and the blind head began questing to and fro.

'My... my lord-in-waiting Petronas Phrax has become unwell, arbitor, as you see,' said Zanti, thinking fast and stepping forward. 'And we made all haste to Hydraphur so that the legacy of the great Hoyyon could be placed in his hands. Once we are able to return my lord to his ship we shall be able to help him rest and regain his strength.'

'This is a travesty!' boomed Simova, striding forward under Zanti's furious gaze. 'That a holy relic of the Emperor should be turned over to such as that? The harbouring of the mutant is an abomination unto the Emperor and this shall not stand!'

'Back in your place, Simova,' Calpurnia warned him. 'You are here on sufferance, not in charge. You.' She pointed at the man with the ruffian's face, and he looked fearfully up at her.

'I am D'Leste, madam arbitor, physician to the Lord Phrax.'

'Does the Lord Phrax have the ability to understand what is going on, for a start? And will the Lord Phrax submit to a genome trial before an Arbites medicae, as we shall demand of his rival?'

'Lord Phrax!' cried the wriggling thing on the bed. 'Yes, Lord Phrax will undergo your genome trial, for the trials that have already been visited on him through his genome have given him no reason to fear one more!' The thing grinned again. One of its lips split open and pinkish fluid began to drizzle out. Behind the carriage the flotilla masters were leaning into an urgent, whispered conversation; by the carriage the veiled heads of the charter's honour guard were turning too.

'A trial by genome is farcical,' declared Simova. 'By the authority vested in me by the priesthood of sacred Terra and the Eparch of Hydraphur I–'

'Back in your place, Simova. Now.' Four armoured arbitrators stepped away from the wall. Simova glared at them and started to back away.

'The Mechanicus will not conduct a gene-trial for us on the occasion of this succession,' Calpurnia told the courtroom, 'but a trial there will be. Trial by genome and trial by testimony. Let the two heirs and claimants come forward. The *two heirs* and claimants, Simova, and you disgrace these proceedings and shame yourself that

I have to say it to you. Restrain him if you need to.' Her voice was ice-cold. Simova of all of them she had expected to know how to behave in a court, but the man was arguing with the arbitrators and shooting glances back over his shoulder at the Sisters Militant, who were looking to Sister Krovedd for direction. D'Leste was guiding the carriage forward to just below the pulpit, beside the charter; the honour guards were following. And with the noise from one and the grotesquerie of the other, it took Calpurnia a moment to notice that Varro Phrax had not moved.

'MOVE IT, VARRO, that's your call. This is as good as over. Look at that joke. The charter's ours, go fetch it.' Domasa's voice was low and pleasant, not carrying even to her guards. She looked at Varro for a moment as he stared at the floor between his feet. He had laced his hands together to stop them shaking.

'I said move. Are you going to make me kick you?' He could feel the Calpurnia woman's eyes on him as well, as cold as Domasa's. And then for a moment it wasn't Domasa he thought of or the little blonde woman in the pulpit, but Ksana, Ksana's beautiful dark eyes looking into his. He looked at the chronometer at his cuff. It was nearly the time they had agreed. Rikah would have things moving by now.

'Varro Phrax,' said Calpurnia, 'as an heir and claimant–'

And Varro stood, and opened his mouth. What came out first was dry and rusty, but then he managed it.

'I am the eldest son of Hoyyon Phrax. I was told his charter was mine. But I have had enough of blood and murder and greed and scheming. If that is the Phrax legacy then I am well rid of it. So, if it please the most learned and respected court: *I will not claim the charter.*'

ATITH AND THE honour guards didn't really register the words. They were focused on the wreck of Petronas, ready for the signal, ready to keep their promises.

D'Leste barely heard it either. He was almost weeping with fear. Petronas dead in the courtroom would mean his own life within the hour, he knew it, and as rune after rune on the diagnostors went into the red he scrabbled through his memory for something, anything that Dyobann had said that might help.

The other flotilla masters heard the words but were too stunned to react to them. The look they exchanged was simple. It said: what does this mean for us now?

Kyorg felt a burst of fear, the sudden certainty that he had taken the wrong bet.

Domasa Dorel felt like a trapdoor had dropped open under her: the lurch in her gut was like falling. She felt her muscles tighten and her third eye start to throb.

'I hope you know you've done it now, you little bastard,' she told Varro aloud. Now that everything had gone in a heap it seemed stupid to care about disrespecting the courtroom. 'You knew what we arranged, and if you think you've seen–' That was when she realised that it might indeed matter what she said there, and without a word she turned and strode out of the courtroom, her two guards falling in behind her. One of them paused by Varro and gave a leer from under his visor and an obscene little fist-in-crotch gesture that Varro did not acknowledge. Then the tall doors swung shut again and they were gone.

'Someone's got to keep an eye on her,' muttered Kyorg to Halpander and hurried out after them. He didn't care if his exit had sounded convincing. By the look of things, points like that were going to be distinctly moot soon.

'On behalf of the departed–' Simova began. He had belatedly remembered that he was here because he had supposedly joined the Phrax entourage as they flew in. He was wondering when Arbitor Calpurnia was going to get things back onto an even keel so that he could begin his arguments. Then Krovedd pushed past him and walked forward level with the carriage.

'Let's neither of us fool ourselves, Arbitor Calpurnia. One heir refuses to claim, the other won't last another day barring the hand of the Emperor Himself touching him. If the charter passes to this Petronas there'll be another hearing soon and, if there's no line, then I think–' but she was interrupted by a scream from the carriage.

'Rogue Trader Petronas!' the thrashing thing howled. The violence of its movements tore its skin in half a dozen places and fluid stained the grey of the coverlet and the white of the cushions. 'Even better! What a time! What timing! Mother, are you listening? Pay close attention, be proud! Rogue Trader Phrax knows no laws, we all learned that, didn't we! Goes where he wants, does the rogue trader! No more sneaking, then!' It snapped upright and suddenly its mummified face was staring point-blank into D'Leste's. His scream cut off as Petronas's split and bleeding hand gripped his neck with terrible, feverish strength.

'Rogue Trader Petronas's first order!' the thing screamed into his face, and D'Leste felt something warm splash out of its throat onto his skin. Something bounced off his lip and onto the bed: a tooth. 'First order is avenging! First order is justice for mother-killers! First order is...'

Petronas stopped. For a moment he had felt wonderful. There had been terrible pain in his hand, but he had felt his fingers sinking into something and his blurred, doubling, tripling vision had shown him the doctor who had done all this, the doctor who had stood over the bed, the doctor, the doctor was dead.

He dimly heard shouts. There were others he had meant to see to, weren't there? The sound of flesh being struck. It sounded good. He could feel his body slumping, hurting, as his tissues rejected once and for all the genetic disguise that Dyobann's brutal experiments had tried to stamp onto them, as his cells blew out and broke down, as his flesh sloughed away. He looked at the doctor's face. He wondered if it still counted as revenge, even though he was the one that this one had hurt and not his mother, and while he was wondering that, he died.

'GONE FEET-UP,' Behaya had said. 'No heir at all, now.'

'If we can get the charter onto the ship,' Galt had muttered, 'we might still have a chance. Get Trazelli.'

So Zanti had left them in the courtroom and hurried out through the doors, their closing swing drowning out the screeching as Petronas finished whatever he was doing to D'Leste. Incompetent idiot. They should never have trusted him to look after Petronas after Dyobann disappeared.

'You.' She snapped her fingers at one of the armoured figures in the corridor. 'Get a message to the boat from the *Callyac's Promise*. The message is–'

'Arbitor Senioris Calpurnia commands us,' the arbitrator told her bluntly. 'Not you.'

'Arbitor Sen–' Anger would not let her finish the sentence, and there were things to do. Red with humiliation, she hurried on until she thought she was in range of the hangar, then keyed the vox in her wrist-amulet. 'Trazelli. We're going to be leaving with the charter soon but things are bad. Has Kyorg reached you yet?'

'I saw him on the dock level,' came Trazelli's voice in her ear, 'but he didn't come here. Not yet.'

Zanti squeezed her eyes shut for a moment and forced clear thoughts through the anger. Waited for connections to click, for data to–

'*Bastard*! Trazelli, four men to meet me at the first set of steps in the courtroom hallway. Now.'

Trazelli knew better than to try and ask why.

ATITH WAS SOBBING as she and Kohze and Trichodi led the charge. They had hidden magazines full of low-density undetectable rounds for their ceremonial rifles, but there was no time to load them as they closed in on the flotilla masters, the people who had betrayed Nils, Nils who was the rogue trader now. Mutiny. Revenge.

Her long dagger was in her hand and red-bearded Halpander was in front of her. He batted her first thrust away with a swipe that laid the back of his hand open along the dagger's edge, bellowed and flicked the sleeves of his coat a certain way. Two shining flaps of micromesh chainmail dropped out, set with odd ridges of metal; then Halpander made fists and the ridges snapped into rows of spines along his now-armoured knuckles.

Next to him, little long-faced Galt flipped up the end of his staff and there was a shimmer in the air as a micron-thin carbon blade took the head off the man next to her. Then Halpander's fist crashed into her mouth and she was on her back. Phyron stepped over her, yelling and swinging his empty gun in an arc that smashed Halpander's collarbone before the microblade in Galt's staff took his arm off.

Sobbing and spitting blood, Atith scrambled back. She wanted to call out to Nils, tell him that they were fighting as he had told them to, but he was limp on his bed. Then she was in a crouch and powering forward and her dagger punched through the flakcloth layers under Halpander's coat, sending him over backwards to sit and gape at the hilt jutting from his sternum.

There was a rapid cracking from behind her: Trichodi had taken the time to find her magazine, load and empty it into Galt's face. That was enough for the Arbites: they had been moving in to break the brawl up with fists and boots and shotgun butts, but after Galt went over without a sound Calpurnia shouted an order as she vaulted the pulpit rail and the arbitrators took aim. Trichodi was knocked three ways at once by blasts of shot – she pirouetted and fell. An Executioner shell smacked into the side of Kohze's head as he tried to load up to get a shot at the fleeing Behaya. Atith scrambled to cover under Nils's bed, and thought she might be about to make it before there were more shots and two bodies collapsed onto her, pinning her to the ground. When she shook them off and stood up again there was an arbitor on the other side of the bed aiming point blank at her and she opened her mouth to say–

TRAZELLI CAME DOWN out of the boat from the *Callyac's Promise* at the head of two dozen armsmen, pounding through the portals along the route that the charter had taken to the courtroom, leaving four armsmen and nine arbitrators lying dead in the boat and on the hangar floor.

'Zanti, sir!'

'What?'

'I just saw Zanti, sir,' said the armsman, 'heading into one of the cross-corridors!'

'Get after her,' Trazelli said, thinking of the last exchange over the vox. 'And you and you and you. Make sure she's all right. Get her into the boat and then wait for my orders.' The four armsmen peeled off and the rest of them ran on.

The hall sloped down into the guts of the fortress, then flattened and widened and rose up in half a dozen broad steps to the double doors of the courtroom. That was where the next garrison of Arbites were. They were just closing ranks across the corridor when the doors swung open and Behaya burst out between them, holding up her skirts and running as fast as her long legs would carry her, as from inside came a roaring chorus of shotgun fire.

'Halt – now!' bellowed an arbitrator in the centre of the line, gold rank-trim glittering as he held up a hand. But one look at Behaya's face was enough to make Trazelli decide. He flung himself flat, high-bore autostubber already whining and clicking as the loader cycled up. Behind them Behaya gave a yell that distracted just enough of the arbitrators for just long enough–

* * *

'KYORG!' IN THE narrow side-passage leading to the dromon docking-sockets, Kyorg jumped guiltily and spun around, his bald head catching the lights. Behind him, Domasa Dorel shuffled a couple more paces back toward the airlock where the *Omicron's Dart* was docked, wishing she'd had the chance to bring the toxin needler with her. She had sent one of the guards ahead into the ship to get a transmission back to the *Gann-Luctis* on what to do with the hostages, and now she motioned for the other one to get between her and the confrontation.

Stamping toward them was a woman in the garb of a flotilla master, a black-haired old biddy with a hawk-beak nose and the shine of augmetic sockets visible under the edge of her hood. Domasa could see the terror of her in Kyorg's eyes. She should probably leave them to it. She backed up a pace more.

'Oh, and didn't I just *know* it would be you, Kyorg, you treacherous little tikk-fondling...' Zanti was spitting with fury, every word flying out like a bullet. 'That's how they knew to send a blood-sample of their own, that's how they knew we were counter-claiming. You told them everything, didn't you. Is that who that freak works for?'

'I was doing what I had to,' Kyorg squeaked, backing away from Zanti. 'You think I didn't know you people had it in for me? You think I didn't know I had no future with the way you all joined against me? Bypassing me, talking about me?'

'You bypassed yourself, you incompetent little tikk! If you'd ever thought of doing your job instead of coasting on Hoyyon's work...' She tailed off as four armsmen in white-grey-green livery came pelting up behind her. 'Ah, good, I don't have to handle all this on my own. I think what I'll do, Kyorg, is drag you back to the *Callyac's Promise* and fly you back with us so we can tell–'

The threat of humiliation before the flotilla did what the other threats had not. Kyorg pistoned out both hands in front of him and his ornate rings flared with energy. Zanti, wise about hidden weapons, backed and turned away in time, and the two hindmost armsmen were protected by their visors. The other two caught the full blast and staggered away, howling and clamping their hands to their faces. Another ring spat a needle-fine laser that lanced through the third man's throat just below his helmet's chin-strap and sent him reeling and choking against the walls.

As Domasa reached the ramp of the *Omicron's Dart* her own guard shoved Kyorg aside and raised a snubby little shotcaster he had drawn from a pouch in the small of his back. His mistake was to pick the last armsman as the major threat: in the time that it took for him to aim and fire, Zanti pinched the front of her floor-length coat firmly in her fingers and flicked it out. The braids of memory-wire woven into the hem curled up for a moment and then whipped savagely back, trying to regain their original shape, and the metal weight in the hem cracked the guard's kneecap. As he lurched and stumbled the second flick hit him between the eyes with more force that any movement that brief should have been able to muster, and the third connected solidly with Kyorg's temple with a sound like an apple hitting concrete. As both men sagged to the floor, Zanti plucked the shotcaster from the guard's limp hand, fired it into the guard's face, checked the load, sighted on Kyorg's head and emptied the rest of the magazine.

ONE OR TWO arbitrators swung around to cover Behaya as she barrelled through the courtroom doors, but most of them were intent on Trazelli's armsmen as they began exchanging fire. Behaya ripped off her heavy uniform medallion and hurled it away, hearing the crack as the casing fragmented then the hiss as the filaments from the xenos weapon they had captured long ago, the filaments it had cost the lives of two techs to extract from the teleporting warrior's strange gun, popped clear.

They touched and tangled and, when the Arbites tried to brush them or pull them away, they cut and bit through armour and into flesh. The air in the hallway was suddenly filled with screams, scarlet droplets and the thick smell of blood.

But three armsmen had fallen to Executioner shells already, and as Behaya ran forward two more were punched off their feet. She raked a hand down the front of her coat, ripping off the ornamental buttons, and scattered them to one side as she ran: a couple were dummies, but more exploded in white heat. Two arbitrators died instantly, arms and faces incinerated and their bodies flash-cooked inside their carapaces; three more staggered and fell as the lethal heat sucked the oxygen out of their lungs. In a few seconds more the tiny incendiary pellets had burned out and Behaya ran on through the smoke and the cauterised blood on the floor.

There were still shapes moving in the thick haze behind her, and the armsmen began a steady suppressing volley. She tried to call to Trazelli, but her voice was lost in the gunshots, the hooting of a fire klaxon and the rumbling of shutters sealing the courtroom off, triggered by the heat and smoke.

'What? Get behind me and speak up, Beyaha.'

'I said everything in there is gone. Zanti and Kyorg are clear, that's all, we have to–'

The first Executioner round came arcing through the smoke and caught her in the small of the back. The impact thrust Behaya's hips forward, then the second round hit the base of her neck and sent her to the deck in an ungainly sprawl of dead limbs. Trazelli bawled a curse and banged off a burst of stubshots into the smoke, barely aware of how many of them were coming back past him in vicious ricochets. It seemed like an hour of firing, rolling, reloading before he realised that nothing in front of him was moving. He stood in the corridor and reloaded in the sudden silence with shaking hands, looking around him at his surviving men, trying to work out what to do. He had walked forward, slowly, picking his way over the corpses, when the courtroom door began to open again.

CHAPTER FOURTEEN

Courtroom, Adeptus Arbites fortress of Selena Secundus, Galata

VARRO PHRAX HAD started for the door after the tall woman in the grey when the brawling changed to shooting. He veered off, hands over his ears, as the Arbites cut down every last one of the white-veiled guard who had inexplicably turned on their masters. Then he heard a clank behind him and looked around: the green-eyed arbitor had vaulted the edge of her pulpit, hung by one arm for a moment, and then slid down the almost-sheer side, hitting the floor and rolling. She disappeared out of sight for a moment behind the box Varro had stood in, and then she was there beside him. There was no malice in her stare, but little pity, either. Still looking at him, she motioned the other Arbites toward the courtroom doors, but as they began to move there was a chorus of shouts from outside, then a storm of gunfire and an odd thumping roar.

'Stand up,' Calpurnia said. He did. She was shorter than he, smaller than he had thought, the three scar-lines running up from her left eye flexing as she scowled.

'You chose not to inherit,' she said. 'Why?'

'I told you,' Varro said dully. 'The things I've seen people do, the things I know people *think*. This can be a terrible universe, Arbitor Calpurnia. Why should I make it worse for myself and my family by putting myself in the middle of... of...' A wave of the hand toward the bed and the corpses summed it all up.

CALPURNIA TILTED HER head as though she were considering another question, and made a statement instead.

'That Navigator wasn't an ally.'

'No.'

'She was using you.'

'Yes.'

'How did you stop her? Stand up to her here?'

'I arranged it with my chief retainer before we came in. He's gone back to the dromon. He has people working to protect my wife and son back on the ship.' Animation started to come back into Varro's voice. 'They're the ones I need to get to. The *Gann-Luctis* was following us in more slowly, that's where they are. They're who I need to get to. Not this charter. We'll go back to Gunarvo, to the house there. Away from this.'

'I don't think you'll be able to get away from this,' Calpurnia told him, 'not now that you're indisputably the only heir. There won't be any getting away from that, not even if you formally renounce your succession. Too many people will want to make you change your mind.'

'Then what do I do?' Varro's voice was low and hopeless.

Calpurnia looked at him for a moment, then stood up and walked across to the dais. Simova was standing over the charter, licking his lips, trying to muster the courage to reach out for it. Calpurnia drew her pistol and knocked him to one side with a sidearm hit to his temple, picked up the book without fuss and walked back.

There was only the faintest shake of her hands as she opened the book to its last page. Varro looked at the marks without really understanding them; Calpurnia stared at them for a long moment before she spoke in an unsteady voice.

'A long time ago, Varro Phrax, the God-Emperor walked across the galaxy choosing men and women to lay the foundations of His Imperium. He came to Hydraphur where there were great fleets ready to strike out into the unknown for Him and He looked at all the masters of spacecraft and who do you think He chose, Varro? He chose the line of Phrax to carry His word and His charter. I don't pretend to know your life or your mind, sir, but I know about family legacies and I know about traditions. Don't drop this burden in the dust. For good or ill, Varro, this is yours as it will be his. The legacy is his and yours and your father's and the Emperor's. Don't betray that.' She looked at his expression. 'Varro, you don't want any part of your legacy to fall into the hands of people like that. Nor do I. I know about minds like that as much as you do. So take the charter. By the authority invested in me, I name you heir. Take the charter and keep it safe from the schemers and the thieves and the murderers. Take it.'

He stared at her for a long moment, another. Finally, his hand reached out, his fingers closed around the plain cloth of the charter cover. They rested there for a moment, then his grip firmed and he took the book from her hands.

'What ceremony do we need for this?' he asked.

'We've had it, I think,' Calpurnia replied. 'You're the Rogue Trader Varro Phrax now.' She stood up. 'And my obligation is to see you safely to your ship and out of Hydraphur. Let's get the flotilla organised and get your wife and child picked up. Get those doors unsealed, please, we're going to the hangar. Sister Krovedd, your bodyguard still have their bolters unloaded? You may give them permission to reload. You Arbites, all of you, with me.' She keyed her vox-torc. 'Culann, vox a message that the escort ships for the *Gann-Luctis* are to stay on heightened watch. Have the *Baron Mykal* stand ready too, we're going to – what? Say again.' She paused glowered again, swore. 'Fine. Have a pinnace ready from the *Mykal*, and fast. We're moving. Varro, come on. Now.'

The doors were opening. Calpurnia walked over to Sister Krovedd and saluted her.

'Let's just abbreviate our whole disagreement, sister. There is not the legal case that Simova thinks there is. The charter has been handed on. This is the Emperor's will as laid down in His law. Will you help us honour it?'

The Sister Pronatus's head bowed, and she murmured something that Varro didn't catch. Calpurnia did, though, and gestured for him to open the book. The Sisters Militant stepped up behind Krovedd and all stared at the marks: the letter, the spot of blood. A single small tear slipped out of Krovedd's eye and down her cheek.

'It's enough,' she said in a small voice, and they turned to go.

The mood was broken an instant later. A moustached man dressed in a flotilla master's uniform stood staring at them, the loader on his autostubber whirring.

Trazelli never pulled the trigger. A shell from one of the Sisters' freshly reloaded bolters took him in the solar plexus, lifting him and carrying him backwards through the air and over the steps before it detonated inside him half a metre above the hallway floor.

'Let's move,' said Shira Calpurnia.

Ecclesiarchal dromon the *Omicron's Dart,* Galata space

As the *Omicron's Dart* closed its hatch on the gun-toting harridan outside and blew itself free from the docking socket, Domasa Dorel found her second guard lying dead outside the cockpit doors, next to the alcove that held controls for the dromon's communications arrays. His helmet was askew and there was a single neat las-burn in his cheek, opening a cauterised tunnel up into his cranium. She had no doubt as to who was to blame. It had been Rikah, the metalheaded no-hoper, on behalf of his worthless, treacherous runt of an employer.

There was no sign of him in the gallery, nor in the central passenger alley as the little ship turned and accelerated up and away from the base. She could not hear him over the soft sound of the ship's systems, and when she made her quiet way through the forward compartments to the cockpit there was no sight nor sound of him. She felt the absence of the needler at her arm, but she was not totally defenceless: she reached up and pushed the hood back from her high-browed head and loosened the headband that bound her warp eye shut.

'Rikah?' she called as she padded along the gallery that ran down the port side of the ship. 'It's over, Rikah. You lost. Come out. It's all done. Just you and me now.' No answer. She wondered if he had taken refuge in the cockpit or the enginarium, but no, she had ordered the crew to seal themselves in.

'We'll be back at our own ship soon, Rikah, and Cherrick is waiting there. You do know you've failed, don't you? Whatever you were planning, I can stop it. Give it up, Rikah, it's over.'

No answer. Domasa shrugged the tension out of her shoulders, looked forward and back, and stalked carefully on through the softly-lit corridors.

* * *

Docking level, Adeptus Arbites
Fortress of Selena Secundus, Galata

ZANTI HAD BARELY survived the dromon's takeoff, scurrying backwards as the sirens went off and the docking seal cracked. She could see the Navigatrix freak silhouetted in the cockpit dormer as the gravity plates powered down and the *Dart* began to withdraw its prow from the docking socket – a dromon was too big to fit in a hangar. The dropping gravity and growing tide of air gave her a moment of utter terror and then she was through the portals and gripping a safety rail as the seals thundered closed.

Zanti didn't bother trying to get to the window to see it climb away. She hung onto the railing, breathing in hoarse gasps, until her heart slowed and her head was clear.

She didn't know how many of the rest were alive, so she didn't think about it, her thoughts stripped to the most simple and brutal. Survive and get out of the fortress. Survive and get to the *Callyac's Promise*. Survive and get to the flotilla. After that there were too many variables. She would deal with it when the time came. And deal with it she would. By then there would be arguing and second thoughts and the kind of woolly thinking that would give Zanti all the opportunities she needed.

She had been too intent on chasing Kyorg down the switchbacking passages between the main hall and the dock to have remembered her way, but it wasn't hard to find her bearings once she concentrated. She hurried back to find her ride back to the *Promise*, the little shotcaster gripped in her hand, and after a few more turns she was close enough to the boat to vox out the name and vector of the *Omicron's Dart* for forwarding to the gunnery officers on *Promise* and the *Bassaan*. She grinned savagely as she ran on towards the boat. See how far the little milksop heir got with his Navigator sidekick dead and his dromon destroyed.

Ecclesiarchal dromon the *Omicron's Dart*,
En route to the Gann-Luctis

THE CAT-AND-MOUSE could not have been going on long, but long enough for Domasa to be struck by the silliness of the image in her mind: the dromon speeding through space, a handful of crew sealed behind blast-doors in each end, and in the long central corridors these two enemies stalking round and round and round. She had found Rikah's cast-off boots in one of the lower galleries – he must have shed them to try and be quieter – and she saw the occasional footprint marked out in sweat, but she hadn't been able to close with him. It had taken effort to keep her mind sharp, to push away idle thoughts like the picture of them chasing each other in circles or the growing temptation to just start stamping down the corridors and galleries yelling his name. That would be the way to walk into an ambush, and yet she had been too keyed up to want to simply wait in ambush herself.

That was when she heard him in the communications alcove. For a moment her heart froze, and then she licked her lips and went towards the sound, tugging the bandanna away from her forehead. Her unveiled warp eye glistened in the low light, looking out into blessedly calm space. Domasa licked her lips as the noises became louder: Rikah's voice and the chitter of message tape. She almost held her breath as she closed on the doorway and then almost laughed when she stood in it.

The idiot must have decided to die. He was turned away from the door, pistol dangling in his hand, the ridiculous silver ruffs on his head quivering as they communicated with the comms panel.

'Sir, you are going to have to change course closer to the formation! They're coming around Galata and from what I can tell they'll be in range. No, not good enough, we can't evade them for long enough to get to the *Gann-Luctis*! Are you even listening to me?'

'Rikah.'

He spun around, eyes wide.

'Domasa, please you have to help, we have to co-operate now.'

'Do we? No we don't. Ask your master about co-operation, Rikah. Do you know what he did? Don't even bother answering, you revolting little insect. Do you know what's going to happen to me? Answer: nothing that can be worse than what I'm about to do to you.'

'LOOK!' Rikah shouted into her face, and despite herself she glanced over at the message tapes in his hand. Most of it was gibberish to her, but she knew enough to pick out authorisation codes for the Phrax flotilla and the Imperial Navy.

'They're going to fire on us!' Rikah yelled at her. 'They're coming around Galata, the whole bloody lot of them! They think Varro's on this ship, or the charter is. They are armed and they are going to try to destroy us! There's a Navy squadron covering us, we need to get into their range! Are you *listening* to me, you stupid woman?'

As they glared at each other there was another chitter from the panel and another tongue of creamy-white tape spewed from an engraved bronze dispenser as the words crackled out of the panel.

'...*Kovash Venator*, ordering you to power down your weapons immediately and redirect to the vector our astropaths are providing. I say again to the Phrax flotilla, this is the Imperial Battlefleet Pacificus warship *Kovash Venator*, ordering you to power down your weapons immediately and redirect onto the vector we are transmitting.'

Domasa leaned over and snaked a long finger out onto the internal vox-switch.

'Maintain course, pilot. Just bob and weave a bit.' They felt the floor start to gently undulate under them as the crew obliged. 'If you can plot a fast course to the *Gann-Luctis* that takes us through Navy cover then do it. If you can't, then don't. We're not going to lose any time.'

'Ships of the Phrax flotilla,' came another crackling voice, 'this is the Battlefleet Pacificus warship *Voice of the Seraph*. Power down your weapons *now*.'

'You heard, Rikah,' said Domasa, turning to face him. 'The Navy are moving on them. We're in the middle of Hydraphur, you stupid man, did you think they would get away with this?'

'We're going to turn in and head for the Navy squadron,' said Rikah, his voice trembling. He had remembered the pistol in his fist and was aiming it at her chest. 'I can tell you what's happened on the *Gann-Luctis*, we saw to you. We had it all worked out before we even reached Hydraphur. So you can, you can just–'

'Did you work out *this*?' asked Domasa, and looked at him.

To Rikah, it suddenly seemed as though a freezing wind laced with sleet and vapour was scouring at him. There was roaring white noise in his ears, and the metal ridges on his head seemed to burn. The augmetic receptors buried in his ears burst into life, registering static that sounded like keening voices, and in his vision the woman's warp eye grew and grew until it filled his sight with purest blackness–

It took a second and a half for her gaze to blow out every synapse in Rikah's brain and send him spasming to the floor. She put a foot on his wrist to make sure the gun could not flail up at her and go off, and waited for the last twitches to subside.

The chatter between the ships had fallen silent, or switched to a different frequency that the *Dart* could not pick up, and there was silence in the alcove now. Domasa grunted to herself and stepped into the corridor. There were viewing ports studding the outer wall of the highest of the galleries, and she headed there to see what she could see.

Just as she was emerging from the stairs all the viewports were lit up with a dazzling yellow-white light as the plasma shells from the *Bassaan's* cannon began to burst around them, and the ship shuddered and bucked under a miss so near that Domasa was catapulted down the corridor.

Ship's boat from the Callyac's Promise, Galata space

ZANTI REACHED THE boat from the *Callyac's Promise* at the same time as Calpurnia, Varro, Odamo and half a dozen arbitrators, and suddenly the plan was in her head as though she had known it for a decade. She made herself nod and smile and bob while they made all their pompous tikk noises about 'by authority of the Adeptus', and let them think they were commandeering the boat to take them to the *Baron Mykal*. She acted horrified by the carnage in the courtroom. It sounded like Galt and Halpander had gone first. Behaya and Trazelli might have had a chance if they hadn't gotten stupid. And D'Leste, D'Leste had deserved every scrap of it.

She fawned and scraped and agreed that of course they must fly to the *Mykal* and then she used her flotilla seal to let herself into the boat's cockpit and told the crew, 'The *Promise*. Dock anywhere but the *Promise* and I gut you.' She knew they would obey, and she knew that once they were back aboard the *Callyac's Promise* things would be different. She knew that once the heir was aboard she could get him into the charter shrine and then who would know, really, what he had to say? She would carry his words out, his orders that the Arbites leave the ship, the orders that the flotilla form up and leave the system, and if he were alive to deliver those orders then fine, and if not, fine too. And then there would be the matter of selecting a new team of flotilla masters, and she had just the people lined up...

'Reverse the order, please.'

Zanti was not used to being in a reverie, let alone having to come out of one, and it took her a moment to realise the green-eyed scar-headed arbitrator woman was standing in front of her, one hand on the butt of her pistol. Varro stood behind her, framed in the arch that led to the boat's main compartment, clutching the charter to his chest and staring. With an effort Zanti pulled her gaze away from the little book and looked the other woman in the eye.

'I gave no order, my esteemed lady justice,' she said, bowing even lower than her stoop normally made her. 'I was ensuring that the crew had the wherewithal and the experience to dock with an unfamiliar craft such as your illustrious warcraft to which you have so wisely redirected–'

'You gave an order for the crew to fly us to the *Callyac's Promise*. Reverse it and maybe I'll try you after this is all over rather than executing you where you stand.'

Zanti stared at her. She could kill the woman easily enough, and then all she had to do was keep Varro from raising the alarm for a ten-minute trip to the *Promise*. Once they were there she would have the resources to take care of the rest. These thoughts took about a second to go through her mind, and then she stepped forward.

Varro saw the grim-faced woman in the cloak-gown grasp the hem of her garment in an odd, tense way and start to move it up and forward, then a pistol-shot made him start. Zanti, pop-eyed with astonishment, doubled over and skidded backwards into the red stain that had appeared on the cockpit doors behind her. As she fell forward onto her knees Calpurnia stepped forward and fired another round into the back of her head, bursting it and sending the metal augmetic plugs popping out of their mounts and scattering across the floor.

As Varro looked on, his face stricken, Calpurnia stepped over to the body and nudged the cape-hem with her foot. It writhed and straightened itself as she pushed a curve into it.

'Memory-wire and weights,' she said. 'Popular blue-blood weapon on Hazhim. You can put a pock-mark into steel plate if you're good enough with it.' She sighed. 'For nothing, too, that was. There are far more of us aboard the *Promise* than I think she knew about.'

She turned back to Varro.

'Make sure the crew get the order that our destination is the *Baron Mykal*. This is your ship now, after all.'

* * *

Near Galata space, Gyre Aurucon, Inner Hydraphur system

THE FLOTILLA HAD come around the curve of Galata, blasting itself forward and out of proximity with its Navy and Arbites shadows. The *Bassaan* and the *Magritta's Arrow*, the two most powerful ships with the most aggressive commands, were the first to surge away after the fleeing *Omicron's Dart*.

The slowest, the *Sounding of Aurucon* and the *Proserpina Dawn*, had it worst as they lumbered about to follow. The Navy had not forgotten the flotilla's conduct on its arrival and when the *Bassaan* powered up and discharged its first burst at the *Dart*, that was enough. The *Voice of the Seraph*, a Furious-class grand cruiser whose gun batteries rivalled those of some battleships, opened up first, using barely half its firepower to cripple the *Proserpina Dawn* outright. As the sleek container craft that had been Halpander's home for nineteen years coasted away from Galata at a drunken angle, bleeding burning air from the wounds in its hull, the light cruisers which made up the *Voice's* squadron-mates equally deftly scythed through the *Sounding of Aurucon's* enginarium with a co-ordinated lance salvo that sent plasma from its drive room coursing through ruptured bulkheads and incinerating three-quarters of the crew.

The *Gyga VII*, the fat nugget of a ship that had housed Magos Dyobann's secret chambers, wrapped itself in layers of void shields that not even the flotilla masters had known it possessed and opened its engines, trying to accelerate through the middle of the flotilla formation and past the Navy ships. But by putting up its shields it made itself a target to one of the few vessels that could both keep pace with it and do it damage. The *Kovash Venator*, a spear-slender Long Serpent-class cruiser with powerful engines, sped out to intercept the *Gyga* and flanked it for another hour, battering at its shields with plasma and macroshells. Finally, its hull crumpled and drives damaged and with another Navy squadron closing in from its patrol route on an intercept course, the *Gyga* accepted its fate, burned retros, dumped off its velocity and prepared to be boarded.

The *Magritta's Arrow* tried to run too, followed by the little escort-sized *Kortika* that had been Zanti's home and domain. *Kortika*, not built for speed, tried to skim over the surface of Galata to hide behind the moon's curve. Her captain realised that Galata was as fortified as every other body in Hydraphur when a great battery of plasma silos in the surface swatted the shields off his ship with contemptuous ease and a trio of giant lance turrets came to bear to finish what the guns had started. *Kortika* blew out in a storm that sent static and interference screaming through unshielded systems for twenty kilometres around.

On the other side of the planet, torpedo bays had slid open their shutters in artificial rift-valleys and six mammoth spikes of adamantium tore through space after the fleeing *Magritta's Arrow*. Two burst as they tried to fly through the heat of its exhaust, and another disintegrated under fire from the *Arrow's* point-defence arrays, but the final three plunged into its hull like lethal hypodermics, exploding deep in the layers of decks they had torn through. The dark, smouldering hulk that had been *Magritta's Arrow* tumbled on through space for another seventy thousand kilometres before four Firestorm escorts drew alongside it and methodically broke the wreck down with their batteries into fragments no bigger than the pulpit Calpurnia had stood on in her courtroom.

Last was the *Bassaan*, which at least had the minor victory of smashing *Omicron's Dart* to pieces with its second and third salvoes before answering fire from the *Baron Mykal* and *Voice of the Seraph* stove in its shields on both sides and left it crippled and fighting to stay functioning.

Aboard the *Callyac's Promise*, stranded above Selena Secundus and cut off from the flotilla, there was a brief and abortive struggle as a third of the crew tried to fight their way through the *tikks* and get the ship out to join their fellows. The Arbites put it down without mercy, and the summary execution of every rebel crewman and the news filtering through of what was happening to the rest of the flotilla was enough to put pay to any more ideas.

There was mopping up, of course, salvage and arrests, damage control around Galata and the recovery of a saviour pod from the *Omicron's Dart* containing a badly injured and barely conscious Navigator who was hastily collected and spirited out of the system by agents of House Dorel. This was generally considered to be the end of the Phrax Mutiny, and that was how it was entered in most of the Imperial records. For Shira Calpurnia, it didn't end there.

* * *

The sanctioned liner *Gann-Luctis*, outer Hydraphur

THE CHARTER LAY on the table, unheeded. Varro Phrax knelt on the floor, Ksana cradled in his arms as Dreyder was cradled in hers. The blood from their death-wounds mingled and pooled under them, and slicked Varro's chest and arms as he tried to hold them both to himself at once. Tears trickled from his face and mingled with their blood.

Shira Calpurnia stood a few paces behind him, hands laced respectfully before her, head bowed. They had passed signs of the fighting, where staff and crew loyal to Varro had tried to wrest the ship from Domasa's agents and the delegation of Gunarvo's governor; that was as much as she had been able to piece together. For the most part they had succeeded, and the *Gann-Luctis* had let the *Baron Mykal* close and the shuttle carrying Calpurnia and Varro to board with no resistance.

They had succeeded except for here.

'Cherrick' had been the name on the tags of the man lying on the floor in the middle of the room with the gunshot hole in his gut. The name was not one that had appeared in any of Calpurnia's dossiers. There was a hellgun lying by his corpse, but when he had come in here to kill Varro's family he had used a knife. She didn't pretend to know why, but that seemed to be what had given Ksana Phrax the chance to draw and fire. She supposed she would never know exactly what had happened here.

Varro wept on and on, the sound with little rise or fall, the low, constant crying of a man whose spirit was broken. He had bent forward over their bodies, his face in his wife's blood-stringed hair.

Calpurnia's vox-torc buzzed, and when she stepped out into the corridor and keyed it open she heard Odamo's voice from the *Baron Mykal*. She turned away, as much so the *Gann-Luctis's* crew waiting outside in the corridor wouldn't see her expression as for privacy of speech.

'Ma'am, you asked for surveillance of the ship.'

'Yes? What of it?' Even as she asked she felt a telltale rumble of power through the deck and the lights for an instant went dim.

'We're picking up power to the drives, ma'am. They're getting ready to move and there's a signature that the auspex crew tells me is consistent with power to the warp coils. We think they're going to try and jump out of the system from here.'

Impossible. That was her thought. She had seen the reports of the state the ship had been in when it came into Hydraphur. And now it was undercrewed, and did they even have a Navigator left after that last voyage?

She rounded on the crewmembers, who quailed under her look.

'Abort this manoeuvre instantly. Now. Get word to the bridge. This ship is not going into warp.'

'Master Phrax gave the order,' said the middle officer defiantly, a rangy man with a cascade of grey hair. 'He gave the order as he was coming up here. He told us that we would break warp for Gunarvo, no matter what the consequences.'

'That's insane,' snapped Calpurnia. 'You of all people know that it's not survivable. This far in-system? With this amount of damage? How could he give the order?'

'He gave it as he came to the stateroom,' the officer said again. 'I think he knew what had happened even then.' The other two nodded agreement.

'Then you know he's not of sound mind. Abort the order. Now.'

'Varro Phrax means more than just a new master to us, ma'am,' said the grey-haired officer with a lift of his chin. 'He risked himself to fight a warp-daemon. He was our luck when we voyaged here. And now he carries a charter signed by the Emperor. We fought for him. We put our trust in him.' The other two nodded their agreement. Calpurnia stared at them for a moment, then strode back through the door and to the kneeling trader.

'Varro? Varro, listen to me. I know what you're feeling. I know what you've been feeling since you did what you did in the courtroom.' He didn't seem to notice her kneeling by his side or her hand on his shoulder. His face was hidden. The smell of blood was thick. The weeping went on and on.

'Varro, you don't have the right to take this whole ship and everyone else on it to a terrible death. They somehow don't believe it will happen, but it will. You owe a duty to the living, Varro. Listen to me!'

Then the ship rumbled with power again, a rumble that rose in pitch as the warp engines struggled to work. Calpurnia's torc buzzed and screeched and through the interference from the charging engines she could hear Odamo's voice frantically calling her name.

It was a decision that she would hate herself for for a long time, but there was nothing else she could do. She stood up.

'Emperor walk with you, then, Varro, wherever you may end up.'

And she ran.

VARRO PHRAX DID not hear the warp engines fire to their highest output, and his only reaction when one of the coils began to flicker and overload and send shudders down the length of the ship was to grip his murdered family tighter and tighter, terrified that the embrace might have to end. He wept, uncaringly, as the proximity alarms went off in response to the *Baron Mykal* passing insanely close to grapple in the saviour pod that Calpurnia had managed to reach before it blasted its way past on full engines and sped out of the danger zone. He wept, unhearing, as the main warp engines, weakened from the terrible strain of the storm, broke and overloaded. He wept, unseeing, as the hole in space opened, not sharp and bullet-precise but a great, ragged, spreading wound into which the ship slid like a reptile into a tarpit.

He kissed his wife's cold cheek as the screams began from the crew, as the Geller field crumpled and the stuff of the hull began to ripple and fray; he stroked his son's hair as the walls of the stateroom began to softly undulate as though they were curtains in a breeze. He did not see the colourless nothingness filling the *Gann-Luctis's* corridors and rooms or the death-throes of the crew as curious, malicious fingers of ether began to pick at their flesh and their minds and finally whirled them out through the disintegrating hull. He heard the whispers at the corner of his mind that got louder and louder until it was a hammering in his skull and he felt the room spin and fade around him and his own flesh teased out into threads and clouds, but he accepted it and rocked his wife and his child. Maybe they would not reach Gunarvo, but maybe he had known this ever since he had seen the faces of the crew when he came off the shuttle with Calpurnia. Maybe he had always known they would never return to Gunarvo, and so all there was to do now was stay here and rock his wife and child until it didn't matter any more.

THE BARON MYKAL sped away from the unholy death of the *Gann-Luctis* with all engines open; it was an hour before its captain felt it safe to shed velocity and start to bring the ship about. No one had any illusions about finding survivors.

Shira Calpurnia went to the bridge and stood there in silence as they passed the spot where the rift had been. After they had passed it, and as Galata loomed large in the forward windows, she left and walked down to the ship's chapel. She did not pray there, but sat in a pew before the golden aquila. She sat with her head bowed in silence, sat there for a very long time.

EPILOGUE

Nobody knows where the story started, nobody knows who is supposed to have seen the events unfold. Some versions tell of a crewman, some of a woman, one last survivor who looked out from a saviour pod and into the wound in reality as it closed. Some are stories of an astropath or a seer somewhere on Hydraphur, or even a nameless rating in an opticon deck aboard one of the ships was in pursuit. The story was rumoured to have been heard in a drinking-nook in the crowded decks of the Bescalion gate-stations, or told to a medicae team aboard the Ring, or whispered to a priest in a shrine somewhere in the Augustaeum, or screamed in desperation in an Arbites cell, or revealed in the Imperial tarot, or printed onto a thousand sheets of grubby paper and pasted onto walls or passed from hand to hand in the lightless alleys of Constanta Hive. The story came from everywhere and nowhere.

But no matter who the witness is supposed to have been, when the embellishments of the various tellers are stripped away the story remains constant. It tells that as the gash in the stars closed, leering and bleeding colours that could corrode the mind, shadowy forms closed on the doomed *Gann-Luctis* as it came apart, closing like sharks on a swimmer, wolves on a traveller, nightmares on a child's bed. They slid around and into the ship like oil flowing into cracks, as the stuff of the hull began to fray and come apart.

Some versions tell of giant talons tearing the *Gann-Luctis* to fragments, or that the edges of the rip sprouted teeth of purest darkness and macerated it like soft meat. There are versions that say that the ship's death-throes were lit by bright hell-light that seemed to come from everywhere and nowhere on the other side of that rent in space, or that the ship disappeared into depthless, mindless patterns of living dark but that images of it still, somehow made their way out, as though the sight of the ship was arriving in the mind without passing through the eyes.

Every form of the story relates that something was left behind when the rip closed and writhed and left nothing but empty starlit space, something that simply passed through the sides of the rip as they closed, or whose presence seemed to push the rip away across space as it shrank. But most of the stories tell instead of a silent howl of pain that came bellowing out of the gap in space, as though some great animal of that other world had tried to grip white-hot metal in its fingers and felt its flesh being burnt away, and that it came hurtling as though its presence in the turmoil on the other side of the rip was unbearable, as though it were poison being spat from a great gullet.

The more restrained storytellers will leave the matter there, and refuse to be drawn on what it might have been that did not follow the *Gann-Luctis* into oblivion. But there are others who insist that that nameless observer saw something drifting past the window of the pod or across the lens of the opticon. They say it was a book, a plain book, cloth-bound, turning end over end in the vacuum. Some go as far as to say that it passed close enough for the watcher's eyes to see the momentum spread the pages, and for light to spill from them, light that died as that observer looked on, as though the discharge from some powerful reaction was only just dying away, light that surrounded a tiny mark like a spot of blood on the final page.

Whether anything really escaped the destruction nobody knows. There are tales that the book flew towards Hydraphur's sun and burns there still, or that it now coasts silently through the vacuum of interplanetary space. Some say that it was caught by a mysterious ship that disappeared like a ghost, or that it flew towards Hydraphur itself and now is locked away in a dark cell beneath the Cathedral, or the Wall, or the Inquisitorial fortress in the planet's furthest land mass. There are stories among the survivors of the flotilla that say that the ghosts of Varro and Petronas Phrax roam the warp around Hydraphur and that one day they will meet and fight for their charter, tales that say that even the memory of the charter is cursed and that every living soul who voyaged with Hoyyon Phrax is doomed.

The last of the flotilla ships has been broken up now, the remnants of the crews imprisoned or dispersed. There is a small memorial garden to Ksana Phrax and her family on Gunarvo, erected by her brothers after the *Gann-Luctis* was lost. All records of the existence of Nils Petronas were erased when he became Petronas Phrax, and he is not now remembered.

The documents of the Phrax succession now lie in one of the archiving houses in a remote corner of the Wall, on a metal shelf in a rockcrete cell, waiting for a servitor to mark and store them. Maybe they will one day be stored, maybe not. Shira Calpurnia, Cynez Sanja, Essach Simova and the others might look back on the strife at Selena Secundus now and again, but there are new challenges, new concerns for all of them now, every day.

And so now the only monument to the ten-thousand-year Phrax succession is legend, the twisted, exaggerated, fanciful tales of heirs and rivals, daemons and poisoned mutants and cold puppeteers, traitors and victims, that travel from ear to ear across Hydraphur to this day. The line of Phrax is gone; this alone is their legacy.

LEGACY

A DOSSIER

A Homily on the Dignity of Obedience

Given by Kostazin Baszle, Eparch of Hydraphur, to a private congregation at the palace of the Monocrat of Hydraphur, on the third eve of Candlemas.

There's a word I'd like to talk to you about this evening. A word and an idea. *Subactima.*

Ah, and I can see some of you nodding. It's a simple concept, isn't it? Such a fundamental part of our spiritual education. Are there any of us who don't know what it means? Of course not. It's a part of the *Principia Magna.* No one deserves [1] full participation in the Imperial congregation if they haven't understood it and shown they can master it.

But even now I'm falling short. Ordinary words must always fall short of the concepts our faith must educate us in, because those concepts come from an immortal, a divine source. But we are charged with preserving and handing down what He on Earth has given us, and our words are tools to do that. So, like D'Oroq pelting the heretics with the rubble of his own altar, let's make use of the tools we have.

We'll better understand the word if we understand that in the traditional High Gothic it is two words: *Subacta Anima.* It refers to a human spirit, with all those things we recognise from our parables, our histories, the lives of our saints and heroes and ourselves: pride, faith, will, ambition, bravery; we all know the qualities. And it refers to a human spirit in its rightful place, quelled and placed in subordination. I've seen plenty of scripture and teachings using exactly those terms, and stronger ones. Some priests I trained with before my days on the pilgrim roads used to talk about brokenness of spirit. They said the natural inclination of our spirits have to be actually destroyed, violently *destroyed*, before we can take our place in the human fold. [2]

I didn't feel that those priests had the right understanding. I didn't then and I don't now. It treats our spirit and all its qualities as something that has to be smashed in order for something else to work, like an augmetist having to knock out a stubborn knob of bone. It denies that the essence of humanity is anything but an obstacle. It reduces the act of devoting ourselves to our Emperor to an act of spiritual brutality, and denies the act of worship of its nobility and beauty, and if there is one thing that bringing ourselves into harmony with our divinity should be, it is beautiful.

How can we be happy if we cannot serve our lord with our whole heart? You've had that question asked in mass, and in devotional classes. And *Every servant has their place, no matter how humble. To excel in it is their greatest glory and their master's satisfaction their greatest reward.* [3] How many times have we all said that in catechism? Too many times to remember? And I'll have recited it more often than you, I'll be bound! *[laughs]*

But think about what I said. Think, really think about this wonderful concept behind the word of *subactima*. Think about that first recitation. So many people think of it as a way to enforce loyalty, but look at the question: it's its own answer, it's talking about how we can be happy. The catechism talks about glory - glory! – to be had in finding the place that has been allotted for us in the great army of humanity that marches in step behind the banner of Earth. When you find that place, it is yours and no other's. In that place no marching feet but yours will properly fit the marching cadence. That place in the cohort is where the Emperor will look, wanting to see your face, knowing it should be there. Your face. No other. Once you know your position and labour it in, then of all the men and women who have ever been born and all the women and men who will ever be born, out of all of them, you are the one the Emperor will want to see when he looks down from the Throne. No other human being in all the past and future of the Imperium can have that particular bond with the Emperor except for you.

Isn't that a beautiful thing? A grand thing? Glorious? To achieve subactima is not about breaking your spirit, and it's not about sullen, defeated acquiescence. True subactima is seeing the dignity in your servitude, and the beauty in your obedience. It's about choosing to have your feet match the marching rhythm of all humanity's, and choosing to keep your gaze upward to where the aquila flies instead of down in the shadows below your feet where the damned rot alive and beg to burn.

I'm not going to say much more on this now, but it's something I'd like you to meditate further on as we come up to Candlemas and our piety oaths for the new year. We'll be finishing the service today with a prayer for clarity [4] and in your evening devotions tonight you may wish to pray the Emperor for a fuller understanding of subactima and the strength to work toward it.

I will certainly pray for that understanding and that strength. They are two weapons we must all possess in our lifelong fight against the shadows that pluck at our heels, whether our allotted place is one that we hold from birth to death *[nods at the Monocrat]* or one of many that the Emperor has planned for us through our lives. Insolence, sullenness, rebelliousness, disobedience, schism, outright heresy - these are the signs we must watch for in ourselves for our imperfect grasp of subactima. [5] And they are the signs we must be vigilant for in those around us, who, if they can't be strengthened in their faith, must be chastised into better behaviour, and who if they cannot be made better through chastisement, must be removed or destroyed.

Do not let rank or pomp blind you to the behaviour of the human spirit behind them. Correct subactima comes not from our allotted place, high or low, but in how we relate to it. A pilgrim walking in the dust at the back of a ceremonial procession with her only shawl and icon clasped to her may show finer subactima than a Rector of the Fleet who poses proudly in front of the admiral's chapel and dreams only of swaggering on to a finer ship and a richer altar. [6]

Now form yourselves to your places, please, and we shall sing our next psalm.

* * *

Interrogator Perelmann's notes
to Inquisitor Zhow

[1] You'll notice the language is delicately specific here. Baszle follows the tougher Opheliate traditions that explicitly refuse congregation to anyone who hasn't passed through formal teachings on each of the *Principia*. He can't come out and be quite that bald about it here because the southern Segmentum doctrines haven't carried as far as Hydraphur, so coming out and saying congregation is impossible risks alienating too many people he needs as supporters. Case in point – the Monocrat's court, which is in my view why he's going softer on it, but trying to seed the idea that anyone who hasn't been schooled in his traditions should be. Religious tutors at the Monocrat's court would be a significant influence-multiplier for the Cathedral at the expense of the Flag.

[2] I've commissioned searches from some of our colleagues in the southern Segmentum and they tell me that if there are indeed any of the Ecclesiarchy who express the sentiments Baszle describes here, they don't represent a school of thought large or organised enough to register on our main dossiers. (And this is after a cross-check on the main enclaves Baszle had con-

tact with in the phase of his career referred to above.) My own thoughts are that either this came up in conversation with one or two colleagues once and he's exaggerating to emphasise the extent of his disagreement, or that he's deliberately using a false position for the same reason, and attributing it to a fictional clique of priests for rhetorical purposes.

[3] He's using an older, core-sector translation from the antique High Gothic here, but I've checked and it doesn't digress from the versions current here in any harmful way. I can make versions of all these texts available if you want to check.

[4] Transcript not included, it was 89 from the *Book of Recitations,* word for word. Baszle has backed right off on trying to introduce the Gathalamor-version prayer books after the Chamber of Exegetors got its back up and he couldn't be sure Theoctista would support him. I'm expecting him to start manoeuvres on this again in time for next year's Mass of Balronas.

[5] It's this sentence that's the meat of this passage, even if the threats that follow it up might be more eye-catching. This is where he makes the firm link between the sort of backtalk the flag-curates have been engaging in with unholiness and unworthiness. You were asking Shengo and me why we didn't think he'd made a direct move against the Fleet's Ecclesiarchal clique yet, and I submit this as some of the evidence of why. He can't take on a power base as entrenched as the Navy's priesthood when he's so newly arrived to Hydraphur, so he's getting ready to outflank them. He's arranging it so that power bloc after power bloc in the system will start to see the way they're carrying on as a liability. And he's careful to do it privately, in high-level closed services like this one. I predict we'll get reports of many more homilies like this over the next year, year and a half or so.

[6] This is as open as Baszle has got yet about walling off the flag-curates in the way I described above. He's trying to ensure that the Hydraphur court see things a very definite way next time there's a conflict between the Cathedral and the Fleet. Also, to use his own words, he's seeding the idea that religious worthiness deserves equal consideration with temporal authority, looking at his choice of a humble pilgrim as a contrasting image. Clever, too, since it's an image we're all so familiar with, and it feeds into the way he's thrown so many resources into building up his own Cathedral as a centre of pilgrimage, bringing him clout within the Ministorum and

perhaps even the civil fleet that lets him outflank the curates from yet another angle.

As per your initial brief to me I do have one concern here, which I intend to discuss with you in person upon your return. I want to bring that contrast in the last main passage to your attention again, with its none-too-subtle suggestion that those in authority might wield it imperfectly and thus be open to question. I don't know if the Eparch has been picking up ideas off this new arbitor senioris, who I understand is from Ultramar where they have some odd ideas about these things, but it's my contention that a highly-placed official of the Adeptus Ministorum who crafts a careful sermon which leaves open the idea that Imperial authority might in some cases be doubted or questioned, bears continued scrutiny and attention. Even commending the engagement of intellect rather than the simple obedience of the body goes against any number of Imperial teachings I can quote. I find it hard to reconcile the thinking behind the latter parts of this homily with the ethos of obedience without stint, question or doubt, which it is the duty of the Adeptus to enforce.

That said, I also suggest that conserving this angle of accusation, for when there looks to be real damage or for when it's otherwise useful to us, is the best course of action here. I'm aware of current thought on local political realignments and there's merit to the argument that the Cathedral's current disposition and agenda are beneficial on a broader scale.

Safe landings, inquisitor, and I shall speak with you again once you are recovered from your journey.

PERELMANN

Morning Devotional Roster for the Chapel of the Martyrs of Delhaad in the Cathedral of the Emperor Ascendant, Bosporian Hive, Hydraphur

Name: Arafino Moyant

Offences: Verbal impiety in the second degree, two offences. Blasphemy in the venial, one offence.

Attended for penance: Yes. *Verified by:* Var Hemry, Deacon.

Details: Supplicant was overheard by two lay confessors to make a sound of pleased amusement upon observing Curate Hindall stumble upon the hem of his robes while walking in procession around the chapel during a morning prayer for the Fourth Seasonal Devotion. He was then witnessed by eleven other worshippers speaking in an impiously jocular manner after the culmination of the prayer, while still within the space of the chapel. Upon being chided for his impieties after leaving the chapel the supplicant was heard to reply 'Does the Saint need you to tell on me for him, then?'

Penance: Supplicant to forfeit three hours of work-shift to walk not more than three, or less than one, pace behind Curate Sloek, fanning him with a feather-fan supplied by the chapel; said fan to have a barbed and abrasive haft to chasten the flesh of supplicant's hands. Wages from said three hours of work-shift to be presented to Cathedral coffers.

* * *

Name: Kaph Tymra

Offences: Petty Simony in the second degree, one offence; impious gluttony in the first degree, one offence.

Attended for penance: Yes. *Verified by:* Akesh Buolon, Assistant Deacon.

Details: Supplicant joined the line to purchase sanctified ashes for the prayer fast on the eve of the Halonic Blessing. Supplicant left the line to attend the latrines, pleading overindulgence at the preceding day's Gifting Feast at the Chapel of Ways at the hive foot. (Verified by chiarograph from Demi-curate Oztanev at time of supplicant's accostal.) Upon returning supplicant was overheard to offer the on-sale of half of her ration of ashes in exchange for her former place in line.

Penance: Supplicant to purge and fast for thirty-six hours before attendance. Supplicant to purchase and ritually burn an illuminated inscription of the Abridged

Prayer of Contrition, ashes from said burning to be retained by the Chapel for blessing and ritual use. Supplicant to purchase a second inscription for prominent display in her dormitory cubicle; this to be verified by unannounced home inspection (Deacon Hemry to randomly determine a date for this within the next two months).

* * *

Name: Adro Corio Yelm

Offences: Culpable spiritual weakness in the fourth degree, one offence. Conduct demeaning to the congregation in the third degree, one offence. Conduct demeaning to the congregation in the fifth degree, one offence.

Attended for penance: Yes. *Verified by:* Akesh Buolon, Assistant Deacon.

Details: Supplicant was witnessed indicating his readiness to allow improper access to the queue for sanctified ashes for the prayer fast on the eve of the Halonic Blessing in exchange for half of a ration of said ashes. Supplicant responded to chastisement from witnesses with demeaning language and began a physical affray against attempts to physically restrain him.

Penance: Supplicant to suffer three strikes of a No. 6 scourge across each set of knuckles, giving thanks in the name of the Emperor with each stroke to the satisfaction of the administering cleric. Supplicant then to perform two Abasing Ascents at the steps to the Chapel, knuckles downward instead of the usual palms, after which he is to spend not less than one hour cleaning the Chapel's stock of scourges, this work to be inspected by the duty curate.

* * *

Name: Vinter Hool

Offences: Blasphemy in the venial, one offence. Wanton irreverence in the fourth degree, one offence.

Attended for penance. Yes. *Verified by:* Chozier Pallom, Chapel demi-rector.

Details: Supplicant had joined a street gathering to observe the parading of the three primary icons of Ushtaf Beatus along the Upper Verdian Road. Supplicant was heard to pass wind as the icon of the Beatus's face passed by; reports were made by congregation members grouped around him and by two junior clerics of the procession itself. Subsequent report was made by Sister Niir of the Sacred Rose, who was stationed atop an Order Rhino at the rear of the parade holding a temple banner and who declared that the supplicant was audible over the parade cymbals and the Rhino engine and treads. Note from same report: supplicant approached the parade without prompting, declared his guilt and begged absolution on the spot.

Penance: Supplicant to fast for one day and ten hours before reporting for penance. Supplicant to have his head ritually shorn while kneeling with his left shoulder toward the Cathedral. Supplicant to purchase two standard measures of vexilbloom incense (the yellow variety is confirmed acceptable by Curate Steeg) and proceed around the Chapel, including all aisles and side cloisters and between the pews, reciting the appropriate contrition prayers from that day's Book of Hours as selected by the duty deacon. Penance to proceed until the incense has been consumed.

* * *

Name: Reave Laesta

Offences: Conduct demeaning to the congregation in the fifth degree, one offence.

Attended for penance: No. *Verified by:* Akesh Buolon, Assistant Deacon.

Details: Supplicant was waiting in line to purchase sanctified ashes for the prayer fast on the eve of the Halonic Blessing. Supplicant claims to have observed fellow congregants preparing to conduct an act of petty simony in interference with the orderly conduct of congregational affairs. Supplicant attempted to physically halt the transaction and entered into a scuffle in the Chapel queue when the other congregants refused his pleas to halt their activities.

Penance: Initial penance: Supplicant to perform three full abasements in the Sabinite side-chapel, followed by one hour of sweeping and general tidying duties in the chapel and vestry. Penance suspended following review by Curate Steeg, given supplicant's zeal in maintaining order and proper pious conduct in the congregation. Supplicant to report to the preacher-in-residence at his scribing-house at the next three prayer shifts to confirm continued good behaviour – sentence to be unsuspended if any concerns are reported. (*Action item:* Asst. Deacon Buolon to confirm name of preacher and arrange surveillance of supplicant.)

* * *

Name: Hlenn Feyneck

Offences: Conduct demeaning to the congregation in the sixth degree, one offence. Failure to report impious thoughts in the third degree, one offence. Failure to report impious actions in the second degree, one offence. Incitement to spiritual weakness in the second degree, one offence. Incitement to impiety in the fifth degree, one offence.

Attended for penance: Yes. *Verified by:* Hestion Liu, Deacon Punitor, Avenue Solar anchor-cells.

Details: Supplicant was observed near the scene of a physical altercation in the line to purchase sanctified ashes for the prayer fast on the eve of the Halonic Blessing.

Supplicant was observed by three congregants and a Chapel lay marshal to cease going about his business of sweeping the lower Chapel steps and instead to attend upon the scuffling. Supplicant was observed to shake his broom in the air and make at least three separate punching motions while audibly whooping and laughing. When questioned by Chapel staff, supplicant admitted seeing the altercation in line but omitted his own behaviour from his account until two congregants from the queue called out descriptions of his actions.

Penance: Supplicant is currently restrained in a declaration cage on the Avenue Solar. Contrition has been stipulated by Deacon-Punitor Liu as two renderings of the Sixth Psalm of Ashes for each offence noted above. Supplicant will be released as per due process for the declaration cages and bring written confirmation of the completion of penance for countersigning by the duty curate at the Chapel.

Evidence for His touch on founding meetings on Hydraphur

Presence on Hydraphur sites? Movements

NO evidence that He set foot on Hydraphur itself. Assertions to contrary in Halum and Klah seem to be based on speculation based on records from early orbital fort constructions. Long gaps, lots of projection. Conclusion may be open? Definite records of His landings and movements at Lembu and Tordisch, no equivalent for H.

~~References w/in extant documents need checking for geog. references – edict of Galata? Further stations?~~ Confirmed. No tangential references either. Phrax, Lhunbond and Kerstoff-Sceis trade charters all illustrate much foundation-level activity in the system over at least half a year, sidereal.

Reprod. Ministorum manuscripts in the D. coll'n show claims of Cathedral founding at same time as planetary succession/administratum foundation. Query with ST! Only claim is w/in Min. documents themselves; no corroboration in other edicts in that period, no references. Materiel tallies actually clash, 2 references to Cathedral site as 'compliance control hq'; references in MS K15-LL to coordinating in 'arcology planning directorate'.

(Terminology check on 'Arcology'.) <————-Got it, early-Imperial term for hive.

Need to verify Ministorum presence dates as from M31? After? Outer religious buildings foundation dates seem to coincide with some period of hostility – temple construction coincides to the month with records of fortification construction and building repair from battle damage. Cross-check with Munitorum archives when/if available at C.

Check on firm dates for foundation and crosscheck with later archives.

New angle: backcheck from later records. Dates get a lot firmer once actual divisions are formalised. Administratum and governorship succession. Actual term 'Arbites' postdates that considerably – arm of administratum? Standardised across multiple locations, correspondence from founding Judges confirms. Imposed from without as a system.

Speech by W and M, references to maintaining order and re-founding (?) Imperial institutions. Context of fragment indicates this was outside of Hyd. Crusade-era? After?

Crusade records confirm Hyd. came into compliance voluntarily; already had shipyards and traffic with nearby systems; Hydraphur's loyalty affirmations copied by other systems. No military action recorded in Imperial foundations at Hyd, at least what records are left. Became military hub for wars of compliance further out; thus shipping nucleus, Rogue Trader warrants.

Documents seem to separate with records of violence just after founding and then much later. Continuity of records gone, several untranslatable. One long period of warfare at Hyd. borders with gap in middle of records, or two conflicts? Speak with Mst Arc.

Internal data requisitions: form №101-1015 ARRQ. Chit for cross-org reqs №EXTD-16-16; personal consult with Praetor at Wall.

Definite records of formal Arbites organisation by second conflict; disjointed structures with early actions. Some separatist trials... attrib. Administratum? Haekulum incident. Surviving court records are third-hand accounts; only confirmed date a hundred years after fact. References to Imperial Judges may have been inserted here; wording style seems to change in these paras. Other docs from equivalent period refer to Administratum tribunals given militant staff & powers...?

Need to request Seg. Solar records; some of W's correspondence suggests this as Segmentum Solar practice imported.

~~*New correspondence file from W with info on structural dating, will*~~

Org References

Planned dedication ceremony for grav-station on the Ring. References to founding & building, some sort of universal Imperial directorate? MS refers to transitions/early days but Arbites cursi & Administratum/Munitorum bureaux already defined by that date, confirmed in 2nd & 4th collections. What???

Conjecture: Imperial organisation laid down in outline by Him but only half-formed when tested by protracted war, at least one, two, generations apart? Immediate survival pressure, design & organisation work unable to continue to broader plan, day-to-day threats and exigencies.

So much potential here!

Appointment: end of week 1745, sub-archivist's chambers. 1 day to collate, draft and prepare 1 day, 1 hour's verbal and be prepared for questions.

Working request: 6 hours time on L8 data-loom and services of 1 bonded savant. Check against schedules.

Exciting!

The above text formed the body of a handwritten and unsigned manuscript found in the carrel stacks at the Trylan Tor facility in Hydraphur's Long Archipelago, to all appearances the notes of someone studying the oldest records available in the Tor archives. The author is unknown. After being found and reported the manuscript was impounded by archive staff and is believed to have been sequestered for data-matching and Verispex work.

BLIND

'Only in your deepest self is the truth of what you can be, and, without a doubt, that truth is terrible to bear.'

– Adeptus Astronomica, *The Book of the Astronomican*

astropath cloisters: the Bastion's watch-hall. In that great, angled space, the voices of the choir were birthed into the air as actual sounds: a complex layer of notes and cries from vox-speakers. Harp strings and metal plates engraved with sensitive wards, tuned to translate the intricate psychic harmonics, fed into them. The shift in the choir's song arrived in the ears of the watch-hall attendants as a rapid string of chimes. They heard a wave of trills and clashing notes before the long notes settled into their new melody.

A skilled watchmaster could read the sounds of the Tower as skilfully as they read the psychic signs, and Watchmaster Chevenne was skilled indeed. He picked up the change in the music, and understood it immediately for what it was. He picked out the nuances that showed him Cantor Angazi's touches on the choir and Astropath Qwahl's clear, disciplined voice reaching out into the warp. Satisfied that he knew all the important details of what was going on in the Firewatch Eyrie, Chevenne twitched his psychic attention away from the sounds and let it drift. As he passed to each new zone of the hall, his mind registered which region of the Tower it represented. He made sure that nothing was wrong, nothing was tainted, that no power was being overused, and no mind overloaded. Unstable psykers who might trigger one another were kept apart by quick orders to their attendants. Minds that were palpably weakening were directed into the cloisters to be meshed to a choir, to cover them with power while they recovered.

The Bastion's watchmaster, hanging in his bronze cage in the centre of the watch-hall, was the constant attendant of the Bastion's pulse. He made sure that the psychic flows never built up here, petered out there, or let a taint spread over there.

Chevenne moved with his hearing and psychic sense over the soft, distinctive tones of Astropath Laris, moving towards the base of the Green Eyrie. He moved over Senior Astropath Thujik's mind as his concordiast helped him through mental exercises to restore tranquillity after his trance in the Eyrie of Bones. Then he found the tightly controlled little psychic sun of Master Otranto himself, walking boldly, unattended but for a vitifer, down the Great Concourse and out beyond the astropath cloisters of the central keep. Chevenne let his mind rest on the Master's for a moment until he heard the old man's querulous psychic voice demanding what he wanted. With the mental equivalent of a shrug and a smile, Chevenne moved on.

* * *

Qwahl reaches out with the net of his mind, sensing the flavour of the message, delicately feeling its contours. He recognises the touch of its sender, Skarant. Astropath Skarant in his colonnaded cell in the high pagoda of Gantia. Skarant whose sendings still carry the scent of conifer-flowers.

Qwahl tightens the skeins of the net, turns the cobweb filaments to something harder, and starts to reel in the message. The great weight, the message, spiky with ciphering and warding, roils up through Qwahl's thoughts like a deadly mine floating up into the shallows of the ocean. It strains the embrace of his mind, swamps it with pain, but will and more still streams in...

DERNESK LEANED OVER Qwahl's body. The astropath's face was contorting and his throat was working as if he was getting ready to scream, or vomit. Dernesk's training kept his own face and mind impassive, even when green-yellow arcs of energy started playing between the cables on Qwahl's skull.

'It's coming,' he said aloud. 'Something big is coming through. Warn the cantor. This is going to hit hard.'

The attendants nodded, and the word went back down the tower. Guaphon moved his control from one bank of psy-instruments to another, keeping them tuned. Angazi led the choir in a change of song, loosening the mesh of minds so that it was no longer a bullet, a psychic pile-driver pushing Qwahl onward. They wove a net, a cloak, surrounding him and warming him, helping to take the strain of the message that had just been sucked into his consciousness, lighting the way back down out of the warp into his body once again.

The message finally reeled in and contained, Qwahl releases his grip and lets his mind fly loose, and pull back.

'HE'S GOT IT,' Dernesk said, but there was no need. The choir was already doing its job, and Guaphon had reported the change in the astropath's life-signs. One of the attendants bent over a particular series of cables, whispering blessings. He was conscious of how the metal was heating, watching the amulet runes dangling from the plugs as they flashed green-ochre-green. The system was ready.

* * *

Qwahl is struggling, reeling backwards. Groping frantically with feather-tendrils at the back of his consciousness, he fights down the panic that wells up in the shadows of his mind. He gropes blindly for his choir, for Angazi. Fleeing back towards his own body, he is dropping into the beautiful cold sanity of the materium. He drops like an overloaded lander towards a planet, flaming down towards his own body. His mind is bulging, smoking, freighted with strange cargo, red veins of information pulsing in the black of his mind that he keeps safe within his soul-bound glow. He has to get it out. He has to push it out. He can feel his soul starting to bleed.

A THIN FILM of blood appeared over Qwahl's lips. With practiced economy of motion, Dernesk crushed a phial of essence, put a taper to it, and dropped the mess into a shallow porcelain dish. He knew that Qwahl responded to essence of epima-oil. He held the dish under the astropath's face, and rested his other hand on the man's brow. The skin flashed hot and cold to his touch, and he began to massage his forehead, chanting a single low note over and over. The attendant behind the chair made a satisfied noise as all the data-runes flickered into the green. The vitifer stood immobile, ready to kill.

Qwahl is being dragged by the choir-song. He is close enough to start picking up traces from his own senses: the scent of epima-oil, a touch on his forehead, a voice humming. He lets go, and plummets.

THE ASTROPATH'S MIND slammed back into his body like a fist into an open palm. The shock of the arrival sent him bucking against the restraints, howling with pain, at the pressure on his distended mind. Dernesk bent over him, shouting out phrases keyed to the deep hypnosis triggers that Qwahl had designed for himself. He tried to help the astropath force his mental defences down on the burning and the strain. Alerted by the sound, the archive-servitor started twitching its pen in readiness. Witchfire was gusting along the eyrie walls in odd patterns that were broken and sucked away by the earths and wards.

Qwahl's mouth was working incessantly now, random syllables starting to spit through the air. The syllables became words, endless strings of words. Dernesk recognised the general form and cadence. It was what they had been expecting – an Imperial message, coded to protect the data. The archive-servitor's pen sprang into life, scribbling and scratching over spooling loops of scrip.

Dernesk bent and listened. He knew Qwahl's voice could slur, the man's facial nerves had been steadily deteriorating since his Binding and his lips didn't move as dextrously as they once had.

Dernesk realised he was sweating. Once they had left the eyrie, it would take hours to get Qwahl's mind relaxed to the point where he'd be able to rest for his next trance. He sighed and mopped his brow.

As the information spewed out, the astropath's struggles eased, and his cries lessened. Something like peace came over his features. His speech was more fluid now, less tortured. Dernesk knew Qwahl, knew how the man thought and associated. He began to whisper trigger-phrases again, fragments of rhyme or scripture or song he knew Qwahl would respond to, his attention dancing between soothing the astropath's mind and manipulating it, gratified when he heard the responding thought-motifs and speech patterns begin to shape Qwahl's talk.

The scrip recordings pouring away from the archive-servitor were being fed down the eyrie's data-sluices, down into the keep, into the maws of the logic mills and data-looms of the tech-shrine where the fortress's cogitators had once turned auspexes out into interstellar space and plotted trajectories and firing grids.

The thick braid of code lit up a bank of chattering cogitators under the watchful eyes of enginseers deputed to the Encryptors' hall. They spooled out under the machine-spirits' precise manipulation, into shipping reports, tithing statistics, demographic data, financial movements, crimes and trials, baptisms, Administratum memoranda. Ream after ream of numbers chronicled the pulse and governance of Gantia for the past month in minute detail. By the end of the month, the Encryptors would have broken down the data to be transmitted to the Administratum at Hydraphur, by bursts small enough to be taken in the astropath's stride. Some of the data would be transmitted on sublight data frequencies, or coded into data-arks. Some would be transcribed onto printouts in the neighbouring Scriptorium and carried in-system by a dromon. To break that mass of data down into transmittable parts would take a week. To transport it from Gantia to Hydraphur on paper would have needed a library lugged in the belly of a transport cruiser.

Other data-skeins had detached from the mass and come in on their own, pulsing angrily with secure-keys and warning codes.

Some were classified Administratum, some Arbites, and some Ministorum. The occasional low-level Battlefleet communiqué was hived off to the Navy offices. There was one strand of note: an Inquisition report bound up in venomous coils of encryption forged to trap and break any unschooled mind that tried to look too closely at them. It was pushed out of Qwahl's mind first, to save his sanity, and carried to the Bastion's autists with hushed respect. The Bastion communed with an Inquisitorial astropath at Hydraphur every twelve hours – now they would have something to give him, and good riddance to it.

High above in the eyrie, Qwahl hovered on the brink of consciousness, dimly aware of the movements and voice of his concordiast, and of the delicious scent of epima-oil. The hypnotic commands had begun the work of gathering up his energies, and his scorched mind was slowly collecting together again. Qwahl was largely beyond coherent thought and would be for hours, but one fragment did bob to the surface of his mind. He vocalised it as slurred words.

'What,' he asked aloud, 'is the Master fighting over?'

No one listened to him. Many astropaths babbled, coming out of their trances. It wasn't usually anything to worry about.

Once, these cloisters had carried munition-carts from the armoured magazines to the weapon batteries, but they are corridors now. The metal floors and steps have been overlaid with layers of soft hessian and synthetic fleeces, to muffle the distracting clang of boots. The armatures for the lumen arrays are high on the inward-curving walls so that their chilly metal will not startle fingertips that brush along the rockcrete of the walls. The lumens are far-spaced and their light is dim – for most who pass this way, sight is far from the most important sense. The intricate veins and whorls carved into the passage sides are polished to a glow by the brushing of eleven centuries of fingertips.

Astropath Kappema's fingertips followed the wall as he shuffled slowly up the passage. He barely needed to touch the wall any more, and as the strain of his duty sapped his body, and his fingers became sensitive, he was more and more thankful for that. He moved with soft, easy steps, slippered feet guiding him up the slope from memory, without the need for sight. Two hundred and eight paces until the turn-off to the stairs that led to the second choir-galleys. Then the slow bend to the right, and another hundred and eighteen paces before the screw-stair up to the maze of access ways leading to the base of his eyrie.

He was barely conscious of the movement of his feet, and the glow of the lumens that fell on his sunken, sightless eyes. The wall that passed his fingertips was alive in his inner senses: he felt the swoops and angles of its carvings as if the air around him had nerves of its own.

Overlaid with the physical layer were the traces and trails of his brothers and sisters, his fellow blind ones passing this way from the cells and chapels of the Curtain and the lower keep, up to the meditation halls, fasting-beds and choir-galleys. Those traces were always there, permeating every part of the Tower where the psykers went, and Kappema, like all the rest, drew comfort from the presence of his companions.

Today, however, he could feel the unease. Thirty-four paces up the passage, where the lines on the wall danced through a series of tight spirals, he passed a scrap of memory left by Senior Astropath Sacredsteel, a brief sound of the old woman's papery voice in his psyker's non-ear, and a sharp stab of resentment left in the air. Sacredsteel had been brooding on the envoy, the man from what she thought of as the Meatsack Masters, the so-called Polarists. This Master Lohjen was corralled up in his dromon at the Tertiary Dock, not deigning to come aboard the station. Kappema felt Sacredsteel's half-day-old outburst of cursing start to form on his own lips. Then he passed the place where the print was strongest, and a reflexive calming exercise helped the outburst slip out of his mind.

With that gone, Kappema was able to focus on a long stream of thought-trail that had the strange dancing cadence of Mehlio's thoughts. Mehlio's focus was good and her discipline strong, and it was unusual for her to leave such a profound sense of herself where she passed. There was apprehension here – Mehlio was unnerved by the envoy where Sacredsteel was angry – but there were tints of disorientation and an almost excited anticipation. Mehlio had been around for long enough to remember Torma Ylante, and she was glad that Ylante was coming back.

Kappema managed a smile, before he had to compose himself and protect his thoughts. A file of choristers was coming down the passage the other way, too lost in the burnt-out mental stink of their own exhaustion to pay him any attention. He felt the puffs and billows of their minds as their handlers yanked on their restraints to urge the chain gang against the far wall. Even then, the passage was so narrow that their shoulders brushed, and Kappema got a quick taste of the mind that they had helped up into the warp scant hours ago. It was a young mind, male, permeated with oddly patterned traces from an unfamiliar psychic choir – an old posting? A message, unciphered, blazed out into the immaterium towards the waiting minds at Darrod and Enla III, a message so simple that fragments of it were still lodged in the choristers' minds: *...arrived, all here... ready begin... functional...*

Kappema moved on up the corridor, his nervousness now entirely his own: bad omens, bad omens. The sloppiness of whoever had allowed the choristers to come down from their post with a message still circling their minds was a small thing, but it added to his unease. The envoy, the infatuation with the new dead-minded Polarist drones, Torma Ylante coming back to the Tower and causing who knew what waves, right down to the little things like this: bad omens.

Was there worse to come? Kappema thought there might be. For some reason, there was a new concept-note coming into his mind, radiating in from somewhere: a tinge of violence? It was a thought-echo of Master Otranto, the image of a judge in black and crimson. It flicked into his mind and was gone. Troubled, Kappema bowed his head and walked on.

Unconsciously, he began counting his paces for the next part of his ascent. Behind him, the soles of his boots padded and muffled so as not to distract the astropath, came his vitifer. His heavy helm and mesh visor hid the scars on his shaven head, mind conditioned out of everything but patience and watchfulness. He shuffled placidly, two paces behind Kappema, a short-barrelled hellpistol in his hand, ready on a moment's warning to take the astropath's life.

THE ENGINARIUM LAY in the heart of the keep, a fortified sanctum in the middle of the fortress. It was a sealed shrine to the Machine-God built around the blazing plasma coils of the station's reactors. Magos Channery of the Adeptus Mechanicus was governing the Enginarium as she had for sixty-seven years.

And as she had done for sixty-seven years, the magos was walking, making an endless pilgrimage around the walkway that led around the equator of the spherical reactor housing. She had long ago slaved her augmetic legs to the walk around and around it. And while her body walked, her mind talked.

Sprouting from the magos's back were twin armatures of black iron, fashioned to resemble a seraph's wings and encrusted with auspexes and voxponders, transmitters linking her in permanent communion with every machine-spirit in her Enginarium. She had sensed the sudden cascade of data down the cables from Qwahl's transmission, as she had sensed the waves of power flooding out of the reactor core and the operation of the psyk-engines installed in the eyrie towers. She was as blind as any astropath, and hadn't used her more elementary senses in decades.

This was something odd, something curious: a ripple of energy through the sinks and wards designed to funnel away any build-up of energy. It was subtle, so subtle, and even as it crossed her senses, it seemed to drop away.

Channery didn't pause in her plodding gait around the walkway. She routed the data from her observations through a savant-servitor and into her records, set a subroutine of her own mind to working to see if it fitted a pattern, and directed her mind elsewhere.

IN THE WATCH-HALL, Chevenne's mind was flickering back and forth through drifts of sound where he hadn't expected to hear any. The notes suggested Master Otranto's mind, but where was it? Ripples were coming through in odd places, thought-notes tinged with fear and rancour, moving into the cloisters, too quick and subtle to get a grip on.

Chevenne was less sanguine about the matter than Channery was. He couldn't locate it, but he didn't dismiss it. He sounded a warning chime of both sounds and mind-waves, and sent a messenger scurrying to Master Warden on post behind his cage.

THE OLD FORTRESS from which the Bastion Psykana had been built had had balconies and panopticon towers and vantage points worked into every level of the design. Command and vantage points should there ever be a mutiny or a boarding, certainly, but even when there was no threat it was still fitting that the high personnel of the fortress, its officers, commissars and preachers, should have strategic high points. They could look out over their command, and could be seen by their subordinates. Like any Imperial building, the structure of the fortress was aimed to make the ideas of authority and hierarchy solid, visual and palpable.

It was wasted on its current inhabitants, whose eyes had looked on the raw glory of Him on Earth and were now darkened forever. So, as the new Bastion was made from the husk of the old fortress, new vantage points were made. Now they were in strange places: in the corners of provision cellars, niches carved out of walls, or platforms swung awkwardly from the walls of the high chambers. They were in places chosen to provide a view for minds, not for eyes.

Teeker Renz stood outside one of those niches, a 'viewing' hole gracelessly chopped into the wall of the Grand Concourse, the high-vaulted walk that ran right through the heart of the keep. He stood and stared. It had been ten minutes since Master Otranto had gone marching down the Concourse. He should have been back by now. This was where he was going to have his meeting with the Ylante woman. Renz knew that, he had ordered the message sent to her himself, although he had protested. He knew the distance Ylante had to walk to get here and knew the route she was coming by. Otranto should have been able to walk there, meet her and come back here. Come back here so that Renz could talk to them both. It would be a terrible meeting, but Renz was determined not to back down.

When they met... Renz stared away down the Concourse again. Why had the old man wheeled and marched off so suddenly?

He started at a movement on the Concourse, but it wasn't the Master. Two uniforms, Battlefleet green and concordiast cream, were walking towards him. His two most trusted associates, Kyto and Dechene.

'Where's Otranto?' he snapped at them. 'He went off in that direction to get this woman of his. Where's he got to?' The tension was getting to him: he was starting to gabble. 'What's she said to him, or done? What's happened?'

Dechene and Kyto looked at one another, and then back at Renz, who began to go pale. Dechene spread his hands and started to say something. Then they heard the warning-bells start to sound in the keep behind them.

* * *

ABOARD THE LOCKED dromon, docked under heavy guard at one of the Curtain's corners, Envoy Lohjen heard the sound of the bells issuing from a silver gargoyle mounted over the document desk in his office aboard the ship. Lohjen's vox-thief bugs, the ones he'd had carefully planted throughout the Bastion, were reporting the sounds.

He didn't panic and he didn't rush. He leaned over the lectern he was working on and keyed a sequence into a caller-amulet. After a moment, the panel began to light up again with wordless confirmation signals as his people moved to their stations at the docking tower, the hangar beneath it, and in the Long Dock Road, the tunnel that circled the entire perimeter of the Curtain and joined the docks together.

As the bells continued to ring, and the first reports from his spies joined the vox-thief recordings, Lohjen got up from his writing desk and started checking the weapons hidden under his loose, rich envoy's robe. If those messages meant what he thought they meant, he'd better be ready for things to go bad, fast.

THE RIPPLES SPREAD and grew stronger. They flowed up to the eyries, and many astropaths who were in communication with the Tower at that moment were bombarded with inexplicable images of anger, pain, flight, black and crimson, and waves of panic. They flowed into the watch-hall and surrounded Chevenne with loud discord from his chimes and frantic, unnerving ghosts from his psyk-senses. They swirled and washed around the choirs and the junior astropaths, and frightened them into fits and spasms – four fell to the guns of their vitifers by the end of the day, their precarious minds caught at exactly the wrong time and unable to recover enough to be proof against the warp.

They found their way into the senior astropaths, who fended them off with will and skill, and even into the minds of the blunts. For months afterwards, there would be non-psykers on the station who'd be haunted by dreams of frantic chasing, wild-eyed violence and pain.

Chevenne wrestled with the psychic spasm for over an hour, ordering psykers to move from one compartment to another as thunderheads of nervous energy built up or dissipated, as some minds spun off their rails and others collected themselves. He juggled wards and cullises and seals, and directed concordiasts and wardens from place to place as parts of the Tower flared in his mind's eye, or calmed.

Chevenne's watch was nearly over and his mind was exhausted by the time he was able to piece together a pattern for the ripples, a path they had radiated out from, and find the taste of the psyker who had left them. It took another half an hour to sound the emergency alarms, break the seals on certain secret orders, and bring long-disused protocols into force. It was two more hours of painstaking orders and oaths, seals and counterseals, before the locks on the heavy armoured door of Master Otranto's chamber could be opened.

After that, it took several whole minutes for the astonished onlookers to properly understand the wound on Otranto's corpse, to realise what it was, and to know that this was no death and no possession. This was murder.

CHAPTER TWO

IN THE SUB-EQUATORIAL deserts of Kleizen Onjere (Shira Calpurnia read from the data-slate), the planet's millennia-old soil conditioning has decayed beyond the inhabitants' ability to restore it. The water table has sunk too low and the earth has broken back down to abrasive orange gravel. At the long day's peak, the desert sweats out pockets of subsurface air, loaded with chemical compounds that sting the eyes and bring rashes to the skin, while bacteria inflame any cut or abrasion. The only refuges are the chains of steep-sided mesas that stand high enough to be clear of the sand-vapour until it cools and sinks away again in the dusk.

The Adeptus arbiters, whose polar training compounds and orbital docks make Kleizen Onjere a nexus point for fleet movements across three sectors, also keep watchtowers across the mesa chains. Moving between them are the convicts, disgraced and sentenced officers of the Adeptus, trekking across the sand barefoot and in coarse prisoners' clothes. They each pull behind them a metal frame that supports a banner-pole, from which hang parchment lists of the convicts' crimes, the dates and particulars of their convictions, the seal of the judge who passed sentence, and the stamps of the

Chasteners who mete out penal labours or floggings as their particular punishment demands.

The crimes that brought this sentence were light ones, all things considered. Calpurnia was aware of this before the scrolling text pointed it out to her. Low-level incompetence in their duties, perhaps, or a speech that a judge had ruled might lead to sedition. It could be impiety, laziness, freethinking, or any of the myriad ways of putting the Emperor behind their personal welfare that the penal codes sum up as 'thoughts of self'.

Whatever the crime, their convictions were judged not to outweigh their ranks, or whatever commendations, ordinations or charters of merit their service might have earned. If there was any question of those weights being equal, the dusty, gasping figure in front of its carriage would be marching into the maw of battle in a Penal Legion uniform, or lying in a red pool in front of an Arbites firing squad. No, the men in the desert were petty criminals.

None of which, Shira Calpurnia decided, was of any real use to her. She rubbed her eyes, and grimaced at the cracking of her jaw when she yawned. As the screen of her slate went black, she slid the data-ark out of its groove, murmured a quick blessing to its anima and returned it to the rack on the cell wall.

Note-sheets lay on the little table in the centre of her cell, neatly stacked and sorted, and covered in annotations and corrections. She had to reposition them every hour or so; the vibration from the dromon's engines was imperfectly damped and whatever she set on the table had a way of wandering imperceptibly if she left it unsecured. Soon after they had left the Incarcery, she had passed a restless evening before sleep prowling about the cell, all three-by-three metres of it, minus the space that the archive-racks, the sleeping pallet and the table took. She had pressed her hand to one wall and then another, trying to work out which way was the dromon's stern by where the vibration was strongest. She hadn't really been able to decide.

She sat down again and looked at the empty paper in front of her without really seeing it, twirling the stylus in her fingers, and wondering whether to write up a summary of the Kleizen Onjere material to look at later. No. It was interesting, certainly, even inspirational in a way: land that had become unusable for anything else becoming, by the Emperor's grace, useful for a just and moral purpose.

She was also struck by the nature of the punishment itself: it resembled one of the heavily symbolic and ritualised retributions of the Adeptus Ministorum, rather than the stern and pragmatic punishments handed out by the Arbites. Back on Hydraphur, she might have chased that thought down, traced the development of the desert as a place of punishment, and studied how Ecclesiarchal customs had blended with the rigid Arbites penal laws. She could debate it with Nestor Leandro at one of the formal commanders' banquets, or delegate Culann or Umry to research and declaim on it; the experience would be good for–

That way, bad thoughts lay. She suppressed them. It simply wasn't much use to her now; that was all. It was a curiosity of a penal world almost a whole segmentum away, and nothing more. She had to concentrate.

She had to prepare for her own trial.

SHE JUMPED AT a booming blow to the cell door. It was not the first time she had heard it, not even the hundredth, but of course it was calculated to startle and unnerve her. Her notes were full of blots and accidental pen-strokes where she had been startled, mid-word.

She had a moment to brace herself between the blow and the bell-toll from behind the vox-grilles in the other walls. The deafening voice of a bell brought its own bad memories. By the time the sound had died away, she was kneeling in what little free space there was in the cell's middle, as law dictated.

The door rumbled open, but she kept her eyes ahead, drill-ground steady, as the two men walked in. The master Chastener raised his staff, brought its metal foot down on the deck with a crash, and the door slid shut. There was silence for the mandated count of eight seconds, and then the two took up their second positions and the staff crashed into the deck again.

Calpurnia's rank allowed her to watch this. More junior arbitors would have had to fall to both knees with heads bowed, or prostrate themselves on the cold metal with the foot of the staff hitting the deck beside their ears. As arbitor senioris, Calpurnia was permitted to remain on one knee, head erect and shoulders back, and look her Chastener in the eye.

Deferring to that same rule, Dast removed his helmet and set it on the table, staring at her over his broken nose and the thick brown beard he had dyed in vertical bands of black to mimic his master Chastener's livery. The fingers that gripped his staff were bright steel augmetics.

Calpurnia kept her eyes on Dast's faded blue ones. Preacher Orovene stood on her right side, four paces away. Calpurnia didn't look at him. The garrison preacher wore a gold-embroidered red sash over his Arbites uniform, and looped around his neck, a narrow strand of parchment with the complete text of the First Lawgiver's Psalm written upon it. As usual, the preacher smelled faintly of lho-smoke.

The staff crashed into the floor again. Calpurnia did not flinch.

'Declare to the Arbites your name.'

'Shira Calpurnia Lucina.' She had been through enough self-denunciation sessions that she no longer had to stop herself from reciting her rank. It had been a close thing, those first few times.

The staff crashed.

'Declare to the Arbites the Emperor's accusations against you.'

'The Immortal Emperor does accuse me, through the vigilance and wisdom of His chosen Adeptus, of the crime of failure in my charged and chartered duties.'

Crash.

'Declare to the Arbites the nature of your failure.'

'By the just and benevolent will of Him on Earth, I bore the office and the duties of arbitor senioris in the service of the *Lex Imperia*. My duty and my orders, given to me in the name of the law by my Emperor-chosen superiors, were to preside and judge on the inheritance of an Imperial Charter. The hearing failed.'

She had been through this many times. Her words no longer caught in her throat when she said them. She liked to tell herself that this was because she had come to terms with what she was saying, and not because she had numbed herself to it. She went on:

'The hearing failed. I was overconfident and I was careless. I failed to plan and I failed to enforce. On Selena Secundus, the very Court of the Arbites broke in bloodshed and mutiny. It succeeded because of my failure. The Battlefleet Pacificus and the Adeptus Ministorum witnessed it, and the law was diminished before them, because of my failure. The Charter was lost and its Emperor-chosen succession ended, because of my failure. Loyal and pious Arbites had their lives ended because of my failure.'

In some of the sessions, she had been required to list their names and ranks, but Dast did not command that of her today. She was glad when she didn't have to name the Arbites who had died at Selena Secundus.

Crash.

'Declare to the Arbites the nature of your weakness.' Calpurnia took a breath.

'I declare myself weak in vigilance, weak in resolve and weak in sternness. That I was not vigilant against the treachery and mutiny of the heirs, blinded by the mask of mourning and duty that they wore, shows my weakness in vigilance. That I was dismayed by the disorder and violence that overcame the hearing, and judged rashly and hastily, not allowing the law to speak through me, shows my weakness of resolve. That the lawbreakers and mutineers were brought to heel and stamped out by the Navy, where the fist of the Arbites should have been seen by all to crush them, shows my weakness in sternness.'

The careful formality of her words was her own choice; Dast had not ordered her to adopt any particular structure or phrasing when her imprisonment had begun. During her career, Calpurnia had attended many self-denunciation sessions, and had presided over more than a few. She had watched cold-eyed as many of the accused had slid into hysterics, into broken weeping at their own failure and disgrace, or into screamed denials that they had done wrong at all. 'None can truly know one's criminality, but for that criminal and Him on Earth,' Chastener Nkirre had told her once on Don-Croix. 'And so for criminals, self-denunciation before the law may be the one service their nature has left them fit to perform.' Calpurnia was proud of the dignity with which she performed that service. She liked to tell herself that her pride had nothing to do with not letting Dast see her break down.

'My weakness caused my failure. My failure is my crime before the law of the Imperium, and in the sight of the Immortal Emperor.'

Crash.

'Declare to the Arbites what punishment you will accept for the crime of failure, and for the sin of incompetence.'

'I will accept the verdict and the punishment brought forth from the magisterium of the *Lex Imperia,* and the judgement of the Adeptus Arbites,' Calpurnia replied. 'It is not my appointed place to accept anything else.'

That last line was one that she had not used before, but it had come to her earlier that day while she was reading trial histories from the Clementia Pacification. She was pleased she had thought of it. She liked to tell herself that it had nothing to do with being a step ahead of Dast in the details of her punishments and self-denunciations.

She remained on one knee with her head high, carefully keeping defiance out of her face – this was for her own good, after all. Dast and Orovene stood over her, impassive as statues, for twenty silent breaths. Then Dast lifted his staff, held it across his body and turned to the door. The lock clanked as the junior Chastener watching them through the internal opticon array worked his controls, and then both men were gone in a clamour of boots on metal decking and a last lingering whiff of lho-ash. Calpurnia met the black-visored gaze of the arbitrator stationed across from her cell entrance, shotgun at arms, for the few seconds more until the door swung shut and locked.

She remained on one knee for a few more moments: leaping straight up and getting back to work would, she thought, show disrespect for the self-denunciation and its objectives. Sometimes, when the sessions came close together, she was barely starting to get up when Dast and Orovene came marching straight back in. Sometimes, when they sprang a session on her in the middle of the sleep shift, she found she stayed kneeling for many minutes longer, floating back into drowsiness, before she could stir herself to lie back down on her pallet. When she had been surprised with a session in the middle of one of her exercise bouts, she could feel her body shaking with the strain of holding the position so soon after she had worked it close to exhaustion.

There was an art to timing self-denunciations, spacing them out over days or packing many of them into half an hour, never letting the accused know how long they must wait before they were forced to survey their crimes again, nor how long each denunciation would last. The techniques had been developed and honed by hundreds of generations of Chasteners, and Calpurnia didn't waste any effort on trying to second-guess Dast's schedule. She stood up, bowed briefly to the aquila on the wall over her pallet, sat down at her table and went back to work.

* * *

THERE HAD BEEN many times, in the little spaceborne Incarcery on the Hydraphur's very outer fringes, that Calpurnia had almost forgotten that she was a prisoner at all. She was on her way back into the heart of the system in the dromon system-runner that held her current cell, and it was harder to forget. Her trial was a matter of weeks away, and the thought of it bearing down on her had sharpened her mind and brought a constant tension to her emotions that she was reluctant to admit to herself.

On good days, she could still lose herself in the reams of data-arks and legal codices, the miniature library that she had been entitled to bring from the Incarcery to prepare herself. Hours would pass when she sat alone over the table, oblivious to the tiny sounds of her breathing and her stylus, and to the distant rumble of the ship's machinery.

Those times helped the memories of Selena Secundus to slip from her mind, and the shadowy dread of her own coming trial lifted a little. She might have been back at the senior inductees' barracks at Machiun, scratching away at one of the rote-tests that every recruit had to pass. She might have been back in one of the great Adeptus libraries on Ephaeda, Ephaeda with its sober, courtly ordinates and priests, and its city-spanning archive banks stocked with the finest wisdom and thoughts in three Segmentae.

Those moods were wonderful when they came, and that was why she worked to resist them, and felt a sharp steel pride in her gut when she did so. She might never be recorded as one of the great Arbites of Hydraphur, her rulings quoted and her wars of enforcement studied by other young recruits from here to the segmentum borders. She might never (and this was a bitter thought to her, more bitter than the first) enter her family annals at Ultramar, her likeness put up in the hearth-house on Iax as an example for future women of the Calpurnii in how to uphold the proud family name.

She was damned, however, if she was going to consider her duty over, simply because her career might be. *Duty is not a word coined in idleness*, she had written down the margin of her notes, deep in one particularly sleepless night, *duty being the first grace the Emperor extends to the newborn, and the last connection with Him to comfort the dying, and so the forsaking of it is damnation in evident form*. Her duty had been to be a strong child of the Calpurnii, and she had upheld it. Then it had been to be a stern and loyal arbitor of the Adeptus, and she had upheld that… until she could uphold it no longer and failure caught up with her.

If she must be a prisoner and a convict, then she would do her duty, as it was expected of a prisoner and a convict. She would not allow herself to forget why she was here. She would meet every demand of the Chasteners, answer strongly and clearly through every self-denunciation, be it a session of a few minutes or twelve hours. She would not seek favours or forgiveness from the law, and she would bow her head to the justice of Imperial punishment. If it were her fate to be a prisoner, then she would bring every scrap of her determination onto this goal: she would be a lesson, an example to the Arbites.

Arbites scholars would write, and instructors would declaim, that if any arbitor should find themselves wanting and face the charge of failure, that if they must bear the punishment of their order in their own turn, then they should look to Shira Calpurnia Lucina, the former arbitor senioris of the High Precinct of Hydraphur. Calpurnia who saw her duty through, whose service to the law did not flinch even as she saw the judgement of law served upon herself, even as she–

She did not weep. She had promised herself that she would not weep. The ink dried unnoticed on her notes, her breath hissed, the stylus shook in her fist and began to crack between her fingers, but her expression did not change and she did not weep.

SHE HAD NO way of measuring time, but she guessed it would be hours before the next staff-blow sounded against the cell door. She had forced herself through the remainder of the treatise on the punishment of erring Adeptus, forced herself through a set of exercises, and prayed before the aquila; that done, she had finally managed to start drifting towards sleep. Then the noise came. Adrenaline snapped her awake with a physical start that the strike on the door had not produced, and she sprang off her pallet and knelt in the middle of the floor without stumbling.

She tensed herself and narrowed her eyes ready for the bell-toll, secretly pleased that she had beaten it to her position even from being half-asleep, and it took her whole seconds to realise that the bell was not sounding. She blinked, her shoulders, already sore from her exercises, twinged as she tensed them. The same tension boiled her gut: was it concluded? She had not expected a summary execution, but she was an arbitrator, not a judge, there could so easily be a provision she was ignorant of that would allow it, and if Dvorov had decided to try her in absentia then–

Then she would meet her fate properly, she told herself, and willed her body to co-operate.

The door clanked open. As always, it was Dast and Orovene – but this time they were different. Dast still carried his staff, but he wore an austere duty uniform and was helmetless. Orovene was in plain uniform, a preacher's red-trimmed white collar, epaulette and shawl over arbitrator black. He was twirling an unlit lho-stick in his fingers.

'Calpurnia,' Dast said without ceremony. He picked up the chair from behind her little table, clattered it to the deck in front of her, and straddled it, facing her. He gave a tilt of his chin, pointing behind her.

Calpurnia remained on one knee, looking up expressionlessly. They stared at one another for a few moments.

'She's waiting for an order, Dast. You're going to have to face up to talking to her sooner or later.' The garrison preacher's voice was smooth and trained, showing only the faintest of rough edges from the lho-smoke.

'Hm.' Dast let the grunt stand as his reply for a few moments more, and then pointed his staff over Calpurnia's shoulder. 'Sit, Calpurnia. This isn't a denunciation. It's not part of any kind of regular procedure.' The distaste in that last sentence dripped from his voice.

Slowly, carefully, Calpurnia rose, backed up to her pallet, and sat down. Dast was staring over at the neat arrangement of her note-sheets on the table. She had the impression that he was enjoying the effort of reading her writing upside-down more than he was enjoying having to talk to her.

Orovene broke the ice.

'How far are you through preparing a defence, Calpurnia?' Dast liked to glare and scowl, but Orovene's face never betrayed much at all.

'With another ten hours' total time,' she answered with a confidence she wasn't sure she felt, 'I should have integrated all the basic precepts into my case. The overall shape of my argument hasn't changed much from my initial premises, but there are rulings and precedents from courts in this segmentum that I've had to familiarise myself with.' She went over Orovene's words again. 'My case will be a true witness against myself, presenting my failures as seen through the eyes of the law, so that both my strengths and weaknesses can be found wanting. The voice of accusation is the voice of the Emperor made concrete through law. It is not for me to "defend" anything.'

'Good.' Orovene nodded. 'Pious, and sound at law. Thank you.' He glanced at Dast again, but the Chastener stayed silent.

'You will not be prevented from completing your studies before your trial,' Orovene went on. 'So don't concern yourself with being denied what you're owed by process. You will be interrupted, however. We have an–' he thought for a moment, 'an *irregularity*. Better you hear it from the master Chastener.'

Dast scowled at the table for a moment longer, glanced at Orovene, and finally swung his head around to Calpurnia, lips tight.

'We're not going to Hydraphur,' he said, and caught himself. 'We're not going *directly* to Hydraphur. Your trial has been deferred. We've all got a duty to attend to before we go any further in-system.'

She sat and waited for his next words. The silence was long enough for her to notice, and wonder. Once she would have been impatient to know more, and would have tried to begin a conversation about the news.

Had all the time in the cell rusted her grip on any words apart from self-denunciation? She knew enough about Chastener work to know that that was often the point of it.

'This isn't about you, Calpurnia, so don't think it is. You're useful, that's all, and so I'm putting you to use as we all do our duty.' Dast stopped to think then snorted and kicked the table leg. One note-sheet skated off the edge and slid back and forth through the air until it rested on the floor.

'You'll have your rank back, Calpurnia, but don't get too attached to it. It's not permanent. This is a brevet, nothing more. It's not a complete one, either, so don't start giving me orders.'

Something inside her clicked and lit up, and suddenly it was an effort to keep control of her expression.

'We're being diverted,' Dast went on. 'The orders came from the Wall, and the Incarcery pilots have passed on a course correction to us. I've given orders for adjustment and burn. We'll be on our new heading in half a day.'

'I know the basic principles of law at work here, master Chastener,' Calpurnia said, 'but I don't yet know the reason. If we're being diverted from a course bound into the system then it means that we're staying out on the fringes, and that means shipboard action or Navy installations. I'm trying to think of an example of either that would cause trouble enough for an Ar– for an accused to have their trial postponed because only they could properly do an arbitor's duty there. Are we on our way to a mutiny, a xenos quarantine...?' She tailed her voice off deferentially, but a little late. The old command was creeping back into it, and there had been a shift in balance, small, but a shift between the three of them nevertheless.

Dast and Orovene had both picked up on it too. Orovene was eyeing Dast, waiting for his reaction.

Dast's reaction was to stand and kick the chair over. It hit the table and, one of Calpurnia's books thudded to the deck, a slew of note-sheets falling after it like a shower of petals.

'Not Navy,' he told her. 'Adeptus Astra Telepathica. Were being diverted into the path of the Witchroost, and we'll dock with it when we rendezvous in three days' time. There will be more personnel on the way, but we'll be arriving there for the moment with nothing, and no more than the personnel on this craft, including you, Calpurnia. You're there as a figurehead. You've got until rendezvous minus four hours to get yourself ready and prepare your uniform. One of the arbitrators will escort you to the cargo racks. I'm sure you can get yourself cleaned up without assistance.'

'I'm sure I can. Master Chastener, why are we docking at the Bastion Psykana?' Mindful of his talk of rank, she carefully avoided belabouring her use of the correct name.

Dast was already banging his staff on the door. Over the noise of the locks and the opening mechanisms, Orovene told her, 'A crime against the Adeptus, Calpurnia. It is a matter of law. Someone has murdered the Master of the Bastion Psykana. We're going to go aboard and find someone who can tell us who it was.'

CHAPTER THREE

'Arm me, please, master Chastener.'

Dast turned and looked at Calpurnia as the distorted bulk of the Bastion Psykana swallowed more and more of the dromon's bridge windows. At first, it had been little more than a silhouette against the stars, but as the distance had shrunk, the fortress had grown into a mosaic of window-lights and oddly angled shadows. They were already more than close enough to see its strange, slumped stature and the incongruous bright spikes of the eyries.

'Throne, Throne look on us,' Orovene had breathed, and he had spoken for all of them. The pilots standing in the scooped control pits had exchanged uneasy glances. Calpurnia and Dast, standing side by side before the captain's pulpit, were the only ones to remain impassive.

Then the transmission had come, asking them to abort their approach. As she looked out at the Bastion, Calpurnia's hand closed on empty air at her belt where the pommel of a power-maul would normally have hung.

'You're not fully reinstated,' Dast said. 'If I'd agreed to your going armed, I would have had you armed already.' He put a hand out to steady himself as the dromon adjusted its trajectory, and the internal gee took a moment to compensate.

'With respect, that will undermine my authority,' Calpurnia replied. 'I'm an arbitrator, I should be armed. You made the point that an arbitor senioris will give weight and fear to an investigation. If that's true, you don't want people looking at me wondering where my maul and pistol are.' She turned her head as a burst of tinny vox-traffic came from one of the control stations in front of them.

'Same message as before, sir and ma'am,' the vox-operator called over her shoulder. 'They ask us to defer our docking and accelerate away on a provided vector, because the docks are not secure.'

'Defer docking, hell!' Dast snarled, and whacked the doorframe behind him with a fist. 'We got here just in time. This is part of it, you wait and see. The bastard witches are trying to pull something.'

'The astropaths don't have operational command of the docks, master Chastener,' Calpurnia corrected him. 'The Navy supplies crews and junior officers to do that. The Telepathica officials may not even know about the order.'

'So it's the Navy that'll be telling us the docks aren't secure?' Dast demanded. 'Why would the Navy do that?'

'I can't tell you until I've found out myself. We don't even know what they mean by not secure. Is it a seal breach? Contamination? Who knows what else there could be?' Calpurnia stepped forwards, peering down at the vox-operator's transmission panel, and then out at the scarred grey flank of the Bastion.

'Send this,' she told the woman. 'We do not accept their deferral of our docking. By the authority of Arbitor Senioris Shira Calpurnia, we *will* dock and we will know the reason why docking is being denied us. If they still try to divert us, they will answer to me. Use those exact words, please.' The vox-woman, back stiffened by her proxy authority, leaned over her mouthpiece again.

'You'll answer for that,' Dast growled. 'You're only to pull rank like that in ways approved by me. You're still an accused, and I'm still your Chastener.'

Calpurnia's reply was cut off by another burst of traffic, boosted by the vox-operator so that they could all hear clearly.

'Hailing the Arbites. Please advise your arbitor senioris that we have, uh, we have problems on the docks. Possible...' there was a brief burst of static, a few moments of dead air, and, '...possible physical danger. Possible danger to the person of the arbitor senioris. Possible, uh... hostile confrontation.' The voice sounded wretched. 'We convey from the dock superintendent...'

'Convey to him our thanks for his concern for my safety,' Calpurnia said, 'and inform him that the arbitor senioris will apply herself to this confrontation as soon as docking is complete.' The woman bent over the controls again, and Calpurnia turned and locked eyes with Dast.

'Something's happening on the docks down there, something violent, by the sound of it. I don't think that young man was making anything up, do you?' Her hand hooked around the empty spot on her belt, again.

'Arm me please, master Chastener.'

He didn't give her a pistol, but that was fine. The maul was a powerful symbol, an arbitrator trademark, and she was more than happy with the heavy-hilted Agni-pattern weapon from the dromon's little armoury.

Clangs and scrapes sounded from outside the ship, the casual music of the docking grapples drawing them in. As she walked towards the hatch, Calpurnia felt the lurch that meant the ship's gravity had aligned with that of the station.

'This is a bad omen,' Dast said aloud. 'Bad. If these witch nests are supposed to be under such tight control, how could there be an open rising like this? Where are our own agents? This is a foul-starred place, I think.'

Calpurnia didn't reply. She had been briefed on the Bastion Psykana when she had taken up her station at Hydraphur, and although she could remember the briefing perfectly well, this didn't seem like the time to share the station's history with Dast. The history included a hellish plasma breach that had gutted the station back in its days as a Naval fortress, and the accidents and ill luck that had dogged efforts to rebuild and reclaim it. It also included legends and ghost-tales that had built up around its lifeless hulk, and had then taken on fresh life when the Adeptus Astra Telepathica had taken possession of the wreck, sealed it, rebuilt it and brought it back to life. It was more than just piety that had sent Orovene to the shrine to pray for them.

'His will,' was all she said, and the other three Arbites echoed her as the hull began to rumble open, and they heard the gunshots.

* * *

Belnove was at the forefront of the mob as they came up the ladderwells. Below them were the metal walkways that crisscrossed just under the hangar bay's ceiling and just above him, the compartment that led into the docking-tower. At the top of the tower stood the dromon, and blessed escape.

Belnove gripped a short-range shotcaster in one hand. It was a powerful weapon, monstrous at two metres, and useless at ten. His face was slick with blood and sweat – he'd been creased by a Navy flechette at some point after they'd rushed the hangar locks. His breaths were deep, even and quiet.

He gave no sign that he had heard the scattered shouts of encouragement from behind him. His attention was on the movements that he could see ahead of him, the glimpses of green uniform turned dark by the orange safety lights.

Above him, Second Petty Officer Roos of the dock sub-command looked out over the long compartment. Behind him were the steep stairs that began the ascent to the docking tower, a guard alcove where two of his men had cover, and the short passage to the cargo lift. He didn't want to look at poor Ostelkoor, lying headless by Laddershaft Four, the victim of some horrible improvised explosive-thrower.

Roos tried to concentrate, but the more he tried to force the shipboard tactical drills from the academy back into his brain the more slippery his thoughts became. He adjusted his grip on his long-barrelled slug-pistol, listening to the soft whine of the loading motor. As soon as the first head came over the top of a laddershaft, the motor could spin the cylinders fast enough to put eight hollowpoints through it in less than a second. He thought of that for reassurance, and prayed for the dromon to abort docking so this might be over. What maniac wanted to disembark into this?

From up above him came the solid clank and the fluid hissing of the final dock-seals going in. The flashing of the lights on the cargo lift changed tempo as the mechanism prepared itself for usefulness.

A roar of 'It's docked! Way's clear, lads!' came from somewhere, and the ladders shook with noise as the mutineers came up them. That was all right. It took all those frightening choices away. Suddenly clear-eyed and steady-handed, Roos locked his body easily into a firing position and took aim.

* * *

Dast was first through the dromon's hatch, and went hammering along the little articulated dock-tunnel with the two arbitrators in tow, breath misting in the chilled air, shotgun unholstered in his hands. Calpurnia, all but shouldered aside, cursed and made to follow before she registered a second set of metallic noises further away. She stepped back and listened: metallic noises. They came from the bottom-most of the three miniature decks, some way back – another tunnel was extending up to kiss the cargo hatch.

She turned to shout after Dast, but the others had already disappeared down the first flight of steps. She grimaced and turned back.

'Intrusion!' she yelled, not sure how many more Arbites were on the dromon to hear her. As far as she knew, she'd been the only prisoner on board – how much of a complement would Dast have brought for just her?

She ran for the screw-stair at the beginning of the dromon's thick midsection. 'Muster at the cargo hatch,' she shouted again. 'Muster for possible intrusion! Orovene, where are you? Arm yourself!'

The first man to pop out of the shaft had thrown a fist-sized chain-link to try and spoil Roos's aim, but he'd just let it clang off the bulkhead, and placed a precise shot a moment later, when the man was too slow ducking. The patch of deck beyond the shaft suddenly glistened red, and the corpse tumbled out of sight to cries and curses from below. Roos worked the speedloader and flicked the cylinder motor down to two-shot as three more men came up through the holes at him.

'I order you to–' he got out before the shattering noise of a shot-caster filled the compartment and Warden Wheyett, who stepped out to meet the charge with a long-handled neural goad, groaned and spun backwards. Roos got one shot off before he had to duck a swinging length of cable, but he was too slow. It scored off his shoulder and the side of his head.

Roos staggered, bounced off a bulkhead and managed a second two-shot through his enemy's thigh, pitching the man over as the shattered limb gave way. The mutineer behind him was already swinging a long-handled wrench. It connected with Roos's gun-arm and numbed it. The other end came around under his jaw, and suddenly Roos was lying across the steps. Someone got a hand on his throat and started squeezing, and he could dimly feel kicks landing on his ribs and hips. Somewhere in the roar of fighting, he heard the sound of the cargo lift opening, but the shouts were all blurring into one another and his hearing was dimming.

BELNOVE JAMMED ANOTHER cartridge into his shotcaster and spared a glance for the brawl around the bottom of the stairs. Someone was throttling the young officer on the steps, while a free-for-all surged around them, fists, bludgeons and blades, and from somewhere in the mess, the dry chatter of a flechette gun.

Screw fighting his way through that. As far as Belnove was concerned, there was no more brotherhood. It was every man for himself. He jinked to his left and down the little passage to the cargo lift. He was a foreman; he knew the codes to that hatch.

In the time that it took for the lift to open, four others had joined him: two came inside with them, and then another two before the hatch closed. Someone outside shouted, 'Come back for us!' and Belnove raised a hand as if he would. Then they were on their way up, packed tight in the little cube, eyeing each other as they ground up towards the dromon's belly.

'Quick and clean, boys, and we need the crew alive,' Belnove told them. They nodded and grunted their agreement, grim-faced. They were past the point of no return. Whoever had brought this little boat in to dock had better damn well do as they were told.

ROOS BUCKED AND goggled, and took a great, harsh gasp for air. The pressure on his neck was gone. The red-shot grey blur in front of his eyes passed a moment later and he began to sit up. Another moment and he managed a word:

'What?'

The big-shouldered man in black and brown didn't reply. He just stepped heavily over Roos and drew his boot back for a kick. Roos realised that the sound he had dimly registered a moment ago had been the butt of the big man's shotgun connecting with the head of the docker who'd been choking him. The kick connected, something in the man's face crumpled, and he went over on his back.

The big man – an arbitor, Roos registered fuzzily, in Chastener's black and brown – fired his shotgun from the hip, catapulting a cleaver-armed docker off his feet and down a laddershaft. As Roos gaped, the Chastener spun on his heel to confront a burly man who was wrestling with Warden Schai for control of a knife, and slammed the stock into the mutineer's head. His target groaned and staggered, and the Chastener finished him off with another swing, turning the movement into another pivot that saw him face the room again, weapon reloaded and ready. The deck lights gleamed off his visor and steel hand.

'Down!' barked a voice behind Roos, and by reflex he dropped his shoulders to the stairs as two more men bounded over him: arbitrators, these, in unbroken black, one with a shotgun, one with a buckler on one arm and a long counterweighted power-maul.

There was barely time for the arbitrators to catch up to their leader before someone shouted, 'We can still take 'em!' and the fighting was on again.

WHATEVER BELNOVE HAD been expecting outside the cargo lift, it hadn't been what he found: the passageway was empty, but for a short woman in black carapace. He had been ready to cut his way through a throng of ships' guards to get at the cockpit, but his mind worked fast enough to change his plan.

'Spin around, girl, and take us to the cockpit. We're not bad men. We only want to keep the lives and souls the Emperor gave us, you understand? So you just–'

That was as far as he got before the upward stroke of a high-charge power-maul blew the shotcaster out of his hands and sent it pin-wheeling into the ceiling. Belnove howled and dropped to his knees, looking at the cooked flesh of his stricken hands, and while the enormity of it was still making its way up his nerves, the maul was in motion again. A low shot, and a man tumbled, his knee exploded and unable to hold him. Another shot, and someone made an ago-nised noise that wasn't quite a scream, because the shock to his sternum had stolen his breath.

'Intrusion!' the woman yelled and swung again. 'Intrusion through the cargo door! Orovene! All hands! I'd better see someone down here damn quick!'

As if in answer, Belnove heard the report of a shotgun behind him. The shot was true, and he was pitched onto his face and wounded hands by the corpse falling full on his back. The impact of his hands on the decking drove the shock of the injuries home, and as it reached his brain Belnove finally began to howl. The shots and power-flares filling the air above him reached a crescendo.

THE SKIRMISH AT the base of the docking-tower stairs didn't last long. The mutineers' morale had dried up in the face of the fresh gunfire: down below the laddershafts, the would-be rioters dropped their improvised weapons and vanished into the docking bay. Those mutineers who'd managed to get up the shafts had their blood up at first, but the arbitrators had tipped that balance back the other way.

'Drop your weapons!' the Chastener was roaring. 'Drop your weapons and submit, you vermin!'

'Rush him!' cried a voice from the back of the mob, as someone tried to make a break for the cargo hatch and was clubbed down. 'He's not station–' another deafening shotgun-blast '–can't order us, they've got no rank here...'

'I am *so* glad to hear someone mention rank,' said a new voice, a woman's voice. Roos, getting unsteadily to his feet, realised that the speaker was walking out of the cargo lift. He heard several sets of footsteps. He looked groggily at the woman as she came out to join the Chastener.

'Rank,' she said, 'and knowing your place. If everyone aboard this station is as conscientious as that on matters of authority and deference, then I shall praise the Emperor for sending me a smooth road to walk. My rank, and pay attention, *my* rank is arbitor senioris of the Adeptus Arbites, arbitor general of the Hydraphur High Precinct. That rank excuses me from having to care why you are trying to fight your way onto an Arbites ship, and cheering each other on to assault an Imperial master Chastener.' She held her buzzing maul directly over her head, so that the glowing indicators on its hilt and the power-flares along its length were visible to the back of the compartment. 'Nothing matters to me, except your obedience. Drop your weapons and submit yourselves to judgement. Don't doubt that that's an order.'

There was a moment's silence. Then the sound of a shotgun being cocked as the Chastener loaded an Executioner shell. One rioter went down on one knee, another following suit. Calpurnia looked at them and nodded, and that was all it needed for half a dozen more to kneel. One man in a grubby mechanician's coverall tried to use the distraction to vault down a laddershaft. Dast calmly shot him down. That did it. Five more seconds and every mutineer was laying face down on the floor, hands stretched out past their heads.

'THEY WERE TRYING to get... onto your... uh, ship,' said one of the Navy men – a boy, Calpurnia realised, who looked barely old enough to have earned his rank pins. His voice was a tortured grate in his throat: his neck was bruised and puffy where someone had been squeezing it in the fighting. 'Trying to get... off station... tried to stop–'

'You did, did you?' said Dast, rounding on the boy and towering over him. The young man swayed in place, staring up at Dast, what little colour he had left in his face, draining away.

Calpurnia turned, leaving them to it. She was looking out over the prisoners, starting to wonder what her next move was, when her vox-torc gave a signal tap on the standard Arbites band and a man's voice spoke to her.

'Arbites? Bastion Psykana garrison to docked dromon, reply. We're approaching your position. Reports are of armed mutiny. Respond. Respond with your status.'

'Status is comfortable enough, thank you, Bastion Garrison,' she replied. 'We are docked and have met the reception you provided for us. I'm pleased to hear that you see fit to follow it and greet us in person.'

There was a pause, and then the man's voice again.

'Arb... arbitor senioris?'

'So you did know we were coming by. Good. Make your way up here, please, whoever you are, and you can identify yourself and explain to me exactly what kind of station you are running here.'

THEY RODE AWAY from the docks on a glide-truck, a long electric corridor-crawler of a kind that Calpurnia had seen in fortresses and space stations across the galaxy. It was little more than two running boards down either side of a long central rail, the whole thing tipped with a sharp-nosed driver's compartment, and rolling forward on thrumming electric wheels.

The truck was almost empty: the arbitrators who'd ridden down on it were still in the docking tower, manhandling the mutineers into shackles and strait-capes. Aedile Bruinann had told Calpurnia that the Bastion Precinct had little cell-space to keep them in, so the prisoners were to be stored in the spare cells on the dromon they had been trying to fight their way onto. It had been fitted out as a flying gaol, after all.

Calpurnia gripped the rail and looked across at the local commander. Joeg Bruinann wore the sparkling green laurels of an aedile majore on his helmet, and the red and gold badge and lanyard of a marshal isolate. He was the officer in charge of a precinct formed under extraordinary circumstances. Bruinann didn't return her gaze, although Calpurnia caught the truck's driver looking steadily at her in the rear-view mirror. Dast stood further back on the truck, with Orovene opposite him. It was hard to tell under the helmet, armour and shawl, but the preacher seemed nervous.

The ride was a short one, even though the truck rarely went above running speed. From the glimpses she got through the thick armourcrys skylights above them, Calpurnia was able to piece together their progress under the outer barbicans, and in under the looming cliff face of the keep wall. We're in, she thought to herself. We're in the Witchroost, and she didn't even notice her own use of the term that she reprimanded others for using. She wondered why the simple fact of her arrival struck her as such a terrible portent.

In the keep, the decking changed from metal to rockcrete, and the bright ceiling panels and skylights ceased. They rode through a dimmer, narrower tunnel. The grates in the arched ceiling were encrusted with fluttering paper prayer seals, their downdraft warm and carrying an odd scent that Calpurnia couldn't place. Finally, the twists and angles of the corridors grew too sharp for the truck to negotiate easily, and they continued on foot through the oddly quiet passageways, boots gritting on the rockcrete. The driver followed them, simply leaving the humming, activated truck behind.

The entrance to the precinct chambers stood in a nest of intersecting tunnels and ways, arched halls marching away at the sides, and staircases and ramps leading from above and below, meeting at a circular floor of plain black metal. Calpurnia craned her head back and peered up the high well above them with its spiral of bright lanterns under eagle-shaped reflectors. Then she looked at the precinct doors, a low tunnel-slot in a black obelisk set into the wall, deliberately dimly lit. It was a good design. The march from a bright, airy space into the close gloom of the portal would put any accused prisoner in exactly the right state of mind.

'These chambers used to accommodate the Battlefleet Commissariat,' said the arbitrator who'd been their driver. She was slightly taller than Calpurnia, wiry and genderless but for her voice. 'The symbolism was cut into the architecture for them. It made it ideal for us, of course.'

'Speech discipline!' snapped Dast as Calpurnia blinked at the woman's informality. They stood in silence, listening to the buzz of the vigil-auspex built into the gates as it read their skin-scent and eye-patterns.

It was some time before the auspex was satisfied, but finally the buzzing ratcheted to a halt, and somewhere, the machine-spirit behind the auspex stirred itself to turn the lock for them. The sound of the gates opening was the same clank and rumble as any heavy blast door across the Imperium, and the familiarity of the sound comforted Calpurnia as they trooped through the passageway.

THE PRECINCT STATION was a block of the keep built around an open well like the one outside, a high narrow space ringed by stacked balconies and walkways. A polished marble eagle hung in a suspensor column below the ceiling, over a judgement pulpit and an old executioner's pit. There was activity, too, boot steps and voices, the smell of gun-oil and armour polish, familiar maxims engraved in the walls. As they emerged from the portal, they passed a plinth holding an ancient data-codex, as long as Calpurnia's arm, wrapped in a blue-black velvet shroud and safely sealed under an armourcrys dome. The front of the plinth was polished mirror-smooth and slightly dished inward from wear. As Dast, Calpurnia and their guides passed the plinth each kissed their fingertips and pressed them to the stone.

Calpurnia noticed that the woman walked in front. The other Arbites made way for her and their salutes in her direction. They did not climb all the way up the spiralling ramp: two turns from the top, where the Calpurnia would have expected the marshal's chamber to be, they stopped at a door no different to any of the others they had passed. Even before she had crossed the threshold, the woman had yanked off her helmet and was scratching in the mop of curly black hair that had spilled out from under it.

The long, angular room was not the austere barrack-room of an arbitrator, nor the crammed library and study-room of a judge, although for a moment that was what Calpurnia took it for. Data-arks and reading slates were scattered across every surface, starting with the untidy bed at the far end of the chamber, and continuing up the long desk and onto the little round table right in front of them. The cushioned chair in the near corner, beneath a powerful blue-white illuminator panel, was clearly intended for reading. It was piled with dossier wallets and rolls of transcripts, all decked out with marker ribbons and note-pins. The gun-rack and shelf of legal books to Calpurnia's left were both small, and she thought she could see dust on them even from here.

A long scriptor-tapestry hung on the opposite wall, and that was far more used. The thick woven fabric hung heavy with circuitry, and the touch-reactive surface was alive with images and letters. Some were obviously uploaded from the data-arks that hung from the tasselled docks along the tapestry's edges, while others were added by touch-stylus in two or three different hands. Calpurnia saw pict-images in that display, and data-runes that would play snatches of vox-recordings captured from spy-circuits.

She'd seen enough to guess what was going on, and when the woman whose room this was – olive-skinned and sharp-eyed under the black curls – turned back towards them, Calpurnia saw the flash of crimson at her throat, and knew that she had guessed right.

THE FOUR OF them sat, the little burner between them warming a jug of recaf infusion whose steam turned the air pungent. Shira Calpurnia, Master Chastener Cholyon Dast, Preacher Orovene, Aedile Majore Joeg Bruinann and Master Detective-Espionist Lazka Rede, in her plain arbitrator uniform and the slender red collar that marked her true rank. Rede was the ranking arbitor aboard the Bastion Psykana. Bruinann, her figurehead, soaked up any outside attention, while Rede presided over her spy-flies, communications taps, webs of informants, and her hypno-conditioned deep agents.

It was a common enough arrangement anywhere that the detectives needed a major presence, but Calpurnia was curious to find it aboard the Bastion.

'It's not the arrangement itself, of course,' she told Rede. 'I understand the need for a high-level detective operation in an environment this complex and this insular.' Bruinann gave a little smile and a heartfelt nod of agreement. 'I'm just interested to know how you maintain the appearances, the Tower being the environment that it is.'

'You're wondering why the witches don't see through us,' Rede said. She was perching in her chair at a crooked angle, one lean leg stretched out straight along the floor. There were circles under her eyes, and she hadn't sounded anything other than tired since they had all sat down. 'I mean, all right, if you want to start with the espionist setup here–'

'*No*' snapped Dast. Bruinann jumped. 'Let's remember the task that brought us here and not deviate from it, in this conversation or anywhere else. A high officer of the Adeptus has been murdered: the Master of the Bastion Psykana. Perhaps that needs to be further forward in our minds.'

'A crime against the Emperor's Adeptus, His law and His Imperium,' Calpurnia agreed as Bruinann and Rede flicked their eyes from one of them to the other. 'We're not rookies here, Chastener. I think we all know our duties. My point was–'

'Misguided,' the Chastener finished for her. 'We'll begin with the murder.'

'Pardon me for a minute,' Bruinann put in. 'I'm not as subtle-minded as Lazka, so help me keep up with you. I had been expecting a taskforce to lock down the Tower under the arbitor senioris's control, not just the three of you. Is there some kind of arrangement here that my simple arbitrator's brain isn't getting a grip on?'

'You would have had the communiqués,' said Dast, 'about the botched trial at Selena Secundus?' Calpurnia saw her hands twitch at Dast's words. She reminded herself that she had no right to protest. It was the truth. 'It may not have been general knowledge that Calpurnia is on trial for her failure as a result,' Dast went on. 'Her authority is suspended and she has been confined in my custody until the Arbitor Majore's verdict is ready.'

'Out in the fringe Incarcery stations?' Bruinann was still addressing Calpurnia, and the warm twinge of gratitude she felt towards him surprised her a little. 'It explains why you were so close at hand. We were wondering how you got here right bang on the heels of the murder.'

'First we were told to hold tight and make no move "Because someone's on the way",' Rede carried on, 'and we'd barely digested that when we got your docking request. Joeg's right, we wouldn't mind knowing what's going on. Is Calpurnia in charge or isn't she?'

'*I* am assuming command of the investigation into the murder of Master Otranto,' Dast declared with perhaps a little more force than was needed. 'Calpurnia has been restored to her former rank on an honorary basis, temporarily and at the pleasure of the master of the Hydraphur Incarcery. Her reduction in rank isn't generally known among Hydraphur's civilians–'

'Not even among Hydraphur Arbites,' commented Rede, to no one in particular.

'–and has not, pending her judgement and sentencing, been widely spread among the Arbites,' Dast continued stiffly. 'Therefore, she will lend her authority to the investigation. The sentiments of the Hydraphur high command are that the presence of an arbitor senioris will extinguish any urge the Adeptus Astra Telepathica might be feeling to try and cover over the circumstances of the murder and address it themselves.'

More nods of agreement. They were all familiar with the fortress mentality that grew in so many Adeptus.

'For the purposes of anyone outside these precinct chambers,' Dast said, 'Calpurnia is still an arbitor senioris, and we proceed by her grace and her authority. In practice, her authority ends with me until such time as I consider the investigation concluded.'

The feeling in Calpurnia's guts took a new twist, and she realised that it was fear. She had been afraid of glancing up, seeing the other two Arbites looking into her face and having to return their gazes. The disgraced commander, reduced to–

She stamped on that thought before it could get a running start, and to prove a point to herself, she forced her eyes up to meet Rede and Bruinann's.

Neither of them was looking at her. They were looking at each other. It wasn't hard to guess what they were thinking. They were wondering what this meant for them. They were wondering if the investigation would turn to examining mistakes of their own. They were thinking that Calpurnia and Dast might be there at first to investigate the Master Astropath's murder, but that they had no reason not to add a pair of Arbites scalps.

So be it, she thought. *Every one of us who breaches the Emperor's trust must answer for it, whether their name is Rede or Bruinann, or Calpurnia.* That thought stayed with her as they turned to the schematics and names glowing on the tapestry, and Rede began to talk about the Master's death. She said nothing aloud, but the thought was never far from her mind for the rest of that day.

CHAPTER FOUR

THE MYSTERY OF the murder of Master Astropath Otranto of the Bastion Psykana was waiting for them in Rede's briefing and her records. Calpurnia and Dast listened to the briefing, shot questions at her like darts, and went back and forth through paper files. They looked into flickering data-slate displays, and pored over output from Rede's menagerie of pict-thieves and eavescopes. They followed her notes and schematics, and weighed up her work, but no matter how rigorously they tested her logic, they found themselves circling around and around the mystery just as Rede had.

Master Otranto had been walking on the promenades over the Grand Concourse of the Bastion Psykana, a thoroughfare outside the astropath cloisters that nearly anyone on the station could go to. He had been conferring with his major-domo and confidante, a herbalist and concordiast named Teeker Renz, and some of Renz's colleagues. He had left that conversation and walked away down the promenade, apparently to a meeting with a new concordiast named Torma Ylante, who had just come to the Bastion from service with the League of Black Ships a station-day before.

From there the trail vanished. All anyone knew for certain was that he had passed into the astropath cloisters – the next sign of him was when the scrying arrays in the watch-hall had picked up a mental cry, alarm, anger or fear. The reports that Rede had been collecting were semi-coherent blends of descriptors that Calpurnia suspected would only make true sense to a psyker. The trail grew clearer after that, as Otranto had careened through the cloisters faster and faster, triggering alarms and defences, until he had been sprinting faster than his aged body should have allowed, racing as if damnation itself was after him. Finally, he had sealed the great psyk-warded door of his rooms behind him.

That, as far as the Bastion Psykana was concerned, had been the end of the old man's life.

That was the top and bottom of the mystery, the start and end of it. Dast gave up, stamped out of Rede's office and left Calpurnia with the records and picts, but even Calpurnia felt daunted by the opacity of it. She had been relying on some insight, something Rede had missed, because she was too closely embedded in the environment, but there were no loose ends for her to worry at. It was insane.

'We're in a tower full of psykers!' she finally snapped at Rede, as the other woman fiddled with the data-tapestry, and the recaf pot went dry again. 'I'm fed up of reading reports about echoes and traces. Half the place seems to know that something was wrong, but whose attention was on the actual crime?'

'The Famous Invisible Traitor,' said Rede, 'that's what we called it at my last post. Everyone sees the flames and the running people, a dozen accounts swear they saw someone running from the scene of the crime, but did anyone see him pitch the bomb, deface the temple, attack the ordinate? Why, no.'

'These are people,' said Calpurnia 'whose vision, by the Emperor's grace, can look through stone and steel, and tracts of space whose distances we have trouble even understanding. Not *one* of them thought to direct their attention to where these damn ripples were coming from? *Nobody* was watching what went on in there?'

'You'll see when you walk through the cloisters, ma'am,' Rede told her. 'It's how they're built. The old fortress walls have been lined with a psyk-cage that's melded into the wards and earths that run through the whole fortress. They're specifically made to contain psyker emanations. They carry them off, fuzz them, and dilute them so that they're not a threat. My understanding is that they're like cooling fins on a hot machine, or earths to carry away electrical power. Get waves of power coming out of their heads and sloshing back and forth in the tower, it gets... overpowering, volatile. They lose control. I've got records from places like this where they lost control. They can unbalance each other, cook one another off like bullets in a fire, or leave themselves open to, well, to...'

'...things not spoken of lightly,' said Calpurnia. 'I understand. So Otranto ran into the cloisters where the defences acting to contain the, what, the overflow of any psychic power actually served to blur his trail. How certain are we of where he went?'

'We know where he entered the cloisters and his path after that.' Rede was running her fingers over the tapestry. 'Those in the watch-hall know where he passed. The path is laid out on the Bastion schematic on the slate there–'

'Thank you. I have it. The trail ends at the door to his chambers. The scryes couldn't follow it inside?'

'Correct,' said Rede. 'The Master is the only psyker on the Tower allowed the privilege of living alone.'

'And his chamber is psychically sealed, armoured against scrying.'

'Yes,' the detective snorted, returning to the table and picking up the recaf pot. 'Psychically speaking, the Master's chambers are a fortress; the psychic protection is even heavier than the physical protection. Even if the rest of the tower turns into a warp-damned nest of, well, we both know what, the Master's chambers are supposed to be his final sanctuary. Whatever happens, he can retreat to his chambers, scream out a message, and still be alive when rescue comes.' She shook the pot, grunted and put it down again. 'And before you ask, the blurring effect of the wards in the cloisters is a hundred times worse in there. The combination of those and the Master's death-shock apparently makes the room next to unreadable. Two senior astropaths tried. They both had to be helped out of there. The death-shock is so overpowering that any fine details that might have been left are blotted out.' Rede shivered. 'The killing had a lot of the astropaths spooked to begin with.'

'They're not the only ones,' said Calpurnia darkly, pushing back from the table. 'I'm the one who fought her way in here through an ignorant pack of rioters who wanted to hijack her ship and escape off-station.'

Rede didn't answer. She just scowled and stared at her boots.

'Our killer is smart,' Calpurnia said, standing up. 'He attacks Otranto somewhere in the fringes of the cloisters, and gets the man's blood up to the point where the Master's panic blurs his own footprints for us. He hounds him through the cloisters, although how this chase ran with no physical witnesses I can't begin to bloody well guess, and chases him into the one place where his death is guaranteed to be almost opaque to psychic probing. A psyker, are we thinking? Or someone who knows psykers well?'

'On this station,' Rede said, 'that's effectively everyone.'

'Very well, I – we, uh, the Chastener and myself – we can't use their senses, so we'll have to use our own. I want to see the cloisters and Otranto's chambers.'

'I thought you might. I've got a detail standing ready. Say the word.'

'I'm saying it now,' Calpurnia growled. She could feel her temper going the way of Dast's. 'We've found a way that doesn't work. Somewhere in this place there's going to be a way that does. Let's go.'

In dim light and with soft sounds, the Arbites made their way through the astropath cloisters. A proctor from the Tower garrison went first, carrying a rod from which the precinct's seal of authority hung on a heavy silver chain. Then came Bruinann, with Rede slightly behind and to his left, once again in her guise as a humble attendant arbitrator. Calpurnia came next with Dast, Orovene and two more arbitrators behind her.

Orovene carried a little reliquary box in cupped hands, a cloisonné cylinder holding scraps of a scroll of decree personally scribed by Grand Provost Marshal Lunkati. Dast had insisted that Orovene bring it from the precinct's chapel, and had been careful to stay within a half-dozen paces of it. Even so, he was ill at ease, twitching his hands and flicking sweat off his brow, even though the air was cool.

The shrouds on their boots had been the first surprise. No trademark hammer of hard Arbites soles here, the traditional warning to the citizenry, *Make way for the law.* Here the astropaths' tight-strung minds needed tranquillity, and they moved with muffling-pads snapped into place over their boots, reducing the proud crash of footsteps to an eerie little soughing sound on the matting.

The astropath cloisters weren't the austere environment of a Navy or Arbites fortress, nor the imposing ceremonial spaces of the

Ministorum. Rede had told her that the old walls had been lined with a psyk-cage and then a layer of rockcrete. The lines of walls and ceiling were rounded, blurring into each other with none of the clean straight surfaces, ornate pillars or vaulting that Calpurnia might have expected. At first, she imagined walking down the smooth bore of some giant gun, but when she peered through the gloom, she realised that the walls were anything but smooth.

Every wall was textured, the rockcrete bearing banks, grooves and whorls that might evoke skin, the contours of clouds, or the print of a finger. Calpurnia found herself wanting to slip off a gauntlet and trail her touch along the wall to feel it under her skin. She blinked and ground her teeth to force herself back into some kind of decorum.

Long pennants of cloth, that looked ragged and grubby to Calpurnia's eyes, hung at every corner and intersection of corridors. They had passed half a dozen of the pennants before she realised why they appeared so slovenly: they were there for the touch, not the eye, and the sigils down their hems were sharp and cleanly embroidered, easily read by questing fingers. Not one of them was frayed or ravelled. The pennants were being maintained in the way that counted.

She noticed something else, too. A fresh patch of rockcrete stood out, as if some damage to the wall had been repaired. The patch was pallid and raw-looking, and around its edges, the wall was speckled and stained.

Calpurnia didn't need to ask what it was. She had seen spray-patterns like that against courthouse walls. The bloodstains were old, long-dried, but they were a reminder where she was and what business had brought her here. Calpurnia set her shoulders, and kept step as they moved on.

NOT LONG AFTERWARDS, they came upon the first astropath that Calpurnia had seen aboard a fortress that was full of them. He was a blot of green robes, in a mass of shadows, where a knot of passages and rampshafts met. Even at first sight, it was obvious that he wasn't well, but the Arbites in front of Calpurnia didn't slow or stop. She took care to keep up with them, keenly aware that she was ignorant about how to behave here.

As they passed, she had a quick impression of a scrawny figure, steadying itself against a buttress with one spidery hand. The hairless ball of his head hung listlessly, his face invisible. The veins on his skull were clearly visible, weaving among skull-plugs and dermal wiring. An attendant in a plain cream-coloured tunic crouched in front of him, holding up a cloth. It was speckled with blood, although Calpurnia couldn't tell where the astropath was bleeding from.

The other attendant, taller, robed and masked, loomed behind the astropath like the figure of Justice in a morality play. He held a silver-chased handgun. A length of crimson ribbon was elaborately knotted around the muzzle, and a small ward-charm hung from it. 'Vitifer', Calpurnia remembered from the briefs.

'The witch is dying,' rumbled Dast.

The walk took them up a short switchback of steps and back past the little tableau, now half a floor up. As they turned down a new passageway, a voice, deeper than Dast's, but hoarse, came up from where the astropath still stooped against the wall.

'Tilting!' was all it said, although the tone was that of a razor-edged parting insult. Calpurnia had no idea what it meant, and in a few moments, the Arbites were gone down the passageway. If the man said anything more, she didn't hear it, and she never saw him again.

THERE WERE ROWS of holes in the floor matting as they came closer to the Master's chambers, set after set of them.

Calpurnia missed the first ones: she had been watching a procession of astropaths ushered past them by two attendants, tailed by another vitifer with his red-ribboned gun. These were junior, less puissant than the man they had passed earlier, with a retinue to himself. They were choristers, not full astropaths. Their green robes were little more than tunics, and their surgery had been brisk and savage, heads cocooned in containment circuitry like bronzed birdcages, held fast by armatures screwed directly into their skulls. They shuffled along, each with a hand on the shoulder of the one in front, the leader holding a rope that an attendant trailed behind him.

For Calpurnia, the sight was almost hypnotically strange, the dim light adding to its power. She was sure she could hear echoes, too, a strange syncopated whispering, counterpointing the choristers' soft steps. In that space, no echo should have been possible. When she saw each of the choristers stumble at exactly the same point, their bare feet catching at a row of gouges in the matting, it was merely one more dreamlike, outlandish touch.

They crossed the second set of holes under an archway hung with three long pennants that they had to push aside like a curtain. However, it was only when they arrived at the third set, on the lip of the little lowered foyer outside the Master's chambers, that she finally asked what they were.

'Witchcullises,' Bruinann told her, indicating upwards. A row of elaborate spearheads jutted out of the ceiling, directly over the punched and torn matting underfoot. Calpurnia winced, wondering how much force the barrier must have come down with, and how many of them she had blithely walked under on the way.

'Part of the defences for when one of them loses control. The cullises stop them from roaming, and hurting too many other people by unbalancing one another. They also cage them if something… taints them.' Bruinann looked edgy. 'The cullises come down around them to contain them.'

'They're blast-doors?' Calpurnia asked.

'No, ma'am. Well, not for that kind of blast. Cage doors, as I say, wards and protections that turn psykcraft back on itself. The same as what lines the walls under that 'crete. Magos Channery and her priests do the forging.'

'Move on,' Dast broke in as she started to speak again. She closed her mouth and followed Bruinann into the Master's chambers.

THE CONVERSATION, EVEN Dast's rebuke, had grounded her a little, broken some of the spell of the cloisters. As they stepped into the anterooms, Calpurnia was looking around her with arbitor's eyes once again.

The outer foyer was a long oval, punctured once at each end and on each side by arched openings, with the black metal spikes of witchcullises poking through the lintels like teeth through gums. Only one of the arches boasted actual doors, although they were barely worthy of the name. A sliding partition blocked the far archway, honey-coloured Hydraphur silk stretched on a frame and lacquered to a brittle stiffness. The frame was broken, and the stiffened silk was ripped and gaping where Otranto had crashed through the partition in his terror.

'How are these fashioned?' Calpurnia asked as they walked down the length of the room.

'As you see them, ma'am,' Bruinann answered. 'Lacquered silk on the wooden frame. You'll see those around the Tower. If you're asking are they like the cullises, they're not. They're purely ornamental. Ma'am?' He had noticed her brief smile.

'It was important. I caught myself looking for designs painted on the doors. How long does it take to get used to living among people whose primary sense you don't share?'

'It's a tough place to get used to, ma'am, in all kinds of ways.' He ended the matter there and walked on, leaving Calpurnia to wonder at the tiredness she had heard in his voice.

She stopped as they made their way past the broken partition and ran her fingers over fabric and frame. The lacquer was rough, the texture of the brush strokes left there deliberately. Patches of screen that must have had especially pleasing textures were polished and stained dark by touch after touch. Calpurnia let her fingers wander over the wood of the frame: lightweight to be sure, but not brittle the way the fabric was. It would have taken quite a turn of speed to break through the frame.

When she stepped through the broken gap into the next room, her first thought was *it's a vineyard*, and for the rest of her time aboard the Bastion that was how she thought of it: Master Otranto's vineyard.

The room was full of ropes and cords. They hung from the ceiling in neat rows, forming aisles like the fruit-vines she remembered on Iax, anchored into the floor by chains and rings that gave each rope a little room to swing. Four lamps shone from mountings in the corners of the room, shaded in silk as golden-brown as that of the door-screens, to give a quality like Hydraphur daylight. Shrouded lanterns hung here and there casting a crazy lattice of rope-shadows across the floor. The shadows fell at all angles beneath Calpurnia's feet, and crisscrossed her legs.

Some of the ropes and cords were woven from rough hemp, some were beautifully brushed silk, or plaited ribbons of velvet. Some were thinner than Calpurnia's little finger, others thicker than her arm. Some had scraps of paper woven into them, holding sayings and devotions that Calpurnia supposed were part of some astropaths' creed, and from others dangled tiny metal chains, chimes, or pendant crystals. There was an elegance about the room that had her smiling again before she realised she was doing it.

The smile flicked off her face when Dast's hand clamped down on her shoulder and he spun her around.

'You broke formation,' he said. His helmet was still on, and she couldn't see his eyes, but there was an ugly, angry twist to his mouth as he spoke. 'We were in formal procession here. You broke the procession and defied my instructions. Remember I have rank here.'

'I fully understand the special nature of my rank, master Chastener,' she told him. 'In fact, that was what motivated me. I'm working on the premise that we're under observation whenever we're outside a sanctuary like the precinct chambers or, or here.' She motioned around them. 'Since my nominal rank is providing the authority for us to launch our investigation, it's important for any observer to conclude that I am still a full arbitor senioris, and that I am in command here. I am conducting myself accordingly.'

I scored a point, she thought, as she watched Dast's expression, and then immediately yanked at the choke chain she kept her thoughts on. She made herself remember that Dast was right. Her duty was to comport herself according to her station.

Without my duty, who am I? she thought. The thought had to fight with a tiny flicker of satisfaction that Dast had taken her point and backed off, but it won comfortably.

'Who am I indeed?' she murmured aloud, and walked through the vineyard to where Rede and Orovene were standing over a tangle of ropes at the far end.

'He got most of the way through the ropes all right, we think,' said Rede as Calpurnia joined them. 'This room was one of his favourites, he knew it very well. Even if he hadn't been pushing out his senses, he wouldn't have needed to think about where anything was. It wasn't until he got right to the end that he got tangled in these two, and he couldn't get out.'

Calpurnia crouched down over the snapped cords. One had been pulled against its rings with such force that they'd given way and broken open, and the rope lay like a kicked-off bed sheet. The other rope was thicker and heavier, trailing streamers of scripture-paper. It had only come loose at the ceiling, but the Master must have become tangled in it. The little chain that anchored it to its floor-ring was pulled taut, towards the doors, and most of the paper had been stripped out of the weave, leaving little stubs like torn-off insect wings. Calpurnia looked around for signs of the torn-out papers, but couldn't see them.

'The Master's close associates had already spent some time in here before we arrived,' said Bruinann as he joined them. 'One of the things they seem to have done was clear away the prayer-papers from that rope. You can see where they were. As we read it, it got wrapped around him as he struggled through here, and the paper ripped out as he tried to get free.'

'Prayer-papers? Is that what these are?' That had caught Orovene's interest. 'Might there be some specific motive in damaging them?'

'They were written by the Master before last,' Rede answered. 'The third most recent, that is. It's a form of meditation for the astropaths who still have enough function left to perform it. They use dense inks that make it easier for a psyker to perceive the words and track them with their minds. It is very slow work, very precise and hard to do without their eyes to guide them. It focuses them, and calms them down when they need it.'

'Who selects the prayers they use?' Orovene asked, but Rede shrugged. Calpurnia leaned carefully over one of the remaining papers until she could read it aloud. The hand was laborious and over-precise, like a child's, and the ink had a strange, laminated gloss.

This Sea does beget Unreason and the Awakening of our Shadows.
Undying Beacon and Protector, to whom we are Bound,
Your Light does ease the Weight of Shackles.
Your Song gladdens our Labours in the Crying Darkness.

'Not any catechism I recognise,' said Orovene.

Rede shrugged again. 'Speak to one of the attendants,' she said. 'I'm sure they'll track it down for you if you feel it's important.' Her tone rankled Calpurnia – the detective seemed oddly detached from an investigation that could land her in the Incarcery, as Calpurnia's neighbour, if the Hydraphur command decided it had been botched.

'We've spent too much time here,' Dast declared. 'Move on.'

BEYOND THE VINEYARD, the Master's chambers were a cluster of low-ceilinged circular silos joined by simple arched doors, their lintels empty of cullis-teeth. Orovene was the first to remark on that.

'None of the individual chambers are separated,' Rede said. 'That's the final defence, over there.' She tilted her head back past them, and the three off-station Arbites turned to consider the door they had just walked through. 'Door' was a mild term, Calpurnia thought as she took a proper look and remembered Rede's remarks about fortification.

The outer defence was a witchcullis like the ones they had already seen, its spikes hung with prayer slips and ceremonial charms. Inside that was the auspex arch, the walls carved into gargoyle faces with sniffers and sensors for eyes. The nozzles of flechette-spitters and acid-misters jutted from mouths, and were clutched in sculpted claws. The whole arch was so shallow that Calpurnia could have crossed it in one long stride, but there was more than enough lethality in the walls to stop an enemy in their tracks. Calpurnia could see that the fittings were chipped and tarnished: these defences had been triggered by Otranto's mind shout against whomever he'd been fleeing. For all the good it had done him.

The final door was a great armoured shutter on its oiled and noiseless slide and hinge. It was an oval slab of adamant, thicker than a hand could span, its surface worked with blessings and wards, crystalline psyk-earths, silver eagle inscribed with holy texts, mag-locks and sliding bolts.

'Stronger than the witchcullis behind it,' Bruinann told them. 'Stronger than most of the containments in the rest of the walls, so I'm advised. It locks physically, with those bolts, as well as magnetically. The Mechanicus has built an engine into the locking mechanism whose spirit can animate a stasis field: the bolt can't move until the correct codes allow the engine to rest. The moving parts are worked with the same witch-wards as the rest of the door and the cullises. The patterns are machined so that when they turn to the locked position, their wards mesh with those of the door and compound the strength of the defences.'

'Something you can put your faith in,' said Orovene. He caught Bruinann's look. 'I'm not making fun, aedile. The works of the Machine come to us by Imperial grace, exactly the way my own sacraments do. The engine-spirit obeys His rule just as the human one does. The Emperor protects. You haven't had that conversation with this Channery yet? No?'

'The magos is not the most approachable,' said Rede. 'She helped us open the door when we got in to find Otranto, and she spoke with the auspexes in the arch there. That was how we confirmed that Otranto used a code to trigger them, and it was just the auspex sniffing a hostile. She did it all through proxies, speaking through servitors, or junior priests slaved to her voice.' Rede's own voice was strained. Mechanicus mysteries could be confronting to people outside the Tech-Priesthood.

Dast had been inspecting the entrance with the practiced manner of one used to working with defended doors, tracing the lines of the wards with his hands, and then inspecting the closing mechanism. Calpurnia walked over and joined him, looking at the micro-detail of the wards, and the powerful closing mechanism that could slam this giant slab shut in moments.

'I'm closing it,' said Dast curtly. 'Check and clear the doorway.'

'Shutter closing!' Calpurnia yelled, back-pedalling to look out of the entranceway. There was no need for the alert: the proctor who'd led them here had positioned the other arbitrators in a cordon line across the vineyard. They did not move from their sentry positions as the door glided along its rails, and swung in and sealed the archway. Calpurnia braced herself for a great clang, but there was only a silky hiss as metal met metal. They came together with the smooth motion that only the meticulous craft of the Mechanicus could perfect. A puff of air, pushed from between door and lintel, brushed their faces, and then they were sealed in at the death-scene.

THE DOOR HAD taken less than four seconds to close, start to finish.

'Whoever was on the Master's tail, as he ran into his chambers, must have been breathing down his neck,' Orovene said. Dast had walked to the door again and was examining the way it sat in the lintel. From what Calpurnia could see, it met the wall so smoothly that there might not have been a join there at all.

'Tripping and tangling on those ropes would have slowed him down. They might have caught him up,' said Calpurnia, but she was frowning as she said it. Rede nodded.

'So it doesn't add up for you either, ma'am. The witchcullises drop in about half the time it takes for that door to close, so whoever Master Otranto was fleeing was right behind him when he came down that passage.'

'Too fast for the archway weapons to catch, too,' Dast put in as he came away from the door. 'The bastard was so hot on Otranto's heels that he sank the knife in as soon as the Master turned around. So what the hell happened when Otranto fell in the ropes outside?'

'That's where our answers dry up,' said Rede. 'Our killer chases Otranto halfway across this fortress. The Master's in a state of mortal terror that sends ripples out across the Bastion even with the containments in place. The killer hounds him so closely that even though the cullises drop and the door slams, he's through without a scratch. Our Verispex tools are crude, but we found no bio-traces anywhere that the pursuer might have been wounded. On the other hand, Otranto tangles himself in rope, falls and lies there struggling, and the killer doesn't strike. He waits until Otranto's free and running again, and then follows him into the inner chambers as the door seals, and does the deed.'

'And,' said Bruinann, 'he's gone. We open the door and Otranto's corpse is alone. No door has opened for the assassin, no cullis has raised. No auspex has sniffed him and no witness has seen him. No psyker-seance can pin him down, and no Verispex can track him.'

The Arbites stood in silence and considered her words.

'I'm very glad you're here to direct us, arbitor senioris,' Rede said, but there was no warmth in her smile at all.

HER ATTENTION OFF the fortified door, Calpurnia could look around the room and see the scars that the Master had left as he fled through it.

The floor matting was finer than outside, straw-like to the eye, but woollen-soft to the touch. The colour was a uniform grey-green from wall to wall, but she could see the weave forming subtle patterns that would tell a barefoot, blind psyker where he was in the room. The walls were finished in panels of dark timber, lightly treated to leave the natural grain exposed and raw to the touch. Braziers had stood on each side of the door, but their slender gold columns had been overbalanced. The burners were extinguished, but Calpurnia could still catch the ghost of a scent, a complex layering of perfumes.

The Master's trail came from the doorway. It seemed to change constantly: now the matting was crushed as if a tank had rolled across it, a pace later it was scorched and the weave pushed outward as if from a red-hot furnace-wind. A pace later and it was whole, but bleached, as if it had sat under a fierce sun for a month. Beyond that, the colour came back, but the pattern of it was ravelled and frayed, the fabric apparently corroded. Above the overbalanced brazier stands, the wooden panelling of the walls was scorched and ragged.

In the dying minutes of his life, Otranto's terror had overwhelmed his control and left its wake through the room. The thought of what it must have been like for him made Calpurnia shudder. Looking around the room from there, she realised that none of the Arbites were standing on the path left through the matting. Without word or direction, they had all instinctively shied away from that patch of floor.

Calpurnia winced at a cramp in her hand and realised that the silver aquila at her throat was pinched between her thumb and forefinger, hard enough to hurt. She released it with an effort of will, and walked through the inner doorway into Otranto's bedchamber, the death room.

The single dusty lumen fitting in the crown of the chamber's ceiling had burst at the moment of the Master's death, and had not been replaced. Instead, the room was full of hot, shadowless light from free-standing Arbites lamp arrays. Calpurnia took in her sparse surroundings, by the lamplight.

The trail through the floor matting faded to scuff marks as it entered the room. Marks that anyone's feet could have left. The bedclothes were lightly tousled from the last time that Otranto had slept – would ever sleep – there. The man had collapsed against the foot of the bed and had died without disturbing the sheets. The mark of his blood still stained the floor beneath the bed.

Six small tripods had held incense burners and chime-boxes, set in a careful circuit around the bed. They had all been knocked over, their legs pointing like fingers, like compass needles, back to the spot where the Master had perished.

THAT WAS ALL. Calpurnia, who had seen murder scenes before, felt the anticlimax as a loosening of her shoulders and a quiet exhalation of breath. She wasn't sure what she had been expecting: the old man's ghost? Some creature made of witch-malice, such as the Navigators were supposed to see out between the stars? She didn't know.

There were two doorways before them, one on each side of the bed, at eleven and one o'clock to the main entrance's six o'clock. One stood dark, the other was softly lit. They were the side-rooms that she had seen on Rede's schematics. She wandered towards the left one, and saw Dast go right.

The dark archway in front of her led into the meditation room: even barer than the bedchamber, a small mat on the naked rockcrete floor the only hint at furnishings. The light from the arc array in the main chamber washed into the little room, enough for her to see the bare walls and high ceiling. She leaned in through the door and–

–back-pedalled frantically out of it, grabbing at the maul-hilt at her belt. She collected herself, ignored a curious glance from Orovene and stepped back inside. The glitter of light from above, when she gave her eyes time to adjust to the shadows came, not from eyes in the dark, but from pale gems. An Imperial aquila adorned the domed ceiling, and the gems picked out its pinions and made a halo around the blind left head.

She took a breath and turned back into the room, conscious of Orovene's eyes still on her. She had the feeling that her moment of fright would cost her with her two jailers when they were back in the Arbites chambers.

Then Dast gave a bellow from the other chamber, and straightaway Calpurnia was running, her maul in her hand. She passed Orovene and ran through to where the master Chastener was glaring over the sights of his shotgun at the grey-haired woman in the concordiast's gown. She sat amid the greenery and regarded the Arbites with no surprise at all.

CHAPTER FIVE

THEY WERE IN the chambers with Ylante.

The halls from the attendants' decks met the astropath cloisters at a broad polished platform underneath high intersecting arches hung with lamps. The Bastion's bells had rung to signal half a dozen transmission-trances in the coming watch, and the air was alive with quiet bustle. Gaggles of housemen and drudges passed this way and that, bent under their loads. Solemn-faced junior apothecaries, with baskets of instruments and medicines, emerged from the stairwells leading to the eastern side of the Second Barbican, ready to join their masters in the keep and assist them in the eyries. Concordiasts and herbalists were passing through from the barrack-decks crowding the sides of the keep. They bore down into the Curtain, on their way to help soothe strained bodies and wrenched minds. Scribes and savants shuffled to their posts in the Encryptors' vault or the Scriptorium.

Teeker Renz, in formal garb that marked out his ranks and offices, stood in the middle of it all. He was well known for prowling the halls, ostensibly so that he could report to the Master that the pulse of the Bastion was beating as it should. More often, he did it so that he could be seen and found, to hold a strolling sort of court in among a pack of his protégés and friends, and anyone who wanted to petition for his favour. Now, he prowled beneath the arches, eyeing the gates that led to the upper keep's stairs, directing baleful thoughts up those stairs to the inner astropath cloisters and the Master's suite.

They were in there with Ylante, these *Arbites,* who had somehow come aboard and marched straight into the middle of all this trouble without Renz being able to do anything about it.

Renz knew about the Arbites, who didn't? Until now, they'd always been an impersonal threat. When the uniforms and grim helmet-plates of Bruinann and his thugs had come down a hall, Renz had always done his best not to look at them.

Now... now he didn't want to think about it. How could they be in there with Ylante when he wanted to be in there talking to the little bi– talking to the woman. Things had to be worked out, but the Arbites were in there. He needed to talk to Ylante, but he–

Where the hell were Dechene and Kyto? They were supposed to be here. Wasn't this their job? To counsel and assist him? So, where the hell were they?

It wasn't much, but it was something for Renz to aim his anger at, and blaming the other two men let him order his thoughts a little and sidle back towards that terrible, central fact: the Arbites. They had no place here. Whoever decided that the Arbites knew anything about... anything? Kyto had said something about how this Calpurnia woman could take command of the Tower if she wanted to. Take command! Run the place just as if she had some damn right to!

What would some clumping-booted arbitor from Hydraphur know about keeping the Blind Tower running?

She wouldn't know them the way Renz did. She wouldn't know that Concordiast Ottre had a mental hide like a trooper's carapace, and could work the most punishing shifts with high-strung astropaths like Jaul and Ankyne without cracking. She wouldn't know that Kyto was the man to ask which astropaths knew the Navy's psykers best and should be on duty in the eyries when a warship squadron was due to pass close by.

She wouldn't know that Astropath Sacredsteel shouldn't be allowed to ascend any further in rank, whatever her nominal level of ability might be, until Angel-of-Auriga had been made Deputy Master of the Watch, because Renz had promised him that. She wouldn't know how the apportioning worked, how the provision orders needed to be... modulated the way Renz had always arranged. She would know nothing of the subtleties of directing assignments and rations to reflect who needed to be kept in their place and who had earned consideration: subtleties with which Renz was perfectly familiar, but which he had never written down.

For a moment, the tension got the better of him and his hands flew to his temples, scrunched the edges of his velvet cap and left it sitting askew on his sweating brow.

How could he explain to some jaw-champing arbitor with planet-dust still on their feet how it worked? These arrangements had just, well, *developed* with time, as Renz had started to interpret and correct the Master's instructions. How could he make them see that the privileges he had slowly drawn about him were rightfully his, see that his friends deserved the places he had carved out for them? It would be so obvious if he could just explain, providing that Ylante didn't get in first. He needed a plan.

Dechene was good at this kind of thing. Where *was* the man?

'THE ARBITES,' SAID Gessante Lohjen, in a low voice that barely ruffled the quiet of the astropath cloister. His hood cast his face into shadow in the dim light, 'Shira Calpurnia and her staff. Remember what I said.'

The posture of the two astropaths he was addressing did not change. They continued to stand, like bookends, slightly turned towards one another, each holding one of the tasselled pennons that hung in a cluster from the ceiling of the intersection. Their fingers worked at the embroidered fabric with eerily identical motions. Their faces, with the care-worn features of long-serving astropaths, remained serene, faintly distracted. Their empty eyes – Brom's lids sewn down over the sockets, del'Kateer's simply shrivelled so deep that they were hidden in the wrinkled skin of the sockets – stared impassively past the Lohjen's shoulders. Standing between them, conscious of the two armed vitifers standing behind him, Attendant Acquerin tried to hide his nerves. He stole a glance at the velvet envelope Lohjen held low to his side, and then made an effort to look away and pretend he hadn't been watching it.

'We'll keep you in mind, sir,' Brom said mildly after a moment, his voice papery-dry. 'But do you really not agree that you're misjudging what we can do for you? We've discussed this.'

'We have, and I don't see the need to repeat myself.' Lohjen began to bow before the two blind men, hesitated, completed the gesture uncertainly and turned away. A moment later, his dove-grey captain's coat was fading into the dim light of the sub-eyrie passages. As he turned a corner, a flash of light turned him briefly into a silhouette, startling Acquerin's eyes, before the light and the man were both gone.

'What was that, a moment ago?' asked Brom in the same mild voice.

'He turned on a lumen, sir. To show his way, I think.'

'Thought so,' said del'Kateer. 'I tasted a change in the air. There's a feel to light, when you know the trick of looking for it.' Acquerin wondered if that last had been for his benefit, if his surprise at the blind astropath noticing the light had been that obvious.

The two astropaths were turning towards him as the thought crossed his mind, and the identical small smiles that flickered across their faces showed that he'd allowed the thought to radiate. He laced his hands in front of him and bowed his head. By the time he had run through ten lines of one of his childhood catechisms, and his mind was calm again, the two old men had passed to either side of him and were shuffling down the passageway to the Green Eyrie. Acquerin waited respectfully until they and the vitifers had passed by, and then turned and took up his proper position, between them and a dozen steps behind, where he wouldn't be in the vitifers' sight line.

Senior Astropath del'Kateer registered the boy as a brief, vivid patch of texture at the fringe of sensing. It settled into part of the pattern, in with the thrum of energy through the Tower's power-conduits, Brom's footsteps and his clinking amulet-chain, and the distant sound of his own feet and staff-tip.

'What do you think of the man?' he asked Brom. The words came out as the barest mutter – but that was all they needed to be. He and Brom were old friends, old colleagues. Where the trailing edges of their minds overlapped, they meshed; the white fires in the centres of their skulls burned and danced to a rhythm so closely that they were effectively one.

Brom picked up the question easily. He just didn't reply.

'I know, friend. Bad times, turbulent, and that Lohjen's just a shadow in the middle of it all.'

Del'Kateer did not say 'shadow'. That part of his sentence was an image-flash through the mind-haze. Lohjen was still a mystery, a blank spot in their knowledge, unpredictable, and dangerous to examine too closely.

Brom's answer was to take that image and turn it. In the experience of astropaths, such vortices would unravel as the currents shifted and weakened. The image of that happening would often be sent from mind to mind to show release, an end to hard times, and a relief of tension.

'Shady or not, I wouldn't have put speaking directly with the Arbites as beyond his capability.' That gave some texture to the meaning of the image Brom had sent: the mystery would unravel, or would be unravelled. Brom was counting on the Arbites to pull apart any danger, any conspiracy.

Del'Kateer considered this.

'Odd how directed they've been. Are you thinking that with me?' The mental image of an astropathic choir, a giant one, such as might stretch even the Blind Tower's abilities to assemble, using all its might to push a routine Administratum surveillance code through clear space. The sense of a powerful force left unused or directed to puzzlingly simple ends.

'You know, we're not the only ones to wonder it.' Brom's reply was entirely verbal, his mind preoccupied with ordering his thoughts, 'Sacredsteel and Thujik, and, well...'

The sentence hung in the air. Del'Kateer adjusted his grip on his staff, leaned on it for a moment and let his mind caress the microscrollwork on its heavy, gilded head. He'd had the staff for eight decades, and the patterns were as delightful to his psychic senses as when he had first been given it. That was back when he had taken ship for Hydraphur, with the pain of the Binding still lingering in his dead eyes, and the new white fire burning deep in him.

'Well. Indeed.' He sighed as the two of them began walking again. Brom had begun to work a stick of worry-wood between his fingers. 'How many are lining up now, then? Who's approached you?'

Brom gave a dry laugh.

'Formally? Nobody. Come on, my friend, would you? Otranto's body is barely cool and his echoes have barely died away. Whatever's left of him is still flying home to the fire.' The twitch of Brom's finger looked like a random gesture to Acquerin, walking behind him.

Del'Kateer, with senses the young attendant did not possess, knew his friend was pointing Earthward, into the light of the Astronomican. 'There's worse trouble ahead before his death's put to rest, and I think I speak both our minds, no?' He paced onwards in silence. Beside him, Del'Kateer's mind had busied itself so deeply on the engravings on his staff that the mental picture of them was radiating off him, as clear to Brom as if he was touching them himself.

'Thujik,' Del'Kateer said at length. 'Hm. He's not been subtle about his ambition the last few years, has he? Just built his power base in the wrong places is all.'

'And made the wrong enemies,' Brom replied.

'Do you think Otranto ever cared? I don't remember him being very exercised about the succession. Big part of why things are as they are now, with this arbitor sitting in his suite. On his seat, too, I don't doubt. Ha.'

'Ha. No, you're right: The whole nub of the problem, really.'

Although neither of the two venerable astropaths spoke much aloud after that, the problem they were both considering stayed fixed in their minds to the point where it even began to form in the mind of their attendant. For no reason that he could think of, Acquerin found himself thinking of Teeker Renz, the murdered Master's high-strung, foul-tempered major-domo. Acquerin disliked Renz, and savoured being far away from him on errands like these, but somehow the man kept bobbing up in his thoughts. He lengthened his steps a little to get closer to the two astropaths, and kept his hearing sharp, remembering Lohjen's instructions:

Bring me back news of everything you overhear after I've done with them. Whatever they say about this Arbites investigation, especially anything they say that they didn't tell me. Whatever they say about the succession to the Master's seat, and whatever they say about who they suspect of Otranto's murder. Especially that, first and foremost that.

THE FIREWATCH EYRIE was so-called because it was most commonly used to speak with the astropathic stations lying towards the Segmentum Solar. It needed its astropath's attention to be turned in the direction of Holy Earth and the great god-furnace of the Astronomican. The Green Eyrie, sitting closer in towards the keep, was so-called because for a long time it had been devoted purely to Naval transmissions, decked out in green Battlefleet livery (to whose colour the astropaths were indifferent, although they knew of it). The base of the Green Eyrie was ringed with the old guard-cells and reinforced psyk-wards that the Navy staff had used to keep control of the movements up and down the column. Now that the old restriction had fallen away, the eyrie was used for the more erratic psykers who needed more careful guarding and containment.

The raw young or the exhausted old, on the other hand, went to the Eyrie of Echoes for their work. Its column stood rooted in old ordnance workshops that had been refitted to hold the extra-large choirs that a less confident mind, or one with a punishing transmission to endure, needed to give it strength. The Lantern Eyrie, far out by the secondary docks, had some of the best-forged mechanisms, and was the best for freeing its occupant's mind from any static or mental wash from other transmissions. That was the place for astropaths standing the Silent Watch, a constant, open listening for transmissions, unscheduled distress calls or warnings, or the trauma of an overloading connection by another astropath.

Then there was the Eyrie of Bones. At the same time that the Green Eyrie had drifted from Navy use to become a workplace for all the Bastion's astropaths, the Eyrie of Bones had begun to fall from favour as a personal eyrie for the Master of the Tower. The Astra Telepathica law that the Master of a place like this had always to be a fully capable astropath in his own right, and to perform his duty regularly, was a given, always. Gonvall, Otranto's predecessor, had never bothered much with a personal eyrie, and Otranto had cared even less. Therefore, the Eyrie of Bones, so close to the corner of the keep that someone in a vacc suit could have spanned the gap with his arms, was there for any astropath who asked to be rostered to it.

That, of course, was highly unbecoming. The position of Master had been allowed to degrade under Otranto – that was the confirmed opinion of Senior Astropath Thujik. Things would certainly change. They could have changed already, but for the wretched motions that had to be gone through by the Arbites, and Thujik's tenure as Master would be to see to that in good order. He promised himself this as he rode the lift up the column to the Eyrie of Bones, an adjutant on one side of him, and a vitifer on the other, with his red-wrapped pistol.

Thujik had been taken aboard the Black Ships at nineteen, with two years' service to his father, whipping the family outposts into shape. He had come out of the Soul Binding, carrying that white fire deep in him, his vision scorched black, but his mind still clear, and his memory too, by the Emperor's grace. Grace it was, and grace with a purpose. So many astropaths had their memories, even their higher cognition, burned away by the trauma of the Binding, but if the Emperor had left Thujik with his skills, wasn't that a sign? He would be the one to get this blasted outpost running properly, just as he had in his youth.

The lift door opened. The passage leading up into the eyrie was ribbed, literally. Human ribs were set into its walls, skulls and spines, and the long bones of arms and legs, marched along the walls in grim symmetry. They were old bones, carefully preserved. Thujik hobbled past, stopping every so often to stretch his humped back and let his adjutant adjust the augmetic splints propping up his withered legs. The astropathic message with Santo Pevrelyi was expected some time in the next two hundred and fifteen hours. He hobbled on, musing.

There was none of Otranto's sloppiness, delegating half the running of the place to his jumped-up little major-domo and his cronies, and there were none of Sacredsteel's idiot pretensions either. Oh, she was devoted, certainly. He would have no hesitation in naming her first among equals when he laid out his circle of senior astropaths. He remained confident, however. He had always known that he was going to succeed Otranto. 'Master of the Tower' was his. He deserved it.

With a sigh, he lowered himself onto a couch and began to run his mind through its exercises. Somewhere below, the Encryptors would be in the last stages of coding and weaving the data to go out to Santo Pevrelyi. They would be encoding it for him to transmit. Then out across space to the waiting minds, in their mountain fort on Pevrelyi's highlands.

MEANWHILE, SENIOR ASTROPATH Sacredsteel was walking in the Smoke Garden.

The garden had no plants or trees. It was an old back vent raking downwards from what had once been gun batteries around the middle tiers of the keep. They had once sucked away exhaust gases from the gun decks and the ordnance launching cradles. Now, the tunnel was again full of smoke, the smoke of incense and aromatic oils, burning and evaporating in precise mixtures, brewed and prepared by Teeker Renz and deployed by his assistants and apprentices.

The floor of the garden hall had two levels. The two outer paths were covered with soft pebbles, rounded, polished silky-smooth, and designed to be walked on barefoot. The centre path, set lower, sat under a layer of the same pebbles, just submerged under ankle-deep water. The water could be made warm enough to steam and add to the texture of the air, or cold enough to cause a shocking, cleansing chill to the skin.

Sacredsteel had come to the Smoke Garden fresh from a turbulent trance in the Eyrie of Echoes. For over three hours, she'd struggled to reel in a maddeningly faint message from the Telepathica matrices at Caruana-IV. She'd strained to snatch compacted notes of thought in her mental fingers and swallow them into her brain. She pushed them firmly enough down into her mind so that she could be sure they wouldn't dissipate like smoke when the trance finished. They hadn't, of course: she knew it was not vanity to consider herself an astropath of the first order. She had imprisoned the melody firmly, and let it out again as words and codes into the ears of the transcriptors and vox-captures as her mind settled back down into the eyrie walls and the bone vault of her skull.

The effort of the session had left her shuddering with exhaustion and alive with psychic echoes. She saw a strange repeating vision of the Judge card of the Emperor's Tarot, splattered with blood and black paint, and a hot sensation danced around the bones of her face and neck.

She was pleased to hitch up her gown and walk barefoot along the path, the cool water soothing her feet (the sensation had gradually died out of her upper body ever since her Soul Binding: her head and shoulders were almost totally numb, but her feet felt the cool water perfectly well). She was dimly aware of the perfumed smokes and steams she was passing through as she walked, but to sharpen her perception of them she would have had to augment her failing sense of smell with psychic perceptions. Marshalling them was an effort she wasn't prepared to make right now. She simply walked.

On one path-bank, shoes rattling in the pebbles, her attendant walked, with the boxy mechanical vox-ear that Channery had consecrated for her. It sucked in the sounds around them and transmitted them to the augmetics that hung from Sacredsteel's ears like vines.

They fed the sounds to her atrophying aural nerves. The astropath's vitifer, or at least the one given to her today, pistol unholstered as always, walked with her. On the other path walked an emissary from Envoy Lohjen.

'Master Lohjen was curious as to whether you had any views on why the Arbites haven't yet approached you about succession,' said the woman, whose name Sacredsteel hadn't bothered to remember.

'It's all one to me,' she replied. 'I've been about my work, no more.'

'With respect, mamzel, I don't believe this hasn't crossed your mind. You're known to be zealous and ambitious. Your calling has marked you, we know as much from your name.'

It wasn't unusual for astropaths to take a new name after their Soul Binding, something reflecting a part of the experience that had moved them. Sacredsteel had rarely seen metal before; she knew that from the murk of half-memories that she had retained from before the white fire had blasted into her.

'No one's spoken to me,' she snapped, breaking the moment's reverie. 'No one's spoken to anyone. They're in the cloisters now. That's all I know. Sniffing around Otranto's rooms, probably.'

'So you are keeping track?' The woman's voice was amused. 'Master Lohjen would like me to–'

There was a spitting crack of feedback from the hearing-box, and the woman broke off, startled. Sacredsteel hid her smile. She had learned the trick of causing those sounds with a tiny wink of mental energy. It was useful for keeping the edge in a conversation.

'Little girl, I don't doubt that you think your errand here is mighty important. I heard you introduce yourself to my assistant as a representative of Envoy Lohjen. Well, if Lohjen is all exercised about the succession here then let him come and talk to me himself. For a formal Astropathica envoy, your master has done an awful lot of lurking on his little boat and not a lot of, well, envoying.'

The woman started to say something, but was silenced by another *zip-crack* from the box.

'Until then, I believe I'll keep my own counsel,' Sacredsteel went on. 'If you know my reputation, then you'll know that pompous oaf Thujik's and you'll know that, oaf he might be, but there's nothing but void between the two of us and any other possible successor. Your master will have plenty of time to talk to both of us, and this arbitor. He can petition me for some time when he feels able to stir himself.'

'My master has–'

Zzip-crack. Sacredsteel's augmetics picked up the woman cursing under her breath.

'That will do for now. Run along and let me be, please. I've to send a cipher to Avignor in twenty-seven hours, and you're not helping me calm down so that I can rest up for it.'

She pushed her psyk-sense out to perceive the woman bowing and loping off down the garden. She grunted and kept walking. The truth was that she was nonplussed by the Arbites, by their tumultuous arrival and by their current seclusion. Weren't all Arbites thugs and idiots? Bruinann and that detective who fancied herself so secret, certainly were. She hoped the investigation wouldn't make any trouble. Sacredsteel was an astropath of the first order, and it was time she had a rank that reflected it. It was well past time that she was made Mastrex, and her patience was running out.

THE MAN WITH the two-coloured beard, who had come storming so loudly into the Master's garden to confront her, was controlling himself rigidly. The anger was clear in his dark eyes and guttural voice. It didn't take Torma Ylante long, however, to see that his shoulders and hands remained steady, the volume of his voice loud, but precisely pitched. How strong must the urge be, she thought, to step forwards and jam the muzzle into her face, her chest, knocking her backward? He controlled it, as he controlled the rest of himself: interesting.

There was a break in the tirade. She wondered how her voice would come out sounding after all this, but it seemed remarkably level. She was rather pleased about that.

'Of course I will identify myself, sir. I am Mamzel Torma Ylante, formerly of the ship's cohort of Captain Galan Vedrier of the League of Black Ships. Lately, I am the Chief Concordiast-Elect of the Master of Hydraphur's Bastion Psykana. Although who knows what will come of that now?'

She met his boiling gaze with the right degree of steadiness.

'As for my business,' she went on, still looking up into his face like a child, as she heard more Arbites enter the garden behind him, 'I am mourning a Master and an old friend. I am simply praying my farewells and putting my spirit at peace.' A whole moment went by without him shouting at her, so she pushed her luck a little. 'To answer your most pressing points, I acknowledge, and have not tried to dispute, that I am under arrest and in whose divine name I am arrested. I very well understand what I have done in coming here.'

'A Master and an old friend.' The Chastener's eyes narrowed and some of the aggression had died out of his voice. 'You were mourning Master Otranto, but who else?' She watched him closely: a slight twitch of the head. 'What other murder are you talking of, woman?'

'Otranto's both of them, Dast. There hasn't been a second death, and I suggest that she no longer needs the gun in her face.' A woman's voice, harder to read than the Chastener's. It was a confident voice in a low alto, used to command, but Ylante heard the tiredness in it.

The man looming over her – Dast – kept the gun in place for a second longer before it spun up and away from her with startling speed, snapping into the scabbard on his armoured back. Chastener Dast, displeasure radiating off him like steam, stepped back.

A woman walked past Dast and dropped to one knee to look Ylante in the eye. This, Ylante thought, must be Arbitor Calpurnia. Five years younger than Ylante herself? Ten? She doubted it. She didn't recognise the badges of rank on Calpurnia's shoulders, but they looked like ones that would take until about Ylante's own age to earn. Three scar-lines ran up from her eye into the woman's unruly dark-blonde hair. The scars themselves were old, just neat lines, but the skin around them looked red and sore as if from constant rubbing.

'You're the one from the Black Ship,' said lady arbitor.

'I am.'

'You came on board to act as some kind of adjutant for this Master Otranto. Concordiast, that was the term you used.'

'The Master of the Tower must serve as an active astropath,' Ylante replied, 'and so he requires me. Or someone like me,' she added, thinking of her one bitter meeting with Teeker Renz. 'The Master reserves the services of a concordiast as part of his own retinue.'

'She has eyes,' put in Dast from over both their heads. 'She's no astropath.'

'Thank you, master Chastener,' Calpurnia replied as she put her other knee on the path and tried to mimic Ylante's posture. She was having a hard time of it – her heavy boots weren't allowing her lower legs to fold in the right ways. 'I have eyes too. I see it. I don't believe that Mamzel Ylante was referring to psyker work.' Her eyes narrowed in imitation of the Chastener's. 'I do need to know what you do. I've seen the rosters of concordiasts in the Bastion precinct files. Here's your chance to educate me, and to convince me, by the way, that whatever a concordiast does, it doesn't involve the murder of their Master.'

CHAPTER SIX

TEEKER RENZ CAME stalking through the downdecks, the stacked compartments around the foundations of the keep. Once the fortress had stored its ratings and indentured stationhands here; now the downdecks were home to the Tower's Naval contingent, officers and midshipmen having to endure the indignity of quarters originally designed for their inferiors.

He found his man striking a louche pose atop a flight of steps, making a show of inspecting the unadorned rockcrete walls, and affecting to ignore the bustle of uniforms around him. Few non-Navy personnel came into the decks without a definite errand, and Dechene, in cream-coloured concordiast's livery of unusually rich cloth and cut, was getting a few curious looks.

Renz got them too, although he was too agitated to notice them. He headed for Dechene, stopped less than a metre away from him, and glared into the man's face.

After a good minute or so, Concordiast Antovin Dechene deigned to notice him.

'See what you think of this,' he said. His voice was low and languid, 'That Navy-girl assembling her shift crew there, outside the archway.' Renz didn't look around, but Dechene went on anyway.

Giving the performance was what counted. 'Had her; still do, if you follow me. Against fleet policy, doing anything with me, that is, non-fleet personnel. She's terrified the Navy will find out. No fleet commissar on the Tower, but plenty in the places they'd send her to if it ever got out. Hah.'

Dechene carefully adjusted the angle of his lean. He inspected the fingernails of his left hand, one after another. The sleeve fell away to show a slender silver chain at his wrist. It was a token from Renz himself, after Dechene had taken care of an unpleasant business before Candlemas. Dechene pointed his chin over Renz's shoulder.

'Now her, the one with the – look where I'm pointing, Teek, just pretend you're looking at something else.' With poor grace, Renz patted his sleeve, looked behind him as if for something dropped, and registered the petty officer with the cropped dark hair.

'Another one of mine,' Dechene said, his smirk as lazily unsettling as his voice. 'Convinced she's my special little thing.' He gave a sidelong glance over Renz's shoulder. 'See the way she's trying not to look at me? She's still at the passionate stage: all het up with the secret romance of it all.' He shifted his attention to the nails of his right hand. 'This is what it's all about, isn't it, Teek? I live for this. Look at the two of them, both trying to catch my eye. Neither one has a clue about the other. Only we know the truth, hey?' He gave a slow, lecherous droop of an eyelid.

'Where the hell have you and Kyto been?' Renz kept enough wits to keep his voice low, but the effort was showing in his face. 'I waited for you for half an hour. Do you think we can afford not to care about what's happening? Nothing's over just because–'

'Relax, Teek. You're driving yourself crazy and you've got no reason to. Why so set on talking yourself into trouble?'

'Talking? I see. Well, at this moment, the Master's suites are full of Arbites and Torma Ylante is in there with them and this arbitor senioris from Hydraphur. The Throne alone knows what–' Renz caught himself, moved closer and lowered his voice. '–what rubbish that woman is stuffing the arbitor's head with. Well? Have you thought about that?'

The pleased expression finally began to slide off Dechene's face. The two of them walked away from the steps, around the circular hall that made a collar between the downdecks and the keep. The crop-haired brunette in the petty officer's uniform was pretty enough, Renz supposed. She gave a shy smile in their direction, which fell away when Dechene ignored her.

Neither man said anything as they made a long clockwise path around the edge of the downdecks and then turned in below one of the great buttresses that ran through the downdecks and then up the side of the keep above them: one of the great pillars that the fortification walls rested on. They turned and made their way through the narrow tunnel through the buttress, under the metal stripe in the ceiling that was the lower edge of a seven-tonne shutter-door. Then they passed the little rat hole guard posts where an armed overseer from the Navy garrison recognised Renz and waved them through.

They were coming into the techmens' quarters, where the lay artisans lived who performed whatever tasks the Mechanicus priests saw fit to delegate outside their own orders. Their workshops surrounded Channery's sealed Enginarium. Renz and Dechene walked through arches carved with barcoded litanies and watched over by skeletal Mechanicus gargoyles, between walls that sloped and swerved. Even through the metal and rockcrete, the sound of machines surrounded them.

A month ago, Renz might have found this exciting. The games and manoeuvres that being Otranto's ear and voice had let him play had been fun, because he knew he was in no danger. Things had changed, dramatically: he and Dechene had come to a place where the rumble and click of machines would make spying hard because, suddenly, it *mattered* that they be hard to spy on. Without the threat of the Master's proxy anger to hold over the heads of anyone who displeased him, Renz had to consider the concept of consequences if his plans went wrong.

He didn't like that sensation at *all*.

'So you're telling me,' said Shira Calpurnia, 'that you have completely free access to the Master's suite? You can come and go as you please?'

Torma Ylante shook her head.

'I have done since Otranto died, whenever the chambers have been unlocked, but I can't open the suite myself. I couldn't get through there now.' She tilted her head towards the massive shutter-door.

They were back in the Master's bedchamber. Calpurnia hadn't wanted to keep Ylante in the garden, where the woman had seemed far too at ease. In the bedchamber, Ylante would be confronted by the bloodstain, the violent echoes of the Master's death. As Ylante had calmly seated herself, Calpurnia had been shocked by the strength of her desire to rattle the other woman, to shake that serenity off her face: to make her eyes widen and get a fear-sweat on that pale forehead.

Be careful, she told herself. *Know the difference between the law's anger and your own.* Oh yes, *the* Lex Imperialis *is the timeless law of the Emperor, not the flickering whim of His servants.* Oh, yes, but the maxims she had mastered back at Machiun and recited so recently in her self-denunciation sessions seemed lighter and more shallow here. They wrestled in her head with bright bursts of temper and a silver lode of migrainous pain.

Do your duty, Calpurnia told herself. *Without duty, what are you?*

'You don't want to make me chase the answers out of you, Mamzel Ylante,' she said aloud. 'Pay attention when I tell you that your best choice is to volunteer everything you know that might bear on what we're asking. I don't doubt that you can sense for yourself what kind of temper I'm in.'

'It isn't hard to deduce,' Ylante answered, her eyes deferentially lowered. 'Well, then, my comings and goings. Chief concordiasts do not work with other astropaths unless the Master orders it, or I – the chief concordiast in question – chooses to, and the Master agrees.' She looked down at her fingers lacing and unlacing in her lap, and Calpurnia took in the movement carefully.

'So, the chief concordiast generally has the freedom of the Master's chambers,' Ylante went on once she had collected her thoughts. 'My own investiture in the position wasn't complete – did I remember to introduce myself as chief concordiast-elect? Not finalised, you see. So by rights, I've the freedom to be here as I wish, but Otranto was to grant me the final keys and pass codes when I formally took on the mantle.'

'Which never happened,' Calpurnia said levelly.

'Which never happened.'

'Because Otranto died on the blade of a filth-hearted murderer,' put in Dast.

'It is as you say,' Ylante answered him.

'Before you had even had the chance to speak with him?' Calpurnia pressed.

'You are correct. I came here from Master Vedrier's Black Ship, three shipboard days ago, but Otranto and I... well, I was to rest after my journey. He was on his way to see me when he died. We never spoke again.' Was that the tiniest tremor in her voice?

'And you were in the concordiasts' cells when he died?'

'Yes. You'll have no trouble verifying that.'

'And how hard will it be,' boomed Dast, 'to *verify* that you are not part of the conspiracy that brought the Master low?'

He was carrying it off a little more theatrically than Calpurnia might have, but he got through to her. The knuckles of her laced hands went white, and she shut her eyes for a long moment.

'I was not Master Otranto's enemy,' she said at last, 'and I'm not frightened of whatever questions you ask about that, because they will show me to be right. Whatever it costs me as a concordiast, when you do know who killed my Master, I beg you the indulgence of letting me be there when you rip the skin off the conspiracy's back and show it to the light.'

THERE WAS SILENCE for moments more. Calpurnia tried to think on Ylante's words, to weigh them up and see if they rang true or whether they were camouflage for a crime.

'Master Chastener Dast. Continue.'

He shot her a sullen look. Calpurnia put her back to him and Ylante, and signalled to Bruinann and Rede to join her in the garden.

Calpurnia looked around – she could see why Ylante had come here to clear her mind. The only seat was a block of rough white stone by a miniature pond, its top carved into a slight bow for the comfort of the sitter. The path from the door to the seat had been cut ankle-deep into the floor and then filled with soft, springy moss, perfect for bare, sensitive feet. Outside the path, the ground was soft sand and carefully cultivated patches of lichen. A cluster of vines rose from the round pond, cable-thick and gnarl-barked, trailing bunches of glossy, narrow leaves as they climbed to a trellis high above. A rill of scented water ran down them, darkening the bark and dripping off the leaves like dew, pattering lightly onto the surface of the pool.

'What is it you need, madam arbitor?' asked Bruinnan.

Calpurnia wondered if his tone was intended to be insolent. He and Rede, she remembered, knew the truth of her position, and Dast's authority over her.

'I've left the Chastener in there to continue the questioning,' she said, 'and to preserve the impression to non-Arbites that I still hold my substantive rank.'

Why was she explaining herself to them? She gave herself a mental kick.

'You briefed me on station personnel, but not really on her. A quick rundown now, please: Ylante's background, and this prior relationship with Otranto that she seems to think is so important. My impression was that she came to the Tower aboard that Black Ship.'

'She *returned* aboard it, yes, when it put in here to provision,' Rede answered. 'Torma Ylante was a concordiast at the Tower in her early life. She was young, and a lot of the astropaths she worked with then are dead now, of course. The ones that she worked with who are still here to welcome her back are tough, the best and most powerful of them. Ylante's got old friends all through the senior tier of astropaths here.'

'Including the old Master,' Calpurnia finished.

'Just so.'

'Are we to trust her word? You've briefed me on what's going on among the astropaths about the succession to the Master's seat, with Otranto being so careless about a nominated heir. Is there a chance that she's the puppet of one of them, or could it be the other way around?'

Rede and Bruinann exchanged a look.

'Arbitor senioris,' Rede began carefully, 'may I respectfully ask how familiar you are with the work of the concordiasts? I wonder if perhaps you have misinterpreted some of your conversation with Mamzel Ylante.'

Calpurnia's flare of anger shocked her, as did the suddenness with which it evaporated and left just a queasy nervousness. She was sure that she could feel a crawling sensation on her skin. She took a moment to listen to the sound of water falling into the pond, and let a breath in and out.

'I don't pretend to be above error,' she said. 'Well, I hardly can, given my status, can I? All right, explain to me what I'm misunderstanding.'

Gracious humility had been the right tack. Rede's manner seemed to thaw somewhat.

'I can tell you, so you have an idea, ma'am, but if I can make a better suggestion: ask Ylante about it. I don't believe that she's our enemy, and she can tell you better than I can, so you understand it down to the bone. Better still–'

'Better still,' Calpurnia finished the thought, 'she can show me.'

MOST OF THE space in the Bastion Psykana had been cannibalised from something else entirely, from back before the old catastrophe had reduced the star fort to a hulk. Sometimes, the new function had some kinship with the old, as when the old Fleet Commissariat offices had become the Arbites precinct, although, Calpurnia or Bruinann, or anyone calling the precinct home, would have bristled at being thought of as another kind of commissar. The living quarters in the downdecks were used much as they always had been, and the Enginarium and the docks ran unchanged, albeit for different masters.

There had been changes too. The promenade decks down which the officers had once strolled beneath tall armoured windows, now held tight-packed chorister astropaths, manacled to their benches, their blind eyes indifferent to the view.

The bridge and Strategium at the keep's summit were now full of elaborate workshops for rendering and brewing oils and essences. Teams of junior concordiasts trained by Teeker Renz laboured over salves, tonics and incense for the concordiasts to use. They brought clarity and energy to their astropaths' minds, and soothed the wounds that the turbulence of the warp would leave in their spirits.

Below them were the staterooms that would have held the gate-captain and his household, now little more than lockers full of shelves and crates. Several of the old magazines had been turned into extra apothecaria, so necessary in a place whose basic work took such a toll on its people. It was odd to see stretcher-beds arrayed along walkways or conveyor racks that had once hefted giant shells for the weapon batteries or flak canisters for the point-defence turrets.

Torma Ylante and Shira Calpurnia walked through all of this, an arbitrator following. Ylante sketched out for Calpurnia the pulse and rhythm of the place, how it laboured, what it demanded. They watched Astropath Brom come down from the Eyrie of Echoes, after a rapid and easy trance. They watched Astropath Ankyne, groaning and lurching, come out of the Green Eyrie, after she had sent a tentative connection southward towards Gathalamor, and had been hit hard by an unexpectedly tough, warp turbulence coming the other way. They saw three members of a choir being rushed into one of the apothecaria, after a momentary spike in an energy flow caused a witchcullis to slam down on them.

Seeing the Bastion from the inside brought it home to Calpurnia: this place was more than just another hive of Imperial functionaries whose noses, as her commander at Don-Croix liked to say, needed forcing a little further into their work. This whole place was an engine, a lighthouse, a junction box, and the green-shrouded astropaths were both its operators and its components. Their minds walked nearly every day in an otherworldly hell storm whose nature Calpurnia barely pretended to understand. It was impossible to treat the place as just another nest of backsliders and suspects, and crash in among them with maul swinging. She might as well scatter a clip of shock-grenades among the enginseers who tended the caged sun at the Bastion's core.

She wondered if Dast understood that. This hunt would be more complex – how could he not see it? The shackle of his authority was maddening; having to play-act at being in charge made it more so. If she had command of this investigation properly and for real, she could…

No. She was in her role by judgement of the Adeptus Arbites, which was the judgement of the *Lex Imperia* and therefore of Him on Earth. Her duty was not to indulge her pride and her fantasies of command; her duty was to serve the law, whatever it required of her. Her duty would not find her wanting. Without her duty, she asked herself, echoing the question that generations of Calpurnii had been taught to ask, what was she?

THEY CAME AT last to the watch-hall and emerged from the claustrophobic entry tunnel onto steps cut into the steep slope of the floor. The watch-hall was a cylinder sweeping up from the long-sealed torpedo magazines at a forty-three degree angle. The sides of the cylinder swept out and away to meet thirty metres above their heads. They shone with a deep glow and lustre. Copper and brass plates rode over and under, and interleaved all across the walls. Their patterns seemed to Calpurnia to be a strange mix of careful symmetry and thrown-together jumble. Here and there, clusters of pennants hung in the tilted tunnel, like the ones she had seen in the corridors, and she saw knotted and braided ropes a little like those in Otranto's pseudo-vineyard. Some held oddly shaped pieces of metal or stonework suspended at their ends, others simply swayed in the breezes from the ventilator holes in the walls.

Sounds surrounded them, shivering out of the air: strange notes like a rubbed wineglass, the plangent sound of harp strings or tuning-fork thrums. As they went further down the steps, sharing them more and more with scurrying young runners and slump-shouldered servitors carrying messages and order seals, Calpurnia started to see the sounds' source. The pitch of the tunnel let her look straight out from the stairs to a swathe of silo roof, and she could see the nests and platforms cut into the silo all around her. Each one was built next to, or was even part of, a web of shining wire, clusters of glass and metal plates. Some put her in mind of wind chimes, some of chandeliers. At some, an operator hung strapped into the array or perched by it, others were tended by flitting servitor-cherubs.

There was something maddening about it: the way that the gong-like note from a hanging copper plate might be slightly, eye-wateringly out of sync with the way the plate moved. The way the sounds seemed to grow louder or softer in ways that bore no relation to the Arbites' movements, or simply that there was no visible force making any of these things vibrate and sound, was disturbing. Part of Calpurnia was enchanted in a way that she rarely allowed herself to be. Part of her was fighting the urge to clap her hands to her ears and run, howling, for an exit.

As Calpurnia twisted to look around her again, cramps ripped up from her thigh muscles and into her belly. She had to wait for the spots to clear from her eyes before she could focus on the next step down.

IN OTRANTO'S ROOMS, Master Chastener Dast was sweating freely. He loathed the feel of it: the slickness of his brow and neck, his sodden garments. He forced himself to breathe evenly, and stood in front of Orovene for more than a minute with his gauntleted hands resting on the reliquary box. Dast was not one for memorised prayers, so he simply concentrated on the lines of the *Auctorita Imperialis* until he brought his thoughts back under control.

Meanwhile, Orovene was working his mouth as if it had gone dry, and was swallowing with a clicking sound. They made a poor picture, the two of them, and a counterpoint to Rede and Bruinann, who were standing cool and at ease on either side of the Master's bed. That triggered a welling of red temper up Dast's throat that it took him whole seconds to suppress. He turned to them, refusing to allow his hands to make fists.

'You've had far more time and access to this chamber than we have,' he said to them. 'Tell me. Run me through the things I've missed. Both of you have been conspicuous by your silence for a while now.' Neither of them, in point of fact, had said a word to him since Calpurnia and Ylante had left them there. Rede and Bruinann looked at one another.

'Are you asking,' Rede began, 'for a recap of the briefings we gave y–'

'Calpurnia may want to sit and shuffle papers until her fingers shrivel,' Dast said. 'I'll use my own eyes.' He caught himself, but they had already heard the contradiction in his words; he could see it in their eyes. He could bring a dozen accusations against them for that – but there would be time for that later. He needed self-control. He exerted it.

'The assassin struck at a distance, not by hand,' he said. 'Respond.'

'The wound in the corpse is that of a blade, a deep and narrow stabbing,' said Rede. 'We read from that and the bloodstain that the weapon came up at an angle, too steep for a projectile unless the killer lay on the floor at his feet. No scorching or blast residue on Otranto's clothes, no projectile in the wound, no scent of gun smoke or las-burn – the sniffers in the air vents system would have picked that up.'

'There are assassin weapons that can strike just that way,' said Dast.

'True,' Rede answered, 'but I have eighty-seven informants under my thumb on this station, and spy craft besides, and I don't believe that any such weapon could have been fired in here, and then smuggled back with none of my cat's-paws noticing. Believe me when I say that they wouldn't lie about it if they had.'

Dast grunted, unconvinced, and a quick spark of anger marked the woman's eye for just a moment. Rede knew her ring of spies and informants through the Tower was sub-par for what a detective-espionist of her rank could be expected to muster, and she knew it would not be long before Dast and Calpurnia knew it too. She had until the Otranto investigation was over to shore her work up until it would pass muster in the arbitor senioris's eyes. She'd had three years of routine reports and communiqués, three years for her to get comfortable, and now this.

Dast had asked something and she had missed it, but Bruinann had stepped in.

'We don't believe the murderer lay in wait here, no. He was able to enter and exit without leaving a trace, but again, the aerator systems would have registered his presence. Magos Channery has charged their machine-spirit to keep itself alive in all the engines across the Tower. It will notice how much air it needs to circulate into a room to keep it fresh. That means that over time it notices the difference between an empty room and one that someone's breathing in.'

'Will it notice that someone in the room has a nurture-mask, or a rebreather mouthpiece?' demanded Dast. 'There are records of assassins entering trances until they wake themselves up and start their work. How many of this station's people – the subjects of your precinct, Bruinann – have been trained by our own holy Adeptus in how to control their bodies and minds?'

'We accept the possibility,' said Bruinann, 'but we know that, although when he left the Concourse Otranto was in a hurry, in the cloisters, he was running as if six colours of xenos hell were after him. You saw how he broke through the furnishings in those outer rooms. It still seems to us that the best conclusion we can make is that Otranto was chased in here by his killer.'

'Who then exited through *that*, locks and seals and all?' Dast swept an arm at the great door, the contempt for their conclusion obvious in his voice.

Rede answered him with careful respect.

'Master Chastener, the man was alive when the door was closed, and dead when it was opened again and he was found. You are left with the fact that the killer escaped from a sealed chamber, no matter how you believe he entered it.'

Dast gave an irritable flap of the hand and went back to inspecting the door. Drops of sweat stood out in his beard. Rede and Bruinann shared a short, sour look.

'Perhaps, sir,' Bruinann said, 'this would be the best time to return to the precinct and review your findings? The verispex reports will be there, and now that we've got some idea of your thinking, we can pick out the reports from Rede's agents and work out who'll be of most value to you. I don't intend any insolence when I say that perhaps you've got as much out of inspecting these rooms as you're going to get, for the time being.'

Dast's shoulders shook, and for the first time since these new Arbites had arrived on the station, Bruinann felt fear, a stab of pure and direct fear. Then the Chastener turned, and startled him by managing a small smile.

'You're correct, of course, aedile, and thank you. I'm a Chastener, not, well, you're right, this place has already been,' he paused for a moment, 'uh, better eyes than mine. You're correct. I realise I have a lot to digest.'

Bruinann wondered whether this was a trick or a genuine effort. It seemed too weird to be a tactic. He'd ask Rede later on, she was better at spotting these things than he was.

'Is the font-water in that garden drinkable?' Orovene managed to get out. His voice was badly parched and cracking.

'No ague in it, or witch-taint?' Dast followed up, twisting his mouth at 'witch-taint'.

'Safe to drink, sir,' said Rede. 'Master Otranto would drink it with his guests sometimes. I'll show you where the ladle is.' She led Orovene into the garden, and Dast turned for the door.

'I'll wait for you outside,' he told Bruinann. 'I'm hoping the air will be cooler in the halls. Seal the door when we leave. Have someone find out where Calpurnia went and get her back to the precinct. She can help me go through these documents of yours.'

The break in the clouds had been brief and the Chastener's old demeanour was creeping back. Bruinann saluted, and waited until Dast was well out of the room and on his way through the vineyard before he broke the salute and went to pass on the orders. You're not out of this yet, he told himself. Be careful.

Dast wondered if the air on his skin as he moved was cooling him, or if it was just a fancy – the rime of sweat seemed so thick that it was sealing him in, as stupid an idea as that sounded. Dashing the water off his skin seemed to make things worse, sending flashes of heat and weird electricity through him. His voice was sounding odd and reedy, and something perpetually dogged the edge of his thoughts, as if he was about to remember or understand something, which never came into focus.

Focus, that was it, he had to focus. As he left Otranto's chambers, he could hear Bruinann passing on his instructions, and an echoing slurping from the garden where Orovene was trying to drain the pool, by the sound of it. It was unbecoming; words would be needed. As far as Dast was concerned, the preacher was part of his command crew, pitiful as that crew was: a preacher who couldn't control his bodily needs, and a disgraced convict dressed in a facade of her former rank.

His thoughts revved feverishly as he walked through the vineyard. They all needed to keep control. Bruinann and Rede knew they were going to face scrutiny. If there was trouble, the off-station Arbites needed to show a united front.

The voices he heard coming from the antechamber startled him out of his thoughts.

'Look, I'm not making trouble, I told you, I'm here on orders.' It wasn't the proctor's voice. Someone seemed to be trying to haggle their way in. 'I'm here to speak with Mamzel Ylante and the arbitor senioris. Orders, see?'

'This is your last chance and your last order,' the proctor snapped back. 'One more attempt to order an arbitor around will see you racked for contempt of law. State your petition or return to your post, and be thankful that we've got better business to attend to than giving you what you deserve.'

'Any petition you have to put to Arbitor Calpurnia, you can put to me,' declaimed Dast, striding out into the antechamber. Humility be damned, Calpurnia might be the figurehead, but he didn't have to pretend that he was powerless. 'I am Master Chastener Dast. I am co-ordinating the arbitor senioris's investigation, and you may salute when y–'

He was halfway through the door to the outer foyer when his mind skidded like a boot on smooth mud. It was enough to throw him physically against the threshold, and when the metal Arbites seal came around like a flail, and crashed into the side of his head, it sent him the rest of the way to the floor, limbs limp and mind black.

CHAPTER SEVEN

'Torma Ylante. Welcome to the watch-hall, concordiast-elect. I hadn't expected to meet you here.' The watchmaster's whisper came when they had barely started down the stone causeway that led to his cage. It should never have been audible to them in the first place, but Calpurnia still heard it clearly.

The watchmaster sat in a sling-chair hanging from the bars, his head nodding under a heavy halo of augmetics and leads. The skin of his hands was as soft and smooth as a child's. He stroked and shuffled the engraved cards of an Emperor's Tarot deck. He had already dealt two cards onto a shelf-like table suspended in front of him.

Calpurnia controlled the urge to peer in and see what cards he'd dealt – bad luck, she'd been told once, to do that.

'Come down and sit with me. One to each side, thank you. There's a symmetry to it. It will be very pleasing. My duty is to be so careful of such symmetries. There, you see?' He seemed to be referring to a quick series of minor-key notes, a slightly clashing arpeggio from a rack of wires and chimes high above them. 'It's so rare to find such a balance. I'd show a card for it, had I one to spare.' The knuckles of his hands grew white on the edges of the ivory tarot cards. Calpurnia half-rose, mouth open, to say something, but on the other side of the cage, Ylante caught her eye and firmly shook her head. An attendant in a dusty-blue veil and gown had come down the walkway, and Ylante curtly beckoned – him, her? – over.

'A bottle of red graft-balm, please,' she said, 'and a gauze wand. Mix Tincture of Unzeo into the balm as you bring it, not more than half a dozen drops.' The attendant blinked at Ylante from under its hood for a moment, and then jumped – Calpurnia guessed that the watchmaster had seconded the command with a thought. As the shrouded figure hurried away, a wheezing sound floated out of the cage: the watchmaster was chuckling.

'How long have you been away, Torma? It gets hard for us to know how time is going, you know, once the fire gets in us, but it's obviously been a long time. It's been a couple of generations of attendants since I've had tincture on my skull. I feel the pressure, Torma, and the weight, and the work of pushing myself out through the plugs, but don't trouble yourself about my skin.' He chuckled again, hard enough to set some of the skull-cables to clinking. 'Let them bring the tincture if it pleases you. Change keeps them attentive.'

'You like catching me out, don't you, Chevenne?' Ylante answered him amiably. 'You always did.'

'These people are not the only ones who have to be kept attentive,' said Chevenne, some of the joking tone evaporating from his voice. 'You're a fine concordiast, Ylante, but your fault was always that you forgot who was the servant. Otranto has a terrible habit of letting his servants act like his peers. That fop who replaced you hasn't been much better. Proper order has been in too short supply here.' He flicked a third card hard down onto the table, and then a fourth. His fingers stroked the images picked out on their rough bone faces. 'Three ascending cards of the Mandatio, a preoccupation with order. I am wandering, and drawing my reading after me: too far unbalanced, no good now.'

Ylante's face remained expressionless as the watchmaster bent his face to the cards. For a moment, Calpurnia was sure that some kind of silvery haze or tarnish passed over the bright sockets around his skull. Then he made a series of quick motions, moving the cards slightly crooked, breaking up their symmetry. Another moment and he had restored them to his deck with deft, practiced darts of his hands.

Two attendants, a man and a woman, had approached down the causeway, shrouded in the same livery as the first. The man hunkered down at the back of the cage, and carefully unstoppered a ceramic jar. The woman leaned against the cage bars, and began rattling off a schedule in a throaty, musical voice.

'Two hours are left on your watch, sir. I am asked to bring to your attention that Cantor Rhyshko is standing down from the Green Eyrie, and Cantor Mecklin is undergoing preparations to replace him. Astropath Ehlin is required to send a message to Xu Primaris station in fifty minutes. He has been preparing with two concordiasts and will be in the Eyrie of Bones in half an hour.'

Through all this, the gangly man was dipping a gauze-wrapped taper into the jar and reaching a lanky arm through the cage bars, dabbing a spicy-smelling ointment onto the watchmaster's scalp around his skull plugs. His attention to the delicate movements of his hand was total.

'Ehlin has asked for Astropaths Slocha and Weth to support him,' the woman went on, 'but Astropath Golan has come out of the Firewatch Eyrie, and from his reports Ehlin will need a full choir behind him to push through as far as Xu. Cantor Angazi is assembling choirs on the third and fourth seclusion decks. Two small choirs will be in communion with the relay at Bescalion, and will shift their attention to Hydraphur proper at the turn of the hour. Astropath Pharnele will spend the second hour in the Eyrie of Echoes to be ready for ciphers coming in from the Obscuras border.'

'Ehm, is Pharnele up to it?' Chevenne's plangent whisper seemed to owe nothing to his physical voice. 'We'll have put him in the Echoes for a reason.'

'He has Arch-Cantor Aderkin preparing him, and both choir-decks at the Echoes are full. The marshal has diverted three junior concordiasts to work with the ciphers, once he has them, but he does suggest–'

'If Pharnele's still going to be riding the warp when I leave the cage, woman, I won't tolerate any risk.' The watchmaster's hands gripped the edge of the shelf for a moment and the head tilted from side to side. 'Close all the inner cullises around the lower Echo. Who's in the Lantern Eyrie?'

'Astropath Ankyn, sir, with two wardens, and Cantor Nyri and one of his acolytes.'

'Peh, that explains a lot. You're lucky you told me about the extra weight on her, straight up. Clear Ankyn out of the Lantern and have her between cullises at the very least by the time Pharnele begins. There's been a leaden cloud over that whole quarter throughout my watch, and I'll damn well have it unravelled before I sleep, do you understand?'

'Yes, watchmaster.' The bumptious tone was gone from the woman's voice.

'Why is Ankyn in the Lantern and not the Green Eyrie?' The watchmaster asked peevishly.

'The marshal's instructions, watchmaster, shall I ask him to–'

'Ask him why that woman's not under guard in the Green Eyrie, and bring me the answer. Your companion there is done, I think.'

The attendant wittered for a moment, and then bowed. It took three increasingly emphatic jabs into the man's shoulder before he started, looked at her and stood up. A minute after that, the watchmaster, Ylante and Calpurnia were alone once again at the tip of the walkway.

'WHAT WAS THAT?' asked Calpurnia after a moment of silence. 'In fact, what is going on here? That conversation? Is there some emergency coming that I need to know about? Watchmaster Chevenne, you're the one who was on, er, watch when the murder took place?' She felt herself start to gabble. Dignity, she told herself.

'Brittle little creature, aren't you?' the watchmaster twanged in her ears. 'Not a match for Ylante at all, in point of fact. I'll have to station you... thirteen metres away and directly opposite her, or slightly above.'

Calpurnia blinked, hard. Her eyes were aching as if she'd been reading all day. Sheer disorientation made her dizzy for a moment, like a diver in deep water loses track of the direction to the surface. She grabbed her thoughts and forced them back into order.

There was a soft, teeth-on-edge buzz from over her shoulder, and she looked around. A servitor-cherub bobbed in the air behind her on wings inlaid with suspensor vanes. Orange-yellow eyes regarded her through the slits in a scowling gargoyle mask grafted to the thing's face.

'You're more distressed than you're admitting,' Ylante observed calmly as Calpurnia shied away from the thing. It glided forwards as she tried to increase the distance between them, staying less than half a metre away from her head. She found herself wanting to bat it away. 'That's why it's marking you,' Ylante said from the other side of the cage. 'Concentrate on controlling your breathing first, and when you've settled into a relaxing rhythm–'

'I *don't* need breathing exercises, Ylante. Have this thing called off, or be ready to have it replaced.' She brought the maul up and thumbed it into action. The hell with formal reserve.

After a moment, she realised that the strange dead leaves-blowing sound was Chevenne laughing.

'Torma, be the obliging concordiast and go to the Marshal's pulpit. Let's identify the marker she complains about so, and gag it. Leave it in place. We'll just do without the voice. Off you go.'

Her composure finally giving way to a slapped expression, Ylante left them, and the watchmaster shifted. That was Calpurnia's overwhelming impression: that he shifted and turned in his cage, his head questing around to her. The impact of his full attention turning to her was like a physical force, but when she looked into the cage, she saw that the man hadn't moved.

'You're an interesting one,' the watchmaster told her. 'Normally I'm better at first judgements. What does *sizzling* mean?'

She was more on guard for the question this time, and didn't let it trouble her. Dvorov, the Arbitor Majore who was her supreme commander on Hydraphur, liked lightning changes of subject like this.

'The word was at the front of your mind for a moment,' said Chevenne when she didn't answer. 'You were thinking about balance.'

For a moment, the air between Calpurnia and the cage darkened. Her eyes seemed to pick out washes of colour in the air: black, purple, a pallid white like unpigmented skin. A quick, stinging ache in her eye and head, and it was gone. 'Then your balance shifted and that was an end to it. Your control is actually rather good. It's a–'

There was a burst of sound from below them. The watchmaster stiffened for a moment. A gluey taste swam across Calpurnia's tongue and the barbed queasiness was back in her gut. Behind her, the cherub shrilled loudly for a moment and fell silent.

'It's a different control from Ylante's,' the watchmaster said through the trills of sound around them. 'Different control from Ylante's,' he repeated as two swirls of corposant orbited his head for a moment, and unbraided themselves into worms of light that crawled along the bars of his cage. 'Different control from Ylante's,' he said a third time a moment later, in a normal voice, 'Tougher, in a way. You exert aggression on yourself, not serenity.'

'I don't appreciate you tunnelling into my mind unasked, astropath,' Calpurnia told him coldly, deliberately demoting him with her address. 'You'll learn better than that, or regret it.'

'There now,' the watchmaster said. 'There was no, hah, "tunnelling", asked for, or otherwise. I don't know that I'd have the strength to bore into you nowadays without a chorus to carry me. It radiated off you, madam arbitrator. Are you…' A pale tongue moistened the thin lips as the watchmaster looked for an analogy, '…are you somehow attacking the sun by feeling the warmth it throws on you?'

'Nevertheless, watchmaster, you can consider yourself on notice. However… *affected* by this environment you might think me, I'll have my office given the respect it's due. Believe me, these are not times when this Bastion can afford to backslide and forget the law.'

'Of course,' said Chevenne, his voice, carefully free of snappishness or mockery. 'You are the Arbitor Senioris Shira Calpurnia, here to punish the murderer of my colleague and friend the Master Otranto, and to command the station while you select his successor. I know.'

'The station command has yet to be settled,' said Calpurnia, too truthful to allow that one past. 'The appointment of a new Master will not be my concern.' By the time that issue came up, Calpurnia would be back at Hydraphur, giving account for the Phrax Mutiny. Perhaps they would try her in the same courtroom on Selena Secundus where that bloodbath had begun. She stamped on the thought.

'I do nothing unasked, madam arbitor,' said the watchmaster carefully, 'but I don't need to *see*, to know that you're troubled here today. Perhaps a rest might–'

'Not your concern,' she snapped. 'We'll continue.'

'As you say,' the watchmaster answered, and fell silent again for a moment, as something seemed to occupy his attention. There were no new chimes or tones, not that Calpurnia could hear, but at the upper edge of her vision, she thought she saw a stirring, a pair of cherubs drifting towards one another to meet at a bell-harp that seemed to be shaking slightly.

'All right, then. That. What was that? This is some kind of giant surveillance auspex, is it not? Do you monitor the voices going to and from the Bastion?'

The pale head shook, and the braided cables rustled and clicked against each other.

'From here, mamzel, I watch *us:* the astropaths and the Bastion. My role is patterns and balances. The watchmaster must make sure that the symmetries that build up in the Tower are rare, and controlled, and coaxed away from the destructive. It is subtle work.'

'Explain,' said Calpurnia.

Torma Ylante had made her way back down the platform to join them; she sat back down on the other little seat, but did not interrupt.

'I can best explain by analogies that would match with your own experiences. If you will allow me to look for an image in you that I might base–'

'No.'

There was a pause.

'Very well. You're familiar with the work of the senior enginseers of the Priesthood of Mars? The ones who tend the plasma furnaces that warm ships and stations like this one?'

'I know a little.'

'My understanding has always been that the balance of forces inside those plasma cages is a delicate thing. There is both a craft and an art to running it smoothly. Well, have you met Magos Channery?'

'No.'

Another pause.

'Smoke,' said the watchmaster. 'Black and crimson. Odd, but then I'll use something more human. There's part of your brain that controls your balance.'

'In the ears, I was once told.' The watchmaster made a small dismissive gesture with one hand, but Calpurnia let it pass.

'Think in a broader sense,' he said. 'Those twists in your brain that tell when you've got a sickness, when and where you're injured. Controls that make you sweat when you're hot, or put a thirst on your tongue when your body feels itself drying out. Do you follow me?'

'Yes.'

The watchmaster hung in silence for a few moments,

'Are you the nerve centre that governs this for the station, watchmaster?' Calpurnia asked. 'Was that why you were talking about a lead weight, something to do with the station's balance?'

The watchmaster gave a tiny, delicate snort, and when he spoke some of the snappishness came back to his voice.

'You're not going to understand the fact of it, judge-woman, because you were born brain-blunted, without what you need to see what I do. Truly see it. Therefore, I'm going to use some ways of talking it out that you will understand, providing that you also understand that I'm scrawling in the mud, trying to draw the stars. Think upon that for a moment.'

'I think I have the idea, watchmaster. Continue.'

'Hm. The watch-hall deals in... movements: energies, patterns and weight. Have you... can you imagine riding on a raft? Imagine the raft rocking on a heavy sea. You share the raft with others, many others, holding torches in their hands, burning. Beautiful white fire...' The words had started to tumble over one another as the watchmaster became more sure of his subject, but for a moment, they tailed off into a sigh. 'If they move too fast on a part of the raft it will tilt, and if they cluster too thickly together the heat of their torches will combine and burn them, and if they are not shepherded by someone who can see the whole raft, feel its tilts and see where the torches are burning dangerously bright...'

'I am starting to see. You are in this room to look out over the raft. You keep it trimmed.'

'Trimming, is that two dimensions, or three? And the forces are mass, gravity, and perhaps a little motion.' The snap of pride was back in his voice. Calpurnia found a moment to wonder about the watchmaster's young days, where he had learned to think of water and rafts before the Black Ships had carried him away. 'There's so much more for me to see, Calpurnia. The fire burned away the lid to a keener eye than any that were taken out of my face, and when it was lit with the fire inside me, it gave me the strength to look out and see things...'

Calpurnia was attuned, now, to the way the watchmaster's moods swung from terse and proud, to dreamy and reflective, and back again.

'The watchmaster directs the movements of psykers, and their placement in the eyries and the choir halls,' Ylante took up when the watchmaster had gone for a dozen breaths without speaking. 'He senses the astropaths' minds and moods. He warns where concordiasts may be needed to soothe, and where the physical proximity of too many astropaths needs to be regulated or broken up. He senses where the distribution of psyker-minds through the Tower is inadvertently forming a pattern that will build reverberations, distil destructive humours into minds, or attract... attention. Astropaths must concentrate on controlling their own minds, keeping their footing on the raft, if you like. Their attention is directed inwards. The watchmaster looks the opposite way.'

'And all of this?' Calpurnia swept an arm around to take in the hall, the ringing, chiming arrays, and the hurrying servitors and orderlies.

'My nerves!' The watchmaster's voice was a bark of amusement that made Calpurnia jump. 'A nerve-centre must have nerves to be at the centre of, mustn't it?'

'They're like a display, an alarm array, what?'

'Consider,' the watchmaster said, and began to talk.

Later, Calpurnia had trouble remembering any one detail of what followed, although she tried hard to bring hard facts and words to mind. The sounds and colours, the watchmaster's words and the odd sensations still haunting her body, each one became a hazy brush-stroke in a soft picture that was all shades of light. He talked about how the sounds corresponded to certain places in the Tower, eyries or choir-halls, passages or stairs. He talked about their significance: what an individual scale meant, or a single trill, or what was signified by a shift of keys, or the sudden clashes or harmonies. He spoke of how the shuffling servitors or gliding cherubs might act as mobile markers, gravitating to a certain point to add warning tones or counter-harmonies to modulate a message. He explained how the vibrations in their air sang in his ears and in his mind, tuning his awareness exquisitely fine, and keeping all the bright psyker-voices of the Tower in harmony and balance.

She took no notes, and she could not remember all the places and names that floated through the watchmaster's conversation. When he asked her if she had heard enough, and she finally nodded in answer, his time in the watch-hall was not due to end, and they left him there, hanging in his harness and cage, the air alive with sound.

As she walked away, Calpurnia was sure that something had slipped her mind. The thought nagged away at her. She tried to place it, as she and Ylante climbed up out of the watch-hall, but failed. The sensation had been dogging her ever since she had arrived in the keep, and by the time they were back out in the cloisters, it had faded into the general mess of sensations that were sleeting through her head.

WATCHMASTER CHEVENNE LET an idle strand of his mind follow the two women away. Most of his physical senses had been deadened many years ago, driven out of his nerve-endings by the great white fire. However, his psychic touch was subtle enough to pick up a hint of scent from the collar of Ylante's gown, the gleam of Calpurnia's carapace, the texture of her hair, and a faint tracery of ghost-pain from her forehead, arm and hip that was so old that she probably didn't even feel it any more.

Chevenne had long since lost any ambition of his own to the Mastership. Some astropaths' minds only grew stronger through years of wrestling their messages across the stars, but his had been stretched thin over all his years in the eyries, with warp-winds trying to buffet his sanity out through his ears. The Master of the Tower had to be a fully empowered astropath, that law was beyond question, but Chevenne had no stomach for that work any more. Hanging in the watchmaster's cage, using the exquisite psychic control he had learned in the eyries, was a calling that he believed would suit him perfectly well, until the furnace the Soul Binding had lit in him guttered out, and his spirit went before the Emperor for the second, and final, time.

The air in the keep tasted of ambition to him now. There was a burred texture in the mesh of minds that would have set his teeth on edge had those teeth not died and dropped out long ago. There were minds in the Tower who looked forward to Mastery, oh yes.

None of them had murdered Master Otranto, Chevenne was sure of it. The thought was intolerable. His dead eyes crimped in pain as he remembered the afterwash, bouncing along the psyk-conduits and echoing like the thunderclaps that had been the terror of his boyhood on the oceans of Chaoku-Minor. Nowhere in that roil had he made out the shape, sound, scent of anyone he knew. The murderer couldn't have been anyone from the Tower. It couldn't have...

That didn't mean that there would be no strife. Many astropaths didn't care about the Mastership, their minds walking in grander places than this little station. Others might covet it, however, now that damnable rumours about the Polarists coming out of the southern segmentum were rife. Then there were genuine ambitions, Sacredsteel's and Thujik's the worst of them, honed sharp by Otranto's odd behaviours, as the Black Ship drew near amid rumours that he was going to step down. The ambitious minds were brought to a frustrated boil when the old man had announced that Torma Ylante would come aboard from the Black Ship as his new concordiast. A more stinging rebuttal to the rumours of his resignation would have been hard to imagine.

What was happening now? Chevenne had taken for granted that Calpurnia was here to seize the Bastion and rule it until the crisis was over – everyone knew that was part of the remit of the Arbites. Telepathica dictates about the Mastership going to an astropath be damned – the *Lex Imperia* could trump that, and Chevenne's masters could say nothing on the subject. He'd heard the stories of Arbites blowing open ancient Adeptus positions when the law told them that those positions had been incompetently filled.

Instead of marching aboard at the head of a taskforce, however, she was sniffing around Otranto's rooms and asking about the watch-hall, marching out and leaving a trail of black and crimson across his mind's eye. Chevenne had wondered about that two-coloured cloud as she had sat beside him, the coiled tension in her mind such a contrast to the symmetry and stillness of Ylante's. Black and crimson: he didn't normally perceive colours like that.

As his awareness reached out to touch the delicate song of the watch-hall, and out past it to the psychic lifeblood of the Tower, Watchmaster Chevenne's fingers kept brushing the topmost card in his Tarot deck, unconsciously tracing the image of the judge. His other hand, tucked deep in his robes, gripped the token that Master Lohjen had given him when he had ordered Chevenne to report everything that he heard or sensed from the arbitor's words and mind.

CONCORDIAST DECHENE WANTED to go hunting for Renz, but didn't want to admit it. Admitting it would have meant admitting that Renz's paranoid stress actually made him feel calmer and more in control himself. That in turn would have meant admitting that he was nervous. He didn't want to admit that he was nervous.

Although, he had a right, everything was so uncertain since the old bastard had been – had died. Who the hell had known that the Arbites would be here so quickly, or that the stakes would rise so high so fast? Hadn't he earned a little nerv–

No! It was fundamental to Dechene's concept of himself: he did not get frightened or uncertain. He caused those feelings in others, but did not accept them in himself. Once his concept of himself started to crack, how could he be sure of anything?

He scowled at Kyto, who had the balls not to flinch. Dechene admired him for that, but it still made him angry.

'So where is he, then?'

'I told you, Dechene, I haven't seen him for two shifts. He was half-gone with neuroses before that Black Ship docked, and he's worse now. You know him better than I do. You tell me where he went. I don't have time to saunter all over the damn tower looking for him.'

The two men kept their voices low as they sauntered, hands behind backs, down the Grand Concourse towards the docks, a servitor trailing them with a lantern held over their heads on a pole. Not many officers of Kyto's rank had the clout to requisition a servitor-adjutant, so it was a useful reminder to anyone who saw them out in public. They were friends and confidants of Teeker Renz, and although the Master who favoured Renz was dead, he and his associates still had influence.

'Well, nor have I,' the concordiast retorted. 'I've been on errands too, you know. Errands of Renz's, and I'd have thought the wittering idiot would have made himself easier to find if it was so important to him.'

'It's a finesse thing,' Kyto said. 'By the accounts I've heard, this woman's a little harder at the edges than that Bruinann fool. Perhaps Renz is making sure that we aren't seen as a group all the time?' He looked at the other man's expression. 'You're young, Dechene. You only really remember Teeker being Otranto's pet, and us being Teeker's mates. That's not always going to be the order of things, unless we all get a bit more careful making it that way. Arbites have a habit of rattling whatever they start stamping around near, this Calpurnia especially. She smashes whatever she touches. Don't you remember how crazy things got after that stupid rogue trader shootout at Galata? And she cost Sambin de Jauncey his gate-captain's commission. His whole family felt that one.'

'I don't care, and you shouldn't talk to me like that.' Dechene's expression had turned petulant.

'It's something you need to hear. It's about time you came up against a problem you couldn't just thug your way past. We need to use our brains, watch what Renz is trying to do and try and learn why he's doing it.'

'The Arbites should be afraid of us, not the other way around,' grumbled Dechene. 'I'm allowed to say it, aren't I?' he added, catching Kyto's reproving look. 'You're not an informant, and neither am I. Anyway, this woman's going to have a bit more to worry about than taking away what's ours.' He managed to grin. 'She deserves it, too. I say they all do.'

CHAPTER EIGHT

MASTER CHASTENER DAST lay on the Apothecarion bed like a stone martyr on a tomb-slab. Orovene, reliquary box finally out of his hands, but the smell of lho-smoke back around him, stood at the foot of the bed, humming soft prayers, as an arbitor medicae ran his fingertips softly over the wounds in Dast's skull and face. The Chastener didn't twitch as the medicae's deft touch probed the crushed parts of his face. His breathing was laboured and there was a bad grey cast to his skin.

The precinct medicae ward was tiny, and Calpurnia, small as she was, had to stand back to make room. She stood with her hands neatly behind her back, fighting the urge to just sag against the wall.

'Master Orovene tells me that he was alone when the attack came,' murmured the doctor, so low that it took Calpurnia a moment to realise that the man wasn't addressing himself.

'Not alone,' Orovene said, 'alone but for his attacker. The rest of us were in the Master's garden.'

'Madam arbitor senioris?' Orovene's expression darkened at the medicae's dismissive tone, but he said nothing.

'I can't add anything,' Calpurnia said. 'I was elsewhere, with Concordiast Ylante. I only just came away and returned directly here.'

She had been walking back through the cloisters when the runner had brought the news; from there, it had been a flat run for the precinct compound. Ylante had kept pace with the scowling, hunched gait of one not used to running.

Still bent over Dast, the medicae looked up at her from under his dark-grey eyebrows. One hand stayed on the Chastener's forehead while the other reached out and finger-walked along a rack of tiny drawers.

'May I ask, madam arbitor senioris, if the watch-hall had noted any kind of discord or alarm while you were there? What did Watch-master Chevenne have to report to you?'

'Nothing.' All that time being lectured about what the watch-hall was for, and she hadn't thought to use it as a detective tool. Well, technically, she'd given a right answer... but no, only cowards hid from their mistakes.

'I didn't ask him. We talked about his work, but the talk went mostly to the nature of his duties.' She thought about it. 'He referred to some of the patterns he was observing in the Tower while I was present, but he didn't volunteer anything about the kind of disturbance a brawl and a death must have created.'

As she spoke, she was trying to replay her surreal visit to the watch-hall in her head: had Chevenne hinted at anything she should have picked up on? Had she heard anything that she should have asked the meaning of?

Orovene was still looking down at Dast and repeating his litany, over and over. Calpurnia recognised it from medicae halls from Hydraphur to Machiun. The words wove between Low and High Gothic, poetry and homily, but the message stayed the same. *The sickbed is poison to us,* she breathed along with Orovene, *grow strong in the name of the Emperor's law and rise from it to your duty. The Emperor's name is your armour; the Emperor's commandments are your strength. The Emperor's voice speaks to turn your wounds to scars and your pain to the cold work of punishment...*

Saying the litany sent memories flitting around her mind like bats startled out of a cave. Without her knowing it, Calpurnia's hand crept to her head, and her fingers began massaging the scars over her eye.

'Do we know what killed the proctor, then?' she asked. 'If that's what he did to Dast with the seal, I have to think that it wasn't the Chastener's response that killed him.'

'The master Chastener didn't respond to the attack at all,' Orovene said, interrupting his monotone. 'It was too quick and hurt him too badly. If he'd had the chance to fight, we'd be sitting in that office upstairs asking him ourselves. Trust me, Calpurnia, when I tell you that the proctor and two more of him wouldn't have bested Dast with his guard up.'

A slightly pained look had crept onto the medicae's face. The man was studiously examining Dast's head wound again. He had already attached a coronet of diagnostor runes to Dast's skull: telltales shone red, and every so often one would give a tiny chime like the watch-hall bells.

Calpurnia caught his expression.

'How well did you know the proctor, arbitor?' she asked him a little more gently. 'Were you friends? And forgive me, I haven't asked your name.'

'Not close, Mamzel Calpurnia,' he said, although he didn't look up from his work, 'but it's too small a garrison for us not to know one another. I knew a little about Proctor Pheissen. He was a good man. I'd give a lot to know what brought him to a death like that.' He paused to secure another diagnostor stud in place, and watched the flicker of its indicator-lights for a moment. 'My name is Scall. Arbitor-Medicae Eschoen Scall, if it please the arbitor general.' His manner was relaxing a little, and Calpurnia allowed herself a flicker of satisfaction. She'd managed to get something right, anyway.

'You know that there have to be questions, Arbitor Scall,' she said, with a soft emphasis on 'arbitor'. 'There are... wrong things about this station, it seems to me, craziness and bad omens ever since I set foot here. A concordiast returns to her old Master's side, and somehow he's dead minutes before they were due to meet again. The Master's murder panics the dock crews into rioting and trying to escape in my ship. A proctor of the Adeptus Arbites attacks the master Chastener from whom he'd been taking orders minutes before.'

'And dies in the doing of it,' put in Orovene, 'in a way we can't yet trace.' Calpurnia nodded.

'Let's not forget Otranto, executed by someone who passed through auspexes, locks, armoured and sealed doors, witchcullises and psyk-wards. He was killed in a station full of seers and psykers who can listen to a pot boil half a sector away, but who haven't one word to say about the killing of one of their own–' She stopped herself. *Not to mention how I came here not being allowed to trust my judgement or my competence,* she had been about to say, *and now I'm having trouble even trusting my body, my mind and my senses.* There were things that an arbitor general, even a disgraced one headed for trial, did not say in company like this.

'Bruinann and Rede have worked hard, Mamzel Calpurnia,' Scall said quietly as his fingers worked the diagnostor studs. 'If the witches have given them nothing then it's not because they've been able to keep secrets. Put an aquila in my hand and I'll swear that the way they've been working has been the best way.'

'There are ways of bringing out the truth that we know they haven't tried,' Orovene said, but Scall shook his cropped grey head.

'If you arrested an astropath and dragged him right off the station, maybe. Even the incarceries in the Kuiper belts might be too close. One of the inner stations, or Galata, might work. Even Hydraphur, they say the Inquisition has a place there where–' He grunted and peered at a telltale. 'The details don't matter. Do it far away from here, is all. No matter how sealed you think you are, something will leak out, like a match into a promethium refinery.'

Orovene was scowling and shaking his head, rubbing the *Auctorita Imperialis* badge at his breast.

'You're walking down a dangerous line of thought, Scall. I don't wonder why your investigation was so moribund. You're lost in witch-shadows.' He made a fist around the badge and glared. 'This is moral weakness. Your preachers will have to answer for your straying as much as your commanders.'

There, it had been said. The whole garrison was potentially on trial for their failings, just as Calpurnia would be for hers. That Orovene had finally put it into words would be all over the precinct compound within half a shift, Calpurnia didn't doubt.

'Tell me again, Arbitor Scall,' she said, 'about why it's so difficult to put an astropath to the torture here. If Bruinann came to that conscious decision then I want to know the thinking behind it.'

'I'm not privy to the aedile's decisions,' Scall told her. His guard was up again.

'I don't need you to be. Just tell me about that promethium refinery remark.'

For the first time since she had come in, Scall straightened up from his stoop over the bed. At full height, he was not much taller than Calpurnia, but with a barrel chest and heavy shoulders that he rolled and stretched.

'If you like the promethium analogy then that's what I'll continue with,' he said. 'A psyker creates a haze around himself. The stronger ones can keep it inside their heads, or hearts or wherever the hell it is that the witch gift touches them, but it's always there. Like sweat, or body heat.

'An individual, a few of them together, you won't notice much, especially if they're properly controlled and damped. I've been to our own astropaths' tower in the Wall back on Hydraphur, which I don't know if either of you have... no?' Calpurnia and Orovene shook their heads, 'You'll barely feel anything there, anyhow. Here, we're well over the critical mass. Even with the rebuilding and the wards, and the watchmasters making sure they don't collect too heavily or move the wrong ways, that spirit-haze drenches everything. I won't try to explain it except in terms of the effects I can see and understand as a medicae, but there's a... a *volatility* you get in that haze.'

'Dangerous,' said Calpurnia, almost to herself, and there was something more than physical danger on her mind. A promethium cylinder slung under a flamer was volatile, but it was an understandable danger. A plasma-furnace had to be constantly tended by its tech-priests and enginseers, but at its heart, such a fire was a gift of the Emperor in his guise as the Machine-God. If the fire turned on its tenders then that was a clean death, an understandable death. The witch-haze, on the other hand, men and women whose minds stretched reality thin and let things start to seep into it that no one short of Him on Earth should have to face...

Calpurnia had been in danger of her life many times – the scars on her body and her grim memories were testament to that. To be in danger of her soul, that was a more frightening thing. Faith was what she needed to shore herself up against those fears, but she'd had faith walking into the courtroom on Selena Secundus, and what had happened? Within hours she–

She bit down on her tongue, not hard, but hard enough to make her wince and flinch, and break out of the trapped loop of thought.

'Dangerous,' agreed Scall. 'Most of us on the station are on a knife-edge because of it, even non-psykers. It's like an ague, or pollution-sickness. A good hard shock like a psyker being tortured is going to touch off something you really don't want.'

'Would the reactions frighten any others into informing?' asked Orovene.

'I'm not talking about a *frightening* reaction, brother preacher,' Scall told him evenly. 'The nightmares you might have had when you last embarked on a warp voyage might have frightened you, but they're a shadow of what a psychic shock will do in a place like this. The arbitor general was right to pick up on my talking about matches. Why do you think that the astropaths take every step at gunpoint? Even the strongest of them can succumb if they let down their guard, or if they're caught by something out there that's stronger than they are. The vitifers are there to put an end to any whose energy gets out of control, before half the witches aboard the Tower go off like bombs, or before something...' he took a breath, 'something goes bad inside them. The smaller enclaves don't need vitifers, but a station this size, funnelling this much power? There are people in the eyries, every moment of every day, arbitor, the power might die down but it never stops. Volatile.' He finished with the needle and reached for another. 'So there are the vitifers. Places like this, that don't have them, don't last long. Don't ever– I mean it's against all the laws of the Astropathica to speak with one, or hinder them. I suggest you bear that powerfully in mind, mamzel, if you find yourself in command and needing to make decisions over the Adeptus Astra Telepathica authorities on board.'

'Vitifers?' asked Orovene, as Calpurnia nodded. The preacher hadn't had the benefit of the tour with Ylante.

'The High Gothic for them,' said Scall, 'because they carry the lives of each astropath in their hands. Ugly word, isn't it?' Scall pressed his fingers against a rune-panel for a moment, murmuring some Apothecarion charm. A pair of slender mechanical arms unfolded from the ceiling, little bundles of surgical tools splaying out from their ends like clawed toes. Scall moved the arms expertly into position, fixing them in place with a soft code word that triggered locking mechanisms in the oiled metal joints.

'I'm ready to begin the next stage of my work, arbitor general,' he said without looking up. 'I respectfully request that you withdraw and make room for my servitors and assistants. Arresting the worst of the damage will take some delicate work and substantial time. Brother preacher, a candle burning in the Chapel for Master Dast would warm my hopes a little.'

'The Emperor protects,' replied Orovene, and Calpurnia repeated the words as they turned to leave.

'SOMETHING'S CHANGED,' WAS the first thing Torma Ylante said when Calpurnia had her brought out of the little attending-cell by the precinct compound doors. The woman had tried to follow them right into the precinct compound, and Calpurnia had rudely shoved her back into the arms of a following arbitrator, and ordered her detained.

'Something's changed,' Ylante said again. 'Your bearing is different. What happened?'

Calpurnia nodded to the arbitrator who'd fetched Ylante from the attending-cell, and he took the concordiast by the elbow and started walking her towards the doors.

'Madam arbitor? Wait, please. May I know what's going on?'

'Master Chastener Dast was the target of an attack,' said Calpurnia. 'Our Apothecarion will restore his strength to do his duty, Emperor willing.'

'Thank you. The Chastener will be in my prayers.' The arbitrator had picked up his pace, and Ylante was forced to conduct the conversation over one shoulder. 'How can I be of further service? I can provide you with a quick survey of – could you slow down, please? – of some of the astropath eyries if you want to familiarise yourself… er…'

'That won't be necessary. My work here is Arbites business, which does not concern you, concordiast.'

'Arbitor Calpurnia, if I'm to guide you properly, I need to be able to–'

'I think you presume a friendship and a favoured position that does not exist, Ylante. Be careful on that score. I don't know how much more indulgence I'll be able to spare you.'

Those words brought them to the compound doors, and Calpurnia nodded to the arbitrator to leave them. Ylante stepped across the threshold, collected herself and turned around, the two women facing each other through the open gates.

'I intended no offence to you, Arbitor Calpurnia, and I apologise for any that I caused.'

'A knowledge of your place is all I'll require of you, that and your duty to law. Your position on Otranto's staff hadn't been fully ratified, is that so? Then you've no formal place in the Bastion. Have you a sleeping-cell? Good. Return there directly and remain there until I, specifically and personally, authorise otherwise. I'll pay you the respect of assuming that I don't need to have you taken there under guard.'

Ylante bowed, a little stiffly, and made a careful sign to the aquila over the precinct doors before she turned away.

Calpurnia watched her go, then spun to re-enter the compound, and almost walked into Rede.

'Watch and follow?' the detective asked. 'I took the liberty of making some arrangements. She isn't as snaky as some of my informants have painted her, but she's too close to the middle of all this not to be watched.'

Calpurnia nodded agreement as they stepped back over the threshold and let the doors swing shut.

'Can you direct a two-level watch? Ylante has to know we're going to keep an eye on her, so let's let her see us doing it. Let's have an eye on her that she doesn't know about, too. I want reports from both of them: level three delegation.'

'Yes, arbitor. Ma'am?' Rede had stopped in the shadow of the doors, and lowered her voice.

'What is it, detective?'

'Does this mean that you're our sole commander now?'

'Does–'

'What happened to the Chastener – you're the arbitor general, ma'am, but we're aware that you came here under a, well, a special situation. With what's happened to Dast, are you our substantive commander now? Your nominal rank came from Dast. Are you still in charge?'

Calpurnia had taken a step back, her hand dropping to the hilt of her maul. A blazing certainty had come out of nowhere: Rede was working herself up to mutiny. She had decided that she couldn't stand the possibility of Calpurnia finding her guilty of incompetence. She was preparing for a murder, just as she'd prepared the murder of–

'I don't intend any disrespect by this, ma'am,' Rede went on, 'but there's not just the murder. There's no successor. Everything that's coming back through my agents is telling me that the whole Tower expects you to annex command and preside over the succession yourself, but no one's seen any signs of it happening.'

'It was the master Chastener's decision,' Calpurnia said carefully, 'that with the, ah, *limited* nature of my office we would keep our work here as narrow as possible. The decisions and plans were his, and I was bound by them. The master Chastener's work is capture and punishment and we see this reflected in his approach.'

'The master Chastener is no longer in command, ma'am. Are we bound to his decisions or to yours? The Emperor's work must be done. I'd know from you, how you want that to happen.'

'Thank you for bringing the matter to my attention, Detective Rede,' Calpurnia answered. The tension had deflated so suddenly that she could swear she had heard it collapse. There had been no mutiny or plot in Rede's words. She had been concerned for the order of things, for the chain of command, and for the rule of law in the Bastion Psykana. Mutiny and murder, what the hell had she been thinking? 'I'll consider my course of action and get whatever advice from the praetory I feel I need. As for you, you have the surveillance instructions. When you're done, I'd like a briefing on exactly why people aboard the Tower are reacting to Ylante the way they are. I know she has a history here, but I need to know what that history is.'

Rede saluted and made to step away, but Calpurnia called her back.

'There is one final matter that I promise I won't keep you on. Medicae Scall made mention that it's the… the *haze* I think he called it. Something about being in a place that's drenched in the energies of so many psykers close together that acts like an ague.'

'Feeling it, are you, ma'am?' Rede stepped back into the gateway recess. Her expression was one of mixed sympathy and a certain professional reserve, a seen-it-before look. 'You're right. Your body plays tricks and your brain does too. Some people can't make peace with it. They have to get shipped out again, and they don't always walk up the boarding ramp, if you get my meaning. The psykers don't care, their minds just float in it like a fish, while we thrash around for air. How bad is it?'

'There's some pain: muscle, joint, head, and some… some oddities in the senses. You're right, I'm having to watch my thoughts, and my temperature perception seems out. Is that unusual for someone new to the station…?'

Rede grunted assent.

'Thank you, detective, I think that's all I needed to know. I won't keep you from your surveillance any longer.'

Rede left her standing at the bottom of the tall well of the precinct compound, head bowed in front of the touch-polished plinth with its ancient, sacred data-ark, deep in thought.

TORMA YLANTE HAD known the watchers were there as she had walked away from the precinct, but they hadn't ruffled her. She had been able to pick two of them out straight away. A houseman overseer plodding behind a whining electric dray, loaded down with soiled bedding. Their laundry run seemed to require an odd, zigzag route that intersected with hers far more often than it should have.

The other one was probably more dangerous: a young woman, an artisan, working her way through the cloisters with a slate and stylus, marking down designs on the pennants. It was a better cover, good enough to work on most. Ylante reckoned she could pick out an armed surveillant when she saw one. If Calpurnia gave the order, that woman was an executioner as well as a watcher.

It was so strange, she thought as she walked. The halls were as she remembered them, but the people had changed. When she had been here so long ago, Chevenne had been in his prime: hawklike, haughty and still fiercely in command of his mind, so different from the files of brain-burned psykers who'd been shepherded alongside him.

Thujik, Thujik had been almost comatose when he arrived, responding to the gentle telepathic questing of the more skilled astropaths, but unable to do anything more sophisticated than add his voice to the very lowest registers of a choir. Now, he was a possible successor to Otranto! She didn't recognise many of the names: Sacredsteel? Ankyne? Del'Kateer? Veterans, apparently, grown old and powerful. So many of the astropaths whose minds she had known almost as well as her own – Tophlio, Light-Of-His-Eyes, Tchangaia – were gone.

Ylante lingered on thoughts of her old colleagues: no matter how strong they had been, how skilled, how faithful or brave in pushing their minds out into that soul-lacerating pandemonium, their calling claimed them eventually. Their brains had burned, their taxed hearts had given out, or their minds had simply worn so thin that they drifted into that grey paralysis that the concordiasts called 'ash-sleep'.

Perhaps something darker had happened, Ylante thought with a shiver, and they had pitched forwards into their own blown-out brains, with the hole from a fire-breaker's bullet in their skull.

In a rare melancholy, she drifted through the twisting cloisters. Her followers were out of sight for a moment, and the only signs of life were muffled footsteps around some distant corner. Something about the silence seemed more poignant to Ylante than the racket of a working dock or the constant sounds of misery aboard the Black Ship.

Was she weakening, she wondered? A younger Ylante would not have let a mood like this interrupt her serenity, but a younger Ylante had been able to work on the Black Ship. She had been able to help control the poor lost souls bound for the furnaces of the Golden Throne, and not let it break her. Was the simple fact that she couldn't face the work any more a sign that her own usefulness was coming to an end? Was the time coming, she wondered, when she couldn't even face her old role with the astropaths and their choirs? She had been a servant to psykers since her fourteenth birthday. What would happen to her when she couldn't serve them any longer?

She realised that she missed the Black Ship, the incense-smoke in the prow chapel, the familiar gargoyles at each passage-head, the black-hooded Inquisitorial wardens, the voice of Galan Vedrier saying her name... No. She had turned her back on that, and she would face the consequences.

Ylante heard a footstep behind her. On her guard, she shot a look over her shoulder, and shied a pace backwards when she saw the figure coming at her. It was just a runner, a thickset man in badly fitting messenger's livery, and in his hand an Arbites icon winked for a moment before he palmed it and shook his head at her, for silence. It only took a moment for the paper to pass from his hand to hers, and then he was a receding shadow, a muffled footstep receding into the cloisters.

Ylante, the paper read. *You were dismissed at our gates to maintain a deception, but your knowledge is needed. Otranto's murderer knows the Bastion too well. Come to the Arbites dromon docked at the tower above the hangar at Prime Dock and we will confer. Tell no one. CALPURNIA.*

There was no formal seal, but a gauntlet-and-laurel design that Ylante had seen on Calpurnia's badges of office had been stamped directly into the paper below the writing. The stamp was crooked, and the pen-strokes were hurried.

She didn't destroy the note, but folded it between her fingers where she could shred and pulp it if she needed to. She held it there as she reversed direction, moving quickly, heading for the docks. She had carefully controlled her emotions about Otranto's death, but in life, he had meant much to her, and the thought of his killer being unmasked lent speed to her step.

CHAPTER NINE

'THEY'RE IN PLACE,' said Rede as Calpurnia sat down opposite her. 'She's spotted two of them, and there's a second level hanging back. There's also one remote drone with one of the lay arbitor-techmen from our shrine. Here, eat.' She put a platter of oily bread-balls and heavy grey nutriate strips on the table between them. 'We tend to find that if the station's getting to you, you deal with it better on a full stomach.'

They were in Rede's long, cluttered office, tables and benches littered as ever with papers and slates.

'This drone, it's come to us from the Mechanicus? How long has it been since its spirit was in service to them, not us?' Calpurnia picked at the nutriates. The headache was going, but her stomach still knotted at the idea of eating.

'Fair question,' said Rede, 'but I think it can be trusted. I was at the ceremony when the Tech-priests forswore the thing over to the Arbites.' Calpurnia nodded her approval, and Rede went on. 'The drone will keep her under watch and I've got half a dozen arbitrators on an ostensible snap inspection of the outer galleries. Their paths won't cross Ylante's, but they can be on her at speed if any of the others report something.'

'Operation leader?' Calpurnia picked off a piece of bread between her fingertips. The oil had a crisp scent.

'Proctor Lagny, the drone operator. She's on a level two delegation from me. She's capable.' Rede picked up a strip of bread for herself and bit off half of it. 'While we're discussing our so-respectable quarry, allow me to direct you to...'

With a gesture, Rede brought up streams of script and images across the tapestry-screen.

'So, the concordiasts,' said the detective, 'attendants, keepers, interpreters. Their job is to know the astropaths well enough to be able to calm them down after their trances, interpret the messages, and talk them back into their own bodies after they've been, you know, out there.' Rede made a flippant wave of her hand, but she put the lie to her casualness by carefully making the sign of the aquila at those last two words. 'A good concordiast is sought after. The bonds they develop with any astropath they work with for any length of time can be quite intense.'

'They're allowed relationships?' Calpurnia chewed cautiously on the bread.

'No,' said Rede. 'Not of the sort I think you have in mind. The bond isn't romantic. It's not dutiful, not religious, and certainly not carnal. The astropaths' metabolisms are so unhinged by what happens to them that as far as I can work out, they're effectively sexless. It's hard to confirm. There are some taboos involved in talking about what they actually go through.'

'Probably because, Detective Rede, what they have been through has taken them onto the very soil of Earth where they touch the presence of the God-Emperor. Even though these people you dismiss as "witches" have stood on such holy ground that the respect of poor sinners like you and I can't bother them any more, I'll still thank you to show a little more reverence.'

'My apologies, ma'am. I forgot myself.' To show that she meant it, Rede took her booted foot down off the table and turned to face Calpurnia face-on. 'All right. In the larger astropath enclaves, with a proper concordiast order on hand, the better ones with the calmest minds will develop working relationships with the senior astropaths. The depth of the bonds that can develop is something blunts like us probably just don't have the – what?' She'd caught

Calpurnia's look. 'Ah, apologies – "Blunt": pejorative term for one without a psyker gift, as employed by those with.'

'Thank you. My interaction with psykers has been limited until now, so bear in mind that I'm relying on you for some pretty elementary bearings.'

'Understood. Where was I? I was at Torma Ylante.'

They turned to regard the portrait in the tapestry's upper corner.

'Just under forty years ago, Ylante was one of the Bastion's senior concordiasts. According to the dossier from the master espionist at that time, she didn't have the hair-trigger emotional sensitivity that some of them have, but she could attune well to body language and speech, and she remembers *everything* she sees and hears. She also has a calmness of mind that apparently makes direct mental contact, which is something not every concordiast is able to handle at all, easy and soothing.'

'And so she became Otranto's favourite?' Calpurnia turned her attention to the portrait below Ylante's. Knowing so much about Otranto's wretched last moments had given her a curiously intimate sense of him, and it was odd to finally see his face. Master Otranto had been a gaunt man, with a good-humoured cast to his mouth that surprised her. The sockets of his dead eyes had been patched over with skin grafts. A tiny gold stud sat in the centre of each one. After peering at the image for a moment, Calpurnia realised that it was an eyeless eagle's head: the part of the aquila that symbolised the Adeptus Astra Telepathica.

'Otranto was a great one to play favourites,' Rede told her. 'He liked having his personal inner circle: the Master of the Bastion, the Master's personal concordiast, the Master's personal herbalist, the Master's personal Naval attaché, the Master's selected senior astropaths. People known to have Otranto's favour also accumulated influence in other ways.'

'Was there a reason for the Master doing this, apart from gratification?' asked Calpurnia.

Rede shook her head. 'Not that I can make out, it was just the way he operated. I'd have known if it was leading anywhere truly criminal.'

The defensive tone told Calpurnia that the woman wasn't as confident as she was letting on. It probably wouldn't make a difference if things came to a trial: influence peddling from an Adeptus office was a crime on multiple levels, and allowing it at all was something that Rede would have to answer for. There was such a thing as taking pragmatism too far.

'So,' Rede went on, 'the precinct records show that three weeks before Candlemas thirty-nine years ago, Torma Ylante left her position within Master Otranto's circle, and her position as concordiast aboard the station. She departed on a Black Ship commanded by one Master Galan Vedrier.'

'Which is the one that just brought her back. What reason was behind all this? How was she even allowed to do it?'

'We don't know. The espionist cell at the time put a fair bit of effort into finding out – there was a covert society operating in several of the Naval stations, called the Chamber of Optika. They were on record as wanting to get at the Blind Tower's officials for reasons of their own. The fear was that this tied in with them somehow, but nothing was ever established. All the Arbites of the time could find out was that there was some kind of falling-out between Ylante and Otranto. Leaving with the Black Ship seems to have been part of the row, rather than solely the result of it.'

'And so, what, thirty-nine years later – really? Thirty-nine years?'

'The astropaths whose bodies can handle the work tend to age pretty well,' Rede said. 'Bruinann says it cures them, like leather. Somehow, I don't think that's exactly how it works, but the ones who survive do seem to toughen up.'

'And Ylante's been warp-voyaging,' Calpurnia mused. 'I doubt that anything like thirty-nine years have passed for her. So, here she is again, returned on the same ship she left on, ready to pick up where she left off.'

'No sooner has she walked onto the station,' said Rede, 'than Master Otranto is–' She stopped, cocked her head, and put a hand to her vox-torc. Calpurnia couldn't make out the voice, but the easy expression dropped out of Rede's eyes and she half-stood.

'Ylante's changed direction,' she said.

'Damn!' Calpurnia was on her feet in an instant. 'Where is she?' She grabbed up her helmet.

'She's dropping onto one of the downward passages to... wait... she's passed through the fourth Manifold Arch.' Rede's brow creased. 'It's one of the ways we came up through, when you arrived. It's on the route to the docks where your dromon's anchored.'

The two women were silent for a moment. Facts and guesses whirled through Calpurnia's head.

'Is there anyone with her?' she asked.

'They... no.' Rede was pacing, scowling at the transmissions she was getting. 'Lagny and Rhiil, that's the agents, both say no. She crossed paths with some message runner a couple of minutes ago, but they're not walking together. She seems in a hurry.'

'Where's the runner now? Can Lagny keep the drone on him?'

'How hidden do you want it to be?' Rede asked by way of a reply. 'It's the size of my fist. It can stay up on the ceilings and not be too obvious in the low light, but the faster it has to move to find him the worse it'll fare.'

'Ideally, this man shouldn't know that we're following him, but following him comes first. Lagny can use her judgement, but it needs to be as quiet as she can make it.' Calpurnia donned her helmet and checked the sit of her maul at her hip.

'Get Bruinann to the gate with a detail to meet us,' she told Rede, 'and with a spare shield for me from the armoury.'

'Ma'am?'

'I gave Ylante a direct order,' Calpurnia growled as she made for the door, 'and what does she do? She turns and wanders off on her own. Keep your surveillance on her, Rede, but I aim to be there when we move in on her. She can explain to my face what brought this on. Who's the arbitrator in charge of that squad you mentioned?'

'Oraxi, ma'am–'

'And is Bruinann on alert? I'm going down there with him and with an escort.' Calpurnia was standing in the doorway, 'the same size again as whatever Oraxi's leading. Send word to the Arbites on my dromon for full lockdown. They stay anchored, but they seal themselves in there.'

Rede nodded and rapid-fired instructions into the vox. Then she looked up at Calpurnia with sharp worry written on her lean brown face.

'What is it?' Calpurnia was gripping the doorframe, ready to propel herself away.

'Order passed on to the dromon crew, but they report in turn. The hangar has just–' she listened to the vox again as Calpurnia fidgeted in the doorway. 'It's shut down. The lights and engines have been put to sleep. They don't know where the command has come from.'

Calpurnia ground her teeth.

'It's either some plot by Ylante or it's an ambush. Either way, I'm in a mood to bust someone's plans wide open. Get whoever you can onto those dock systems; I don't care if we have to drag Channery out of the Enginarium by her collar. Wake those machines up and find out who put them to bed. We're on the move.'

IT HAD BEEN a shock when the lights cut off. Dechene was not used to being in darkness, and he wasn't sure he could remember the last time he had been on the Bastion's docking hangars. Suddenly, the big metal space he'd been skulking through was a black maze, hard metal shapes all around him, cables, steps and ridges, making his footing treacherous. He'd spotted dead Otranto's precious little pet concordiast in the cloisters, and had been curious to see what she had been in such a hurry for. At the worst he had expected that to lead to Renz snarking at him for wasting some time. He hadn't bargained on this.

Still, he was rather pleased with the perch he had found for himself. Once his eyes had adapted a little, Dechene had managed to get his bearings and climb up onto an elevated lifter-tray. From here, by the pallid light coming in from the lit passageways at the rear of the hangar, he could see Ylante in her cream gown. She'd been as spooked as he was by the darkness, and was looking around her. Dechene hunkered down to make sure she didn't see him and then caught his breath. The movement behind Ylante hadn't been his imagination. He froze, watched and concentrated. Quick, furtive figures, four of them, slipped easily through the darkness.

Dechene was sure that they were people from Lohjen's ship. Hard to keep track of – they seemed to lose definition in the shadows, somehow. He was glad they didn't think to look up. Ylante's pale clothes glimmered in the dark. Dechene, dressed in the same shade, would stand out like a, well, like something he didn't want to be, because it would, most likely, get him shot. Ylante, shivering, had put her back to a lifter-column. He watched and waited, wondering when one of the figures would make a move.

'Mamzel Ylante, to us!'

The shout made Dechene jump, enough to set the lifter tray swinging gently. He gritted his teeth – what if someone heard the chain squeaking? No. He heard two sets of footsteps, no effort at quiet, clattering in from the keep, a wiry dark-haired woman in an artisan's bodyglove and... and a *houseman*? A damn laundry cart pusher with his drudges trotting along behind him! Dechene wanted to laugh out loud. Who the hell had sent these people in for the rescue?

'Mamzel Ylante,' called the woman again. 'You're in danger. Please come and stand by us!' The houseman motioned to his drudges, and one of them directed a heavy hand-lumen into the hangar.

The hot white beam swung back and forth through the shadows underneath Dechene for a moment, and just when he was sure it would fan up and reveal him, the first two shots went by underneath, snuffing out the light and the boy who held it.

The house crew scattered, sprinting sideways and forwards into the shadows, as whispered words of combat-cant came up from behind him. Another shot, stub, not las. Dechene inched himself backwards so that the platform wouldn't sway, and pressed his head down. This would do him fine until the shooting had died down – Dechene could be arrogant, but he wasn't stupid.

THE SPOTLIGHT DROPPED and crashed, and its carrier fell dead on top of it. Suddenly, Torma Ylante was groping through a green-purple haze, a stabbing, pulsing after-image right in the centre of her vision. She squeezed her eyes shut and opened them again, trying to focus on her outstretched hand through the throbbing nova in front of her eyes. Behind her, someone shouted her name again. Ylante gritted her teeth and started towards the sound, sure that, at any moment she'd brain herself on an overhead rail, or break her outstretched fingers on a stanchion. What was going on? She thought she recognised one of the silhouettes as the houseman she had spotted watching her. But that light – had they been looking for her, or deliberately trying to blind her?

She spotted a shadowy shape in front of her in time to sidestep it and get around it – some kind of machinery, too indistinct for her to get a clear idea of what it was. She wondered if she was safe here. No, wherever the shots had come from, it had been somewhere in the dark. She had to keep moving. She closed her eyes for a moment, opened them, and could see a little better. Move on and just perhaps she could get to cover. That or stay where she was, marooned and alone. No.

She took a step and her foot came down askew onto a thick snaking cable that sent her staggering sideways, twisting her knee and ankle. Torma Ylante dropped to one knee, fighting to keep in the cry that she knew would bring a bullet out of the darkness.

'TORMA YLANTE! WE'RE here to keep you safe!' shouted Hasta Rhiil, and then immediately danced three steps sideways, scanning the hangar through the tiny darklight monocular that Rede had issued to her. A long-barrelled silenced dartcaster jutted from each sleeve, the spots of light from the black-laser targeters skittering back and forth over the bay, visible only to her. Where the hell had the woman gone? And where were the bastards who'd shot that poor kid with the lamp? She couldn't see anything moving in the lilac-tinted image the monocular fed her. Were they cowards, or they just smart?

She darted forwards between two crates, kicked one loudly and cursed theatrically, and then doubled back and around. Nobody seemed to be moving on her. Moans and shouts came from where she had been standing: the rest of those boys were trying to drag their dead companion to cover.

She tried to let the training take over – the combat training from the arbitrator range, not the endless classroom exercises of the Espionist schools and let her skills work for themselves.

Throne alone knew what the houseman made of what was happening, but he was being stupidly, loudly brave, helping his crew drag their dead friend behind a track-loader, bawling for the murderer to come out and face him man to man. Rhiil pushed deeper into the hangar, among half-filled containers and abandoned trucking equipment. Where had the woman gone?

There was a dark human figure against a paler spot of half-shadow, and Rhiil's arm snapped straight. The point of violet light dropped neatly to the base of its neck and her dartcaster made its barely-there *shikshikshik*. The figure reeled and clutched at where the shots had hit, but it didn't fall.

Rhiil's eagerness betrayed her. Suddenly, all she could think about was riding her kill and standing over his corpse. She'd save Ylante and hello, full espionist rank, and she could finally wear a proper black carapace again with that wonderful red collar. She ran a few silent paces forwards, but the second assassin had been ready for her and the las-shot exploded in Rhiil's shoulder, spun her around in mid-stride and mid-air, and dumped her hard on the metal deck as her vision went from purple-shaded dark to utter black.

YLANTE HEARD THE crack of the las-round's superheated trail and then the ugly sound of a human body falling. She hobbled three steps to another stanchion, but she was clumsy with panic and fell heavily against it, shoulder-first. She slumped there for a moment and then plunged on through the dimness. Stupid, stupid! How had she trusted the letter, but then how could she have known?

Her chest hit a diagonal support and she grunted, gripped it and lowered herself down, thinking that she could crawl under it and get her breath. Her vision was starting to come back, shapes and distances visible around the livid after-image. If only they could keep fighting each other behind her for just a minute more.

That was the moment that the gun-barrel hit the back of her head and bounced her off the support. Before her knees had even fully buckled, the man behind her had a fistful of her hair, and she was half-stumbling, half-crawling to try to keep up, as he dragged her away.

BELLO WAS DEAD. The poor slack-witted boy hadn't understood why they had come running down to the hangar, but he'd been so proud when he'd been given the lamp to hold, and now he was dead.

Goll Rybicker hammered his great fists on the metal deck. He had chosen Bello to hold the lamp, and now Bello was dead. Goll looked at the hole in the boy's tunic and all he could think was *Emperor, please, how can I make this not happen?*

Goll was not bright. He didn't really understand all the things the Arbites had said to him, that time when he had obeyed his foreman and helped carry some barrels to a storeroom away from the usual commissary compound. He hadn't understood what was wrong with that, but suddenly there had been Arbites there and his foreman hadn't ever been seen again, and then people had talked at him in a dark little cell. It had all meant that he had to do things that the secret Arbites messengers wanted him to do, or he would disappear too. That had been about as much sense as he could make of it.

Goll roared and struck his fists against his face. His voice drowned out the weeping of the other boys. He wanted to get the coward with the gun, but if he ran out, he would be shot, just like Bello. In his rage, dying was something Goll could shrug off, but dying without avenging his boy – a hateful idea!

Maybe, maybe if he was fast and loud? The shooter was a coward, killing boys and hiding in the dark. Surely, the sight of Goll running at him would make him drop the gun and wriggle away like the worm he was, and Goll could run fast. Right now, he knew he could run like the wind.

He began to take great, whooping breaths, building himself up for the rush, but already the other boys were looking up from their dead crewmate, as the racket of arbitrator boots came booming down the steps.

Lead Arbitor Oraxi spared the little knot of people huddled behind the truck. He had more important things to worry about than a handful of cowed drudges, and the paunchy man baying at the hangar roof. The transmission from Rede had instructed them to catch the concordiast, and the last frantic vox from Rhiil said that there was already shooting. That was fine by Oraxi. For the first time in a mind-numbing twenty-one months at the Tower, he had a real operation to lead.

There were clicks and clanks from above them as the lighting arrays started to warm up. Oraxi and his five arbitrators prowled forwards in three pairs, beams from their shoulder-lumens criss-crossing. The lead arbitor in each pair was ready to volley scattershot, and the man behind him had a body-seeking Executioner round loaded. They advanced through the brightening hangar bay easily and wordlessly, covering open spaces and taking control of sight lines.

Then the lights began to go out.

Oraxi had served longer than Rhiil, and his preservation reflexes were better: his legs had already propelled him into cover behind a stack of rolled freight-slings before he looked up. There was nothing broken that he could see, no shots shattering the floodlight glass. They were simply shutting down. Either they were up against some-one who could poison the minds of the machine-spirits against them or… but that thought was bad enough, so Oraxi left it there. He listened for a moment, heard no attacks and moved out again, lumen activated, motioning the others forwards. Arbitrator Arkepp prowled at his side, hunting.

* * *

One of her attackers was hurt or dead. Ylante's head was still ringing, and the blow had sent her vision into blurs and spots again, but the fitful on-off patches of light appearing in the hangar let her see what her captors were doing. Whoever was yanking her along had had to stop while one of his companions, also bodygloved and masked, hoisted a third limp form onto one shoulder.

'Move it, murderess,' her captor ordered, through a vox-masker that turned the voice into a genderless rasp. 'You're in our power. Forget that for a moment and–' it pushed the gun-muzzle against her forehead, hard enough to make her flinch. 'No sound, just obey.'

Ylante's thoughts were too jumbled to question the weapon pointed at her face, and she mutely let them hustle her on. A fourth figure came ghosting out of the shadows to join them. It was dark-shrouded, like the others, but she had enough wit and skill to recognise the man's build, his moves and his walk. It was the man who'd come to her with the fake letter.

Suddenly the hurt one, the one who was being carried, began to spasm and buck. The others frantically grabbed at it, but all hope of stealth was gone when it gave a wet, rattling wail and finally went limp. Its carrier staggered for balance under the now truly dead weight, and a moment later there was a double-clap of sound from somewhere behind them. The screams of the guided shells passing over her were gone almost before she heard them, but Ylante would remember the sound of them thudding into the meat of the dead kidnapper's carcass, for the rest of her life.

The corpse stopped the shells. The body thudded to the deck as the kidnapper carrying it let it slide off his shoulders. Something passed between the three surviving shadow-figures, and then two of them were returning fire with las-shots and curses that their vox-maskers turned frighteningly flat and metallic. The third stared expressionlessly down at Ylante for a moment, and then disappeared into the dark.

A thought forced its way up through the pain-fog and into her brain: *she had a chance – as much of a chance as she was ever going to have*. She managed to get to her hands and knees, as her captor swayed to the side and a whicker of shot shredded the air above and behind her. The racket of the shotguns was infernal, impossible, after the quiet snap of the las-rounds. Ylante looked around, and tested her ankle. She thought she could trust it for a few paces, enough to get her far enough away so that they would have to turn their backs on the Arbites to chase her. If they responded too quickly then she could hit the second one's knees with her shoulder and maybe she could buy herself a couple of seconds before the las-beam came through her shoulders.

She thought of Calpurnia, and of what the grim little woman would say to her if they ever met face to face again. That was a problem to look forward to, she told herself, and began to crawl again.

CHAPTER TEN

'Talk to me.'

Calpurnia was first down off the glide-truck, shield in place and maul at the ready. Bruinann came behind her at the head of a pack of Arbites, weapons at the ready. The dim expanse of the hangar spread out in front of her. She could see the lamps clipped to the shoulders and shields of Oraxi's squad, swinging back and forth.

'Three exchanges so far,' came the lead arbitor's reply over the vox. 'Las-fire, maybe some kind of silenced slug thrower, but they've gone quiet. I think we've pushed them out of whatever position they were trying to hold. Instructions?'

'Bear to your three,' ordered Bruinann, after Calpurnia signalled him to speak. 'We're coming in behind you. Advance pattern scale-two, your lead.'

'Affirm,' he replied. Calpurnia fell in beside Bruinann as they jogged forwards.

'Rede?' she voxed, 'Rede, come in. The lights are coming and going on us. Who's got control?'

'We're trying to trace the countermands through the code-channels,' the detective replied, 'but we haven't pinned down the source yet. Someone's working against us, and they're getting the machines' attention better than we are. Their codes are trumping ours. We can fire up the lights, but we can't keep them on.' On cue, the overhead arrays clanked, and the haphazard columns of light died away. Calpurnia, Bruinann and their squad lit their own lanterns and formed a line with Oraxi's squad, spreading out further in the dark.

A shotgun blasted somewhere to Calpurnia's right, and she snapped her head around, breathing softly, leaving the vox open for a report. There was another blast.

'Got a–' came a voice. 'No, there's, damn! Quick contact, hard to see. Maybe masked somehow. Don't think I connected but–' There was the snap of a las-shot and a burst of yelling, followed by two more answering shotgun blasts. 'Forward, it's moving! Bearing right, right of file, 'ware movement!' The enemy was coming past her. Calpurnia set her grip on her maul and got ready to charge.

THEY WERE ALMOST at the edge of the hangar when Ylante finally recognised the broad square entranceway ahead of her and began to fight in earnest. When the shadowy killers had grabbed her again, she had held herself back, certain that at any moment there would be Arbites to rescue her, and determined to be ready when the moment came. As she struggled along in her captor's grip, her injured leg throbbing in time to her hoarse breathing, she realised that they were about to enter the Long Dock Road, the passage that skirted the Curtain and connected the three dock assemblies. They were on their way out of the hangar, and the Arbites were getting no closer. Bitter despair gnawed the back of her mind as they closed on the entranceway without a shot, a shout or a light coming after them.

Then the lights came on. She saw who was holding her, for the first time, and lashed out with bright, wordless terror.

When they were in the dark, their bodies had been the soft black of the shadows. When the lights began to come up, their forms had started to ripple with the same grey as the half-light around them, and now...

They skirted a lifter pillar, and the yellow and black livery of the engine flickered briefly across their bodies. They passed the pulpit, and yanked her over a bundle of power conduits that swarmed up a buttress towards the ceiling. Traces of the conduits' red coating flamed around their feet and shins for a moment before it passed away. Now that they were getting close to the Road, its fat support arches processing away before them, their bodies were picking up the yellowish cast of the Road's lamplight.

Ylante had heard ships' tales of xenos who cloaked themselves in mirror-shard colours and vanished into the air of the strange worlds they called home, but the fragments of those stories didn't stay in her head for long; not when she looked at the faceplates the figures wore, and saw the chameleon colours fading around them. She had seen that design before, in her old days in the Hydraphur system. She did not think any xenos would ever wear one.

She mock-stumbled and let the chameleon-figure drag on the sleeve of her gown. Then she pushed herself quickly straight, trying to twist its arm around so that she could lock it, but she was too clumsy, and the man countered it easily. He simply yanked her towards him while her balance was still compromised. Her forehead met his, but his was shielded by the dull ceramite of his faceplate. There was no contest. He dragged her for another half a dozen paces before the grogginess faded again and she was able to get her feet under her. The other figure, lithe and snake-hipped in its shifting colours, grabbed a handful of her hair and helped to pull her along.

Ylante panicked again as they passed through the archway. Whatever they could do to her in a fight, it couldn't be worse than what they would do to her when they got her somewhere that they controlled. She tried to scream – it came out as a wheezing old woman's groan – and she beat frantically at the hand holding her hair.

'Throne *alone*,' said the voice in front of her. 'Are we really going to be able to get her back down this thing?'

'Voice.'

'Ah, piss on voice-discipline, who's here to hear us? Apart from her, and you're going to have to talk to the damn murderess eventually. Can't we just drug her until then? Let me crease her grey head for her. Dead weight would be easier than this, and I know what I'm talking about.' The slim figure still had the corpse of its companion over its – her? – shoulders.

'Not... murder...' Ylante managed to get out.

'It talks!' The woman had released Ylante's hair to adjust the position of the corpse on its back.

'I'm going to be generous, and put this incessant jabbering down to an adrenaline high from the fight. That had better be all it is, too.'

'Relax, *sir*, I've been ordered off the battle-dope and I will stay off it. Give me a little credit.'

'I'll five you all the credit you want, as long as you full-mask your vox and switch to your silent channel before you utter another misbegotten word.'

'Misb–' and the voice cut off from Ylante's hearing as the speaker obeyed the order.

'Come on, not-murderess, move yourself and I won't give you a kicking. I'll have your face in front of me when we mourn my comrade-in-arms at the next Funeral Lighting, woman, so don't give me any more cause to dislike you.'

'I'm not a murderess,' Ylante gasped again. Please, she thought, just keep talking. Give away something that I can draw you about, or just give away your position to someone. Just talk some more. She stumbled again, a real accident this time, and moaned as her shoulder caught the corner of a high rockcrete support. The man released her arm and gripped her hair, the way the woman had. They proceeded for another twenty paces before the hunched posture she was being pulled along in, cramped Ylante's lungs too much and she sagged onto her knees to pant. He allowed her a moment or two, and just as she was wondering about filling her lungs to yell for help – he gave a curt one-two tug on her hair.

The woman with the corpse had drawn ahead again. She would be the tough one, thought Ylante. The man who was dragging her – she had no option but to take a chance on him.

'The Funeral Lighting,' pitching her voice as low and unthreatening as she could with her control of it reduced to stumbling gasps. 'It's a Hydraphur ceremony... ceremony for pil-*uhh*, pilgrims. You're not from here.'

He made no reply except a savage wrench at her hair.

'If you're from outside the Tower then you won't know me,' she tried to press on. 'You won't know that I'm not a murderess! Otranto's room was sealed when he was killed, a seal nobody could get through! I was on my way to meet him, but I never *uhh* never did, how can I be–' She shut up as they came to a set of steps, up and over a switching-circle for the Dock Road's little railcars. It took an effort of concentration to place her feet so that her injured leg didn't misstep and crumple. There was a buzz and tick from the faceplate above her as the man enabled his vox again.

'The Arbites were after you for it,' grunted the flat pseudo-voice. 'They were watching you. Good enough for them, good enough for–' He caught himself, and the vox clicked off again, but it was a crack, a crack that Ylante surveyed and went to work on.

'I've spent hours with the arbitor senioris. She's a troubled woman, but I believe she knows what she's doing.' A part of her wondered about this even as she said it. Even without the psyker-static of the Tower taking its toll, Calpurnia had seemed fogged by self-doubt and a strange, deferential hesitation that Ylante had found hard to interpret. 'If she suspected me, why would she release me?' She wanted to keep him talking. She whipped her thoughts into line as the man's vox ticked.

'She's waiting for you to destroy yourself, waiting for you to kill another one. Astropaths are sacrifices the day they stand for Binding. She decided another astropath was a fair trade for catching you with blood on your hands.'

'*Talk* to her, then, let her stand me up there and accuse me, if that's what she wants to do. Then you can hear it for yourself, not just take guess. What can it cost you to talk to her?' She was shouting. Part of it was panicky despair, part of it was trying to be crafty, sending echoes up and down the Dock Road. She could no longer hear gunfire from behind her. Perhaps someone was following? Or maybe there would be workers somewhere ahead on the Road? *Where was everyone?* Just a single answering voice, she prayed, a single hand raised for her, a single watching pair of eyes...

TORMA YLANTE HAD only the smallest part of her wish. One pair of eyes was watching her stumbling progress along the Dock Road, but there would be no hand or voice raised for her.

When the cat-and-mouse firefight in the hangar had kicked up a gear, Dechene had finally moved, pushing himself off his platform and scrambling away. He congratulated himself on his escape and headed for the Long Dock Road as fast as he dared – once those brawling fools finished what they were doing, they might start looking through the rest of the hangar. This was a time to hedge bets. Then the flicker of movement had caught his eye ahead of him and, entering the Dock Road and flitting from one arch to the next, he had started following.

It was starting to dawn on Dechene that he was painfully exposed, moving down a wide lit passageway after two targets that were lethally intent on remaining undisturbed. He stayed back as far as he dared, trying to make sure that he was safely behind a column when either blurry figure looked like turning. He had caught one glimpse of the bland pale faceplate floating at the top of the indistinct body, and something about the expressionless pale-yellow eye scopes had chilled him to his feet.

He had to know. Had the Arbites really arrested Ylante or were they in league somehow? Was Ylante steering the seizure of the Mastership? Would she steer the appointment of the next true Master when the arbitor considered her work done? Were these her agents? The dromon that had brought this so-called Astropathica envoy, Lohjen, had arrived before the Arbites, but that didn't mean they weren't in league.

If they were her agents, then this would be something that she and Rede had cooked up.

He couldn't hear, however, and he couldn't get close enough. They were coming up on the first Knot, the defensive switchback of fortified passageways. From there they might continue on to the next dock where the envoy's dromon sat, or they might detour into the station – to the Arbites compound?

He peered out from behind an arch, watched the watery outline of Ylante's captor bend over her as they exchanged words, and then ducked forward one-two-three archways instead of one, his heart in his mouth and his heartbeat in his ears. Then he was in cover again, straining to catch what scraps of words he could from them.

'Arbites…' from a flat inhuman voice that seemed to float out of the air over Ylante's head. '…killed? …know everything.' Dechene's eyes narrowed.

'… can't, don't you…' from Ylante. Then something that might have been 'Master' or 'after'. 'Psyker'. He heard that very clearly, and then again, '…cret psyker.'

What was she admitting to? Who was she accusing? Dechene weighed his choices. He had seen the kidnappers in action – they weren't amateurs, caught by surprise, and their defences would be tough. Then Dechene thought about the hangar, which made him remember something else that he had seen there: a weapon, maybe. He didn't have to deal with this on his own.

Dechene wore the badge and livery of a concordiast over the mind of a bully and a thug. He wasn't crafty or patient. Whatever was taking shape, it wasn't something he could easily manipulate or spy out. The answer was easy. Do what comes naturally. Smash it. Renz wouldn't like it, but Renz was a wittering idiot, and Kyto was a purse-lipped coward with sinews like wet paper. Dechene would smash it all up, and trust to his wits and guts to look after the pieces wherever they might land.

Calpurnia came around, and through the gap between a thicket of winch-chains and a generator trunk, running fast and low, she took the first las-shot on her shield. The skulking bastard who'd shot at her hadn't been expecting a rush, and went scrambling backwards, dodging around a stanchion a split-second ahead of her maul-stroke.

'Contact!' she shouted, as a shot cauterised the air by Calpurnia's ear. She ploughed on without breaking step. Masked, half-visible killers shooting at her from shadows – she'd been there before. She lunged and swiped with her maul, and as she followed her target backwards, she stepped straight into the grenade burst.

It was a pellet-bomb, not enough to knock her flat, but the concussion was out of all proportion to the bomb's tiny size, and the shock left her off-balance. As she went down on one knee, retching and dragging her shield in front of her, the lights clanked on above her and shone on empty space.

Bruinann and his squad were by her side a moment later, two Arbites with their own shields closing in on either side of her. Calpurnia managed to stand and make up the centre of a rough shield-wedge, just as a burst of shooting came from back along their left flank. Oraxi's squad had pushed forwards again and made contact. The shadows in the hangar were shrinking to islands and pockets as somewhere the Arbites started to win the battle for the lights. The hunt started to speed up among the parked trucks and loaders, and the marching rows of overhead columns from which the hangar's conveyor cables hung.

There was another grenade-blast and puff of smoke up ahead, but the Arbites were savvy enough to scan around them for a diversion as well as an assault. They quickly spotted the blur of movement by the hangar wall, slipping away from the blast, towards a heavy bank of motivator machines. Three Executioner shells chased it as it dived, but their trajectories swayed in the air, their target-sense blunted. They punched the hangar wall instead, and the snaking blur disappeared in among the mechanisms.

The Arbites came forwards cautiously, bounding pairs of shotgun arbitrators with Calpurnia's shield-wedge at their front, covering the ends of the machine housing and ready for another grenade or shot, at any moment.

The shots didn't come.

The synthetic screech of alarms tore through the vox system, a fast-pulsing siren, code for a shipboard alarm. On its heels, a voice, indistinct through static, shouted the code for the prison dromon docked high above them.

'...igh alert, urgent, we need rein...' The voice swam in and out of vox-noise as if through a damaged transmitter; there was the repeated loud cracking of a power-maul somewhere near the transmitter. '...break, rioters are... all the cells opened, we're overw...'

Calpurnia went cold. That was why the lights had come back on. Whoever had tampered with them had found a better machine to seduce. They had unlocked the cell doors. The mob she had suppressed in this very dock was rampaging through her dromon.

'Keep him penned,' she said into her vox, snarling with frustration. 'Oraxi, you and your squad, keep him penned and flush him. Bruinann and the reinforcements, with me, time you got your own crack at these bastards. Let's rescue that ship.'

THEY SEEMED TO think they were being followed, Ylante's two captors, until they reached the first Knot in the dock road. There, they waited silently around a loop of corridor with weapons ready. At the six-minute mark, the woman flitted back along the passageway, her chameleon clothes wriggling with shades, and was gone for four minutes. From the way they had hesitated and cocked their heads towards one another, it was obvious that they were conferring.

Then they moved again, double time, this time with the man carrying their dead comrade and the woman goading Ylante with a pricking blade in her back. Ylante was looking wildly around. Where were the crews? Even off shift, the Curtain passages were popular for drinking, settling fights, clandestine dice-games or trysts. Why was it empty now?

It was another fifteen minutes of painful stumbling before they exited the passage. Their destination was not like the slender spike that Calpurnia's dromon was anchored to, but a broad little ziggurat, able to provide an open hangar and a ramp up to the dromon's flank. Her welcomers stood at the foot of the ramp: a grizzled man in the white and green of an Astropathica envoy and a Battlefleet officer, the badges and chain of a fore-ensign catching the light against his emerald coat.

'Get the murderess into the ship,' said Envoy Lohjen, 'and notify Hydraphur that we have her. We'll uncouple and be on our way as soon as we're all back and aboard.'

Torma Ylante was starting to realise exactly how badly things had gone for her.

GOLL RYBICKER WAS beyond shouting. His head hurt and his fists throbbed. His legs ached as he hurled himself through the passages that flanked the Long Dock Road. There was little conscious thought left in his head. He was going to kill someone.

That someone was in front of him, their outline shimmering and shifting, a blur that tickled him deep inside his head, but in the edge of his vision, it was clear enough. A man in the bodyglove and tabard of the wardens who'd made Goll's old life on the Bescalion docks a misery for years.

Goll didn't wonder how a Bescalion warden had come onto the Bastion Psykana. Who cared, there he was! This was one of the sneering bastards in his red-bordered tabard, calling his name, mockingly, just like when they baited him for his slow wits. The cur was waving Bello's khaki uniform sash over his head, and Goll could see the pistol in the murderer's hand. He was sure he could hear Bello's voice: 'Goll, he killed me. You gave me the lamp to hold so he killed me! Goll, I forgive you, Goll, but you have to kill him. Goll, my ghost will rest when you've killed them all.'

If Goll could actually feel the pressure on his mind, easing it off its hinges, well, maybe he didn't care; maybe he welcomed it as a mercy. By the time he burst into the docking ziggurat, his conscious thoughts were gone forever. He saw, without really seeing, the figures ahead of him: the odd ones whose colours kept changing, the grey-haired woman slumped between them, the two richly dressed men.

They were all just obstacles to be knocked down. He threw his thick arms wide and screamed his rage at the murderer's friends. His mind a single red loop of revenge with Bello's ghost-voice at its centre, Goll launched himself forwards to begin his work.

HER SHIELD ON her back, Calpurnia drove herself up rattling metal stairs, so steep that she could put her hands on the steps in front of her and climb them like a ladder. Behind her, the compartment that Dast and Roos had defended from the riot was full of the grim clatter of boots and weapons.

'Calpurnia to dromon. Calpurnia to any arbitor alive in the dromon.' She tried to keep the desperation out of her voice as they charged up the articulated pipe to the airlock. It was closed, and she resisted the temptation to grab her maul and beat wildly at the metal. There was no response over the vox.

'Bruinann!' she snapped over her shoulder. 'Where the hell are you? If you don't have the rank to override the hatch-seals, get Rede on the vox.' She was unlimbering her shield as she spoke, and the other two shield-bearing Arbites pushed forwards through the tunnel to join her, walling off the tunnel against whatever might come out of the opening hatch. The walls were already running with the condensation of their breath. Bruinann was muttering into his vox-torc, ordering the transmission of overrides down through the dock, to bring the machine of the hatch-lock to heel. Calpurnia couldn't order those codes: she was still accused, and this ship was still her cell.

There was a hiss and a puff of warm air from the hatch as Calpurnia's vox squawked into life.

'Who goes there! Party at hatch identify yourselves immediately, on pain of armed response!' It was the vox-operator that Calpurnia had stood behind when they docked. Her voice was startled, but not battle-frightened.

'This is Shira Calpurnia,' was her retort, 'coming aboard with reinforcements. Report on the cell-break status.'

There was silence, and Calpurnia feared the worst when the hatch slid up, but instead of a criminal mob ready to reverse their defeat on her, the passageway simply held an arbitrator, hastily pulling his helmet into place, although not in time to hide his surprise.

'Uh, welcome back aboard, mamzel, and aedile majore.' He blinked, looked at the shield wall and the shotgun muzzles, and heard the click of pistol actions and the buzz of mauls. 'Is something wrong?'

It was quiet in Lohjen's dromon, the hangar and the Long Dock Road still deserted from the spurious stand-down order. Someone would be on his way to the Dockmaster's suite to find out who'd given that order. Oraxi didn't envy whoever was to blame. Bruinann might be sloppy, but Rede was sharper, and Calpurnia was as cold as space-chilled iron. Rumour was, she hadn't even argued her own case in the indictment after the Phrax Mutiny, to set an example that nobody should presume themselves above the law. Oraxi didn't know whether to fear that kind of mind or admire it. From her reputation, Calpurnia would only show mercy if the Emperor Himself called her before the throne and ordered her to, and she wouldn't be happy about it, even then.

'Sir? Master arbitor?' Oraxi was jerked from his thoughts as the twitching man who'd hailed them in the Long Dock Road motioned him across the hangar and towards the ramp. He gave a discreet hand-signal for his team to divide and disperse, and heard two of them take up positions at the ramp, while two more walked up behind him into the dromon. Stay sharp, he reminded himself. Their quarry in the hangar had been flushed out and battered senseless, but they knew he had friends who'd slipped the fighting. His mission wasn't over y–

Ah. Well, maybe it was.

Oraxi was too good an arbitrator to utter the oath that sprang to his lips, but Dolan's balls, what had happened here? He stepped through the miniature slaughterhouse of the dromon's lock and tracked blood into its compartment, gun ready, another arbitrator behind him.

'It was, ah, I can't describe it, it was a terrible spectacle, before the Golden Throne it was!' came the voice of the man who'd come shouting for them, the jittery man in grubby concordiast clothes. 'He was insane, just berserk! What drove him to this, the poor Emperor-fearing man?'

'Quiet,' Oraxi called. He peered forwards. This wasn't a standard dromon. He hadn't seen an interior like this before, instead of the three-levelled passage decks, it was a single high-roofed space, overhung with rich curtains that could drop down to create makeshift rooms. Oraxi smelled scent in the air, could hear music playing when he came up the ramp. He could see racks of books and data-arks, and a table with a reader and a script-book, strapped down for stability in flight. An envoy's ship to be sure, Oraxi thought a little bitterly, not a working one. Well, it shouldn't be hard to clear it out, if there was anyone hiding in here.

'Lead arbitor?' asked Arbitrator Lianch's, over the vox.

'Stand ready. Get Shanizad in here, leave Smey on the ramp to call a second squad and wait for them. We're closing the hatchway, and we'll clear them on a standard three-and-one. On my–'

'Lead arbitor!'

Oraxi bit off the curt reply: the nerves in Lianch's voice had been unmistakable. Keeping his shotgun at his shoulder, he moved back to the bodies in their congealing sheet of blood.

'What is it, arbitrator? Got a live one?'

'No sir. Got *that*.' Lianch was pointing at something that Oraxi had missed. The lead arbitor bent over for a closer look, and then stood up quickly before shock could take his balance away. He tried to swear, as he hadn't let himself do before, but the word came out as nothing more than a soft indistinct breath of air. The two of them stared down at the dead envoy, the velvet envelope that had fallen from his sleeve and the Inquisitorial rosette lying on the deck. With some distant part of his mind, he realised that the concordiast was still on the ramp, looking in, grinning.

'This is just *terrible*,' said Antovin Dechene.

CHAPTER ELEVEN

THEY SAT AROUND Rede's table, the Ordo Hereticus rosette between them, staring at it in silence: Shira Calpurnia, Lazka Rede, Joeg Bruinann and Orovene, who constantly took sips of water from a chilled flask. The preacher couldn't shake the feeling that his clothes were too tight, although he had worn them in perfect comfort at the Incarcery. He also felt that someone in the next chamber was shouting and weeping, although the walls were too strong to carry such sounds.

'I don't understand what he was doing here if not investigating the murder,' Bruinann said. He had been repeating variations on this theme since the gloomy, stop-and-start attempt at a conference had begun an hour ago.

'He couldn't have come here for that. He was here a full day before Otranto was killed.' Rede had answered Bruinann with that, more or less, every time he had brought the subject up. Neither of them looked up from the intricate little thing on the table between them.

Calpurnia felt a little like that herself. Coming back to the precinct compound, she had been trying to work out how long she had been aboard the Bastion Psykana, and how long it had been since she had slept. It was hard to keep a feel for time, here: the shifts were of odd lengths and the lighting levels never varied – the inhabitants for whom the place was run didn't care about them.

'What I don't understand,' she said, 'is why he didn't reveal himself. It's impossible that he didn't know about the murder. It's doubtful that he was unaware of what's been happening since the murder. We know he had a damn fine informers' network for only a few days' work.'

'An Inquisitorial rosette will do that, ma'am.' Rede's tone was defensive, sensing the criticism of her system. Her efforts to roll up the dead 'envoy' Lohjen's network had borne some fruit: they knew about the Navy moles who'd stood down the hangar crews and tampered with the hangar lights, but the wilier agents had dived down deep, and the Arbites themselves were stymied by the question of authority. If the man who'd posed as an inter-sectoral Astropathica envoy had done so under the aegis of the Inquisition, then did they even have the right to root out his spies?

'It's naive to expect that he would,' said Bruinann. 'Reveal himself, that is. We all know the stories, the inquisitor marching out with his polished armour blazing, declaring his condemnations.' Calpurnia thought of Stefanos Zhow, the inquisitor who'd appointed himself to hunt the psyker assassin sent after her when she'd arrived on Hydraphur: Zhow, with his bright green armour, his retainers and guards, and his silent Inquisitorial troopers. 'I think we know better, and I think we know better than to think that Lohjen's presence was anything to do with Otranto.'

Calpurnia found herself nodding with the rest of them. The Inquisition used the fear that their name created exactly as the Arbites did. That treacherous, so-useful bit of doubt – would you leave after you had done what you said you'd come for, or were they your quarry too? Plant the seed and watch what grew; nervous consciences gave a lot away.

Orovene croaked, took a gulp of water and tried again. 'Where's the seal, then? We see his rosette, but where's the Inquisitorial seal? That's the true mark.'

The other Arbites looked at one another. All three of them had boarded Lohjen's ship. 'It would be well hidden if he had to hide it, but I'd be surprised if it was too far away from him. He carried the rosette hidden, I'm betting in case he needed to produce it in an emergency. I think that's what he was trying to do when that maniac attacked them. So if he was that careful about having his rosette to hand, why not the seal?'

'I don't understand,' said Bruinann. Frustration made his voice brittle. 'What you're saying makes sense, but we found no seal on the man, nothing. Two concealed blades, a needle pistol and that.' He pointed to the rosette, diffidently, as if it could order him shot simply for the gesture.

'I do,' said Rede. 'There is a difference between a seal and a rosette. A rosette can be carried by Inquisitorial agents as a badge of authority from their master, but you'll never see a seal on any finger but an inquisitor's. Arbitor senioris, do you agree?' Calpurnia nodded.

'I think you're right,' she said. 'I think Lohjen wasn't a full inquisitor. He was sent here in disguise on behalf of one, on what business I don't know. He didn't have an inquisitor's authority to simply commandeer us–'

'I wouldn't have argued with the rosette,' Bruinann observed, 'but I see what you're saying.'

'–and so he just watched and waited,' Calpurnia finished. 'I think if we dig a little, we'll find at least one message back to Hydraphur from that dromon, astropathic or machine-call, if he's got a broadcaster strong enough and a cogitator-spirit cunning enough to wrap it up in a good cipher. I don't think Lohjen was prepared for the Master's death, and he didn't know what to do when it happened.' She said it with a certain pleasure. The Arbites had gone about their work while an agent of the Inquisition had sat on his hands, unsure. Only an agent, certainly, but Calpurnia was prepared to take her reassurances where she found them.

'So what was he doing here?' asked Orovene, looking around at the others. 'If he wasn't here for the Master's death, then what was he doing? I think we need to know, if we're to do our duty.'

There was another moment of silence. Calpurnia found the rosette on the table, holding her gaze like an eye.

'We can't know it,' she said finally, 'and that's the sticking point. We can't know he wasn't here for Otranto's death. Not to investigate it, but...' She let the words hang in the air. Otranto had been killed by an assailant who'd slipped out of the room like a ghost, through a locked and sealed door, and Lohjen had brought agents with him with chameleon suits. They knew about of locks and warding, and ways to overpower systems and make false messages and alarms. If the murder-trail led back to the Inquisition...

'Was he here to do something to the Master?' Bruinann wondered, backtracking along Calpurnia's train of thought. 'Or was it about Ylante all along, something to do with the Black Ship? Or did, no, that's stupid... I was going to ask, did his dromon simply need a refit as it passed? Hah.'

'The idea's a sound one, though' Rede said. 'Inquisitors have strange, quiet ways, and so do their servants. We may be presuming too much by just thinking he had an errand that we can make sense.'

'We haven't tied Ylante in with anything, either,' Bruinann took up again. 'Otranto was on his way to meet her for the first time when he died. I can't let go of that. If Lohjen had these spies and tools, and he went after her, shouldn't we pay attention?'

'I'll tell you what I can't let go of,' said Calpurnia. 'The way that an admittedly big man managed to sprint through all that empty corridor, home in unerringly on the point where Lohjen's doors were open to let his own people back in, and then massacre the agent, that fore-ensign and two of the warriors who gave us such a bastard of a time in the hangar.' Her gorge rose slightly at the memory. 'Think what he did to those people, with his bare hands, and with those injuries in him. What got him to that state?'

'Scall told us that the verispex tests found no combat juice in the corpse,' said Rede, 'no frenzon or any of its variants.' She looked at the slate again. 'He was a pretty mediocre mole. He never asked questions, but he wasn't violent, either.'

'The Tower didn't get to him, you don't think?' Calpurnia thought about what the place had done to her own mind, and shot a look over at Orovene.

'There are some who turn violent under it, ma'am, but to cook off like that? No. I don't know what pushed him.'

Silence. The rosette glimmered at them from the table in mute accusation. Calpurnia closed her eyes and listened to the churn of her thoughts. She was sure that she could feel them in her head. The sensation wasn't of fireworks any more, but of some kind of red, feverish jelly in her skull, stirring and slowly bubbling. The more she listened, the more the sound actually seemed to be out there beyond her ears, hypnotic.

She snapped her eyes open.

'Rede,' she said, 'do you have a nexus of reports and alarms coming in? Do informants provide those?'

'No need for informants,' Rede said, plucking a data-slate off the table. 'Any alert or station action is reported to us formally, and, well,' she added, 'I verify them through my own sources, of course.'

Of course, Calpurnia thought. For a moment, the rhythm of the flickering slate-light on Rede's face exactly matched the rhythm of the throb in Calpurnia's head, and she had to squeeze a hand over her eyes for a moment.

'Survey the docks and the surrounding passages, please. We've had tunnel vision from that bastardry with the hangar controls and the fake alarm from the dromon. We should have been looking wider. Any other incidents of violence, unauthorised access, hell, I don't know, pollutant leaks, anything that might have got a hook into Rybicker?'

'There's... no. The systems in the–' Rede's narrow forehead knitted in a frown. 'Wait.' *Flick-flick* from the slate display, before Rede walked over and hooked it to her tapestry, respectfully touched the Mechanicus scripture across the top, and brought the display to life. 'Watch this. This is the projected path that Rybicker took from the first hangar, around the edge of the Curtain to Lohjen's hangar.' A schematic flared, and a crude red line began to follow Rede's fingers. She murmured to the slate and made a gesture. 'Look at these.' Along the base of the keep came a series of tiny white glows, flaring like match-heads. 'You can't see the detail, and this map collapses it into two dimensions, but it's... strange.'

'What are we looking at, Rede?' Calpurnia asked.

'Cullises. Each of those flashes marks a closure, ordered from the watch-hall. As Rybicker was racing along those corridors, the watch-hall was sensing him.'

Calpurnia shook her head. 'I don't understand. Slamming down cullises is a hell of a reaction. Look how far the edge of the keep is from those passages. Let's grant that Rybicker was unhinged enough to sing out to the astropaths in the cloisters – not hard to believe, if he managed to tear four people apart while they were shooting and stabbing him. Why didn't the watchmaster try and contain him further out?'

'The psyk-wards, at least those damn great cages and sinks they have all through the keep, they end at the cloisters, ma'am,' said

Rede. 'Rybicker was going off in the senses of a lot of the astropaths, it seems, but the only psyk-scryers that would have seen him were over on that side of the keep. Likewise, the only doors that Watchmaster Voices-In-The-Fire could have closed by direct order.'

'Ah. *Ah.* Stupid.' Calpurnia's tone was dry and matter-of-fact. Thoughts were bursting in her brain in brisk succession. She smiled. 'Don't panic, Rede, not you, me. Stupid: I should never have needed this pointed out to me.'

'I don't follow, ma'am.'

'Why were the psyker-scryes in the cloisters unsuccessful in reading Otranto's death exactly?'

'The way that the wards and sinks blurred the traces, they drain away the prints that the witches leave, and – *Ah*.'

'You're going to do another scry,' said Bruinann.

'I am. Out in the docks, where the wards won't break up the trail. Let's find out exactly what pumped up our late houseman into such a killing machine, and I have another idea besides.'

'I'll prepare a representation,' said Bruinann. 'The three watchmasters have been improvising the allocation of astropaths without a new Master to direct them, so they're the ones who can help us find someone who'll do the – ma'am?' Calpurnia was shaking her head.

'No representations, Bruinann, no polite requests. I've had enough. There are too many loose ends, too many shadowy half-answers. It's time to do what I should have done right from the start.'

'IT'S HAPPENED!' SAID Teeker Renz, his voice almost a wail. Dechene ignored the sound, and kept admiring himself in the mirror.

'I said it's happened, Dechene, and I blame your stupid idiotic stunts. Going down into the hangar, like that! Stamping about with the Arbites! And Kyto… Kyto…'

'He might always be alive, Teek,' Dechene said through a sneer. He'd washed and scented himself, and changed the filthy jacket he'd been crawling about in for a fresh one. Considering himself entitled to a little insolence was Dechene's default state of mind, but never more so than after a busy day like today.

'Anyway,' he went on, leaning this way and that, and studying the hang of the coat, 'I don't see the problem. Whatever Ylante thinks she's been up to, I think we can see to it that her reputation's blighted. Look at how everything's gone to crap since she got here. Everyone was ready to believe the worst of her before she ever stepped off that tub of Vedrier's, not just you.' He turned away from the mirror and stared directly into Renz's eyes.

Renz wasn't used to that, certainly not from a man he'd personally promoted up from an indentured serf ship. He tried to return Dechene's gaze, but couldn't.

'I just think it's more than just Ylante now, Dechene,' said Renz without looking up. 'You don't think about this kind of thing. That's fine, it's not, well, you know, I, uh, I'm not criticising you for it, but I need to think about how we're placed. She's done it. That little arbitor woman has done what everyone was saying she was going to do right from the start. She's seized the office of Master. It's what the Arbites do when there's been a crime like this. We can't just rely on Ylante shouldering the trouble for Otranto's death. Someone's in charge who we haven't even met. We need to decide what to do! Do you... does this make sense? Am I making sense?'

Only a grunt, and it hit Renz then with appalling force: he was waiting on Dechene for an answer. He was waiting like a retainer, just as he'd waited on Otranto, asking, with a disgusting pleading tone in his voice, for Dechene to deign to answer him.

A new insight followed, a second horrified shock: *There was nothing he could do.* He had been conning himself. He had been powerful, yes, but he had been powerful as the personal attendant of a man too keen to delegate. It was not because he could outwit someone as crafty as Thujik, not because he had the unimaginable knowledge and experience of someone like Chevenne. He didn't have the strength of will of Sacredsteel, and he didn't even have the stubborn thuggery of Dechene. He had been lucky. He had charmed his way into Otranto's good books through a superficial wit and a talent for his chosen craft, and he had benefited from it. However, everything he thought he had built for himself aboard the Tower, the power base, the network of dependents all greedy for his patronage, the position of influence from behind the Master's seat, the centre of gravity for the Bastion Psykana's power politics...

It was all show: painted paper with the presence of Master Otranto over his shoulder to give it solidity. Renz twisted and spun the thought in his mind, trying to find an upside, some way he could profit. No, he realised with another wave of breathless sickness, the time for thinking like that was over. It was time to look for some way that he could simply hold on to a fraction of what he had. As he spun the realisation ever faster, every turn of it seemed to whip around and crack across the back of his head like a flail. He tried to tell himself that he was being stupid, that he was just gripped by useless fever-ghosts. It took more strength of mind than he had, and he slumped back down into shocked despair. This was how it felt, he thought, to stand hooded and manacled on the scaffold and hear the sound of the executioner's flamer igniting behind you.

'We don't need to care,' Dechene said, running a hand through his hair and grinning at his reflection. 'We just don't, Teek. Even if Kyto's dead, what does it matter? We're important people. There'll be somebody else like Kyto along. You said so yourself. What was it you said?'

'But if we're going to make the best–'

'No, no, come on, Teek. Tell me what it was you said, remember, when we thought Kyto might be ready to spill something about some of our arrangements?'

So Dechene knew as well. Renz's spirits slumped down further. He should have expected it. The man was a thug, but he was a crafty thug.

'I said that Kyto was an ambitious young hot-burning rocket of an officer with plans for himself and his family in the Battlefleet.'

'What was the next bit? The next bit was important.'

'I said that hot-burning rockets of officers weren't hard to come by in Hydraphur,' Renz said, defeated. 'I said that the Daradny academies churn them out by the thousands every generation, and that the day we couldn't replace Kyto was the day we might as well walk down to the docks and pick up a scrubbing-ram for our trouble.'

'There you are, then. You know what? I don't care who the new Master is. I just don't. We're going to do fine, Teek, even without the Navy stooge. Too many people depend on us to look after their little perks and rackets. We're strong.' Dechene thought about that and said something that chilled Renz to the core. '*I'm* strong. It'll be nice not to have to piss about and hide it. Whoever thinks they're going to supplant us has got another think coming.'

He turned from the mirror and gave Renz a sunny smile.

'Who tonight, then?' he asked. 'The tall redhead from the food depots? That little one from the Encryptors' chambers with the hips?

Or the brunette from the auspex silos? She might be fun.' He clapped Renz on the shoulder and pretended not to notice the herbalist cringe. 'If you like, I'll let you watch.'

WATCHMASTER CHEVENNE WAS tired, but not unpleasantly so. He was sitting on the side of a gently rocking sling-bed in his quarters. A delicate spiced scent floated through the room. The mild soporific was aiding the mantras that were taking the restless edge off his mind. The embroidered silk and paper hangings around the walls had been hung a precise distance from the rockcrete, the relationship of soft fabric to hard, dense wall and the space between them finely calculated to be pleasing to a psyker's awareness. The only jarring element was the masked vitifer standing by the door, bare hand gripping his gun.

Chevenne let his senses roam around the room for a moment more, and then focused on a series of beads hanging over the door. Fixing on two, he pushed a tiny thought-echo into them and set them resonating in a particular way. A moment or two later a tray-table, like the one in the watch-hall cage, lowered itself down in front of him with a soft ratcheting click of its chains. His tarot cards were already in his hands, and his mind was on the pleasant down slope towards rest where tiredness was relaxing, not burdensome.

In his days as an active astropath, Chevenne had endured fatigue in his body and soul that would have simply wrung the life out of the proud young Chevenne who'd gone into the furnace of the Soul Binding. The bloom of white fire that the Binding had planted was what had sustained him, body and soul. Even so, as the years had gone on, the nightmare of the warp had begun to eat away at his strength. The messages and ciphers he jammed into his mind and pushed out of it again had begun to strain and deform his mind. They had torn at his mind, worn him thin until he had sometimes felt that his whole consciousness was nothing more than a threadbare grey cobweb stretched across that furnace-fire. With every load of information that the cobweb groaned under, somewhere in his mind, another strand or two would part.

Chevenne sometimes thought that he had yearned for that to happen. From the beginning, back aboard the Black Ship itself, the Adeptus had started schooling them in acceptance of death. *An astropath walks from the Throne Room on a circular road,* they had said.

You walk out of here touched by Him, but that touch marks you. It will bring your soul back here to Him before long. For so many of Chevenne's companions that had been true. Over a dozen had died as the furnace-light had come over them like a storm-front. As the fire had filled every corner of his skull with his own screams, and his eyesight had guttered and died, the senses inside him, which had been wrenched into glaring wakefulness, had felt lives around him buckle and flutter, and end from the strain. His had not. Like Thujik and Otranto, and a handful of others among the thousands of astropaths who lived and died around them, the work had cured him like leather, and tempered him like metal.

It had taken a long time for the wear to start to show, a long time for the control that he had learned in the eyries to lead him to semi-retirement in the safer seat of the watch-hall. Was he luckier than the ones who'd burned out under the strain in their first years? Was this better than being battered into idiocy and left as an empty pool of energy in a lifeless meat shell? Would it have been worse if he were able only to blast out a single note into a choir, in response to the crudest stimuli of the cantors' goads? When the white fire in the centre of his mind flew free, how much of his soul would be left for it to carry back to the Throne?

Almost unconsciously, his hands shuffled the cards, cut the deck, and turned them in his hands. Idly, he laid the two halves of the deck down. He had brought no focus onto them, made no attempt to push his energy into the cards, but the images he turned up gave him pause when he let his fingertips and psychic-sense settle onto them.

The Mountain, inverted. Next to it, the card that had appeared in every reading he had done since Otranto had died: the Judge. Chevenne's fingers traced the outlines of the wires and the delicate glass inlays that made up the picture he had never truly seen. Something was building.

That was why, when his chief attendant's voice came through the grille in the door that he must rouse himself, there were Arbites at the door of his rooms ordering his attendance upon Arbitor Calpurnia, Chevenne failed to feel any real surprise at all.

CHAPTER TWELVE

'SHE'S OVERSTEPPED HER authority,' said Preacher Orovene, looking up at frantic Scriptorium stacks. He had an unlit lho-stick in his fingers, turning it over and over. 'She's acted without even the stamp of the Praetory,' he went on. 'An astropath should have been deputed to transmit the facts and postulations of the case back to Hydraphur.'

Orovene rubbed his jaw. He wondered if he would ever get his voice back properly. He remembered being very proud of his voice, but since he'd been here he'd had trouble calling to mind exactly how it had sounded. He was having trouble remembering his rooms at the Incarcery, for that matter, or the face of the Praetor Primaris. He didn't like to dwell on the way his memories were feathering and greying out.

'What's your point?' asked Rede. She hadn't much taken to Orovene. She knew as well as any non-psyker what the soaked atmosphere of the Tower could do, but she had trouble respecting the way Orovene seemed to be at the mercy of the witch-fog. At least Calpurnia had the guts to fight it. Rede was so used to the marks that the Bastion had left on her that she sometimes wondered how life would feel without them.

'Just that I trust you to pay attention, detective-espionist. You may need to testify to it at Hydraphur.'

'I don't–' Rede snapped, and caught herself and pitched her voice below the background droning of the autists, and the buzzing and rattling of their machines. 'I don't object to doing my duty, preacher, and thank you for pointing it out, but I wonder, did you mention my rank and title loudly enough? I know your voice isn't what it should be, but try harder. Perhaps with an effort, you can even communicate to the autists that I'm not what I seem to be.'

Orovene flushed, but stayed next to Rede, rocking on his heels, his grip constantly shifting on the tall staff he had carried.

The Scriptorium had once been a hangar for the Fury interceptors housed in the station. The fighters had roosted on adamantium shelves around the walls, lifted to the launch bay by crane. Now, those shelves, each the width of an Arbites drill-square, were crowded with narrow lectern-desks. An autist-scriptor was bent over each, the overhead lights glinting off their shaved scalps and optical augmetics. Data-sluices hung in clusters and tangles from the ceiling, and trailed out to each lectern, spewing readout onto green-glowing screens, or up cables and straight into the autist's brain.

This was the antithesis of the hushed, solitary work of the astropaths. Every deck bustled as scribes frantically fielded the information pouring down the sluices. The information chattered into transcription slates or ribbons of printout, before being grabbed up by stooping, scurrying drudges, who milled between the desks, and bore off transcript like harvester ants carting away their leaf-cuttings.

Some data came from attendants in the eyries, frantically scrawling on slate-screens or tapping keys. All astropaths transmitted and received messages differently. For many, the information came across as symbols, images, sensations – while others would relay strings of words or numbers. It was meaningless to them, but recorded by the nimble pen-fingers of an archive servitor and fed into a cogitator, real information would emerge.

The most demanding and dangerous transmissions came through the Encryptors' Chamber, vital messages wrenched out of the immaterium by the most skilled and powerful astropaths working in choir, carried down through minds groaning with the strain.

Part of the Scriptorium had found a different use, now. Seven arbitrators prowled the lowest of the deck-shelves, shouldering gaps in the press of messengers and drudges. They nudged the runners to run faster, and stepped up to random lectern-desks for spot-checks on the autists' speed and focus. Rede found herself wondering, with all due respect for her fellows, how useful they were actually being to the scriptor crews.

They were useful, she conceded, in a larger sense. Since Calpurnia had finally issued her decree, the free-floating malaise that had settled into the whole Tower had evaporated. Few liked it – Rede was well briefed on the complaints – but Emperor's teeth, they knew someone was in charge, now.

Rede carefully policed her thoughts, as a detective must always do. No lying: she resented Calpurnia. She had been carefully priming the investigation of Otranto's murder – ready to start any day – and then someone had noticed an arbitor senioris in transit near the Bastion and had decided that an arbitor general's presence would be the perfect thing to keep delicate Astropathica sensibilities in line; tainted as that arbitor general might be.

That was what really rankled: Rede's chance of a commendation, and the chance to haggle herself a post back on Hydraphur, stamped out by someone who didn't have any damn right to be in uniform, if what she'd heard was true. A ten thousand-year-old ceremonial tradition was in ruins, a bloodbath had occurred right inside an Arbites court. Rede knew her work here had shortcomings, but all she needed was the chance to put her case, and not to some woman on her way to her own trial, who shouldn't even be–

She kept control, and when Orovene glanced over at her, it was hard for him to tell that she was thinking anything at all.

THE RUNNERS LUGGED their panniers out through the arched doors, through the maze of sorting-rooms and archivists' cells and out into the keep. They toiled along its passages, skirting the astropath cloisters and the outer walls of the Enginarium, to the Arbites' doorstep. The bright chamber outside the precinct doors was alive with voices as praetores and Rede's analyser teams directed the runners to-and-fro, rifled through their panniers, and passed printout and data-slates from hand to hand.

Praetor Secundus DeMoq had taken up post in the doorway. His head was bowed under the low ceiling, surveying the documents that the analysers brought to him, making the occasional careful note of his own. Only a handful of pages or slates made it past him. Looking at the latest slate to be pushed into his hands, he pursed his lips, murmured a few orders and carried the little green-lit tile back through the doors.

CALPURNIA HADN'T STAYED in the Scriptorium. Unlike Rede, she hadn't found much to watch there. Once the staff whose labour she'd commandeered understood her needs, their minds had utterly bent to their work, and beyond that moment, she had become scenery to them. Anyway, she had somewhere else to be. Chevenne and his assistant would be ready before long.

'Arbitor senioris!' Bruinann's voice, hailing her for the third time. 'DeMoq thinks he might have found something.'

'It took a while for the breakthrough, mamzel,' said DeMoq. 'These ones have wonderful nimble minds, Emperor's grace, but they, well, they're delicate. I think being here doesn't do them any good.'

'Being here hasn't done me any good either, praetor,' Calpurnia replied. 'My patience, for example, well, that's just about been eaten away to nothing.'

The praetor blinked.

'Well,' he said, 'the autists began by using Detective-Espionist Rede's formulae...'

Calpurnia's eyes narrowed. The more she was finding out about the limits of Rede's knowledge of Bastion affairs, the lower her opinion of the detective got.

'...but now we're moving them onto broader datasets and allowing them to draw their own connections.'

'And? You'll have come up from the doors to tell me something, praetor.'

'And there are correlations. Large spikes of correlations. Once we abandoned our sifting formulae with this "Polarist" term, and simply used Lohjen's informants as determinants, the recovery patterns changed completely.'

'How much of the Scriptorium is working on this now?' Bruinann asked. Calpurnia wondered what he meant. Was he questioning her diversion of the Tower's resources?

'One tier,' DeMoq told him, 'about five dozen autists,' and as Bruinann grunted a reply, she could hear them starting to shut her out, starting to turn on her, starting to undermine her.

Calpurnia grabbed a jug of water off the chill plate by the wall and dumped a glassful down her throat. It tasted bitter and recycled, but the cold was what she wanted, driving the cobwebs out of her head. Was she getting that paranoid? Was this blasted fug getting that far into her brain?

'The cold helps clear the head, doesn't it?' Bruinann said to her with no trace of anything but sympathy. Calpurnia allowed herself a small smile back at him and then looked at DeMoq.

'Pardon my being distracted, praetor. Continue, please.'

'As you ordered, ma'am, we haven't attempted to open any of Lohjen's records, just sealed them back in the dromon once the dead and injured were out. If I may be permitted, ma'am, using the records Lohjen was keeping for himself would have given us a real flying start.'

'And a flying finish, too, DeMoq, straight out of the airlock when the rest of the Inquisition found out. Trust me, we're better off not touching those until someone with a rosette picks them up and hands them to us. I'm unpopular with the Inquisition on Hydraphur as it is.' She was exaggerating, but the bravado worked. DeMoq did an impressed double take and got back onto the subject.

'The people that Lohjen went to the most effort to cultivate are one Sanxier Acquerin, an aide and minor-domo to three of the senior astropaths, Vald Kyto, that senior Battlefleet ensign – he also seems to have been some kind of attaché to the Master's staff, and one ordained lay tech-preacher Jagill.'

Two familiar names: Jagill had been the man who'd misdirected the lights in the hangar, and Kyto had been with Lohjen when the berserk Goll Rybicker had taken the whole gang of them off-guard. His corpse was in a vault in the Navy bunker waiting for a Battlefleet funeral detail.

'I know Acquerin,' said Bruinann. 'The boy's so inoffensive that it's almost comical, Lohjen probably just monstered him for a few minutes until he gave in. He hasn't got the stomach for rackets or powerplay. That cut him off from anyone who mattered.'

'As opposed to the astropaths, Bruinann, who apparently don't matter here at all?'

'I'll clarify.' Bruinann's tone had stiffened a little. 'A place like this, well, you've seen some of the briefs, ma'am: politics over the pissiest things. Who can get the Naval procurators to slant their inventories so that one section gets an extra ration of seasoning sticks? Who controls privileges to walk on the upper galleries where the viewing ports are clearest? It's that kind of thing. The astropaths mostly don't give a damn, but there's a lot of people who do. I'm sure you know what I'm trying to say.'

'I know what you're talking about, Bruinann. All games, isn't it? No one seems to care about simple pleasures, Bruinann. Duty and service. No, they play games instead, and people die of them.' For a moment, her thoughts seemed to be elsewhere, and then she locked eyes on DeMoq again.

'Get Acquerin in a cell, anyway. If he's that harmless, he'll be easy to crack for whatever we can get. We'll add anything useful to whatever Rede's dossiers manage to actually tell us.'

Her tone was more acidic than she'd intended, and from Bruinann's pained expression, Calpurnia was suddenly sure of something that she had previously only suspected: Bruinann and Rede were more than just fellow Arbites. Now, or some time in the past, they had struck up something more. She made a note to double-check the pair's judgement in any matter she had to raise with one about the other.

It wasn't until later that she realised how changed she was from the accused Calpurnia in the cell on the dromon, the doubt-gnawed Calpurnia who'd have denounced herself as unfit to check anyone's judgement.

'Kyto, then,' she said. 'The Navy man, the one with friends in high places.'

'Kyto was a regular associate of, well, not Master Otranto, but of Otranto's staff, the ones who had a lot of that day-to-day power,' answered DeMoq. 'Perks and privileges, the sort we were talking about? A great many came indirectly from the Master, directed by this clique according to their own systems of favourites. Kyto was one of the inner circle. He used his Navy position to tweak supply and crew allocations, in exchange for various little luxuries that the Navy didn't provide for him.'

'Games, games and self-indulgence.' Calpurnia scowled and rubbed her forehead again. 'What about his associates?'

'Renz, Teeker Renz, Otranto's old major-domo and personal herbalist, he's not well liked, but he has genuine skill at his job and he performs genuine work. A lot of his associates and designated favourites, well, the sifting of the station records is–'

'Long overdue,' said Calpurnia. 'Rede has been lax.' She noted that expression from Bruinann again.

'So,' said DeMoq, looking uncomfortably from one of them to the other. 'We've got a couple of other Navy types whom Kyto was helping to feather nests, and several attendants and wardens owing all sorts of perks to favour-trades with Renz. No concordiasts, thank the Emperor, and the Wardens and the vitifers are oath-bound. They wouldn't be touchable.'

'No concordiasts?' Bruinann asked. 'Not one?'

'Actually, one, you're right.' Green light flickered off it as DeMoq scrolled. 'One of Renz's clique, Antovin Dechene, brought up a couple of flags in the records. A lot of movement through the station, fraternising with all sorts of personnel, although he hasn't done any actual concordiast work for a very long time. There doesn't seem to be much indication of what he does do.'

'But he had close access to Otranto?' Calpurnia put in.

'Through Renz, yes.'

'I see.' She drummed her fingers on Rede's table for a moment. 'But his good life came from Otranto. Ditto this herbalist. They have to have wanted Otranto alive for his patronage to continue. That might sharpen their minds on how the murder might have come about, don't you think? Put Renz and that other one, the concordiast, on notice that I'll want to see them soon.'

'Soon?' Bruinann asked.

'Soon, not now. Now, you and I are both going to keep another appointment that's just as overdue.'

'Arbitor senioris,' put in DeMoq, 'there's a final point, a direct message I was given for you. Watchmaster Chevenne is on his way out of the cloisters, I'm told, with his staff and an astropath accompanying them'

'And there it is. DeMoq, the job of bringing in Renz and Dechene is yours. Bruinann, you're in charge here. I went out on a limb taking command so I could order Chevenne to do this. I want to be there when he does.'

BURSTING OUT OF *his skull as if his thoughts were stretched across the front of a rocket launched from a Titan's fist, riding the towering white fire in the heart of his consciousness, riding it up and out as reality falls away and shows the clamouring black tide of power behind everything...*

'Is he under control? Get him under control.'

'Calm yourself, Arbitor Calpurnia.' What seemed to be random jitters in Concordiast Angazi's eyes were anything but. He took in everything: the runes and colours in the glass armature surrounding Astropath Anschuk, the threadlike connectors coming out of Anschuk's and Chevenne's heads, the way the tics and jerks in their bodies were gradually synchronising, as was their breathing; and even the breeze that seemed to come from nowhere to stir the air around them.

...and the lights swimming around like the lanternbugs of the wetlands of home, just like the old days before the masked men took him away, and for a moment the living hammer beat surrounding his thoughts tries to trick him, carving their likeness from the frothing blackness and could this be them, here with him now? But...

The two psykers sat on chairs anchored to the back of a flatbed glide-truck, parked in the Long Dock Road with a vitifer each side. Calpurnia had wanted to set them up in the hangar where Rybicker had killed and died, but Chevenne and Angazi had talked her out of it. Being right in the hot swamp of the man's rage would drown any evidence beyond even Chevenne's rarefied senses. This was as close as they could get to begin the trance.

...but their beloved faces begin to leer and snap with teeth in their eyes, in their tongues, on the hands that grow from the sounds of their voices, as the force of their approach presses like a water-current. Then his mind finds the white fire inside it and the delicate touch of its companion, anchoring the sense-blizzard in the metal chamber that part of him has been left in. He has his footing now, in harmony with the other mind that's looking through him as if he was a lens...

'They're in concert,' said Angazi, nodding to a flicker of colour through the glass and a shifting pair of runes that Calpurnia couldn't interpret.

'Thank you, concordiast. Can they hear us?'

'We can.' As before, Chevenne's answer came partly through Calpurnia's ears and partly through her hindbrain, bringing layers and textures that seemed wrong for a human voice. She felt a soft, feather light crawling across her skin.

...a lens focusing, tightening its vision at the same time as it spins deliriously, feeling the sounds of voices, seeing the hard texture of metal walls, scenting the arbitor's troubled thoughts and the ward-armoured minds of the vitifers. Spinning, spinning, the centre cannot hold until a hot surge from nerve-endings breaks the spell...

'What just happened?' asked Calpurnia. Angazi didn't look up from the rune-bank, either at her or at where Anschuk had jolted with some kind of shock.

'It's a small phrenological manipulation. Anschuk isn't used to this work. Even with Chevenne guiding him, he needs help. Stimulus to certain cerebral nerves can divert high-beating strands and aid with the dive.' Calpurnia was about to ask what the hell that meant, but thought better of it. Angazi seemed unworried: time to show a little trust.

...breaks the spell and the faces melt away, no more the promise of the delicious pain of the bites they promised him. The two minds focus the lens and are penned between their own interleaved wills, like water slamming down a sluiceway...

'What are they seeing?'

'A moment more, arbiter, be patient. I won't have a mind pop its seams on my watch.'

...a sluiceway that carries their sight through all the layers, the ghosts, the ages mixed, brewed, grown together like vines: a hard shape, a slab of metal and stone in space with the towers above and below it. A proud fortress full of warriors attended by ships of war: a black and twisted wreck against the black sky, where only vacuum walks in the halls, a nest of witches and seers alive with thoughts singing through the great boiling black. A white-hot fireball crumpling in on itself as the little sun inside reaches out through the bars of its cell, blue-hot majesty drowning out the cries...

Calpurnia saw the runes change, and couldn't stop herself glancing nervously at the vitifers. Neither one had moved. She could see black glass glinting from under their hoods, visors or augmetics. She realised that her hand was sticky on the butt of the pistol that she had finally started carrying again.

...the cries that fill this metal space as the lens of two minds flies down the passages, weaving through space (metal walls no barrier, gossamer, shadow, a laughable abstraction), weaving through time, as a bright trail of pain lights up and sings back to their mind, eye, voice, and leads them down to it, leads them on...

'We have it,' said Chevenne, his voice papery with its deep soul-echo. 'We have the dead man's trail, Eagle's cry, but there's pain here, soul stoked 'til it burned. What could do this?'

'Read it and tell me, watchmaster,' Calpurnia replied. 'I need to know.'

...leading them on down into the wake of the pain's passing, where the thoughts still swim in the air. Raw memories and howling guilt spin around one another like the Brownian dance of particles, the footsteps glowing cherry-red with the heat of anger, grief...

'Wait.' The word came from two throats at once, each voice flavoured with the sound of the other. Chevenne's chair edged a millimetre forwards.

...the footprints float, disconnected. The path flows, focuses, narrows as the hate is always fixed ahead. The hate, rage, grief flowing with a Mobius twist, back on itself, a circle shrinking like a contracting pupil. In, not out, closing in on the figure dancing like a mirage, a slim mocking figure flaunting a scrap of khaki cloth. A figure with no wake, no weight, no print: a phantom mirage that breaks in the grip of the lens-vision like a reflection that won't allow itself to be clawed off the surface of a pond...

'He was ghost-chasing.' The words came from Chevenne, utterly clear and confident, and free of the wrapping of psyk-shadows. 'Something seeded him. He was... he... was spider-netted and pulled.'

'I don't understand,' said Calpurnia.

'Something was used to draw the man's thoughts onwards,' Angazi said, his face still turned to the flickering glass rack behind Anschuk. 'It was a light touch on his mind, but one that stuck, like a cobweb.'

'You can pick that up from his trail?'

'We see in his wake the shape of what made it,' said Anschuk in Chevenne's voice. 'We see the trail he was following. We... dance behind... the shadow... man... in red and... grey... battlements break when the star dies... his tabard...'

'Red and grey tabard, they're not Bastion colours. That's one of the in-system dock wardens. Battlements?'

'Star coming down,' said Chevenne, his lips moving soundlessly, and the words arriving in her brain in Anschuk's voice a second later. 'Coming down!'

'Star coming... Bescalion. That's it: their badge is a battlement split by a comet.' Calpurnia blinked and concentrated. 'Why would he be seeing that?'

'Not real,' said Chevenne. 'Old, but not real. Caught in the cobweb, star coming down, caught and netted...'

'Old but not real,' Angazi said. 'In the past, then, but it hasn't left any substantial imprint in reality that they can see now: someone's memory.'

The response from the two psykers was a headshake, a deep rumble of negation, a chilly shock to the skin. Neither said 'no', but neither needed to.

'No weight to it. No...' Angazi concentrated for a moment. 'The image I'm getting is an umbilicus to a baby in the womb, arbitor. Whatever ghost he was chasing, it wasn't something firmly grounded in his mind. Drawn from it, but that's all, just a phantom.'

'What else?' Calpurnia asked. Her question was to Angazi, but Chevenne answered.

'Nothing else. Not here. Too slick to the touch. Too deep.'

Angazi already had a vial in his hands, reaching for a drip-tube that snaked into Angazi's scalp.

'I'll begin rousing them, ma'am. We shouldn't move them for a while. They got a hard sting off those emotions they read, and their life-signs are both...'

'We're not done,' said Calpurnia. Angazi frowned at her. Anschuk's mouth hung wetly open. The wooden plugs sitting in his empty sockets made his stare blank, disturbing. Chevenne's mouth twitched with amusement as if he'd expected this. The vitifers stood like statues.

'Turn around,' Calpurnia told them, 'and send your minds up to the Grand Concourse. The test has worked. Let's play the main game. Otranto was last seen on the Concourse before he entered the astropath cloisters. There are no wards or psyker-cages there to blur his trail. Bring the scent of that trail to me.'

AND SO, THEY *swoop up into the heart of the Tower. A white shimmer of delight, this place so rarely seen with an unfettered spirit-eye, and here truly is a fortress made for a mind. Here the runnels on the walls dance in their thoughts, veins of glass and crystal bearing intoxicating rapids of energy; a beautiful mist of mind and energy...*

'We're taking a risk,' said Angazi. 'Chevenne's skilful, but weak, and Anschuk lends the seance power, but he's not experienced. Their harmony will strengthen them, but pushing them will strain them and leave them vulnerable.'

'Then we release them from life and mourn their souls. We all owe the Emperor a death, Angazi. If their debt falls due today then the will of Him on Earth be done. The burden is to see that their lives are spent wisely, and that's mine, not yours. Carry out my orders.'

...mind and energy melded into one the lens, duet, eye wheels and dives through the keep, past the edge of the chamber at the Tower's centre where the power-shocks radiate off the blue-hot fire; through the sluices, pouring data changed from warp-patterns to electron-patterns; down to the Great Concourse. Straight into a shocking tangle of violence and pain, not the simple red hurt of the docks, but a wiry cats-cradle of shining nerve-pain and deep-flowing soul-pain. Mind sparks bound together by arcing bands of aggression, greenish-black and crack stinging like sandpaper lashes as images spin, green and cream, and steel, and harsh laughter. A voice rises and wails in their consciousness...

'Guilliman's blood, what was that?' Calpurnia had drawn her pistol when the terrified scream had boiled out of the air.

'Something from the reading, something they're getting out of the air of the Concourse.' Angazi's voice was tight with fear. 'We have to stop this. I've got drugs that will break the trance–'

'No! We're too close.' Calpurnia's eyes were alight. 'I was right, perish it, I was right! Make them follow. What can they read?' Ice was forming on the bed of the truck. The air between the psykers was filling with rainbows as if there was water in the air, but those rainbows were of shifting colours, too bright or too dull, sickening the eye.

...wailing in their consciousness, ghosts rising out of the air, the deck, and the past. Shuddering bundles of thoughts held in formation with rough willpower, or the steel bolts of faith: not the cool symmetries of psyker-discipline or the painless white throne-fire of Soul Binding. A bank of razor blades heated to cherry-red, clicking open and shut like teeth –fearful jealousy wanting to spend itself in violence. There are air-movements of braggadocio, savage arrogance kept in check, and there is, there is, there is a bound-up thought-trail that is so hard to pick apart. A man? A woman? A master and his woman? Thin keening, like an angry ghost, the memory-flash of a blade – how does it look, how does it look? All so cobweb-fine, all lost in a moment, tossed away by the violence of its own wake as the psyk-scent wavers...

'Arbitor...' said Chevenne, and the rainbows rippled. His next words were slurred, but something danced in the images: the rainbows knitted for a moment to make a flash of blade-metal.

'Yes. *Yes*. We're onto it.' Calpurnia was breathing hard. Exhilaration was a drug.

...scent wavers maddening, whisper-faint, twisting through the corridors like wind, now scraping against the wards and the cages whose hexagrammatic bars glitter like imprisoning ice under the insubstantial rockcrete of the walls. The scent is here like a last scrap of moonlight, the soft sound of running footsteps, the after-image of a strange mind flow, snapping out to see the walls and cullises ahead of it. Turned in somehow, perceptions trapped in recursive folds, and there's familiarity here, a song they know. The other images radiate off it like flares off a dying sun, a corkscrewing bitter vacuum around it, which he is only starting to guess is the oncoming of death. A flash of a grey-haired head surrounded with doomed regret, the stained-glass image of a judge in black and crimson. Then they are fighting to release it as the fear grows and hungers, and starts to fray their minds at the edges. Their guard starts to fray and the frothing blackness outside chills them with brass and rot and pink and blue flames. They have to escape, they break, they break...

'Saints and primarchs, arbitor, we've got to put a stop to this, now. Their minds have hit some kind of synergy that I can barely measure. They're running too hot and too fast!'

'Do we have everything we need?'

'Pity's sake, ma'am, trust me, break the trance now!'

...they CAN'T break, because now something has them, a soft tripping strand across their way that takes their balance, so they tumble and spin, and their harmony breaks. A sharp taste, predatory, acidic, a growing stain, darkening, and...

'Break it. Bring them out. Fast as you can.'

...and shocks begin, blearing hazes begin. The grey weight of suppressors begin as Angazi starts to work his machines and the senses drift up from their crude meat-bodies so far away. The harmony is gone. The harmony is broken and Chevenne's mind goes sleeting away as he withdraws into his barrier of will-shield, and prayers. Anschuk is left alone, unable to hear Angazi's voice as he tries to begin a focusing litany; unable to find his path home, and it is what he had always feared. His terror, the terror that one day, the last of his senses would snuff out, leaving his mind drifting and anchorless, fraying, trapped between witchcullises that were like hot jagged glass on his thoughts. There, or at the mercy of the boiling dark...

Chevenne had sat up, his face working, his voice joining Angazi's in incantation. Anschuk bucked in his chair, blood seeping past the plugs in his eyes and from under his brittle fingernails.

Calpurnia recoiled at the stink, the acrid smell: Anschuk's gown had started to char and burn. He bucked again, jumped half off the chair, and then remained there, floating in a position that his body could never have supported...

(As Angazi yelled in outright fear, Calpurnia was knocked dizzy by a vicious psyk-surge, and Chevenne scrabbled at the leads in his head).

(As ugly clashes of warning-bells sounded in the watch-hall and Watchmaster Voices-In-The-Fire twitched in her harness and shot out a frantic burst of orders, the knot of force gathering in her mind-vision).

(As the cantors and concordiasts of the astropath choirs beneath the eyries saw the runes light on the warning panels and urged their choirs to redouble their song, sending waves of power up the eyrie, and steeling themselves and their psykers for whatever was about to happen).

(As a quick hail of images ghosted out through the geography of the Tower, some gone faster than they could be sensed, others flicking into the minds of astropaths for a nonsensical moment. Kappema saw acid raindrops condensing in a sky that he'd never seen. Thujik saw an acrid smoke-trail through clear air, and felt a terrifying tip in his balance. Astropath Ankyn howled as the shape of a witchcullis branded itself across her raw consciousness. In the Firewatch Eyre, Astropath Ehlin found the word-thought *Judge in black and crimson* caught up in his mind, and blasted out and away towards a star whose light could barely reach the Tower at all).

...and then the gunshot.

It ended. Anschuk made a tangle of limbs and green robes in his chair. The vitifer whose name the psyker had never known calmly lowered his pistol, and took up his vigil again.

CHAPTER THIRTEEN

THE WARDENS AND apothecaries had drawn back when the seance began, withdrawing until they were far enough away not to disturb the delicate interweaving of the psykers' minds. When the spidery metal charms etched onto their phylacteries began to warm to the touch, and when the warning augurs started to hum like tuning forks, they began to shift and fuss. They double-checked protective seals and kit, and when the frantic messages came from the watch-hall that the seance had bolted out of control, they were in motion in a moment.

They burst out onto the Long Dock Road as Calpurnia held Chevenne's shoulders down and Angazi desperately worked the drug-pumps and neuro-electrical sleep-rams. They surrounded the truck with a punchy, economical precision bred over hundreds of hours of drill, and bitter practical experience.

Three long staves were driven against Chevenne's chest, hypodermal spears jabbing out of their ends and dosing the thrashing little man with a flood of psyk-suppressants and anti-cognitive serums. A warden dodged around the vitifer, who had his pistol levelled at Chevenne's head, leaned in and clicked a wand home into one of the watchmaster's skull-plugs. The twisting patterns up the wand's length began to glow as it drained off the saturating warp-energy whirling around Chevenne's brain, and after a moment, the palpable haze around the watchmaster began to dissipate.

Then the warden who'd planted the wand in Chevenne's skull danced forwards again, a skein of wire looped up one arm. He flicked his hand out and let his net uncurl in mid-air. It was memory-wire, coded to its shape at molecular level and imbued with nano-particles of psyk-resonant crystals. As it snapped into position, the particles assumed their proper symmetries. Chevenne collapsed like a rag doll, breathing hoarsely, tendrils of corposant still drifting from his ears and skull-sockets. At the opposite chair, the warden was already kneeling beside Anschuk's corpse. He and Angazi were lashing ribbons woven from more of the imbued wire around the dead limbs in careful crisscrossing patterns.

'Move him,' said a woman's voice.

Calpurnia, down off the truck to give them space to work, couldn't tell who'd spoken: the wardens were near identical under their dark coats and armour. Their visors, like the vitifers', were made of layers of filigree, breathtakingly fine, that made up hexagrammic symmetries in three dimensions. Their faces were invisible behind them. As the wardens and vitifers made a ring around the truck, one of them at the tiller started it rolling.

On the bed of the truck, the apothecaries went to work, cutting Chevenne's clothes free and jabbing diagnostor pins into his skin. Runes and chimes began to sound. Chevenne had fallen silent, but his limbs were still twitching. Each lumen they passed under flickered in an odd, syncopated rhythm, and crackling frost was forming in sharp-edged patches on the rough plastic truck-bed.

One vitifer was still up on the truck, his pistol drawn. The other had dropped down to the deck, and was part of the ring of jogging wardens. Calpurnia kept pace behind them, keeping her distance and letting them work. After a moment, she noticed that she was running alongside a trail of red spots on the deck where the blood from Anschuk's burst head was dripping off the truck's edge.

She had barely had time to register it when she dodged something in her path by reflex, a torn piece of bloody cloth the same green as Chevenne's garments.

'Speed up!' The truck began to accelerate, the wardens picking up their pace to a run. Calpurnia gritted her teeth and stretched her stride, racing to catch up and see what had happened. She was on the outside as they rounded into the hangar and swung around to the passageway up into the keep. For a moment, she had to pour on even more pace to keep up, as a second blood-sodden length of cloth was cast off the truck and splatted onto the deck in front of her.

She drew level with it, jinked inwards and slid between two wardens so that she was running inside the circle. Anschuk's corpse was a barely-recognisable tangle in one seat, and in the other the apothecaries had sliced Chevenne's tunic open up its front so that they could work.

After a moment more, what she was seeing sank in, and the shock took all the speed out of her legs. She dropped to half-pace as the wardens dodged, cursed and passed her, leaving her behind as they spirited Chevenne up the passage towards the medicae halls. Her helmet off, breathing hard, Calpurnia walked back down the corridor alone, to where that second piece of cloth lay in its red stain. She stood over it for a long time, her face solemn, eyes opaque, her mind whirling.

Torma Ylante had to lie on her side on the bed that the Arbites doctor had given her. The screaming giant who'd torn into her captors had grabbed her by one arm as she had gone to flee, and wrenched her around in a circle that had sent her through the air and into the side of the dromon, barely conscious. She believed that falling down past the ramp where the giant couldn't see her had saved her life. The next people his eye had fallen on had been Lohjen and the Navy man, and her last memory from that hangar had been of wet, cracking, ripping sounds as the man had got his hands on them.

She lay on her side in a futile attempt to keep her shoulder comfortable, throbbing as it was after the arbitor medicae's quick and brutal repairs to the joint. Moving sent bursts of pain scrubbing up and down her arm like razor wire. She tried to keep her eyes closed, concentrating on breathing exercises and stillness.

She jumped at Calpurnia's voice, and moaned aloud as her patched-up shoulder twitched and flashed with agony.

'Lie down, Ylante. Wait a moment and let it die down.'

'Thank you, arbitor.' Ylante's voice was as strained as her face. Sweat had started up on her forehead.

'No need for the tone. I've been through worse than what ails you and I know what I'm saying.'

'Well, thank you. I suppose I'm just having a little trouble resting.'

'I had Scall dose you with stimulants,' said Calpurnia, 'and some fairly specific pain suppressors. I need you alert and able to talk.'

'I… see. May I ask what happened to me? Who was the screaming man? Who were the people–'

'No.'

The two women stared at each other for a moment.

'Tell you what, Ylante,' said Calpurnia. 'I'll start by making an admission to you. We're running low on time. The succession issue is making the senior astropaths fractious, and the operation of the eyries is starting to suffer. This Bastion has too important a place for me to allow that. Whoever else Lohjen was, he was Inquisition, and I need to know how he was involved in this before one of his friends or masters shows up. My own time on the Tower may not be long, and I *will* have Otranto's murderer by the time I leave.' She caught herself, the next moment and shut her mouth. She had been about to say why, to tell Ylante what had happened at Selena Secundus, and confess that another failure flapped in her wake, another burden of duty had slipped through her fingers onto the floor, and that really would be more than she could bear.

'And so now I need your advice,' she said. 'I need your explanations. I can feel the door of this thing almost open, and I need your hand on the pry bar.'

After a moment, Ylante made a small motion of her eyes that was close enough to assent. Calpurnia forced her hand away from her forehead, and forced her thoughts into an orderly queue.

'When we were walking in the medicae chambers,' she said, 'we saw several astropaths come in, three of them I think, with injuries, similar injuries.'

'I remember them. The choristers: they were walking too fast and the lead one ran into a witchcullis. Their attendant should have been more careful.'

'They didn't have separate attendants?'

'Choristers are the small cogs, arbitor,' said Ylante with the hint of a smile. 'On their own, their powers are limited. It's en masse with their song poured into another psyker's trance that they're powerful.'

'Too weak to deserve individual staff, you're saying.'

'Too weak, or too exhausted, or their mind or sanity has been too damaged by their Binding. An astropath's spirit has felt the tread of the Emperor, ma'am, and the Emperor does not tread lightly.' Ylante shifted a little and grimaced. 'Was that your question?'

'No. Tell me why contact with a cullis is going to have that effect. They're wards. They contain a psyker, do they not? If containment causes injury, why aren't I struck permanently deaf if I put shooters' plugs in my ears when I'm at the range?'

'It's commonplace to believe one's body and mind are separate,' said Ylante, 'linked almost by coincidence. Whether or not you believe it, it's not true of psykers. For them, the energy washing out of their minds, it fills them, like blood.' Ylante shuddered at the words.

'So if there's a bond between their bodies and minds–' Calpurnia began, frowning.

'So there is,' said Ylante, 'but not an equal one. Their bodies can become an afterthought to their minds. The old ones can be almost hollowed out by it. They need powerful wills and containing, and constant attention from their concordiast, to stay anchored in their bodies at all.'

'The older they are the worse it gets?'

'Once in the Adeptus, yes, but also the young ones whose gifts have started to eat into them before they can be trained to contain it. We saw it aboard the Black Ship.' Her eyes were haunted, 'Constantly.'

'So the young man we saw was burned,' Calpurnia said, feeling haunted and wanting the conversation on a new track. 'He hit the wards of the cullis, which are made to cage and repel energies like the ones that flow all through him...'

'...and the wards threw him back and burned his mind,' Ylante finished. 'That's what makes the cloisters so dark and narrow: they're completely enclosed in psyk-cages, sealed in with rockcrete so the astropaths can find their way by touch and not hurt themselves.'

'So the wards burned his mind, but they also burned his body, because his body is so powerfully slaved to his mind,' said Calpurnia. 'His body burned where it touched the cullis, and... All right then. There were three of them: the two who'd been walking along with him. I remember this: lighter burns, just welts and lesions.'

'They'd have been walking behind him,' said Ylante, fidgeting on the bed and grunting with discomfort. 'The cullis would have broken up the forwards wash of his pain, but they would have had less protection.'

Calpurnia closed her eyes and ran her fingertips over her forehead. She could feel it coming, that final click of the lock opening, that grinding that meant the door was finally leaving its hinges.

'They felt the pain in their minds,' she said. 'The pain manifested in their minds, and their minds made that pain burst out onto their bodies.'

'You have it.'

'I have it,' Calpurnia repeated. 'All right, then. The scrying I've just come from had a concordiast helping it. You've done that?'

'Once or twice,' Ylante said cautiously, 'in my time.'

'Can you describe the process? How might we get detailed pictures of something, something I can use the Scriptorium's systems to put in a form I can see for myself?'

'It would be hard, ma'am. Bear in mind, I'm no psyker myself. We're talking about this like two blind pilgrims trying to discuss the colours of a temple fresco. Seance images are rarely like your detectives' pict-captures. You can't make a clear portrait out of them. If you know in advance the man or woman you're scrying, you can bring them into focus, because your own knowledge of them, your memories of them, provides a kind of lens.'

'So, a mind scrying a thing that mind knows...'

'...will do so more powerfully and more dangerously, too. Vedrier once described a seer becoming a still pool: something attuned to event-echoes – the finer the seers' control, the narrower the set of events they can attune themselves to. They also have to let those echoes imprint on their consciousness. Do you understand? Let some of that echo into them. It takes an excellent mind to withstand that for scry after scry. Most psykers who attempt seeings do it in choirs, or through a focus like the Imperial Tarot, and with the most puissant prayers and blessings, they can surround themselves with. Scrying can hurt. Even a soul-bound astropath isn't immune.'

I won't have a mind pop its seams on my watch, Calpurnia thought, and felt a stab of guilt. Chevenne had seemed confident when she had asked it of him. The strength of a single powerful astropath in choir with Chevenne's own fine control, but something had happened nevertheless.

'I'll put it another way,' said Ylante, mistaking Calpurnia's thoughtful look for puzzlement. 'Scrying isn't passive, arbitor. It's not like an eye taking in light that's fallen on an inanimate book. Astropaths exert power in scrying, and what they look at isn't lifeless. It must have been explained to you why the structure of the Bastion's been engineered to break up psyk-traces? It's so that sensitive psykers don't travel across a point where something terrible happened and look into it accidentally, experience it all over again in their minds. Why are you smiling, madam arbitor?'

Experience it again in their minds. I'm right, I know I am. I have to be.

'No reason, Ylante. Tell me why the scryes of Otranto's path report a man and a woman.'

Ylante blinked and gasped, first in astonishment and then in pain.

'A man and a woman,' Calpurnia said, looking at her, 'a *master* and his woman. When the psykers who did try to scry Otranto's path came out of it, they reported seeing a man and a woman, and sensations of fear. Why would they all talk about a master and his woman, Ylante? It's hard to avoid thinking that they were talking about Master Otranto and his new Concordiast Torma Ylante. It's hard to avoid thinking that the fear and his death were because she came off her Black Ship unhinged. She was angry about her parting from this Master Vedrier whom she apparently cared about, and stabbed the master through the heart. Why would they talk about a master and his woman if they couldn't see your faces, Ylante? Is that why you were trying to talk me out of working to find out who the images were of?'

Ylante had rallied magnificently, but then, thought Calpurnia, she had been trained to control her emotions.

'I submit, arbitor, that you're misunderstanding scrying,' said Ylante with great care. 'Things become apparent in it that would not be so for the rest of us: emotions, power, patterns, relationships, symbols, change, all in intersecting layers. One of my old astropaths once tried to explain it to me. He said, "Take the incident you're scrying, interpret it in as many poetic, allegorical, symbolic ways as you can, put each of those into a stained-glass window, put all those windows in front of each other and shine a stablight through them. Now, stand in front of that array and look at all the pictures at once, try to untangle them and arrive at a meaning." That's the closest he could come.

Except for a psyker, often the meanings arrive far more tangled than that, and with the force of a bullet between the eyes. So much of their training is about calming and controlling their minds, because what comes into them will knock their minds off their hinges if they don't tease out the meanings and move to–'

'Shit the information out of their brains,' Calpurnia finished, and Ylante blinked at the crudity. 'Hm. Who's this other astropath you referred to? He sounded good at putting these concepts into words.'

'Five years dead, madam,' Ylante told her with a touch of coldness. 'Suffice to say that something got into his head that had no right to be there.'

'I see. I'm... sorry for an untimely death.'

'Thank you.' There was a pause. 'Arbitor? Those people in the dromon I was... taken to. They were Inquisition, weren't they? I recognised the faceplate design from other agents of theirs we've met.'

'Yes.' Calpurnia took a breath. 'Yes, Inquisition, you're correct.'

'Were they Polarists?' Calpurnia felt a chill at Ylante's question. The concordiast's face wore a look of naked disdain.

'How do you know that term, Ylante? Your chances just took a turn for the worse, unless you can come up with a damned good explanation.'

'The Polarists,' Ylante said, 'are spreading everywhere. There are some in the Astropathica, not many, but there are many in the Navy, and the Ecclesiarchy around Chiros is rotten with them. It's said that it's a growing blight in the Inquisition too, with Tonnabi's monograph spreading like a brushfire. Vedrier even said he'd met the master of another Black Ship at Coellow Quintus who'd fallen in with them.'

'Back up, Ylante. The Polarists: start at the beginning.'

'Polarists: believers in the polarity between human and psyker. The monograph by Eparch Kvander Tonnabi is being spread by some in the Missionaria Galaxia, if you care to read it, but promise me you won't swallow his ravings.' Ylante was breathing hard, clearly in pain. 'The Emperor, so they say, is divine, transcendent. The only place where human and psyker can meet is in the Godhead, and He holds humanity and witchery in his hands as proof of His godhood. In any mortal, the combination of human and psyker is a mockery. The polarity must be enforced: either a human is a human, and walks and talks, and prays; or it's a psyker and it can't be allowed to have any humanity at all. Astropaths that Polarists get their hands on are trepanned, lobotomised, reduced to no more than servitors. They say that the poor ones who're brain-burned by their Soul Binding are the right ones, that that's what the Emperor means to do. The ones who come out still proud and strong are the aberrations, and we must serve the Emperor by completing His plan and reducing them to… '

A tear leaked out of the corner of Ylante's eye. 'They can barely make a choir. Ciphers are pumped into their heads and some idiot blunt plays them like an organ. Orders them around like a servitor. All that holiness and knowledge gone: just a lump of meat on an eyrie couch. They can't handle a millionth of the work someone like Chevenne could, but the Polarists say it's the Emperor's will. How could the Emperor will this? I am dutiful before Him, but how could He will that? It can't be right.'

'I don't believe Lohjen was a Polarist,' Calpurnia said. 'The word appears in what we know about some of his conversations here, but whether he was a full inquisitor or an agent, he spent a lot of time talking with astropaths, and there's no trace in our reports of… of what you describe.'

Calpurnia wondered why it seemed so important to comfort Ylante all of a sudden. 'He may have been warning them, or he may have been part of a backlash, who knows? But no, I don't think he was one of them.'

Ylante lay still, staring past Calpurnia in silence.

'Do you still suspect me?' she asked after a moment.

'No,' said Calpurnia. 'By rights I shouldn't reassure you, but no, I don't. I do think that the master-servant pairing in the scryes was you and Otranto, but you didn't kill him.'

'I don't understand.'

'That's all right,' said Calpurnia, 'I do. You'll excuse me. I've got work to do.'

THE STATUES OVER the stairs up the Grand Concourse had once been heroic. This had been the ceremonial entrance to the station, when it had been a military fortress: the glorious entryway to the keep where important arrivals would process up from the docks. Passing through the outer arch, carved with intricate patterns representing every system in which Battlefleet Pacificus had fought as seen from Hydraphur, the new arrivals would look up and see a three-sided frieze, a mass of statues, staring down at them. Heroes of the Navy, representations of real commanders and of romanticised lower crewmen with clean augmetics and chiselled chins, vanquishing hideous leering heretics.

The statues had been devastated by time: once clean lines roughened and corroded, smooth stone, chipped and soiled.

Like me, Teeker Renz thought, looking up at the statues through a mist of self-pity, just like me.

He watched Thujik's back disappearing down the Grand Concourse. The man's little procession passed through the shadows of the processional arches, light and dark and light, the fixtures on his head gleaming like the gun the vitifer next to him carried. The pompous bastard, all that show. Thujik wouldn't have dared behave like this if Renz was still… If Renz still had… If Otranto…

Renz gave a little moan as anger fought with self-pity, and dropped his eyes to the strange patterns on the Concourse floor. Renz could see his dim reflection in it, see how gaunt he was getting, how ratty his hair and clothes. He shouldn't have to put up with this.

'Don't even bother trying it, Renz,' Thujik had told him with every sign of enjoyment. 'Too little, too late. Were you so coddled by Otranto that you've lost all grip on diplomacy? Once you wouldn't have been stupid enough to ever try this. Perhaps if the Polarists suck out my ability to think through a straw, I'll be as stupid as you one day, but no. You're wasting your time.'

'You're going to recruit Ylante?' Renz had asked, horrified, and Thujik had cackled aloud.

'So you admit it, then? This pestering me for a meeting, all your extravagant compliments: you admit the whole thing was about slipping into a position by my side? Too little, too late, and it would never have been enough anyway. I don't approve of you, Renz, and I don't approve of how Otranto let you get your hooks into this place. When I'm Master of the Tower, you're finished. Stand there in that cloud of sickly fear I can feel radiating off you, and think on that. Since you've been so careless as to allow Sacredsteel to float to the front of your mind, I'll advise you, gratis, that she may not like me, but she loathes you even more than I do.'

Renz had tried to plead, then to lecture, and then to at least manage a civil goodbye, but Thujik had not even allowed him that, having his servitor spin his chair and wheel him away.

Just like me, he thought, looking up at the broken and defeated statues.

It took him a moment even to register the sound of boot soles on the stairs behind him, but when he did and turned around, the fresh weight of fear fell on him as if one of those broken carvings had dropped onto his head.

'Teeker Renz?' said Lead Arbitor Oraxi at the head of his squad. 'By order of the arbitor senioris, Renz, you're coming with us.'

SECOND PETTY OFFICER Roos was frightened of Antovin Dechene, and fighting not to show it. This was his home turf, after all: the sneering concordiast was standing in one of the officers' staterooms in the keep's Naval quarters, well away from the attendant's chambers where he was supposed to remain. The warden still found it hard to look him in the eye, however.

Many of the Navy crews and lower-echelon attendants aboard the Bastion found Dechene unnerving, but few could have said why. Perhaps it the unthinking arrogance of his demeanour. Or, it could have been as simple as the well-known way in which people aboard the Bastion Psykana, both within the Naval contingent and out of it, found their careers withering after they crossed the little power-clique of which he was a part. The station had its share of dead-enders with little ambition to stir them. The ambitious officers usually gravitated to the war fleets, constantly sailing the warp into and out of the system. However, it also played host to a few young lions of Battlefleet Pacificus: young officers with the favour of their superiors for whom a posting to an exotic setting like this was intended to round out their early careers and experiences. They were the sort of people who learned that Antovin Dechene was someone to try to stay on the right side of.

'I'm not sure I understand why you think I *care* where Renz is,' Dechene snapped. 'I don't like being interrupted when I'm sure I intended to be private for a couple of hours.'

Roos, looking past his shoulder through the partly open partition-door, caught sight of the shivering naked woman in the bed behind Dechene. Something about Dechene's eyes reminded him of the reptiles he had once seen in Commodore Vlassion's menagerie at the High Septacian station.

'Master Dechene, he instructed me to tell you the Arbites were taking him to the Master's suite. They were marching with him, sir. He said to tell, uh, he said that you would know what he meant.'

'He sent you to tell me that, did he?'

'He, uh, said it to me when I asked him if I sh–'

'Shut up.' Dechene spared a quick backwards glance for the woman on the bed and gave a dismissive grunt. 'All right. Get your gibbering face out of mine.' He pushed through the door and let it slide shut behind him. 'Master Renz hasn't been himself, you know. He's probably desperate for me to go looking out for him... again. He'll be his usual self when I've pulled him out of trouble, I'm sure, the ungrateful worm.' Dechene ran a final hand through his hair and threw his jacket over his shoulders. 'You never know,' he said, to himself as much as to anyone else. 'This might even be fun.'

STANDING NEXT TO Orovene at the foot of Dast's bed, Shira Calpurnia could feel her nerves stretching. Nothing to do with the psychic fog of the Bastion, this was simple fear. Fear at the slender limb she had gone out on, fear that this might be another monstrous mistake, fear that simply became colder and deeper, because fearing her own decisions was something she had never had cause to do.

Her orders had gone out and her orders had been obeyed. Things were in motion and it was simply too late for second thoughts. That was a thought that was more frightening to her than it ought to have been. To stop it from crawling too far forwards into her mind, Calpurnia concentrated on her prayers. Her hand was up over her heart, fingers stiff and thumb curled into her palm: an eagle's wing, a pious gesture that she hadn't used since childhood. She held it over her arbitor senioris rank badge.

Cerebrally, rationally, Calpurnia knew where the fear had come from. It was the memory of the hearing at Selena Secundus, the ugly shrapnel-bomb of a disaster that she had so cheerfully walked into, so full of her own prowess – Shira Calpurnia, the fierce new arbitor general, the woman who'd broken the conspiracy dogging the Mass of Balronas, and foiled the escape of Ghammo Stroon, what could go wrong?

She'd had all the time she could want in the Incarcery, enough time and Chasteners and self-denunciations to drive home what had gone wrong, but the self-loathing she had felt wasn't the surprise. Neither was that constant yawning emptiness she felt over her shoulder all the time, the gap in herself: if she couldn't trust herself to succeed in her duty, what could she believe about herself any more? What was left of the Shira Calpurnia she had thought she was for nearly forty years?

What really took her by surprise was the terrible anger she felt: a part of herself that she had never expected would get so bold. She had been in peril of her life from a dozen different kinds of enemy over and over again since she had left Machiun, but the anger she felt had always been a tight, cold thing: anger with a razor-edge of bright Ultramar steel, not this thrashing red animal.

'What are you praying for?' Orovene asked next to her, his breath coming out as a puff of lho-smell.

'Shall I tell you the truth, preacher?'

'We've come too deep into this for anything else. We're both too wretched for lies.' The weariness in Orovene's voice startled her.

'The truth, then: I was praying to the Emperor for strength for our brother. Dast is my Chastener and I owe him my prayers. Except that, I was also praying for the Emperor to grant something to me. I was praying that he let Dast lie for just a few more hours. I was praying that the Chastener stay asleep and not retake my command, so that I can see this matter through. I need to do this, Orovene. I need to stand before my conscience and my Emperor, and declare that I did this one thing well, for Him.' The preacher nodded silently. 'You?' she asked him.

'In truth, Calpurnia? For the same: for one chance to show strength. I've failed too. I came on that dromon as your preacher, confessor and spiritual guide. Then, when He tested us with this, you were my guide. I haven't walked before you to lead. I haven't walked beside you to inspire. I've trailed you and been mute. I've learned from you, Calpurnia. I wandered in the witch-fog that I didn't have the strength to fight, while you did the Emperor's work. Punished I may be, but I want the chance to restore my faith too.'

'Well then, Preacher Orovene,' said Calpurnia, 'walk with me. The Emperor knows us by our deeds. Let us, by our deeds, show that we deserve what we've asked of Him.'

CHAPTER FOURTEEN

'THE SUCCESSION?' RENZ asked, 'The succession for Master?' He was staring ahead, through the archway into the oval antechamber outside the Master's suite, towards the broken silk partition at the far end that still hadn't been repaired.

'The succession, Master Renz, or should I say Master Concordiast Renz? Master Herbalist Renz? You have had a number of titles. You'll have to take pity on my poor attempts to understand all the protocols of your Blind Tower.' Calpurnia wondered for a moment if she was playing the baffle-witted act a little too heavy. She was painfully aware that deception fitted her about as well as a suit of Astartes armour. Back in the heart of the cloisters, her senses were playing up again and it was difficult to concentrate.

'I had to take over command here, you see, as a matter of duty. Now, I have to establish a succession to poor Master Otranto, and of course, I will depend on your guidance. I know you were the Master's major-domo and chief of staff. You've made yourself central to the running of the Bastion.'

'You flatter me, mamzel arbitor. I saw to it that the mundane life of the Tower ran smoothly, to free up my Master's attention. That was all.' Renz was frightened and wary, but fear hadn't made him stupid. If Calpurnia knew he was at the centre of so much of the Bastion's activities, what else might she have found out?

Time to make sure he didn't dwell on that. She ushered him down out of the passageway and into the room, and sat him on a hassock that she'd brought out of Otranto's bedchamber. He didn't remark on Bruinann and Orovene standing in one of the side arches, or the pistol and maul Calpurnia wore.

'You're ready... to look to the succession?' he asked finally. 'To take full command?'

'I aim to have the matter settled by the time my colleagues arrive from Hydraphur,' Calpurnia told him. 'I will have to leave the station once Otranto's murderers have been neutralised, and it would be poor indeed of me to leave a mess to be cleaned up after me.'

'Who's coming? What?' Renz's eyes flicked to the other two arbitrators, watching him impassively from the passage. 'How long has this been known?'

'The Bastion is no easy destination,' Calpurnia told him smoothly. 'Have you forgotten how far out from Hydraphur you orbit? The Bastion's own orbit has been threaded through the gravity wells of planets in both ecliptics. It's hard to intercept, that's the whole point. It's taking time for the follow-up taskforce to reach here, but I'm sure, with your help, I'll be able to organise their visit so it's not disruptive. Their task won't be complex, after all. Just collect the corpses of Kyto and that inquisitor and the Ylante woman, and cart them off for destruction, and the investiture of the new Master. I imagine you're looking forward to your days returning to normal.'

Renz jerked forwards, and then stood up in a clumsy attempt to hide the reaction.

'Kyto and the inq–'

'Don't fear, Master Renz, please don't trouble yourself. It can't have been easy for you, finding that someone so close by has it in them to commit such terrible crimes, but there's not a place under the Emperor's sun that's free of human folly, aren't we taught that? It was a stroke of justice, that madman catching all three conspirators together. We've got some work ahead of us, piecing together the details of their plot, but if you feel up to– well, no, I won't trouble you with such disturbing work, sir.'

'Oh, no,' exclaimed Renz. He had almost started to smile. 'No, I will do what I must! Torma Ylante, well, she, she obviously was a superb concordiast in her day, of course.'

'Of course.'

'She lacked some of my own skills, though I tell you it myself, she hadn't the, er, the far more onerous range of tasks that I do.'

Throne, he was a smug bastard, but talking about himself was getting him gabbling. Calpurnia shook off the buzz in her head and concentrated on his words. 'But to leave the station addled by this Master Vedrier, as she did! Who knows why, really, why she left, but the Black Ships have a dark reputation, mamzel, and perhaps, well, you yourself won't need telling about the vermin that can slip through the cracks of the Imperium. You said so yourself. Perhaps the inquisitor was attempting to unmask her when her assassin killed him? Ylante, well, name the service I can render to condemn the woman, and I'll do my duty, arbitor.'

'Without duty, what are we?' Calpurnia asked.

'What indeed, madam arbitor senioris, and it is only proper of you to say so.'

'To think Ylante was on her way back here to replace you.'

'Replace?' Renz made a nervous flapping gesture of his hand. 'Ylante was no threat to my position, I assure you, mamzel. My wide range of duties for Master Otranto has required me to become skilled in–'

'I've been misinformed then,' said Calpurnia a little curtly. 'There was no tension between you and the Master over Ylante's return to the staff?'

'Oh, well, mamzel, I did try to point out to the dear Master that the woman couldn't be trusted. I'd seen through her, you see.'

'Ah, well,' Calpurnia said with a bow. 'I'll double-check your reports to Arbitor Bruinann on the matter. I have no doubt you were thorough in setting out your suspicions before the law.'

There were footsteps in one of the other passages, movements. More Arbites: Rede, this time, with a second arbitrator and a concordiast in tow. He was quiet, saturnine, his dark hair heavy over his forehead.

'Reports. Well. My suspicions. I–'

'Or did you discuss them with the inquisitor directly? I commend your intelligence in doing so, Master Renz. You weren't to know that he was in league with Ylante. Was Kyto aboard his ship as your representative?'

Renz was actually almost panting with the effort of steering his thoughts through the swerves she was throwing him. Too much agreement and he might be trapped in a lie, too little and he might look guilty: time to let out the leash a little.

'I apologise, Master Renz,' she said. 'I shouldn't press you so at a time like this. Shall I talk to your assistant while you clear your head for us to talk about the succession? With Kyto dead, the only testimonies I have of the Master's last sightings will be from the two of you.'

'And whoever killed him,' drawled the other concordiast from the passageway. He made to walk forwards and Rede blocked him.

'Of course,' said Calpurnia. Renz was twitching again. *Come on*, she thought. *Come on and lie. Show me you know better.*

'Thanks to you, that is all over,' Renz burst out. 'We now know it was Ylante who struck him down in his room. What a foul act!'

A flash of satisfaction helped clear Calpurnia's head. He had looked towards Dechene as he said it. He wasn't agreeing with her, he was bringing Dechene up to speed on the lie.

'And cunning, too,' Calpurnia replied. 'Think of it, Otranto perishing inside his own sanctuary, whose seals and guards were made to keep him safe.'

'Yes,' said Renz uncertainly.

'And then escaping! Look through there at that door! As Otranto's assistant, you must have known how formidably secure his chambers were. We couldn't understand how an assassin had got in, but it's almost as hard to understand how Ylante escaped it!'

'She's a cunning woman,' Renz said, his eyes sliding back and forth, 'and savage. Such an attack! I had heard reports of how deep the knife went.'

Calpurnia took a couple of idle steps towards the passage they'd entered by.

'It was a fierce attack, you're not wrong,' she said. 'Watchmaster Chevenne read a trace of it in his scry, and even the memory of it hurt him grievously.'

'I am sorry for it,' Renz said with a bowed head. He took a pace to keep level with her. 'The memory must have been very painful.'

'It was. It was vivid, almost alive. So vivid that it printed itself on his mind, and because a psyker's mind suffuses his body so powerfully, it printed itself on his body, too. You're a concordiast, Renz, you must know about image stigmata. A psyker can be made to relive something, or imagine it, so powerfully that they experience it. Come and let me show you what we found.'

The smell of Renz's sweat was rank and piercing. His eyes rolled, but he walked with her, hesitantly, like a child, to the empty archway.

'A psyker can form lesions on their skin when their companion burns themselves on a witchcullis. A psyker can experience an injury that comes to life in a memory they read.' She had Renz's arm and was walking him. There was no time to lose.

'A psyker can be made to feel an imaginary wound if the thought of it is driven into his mind,' she said, and Renz groaned aloud. Her hand on his arm grabbed hard at his sleeve and she slipped her hip under his, rocked him off balance and sent him pitching forwards into the passageway. As he screeched and tried to scramble up, tangling himself in his robes and stinking of panic, Calpurnia jumped back and slapped an amulet on her vox-torc. Witchcullises at each end of the passage slammed down. Calpurnia, in the antechamber, looked in at Renz, trapped and alone between sets of hexagrammic filigree and ward-etched bars.

'Someone did exactly that, didn't they Renz?' she asked him coldly. From behind her, she could hear boot steps as Rede and Bruinann came into the antechamber.

'Rybicker, the madman, he was driven mad,' she said to the quivering Renz. 'He was driven mad by an illusion, something someone spun in his head to fuel what he felt for his dead drudge. They snared him with that and made him chase a phantom. Chevenne was able to tell me that.'

Renz sat on the passage floor staring up at her, wide-eyed.

'I'll guess that's what we'll find killed Anschuk and Proctor Pheissen, isn't it, Renz? Something got into them, toppled them off balance and turned their minds in on themselves. Isn't that right?'

He stared at her, dumbly.

'I don't need to guess about Otranto, Renz. He died in the cloisters, but he left a psyk-trail through the Concourse where there are no wards to break it up. Chevenne read that trail, Renz, and he found exactly the same inward-twisted images that he found in poor Rybicker's trail. The same thing: the same imaginary ghosts.'

She stepped right up to the bars and stared at him.

'Otranto was killed because someone caught him off-guard, someone with a psyker-gift they'd Emperor-knows-how managed to hide.'

Renz had raised a hand, pointing or beseeching, she couldn't tell.

'Was it just a quarrel, Renz? Was it just that he wouldn't turn Ylante away and leave you with all your influence? You lashed out, didn't you? Why not confess?'

He was shaking his head.

'Ylante didn't stab Otranto in his chamber, or out of it. Not a living soul took a knife and stabbed him through the heart. Otranto was stabbed in the soul.'

'No…' Renz whispered.

'Yes, Renz. In the soul,' said Calpurnia. 'You know it. You know how to drive your enemies mad by bringing nightmares to life inside their skulls. You brought a nightmare to life for Otranto. You hammered the illusion into his head that what you wished for was true. Ylante had come back from the Black Ship meaning him harm, with a knife ready for him. That's what he was fleeing, a murderess he couldn't escape, because she was in his thoughts with him. Fleeing and bringing down the defences against someone who didn't care about defences, because she wasn't there, until he was locked away and alone, and the fantasy completed itself. The stigmata: the death-wound he was convinced he'd been dealt. Otranto was a powerful psyker, his mind and his body: no contest. His mind knew it had been dealt a death blow and his body manifested the wound.'

'Someone put that phantom in his head before he went running into the cloisters. Someone he trusted and let get close to him with no wards or psyk-suppressors nearby. You argued over Ylante's return and you were standing in the Concourse at the spot where Otranto started his last run.'

'Where do you actually think there's a chink in the case against you, Renz? Where? Why not confess?'

Renz sat and gawped, tears in his eyes, and breath heaving. His hand was still out. It wasn't a beseeching gesture, or a fending off, or a symbol of defiance. His thumb was curled in and his fingers out, the eagle-wing charm.

He wasn't pointing it at Calpurnia. He was pointing it past her, into the antechamber where Dechene was standing.

'Did you seriously think he did it?' chuckled Dechene. 'Look at him, the worm. How could he ever stand up to Otranto? I'll tell you, he didn't.'

Bruinann stepped in and whipped the butt of his shotgun around in a curt, ferocious movement, ready to leave Dechene sprawled on the floor with a fractured skull. Things went slick under his mind and *every time Bruinann had shared Lazka Rede's bed, he knew it was a mistake. The detectives were snakes with ice in their hearts, every arbitor knew that. The tenderest of emotions were fodder for their dossiers, levers and nothing more. He'd been a fool to think that he was anything more than that to Rede. He had known she wanted to return to Hydraphur and leave the Tower, but he had never expected this. Never expected her to open her dossiers to show Calpurnia all his mistakes, all his little laxnesses, all the things he had whispered to her in the night that she thought were secret. Now here they were on parchment banners, fluttering from scaffolding on which he was to hang, stripped and beaten, and branded with symbols of condemnation. Rede was laughing at him, Calpurnia and Oraxi and every arbitor he had ever known was laughing at him, here atop the Wall under the warm Hydraphur sun, handing him the shackles that he was to use, to fix himself to the beam that would lift him high in the air to hang until he died…*

Bruinann's face was waxy and vacant. His swing missed and tipped him off balance, and he skidded to one knee. A low moan trickled from his mouth.

'He whimpered and begged,' said Dechene. His face was flushed, his pupils so dilated that even the low light of the antechamber should have been dazzling. 'Renz almost got down and grabbed the old man's skirts. Pathetic.'

A point of scarlet light flicked into existence on Dechene's temple. Rede's sight had come on as soon as she'd drawn her own gun, and she held it unerring. She did not pull the trigger. Her finger didn't move, because *even with him dead there were too many more out there, the witches the psykers the shivering twitching forms that anchored the minds whirling outside in the warp. Rede was trapped here, sealed in this tomb, so far out that she could barely see the sun she missed so. Locked in here with these people whose minds were eating them from the inside. She couldn't kill them; they were already dead. She'd never get past them, never get out, she would stay here all her life. She knew this now: she was doomed to be trapped among the witches for all the years she had left. Suddenly, that thought weighed too much, suddenly she simply broke. Stupid woman, why not spare the poor wretch's life when she knew which life really needed to end...*

Orovene launched himself across the antechamber without a word, trailing a hoarse cry in the air. Rede's arm was curling, coming around, her mouth opening to take the barrel of her pistol, until the preacher cannoned into her, knocking her sprawling and wrenching her gun-arm down. Rede squalled and struggled in his grip, fighting to get the pistol back up to her head. Somewhere, a klaxon started to sound, as Calpurnia punched the amulet on her torc a second time. Every other cullis around the chamber smashed down. Dechene was contained.

But she was contained in here with him.

'Otranto didn't need begging,' said Dechene, stepping daintily away from the brawl on the floor. His coat was rippling as if in a breeze. 'Otranto needed telling. Too many people think they don't need telling. I like telling.'

The air between them vibrated. The witchcullises rattled in their mounts.

'Had two long good years since this little talent woke up,' said Dechene. 'Otranto was the first time I really opened up and pushed it: stupid old man. Who'd have thought I'd give him a slap and he'd feel a punch?'

Calpurnia's grip closed on her gun, but then it hammered into her and her thoughts blurred for a moment, before *she fumbled and only managed to flip the pistol out of its holster onto the floor. She grabbed for it, comically, her co-ordination gone, and then Dechene's open-handed slap knocked her onto her back with her gun on the padded floor a metre away from her hand. A little woman like her had never stood a chance against someone like Antovin Dechene. She should have known never to stand up to someone like him. It was no use fighting him; she should just lie there and...*

...and the gun came free of the holster. Calpurnia realised that she was breathing in gulps, her legs shaking. Dechene's face was purple with the strain. A thread of blood ran from his nose.

'No good,' she managed to gasp. 'Arbitor senioris, Daughter of Ultramar: no good thinking I'll fold in a fight.' They circled each other. On the floor, Rede and Orovene fought on.

'Guess not,' he panted back. 'A pity.' He wiped blood off his lips with a creamy linen sleeve. 'So you can fight, can you? Well...' Then the wrecking-ball came through the front of her skull, and although she had raised her gun...

...against Dechene, now she heard the racking of the shotgun and she leapt, twisted catlike in the air and landed in a perfect roll. Spinning, she deftly shot the gun out of the astonished Bruinann's hands, and put the second round between his eyes. Orovene, standing, drew on her, but her maul was out and she crushed his skull. Then she leapt into the air and sent Rede choking with a lightning-fast flying kick into her throat. Calpurnia landed in a perfect warrior's crouch as the cullises raised and the other arbitrators poured in. She met a shouting Chastener Dast maul to maul. The big man tried to drive her back in a flurry of strokes, but she parried each one easily, numbed his arm with a skilful counter swing. She ducked under his clumsy riposte, destroying his throat and neck with the power-flare off the maul's tip. Before his body had even began to fall, she was turning a cartwheel, firing shot after shot with deadly accuracy as she pin-wheeled upside-down through the air. The other Arbites flailed and fell back onto the polished floor...

What the...

'...hell is going on?' She was in front of him again, her vision dark with swarming spots and her mind blessedly her own again. As Guilliman help her, she could even feel a chuckle on her lips.

'If you wanted to lose me in some ridiculous battle-fantasy, Dechene, you never had a hope. Did you think that would sit properly in the mind of anyone who's ever really held a gun?' She put spite into the words, and tried to hold his attention on her voice while she shuffled forwards, 'A boy drooling over a Commissar Cain propaganda-poster, maybe, but me?' She saw a flash of anger in his eyes. Good: get him angry and stop him concentrating. Her gun felt lead-heavy, but it was raised halfway now.

'Oh, well, yes, little miss warrior, I should have known you wouldn't accept a dream of a battle you were winning: little thing like you, and not as young as you were, either, by the look of you, and oh, those scars, too. Ehh, look at those.' Calpurnia felt as if she was floating, her legs barely strong enough to hold her down. One knee shook and buckled and she half-staggered against a rough concrete wall. Dechene's laughter was ragged at the edges, rising into whoops and cries.

'Memories are harder than fears, harder to bend. Let's see how hard yours are.' She managed a step and started to raise the gun when a sick sensation welled up inside her, because she was back there. She was back in the place she sometimes dreamed about. She was wide awake and yet she was back there still, back *there behind her they all were, dead limbs tangled with the hard white lights coming off the carapace armour. The smell of their blood welled up and mixed with the stink of the gun smoke and the scorched reek where las-fire had hit the flaking metal walls. There was another smell, a weird sharp chemical stink as organic, but as inhuman as the voice in her ear and the limbs gripping her shoulder and her head. The sound of leather parting as a serrated dagger edge sliced through her chinstrap and the helmet dropped off her head. 'A little poetic, this,' says that voice, 'one and one, down to us with all the blood on the floor. That's the end of it. That's the end of the poetical little duel, and in a moment I'll be here all on my own…' and she knows the knife-blade is coming around to cut her throat, but it's shifted its balance to make the cut clean, and she can see the proctor's wide-bore stubber in front of her. She stamps backwards. The leg behind her is all wrong in the length so she misses the joint, but now the balance is gone and she drives herself forwards, wrenching her head forwards against the claw. The points are driven into her eyebrow, ripping three sizzling lines of pain up into her scalp. She's fallen flat. The gun is in her hand and she's rolling over, one eye already filling with sticky blood. She's firing, firing and her cries mix with the scraping shriek of agony from the shape above her…*

That flash in Dechene's eyes wasn't anger any more. It was fear. She wondered if he had even admitted that to himself yet.

'Didn't die then,' she said. Her voice seemed as strange and distant as her limbs. 'I won't die now.' Her chest felt cramped and her breath short, and she just had time to mutter *the Emperor is my–*, before it hit her again. It wasn't a blow, but something softer and more sickening, crawling over her like an amoeba. It found the chinks in her thoughts with sly little fingers and fanned her memories out like cards, searching for pain, searching for hurt…

…struggling up a silica slope on Hazhim under the hard low constellations of the orbital forges, until the shell hits her and cracks her carapace apart. She's airborne for whole seconds before she drops into the scorching dust and…

…and in the chilly claustrophobia of the drain ways. They know they're just mopping up and so they're too confident to stay away from

the sieve-grate that's suddenly punched clean across the drain way. The thing comes out all glistening, without even breaking step, and before she can cry out an order, a great wedge of flesh has been scissored out of the front of her hip. There's an artery in there somewhere and she's painting the wall of the drain way red as she collapses in shock. The shotguns open up behind her...

...and she's walking, trying to walk up the steps, the silent bulk of the thing behind her. Its crusher-claw and the drills and chainblades are slick with the gore of Arbites and sisters. Her arm and shoulder a slumped and wrecked ruin, in agony. She can barely walk, but for the thing behind her that has been told to bring her to the very top of the stairs to die...

The gun was still only half-raised and the shot just creased the side of Dechene's leg. He wasn't used to pain, he didn't expect it, and he screamed and tottered. The fear in his eyes was real. *Focus on that,* she told herself, forcing her mind through the last wispy dregs of the delusion. *He's weakening, press him.*

'Pain is an... illusion of the... senses...' she said. 'Despair... illusion... of the mind.'

'What does it take for you?' hissed Dechene, panting. A red haemorrhage was blooming in his right eye. He seemed oblivious to the insanity of putting the question to her. 'What does it take to... oh, now. Oh, wait.' He managed a giggle. 'Oh, of course, it's not pain that frightens you, is it? It's not hurt or fear. They're too *crude* for you.' The crawling was starting again and his voice was becoming flat and colourless in her ears. 'If I can't make you afraid, then what is it, what is it, what is it that can make you *despair*?'

Inside her mind those crawling, violating amoebic fingers found their weak chink, slid home, and squeezed.

Shira Calpurnia Lucina grunted as she clambered off the bunk, already nervy, and shooting her eyes around to see what she'd missed. The morning shift alarms were already half through – in a moment, the daily reading from the Book of law would begin through the vox-horns. From there, she had minutes to get to the mess before the reading was followed up with the daily sermon.

She hauled on her uniform breeches – they were tight, harder to get on than they should have been. She'd been disciplined for her physical condition already this month – and shoved her feet into her boots. She scrabbled with her armour as the sermon began, and someone dropped her helmet onto her head. She didn't know who. Her barrack-mates had received enough group punishments for her errors to have learned to cover for her.

The reading was a homily against allowing seditious speech to go unchallenged. It lasted four minutes, bellowing over the vox-horns in every room, and from the boxes slung under the arms of the proctors who prowled through each barrack. Proctor Todzaw's gaze passed over her, and the man kept moving down their hall and away. She was clear for the moment.

She was half a pace behind as they ran out of the long barrack halls, and three paces behind and out of breath when they went up the steps into the mess. Half an hour later she was trailing out towards the gate hangars and moaning softly under her breath: she had spilled protein meal onto her chest and onto the eagle embroidered over her heart. Staining a holy symbol: two strikes from the proctor's maul on its lowest setting, and she had been sent to the barracks to change. She had a clean tunic, but she hadn't pressed it, she had meant to, but she just hadn't. She hoped it wouldn't show with her armour on top of it.

Hers was the last squad to climb into their Rhino: they had been waiting for her. There were no oaths or complaints, and no insults. They all knew that she knew what they thought of her. She slumped down into her place as the engine gunned.

The ash-clouds were low this afternoon, and they turned Drade-73's sky lush like a bruise. The pumice slicks on the canals clicked and ground, and the sulphurous breezes blew flakes of hot ash down the street.

It was her squad's off day for formation and range drill, which meant a long patrol loop instead. First to the labour-gangs hauling slag panniers up towards the mills for a surprise inspection of the local enforcers' prisoner handling. Calpurnia handled that well enough, since all she had to do was stand in formation. They were back on the move before her arms had started to ache too much with the shotgun, on to one of the syndarchs' plazas where the detectives' pict-spies had shown too many citizens loitering without authorisation. A slow sweep of the plaza on foot, the city folk hurriedly finding ways to look busy, but then the handful who were loafing about the water-still in the central obelisk started eyeballing them. Calpurnia saw it first, and her mind froze: should she fire a warning shot? Fire at them? Warn someone? She had made up her mind to fire a warning shot, moved her gun, and then the proctor had pointed his maul at them and roared for them to disperse or face the consequences.

'Thank you for your signal, arbitor, but I saw them,' he had muttered to her as they had boarded the Rhino again. She hadn't known whether to be ashamed or thrilled – she had meant to fire, but had just waggled her gun. He had thanked her. He had thought she was doing well.

The thought of doing anything to make that compliment go sour terrified her, and so, of course, she did. She moved too clumsily when they were disembarking again, and got someone's shoulder in the chest for it. She grabbed at the hull and steadied herself before she fell, and swallowed the humiliation: she had done that so many times that she barely noticed herself doing it. The shove probably hadn't been intentional anyway. The squad was past bothering to do things like that to her now.

A long foot patrol through the avenues and back streets of the Seventeenth District. Poor temple attendance and slipshod labour performance had shown up in the courthouse compound's reports once too often, and it was time to put the record straight.

By the second hour, Calpurnia's feet were aching and her muscles were sore. She tried to disguise it, stopping and staring down alleyways while she shifted her weight from one bruise-soled foot to the other, or kneeling as if to check a sightline while she vainly hoped for the energy to return to her legs, when a voice came over her torc: 'You're not fooling us, woman.' After that, a little scrap of pride made her try to keep up for another half hour, but soon, even that was gone and she was walking flatfooted, her shotgun hanging from her arms. She was almost too tired to care that she looked such a disgrace, but not entirely, so that was one more thing that hurt when she caught up to the squad by the aqueduct steps.

'Punishment vigil tonight, Cal, forty minutes,' Nalbern muttered – a message from the proctor, who'd turned his back on her. She nodded. It had been about what she'd expected.

Back in the Rhino some of them risked jokes about what would happen to the officials who'd let Seventeen slide into that state. Two had already been arrested. The lead arbitor sprang a test on them, demanding that they quote the laws and citations under which the arrests could take place. The others shot out the passages of the Lex Imperica almost in unison. Calpurnia moved her lips randomly a moment behind them, pretending she remembered the answers too. She didn't think anyone was fooled.

On the range that afternoon, her body was clumsy. Her hit rate was tolerable, so no additions to her penance today. She looked at the other enforcers as the guns danced through their hands, out of scabbard, in, out of holster and in, fire, and reload. Their hands were quick and methodical, and she knew how she looked: the chunky woman with her feet planted wrong, never quite getting the knack of wearing the recoil-kick, the shells and magazines still apparently slippery in her hands. She stripped and cleaned her weapons with the rest of them, scrabbling to finish in time, and walked back to the barracks with her head down.

Her punishment vigil was on the chapel steps, where she knelt outside the doors with her eyes on the broad steel aquila inside. She wasn't so vain as to think that its eyes were on her, nor the eyes of the Emperor it embodied. Her own eyes blurred and stung and her voice hitched and stumbled over her prayers. In the barracks, they would be reading passages from law and scripture, arguing and testing one another: laws, weapons, Arbites history, tactics, and judicial theology. She wasn't missing much. She never tried to speak there any more, not when she struggled to remember the passages the others quoted, confused names, misquoted laws, in her timid little voice that so often got lost under someone else's anyway. They were better off with her out of their way.

Her vigil came to an end, eventually, and the preacher came to lock the doors as she clambered up off her raw knees. He didn't greet her. They were used to seeing each other here.

She stumbled on her way back into the barracks as she usually did, no matter how well she thought she knew the way. Tonight there was only one curse from someone down the hall who didn't know about old Calpurnia and the noise she always made coming in from her punishment details. She made her way through the others as they sat and talked and ignored her. She dropped onto her bunk, exhausted, knowing she should undress, that there would be trouble for it tomorrow, but all she wanted to do was sleep and not think about it, just sleep and maybe tomorrow it would be all right.

Anything was better than having to think about this place, this baking, ashy reeking world that she had always meant to be the first posting in her grand career. This first posting where she'd been for nearly twenty years, still an entry-rank arbitrator, no closer to even a lead arbitor's pins than she had been the day she left Machiun. No closer to joining the noble Calpurnii whose portraits and statues she'd stared at on Iax, no closer to bringing her own distinctions on her family. A dead-end, a cast-off, nothing to the Arbites and nothing to the Calpurnii: she was smart enough to know the truth of it.

For twenty years, whole generations of enforcers had come here, served alongside her, learned more than her and moved on. They had quickly learned to ignore her, ignore the dead-end woman stuck in the corner bunk. There was one like her in every garrison, man or woman.

She put her fists to her face. This was how it was and it wasn't going to change. If she'd had the power to change it, she would have changed it by now. So this was it, she told herself, this was her life, this was the place where this seed of the Calpurnii would never bloom. She wanted to drink to forget, but the others always drank her liquor ration, and she wasn't brave enough to argue when they took it and sneered at her. The last time she'd had a bottle in her hand was in the garrison festivities after Candlemas, when Nalbern had got drunk too and had come back to her bunk with her. She was years older than he was and the years had not been kind ones, she knew he came to her with no real desire, she had known as soon as they'd finished that it had only been sympathy. He had felt sorry for her, and nobody had even bothered teasing her about it...

She lost control then, and the worst of it was this: still nobody cared, because this happened so many nights that it was just another part of the joke, just another night of Fat Cal blubbering herself to sleep in the corner bunk, just another waste of space.

After a time, she sat up. Tears were still sticky on her cheeks. Talk and laughter from the other end of the room swirled around her. She looked dully down at the boots sitting by her bunk, the boots that never seemed to have as much of a shine on them as anyone else's no matter how hard she worked on them.

Fine, she'd work on them now. She wasn't going to sleep any time soon. She might as well give her hands something to do. She angrily dashed the tears away. She promised herself that it would be the last time, but she had promised that many times before.

Working the polisher over the boot felt odd. The sound of the others talking was flat in her ears, as if the pressure in the room had changed. She ignored it and concentrated, although the feeling only intensified. Just keep working, she told herself. You can at least do this much. You can work at this. Twenty years an arbitrator and you're just learning to polish a boot properly.

Fine, then, she snapped back at herself. Twenty years an arbitrator and learned to polish a boot. If it takes another twenty to master the Thirty Maxims and another twenty to do disembark drill without stumbling, then fine. The lights flickered for a moment. She ignored them. If those are all the skills I learn in sixty years, then those are the skills I learn, she told herself, and that will be fine, because I will have spent my life...

…she closed her eyes under a wave of dizziness…

…working at my duty. Working at my duty. The thought seemed to firm her and she thought it again, said it aloud. No matter what, I'll spend my life working at my duty.

She put the boot down without really looking at it. Her feet seemed to rest lightly on the floor as she stood. The talk from the lit end of the room seemed forced, tinny.

I don't understand why I've been in such misery these twenty years, she thought. I don't understand why I haven't understood this before. The Emperor wants me here. The Emperor wants me doing this. My duty, my duty… however humble, how can I be unhappy if I am embracing my duty with my whole heart?

The shadows of the bunks and lockers were strange, the angles of the partitions leaning in a way she didn't remember, and why did her memories of this place feel so old? Why did she remember giving orders to Nalbern, not, not…

She walked slowly into the knot of talking, laughing enforcers. None of them paid attention to her; she might have been a ghost. The room seemed to spin lazily around her. She closed her eyes and spoke to herself again, made it a prayer.

God-Emperor on your Throne, if it is my duty to live and die here, then hand me the cup and I will drink from it. Your laws: your will.

The words were coming into her head as if she had newly thought of them, but even as she discovered each concept afresh, it was as if she had embraced it all her life.

My place is where my duty is. My achievements are what my duty provides. My life is what my duty makes it. I am Shira Calpurnia Lucina of Ultramar and I will do my duty with all my heart, I am Shira Calpurnia, I am… I…

I am not this woman.

The floor seemed to be heaving under her, and when she opened her eyes the lamps and the other men and women, and the shadows, and everything were just a blur, ghost-weak, a meaningless pattern turning around and around her. A poor stage-backdrop was painted around her, painted on eggshell, and it seemed that all she had to do was reach out to push against it…

…and she felt this shell-world lurch and spin…

…and then… it…

…CRACKED.

EPILOGUE

THE ORDO HERETICUS came first, and Calpurnia wasn't surprised, riding aboard a sleek Battlefleet Pacificus cruiser that they had commandeered at High Septacian. Inquisitorial troopers in stern grey cloaks filled the hangar – everything that moved did so under the scrutiny of red-eyed targeters and pale ceramic faceplates, like the ones Lohjen's chameleon-armoured agents had worn.

After the storm-troopers came the sisters, nine of them, in the white livery of the Sacred Rose, faces rigid with disapproval that they had been ordered to come to this place. Two stood back with long ceremonial sarissae crossed over the ramp; the rest surrounded the stasis-cage that carried Antovin Dechene onto the ship. Within the field, light grew murky, but Calpurnia could just make out Dechene's face. His mouth was still in the gape of horrified denial that he had worn when she hatched out of the fantasy. 'You can't,' he had said, and 'No one could,' and 'No one has *ever*…' before she shot out his brains.

'They say that not even the Black Ships see every one of them,' said Rede from next to her.

Rede had ceased to hide her rank. She wore the black arbitrator uniform she always had, but with her red collar, and a red sash, lanyard and epaulette, openly displayed. Calpurnia, somewhat to her amusement, had been able to tell which of the Navy contingent knew about Arbites ranks by the way they had started to shy away from her. Ylante had been indifferent, but then Ylante had a lot on her mind, marshalling the concordiasts and counselling Dast about the astropaths who might ascend to the Mastership. She and Calpurnia had avoided one another for the most part. None of the astropaths seemed to care about Rede's rank, and that hadn't surprised Calpurnia at all.

'I've heard stories of witches who make it into the Administratum, the Guard, who knows where else,' Rede went on. 'They can go for years without being discovered. How do you think they do it? How do you think they believe they'll get away with it?'

'I'm no inquisitor, detective,' said Calpurnia with a shrug, not taking her eyes off the cage and the ring of white-armoured sisters around it. 'All I care to point to is experience. It seems to me that the power in Dechene was starting to work on him by the end.'

'That does trouble me,' said Rede with a shudder. 'The idea that that could happen and the watch-hall not register a single note of it–'

'I understand you, but it's not what I meant,' said Calpurnia. 'I don't believe anything, any kind of... shadow entered him. I think that when a power like that grows in your mind it pushes other things aside to make room for itself. Your own reports show that Dechene was always a cruel man, a criminal bastard in the making, but when that power in him woke up, it expanded his psyche like a balloon. It distorted him even further. It's no wonder Renz wasn't able to control him in the end.'

'Huh, Renz.' There hadn't been any need to hold Renz's trial over for conducting at the Wall. Rede had sat him in the execution range and simply read from her dossier, DeMoq had interjected with the formal citations for his crimes, and Calpurnia had pulled the trigger. The whole affair had taken less than two hours.

However, Calpurnia had gone straight to the chapel afterwards, and Rede had gone with her. The two women hadn't spoken to each other, but they had both prayed there for a long time. The trial and execution – and the knowledge that there would be more to follow as Rede uprooted the rackets that Teeker Renz's little clique had been running – had focused their minds.

'Arbitor senioris, I...' Rede began, and faltered. The wheeled cage with Dechene's remains had reached the bottom of the ramp, and a man in a grey cloak like the storm-troopers' was talking with the Sister Palatine leading it. Calpurnia watched as the man finished and walked towards them.

'I'll be coming to Hydraphur myself when my work here is finished,' said Rede, 'to account for the shortcomings in my own work here.' There was regret in her voice, but no rancour. It would be hard for Rede to sound wounded about going on trial for failure given who she was talking to, Calpurnia thought ruefully. 'I shall see you when I'm called by the Arbitor Majore to testify about you, I think. Dast and Orovene have both gone into detail about that. They're having several of your actions here added to the trial charges.'

Calpurnia allowed herself a little smile. Dast had regained consciousness a day before. His first action had been an order that he be wheeled into Rede's room so that he could start going through the reports. His second had been to declare the investigation over and hold his hand out for Calpurnia's arbitor senioris pins. Handing them over had hurt far less than she'd expected.

Dast's old bed in the Precinct Apothecarion was taken by Bruinann, brain-burned by one of Dechene's strongest attacks, and barely coherent. When the Arbites ship arrived to take Calpurnia away, Bruinann would ride with them to the Apothecarion at the Wall.

'Orovene says he hated working to add to the charges on you,' Rede said, 'if you can imagine that. I wanted to say that I'll tell the Arbitor Majore–'

'The truth,' said Calpurnia. 'You'll tell him the truth exactly as you recall it from the events that happened here.'

She saw the other woman turn to stare at her.

'I'm not afraid of my duty, detective-espionist, not any more. I'll meet my duty no matter what it requires of me, because that's the Emperor's will. It took a strange kind of teacher to teach me that, but I'm holding onto the lesson with both fists. My duty as an arbitor... it's what I am. Good or bad.'

'Arbitor Calpurnia?' said the young man in the grey cloak. A black velvet cap on his head didn't quite hide the augmetic inlays, and one of his eyes was a clear green graft that shone like glass. A rosette was pinned at his breast.

'We are passing on now, arbitor. Ah, Arbites,' he corrected himself with an easy smile and a nod at Rede. 'We've got the body and our agents are already at work within the Tower. We'll have cause to confer with Detective Rede before long, but for now–'

'I understand, sir. Thank you for coming to appraise us.' Calpurnia gave a click of her heels and a small bow. The man returned it, still smiling.

'Forgive the departure from protocol, but I'm specifically charged to say this. Inquisitor Stefanos Zhow extends his commendation for your work, and declares that although he will by no means press the matter he would be pleased to offer you passage to Hydraphur aboard the *Aeon Aquilifer*.'

Rede's eyes widened, but Calpurnia only smiled.

'Please present the inquisitor with my thanks and my compliments in return,' she told him, 'but my duty commands the protocol of arrest, and without duty...'

'...what are we?' said the man, and bowed again. 'I am pleased to have spoken with you, arbitor. I understand an Arbites cruiser is closing to dock when the *Aquilifer* casts off – reinforcements for your purge, I believe, mamzel detective? – I doubt you'll have too long to wait for your departure. For what it is worth, I hope that your duty will not call you to the execution cell quite yet, and I speak on more than my own behalf.' He spun on his heel and marched away without looking back.

'You have work to do, detective,' Shira Calpurnia said. 'I won't keep you. For the moment I think I'll just wait here in peace.'

Rede started to say something, but thought better of it. She saluted, and walked away without looking back. Calpurnia turned and watched the sisters walk up the ramp. The airlocks began to stamp closed.

It wouldn't be long now. She would take ship for Hydraphur, and she would stand her trial. Her trial no longer frightened her, and nor did anything that might come after it. She didn't doubt herself any more. She had seen herself stripped down to the core, and she knew better than to be afraid.

I'm ready, she thought to herself. *I'm ready to go home.*

BLIND

A DOSSIER

Selected excerpts from the monograph *A Declaration of the Polarity of Human Disposition* by Inquisitor Kvander Tonnabi, privately published on Gathalamor and subsequently reprinted and distributed through various Ministorum and Munitorum channels. Page numbers in the following excerpts are based on the edition distributed in the port-hives of Marentull Secundus, financed by an anonymous patron referred to in the cover notes as 'A Pious Lady of the Spires'. Readers should note that most copies of this edition were confiscated and destroyed by the planetary governor's own political cadres after extensive pressure by representatives from the League of Blackships and the Navis Nobilite. Reports of an exchange of assassinations within the sector's Inquisitorial Conclave over the issue have yet to be verified.

Page 3

At its essence, humanity is noble.

This I believe. This I *know*. This knowledge comes to me in revealed truth through my faith in Him on Earth and in received truth enshrined in the teachings of His Adeptus. The work of the Adeptus shows me human nobility every day, in every manner, the humbling power of the human mind and soul. The capacity of my species for faith, obedience and tradition. To be a human being, intelligent and ensouled with our minds and souls a reflection of His: simply to be born thus is already the greatest honour that the galaxy can bestow on us.

It follows that if what ennobles us is our mind, which allows us to understand our place and duty and to guide our actions to what is right, and our soul, which allows us the blessings of faith, reverence and righteous hate, then the defiling of our human mind and soul must be paramount in our understanding here. The human form has dignity as an echo of His own form, and its genetic purity is fundamental to the great work of Humanity. Its preservation is a rightful and righteous part of the divine Imperial mandate.

However, the purely physical body may be made the subject of human works, built on and shaped by the human mind. We know that the augmetic and the flesh-graft fall within that mandate: we can see such works upon the bodies of the Adeptus back through hundreds of generations and can therefore infer rightness by tradition. Progressing to more emphatic examples, we can see the human form worked upon for a greater purpose in the creation of the servo-skull and the luminant, let alone the arco-flagellant, or in the genesis of each warrior of the Adeptus Astartes. The servitor provides the most powerful argument, in both its cultured and rendered forms. The cultured servitor shares a human gene and form but has lacked the ennobling mind and soul from its creation; the rendered servitor had the superficial appearance of a full human, being able to act and speak as one, but demonstrated their flaw through wrongdoing, and rendering brings their outward physical nature into alignment with their essential nature. Both kinds of servitor are worked upon to create the physical form that their duties demand of them.

This bears upon the insight that my prayers and meditations brought me. It is the human mind and soul that are the vessels for the Emperor's light. The human body, while deserving of respect, is subordinate to the demands that duty places upon it. It follows that the interaction of base flesh with the attributes of warpcraft, while presenting dangers that we must never underestimate, is not intrinsically morally repugnant. A nominally human body devoid of mind or soul but which interacts with the warp is a necessary danger. It is the cohabitation of our gifts of mind and soul with the warp-touch which constitutes an affront. That is the affront to which the duties of the Ordo Hereticus and the blessed Ministorum must be directed toward remedying.

Page 12

The counter-claims are not new to me. I have been the victim of many an attack by the backslider, by the morally lazy, by the unworthy. Must I elaborate upon the moral slackness that has made room for the human pollution of the psykers that surround us even in the Adeptus, even in the Inquisition?

I must.

I have been accused of short-sightedness and have been told that I have no understanding. I have been accused of a deliberate effort at sabotage, a charge that stops not far short of outright treason against the blessed Adeptus. I wear these attacks with contempt. They are falsehoods. How can I be guilty of what these empty broadsides claim when all my work is to bring the Imperium just a little closer to what it was created as, and what it has fallen so far from?

I shall state again the cause of the fall. We cannot, for a moment, fail to keep our eyes on our enemies. Let me repeat it. The crumbling of our moral strength comes from our willingness to tolerate the poison mix of human mind and psyker affinity.

The sap of the Golden Diomede is sweet, and the juices of its berries harmless; it is only their mixture which turns them into the toxin whose potency is legendary in a dozen sectors across the Segmentum Pacificus, and has made 'double-shade deadly' such bywords along the sectors of the Anyen Gulf. Take this as your conceit: the ability to exert the force of our mind and faith upon this universe and the ability to exert the force of our will upon the other universe; both of these are at their heart blessings, for all that our history shows us that either of them can be turned to poisonous ends. It is the mixing of them that produces the poison, the damnable alchemy that was not there before. I write this treatise for readers who will not need reminding of the terrible scars that that poison has left upon our Imperium, but let me make sure that the magnitude of the issue is understood. I refer to Kota-Tchera and the fall of the continents of Gelro. Reader, whether you are a companion of mine in the Inquisition, or serve in the Imperial Navy or carry the vows of the Ministorum, you will know these names and know where tolerance leads.

Even if the poison were not obvious in its effects, it must surely be obvious in the blasphemy of its very concept. This is one of the most potent ways in which the Emperor has made His divinity known to us, for He and He alone has shown that he can take up the dreadful gift of the psyker and remain untainted; proof of his divine nature that he transcends the principles I have outlined heretofore, by which His mortal servants are bound. Mind and psyk contained in one being; this is a template of purest divinity which suffers mockery and blasphemy when slack-spined, backsliding fools allow the freak of a cognizant psyker to exist, blind to the disgrace they have created.

Page 16

Simple foolishness is simply corrected. The most dangerous of these spiritual cripples are the ones wit enough to comprehend but who have wilfully blinded themselves for expediency and profit. Simple blindness can be corrected when eyes are opened, but even as I write these words the wilfully blind are working all around me to bury my truths.

Costly, they claim. Unworkable, they claim. Because a psyker in its rightful state must be teamed with others and controlled more tightly, even as a servitor must be programmed and handled rather than turned loose in violation of all our purest instincts toward hierarchy. Because they say I cannot justify the drain on Imperial resources for the tending wards for psykers stripped of the minds that rightfully belong to their betters. Even the weakest-minded psyker, I have been told, can manage a million times and more the labour of its cured companion. They say I will make the Navigator's vision murky, reduce the song of the astropath to a mumble, require a regiment of my 'husks' to do the work half a dozen abominations could do.

Costly.

Unworkable.

Because allowing mockeries of the dual face of the Godhead, corroding our morals and weakening our Imperium, of *course* this must take second place to some lazy and faithless adept's *convenience*.

Dangerous, they claim. Wrong, they claim. Because a mind that is conscious and wills itself to be strong is supposedly a defence against the great Enemy that always watches us from the shadows beyond the Emperor's light. Because we are supposed to believe a psyker is a full and ensouled human with a gift, with a right to serve according to their lights as much as any of us.

Dangerous.

Wrong.

Because we are expected to gut our moral understanding and turn it inside out, congratulating ourselves on our wisdom as we greet as human a psyker-thing that was never meant to speak and think, and has sprouted like a tumour a false mockery of an intellect it was never meant to have. So, then, shall I next appoint as human the mound of slops and offal under my hive wall's midden-chutes?

Page 27

The psyker can make thoughts, and the psyker can make words. Neither is an argument for humanity. Servitors can be programmed with the ability to speak. Animals can mimic our sounds. Xenos can present the appearance of true life that a human soul imparts, but a xenos that can make human words is still an empty sham of humanity, trash and obstacles fit only to be swept aside. We must look past appearances. The psyk-presence in a human-shaped shell leaves no room for the soul. Whatever mannerisms a psyker might present that seem to be human virtue or emotion are mimicries wrapped around a core that is alien to us, knowable only to Him on Earth. The servitor trudging in the street might seem bowed under its load but to extend compassion or human fellowship to it is sentimental folly fit only for children. So it is for a psyker which may be able to mouth the sounds of faith, duty and loyalty but which will never have the human essence that gives those words meaning.

Page 31

This challenge is not insurmountable. However sheer the mountain in front of us may appear, stone can be chipped, then drilled, then shattered. We can only fail in this great work if we first fail in our faith and resolve.

And the great work has already begun. The year before last I could count a dozen victories, ships and stations who remade their psykers according to true moral principles. The past year, twice that many again on Gathalamor alone, and now the work is beginning further across the system. As I write this my staff bring me messages from as far away as Hydraphur, affirming their understanding and pledging themselves to the restoration of the great order. A surgical mill has been founded on Chelm and I have high hopes that another will be under way on Sephorda by Candlemas.

Once the shield has been breached the barrier cannot help but perish. Now the chink has been made in the rusting, rotting armour that has protected the corruption underneath. This is our hour.

Humanity is noble.

Humanity will prevail.

• A Letter from •
House de lo Piriya

My dearest Big Sister!

It is too long since I heard from you, and even with all this grim news and distress it was still a joy when the packet was handed me. We had heard of a grey current enveloping much of the middle part of your route but I scolded Uncle when he tried to tell us we should have mourning hoods at the ready. Your Eye has always been keener than his!

I only wish I could say the same for your wits! (Oh, I know you, Big Sister, I can just tell you're making that face at my letter right now and wishing I were there so you could shout at me so. Why can you never see that I'm joking at you?) But all this fluttering about this silly delay at Hougeran? How so very like you! If I were there with you, perhaps I could make you explain to me what's worth all the fuss over some thick-clotted blunt of an Arbitor who decides he wants a glimpse of how his betters live.

It should be all one to us, I'm sure Mother told you that as she did me. (Oh, and I must write this down while I remember, my sister, she has sent word to me just yesterday that her petition is to be carried to the Paternoval Court as soon as the skeinflows below the Coronet Nebula reach the right tide! Soon I think that House de lo Piriya is to have such exciting news!) They really don't like us, of course they don't. All the other Adeptus. Of course they know they must stay out of our way, except for the filthy Inquisition, you remember how Grandfather would always call them that? They don't like our Eyes and they don't like the way we can do as we want and not drag around these rules like manacles all the time. And they certainly don't like the way we can provide so well for ourselves! It's just a little price to pay, Big Sister, that every so often some stupid little man comes stamping about trying to show us he's not afraid of us and he doesn't envy us. Just think of that the next time one of these Arbites ships boards one of ours. They can't do a thing! Watch them scurry about pretending they're not powerless! You'll find it as funny as I do, what laughs we shall have together when I meet you next!

The only thing I can think as I reread your letter is that Markov has been putting thoughts in your head again. I hope I told you how that whole affair with the Victory at Jantespont finished, but now I can't recall and so I shall tell you again. The problem was those two priests making such a fuss at the way station, remember? Well, it turned out one of the witnesses Markov had to clean up was an Adeptus, which was why everything had to be done so secretively. But still, even though it was such a menial, trivial little person, you know if it's an Adeptus then the Arbites get involved. How they must hate having such work put to them for such an unimportant death! Anyhow, Markov got suspicious that the Arbites had tried to get one of these so-called Detectives in to spy on what we were doing with the Victory, and so of course he had his suspects out in short order. Now listen to me, Big Sister, because I can tell you that I used my Eye on them myself! You always did say I was the best at the practical stuff, and you would have been so proud of me! But Markov knows about information and he said that if these people were still not letting slip even after what I did to them then that meant there was no Detective on board. He spent quite the time explaining to me and I thought it should be so very dull, but I'm sure that Markov knows more about the work of the Detectives than they would allow him to know, ha!

He told me he had personally 'rolled up' (this is what he likes to say) a network that some Arbites Detectives had set up right along the Kyryde-Zenj route to track some sort of behaviour by a ship that Uncle was navigating. He said that some of the people he killed were Arbites themselves but many of them weren't. I had no idea! He said that the Detectives aren't like the stupid man and his arbitrators who boarded you. He said that they are supposed to be very proud of how they can watch and infiltrate anywhere, and often they use these networks and devices so they can make these enormous files on anyone at all. He said that sometimes they'll use their networks to push people into committing crimes so they can arrest them, just to show that they were criminal types who needed to be punished. Perhaps there's one watching you read this right now, ha!

Anyway, Markov said that the Detectives are never as clever as they think they are, and they're never as clever as him. He spent a lot of time telling me about all the ways he can tell when there's an Arbites Detective trying to monitor an operation he's running for us and he kept telling me that there simply couldn't be a danger to you. If there had been Arbites agents digging around the details of what your ship is really going to be carrying into the Pacificus, why then Markov would have found them and killed them. Of course he would! They wouldn't be alive to tell this clot you wrote of to come and strut about as though you owed him something. Now if the Arbites had people working for them who were as clever as our Markov then perhaps even you and I would need to start being careful! But since they don't, Big Sister, all you need do is hold your nerve and keep your lovely keen Eye to the bow. After we get this plan into motion the whole Eilgard system will be a wreck and House Chiban with it, and House Dorel will realise that they must support our bid. What a pity Great-Grandmother didn't live to see so many Ferraci contracts fall open!

By the time you read this the Moon of Niccolo will be in dock and you will be enjoying a wonderfully earned rest. I hope this letter brings you some pleasure and reassurance before you move our plan on to its next stage! Ignore those ridiculous Arbites, and ignore that certain General You-Know-Who! He shan't be much of a problem for us in a very short while!

Your dearest Sister!

Addendum: Letter intercepted and recorded by [SECURE – REDACTED], agent of Detective-Espionist Seyrigg of the Doneck-Elan Precinct. Using a dossier including this letter, as well as private conversations intercepted by vox-thieves planted aboard the *Moon of Niccolo* during a decoy arbitrator boarding and inspection, Arbites of Doneck-Elan and Hydraphur were able to break an assassination conspiracy against General Kersh of the 417th Segmentum Pacificus Imperial Guard Expeditionary Command. Navigator House de lo Piriya cited immunity from the operation, but several family members were publicly disowned by the House in the aftermath of the affair and subsequently murdered by persons unknown.

Act IV scIII from 'A Judge in Black and Crimson, or, Fair Price for Mutiny', a short play produced with the patronage of the Monocrat of Hydraphur and first presented to an invited audience of dignitaries from the Bosporian, Constanta and Estann Hives.

Enter the JUDGE.

JUDGE: The line is gone, in procession, before my eyes. The Trader bore the torch into the shadows, and beckoned the way, and the False Heir and the True Heir have alike walked down the turning path to follow him. Emptiness! Emptiness and shadows now!

CHORUS: Empty the Trader's house stands, shadowed his deed and line!

JUDGE: Upon whom now does my word fall? Must my judgement stand empty?

CHORUS: What is left in the winged gauntlet's grasp? Has the wind carried the last mortal dust between its fingers?

Enter the TRUE HEIR and the FALSE HEIR, as apparitions.

TRUE HEIR: Brother to me you never were in life, brother to me you never could become. Mock-brotherhood drove you further from my flesh and blood than you could ever have gone by simple act.

FALSE HEIR: Death changes as the dusk to the dawn, and the new light makes new the landscape. Only death can make us brothers where life must recoil from the thought.

CHORUS: Let the sun move again, dusk and dawn, and the eyes of the living and dead alight.

The JUDGE kneels and bows her head. Enter the PRIEST, the SISTER, the CAPTAIN OF THE FLEET, and a JUDGE IN BLACK, hooded.

PRIEST: Though we crave the shelter of the aquila's shining wings, an eagle's claw cuts to the soul's quick.

CHORUS: What shall our wounds be worth?

CAPTAIN: Glorious is the sign of the aquila upon the shoulder, heavy the grip of its talons.

CHORUS: What shall be the judgement when our blood paints the scales?

SISTER: Faith makes joy of the weight of duty; devotion brings gladness from the pain of judgement.
CHORUS: The great engine of judgement makes ephemera of the stars in their courses.

HOODED JUDGE: And so must every soul walk before the Throne to bow to the consequences of its deeds.

CHORUS: Beneath the ecliptic wings, let her raise her hand! If she has will to do it, let her raise her hand! If she is true to her burden, let her raise her hand!

The JUDGE stands and extends her hand.

JUDGE: I march in the cohorts of the Throne. My heartbeat is the beat of the aquila's wings. I will be proved!

FALSE HEIR (to the JUDGE): Such a great freight for your shoulders! Have you not earned the surety of forgiveness if your burden should touch the dust?

TRUE HEIR: (to the JUDGE): In every mortal soul is the sweet cool shadow that whispers to our weakest selves! Take the measure of yourself, and ask what there is to spare once you have let the core of you be ravelled away?

JUDGE: There is blood on the altar of Law. The stink of murder arrests the senses of bright Galata. Corpse-ash on the solar wind dulls golden wings. My ark, my task, lies spilled in the dust and I with it. To let my eyes close, to let my will sleep; will dereliction keep its sting once my conscience's anchor is cast off?

FALSE HEIR: If your knee bends under the weight, is that not a worthy submission? If your head bows and your eyes sink from the star of Terra to the dark below, can you not rest a while in your course? All the hosts that surround and follow you in the wake of His banner, how light all their hands will make this!

JUDGE: When we speak of duty's end, do we speak of the death of flesh, or the death of will? My will is hollow. I am afraid.

TRUE HEIR: Your oath takes your flesh from you, bones, breath and will all. The blood in you does not flow for you, but is sworn to Him. You no longer boast of your sinews' strength because their every motion is for His end, not yours. What is pain, what is weariness, of a body that you only borrow for so long as He has duties to exact of you? Lighter than a moth's fluttering against a bastion. Only make of yourself that bastion and the fear can never breach you.

JUDGE: When the air flees a breached ship, only vacuum remains. As I bleed my veins of the fear they do not rush again with hope. I have seen the deepest tide fill the channels of a ship with poison that will blacken the soul that it touches. What hope have I to relight the beacon in me, to rekindle my fortunes and brighten my path to the Throne?

TRUE HEIR: Trinkets and false starlight! Put away from you such foolishness, shallow hope and the childish fancies of self. Regard yourself and your eyes fall from His banner to your own imperfect flesh. Admire yourself and you steal what is rightfully His, usurp His privilege and send your feet from His track. What spirit is so weak it will let weariness pull it over the precipice's lip?

CHORUS: Choices part as before the edge of a sword. How shall our fate be cut?

JUDGE: Then let my voice speak not for me but for my office. Then let my hands move not by my direction but by that of my office. Let my will be for my will to be yoked to duty in the name of Him on Earth. Let me step upon the rack, let me carry the signs and markers of all this undoing, to place upon the Chapel step.

HOODED JUDGE: The will of the Adeptus stays its course, the will of the Throne is carried forward.
Exit.

JUDGE: Upon my oath, I will not be found wanting. By the twice-gazing aquila, by the singlefold spire and the threefold palace, by all the songs and deeds that rise like firelight from the Augustaeum, I shall not be found wanting.

SISTER: We who carry forward the banner of Earth see it unfurl anew, and our duty vindicated.
Exit.

JUDGE: Not my will, but the law's, be done. Not my will, but the Throne's, be done.

CAPTAIN: The macroshell, the plasma shell, the las-beam are ranked behind the adamantine ram and mine to command, and yet who can master the weapons at our hands while rebellious will runs free? I salute the human will re-mustered.

Exit.

JUDGE: Not my will, but the Emperor's, be done.

TRUE HEIR: The great march continues on through the ashes, and the shadow is fleeting, the colours of humanity fly unblemished, the Throne is borne up and glorified!

FALSE HEIR (drawing a veil over his face): I find no purchase on faith, I make no mark on duty though my throat gasps and my fingers bleed at its face. Alone I walk the path into shadow, unmourned I turn my back on human works and give over my soul to the emptiness.

PRIEST: Begone, shades, weave no more cares into the path of the pilgrim, the path of the faithful!

Enter the HOODED JUDGE.

See now, this is not the hour of words and phantoms, but of the iron of law and the adamant of judgement.

Exeunt the PRIEST, TRUE HEIR and FALSE HEIR.

HOODED JUDGE: The tread of the cohorts rings like a hammer upon armour. The beauty of the law's progress stands across the firmament like the Ring against the stars. Mutiny, rebellion and apostasy, all overthrown and trampled upon the ground. They lie in the shadow of Law, Duty and Faith, beneath the gazes of the saints and the aquiline wings. Let all heads bow to verdict. Let penance close the ranks of the Great Work. Let the proudest soul bow before the Throne and the Emperor reign in light, blessed and glorified, forever.

For Justice is worked as the Throne commands,
So Justice shall be work'd by all our hands.

Exeunt the JUDGE and the HOODED JUDGE.

Finish.

ABOUT THE AUTHOR

Matthew Farrer lives in Australia, and is a member of the Canberra Speculative Fiction Guild. He has been writing since his teens, and has a number of novels and short stories to his name, including a story for the Horus Heresy anthology, *Tales of Heresy*.

Buy these books or read free extracts at *www.blacklibrary.com*

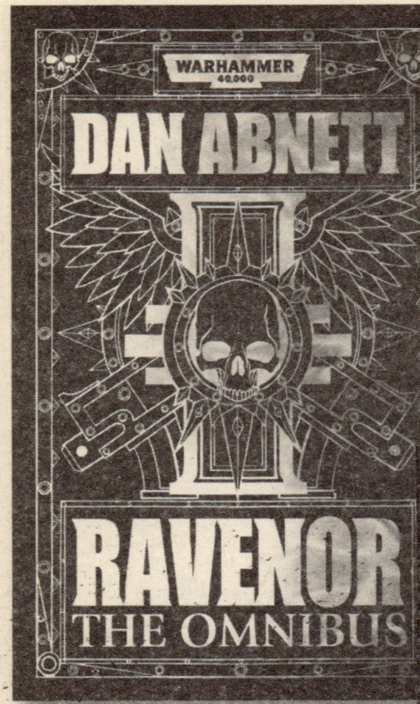

UK ISBN: 978-1-84416-736-4
US ISBN: 978-1-84416-736-1

ISBN: 978-1-84416-156-0

UK ISBN: 978-1-84416-374-10
US ISBN: 978-1-84416-375-7